take the
chance

BRITTAINY CHERRY • EMMA SCOTT
MELANIE HARLOW • HELENA HUNTING

Take the Chance

The Gravity of Us
Copyright © 2017 by Brittainy C. Cherry
All rights reserved.

Without limiting the rights under copyright reserved above, no part of this publication may be reproduced, stored in or introduced into a retrieval system, or transmitted, in any form, or by any means (electronic, mechanical, photocopying, recording, or otherwise) without the prior written permission of the author of this book.

This is a work of fiction. Names, characters, places, brands, media, and incidents are either the product of the author's imagination or are used fictitiously. Any resemblance to actual events, locales, or persons, living or dead, is coincidental.

Editing: Editing by C. Marie, Ellie at Love N Books
Proofreading: Virginia Tesi Carey, Lawrence Editing, Alison Evans-Maxwell-Red Leaf Proofing

Forever Right Now
Copyright © 2017 Emma Scott

All rights reserved

This is a work of fiction. Any names or characters, businesses or places, events or incidents, are fictitious or have been used in a fictitious manner. Any resemblance to actual persons, living or dead, or actual events is purely coincidental.

After We Fall
Copyright © 2016 by Melanie Harlow
All rights reserved.

No part of this book may be reproduced in any form or by any electronic or mechanical means, including information storage and retrieval systems, without written permission from the author, except for the use of brief quotations in a book review.

Editing: Tamara Mataya
tamaramataya.blogspot.com

Pucked Love
Copyright © 2018 Helena Hunting
All rights reserved
Editing by Jessica Royer Ocken

Pucked Love is a work of fiction. Names, characters, places, and incidents are all products of the author's twisted imagination and are used fictitiously. All references to the NHL are fictitious and that there is no endorsement by the NHL. Any resemblance to actual events, locales, or persons, living or dead, is entirely coincidental.

Except as permitted under the US Copyright Act of 1976, no part of this publication may be reproduced, distributed or transmitted in any form by any means, or stored in a database or retrieval system, without the prior written permission of the author.

the gravity of us

Book Four in the Elements Series

BRITTAINY C. CHERRY

dedication

To love,
and all the heartache that weighs it down.

To love,
and all the heartbeats that lift it up.

prologue

Lucy
2015

Before Mama passed away five years ago, she left three gifts for my sisters and me. On my sister Mari's front porch sat the wooden rocking chair Mama gave her. Mari received the rocking chair because Mama always worried that her mind was always on the go. Mari was the middle child and had a way of constantly feeling as if she was missing out on something in life, which led to her oftentimes living in limbo. "If you don't stop overthinking things, you're going to put your brain into overdrive, baby girl. It's okay to go slower sometimes," Mama would say to her. The rocking chair was a reminder for Mari to slow down and take a few moments to embrace life, to not let it pass her by.

Our oldest sister, Lyric, received a small music box with a dancing ballerina. When we were children, Lyric dreamed of being a dancer, but over the years, she packed that dream away. After growing up with Mama, who was a lifelong wild child, Lyric began to resent the idea of a career based on passion. Mama lived her life in the most passionate way, and at times, that meant we didn't know where our next meal would be coming from. When the rent was due, we'd be packed up and off on our next adventure.

Lyric and Mama fought all the time. I believed my sister felt responsible for us all, feeling as if she had to mother her own mother. Mari and I were young and free; we loved the adventures, but Lyric hated it. She hated not having a solid place to call home, hated the fact that Mama had no structure in her life. She hated that her freedom was her cage. When the opportunity came for Lyric to leave, she left our sides and went off to become a fancy lawyer. I never knew what happened to the small music box, but I hoped Lyric still held on to it. *Always dance, Lyric*, Mama used to say to my sister. *Always dance.*

My gift from Mama was her heart.

It was a tiny heart-shaped gem she'd worn around her neck since she was a teenager, and I felt honored to receive it from her. "It's the heart of our family," she told me. "From one wild one to another, may you never forget to love fully, my Lucille. I'll need you to keep our family together and be there for your sisters during the hard times, okay? You'll be their strength. I know you will because you already love so loudly. Even the darkest souls can find some kind of light from your smile. You'll protect this family, Lucy, I know you will, and that's why I'm not afraid to say goodbye."

The necklace hadn't left my neck since Mama passed away years ago, but that summer afternoon I held it tighter in my hand as I stared at Mari's rocking chair. After Mama's death, Mari was shaken to her core, and every belief she'd been taught about spirituality and freedom felt like a lie.

"She was too young," Mari told me the day Mama passed away. She believed we were supposed to have time that was closer to forever. "It's not fair," she cried.

I was only eighteen when she passed, and Mari was twenty. At the time, it felt like the sun had been stolen away from us, and we didn't have a clue how to move forward.

"Maktub," I whispered, holding her close. The word was tattooed on both of our wrists, meaning 'it is written.' Everything in life happened for a reason, happened exactly how it was meant to, no matter how painful it seemed. Some love stories were meant to be forever, and others just for a season. What Mari had forgotten was that the love story between a mother and daughter was always there, even when the seasons changed.

Death wasn't something that could alter that kind of love, but after Mama had passed away, Mari let go of her free-spirited nature, met a boy, and planted her roots in Wauwatosa, Wisconsin—all in the name of love.

Love.

The emotion that made people both soar and crash. The feeling that lit humans up and burned their hearts. The beginning and ending of every journey.

When I moved in with Mari and her husband, Parker, I knew it wouldn't be a permanent situation, but I was completely thrown off when I caught him leaving that afternoon. The late summer air was sharp with the scent of autumn's chill waiting in the shadows. Parker hadn't heard me walk up behind him—he was too busy tossing a few pieces of luggage into his gray sedan.

Between his tight lips sat two toothpicks, and his navy blue designer suit lay perfectly flat against his skin with his folded handkerchief in the left breast pocket of his blazer. When the day came for him to die, I was certain he'd want to be buried with all his handkerchiefs. It was an odd obsession of his, along with his collection of socks. I'd never seen someone iron so many handkerchiefs and socks before I met Parker Lee. He told me it was a common practice, but his definition of common differed from mine.

For example, having pizza five days a week was a common practice to me, while Parker saw it as unnecessary carbohydrates. That should've been a big warning sign when I first met him. He had many red flags along the way. A man who didn't like pizza, tacos, or pajamas on Sunday afternoons wasn't someone who was meant to cross my path.

He bent forward into his trunk and started shifting his suitcases around to make more room.

"What are you doing?" I asked.

My voice threw him off kilter and he jumped a few inches into the air, banging his head against the hood. *"Shit!"* He stood up and rubbed the back of his head. "Jesus, Lucy. I didn't see you there." His hands ran through his dirty-blond hair before he stuffed them into his slacks. "I thought you were at work."

"The boys' dad came home early," I said, referring to my nanny job as my eyes stared at the trunk of his car. "Do you have a work conference or something? You should've called me. I could've come back to—"

"Does that mean you're losing pay for today?" he asked, cutting me off and avoiding my question. "How are you going to help with everything? With the bills? Why didn't you pick up more hours at the coffee shop?" Sweat dripped from his forehead as the summer sun beat down on our skin.

"I quit the coffee shop weeks ago, Parker. I wasn't exactly bringing home the bacon. Plus, I figured if you're working, I could be helping more here."

"Jesus, Lucy. That's so like you. How could you be so irresponsible? Especially with everything going on." He started pacing, tossing his hands around in anger, pissing and moaning, confusing me more and more each second.

"What exactly *is* going on?" I stepped toward him. "Where are you going, Parker?"

He stood still and his eyes grew heavy. Something shifted inside him. His state of annoyance transformed to reveal his hidden remorse. "I'm sorry."

"Sorry?" My chest tightened. "For what?" I didn't know why, but my chest began to cave in as an avalanche of emotions overtook my mind. I was already predicting the doom of his next chosen words. My heart was set to break.

"I can't do it anymore, Lucy. I just can't do it."

The way the words burned from his lips made my skin crawl. He said it as if he felt guilty, but the bags in his car showed that even with that guilt, he'd decided. In his mind, he was far gone.

"She's getting better," I said, my voice shaky with unease and fear.

"It's too much. I can't…she's…" He sighed and brushed the back of his palm against his temple. "I can't stay and watch her die."

"Then stay and see her live."

"I can't sleep. I haven't eaten in days. My boss is getting on my case because I'm falling behind, and I can't lose that job, especially with the medical expenses. I worked too hard to get everything I have, and I can't lose it because of this. I can't sacrifice anymore. I'm tired, Lucy."

I'm tired, Lucy.

How dare he use those words? How dare he claim to be exhausted as if he was the one going through the hardest fight of his life? "We're all tired, Parker. We're all dealing with this. I moved in with you two so I could look after her, to make it easier for you, and now you're just giving up on her? On your marriage?" No words from him. My heart…it cracked. "Does she know? Did you tell her you're leaving?"

"No." He shook his head sheepishly. "She doesn't know. I figured this would be easiest. I don't want her to worry."

I huffed, shocked by the lies he was throwing my way, even more stunned by how he somehow believed those words to be true.

"I'm sorry. I left some money on the table in the foyer. I'll check in with you to make sure she's okay, to make sure she's comfortable. I can even wire you more money if you need it."

"I don't want your money," I said, my voice unsympathetic to his pained expression. "We don't need anything from you."

He parted his lips to speak but shut them quickly, unable to form any sentences that could make the situation any easier. I watched every step he took to reach his driver's side door, and when he did, I called his name. He didn't turn to look at me, but his ears perked up, waiting.

"If you leave my sister right now, you don't get to come back. You don't get to call when you're drunk or check in when you're sad. When she beats this cancer—which she *will*—you don't get to step back in and pretend you love her. Do you understand?"

"I do."

Those two words were the same he'd used to promise himself to Mari through sickness and in health. Those two words were now forever drenched in agony and filthy lies.

He stepped into his car before driving off without once hitting his brakes. I stayed in the driveway for a few moments, unsure of how to walk inside and tell my sister that her husband had abandoned her during her storm.

My heart cracked again.

My heart broke for my sister, the innocent one in a world full of ruthlessness. She'd given up her free spirit life to live a more structured one, and both worlds had turned against her.

I took a deep breath and placed the palm of my hand around my heart-shaped necklace.

Maktub.

Instead of running like Parker, I went to see Mari. She was lying in her bed resting. I smiled her way, and she smiled back at me. She was so skinny, her body pushing each day to fight against expiration. Her head was wrapped in a scarf, her once long brunette hair now nothing more than a memory. It made her sad at times, staring into the mirror, but she didn't see what I saw. She was so beautiful, even in sickness. Her true glow couldn't be stolen away by such changes to her body, because her beauty stemmed from her soul, where only goodness and light resided.

She'd be okay, I knew she would, because she was a fighter.

Hair grew back, bones regained strength, and my sister's heart was still beating, which was reason enough to celebrate each day.

"Hey, Pea," I whispered, hurrying over to the bed and crawling into it to lie beside her. I lay on my side, and she turned on hers to face me.

Even in her weakness, she found a way to smile each day. "Hey, Pod."

"There's something I need to tell you."

She shut her eyes. "He's gone."

"You knew?"

"I saw him packing when he thought I was sleeping." Tears started rolling from the corners of her eyes, which she kept closed. For a while, we just lay there. Her sadness became my tears, and her tears articulated my sadness.

"Do you think he'll miss me when I die?" she asked me. Whenever she brought up death, I wanted to curse the universe for hurting my best friend, my family.

"Don't say that," I scolded.

"But do you think he will?" She opened her eyes, reached across to me, and held my hands in hers. "Remember when we were kids and I had that awful dream about Mama dying? I spent the whole day crying, and then she gave us all a talk about death? About how it isn't the end of the journey?"

I nodded. "Yes, she told us we'd see her in everything—the sunbeams, the shadows, the flowers, the rain. She said death doesn't kill us, it only awakens us to more."

"Do you ever see her?" she whispered.

"Yes, in everything. In absolutely everything."

A small whimper fell from her lips, and she nodded. "Me too, but mostly I see her in you."

Those words were the kindest I'd ever had delivered to me. I missed Mama every second of every day, and to have Mari say she saw her within me meant more than she'd ever know. I moved in closer to her and wrapped her in a hug. "He'll miss you. He'll miss you while you're alive and healthy, and he'll miss you when you're a part of the trees. He'll miss you tomorrow, and he'll miss you when you become the wind brushing against his shoulder. The world's going to miss you, Mari, even though you'll still be here for many years to come. The second you're better, we're going to open our flower shop, okay? You and me, we're going to do it."

All our lives, my sister and I had been in love with nature. We always had a dream to open a floral shop, and even went so far as to attend Milwaukee's School of Flower Design. We each earned degrees in business so we'd have all the knowledge available to us. If it weren't for the cancer, we would've had our shop. So, once the cancer was gone, I planned to do everything in my power to bring that shop to life.

"Okay, Mari? We're going to do that," I said once more, hoping to sound more convincing, hoping to bring her ease.

"Okay," she said, but her voice dripped with doubt. Her brown doe eyes, which were shaped like Mama's, were filled with the deepest look of sorrow. "Can you get the jar? And the bag of coins?"

I sighed, but agreed. I hurried to the living room where we'd left the jar and the bag of change sitting the night before. The Mason jar was wrapped with pink and black ribbon, and it was almost full of coins. We had started the jar when Mari was diagnosed seven months ago. The jar had the letters NT written on the side, which stood for negative thoughts. Whenever one of us had a bad thought race through our minds, we'd place a coin in the jar. Every negative thought was leading to a beautiful outcome—Europe. Once Mari was better, we'd use the money to go toward us backpacking across Europe, a dream we'd always wanted to bring to life.

For every present negative thought, the coins were a reminder of better tomorrows.

We had eight jars filled to the top already.

I sat back down on Mari's bed, and she pushed herself up a bit then grabbed the bag of change.

"Pod," she whispered.

"Yes, Pea?"

Tears raced down her cheeks faster and faster as her small frame was overtaken by emotion. "We're going to need more change."

She poured all the coins into the jar and when she finished, I wrapped her up in my arms where she continued to fall apart. They had been married and healthy for five years and it only took seven months of sickness to make Parker vanish, leaving my poor sister brokenhearted.

"Lucy?" I heard as I sat on the front porch. I'd been sitting in the rocking chair for the past hour as Mari rested, trying my best to understand how everything that unfolded was destined to happen. When I looked up, I saw Richard, my boyfriend, hurrying my way as he leaped off his bicycle and then leaned it against the porch. "What's going on? I got your text message." Richard's shirt was covered in paint as always, a result of him being the creative artist he was. "I'm sorry I didn't answer your calls. My phone was on mute while I drank my sorrows away about being declined an invite to yet another art gallery."

He walked up to me and kissed my forehead. "What's going on?" he asked again.

"Parker left."

It only took two words for Richard's mouth to drop. I filled him in on everything, and the more I said, the more he gasped. "Are you kidding? Is Mari okay?"

I shook my head; of course she wasn't.

"We should get inside," he said, reaching for my hand, but I declined.

"I have to call Lyric. I've been trying to for hours, but she hasn't answered. I'm just going to keep trying for a while. Do you think you can go check on her and see if she needs anything?"

He nodded. "Of course."

I reached out and wiped some yellow paint from his cheek before leaning in to kiss him. "I'm sorry about the gallery."

Richard grimaced and shrugged. "It's okay. As long as you're okay with dating a turd who's not good enough for his work to be showcased, then I'm okay with it."

I'd been with Richard for three years now, and I couldn't imagine being with anyone other than him. I just hated how the world hadn't given him a chance to shine yet; he was worthy of success.

But, until it came, I'd stand by his side, being his biggest cheerleader.

As he went inside, I dialed Lyric's number one more time.

"Hello?"

"Lyric, finally." I sighed, sitting up straighter as I heard my sister's voice for the first time in a long time. "I've been trying to reach you all day."

"Well, not everyone can be Mrs. Doubtfire and work part-time at a coffee shop, Lucy," she said, her sarcasm loud and clear.

"I actually only nanny now. I quit the coffee shop."

"*Shocking,*" she replied. "Listen, do you need something, or were you just bored and decided to call me repeatedly?"

Her tone was the same one I'd known for most of my life—complete disappointment in my entire existence. Lyric had a way of putting up with Mari's quirks, especially since Mari had finally settled down with Parker. Lyric was, after all, the one who introduced the couple to one another. When it came to my relationship with my eldest sister, it was the complete opposite. I often thought she hated me because I reminded her too much of our mother.

As time went by, I realized she hated me because I was nothing more than myself.

"Yeah, no. It's Mari."

"Is she okay?" she asked, her voice drenched with fake concern. I could hear her still typing away on her computer, working late into the night. "She's not...?"

"Dead?" I huffed. "No, she's not, but Parker left today."

"Left? What do you mean?"

"He just left. He packed his bags, said he couldn't deal with watching her die, and drove away. He left her alone."

"Oh my God. That's insane."

"Yeah, I agree."

There was a long moment of silence and me listening to her type before she spoke again. "Well, did you piss him off or something?"

I stopped rocking in the chair. "What?"

"Come on, Lucy. Since you moved in to help, I'm sure you haven't been the easiest person to live with. You're a lot to handle." She somehow managed to do what she always did when I was involved in any situation—she made me the villain. She put me at fault for a coward walking out on his wife.

I swallowed hard and ignored her comment. "I just wanted you to know, that's all."

"Is Parker okay?"

What? "I think what you meant to say was 'Is Mari okay,' and no, she's not. She's dealing with cancer, her husband just left her, and she hardly has a penny to her name, let alone the strength to keep going."

"Ah, there it is," Lyric murmured.

"There what is?"

"You're calling me for money. How much do you need?"

My stomach knotted at her words and a taste of disgust spread on my tongue. She thought I'd called her because I wanted money? "I called you because your sister is hurting and feels alone, and I thought you might want to come see her and make sure she's okay. I don't want your money, Lyric. I want you to start acting like a freaking sister."

Another moment of silence passed, along with more typing.

"Look, I'm swamped at work. I have these cases coming up for the firm, and I can't be pulled away from them right now. There's no way I'd be able to get by her place until maybe next week or the week after."

Lyric lived downtown—a short twenty-minute drive away—but still, she was convinced it was too far away.

"Never mind, okay? Just pretend I never called." My eyes watered over, shocked by the coldness of someone I'd once looked up to in my life. DNA told me she was my sister, but the words she spoke conveyed that she was nothing more than a stranger.

"Stop it, Lucy. Stop with the passive aggressive approach. I'll drop a check in the mail tomorrow, all right?"

"Don't, seriously. We don't need your money, and we don't need your support. I don't even know why I called you. Just mark it down as a low point of mine. Goodbye, Lyric. Good luck with your cases."

"Yeah, okay. And, Lucy?"

"Yeah?"

"You might want to get that coffee job back as soon as possible."

After a while, I stood up from the rocking chair and walked to the guest room where I'd been staying. I shut the bedroom door, held my hand around my necklace, and shut my eyes. "Air above me, earth below me, fire within me, water surround me…" I took deep breaths and kept repeating the words Mama had taught me. Whenever she'd lose her balance in life and feel far from grounded, she'd repeat that chant, finding her inner strength.

Even though I repeated the words, I felt like a failure.

My shoulders drooped and my tears began to fall as I spoke to the only woman who had ever truly understood me. "Mama, I'm scared, and I hate it. I hate that I'm afraid, because that means I'm somewhat thinking what Parker was thinking. A part of me feels like she won't make it, and I just feel terrified each day."

There was something so heartbreaking about watching your best friend fall apart. Even though I knew death was simply the next chapter in her beautiful memoir, it didn't make it any easier for me to grasp. In the back of my mind, I knew each hug could be the last, knew each word could be goodbye.

"I feel guilty, because for every good thought I have, five negative ones pass through. I have fifteen coin jars filled in my closet that Mari doesn't even know exist. I'm tired, Mama. I'm exhausted, and then I feel guilty for almost falling apart. I have to stay strong, because she doesn't need anyone falling apart around her. I know you taught us girls not to hate, but I just hate Parker. God forbid, but if these are Mari's last days, I hate that he tainted them. Her final days shouldn't be filled with the memory of her husband walking out on her."

It wasn't fair that Parker could pack his bags and just escape to a new life without my sister. He might find love again someday, but what about Mari? He'd be the love of her life, and that hurt me more than she'd ever know. I knew my sister like the back of my hand, knew how gentle her heart was. She felt every hurt ten times more than most people. Her heart resided on her sleeve, and she allowed everyone to listen to its beautiful heartbeats—even those who were undeserving of hearing the sounds. She prayed they loved her heart's sounds, too. She always wanted to feel loved, and I hated that Parker made her feel like a failure. She'd leave the world feeling as if she had somehow failed her marriage, all in the name of love.

Love.

The emotion that made people both soar and crash. The feeling that lit humans up and burned their hearts. The beginning and ending of every journey.

As the days, months, and years passed by, Mari and I heard less and less from both Parker and Lyric. The pity check-ins grew less frequent, and the guilt-driven checks stopped coming through the mail. When the divorce papers landed in the mailbox, Mari cried for weeks. I stood strong for her in the light, and teared up for her heart in the shadows.

It wasn't fair how the world took Mari's health and then had the nerve to come back to make sure her heart was shattered into a trillion pieces too. With every inhale, she cursed her body for betraying her and ruining the life she'd built. With every exhale, she prayed for her husband to return home.

I never told her, but with every inhale, I begged for her healing, and with every exhale, I prayed for her husband to never come back.

chapter one

Graham
2017

Two days before, I'd bought flowers for someone who wasn't my wife. Since the purchase, I hadn't left my office. Papers were scattered all around—notecards, Post-It notes, crumpled pieces of paper with pointless scribbles and words crossed out. On my desk sat five bottles of whisky and an unopened box of cigars.

My eyes burned from exhaustion, but I couldn't shut them as I stared blankly in front of me at my computer screen, typing words I'd later delete.

I never bought my wife flowers.

I never gave her chocolates on Valentine's, I found stuffed animals ridiculous, and I didn't have a clue what her favorite color was.

She didn't have a clue what mine was either, but I knew her favorite politician. I knew her views on global warming, she knew my views on religion, and we both knew our views on children: we never wanted them.

Those things were what we agreed mattered the most; those things were our glue. We were both driven by career and had little time for one another, let alone family.

I wasn't romantic, and Jane didn't mind because she wasn't either. We weren't often seen holding hands or exchanging kisses in public. We weren't into snuggling or social media expressions of love, but that didn't mean our love wasn't real. We cared in our own way. We were a logical couple who understood what it meant to be in love, to be committed to one another, yet we never truly dived into the romantic aspects of a relationship.

Our love was driven by a mutual respect, by structure. Each big decision we made was always thoroughly thought out and often involved diagrams and charts. The day I asked her to by my wife, we made fifteen pie and flow charts to make sure we were making the right decision.

Romantic?

Maybe not.

Logical?

Absolutely.

Which was why her current invasion of my deadline was concerning. She never interrupted me while I was working, and for her to barge in while I was on a deadline was beyond bizarre.

I had ninety-five thousand more to go.

Ninety-five thousand words to go before the manuscript went to the editor in two weeks. Ninety-five thousand words equated to an average of six thousand seven hundred eighty-six words a day. That meant the next two weeks of my life would be spent in front of my computer, hardly pulling myself away for a breath of fresh air.

My fingers were on speed, typing and typing as fast as they could. The purplish bags under my eyes displayed my exhaustion, and my back ached from not leaving my chair for hours. Yet, when I sat in front of my computer with my drugged-up fingers and zombie eyes, I felt more like myself than any other time in my life.

"Graham," Jane said, breaking me from my world of horror and bringing me into hers. "We should get going."

She stood in the doorway of my office. Her hair was curly, which was bizarre seeing as how her hair was always straight. Each day she awoke hours before me to tame the curly blond mop upon her head. I could count on my right hand the number of times I'd seen her with her natural curls. Along with the wild hair, her makeup was smudged, left on from the night before.

I'd only seen my wife cry two times since we'd been together: one time when she'd learned she was pregnant seven months ago, and another when some bad news came in four days ago.

"Shouldn't you straighten your hair?" I asked.

"I'm not straightening my hair today."

"You always straighten your hair."

"I haven't straightened my hair in four days." She frowned, but I didn't make a comment about her disappointment. I didn't want to deal with her emotions that afternoon. For the past four days, she'd been a wreck, the opposite of the woman I married, and I wasn't one to deal with people's emotions.

What Jane needed to do was pull herself together.

I went back to staring at my computer screen, and my fingers started moving quickly once more.

"Graham," she grumbled, waddling over to me with her very pregnant stomach. "We have to get going."

"I have to finish my manuscript."

"You haven't stopped writing for the past four days. You hardly make it to bed before three in the morning, and then you're up by six. You need a break. Plus, we can't be late."

I cleared my throat and kept typing. "I decided I'm going to have to miss out on this silly engagement. Sorry, Jane."

Out of the corner of my eye, I saw her jaw slacken. "Silly engagement? Graham…it's your father's funeral."

"You say that as if it should mean something to me."

"It does mean something to you."

"Don't tell me what does and doesn't mean something to me. It's belittling."

"You're tired," she said.

There you go again, telling me about myself. "I'll sleep when I'm eighty, or when I'm my father. I'm sure he's sleeping well tonight."

She cringed. I didn't care.

"You've been drinking?" she asked, concerned.

"In all the years of us being together, when have you ever known me to drink?"

She studied the bottles of alcohol surrounding me and let out a small breath. "I know, sorry. It's just…you added more bottles to your desk."

"It's a tribute to my dear father. May he rot in hell."

"Don't speak so ill of the dead," Jane said before hiccupping and placing her hands on her stomach. "God, I hate that feeling." She took my hands away from my keyboard and placed them on her stomach. "It's like she's kicking me in every internal organ I have. I cannot stand it."

"How motherly of you," I mocked, my hands still on her.

"I never wanted children." She breathed out, hiccupping once more. "Ever."

"And yet, here we are," I replied. I wasn't certain Jane had fully come to terms with the fact that in two short months, she'd be giving birth to an actual human being who would need her love and attention twenty-four hours a day.

If there was anyone who gave love less than I did, it was my wife.

"God," she murmured, closing her eyes. "It just feels weird today."

"Maybe we should go to the hospital," I offered.

"Nice try. You're going to your father's funeral."

Damn.

"We still need to find a nanny," she said. "The firm gave me a few weeks off for maternity leave, but I won't need all of the time if we find a decent nanny. I'd love a little old Mexican lady, preferably one with a green card."

My eyebrows furrowed, disturbed. "You do know saying that is not only disgusting and racist, but also saying it to your half-Mexican husband is pretty distasteful, right?"

"You're hardly Mexican, Graham. You don't even speak a lick of Spanish."

"Which makes me non-Mexican—duly noted, thank you," I said coldly. At times my wife was the person I hated the most. While we agreed on many things, sometimes the words that left her mouth made me rethink every flow chart we'd ever made.

How could someone so beautiful be so ugly at times?

Kick.

Kick.

My chest tightened, my hands still resting around Jane's stomach.

Those kicks terrified me. If there was anything I knew for certain, it was that I was not father material. My family history led me to believe anything that came from my line of ancestry couldn't be good.

I just prayed to God that the baby wouldn't inherit any of my traits—or worse, my father's.

Jane leaned against my desk, shifting my perfectly neat paperwork as my fingers lay still against her stomach. "It's time to hop in the shower and get dressed. I hung your suit in the bathroom."

"I told you, I cannot make this engagement. I have a deadline to meet."

"While you have a deadline to meet, your father has already met his deadline, and now it's time to send off his manuscript."

"His manuscript being his casket?"

Jane's brows furrowed. "No. Don't be silly. His body is the manuscript; his casket is the book cover."

"A freaking expensive book cover, too. I can't believe he picked one that is lined with gold." I paused and bit my lip. "On second thought, I easily believe that. You know my father."

"So many people will be there today. His readers, his colleagues."

Hundreds would show up to celebrate the life of Kent Russell. "It's going to be a circus," I groaned. "They'll mourn for him, in complete and utter sadness, and they'll sit in disbelief. They'll start pouring in with their stories, with their pain. 'Not Kent, it can't be. He's the reason I even gave this writing thing a chance. Five years sober because of that man. I cannot believe he's gone. Kent Theodore Russell, a man, a father, a hero. Nobel Prize winner. Dead.' The world will mourn."

"And you?" Jane asked. "What will you do?"

"Me?" I leaned back in my chair and crossed my arms. "I'll finish my manuscript."

"Are you sad he's gone?" Jane asked, rubbing her stomach.

Her question swam in my mind for a beat before I answered. "No."

I wanted to miss him.

I wanted to love him.

I wanted to hate him.

I wanted to forget him.

But instead, I felt nothing. It had taken me years to teach myself to feel nothing toward my father, to erase all the pain he'd inflicted on me, on the ones I loved the most. The only way I knew how to shut off the hurt was to lock it away and forget everything he'd ever done to me, to forget everything I'd ever wished him to be.

Once I locked the hurt away, I almost forgot how to feel completely.

Jane didn't mind my locked-away soul, because she too didn't feel much either.

"You answered too quickly," she told me.

"The fastest answer is always the truest."

"I miss him," she said, her voice lowering, communicating her pain over the loss of my father. In many ways, Kent Russell was a best friend to millions through his storybooks, his inspirational speeches, and the persona and brand he sold to the world. I would've missed him too if I didn't know the man he truly was in the privacy of his home.

"You miss him because you never actually knew him. Stop moping over a man who's not worth your time."

"No," she said sharply, her voice heightened with pain. Her eyes started to water over as they'd been doing for the past few days. "You don't get to do that, Graham. You don't get to undermine my hurt. Your father was a good man to me. He was good to me when you were cold, and he stood up for you every time I wanted to leave, so you don't get to tell me to stop moping. You don't get to define the kind of sadness I feel," she said, full-blown emotion taking over her body as she shook with a flood of tears falling from her eyes.

I tilted my head toward her, confused by her sudden outburst, but then my eyes fell to her stomach.

Hormonal mess.

"Whoa," I muttered, a bit stunned.

She sat up straight. "What was that?" she asked, a bit frightened.

"I think you just had an emotional breakdown over the death of my father."

She took a breath and groaned. "Oh my God, what's wrong with me? These hormones are making me a mess. I hate everything about being pregnant. I swear I'm getting my tubes tied after this." She stood up, trying to pull herself together, and wiped away her tears as she took more deep breaths. "Can you at least do me one favor today?"

"What's that?"

"Can you pretend you're sad at the funeral? People will talk if they see you smiling."

I gave her a tight fake frown.

She rolled her eyes. "Good, now repeat after me: my father was truly loved, and he will be missed dearly."

"My father was truly a dick, and he won't be missed at all."

She patted my chest. "Close enough. Now go get dressed."

Standing up, I grumbled the whole way.

"Oh! Did you order the flowers for the service?" Jane hollered my way as I slid my white T-shirt over my head and tossed it onto the bathroom floor.

"All five thousand dollars' worth of useless plants for a funeral that will be over in a few hours."

"People will love them," she told me.

"People are stupid," I replied, stepping into the burning water falling from the showerhead. In the water, I tried my best to think of what type of eulogy I'd deliver for the man who was a hero to many but a devil to myself. I tried to dig up memories of love, moments of care, seconds of pride he'd delivered me, but I came up blank. Nothing. No real feelings could be found.

The heart inside my chest—the one he'd helped harden—remained completely numb.

chapter two

Lucy

"HERE LIES MARI JOY PALMER, A GIVER OF LOVE, PEACE, AND HAPPINESS. It's a shame the way she left the world. It was sudden, unspeakable, and more painful than I'd ever thought it would be." I stared down at Mari's motionless body and wiped the back of my neck with a small towel. The early morning sun beamed through the windows as I tried my best to catch my breath.

"Death by hot yoga." Mari sighed, inhaling deeply and exhaling unevenly.

I laughed. "You're going to have to get up, Mari. They have to set up for the next class." I held my hand out toward my sister, who was lying in a puddle of sweat. "Let's go."

"Go on without me," she said theatrically, waving her invisible flag. "I surrender."

"Oh no you don't. Come on." I grabbed her arms and pulled her to a standing position, with her resisting the whole way up. "You went through chemotherapy, Mari. You can handle hot yoga."

"I don't get it," she whined. "I thought yoga was supposed to make you feel grounded and bring about peace, not buckets of sweat and disgusting hair."

I smirked, looking at her shoulder-length hair that was frizzy and knotted on top of her head. She'd been in remission for almost two years now, and we'd been living our lives to the fullest ever since then, including opening the flower shop.

After quick showers at the yoga studio, we headed outside, and when the summer sun kissed our skin and blinded us, Mari groaned. "Why the heck did we decide to ride our bikes here today? And why is six AM hot yoga even a thing we'd consider?"

"Because we care about our health and well-being, and want to be in the best shape of our lives," I mocked. "Plus, the car's in the shop."

She rolled her eyes. "Is this the point where we bike to a café and get donuts and croissants before work?"

"Yup!" I said, unlocking my bike from the pole and hopping onto it.

"And by donuts and croissants do you mean…?"

"Green kale drinks? Yes, yes, I do."

She groaned again, this time louder. "I liked you better when you didn't give a crap about your health and just ate a steady diet of candy and tacos."

I smiled and started pedaling. "Race you!"

I beat her to Green Dreams—obviously—and when she made it inside, she draped her body across the front counter. "Seriously, Lucy—regular yoga, yes, but hot yoga?" She paused, taking a few deep breaths. "Hot yoga can go straight back to hell where it came from to die a long painful death."

A worker walked over to us with a bright smile. "Hey, ladies! What can I get for you?"

"Tequila, please," Mari said, finally raising her head from the countertop. "You can put it in a to-go cup if you want. Then I can drink it on the way to work."

The waitress stared at my sister blankly, and I smirked. "We'll take two green machine juices, and two egg and potato breakfast wraps."

"Sounds good. Would you like whole wheat, spinach, or flaxseed wraps?" she asked.

"Oh, stuffed crust pizza will do just fine," Mari replied. "With a side of chips and queso."

"Flaxseed." I laughed. "We'll have the flaxseed."

When our food came out, we grabbed a table, and Mari dived in as if she hadn't eaten in years. "So," she started, her cheeks puffed out like a chipmunk. "How's Richard?"

"He's good," I said, nodding. "Busy, but good. Our apartment currently looks like a tornado blew through it with his latest work, but he's good. Since he found out he's having a showcase at the museum in a few months, he's been in panic mode trying to create something inspiring. He's not sleeping, but that's Richard."

"Men are weird, and I can't believe you're actually living with one."

"I know." I laughed. It had taken me over five years to finally move in with Richard, mainly because I didn't feel comfortable leaving Mari's side when she got sick. We'd been living together for the past four months, and I loved it. I loved him. "Remember what Mama used to say about men moving in with women?"

"Yes—the second they get comfortable enough to take their shoes off in your house and go into your fridge without asking, it's time for them to go."

"A smart woman."

Mari nodded. "I should've kept living by her rules after she passed away—maybe then I could've avoided Parker." Her eyes grew heavy for a few seconds before she blinked away her pain and smiled. She hardly talked about Parker since he'd left her over two years ago, but whenever she did, it was as if a cloud of sadness hovered above her. She fought the cloud, though, and never let it release rain for her to wallow in. She did her best to be happy, and for the most part she was, though there were seconds of pain sometimes.

Seconds when she remembered, seconds when she blamed herself, seconds when she felt lonely. Seconds when she allowed her heart to break before she swiftly started piecing it back together.

With every second of hurt, Mari made it her duty to find a minute of happiness.

"Well, you're living by her rules now, which is better than never, right?" I said, trying to help her get rid of the cloud above her.

"Right!" she cheered, her eyes finding their joy again. It was odd how feelings worked, how a person could be sad one second and happy another. What amazed me the most was how a person could be both things all within the same second. I believed Mari had a pinch of both emotions in that moment, a little bit of sadness intermingled with her joy.

I thought that was a beautiful way to live.

"So, shall we get to work?" I asked, standing up from my chair. Mari moaned, annoyed, but agreed as she dragged herself back out to her bicycle and started pedaling to our shop.

Monet's Gardens was mine and my sister's dream come to life. The shop was fashioned after the paintings of my favorite artist, Claude Monet. When Mari and I finally made it to Europe, I planned to spend a lot of time standing in Monet's Gardens in Giverny, France.

Prints of his artwork were scattered around the shop, and at times we'd shape floral arrangements to match the paintings. After we signed our lives away with bank loans, Mari and I worked our butts off to open the shop, and it came together swimmingly over time. We almost didn't even get the shop, but Mari came through with a final loan she tried for. Even though it was a lot of work and took up so much time I never even considered having a social life, I couldn't really complain about spending my days surrounded by flowers.

The building was small, but big enough to have dozens of different types of flowers, like parrot tulips, lilies, poppies, and of course, roses. We catered to all kinds of functions too; my favorites were weddings, and the worst were funerals.

Today was one of the worst, and it was my turn to drive the delivery truck to drop off the order.

"Are you sure you don't want me to do the Garrett wedding and you do the Russell funeral?" I asked, getting all the white gladiolus bulbs and white roses organized to move into the truck. The person who'd passed away must've been very loved, based on the number of arrangements ordered. There were dozens of white roses for the casket spray, five different cross easels with sashes that said 'Father' across them, and dozens of random bouquets to be placed around the church.

It amazed me how beautiful flowers for such a sad occasion could be.

"No, I'm sure. I can help you load up the van, though," Mari said, lifting up one of the arrangements and heading back to the alleyway where our delivery van was parked.

"If you do the funeral today, I'll stop dragging you to hot yoga each morning."

She snickered. "If I had a penny for every time I'd heard that, I'd already be in Europe."

"No, I swear! No more sweating at six in the morning."

"That's a lie."

I nodded. "Yeah, that's a lie."

"And, no more putting off our trip to Europe. We are officially going next summer, right?" she asked, her eyes narrowed.

I groaned. Ever since she got sick two years ago, I'd been putting off taking our trip. My brain knew that she was better, she was healthy and strong, but a small part of my heart feared traveling so far from home with the possibility of something going wrong with her health in a different country.

I swallowed hard and agreed. She smiled wide, pleased, and walked into the back room.

"Which church am I even going to today?" I wondered out loud, jumping onto the computer to pull up the file. I paused and narrowed my eyes as I read the words: *UW-Milwaukee Panther Arena.*

"Mari," I hollered. "This says it's at the arena downtown…is that right?"

She hurried back into the room and peered at the computer then shrugged. "Wow. That explains all the flowers." She ran her hands through her hair, and I smiled. Every time she did that, my heart overflowed with joy. Her growing hair was a reminder of her growing life, of how lucky we were to be in the place we were. I was so happy the flowers in the truck weren't for her.

"Yeah, but who has a funeral at an arena?" I asked, confused.

"Must be someone important."

I shrugged, not thinking too much of it. I arrived at the arena two hours before the ceremony to get everything set up, and the outside of the building was already surrounded with numerous people. I swore there had to be hundreds crowding the downtown streets of Milwaukee, and police officers paced the area.

Individuals were writing notes and posting them on the front steps; some cried while others were engaged in deep conversations.

As I drove the van around to the back to unload the flowers, I was denied access to the actual building by one of the arena workers. He pushed the door open and used his body to block my entrance. "Excuse me, you can't come in here," the man told me. "VIP access only." He had a large headset around his neck, and the way he slightly closed the door behind him to avoid me peering inside made me suspicious.

"Oh, no, I'm just dropping off the flowers for the service," I started to explain, and he rolled his eyes.

"More flowers?" he groaned, and then he pointed to another door. "The flower drop off is around the corner, third door. You can't miss it," he said flatly.

"Okay. Hey, whose funeral is this exactly?" I asked. I stood on my tiptoes and tried to get a peek of what was happening inside.

He shot me a dirty look filled with annoyance. "Around the corner," he barked before slamming the door shut. I yanked on the door once and frowned. Locked.

One day I'd stop being so nosey, but obviously that day wasn't today.

I smiled to myself and mumbled, "Nice meeting you, too."

When I drove the van around the corner, I realized we weren't the only floral shop who'd been contacted for this event. Three vans were in line before me, and they weren't even able to go inside the building; there were employees collecting the flower arrangements at the door. Before I could even put the car in park, workers were at the back, pounding on the back doors for me to open it up. Once I did, they started grabbing the flowers without much care, and I cringed at the way one of the women handled the white rose wreath. She tossed it over her arm, destroying the green Bells of Ireland.

"Careful!" I hollered, but everyone seemed to be deaf.

When finished, they slammed my doors shut, signed my paperwork, and handed me an envelope. "What's this for?"

"Didn't they tell you already?" The woman sighed heavily, then placed her hands on her hips. "The flowers are just for show, and the son of Mr. Russell instructed that they be returned to the florists who delivered them after the service. Inside is your ticket for the event, along with a pass to get backstage afterward to collect your flowers. Otherwise they will be tossed."

"Tossed?" I exclaimed. "How wasteful."

The woman arched an eyebrow. "Yes, because there was no possible chance the flowers wouldn't have died all on their own," she stated sarcastically. "At least now you can resell them."

Resell funeral flowers? Because that wasn't morbid.

Before I could reply, she waved me off without a goodbye.

I opened an envelope and found my ticket and a card that read, "After the service, please present this card to pick up the floral arrangements; otherwise they will be disposed of."

My eyes read the ticket repeatedly.

A ticket.

For a funeral.

Never in my life had I witnessed such an odd event. When I rounded the corner to the main street, I noticed even more people had gathered around and were posting letters to the walls of the building.

My curiosity hit a new high, and after circling around a few times in search of parking, I pulled into a parking structure. I parked the van and climbed out to go see what everyone was doing there and whose funeral was taking place. As I stepped onto the packed sidewalk, I noticed a woman kneeling down, scribbling on a piece of paper.

"Excuse me," I said, tapping her on the shoulder. She looked up with a bright smile on her face. "I'm sorry to bother you, but…whose funeral is this exactly?"

She stood up, still grinning. "Kent Russell, the author."

"Oh, no way."

"Yeah. Everyone's writing their own eulogies about how he saved their lives and taping them to the side of the building to honor his memory, but between you and me, I'm most excited to see G.M. Russell. It's a shame it had to be for an event such as this one, though."

"G.M. Russell? Wait, as in the greatest thriller and horror author of all time?!" I gushed, realization finally setting in. "Oh my gosh! I love G.M. Russell!"

"Wow. Took you long enough to connect those dots. At first I thought your blond hair was dyed that color, but now I see that you are actually a true-blue blonde," she joked. "It's such a big event because you know how G.M. is when it comes to public appearances—he hardly makes them. At book events, he doesn't engage with the readers except for his big fake grin, and he doesn't ever allow photographs, but today we'll be able to take pictures of him. This. Is. Big!"

"Fans were invited to attend the funeral?"

"Yeah, Kent put it in his will. All the money is being donated to a children's hospital. I got solid seats. My best friend Heather was supposed to come with me, but she went into labor—freaking kids ruin everything."

I laughed.

"Do you want my extra ticket?" she asked. "It's super close up front. Plus, I'd rather sit beside another G.M. fan than a Papa Russell fan. You'd be shocked by how many people are here for him." She paused, cocked an eyebrow, and went digging through her purse. "On second thought, maybe not, seeing as how he was the one who croaked and all. Here you go, they're opening the doors now." She handed me her spare ticket. "Oh, and my name's Tori."

"Lucy," I said with a smile. I hesitated for a moment, thinking how weird and out of the ordinary attending a stranger's funeral in an arena was, but then again…G.M. Russell was inside that building, along with my flowers, which were going to be tossed in a few hours.

We made it to our seats, and Tori couldn't stop snapping photographs. "These are amazing seats, aren't they? I can't believe I snatched this ticket up for only two thousand!"

"Two thousand?!" I gasped.

"I know, right? Such a steal, and all I had to do was sell my kidney on Craigslist to some dude named Kenny."

She turned to the older gentleman sitting on her left. He had to be in his late seventies, and was handsome as ever. He wore an open trench coat, and underneath it, a brown suede suit with a polka dot blue and white bowtie. When he looked our way, he had the most genuine smile.

"Hey, sorry, just curious—how much did you pay for your seat?"

"Oh, I didn't pay," he said with the kindest grin in the world. "Graham was a former student of mine. I was invited."

Tori's arms flew out in a state of complete and utter shock. "Wait, wait, wait, time out—you're Professor Oliver?!"

He smirked and nodded. "Guilty as charged."

"You're like...the Yoda to our Luke Skywalker. You're the Wizard behind Oz. You're the freaking shit, Professor Oliver! I've read every article Graham ever wrote and I must say, it's just so great to meet the person he spoke so highly of—well, highly in G.M. Russell terms, which isn't really highly, if you know what I mean." She chuckled to herself. "Can I shake your hand?"

Tori continued talking through almost the whole service, but stopped the moment Graham was called up to the stage to deliver the eulogy. Before his lips parted, he unbuttoned his suit jacket, took it off, unhooked his cuffs, and rolled up his sleeves in such a manly-man style. I swore he rolled each sleeve up in slow motion as he rubbed his lips together and let out a small breath.

Wow.

He was so handsome, and effortlessly so, too.

He was more handsome in person than I thought he'd be. His whole persona was dark, enchanting, yet extremely uninviting. His short, midnight black hair was slicked back with loose tiny waves, and his sharp square jaw was covered with a few days' growth of beard. His copper-colored skin was smooth and flawless, not a blemish of imperfection anywhere to be found, except for a small scar that ran across his neck, but that didn't make him imperfect.

If I'd learned anything about scars from Graham's novels, it was that they, too, could be beautiful.

He hadn't smiled once, but that wasn't shocking—after all, it was his father's funeral—but when he spoke, his voice came out smooth, like whisky on the rocks. Just like everyone else in the arena, I couldn't tear my eyes from him.

"My father, Kent Russell, saved my life. He challenged me daily to not only be a better storyteller, but to become a better person." The next five minutes of his speech led to hundreds of people crying, holding their breaths, and wishing that they, too, were kin to Kent. I hadn't ever read any of Kent's tales, but Graham made me curious to pick up one of his books. He finished his speech, looked up at the ceiling, and gave a tight grin. "So, I'll end this in the words of my father: Be inspiration. Be true. Be adventurous. We only have one life to live, and to honor my father, I plan to live each day as if it's my final chapter."

"Oh my gosh," Tori whispered, wiping tears from her eyes. "Do you see it?" she asked, gesturing her head toward her lap.

"See what?" I whispered.

"How massive my invisible boner currently is. I didn't know it was possible to be turned on by a eulogy."

I laughed. "Neither did I."

After everything finished, Tori exchanged numbers with me and invited me to her book club. After our goodbyes, I made it to the back room to collect my floral arrangements. As I searched for my roses, I couldn't help but think how uncomfortable I felt by the lavishness of Kent's funeral. It almost seemed a bit…circus-like.

I wasn't one who understood funerals, at least not the typical mainstream ones. In my family, our final goodbyes normally involved planting a tree in our loved one's memory, honoring their life by bringing more beauty to the world.

As a worker walked by with one of my floral arrangements, I gasped and called after her. "Excuse me!" The headphones in her ears kept her from hearing me, though, so I hurried, pushing my way through a crowd, trying to keep up with her. She walked up to a door, held it open, and tossed the flowers outside before shutting the door and walking off dancing to the sound of her music.

"Those were three-hundred-dollar flowers!" I groaned out loud, hurrying through the door. As it slammed, I raced over to the roses that had been tossed into a trash bin in a gated area.

The night's air brushed against my skin, and I was bathed in the light of the moon shining down as I gathered the roses. When I finished, I took a deep inhale. There was something so peaceful about the night, how everything slowed a bit, how the busyness of the day disappeared until morning.

When I went to open the door to head back inside, I panicked.

I yanked on the handle repeatedly.

Locked.

Oh crap.

My hands formed fists and I started banging against the door, trying my best to get back inside. "Hello?!" I hollered for what felt like ten minutes straight before I gave up.

Thirty minutes later, I had sat down on the concrete and was staring at the stars when I heard the door behind me open. I twisted myself around and gasped lightly.

It's you.

Graham Russell.

Standing right behind me.

"Don't do that," he snapped, noting my stare glued to him. "Stop noticing me."

"Wait, wait! It—" I stood up, and right before I could tell him to hold the door, I listened to it slam shut. "Locks."

He cocked an eyebrow, processing my words. He yanked on the door then sighed heavily. "You have got to be kidding me." He yanked again and again, but the door was locked. "It's locked."

I nodded. "Yup."

He patted his slacks pockets and groaned. "And my phone is in my suit jacket, which is hanging on the back of a chair inside."

"Sorry, I would offer you my phone, but it's dead."

"Of course it is," he said moodily. "Because the day just couldn't get any worse."

He pounded on the door for several minutes without any results then started cursing the universe for an extremely sucky life. He walked over to the other side of the gated area and placed his hands behind his neck. He looked completely exhausted over the day's events.

"I'm so sorry," I whispered, my voice timid and low. What else could I say? "I'm so sorry for your loss."

He shrugged, uninterested. "People die. It's a pretty common aspect of life."

"Yes, but that doesn't make it any easier, and for that, I'm sorry."

He didn't reply, but he didn't have to. I was still just amazed to be standing so close to him. I cleared my throat and spoke again because being silent wasn't something I knew how to do. "That was a beautiful speech." He turned his head in my direction and gave me a cold hard stare before turning back around. I continued. "You really showcased what a kind, gentle man your father was and how he changed your life and the lives of others. Your speech tonight...it was just such..." I paused, searching my mind for the right words to describe his eulogy.

"Bullshit," he stated.

I stood up straighter. "What?"

"The eulogy was bullshit. I grabbed it from outside. A stranger wrote it and posted it on the building, someone who'd probably never spent ten minutes in the same room as my father, because if they had, they would've known how shitty of a person Kent Russell was."

"Wait, so you plagiarized a eulogy for your father's funeral?"

"When you say it like that, it sounds awful," he replied dryly.

"It probably sounds that way because it kind of is."

"My father was a cruel man who manipulated situations and people to get the best bang for his buck. He laughed at the fact that you people paid money for his pile of shit inspirational books and lived your lives based on the garbage he wrote about. I mean, his book *Thirty Days to a Sober Life*? He wrote that book drunk off his ass. I literally had to lift him up out of his own vomit and filth more times than I'm willing to admit. *Fifty Ways to Fall in Love*? He screwed prostitutes and fired personal assistants for not sleeping with him. He was trash, a joke of a human, and I'm certain he didn't save anyone's life, as many have so dramatically stated to me this evening. He used you all to buy himself a boat and a handful of one-night stands."

My mouth dropped open, stunned. "Wow." I laughed, kicking around a small stone with my shoe. "Tell me how you really feel."

He took my challenge and turned slowly around to face me, stepping closer, making my heart race. No man should've been as handsomely dark as he was. Graham was a professional at grimacing. I wondered if he knew how to smile at all. "You want to know how I really feel?"

No.

Yes.

Um, maybe?

He didn't give me a chance to answer before he continued to speak. "I think it's absurd to sell tickets to a funeral service. I find it ridiculous to profit from a man's death, turning his final farewell into a three-ring circus. I think it's terrifying that individuals paid extra to have access to a VIP gathering afterward, but then again, people paid to sit on the same couch Jeffrey Dahmer sat upon. I shouldn't be surprised by humans at all, but still, each day they tend to shock me with their lack of intelligence."

"Wow…" I smoothed out my white dress and swayed back and forth. "You really didn't like him, did you?"

His stare dropped to the ground before he looked back up at me. "Not in the least."

I looked out into the darkness of the night, staring up at the stars. "It's funny, isn't it? How one person's angel could be another's biggest demon."

He wasn't interested in my thoughts, though. He moved back to the door and started banging again.

"Maktub." I smiled.

"What?"

"Maktub. It means all is written, that everything happens for a reason." Without much thought, I extended my hand out toward Graham. "I'm Lucy, by the way. Short for Lucille."

He narrowed his eyes, not amused. "Okay."

I giggled and stepped in closer, still holding my hand out. "I know sometimes authors can miss out on social cues, but this is the moment when you're supposed to shake my hand."

"I don't know you."

"Surprisingly, that's exactly when you're supposed to shake a person's hand. "

"Graham Russell," he said, not taking my hand. "I'm Graham Russell."

I lowered my hand, a sheepish grin on my lips. "Oh, I know who you are. Not to sound cliché, but I'm your biggest fan. I've read every word you've ever written."

"That's impossible. There are words I've written that have never been published."

"Perhaps, but if you did, I swear I'd read them."

"You've read *The Harvest*?"

I wiggled my nose. "Yes…"

He smiled—no, it was just a twitch in his lip. *My mistake.*

"It's as bad as I think it is, isn't it?" he asked.

"No, I just…it's different than the others." I chewed my bottom lip. "It's different, but I can't put my finger on why."

"I wrote that one after my grandmother passed away." He shifted his feet around. "It's complete shit and should've never been published."

"No," I said eagerly. "It still stole my breath away, just in a different kind of way—and trust me, I'd tell you if I thought it was complete trash. I've never been a good liar." My eyebrows wiggled and my nose scrunched up as I moved on my tiptoes—the same way Mama used to—and went back to staring up at the stars. "Have you thought of planting a tree?"

"What?"

"A tree, in honor of your father. After someone close to me passed away, she was cremated, and my sister and I planted a tree with her ashes. On holidays we take her favorite candy, sit beneath the tree, and eat the candy in her honor. It's a full circle of life. She came in as energy of the world, and went back into it as the same."

"You're really feeding into those millennial stereotypes, aren't you?"

"It's actually a great way to preserve the beauty of the environment."

"Lucille—"

"You can call me Lucy."

"How old are you?"

"Twenty-six."

"Lucy is a name for a child. If you ever truly want to make it in the world, you should go by Lucille."

"Noted. If you ever want to be the life of the party, you should consider the nickname Graham Cracker."

"Are you always this ridiculous?"

"Only at funerals where people have to buy tickets."

"What was the selling price?"

"They ranged from two hundred to two thousand dollars."

He gasped. "Are you kidding me? People paid two thousand dollars to look at a dead body?!"

I ran my hands through my hair. "Plus tax."

"I'm worried about the future generations."

"Don't worry, the generation before you worried about you, too, and it's obvious you're a bright, charming personality," I mocked.

He almost smiled, I thought.

And it was almost beautiful.

"You know what, I should have known you didn't write that eulogy based on how it ended. That was a huge clue that it wasn't written by you."

He cocked an eyebrow. "I actually did write that eulogy."

I laughed. "No, you didn't."

He didn't laugh. "You're right, I didn't. How did you know?"

"Well...you write horror and thriller stories. I've read every single one since I was eighteen, and they never ever end happy."

"That's not true," he argued.

I nodded. "It is. The monsters always win. I started reading your books after I lost one of my best friends, and the darkness of them kind of brought me a bit of relief. Knowing there were other kinds of hurts out in the world helped me with my own pain. Oddly enough, your books brought me peace."

"I'm sure one ended happily."

"Not a single one." I shrugged. "It's okay. They are all still masterpieces, just not as positive as the eulogy was tonight." I paused and giggled again. "A positive eulogy. That was probably the most awkward sentence I've ever said."

We were silent again, and Graham went back to the banging of the sealed door every few minutes. After each failed attempt, he'd heavily sigh with disappointment.

"I'm sorry about your father," I told him once more, watching how tense he seemed. It'd been a long day for him, and I hated how clear it was that he wanted to be alone and I was the one standing in his way. He was literally caged with a stranger on the day of his father's funeral.

"It's okay. People die."

"Oh no, I'm not sorry about his death. I'm one of those who believe that death is just the beginning of another adventure. What I mean is, I'm sorry that for you, he wasn't the man he was to the rest of the world."

He took a moment, appearing to consider saying something, but then he chose silence.

"You don't express your feelings very often, do you?" I asked.

"And you express yours too often," he replied.

"Did you write one at all?"

"A eulogy? No. Did you post one outside? Was it yours I read?"

I laughed. "No, but I did write one during the service." I went digging into my purse and pulled out my small piece of paper. "It's not as beautiful as yours was—*yours* being a stretch of a word—but it's words."

He held his hand out toward me, and I placed the paper in his hold, our fingers lightly brushing against one another.

Fangirl freak-out in three, two...

"*Air above me, earth below me, fire within me, water surround me...*" He read my words out loud and then whistled low. "Oh," he said, nodding slowly. "You're a hippie weirdo."

"Yes, I'm a hippie weirdo." The corner of his mouth twitched, as if he was forcing himself not to smile. "My mother used to say it to my sisters and me all the time."

"So your mom's a weirdo hippie too."

A slight pain hit my heart, but I kept smiling. I found a spot on the ground and sat once again. "Yeah, she was."

"Was," he murmured, his brows knitting together. "I'm sorry."

"It's okay. Someone once told me people die, that it's a pretty common aspect of life."

"Yes, but..." he started, but his words faded away. Our eyes locked and for a moment, the coldness they held was gone, and the look he gave me was filled with sorrow and pain. It was a look he'd spent his whole day hiding from the world, a look he'd probably spent his whole life hiding from himself.

"I did write a eulogy," he whispered, sitting down on the ground beside me. He bent his knees and his hands pushed up the sleeves of his shirt.

"Yeah?"

"Yes."

"Do you want to share it?" I asked.

"No."

"Okay."

"Yes," he muttered softly.

"Okay."

"It's not much at all..." he warned, reaching into his back pocket and pulling out a small folded piece of paper.

I nudged him in the leg. "Graham, you're sitting outside of an arena trapped with a hippie weirdo you'll probably never see again. You shouldn't be nervous about sharing it."

"Okay." He cleared his throat, his nerves more intense than they should've been. "I hated my father, and a few nights ago, he passed away. He was my biggest demon, my greatest monster, and my living nightmare. Still, with him gone, everything around me has somehow slowed, and I miss the memories that never existed."

Wow.

His words were few, yet they weighed so much. "That's it?" I asked, goose bumps forming on my arms.

He nodded. "That's it."

"Graham Cracker?" I said softly, turning my body toward him, moving a few inches closer.

"Yes, Lucille?" he replied, turning more toward me.

"Every word you've ever written becomes my new favorite story."

As his lips parted to speak again, the door swung open, breaking us from our stare. I turned to see a security guard holler behind him.

"Found him! This door locks once closed. I'm guessing he got stuck."

"Oh my God, it's about freaking time!" a woman's voice said. The moment she stepped outside to meet us, my eyes narrowed with confusion.

"Jane."

"Lyric?"

Graham and I spoke in unison, staring at my older sister, who I hadn't seen in years—my older sister who was pregnant and wide-eyed as she stared my way.

"Who's Jane?" I asked.

"Who's Lyric?" Graham countered.

Her eyes filled with emotion and she placed her hands over her chest. "What the hell are you doing here, Lucy?" she asked, her voice shaking.

"I brought flowers for the service," I told her.

"You ordered from Monet's Gardens?" Lyric asked Graham.

I was somewhat surprised she knew the name of my shop.

"I ordered from several shops. What does it matter? Wait, how do you two know each other?" Graham asked, still confused.

"Well," I said, my body shaking as I stared at Lyric's stomach, and then into her eyes, which matched Mama's. Her eyes filled with tears as if she'd been caught in the biggest lie, and my lips parted to speak the biggest truth. "She's my sister."

chapter three

Graham

"Your sister?" I asked, repeating Lucy's words as I stared blankly at my wife, who wasn't speaking up at all. "Since when do you have a sister?"

"And since when are you married and pregnant?" Lucy questioned.

"It's a long story," she said softly, placing her hand against her stomach and cringing a bit.

"Graham, it's time to go. My ankles are swollen and I'm exhausted."

Jane's eyes—*Lyric's eyes*—darted to Lucy, whose eyes were still wide with confusion. Their eyes matched in color, but that was the only resemblance they shared. One pair of chocolate eyes was ice cold as always, while the other was soft and filled with warmth.

I couldn't take my stare off Lucy as I searched my mind, trying to understand how someone like her could've been related to someone like my wife.

If Jane had an opposite, it would be Lucy.

"Graham," Jane barked, breaking my stare from the woman with warm eyes. I turned her way and arched an eyebrow. She crossed her arms over her stomach and huffed loudly. "It has been a long day, and it's time to go."

She turned away and started to walk off when Lucy spoke, staring at her sister.

"You kept the biggest parts of you secret from your family. Do you really hate us that much?" Lucy asked, her voice shaking.

Jane's body froze for a moment and she stood up straight, yet didn't turn around. "You are not my family."

With that, she left.

I stood there for a few seconds, uncertain if my feet would allow me to move. As for Lucy, I witnessed her heart break right in front of me. Completely and unapologetically, she began to fall apart. A wave of emotion filled those gentle eyes, and she didn't even try to keep the tears from falling down her cheeks. She allowed her feelings to overtake her fully, not resisting the tears and body shakes. I could almost see it—how she placed the entire world on her shoulders, and how the world was slowly weighing her down. Her body physically bent, making her appear much smaller than she was as the hurt coursed through her. I'd never seen someone feel so freely when it came to emotions, not since…

Stop.

My mind was traveling back to my past, to memories I buried deep within me. I broke my stare away from her, rolled down my sleeves, and tried to block out the noise of the pain she was feeling.

As I moved toward the door—which the security guard was still holding open—I glanced back at the woman who was falling apart and cleared my throat.

"Lucille," I called, straightening my tie. "A bit of advice."

"Yes?" She wrapped her arms around her body and when she looked at me, her smile was gone, replaced by a heavy frown.

"*Feel* less." I breathed out. "Don't allow others to drive your emotions in such a way. Shut it off."

"Shut off my feelings?"

I nodded.

"I can't," she argued, still crying. Her hands fell over her heart, and she shook her head back and forth. "This is who I am. I am the girl who feels everything."

I could tell that was true.

She was the girl who felt everything, and I was the man who felt nothing at all.

"Then the world will do its best to make you nothing," I told her. "The more feelings you give, the more they'll take from you. Trust me. Pull yourself together."

"But…she's my sister, and—"

"She's not your sister."

"What?"

I brushed my hand against the back of my neck before placing my hands into my pockets. "She just said you're not her family, which means she doesn't give a damn about you."

"No." She shook her head, holding the heart-shaped necklace in her hand. "You don't understand. My relationship with my sister is—"

"Nonexistent. If you loved someone, wouldn't you speak their name? I've never once heard of you."

She remained silent, but her emotions slowed down a tad as she wiped away her tears. She shut her eyes, took a deep breath, and began to softly speak to herself. "Air above me, earth below me, fire within me, water surround me, spirit becomes me."

She kept repeating the words, and I narrowed my eyes, confused about who Lucy truly was as a person. She was all over the place: flighty, random, passionate, and emotionally overcharged. It was as if she was fully aware of her faults, and she allowed them to exist regardless. Somehow those faults made her whole.

"Doesn't it tire you?" I asked. "To feel so much?"

"Doesn't it tire you to not feel at all?"

In that moment, I realized I'd come face to face with my polar opposite, and I didn't have a clue what else to say to a stranger as strange as her.

"Goodbye, Lucille," I said.

"Goodbye, Graham Cracker," she replied.

"I didn't lie," Jane swore as we drove back to our home. I hadn't called her a liar, hadn't asked her any questions whatsoever about Lucy or the fact that I hadn't known she existed up until that evening. I hadn't even shown Jane any kind of anger regarding the issue, and still, she kept telling me how she hadn't lied.

Jane.

Lyric?

I didn't have a clue who the woman sitting beside me was, but in reality, had I really known who she was before the sister revelation that evening?

"Your name is Jane," I said, my hands gripped the steering wheel. She nodded. "And your name is Lyric?"

"Yes..." She shook her head. "No, well, it was, but I changed it years ago, before I even met you. When I started applying to colleges, I knew no place would take me seriously with a name like Lyric. What kind of law firm would hire someone named Lyric Daisy Palmer?"

"Daisy," I huffed out. "You've never told me your middle name before."

"You never asked."

"Oh."

She raised an eyebrow. "You're not mad?"

"No."

"Wow." She took a deep breath. "Okay then. If it were the other way around, I would be so—"

"It's not the other way around," I cut in, not feeling like speaking after the longest day of my life.

She shifted around in her seat, but remained quiet.

The rest of the way home, we sat in silence, my head swirling with questions, a big part of me not wanting to know the answers. Jane had a past she didn't speak about, and I had a past of the same kind. There were parts of all lives that were better left in the shadows, and I figured Jane's family was a prime example. There was no reason to go over the details. Yesterday she hadn't had a sister, and today she did.

Though I doubted Lucy would be coming over for Thanksgiving any time soon.

I headed straight into our bedroom and started unbuttoning my shirt. It only took her a couple seconds to follow me into the room with a look of nerves plastered on her face, but she didn't speak a word. We both started undressing, and she moved over to me, quiet, and turned her back to me, silently asking for me to unzip her black gown.

I did as she requested, and she slid the dress off her body before tossing on one of my T-shirts, which she always used as her nightgowns. Her growing stomach stretched them out, but I didn't mind.

Minutes later, we stood in the bathroom, both brushing our teeth, no words exchanged. We brushed, we spat, we rinsed. It was our normal routine; silence was always our friend, and that night hadn't changed anything.

When we climbed into bed, we both shut off the lamps sitting on our nightstands, and we didn't mutter a word, not even to say good night.

As my eyes closed, I tried my best to shut my brain off, but something from that day split my memories open. So, instead of asking Jane about her past, I crawled out of bed and went to my office to lose myself in my novel. I still needed about ninety-five thousand words, so I decided to fall into fiction in order to forget about reality for a while. When my fingers were working, my brain wasn't focused on anything but the words. Words freed me from the confusion my wife had dumped in my lap. Words freed me from remembering my father. Words freed me from falling too deep into my mind where I stored all the pain from my past.

Without writing, my world would be filled with loss.

Without words, I'd be shattered.

"Come to bed, Graham," Jane said, standing in my doorway. It was the second time in one day that she'd interrupted me while I was writing. I hoped it wasn't becoming a common thing.

"I have to finish up my chapter."

"You'll be up for hours, just like the last few days."

"It doesn't matter."

"I have two," she said, crossing her arms. "I have two sisters."

I grimaced and went back to typing. "Let's not do this, Jane."

"Did you kiss her?"

My fingers froze, and my brows lowered as I turned to face her. "What?"

She ran her fingers through her hair, and tears were streaming down her face. She was crying—again. Too many tears from my wife in one day. "I said, did you kiss her?"

"What are you talking about?"

"My question is pretty simple. Just answer it."

"We're not doing this."

"You did, didn't you?" she cried, any kind of rational mindset she'd previously had now long gone. Somewhere between us shutting off our lights and me heading to my office, my wife had turned into an emotional wreck, and now her mind was making up stories crafted completely of fiction. "You kissed her. You kissed my sister!"

My eyes narrowed. "Not now, Jane."

"Not now?"

"Please don't have a hormonal breakdown right now. It's been a long day."

"Just tell me if you kissed my sister," she repeated, sounding like a broken record. "Say it, tell me."

"I didn't even know you *had* a sister."

"That doesn't change the fact that you kissed her."

"Go lie down, Jane. You're going to raise your blood pressure."

"You cheated on me. I always knew this would happen. I always knew you'd cheat on me."

"You're paranoid."

"Just tell me, Graham."

I threaded my fingers through my hair, uncertain of what to do other than telling the truth. "Jesus! I didn't kiss her."

"You did," she cried, wiping away the tears from her eyes. "I know you did, because I know her. I know my sister. She probably knew you were my husband and did it to get back at me. She destroys everything she touches."

"I didn't kiss her."

"She's this—this plague of sickness that no one sees. I see it, though. She's so much like my mother, she ruins everything. Why can't anyone else see what she's doing? I can't believe you'd do that to me—to us. I'm pregnant, Graham!"

"*I didn't kiss her!*" I shouted, my throat burning as the words somersaulted from my tongue. I didn't want to know anything more about Jane's past. I hadn't asked her to tell me about her sisters, I hadn't dug, I hadn't badgered her, but still, we somehow ended up in an argument about a woman I hardly knew. "I have no clue who your sister is, and I don't care to know anything more about her. I don't know what the hell is eating you up in your head, but stop taking it out on me. I didn't lie to you. I didn't cheat on you. I didn't do anything wrong tonight, so stop attacking me on today of all days."

"Stop acting like you care about today," she whispered, her back turned to me. "You didn't even care about your father."

My mind flashed.

Still, with him gone, everything around me has somehow slowed, and I miss the memories that never existed.

"Now's a good time to stop talking," I warned.

She wouldn't.

"It's true, you know. He meant nothing to you. He was a good man, and he meant nothing to you."

I remained quiet.

"Why won't you ask me about my sisters?" she asked. "Why don't you care?"

"We all have a past we don't speak about."

"I didn't lie," she said once again, but I had never called her a liar. It was as if she was trying to convince herself she hadn't lied, when in fact, that was exactly what she'd done. The thing was, I didn't care, because if I'd learned anything from humans, it was that they all lied. I didn't trust a soul.

Once a person broke trust, once a lie was brought to the surface, everything they ever said, true or false, felt as if it was at least partially covered in betrayal.

"Fine. Okay, let's do this. Let's just put it all out there on the table. Everything. I have two sisters, Mari and Lucy."

I cringed. "Stop, please."

"We don't talk. I'm the oldest, and Lucy is the youngest. She's an emotional wreck." It was an ironic statement, seeing as how Jane was currently in the middle of her own breakdown. "And she's the spitting image of my mother, who passed away years ago. My father walked out on us when I was nine, and I couldn't even blame him—my mother was a nutcase."

I slammed my hands down on my desk and flipped around to face her. "What do you want from me, Jane? You want me to say I'm pissed at you for not telling me? Fine, I'm pissed. You want me to be understanding? Fine, I understand. You want me to say you're right for ditching those people? Great, you're right for ditching them. Now can I please get back to work?"

"Tell me about yourself, Graham. Tell me about your past—you know, the one you never talk about."

"Leave it alone, Jane." I was so good at keeping my feelings at bay. I was so good at not getting emotionally involved, but she was pushing me, testing me. I wished she would stop, because when the feelings unleashed from the darkness of my soul, it wasn't sadness or misery that came shooting out.

It was anger.

Anger was creeping up, and she was mentally slamming a sledgehammer against me.

She was forcing me to turn back into the monster she hadn't known she lay beside each night.

"Come on, Graham. Tell me about your childhood. What about your mom? You had to have one of those, right? What happened to her?"

"Stop," I said, shutting my eyes tight, my hands forming fists, but she wouldn't let it go.

"Did she not love you enough? Did she cheat on your father? Did she die?"

I walked out of the room, because I felt it climbing to the surface. I felt my anger getting too big, too much, too overbearing. I tried my best to escape from her, but she followed me through the house.

"Okay, you don't want to talk about your mom. How about we talk about your dad? Tell me why you despise your father so much. What did he do? Did it bother you that he was busy working all the time?"

"You don't want to do this," I warned once more, but she was too far gone. She wanted to play nasty, but she was playing with the wrong person.

"Did he take away your favorite toy? Did he not let you get a pet as a child? Did he forget your birthday?"

My eyes grew heavy, and she noticed it as my stare met hers. "Oh," she whispered. "He missed a lot of birthdays."

"*I kissed her!*" I finally snapped, turning to face my wife, whose jaw was hanging open. "Is that what you want? Is that the lie you want me to tell?!" I hissed. "I swear you're acting like an idiot."

She slammed her hands against me.

Hard.

Each time she hit me, another emotion started coming to the surface. Each time she slammed, a feeling hit my gut.

This time, it was regret.

"I'm sorry," I said on an exhale. "I'm sorry."

"You didn't kiss her?" she asked as her voice shook.

"Of course not."

"It's been a long day and—ow," she whispered as she bent over in pain. "Ouch!"

"What is it?" When my eyes met hers, my chest caved in. Her hands clutched her stomach, and her legs were soaking wet and shaking as she stood in my stretched-out T-shirt. "Jane?" I whispered, nervous and confused. "What just happened?"

"I think my water broke."

chapter four

Graham

"It's too early, it's too early, it's too early," Jane kept whispering to herself as I drove her to the hospital. Her hands rested on her stomach as the contractions kept coming.

"You're fine, everything's okay," I reassured her out loud, but in my mind, I was terrified. *It's too early, it's too early, it's too early…*

Once we made it to the hospital, we were rushed into a room where we were surrounded by nurses and doctors asking questions as they tried to figure out what had happened. Whenever I asked a question, they'd smile and tell me I'd have to wait to speak with the attending neonatologist. Time passed slowly, and each minute felt like an hour. I knew it was too early for the child—she was only at thirty-one weeks. When the neonatologist finally made his way to our room, he had Jane's chart in his grip and a small smile on his face as he pulled up a chair to the side of her bed.

"Hey there, I'm Doctor Lawrence, and I'll be the one you get sick of soon enough." He started flipping through his folder and brushed one of his hands against his hairy chin. "It looks to me like your baby's giving you quite the fight right now, Jane. Being that it's still so early in the pregnancy, we are concerned about the safety of performing a delivery with there still being a good twelve weeks left until you're due."

"Nine," I corrected. "There are only nine weeks left."

Dr. Lawrence's bushy eyebrows lowered as he went flipping through his paperwork. "No, definitely twelve, which brings about some pretty complex issues. I know you've probably been going over all of these questions with the nurses already, but it's important to know what's going on with you and the child. So first, have you been under any kind of stress lately?"

"I'm a lawyer, so that's the definition of my life," she replied.

"Any kind of alcohol or drugs?"

"No and no."

"Smoking?"

She hesitated.

I raised an eyebrow. "Come on, Jane. Seriously?"

"It's only been a few times a week," she argued, stunning me. She turned to the doctor and tried to explain. "I've been under a lot of stress at work. When I found out I was pregnant, I tried to quit, but a few cigarettes a day was better than my half a pack."

"You told me you quit," I said through gritted teeth.

"I tried."

"That's not the same as quitting!"

"You don't get to yell at me!" she bellowed, shaking. "I made a mistake, I'm in a lot of pain, and you yelling at me isn't going to help anything. Jesus, Graham, sometimes I wish you could be more kind like your father."

I felt her words deep in my soul, but I did my best not to react.

Dr. Lawrence grimaced before finding that small smile again. "Okay, smoking can lead to many different complications when it comes to childbirth, and although it's impossible to know the exact cause of it, it's good that we have this information. Seeing as how you're so early and are having contractions, we are going to give you tocolytic medicines to try to stop the premature labor. The baby still has a lot of growing to do, so we'll have to do our best to keep her inside for a bit more. We'll keep you here and monitored for the next forty-eight hours."

"Forty-eight hours? But what about my job…"

"I'll write you a very good doctor's note." Dr. Lawrence winked and stood up to leave. "The nurses will be back in a second to check on you and start the medicine."

As he left, I stood quickly and followed him out of the room. "Dr. Lawrence."

He turned back to me and stepped my way. "Yes?"

I crossed my arms and narrowed my eyes. "We got into a fight, right before her water broke. I yelled and…" I paused and ran a hand through my hair before crossing my arms once more. "I just wanted to know if that was the cause…did I do this?"

Dr. Lawrence smiled out of the left side of his mouth and shook his head. "These things happen. There's no way to know the cause, and beating yourself up isn't going to do anyone any good. All we can do right now is live in the moment and make sure to do what's best for your wife and child."

I nodded and thanked him.

I tried my best to believe his words, but in the back of my mind, I felt as if it was all my fault.

༄

After forty-eight hours and the baby's blood pressure dropping, the doctors informed us that we had no other choice but to deliver the baby via C-section. It was all a blur once it happened, and my heart was lodged in my throat the whole time. I stood in the operating room, uncertain of what to feel once the baby was delivered.

When the doctors finished with the C-section and the umbilical cord was cut, everyone hurried around, shouting at one another.

She wasn't crying.

Why wasn't she crying?

"Two pounds, three ounces," a nurse stated.

"We're gonna need CPAP," another one said.

"CPAP?" I asked as they hurried past me.

"Continuous positive airway pressure, to help her breathe."

"She's not breathing?" I asked another.

"She is, it's just very weak. We're going to transfer her to the NICU, and we'll have someone contact you once she's stable."

Before I could ask anything else, they were rushing the child away.

A few people stayed to take care of Jane, and once she was moved to a hospital room, she spent a few hours resting. When she finally awoke, the doctor filled us in on the health of our daughter. They told us of her struggles, of how they were doing their best to care for her in the NICU, and how her life was still at risk.

"If anything happens to her, know that it was your fault," Jane told me once the doctor left the room. She turned her head away from me, toward the windows. "If she dies, it isn't my fault. It's yours."

∽

"I understand what you're saying, Mr. White, but—" Jane stood in the NICU with her back to me as she spoke on her cell phone. "I know, sir, I completely understand. It's just, my child's been in the NICU, and…" She paused, shifted her feet around, and nodded. "Okay. I understand. Thank you, Mr. White."

She hung up the phone and shook her head back and forth, wiping at her eyes before she turned back toward me.

"Everything all right?" I asked.

"Just work stuff."

I just nodded once.

We stood still, staring down at our daughter, who was struggling with her breathing.

"I can't do this," Jane whispered, her body starting to shake. "I can't just stay here doing nothing. I feel so useless."

The night before, we thought we'd lost our little girl, and in that moment, I felt everything inside me begin to fall apart. Jane wasn't handling it well at all, and she hadn't gotten a minute of sleep.

"It's fine," I said, but I didn't believe it.

She shook her head. "I didn't sign up for this. I didn't sign up for any of this. I never wanted kids. I just wanted to be a lawyer. I had everything I wanted. And now…" Jane kept fidgeting. "She's going to die, Graham," she whispered, her arms crossed. "Her heart isn't strong enough. Her lungs aren't developed. She's hardly even here. She's only existing because of all of this"—she waved at the machines attached to our daughter's tiny body—"this *crap*, and we're just supposed to sit here and watch her die?! It's cruel."

I didn't reply.

"I can't do this. It's been almost two months in this place, Graham. Isn't she supposed to start getting better?"

Her words annoyed me, and her belief that our daughter was already too far gone sickened me. "Maybe you should just go home and shower," I offered. "Take a break. Maybe go to work to help clear your mind."

She shifted in her shoes and grimaced. "Yeah, you're right. I have a lot to catch up on at work. I'll be back in a few hours, okay? Then we can switch, and you can take a break to shower."

I nodded.

She walked over to our daughter and looked down at her. "I haven't told anyone her name yet. It seems silly, right? To tell people her name when she's going to die."

"Don't say that," I snapped at her. "There's still hope."

"Hope?" Jane's eyes filled with confusion. "Since when are you a hopeful man?"

I didn't have an answer, because she was right. I didn't believe in signs, or hope, or anything of that nature. I hadn't known God's name until the day my daughter was born, and I felt too foolish to even offer him a prayer.

I was a realist.

I believed in what I saw, not what I hoped might be, but still, there was a part of me that looked at that small figure and wished I knew how to pray.

It was a selfish need, but I needed my daughter to be okay. I needed her to pull through, because I wasn't certain I'd make it through losing her. The moment she was born, my chest ached. My heart somewhat awakened after years of being asleep, and when it awakened it felt nothing but pain. Pain of knowing my daughter could die. Pain of not knowing how many days, hours, or minutes were left with her. Therefore, I needed her to survive so the aching of my soul would disappear.

It was much easier to exist when it was shut off.

How had she done that? How had she turned it back on merely by being born?

I hadn't even spoken her name...

What kind of monsters were we?

"Just go, Jane," I said, my voice cold. "I'll stay here."

She left without another word, and I sat in the chair beside our daughter, whose name I, too, was too nervous to speak out loud.

I waited hours before trying to call Jane. I knew at times she'd get so wrapped up in her work, she'd forget to step away from her office, the same way I did when I was wrapped in my writing.

There wasn't an answer on her cell phone. I called again for the next five hours with no reply, so I went ahead and called her office's front desk. When I spoke to Heather, the receptionist, I felt gutted.

"Hi, Mr. Russell. I'm sorry, but, um…she was actually let go earlier this morning. She's missed so much, and Mr. White let her go…I figured you would know." Her voice lowered. "How is everything going? With the baby?"

I hung up.

Confused.

Angered.

Tired.

I tried Jane's cell phone again, and it went straight to voicemail.

"Do you need a break?" one of the nurses asked me, coming to check on my daughter's feeding tube. "You look exhausted. You can go home and rest for a bit. We'll call you if—"

"I'm fine," I said, cutting her off.

She started to speak again, but my stern look made her shut her lips. She finished up checking all the stats, and then she gave me a small smile on her way out.

I sat with my daughter, listening to the beeping machines working, waiting for my wife to come back to us. As hours went by, I allowed myself to go home for a shower and to grab my laptop so I could write at the hospital.

I made it quick, jumping into the steaming water, letting it hit me and burn my skin. Then I got dressed and hurried to my office to grab my computer and some paperwork. That was when I noticed it—the folded piece of paper sitting on my keyboard.

Graham,

I should've stopped reading there. I knew nothing good could come from her next words. I knew nothing good ever came from an unexpected letter written in black ink.

I can't do this. I can't stay and watch her die. I lost my job today, the thing I worked hardest for, and I feel as if I lost a part of my heart. I can't sit and watch another part of me fade away, too. It's all too much. I'm sorry. -Jane

I stared at the paper, rereading her words multiple times before folding the paper and placing it in my back pocket.

I felt her words deep in my soul, but I did my best not to react.

chapter five

Lucy

"I COMPLETELY BLANKED," THE STRANGER TOLD ME, HIS VOICE SHAKY. "I MEAN, we were both swamped with exams, and I'm just trying to keep my head above water, and I totally forgot about our anniversary. It was a given that she hadn't when she showed up with my gifts and dressed for the dinner date I forgot to book."

I gave the guy a smile and nodded as he told me the full saga of why his girlfriend was currently pissed off at him.

"And it doesn't help that I missed her birthday too, seeing as how I'd just gotten rejected from med school the week before. That put me in a big funk, but, man. Okay, yeah, sorry—I'll just get these flowers."

"Will that be all?" I asked, ringing up the dozen red roses the guy had picked out as an attempt to apologize to his girlfriend for forgetting the only two dates he really had to remember.

"Yeah, do you think it's enough?" he asked nervously. "I just really messed up, and I'm not sure how to even start apologizing."

"Flowers are a good start," I told him. "And words help, too. Then, I think your actions will speak the loudest."

He thanked me as he paid and walked out of the shop.

"I give them two weeks before they break up," Mari said with a smirk on her lips as she trimmed a few tulips.

"Ms. Optimist." I laughed. "He's trying."

"He's asking a stranger for advice on his relationship. He's failing," she replied, shaking her head. "I just don't get it. Why do guys find the need to apologize *after* they screw up? If they could just *not* screw up, there wouldn't be anything to apologize for. It's not that hard to just…be good."

I gave her a tight smile, watching her cut the flower stems aggressively while her eyes filled with emotion. She wouldn't admit to the fact that she was currently taking her pain out on the beautiful plants, but it was clear that she was.

"Are you…okay?" I asked as she picked up a handful of daisies and shoved them into the vase.

"I'm fine. I just don't understand how that guy could be so insensitive, you know? Why in the world would he ask you for advice?!"

"Mari."

"What?"

"Your nose is flaring and you're waving scissors around like a madwoman because a guy bought his girlfriend flowers for forgetting their anniversary. Are you really upset about that or does it have something to do with today's date? Seeing as how it would've been your—"

"Seven-year anniversary?" She chopped up two roses into tiny pieces. "Oh? Is that today? I hardly noticed."

"Mari, back away from the scissors."

She looked up at me, and then down at the roses. "Oh no, am I having one of those mental breakdown moments?" she asked as I walked over and slowly removed the scissors from her grip.

"No, you're having one of those human moments. It's fine, really. You're allowed to be angry and sad for as long as you need to. Remember? Maktub. It just becomes an issue when we start destroying our own things over asshole men, especially flowers."

"Ugh, you're right, I'm sorry." She groaned, placing her head in the palms of her hands. "Why do I still care? It's been years."

"Time doesn't just shut off your feelings, Mari. It's fine, but it's also fine that I booked you and me a date for tonight."

"Seriously?"

I nodded. "It involves margaritas and tacos."

She perked up a bit. "And queso dip?"

"Oh yeah. All the queso dip."

She stood up and wrapped me in a tight hug. "Thank you, Pea, for always being there for me even when I don't say I need you."

"Always, Pod. Let me go grab a broom to clean up your anger management mess." I hurried into the back room and heard the bell ring at the front of the store, announcing a customer's arrival.

"Hi, uh, I'm looking for Lucille?" a deep voice said, making my ears perk up.

"Oh, she just went in the back," Mari replied. "She'll be out in a—"

I hurried out to the front of the shop and stood there, staring at Graham. He looked different without his suit and tie, but still, somewhat the same. He wore dark blue jeans and a black T-shirt that hugged his body, and that same cold stare lived in his eyes.

"Hi," I said breathlessly, crossing my arms and walking farther into the room. "How can I help you?"

He was fidgeting with his hands, and whenever we made eye contact, he looked away. "I was just wondering, have you seen Jane lately?" He cringed a bit and cleared his throat. "I mean, Lyric. I mean, your sister. Have you seen your sister lately?"

"You're Graham Cracker?" Mari said, standing up from her chair.

"Graham," he said sternly. "My name is Graham."

"I haven't seen her since the funeral," I told him.

He nodded, a spark of disappointment making his shoulders round forward. "All right, well, if you do..." He sighed. "Never mind." He turned to leave, and I called after him.

"Is everything okay? With Lyric?" I paused. "Jane." My chest tightened as the worst possibilities shot through my mind. "Is she okay? Is it the baby? Is everything all right?"

"Yes and no. She delivered the baby almost two months ago, a girl. She was premature and has been at St. Joseph's ever since."

"Oh my gosh," Mari muttered, placing her hand over her heart. "Are they doing better?"

"We..." He started to answer, but the way his words faded showed his doubt, the same way his heavy eyes displayed his fears. "That's not why I'm here. I'm here because Jane is missing."

"Huh?" My mind was racing with all the information he was giving me. "Missing?"

"She left yesterday around twelve in the afternoon, and I haven't heard from her since. She was fired from her job, and I don't know where she is or if she's okay. I just thought perhaps you'd heard from her."

"I haven't." I turned to Mari. "Have you heard from Lyric?"

She shook her head.

"It's fine. Sorry I stopped by. I didn't mean to bother you."

"You're not a—" Before I could finish my sentence, he was out the door. "Bother," I murmured.

"I'm gonna try to call her," Mari said, racing to her cell phone, her heart probably racing at the same speed as mine. "Where are you going?" she asked as I headed for the front door.

I didn't have time to reply as I left in the same hurry Graham had.

"Graham!" I called, just seconds before he stepped into his black Audi. He looked up at me, almost as if he was confused by my entire existence.

"What?"

"I...what—you can't just barge into my shop, drop all of this information, and then rush off. What can I do? How can I help?"

His brows lowered and he shook his head. "You can't." Then he climbed into his car and drove off, leaving me baffled.

My sister was missing and I had a niece fighting for her life, and there was nothing I could do to help?

I found that hard to believe.

"I'm going to go to the hospital," I told Mari as I stepped back inside the building. "To check in on everything."

"I'll come too," she offered, but I told her it was best if she kept the shop up and running. There was too much to do, and if both of us left, we would fall too far behind on everything.

"Also, keep trying to get a hold of Lyric. If she's going to answer for one of us, it would be you."

"Okay. Promise to call me if anything goes wrong and you need me," she told me.

"Promise."

∽

When I walked into the NICU, I noticed Graham's back first. He was sitting in a chair, hunched over, his eyes glued to the small crib that held his daughter. "Graham," I whispered, making him look up. When he turned to see me, he looked hopeful, almost as if he thought I was Jane. The flash of hope disappeared as he stood up and stepped closer to his daughter.

"You didn't have to come here," he told me.

"I know. I just thought I should make sure everything was okay."

"I don't need the company," he said as I stepped in closer. The closer I got, the more he tensed up.

"It's okay if you're sad, or scared..." I whispered, staring at the little girl's tiny lungs working so hard to breathe. "You don't have to be strong at all times," I said.

"Will my weakness save her?" he snapped.

"No, but—"

"Then I won't waste my time."

I shifted around in my shoes. "Have you heard from my sister?"

"No."

"She'll be back," I said, hoping I wasn't a liar.

"She left me a note that said otherwise."

"Seriously? That's..." My words faded away before I could say it was shocking. In a way, it wasn't. My oldest sister had always been a bit of a runner, like our father. I shifted the conversation. "What's her name?" I asked, looking down at the tiny girl.

"There's no point in telling people if she's going to..." His voice cracked. His hands formed fists, and he shut his eyes. When he reopened them, something about his cold stare shifted. For a split second, he allowed himself to feel as he watched his child trying her best to live. He lowered his head and whispered, "If she's going to die."

"She's still here, Graham," I promised, nodding her way. "She's still here, and she's beautiful."

"But for how long? I'm just being a realist."

"Well, lucky for you, I'm a hope-ist."

His hands were clenched so hard, forcing his skin to turn red. "I don't want you here," he told me, turning my way. For a moment, I considered how disrespectful I was, staying when I wasn't welcome.

But then I noticed his shaking.

It was a small tremble in his body as he stared at his daughter, as he stared at the unknown. It was right then that I knew I couldn't leave him.

I reached out and unwrapped his fists, taking his hand into my hold. I knew the child was fighting a hard battle, and I could tell Graham was also at war. As I held his hand, I noticed a small breath release from between his lips.

He swallowed hard and dropped my hand a few seconds later, but it seemed to be enough to make him stop shaking. "Talon," he whispered, his voice low and frightened, almost as if he thought telling me her name meant kissing his child with a death wish.

"Talon," I repeated softly, a small smile spreading across my lips. "Welcome to the world, Talon."

Then, for the first time in my presence, Talon Russell opened her eyes.

chapter six

Graham

"Are you sure you're okay?" Lucy asked, unaware she'd overstayed her welcome at the hospital. She'd been to the hospital every day for the past two weeks, checking in on Talon, checking in on me. As each day passed, I grew more and more irritated by her persistence in showing up. I didn't want her there, and it was clear that my stopping at the floral shop in search of Jane had been a bad idea.

The worst part of it all? Lucy never shut up.

She wasn't one to ever stop talking. It was as if every thought she ever had needed to pass through her lips. What was worse was how each word was filled with positive hippie mumbo jumbo. The only things missing from her speeches were a joint, rock crystals, and a yoga mat.

"I can stay, if you need me to," she offered once more. Talon was getting her feeding tube taken out and the doctors felt confident she'd be able to start eating on her own, which was a step in the right direction after months of uncertainty.

"Really, Graham. It's no problem for me to stay a few more hours."

"No. Go."

She nodded and finally stood up. "Okay. I'll come back tomorrow."

"Don't."

"Graham, you don't have to do this alone," she insisted. "I can stay here and help if—"

"Don't you see?" I snapped. "You're not wanted. Go bother someone else with your pity."

Her lips parted, and she took a few steps backward. "I don't pity you."

"Then you must pity yourself for not having a life of your own," I muttered, not making eye contact with her yet still seeing the pained look on her face out of the corner of my eye.

"There are moments when I see you, you know—when I see how hurt you are, when I see your pain and worry, but then you go ahead and cancel it out with your rudeness."

"Stop acting like you know me," I told her.

"Stop acting like you're heartless," she replied. She went digging into her purse and pulled out a pen and paper then scribbled down her phone number. "Here, take this, in case you need me or you change your mind. I used to be a nanny, and I could give you a hand if you need it."

"Why don't you get it? I don't need anything from you."

"You think this is about you?" She snickered, shaking her head as she wrapped her fingers around her heart-shaped necklace. "It seems your egotistic ways are getting in the way of you realizing the truth of the matter. I'm not here for you. I hardly know you. The last thing my mother asked from me was to look after my sisters, and seeing as how Lyric is missing in action, I find it important for me to look after her daughter."

"Talon is not your responsibility," I argued.

"Maybe not," she said. "But like it or not, she is my family, so please don't let your pride and misplaced anger keep you from reaching out if you need me."

"I won't need you. I don't need anyone," I barked at her, feeling annoyed by her giving personality. How ridiculous it was for her to give so much of herself so freely.

Her eyes narrowed and she tilted her head, studying me. I hated the way she stared at me. I hated how when our eyes locked, she stared as if she saw a part of my soul that I hadn't even discovered. "Who hurt you?" she whispered.

"What?"

She stepped in closer to me, unfolded my clenched hand, and placed her number in my grasp. "Who hurt you so bad and made you so cold?"

When she left, my eyes followed her, but she didn't once look back.

Three weeks passed before the doctors and nurses informed me it was time for Talon and me to go home. It took me over two hours to make sure the car seat was installed properly, along with having five different nurses check to make sure it was securely fastened.

I'd never driven so slowly in my life, and every time I turned to check on Talon, she was sleeping peacefully.

I'm going to fuck this up.

I knew I would. I knew nothing about being a father. I knew nothing about taking care of a child. Jane would've been great at it. Sure, she never wanted children, but she was a perfectionist. She would've taught herself to become the best mother in the world. She would've been the better option when it came to one of us caring for Talon.

My having her felt like a cruel mistake.

"Shh," I tried to soothe her as I carried the car seat into the house. She'd started crying the moment I took her out of the car, and my gut was tightened with nerves.

Is she hungry? Does she need a diaper change? Is she too hot? Too cold? Did she just miss an inhale? Are her lungs strong enough? Will she even make it through the night?

Once Talon was in her crib, I sat on the floor beside it. Any time she moved, I was up on my feet, checking on her. Any time she didn't shift, I was up on my feet, checking on her.

I'm going to fuck this up.

The doctors were wrong. I knew they were. They shouldn't have sent her home yet. She wasn't ready. I wasn't ready. She was too small, and my hands were too big.

I'd hurt her.

I'd make a mistake that would cost Talon her life.

I can't do this.

Pulling out my cell phone, I made a call to the number I'd been calling for weeks. "Jane, it's me, Graham. I just wanted to let you know…Talon's home. She's okay. She's not going to die, Jane, and I just wanted to let you know that. You can come home now." My grip on the phone was tight, my voice stern. "Come home. Please. I can't…I can't do this without you. I can't do this alone."

It was the same message I'd left her multiple times since the moment the doctors told me Talon was going to be discharged. But still, Jane never came back.

That night was the hardest night of my life.

Every time Talon started screaming, I couldn't get her to stop. Every time I picked her up, I was terrified I'd break her. Every time I fed her and she wouldn't eat, I worried about her health. The pressure was too much. How could someone so small rely on me as her life support?

How was a monster supposed to raise a child?

Lucy's question from the last time I saw her played over and over again in my head.

Who hurt me so bad and made me so cold?

The 'who' part was easy.

It was the reason that was blurred.

chapter seven

Eleventh Birthday

THE BOY STOOD STILL IN THE DARKENED HALLWAY, UNSURE IF HIS FATHER WANTED HIM TO be noticed. He'd been home alone for some time that night, and felt safer when he was the only one there. The young boy was certain his father would come home intoxicated, because that was what the past had taught him. What he wasn't certain of was which drunken version would walk through the front door this time.

Sometimes his father was playful, other times, extremely cruel.

His father would come home so cruel that the boy would oftentimes close his eyes at night and convince himself that he'd made up the actions of the drunken man, telling himself his father would never be so cold. He'd tell himself no person could hate his own flesh and blood so much—even with the aid of alcohol.

Yet the truth of the matter was, sometimes the ones we loved most were the monsters that tucked us in at night.

"Come here, son," the grown man called, making the boy stand up taller. He hurried himself into the living room where he spotted his father sitting with a woman. The father grinned as the woman's hands rested in his hold. "This," he said, his eyes light, practically shining, "is Rebecca."

The woman was beautiful with chocolate hair that fell against her shoulders and a slender nose that fit perfectly between her brown doe eyes. Her lips were full and painted red, and when she smiled, she kind of reminded the boy of his mother.

"Hello there," Rebecca said softly, her voice brimming with kindness and misplaced trust. She extended her hand toward the boy. "It's wonderful to finally meet you."

The boy stayed at a distance, uncertain of what he should say or feel.

"Well," his father scolded. "Shake her hand. Say hello, son."

"Hello," the boy said in a whisper, as if he was worried he was walking into his father's trap.

"Rebecca is going to be my new wife, your new mother."

"I have a mother," the boy barked, his voice louder than he meant it to be. He cleared his throat and returned to his whispering sounds. "I have a mom."

"No," his father corrected. "She left us."

"She left you," the boy argued. "Because you're a drunk!" He knew he shouldn't have said it, but he also knew how much his heart hurt thinking that his mother would walk out on him, leaving him with the monster. His mother loved him—he was certain of that. One day she just got too scared, and that fear had driven her away.

He often wondered if she realized she'd left him behind.

He often prayed she'd come back some day.

His father sat up straighter, and his hands formed fists. As he was about to snap at his loud-mouthed son, Rebecca placed her hand on his shoulder, soothing him. "It's okay. This is a new situation for all of us," she said, moving her hands to rub his back. "I'm not here to replace your mom. I know she meant a lot to you, and I'd never want to take her place. But, I am hoping that someday, you'll somehow find a place for me in your heart, too, because that's the thing about hearts—when you think they're completely full, you somehow find room to add a little more love."

The boy remained silent, unsure what he should say. He could still see the anger in his father's eyes, but something about Rebecca's touch kept him calm. She seemed to be the beauty that somehow tamed the beast.

For that reason alone, the boy secretly hoped she'd stay the night, and perhaps the morning, too.

"Now, on to the fun things," Rebecca said, standing up and walking over to the dining room table. She came back with a cupcake in her hand, and it bore a yellow and green striped candle. "Rumor has it that it's your eleventh birthday. Is that true?"

The boy nodded warily.

How had she known?

His own father hadn't even mentioned it all day.

"Then you must make a wish." Rebecca smiled big, like his mother used to do. She reached into her purse, pulled out a lighter, and flicked on the flame. The boy watched as the candle wick began to burn, the wax slowly dripping down the sides of the candle, melting into the frosting. "Go ahead, blow out the candle and make your wish."

He did as she said, and she smiled even wider than before.

The young boy made a mistake that night, and he didn't even notice. It happened so quickly, between the moment he opened his mouth to blow out the candle and the moment when the flame dissipated.

In that split second, in that tiny space of time, he accidentally opened his heart and let her in.

The last woman to remember his birthday was his mother, and how he loved her so.

She reminded him so much of his mother, from her kind smile and misplaced trust, her painted lips and doe eyes to her willingness to love.

Rebecca wasn't wrong about hearts and love. Hearts were always welcoming to new love, but when that love settled in, heartbreak sometimes began to creep in the shadows as well.

In the shadows, heartbreak poisoned the love, twisting it into something darker, heavier, uglier. Heartbreak took love and mutilated it, humiliated it, scarred it. Heartbreak slowly began to freeze heartbeats that had once been so welcoming to love.

"Happy birthday," Rebecca said, taking a swipe of frosting from his cupcake with her finger and placing it in her mouth. "I hope all of your wishes come true."

chapter eight

Lucy

It was the middle of the night when my cell phone started ringing. I rolled over in my bed in search of Richard, but he wasn't there. I glanced toward the hallway, where a light shined and light jazz music was playing, which meant he was up working on his artwork. My phone kept ringing, and I rubbed my eyes as I went to answer. "Hello?" I yawned, trying my best to keep my eyes open. The shades were drawn in my room and no sunlight was peeking in, clearly indicating that it was far from morning.

"Lucille, it's Graham. Did I wake you?" he asked, his voice shaky.

I heard a crying baby in the background as I sat up in my bed and yawned once more. "No, I'm always awake at three in the morning." I chuckled. "What is it? What's wrong?"

"Talon came home today."

"That's great."

"No," he replied, his voice cracking. "She won't stop crying. She won't eat. When she's asleep, I think she's dead, so I check her heartbeat, which in turns wakes her and leads to the crying again. When I put her in the crib, she screams even louder than when she's in my arms. I need…I—"

"What's your address?"

"You don't have—"

"Graham, address, now."

He complied and gave me directions to his house in River Hills, which told me at least one thing: he lived a comfortable life.

I got dressed fast, tossed my messy curly hair into an even messier bun, and hurried into the living room where I saw Richard sitting. He was intensely staring at one of his charcoal drawings.

"Still working?" I asked.

His eyes darted to me, and he raised a brow. "Where are you going?" His face was different, his full beard shaven, leaving only his mustache.

"You have no beard," I commented. "And…a mustache."

"Yeah, I needed inspiration, and I knew shaving my face would bring about some kind of expression. You like it?"

"It's…" I wiggled my nose. "Artistic?"

"Which is exactly what this artist strives for. So wait, where are you going?"

"Graham just called me. He brought Talon home from the hospital and is having a lot of trouble with her."

"It's…" Richard glanced at his watch with narrowed eyes. He'd lost his glasses somewhere in the mess of his creation, I was certain. "Three in the morning."

"I know." I walked over to him and kissed him on the top of his head. "Which is exactly why you should get some sleep."

He waved me off. "People who get showcases at museums don't sleep, Lucy. They create."

I laughed, walking to the front door. "Well, try to create with your eyes shut for a bit. I'll be back soon."

As I pulled into Graham's driveway, I was stunned by the size of his house. Of course, all the mansions in River Hills were stunning, but his was hauntingly breathtaking. Graham's property was much like his personality—secluded from the rest of the world. The front of the house was surrounded by trees, while the backyard had a bit of open land to it. There were pebbled pathways that marked the areas that were supposed to be made into gardens, but the wild grass just grew high in those areas. It would've been great for a beautiful garden. I could envision the types of unique flowers and vines that could exist in the space. Behind the patch of field were more trees that traveled far back.

The sun hadn't risen yet and his house was dark, but still so beautiful. In front of his porch sat two huge lion statues, and on his rooftop were three gargoyles.

I walked up to his door carrying two cups of coffee, and right as I was about to ring the doorbell, Graham was already there, rushing me inside.

"She won't stop screaming," he said, not greeting me, just hurrying me into the house with the crying baby. The house was pitch-black, except for a lamp that sat on the living room table. The draping on all the windows was heavy red velvet, making the home feel even darker. He led me to Talon's room, where the tiny girl was lying in her crib, her face red as day as she hollered.

"She doesn't have a temperature, and I laid her on her back, because you know…" He shrugged. "I read up a lot about SIDS, and I know she's not able to roll, but what if she does by mistake? And she's not eating much. I'm not sure what to do, so I was going to try kangaroo care."

I almost laughed at his nerves, except there was the issue that Talon was in distress. I looked around the room, noting that the little girl's bedroom was two times the size of my own. Scattered across the floor were dozens of parenting books opened to certain pages, with other pages folded down so he could return to them at a later time.

"What's kangaroo care?" I asked.

When I looked up from the books, I noticed a shirtless Graham standing before me. My eyes danced across his toned chest and caramel skin before

I forced myself to stop gawking at him. For an author, he was unnervingly good-looking and fit. A tattoo traveled up his left arm, wrapping around to the back of his shoulder blade, and his arms appeared as if his biceps had their own biceps, who had then given birth to their own biceps.

For a moment, I considered if he truly was an author and not Dwayne Johnson.

After he took off Talon's onesie, leaving her in only a diaper, he reached into the crib, lifted the crying baby into his muscular arms, and started swaying back and forth as her ear lay against his chest, over his heart.

"It's when the parent and the child have skin-to-skin contact to form a bond. It works best for mothers, I believe, though the nurses told me I should try it, which seems pointless," he grumbled as the crying continued. He held her as if she was a football and swayed frantically, almost as if he was falling apart from not being able to calm her.

"Maybe we should try feeding her again," I offered. "Do you want me to make a bottle?"

"No." He shook his head. "You wouldn't know how warm it would have to be."

I smiled, unbothered by his lack of faith in me. "That's fine. Here, hand her over and you can go make the bottle." His brows furrowed and doubt crept into his frown, deepening it. I sat down in the gray gliding chair in the corner and held my arms out. "I promise to not let her go."

"You have to protect her head," he told me as he slowly—*very slowly*—placed Talon in my arms. "And don't move until I'm back."

I laughed. "You have my word, Graham."

Before he left the room, he glanced back at me, as if he expected the baby to be on the floor or something ridiculous. I couldn't fault him for his fears, though; it seemed Graham had a hard time when it came to trust, especially after my sister walked out on him.

"Hello, beautiful," I said to Talon, gliding her in the chair, holding her close to me. She was beautiful, a work of art almost. A few weeks ago she had been a tiny peanut, and since the last time I saw her, she had gained five pounds. She was a survivor, a beacon of hope. The more I glided in the chair, the more she seemed to calm down. By the time Graham returned to the room, she was sleeping peacefully in my arms.

He cocked an eyebrow. "How did you do that?"

I shrugged. "I guess she just really loves this chair."

He grimaced and reached for Talon, taking her from my hold and placing her sleeping self into the crib. "Leave."

"What?" I asked, confused. "I'm sorry, did I do something wrong? I thought you wanted—"

"You can go now, Lucille. Your services are no longer needed."

"My services?" I remarked, stunned by his coldness. "I just came to help. You called me."

"Now I'm uncalling you. Goodbye."

He hurried me to the front door and ushered me out without another word. Not even a thank you was mentioned before he slammed the door in my face.

"Don't forget to drink the coffee I brought you that's sitting on the counter!" I hollered, banging on his door. "It's black—ya know, like your soul."

※

"He called you over at three in the morning?" Mari asked, unlocking the shop the next morning. We were closed on Sundays, but we went in to prep for the following week ahead. "Granted, I was happy when you didn't come to wake me at five in the morning for hot yoga, but I was wondering where you were. How's the baby?"

"Good, she's doing well." I smiled as I thought about her. "She's perfect."

"And he's…handling it all by himself?"

"The best he can," I said, walking inside. "He's struggling, I think. Him calling me was a big deal, I could tell."

"That's so weird that he'd call you. He hardly knows you."

"I don't think he has family of his own. I think his father was the last family he had. Plus, I gave him my number in case he needed the help."

"And then he kicked you out?"

"Yup."

Mari rolled her eyes. "That totally seems like a stable living arrangement for a child. I could tell when he came into the shop that he had an edge to him."

"He's definitely rough around the edges, but I think he really wants to do right by Talon. He was forced into a situation and thought he'd have a partner to help him, but now he's doing it all on his own."

"I couldn't imagine," my sister said. "I can't believe Lyric just left him. You'd think she'd be more thoughtful after she saw what went on with Parker and me."

"She abandoned her newborn baby in the hospital, Mari. Any thoughtfulness we thought Lyric possessed went straight out the window and is now void." It was crazy how you could know a person your whole life and then realize you knew nothing about them at all.

Time was a curse, the way it slowly morphed relationships into foreign affairs.

Mari shook her head. "What a mess. But, on a brighter note, I have a surprise for you."

"Is it a green smoothie?"

She cocked an eyebrow. "I said a surprise, not a disgusting ground-up plant.

We are officially hiring an additional florist! I'm interviewing a few people over these next few weeks."

Since opening our floral shop, we'd always talked about hiring on more staff, but we hadn't had enough profit to actually do it. So, the fact that we were now at that stage where we could afford to bring on more staff was exciting. There was nothing more exhilarating than watching your dream grow.

As I went to reply, the bell over the front door rang, making us both look up. "Sorry, we're not actually open tod—" I couldn't even finish my sentence when I saw who was standing there with a bouquet of roses.

"Parker," Mari said as she breathed out, her strength dissipating as his name rolled off her tongue. Her body physically reacted to him as her shoulders drooped and her knees buckled. "Wh-What are you do-doing here?" Her voice trembled, and I wished it hadn't. It gave away the effect he had on her—the effect he obviously wanted to have.

"I, um…" He chuckled nervously and looked down at the flowers. "I guess it's a little stupid to bring flowers to a flower shop, huh?"

"What are you doing here, Parker?" I said, my voice much more stern than my sister's. I crossed my arms and didn't look away from him for a second.

"It's good to see you too, Lucy," he remarked. "I was hoping to speak to my wife for a minute."

"You don't have a wife anymore," I told him. Every step he took toward Mari, I interfered. "You lost her when you packed your bags and left all those years ago."

"Okay, okay, fair enough. I deserve that," he replied. Mari murmured something under her breath, making Parker arch an eyebrow. "What did you say?"

"I said you don't deserve shit!" Mari barked out, her voice still shaky, but louder now. Mari wasn't one to ever curse, so when the last word flew off her tongue, I knew he had her really shaken up.

"Mari," Parker started. She turned her back to him, but he kept talking. "It would've been seven years a few weeks ago."

She didn't turn to face him, but I saw her body react.

Stay strong, sister.

"I know I screwed up. I know it seems like a real shitty thing to do to show up here after all this time with some crap flowers, but I miss you."

Her body reacted more.

"I miss us. I'm an idiot, okay? I made a lot of shitty mistakes. I'm not asking you to take me back today, Mari. I'm not asking you to fall in love with me. I'm just a boy, standing in front of a girl, asking her to get coffee with me."

"Oh my gosh," I groaned.

"What?" Parker asked, offended by my annoyance.

"You stole that line from *Notting Hill!*"

"Not exactly! Julia Roberts asked Hugh Grant to love her. I just asked for a cup of coffee," Parker explained.

I couldn't roll my eyes hard enough. "Whatever. Leave."

"No offense, Lucy, but I didn't come here for you. I came for Mari, and she hasn't told me to—"

"Leave," Mari said, her voice rediscovering its strength as she turned back to face him. She stood tall, like a strong oak tree.

"Mari..." He stepped closer to her, and she held up a hand to halt him.

"I said go, Parker. I have nothing to say, and I want nothing to do with you. Now just leave."

He hesitated for second before he placed the flowers down on the counter and left.

The moment the door shut, Mari released the breath she'd been holding, and I hurried to the back room.

"What are you doing?" she called after me.

"Getting the sage stick," I hollered back. When we were kids, Mama kept a sage stick in our house that she'd burn whenever there was an argument of any kind. She always said fights brought bad energy to a space, and it was best to clear it out right away. "There's nothing good about Parker's energy, and I refuse to let his negativity seep into our lives again. Not today, Satan." I lit the sage and walked through the shop, waving it.

"Speaking of Satan," Mari mentioned, picking up my cell phone when it started ringing.

I reached over for it, and Graham's name flashed across the screen.

Warily, I answered, passing the sage stick to my sister. "Hello?"

"The chair doesn't work."

"What?"

"I said the chair doesn't work. You told me she liked the gliding chair, and that's how you got her to sleep, but it's not working. I've been trying all morning, and she won't sleep. She's hardly eating and..." His words dropped off for a moment before he softly spoke again. "Come back."

"Excuse me?" I leaned against the counter, flabbergasted. "You shoved me out of your house."

"I know."

"That's all you can say? That you know?"

"Listen, if you don't want to come help, fine. I don't need you."

"Yes, you do. That's why you're calling." I bit my bottom lip and closed my eyes. "I'll be there in twenty minutes."

"Okay."

Again, not a thank you.

"Lucille?"

"Yes?"

"Make it fifteen."

chapter nine

Graham

Lucy pulled up to my house in her beat-up burgundy car, and I opened the door before she even climbed out of her vehicle. I held Talon in my arms, rocking her as she cried from discomfort.

"That was twenty-five minutes," I scolded her.

She just smiled. She was always smiling.

She had a smile that reminded me of my past, a beautiful smile filled with hope.

Hope was the weak man's remedy to life's issues.

I only knew that was true from the past I'd lived.

"I like to call it fashionably late."

The closer she got, the tenser I became. "Why do you smell like weed?"

She laughed. "It's not weed, it's sage. I was burning it."

"Why were you burning sage?"

A sly grin found her and she shrugged. "To fight off negative energy like yours."

"Oh right, hippie weirdo. I bet you travel with crystals and stones with you, too."

With no effort at all, she reached into her over-the-shoulder purse and pulled out a handful of crystals.

Because *of course* she did.

"Here." She reached out, took Talon from my hands, and began rocking her. "You need rest. I'll watch her." The guilt I had from the fact that Talon so effortlessly seemed to calm down when she was in Lucy's arms was strong.

"I can't sleep," I told her.

"No, you can. You're choosing not to because you're paranoid that something might happen to your daughter, which is a very reasonable reaction that I'm sure a lot of new parents go through. But, you're not alone right now, Graham. I'm here."

I hesitated, and she slightly nudged me in the shoulder. "Go. I can do this."

"You said you've nannied before, right?"

"Yes, a set of twins and their little brother. I was there from the first week up until they went off to school. Graham, I promise you, Talon's okay."

"Okay." I brushed my hand over my hairy chin and started in the direction of my bedroom. A shower sounded nice. I couldn't remember the last time I'd showered—or eaten. *When was my last meal? Do I even have food in my fridge? Is my fridge even still running?*

Bills.

Did I pay my bills? My phone hasn't been shut off yet, which is a good sign, because I have to call Talon's pediatrician in the morning.

Doctor.

Doctor's appointment—I have to set up doctor's appointments.

Nanny? I need to interview nannies.

"Shut up," Lucy barked at me.

"I didn't say anything."

"No, but your mind is spinning with everything you could be doing instead of sleeping. Before you can be productive, you gotta rest, and, Graham?"

I turned to see her kind eyes staring my way. "Yes?"

"You're doing everything right, you know, with your daughter."

I cleared my throat and stuffed my hands into my jeans pockets. *Laundry—when was the last time I did laundry?* "She cries all the time. She's not happy with me."

Lucy laughed, the kind of laugh where she tossed her head backward and her smile stretched so far. She laughed too loud, and at the wrong times. "Babies cry, Graham. It's normal. This is all new for both of you. It's a brand-new world, and you both are doing the best you can to adjust."

"She doesn't cry with you."

"Trust me." Lucy grinned, looking down at the somewhat calm Talon in her hold. "Give her a few minutes and I'll be begging for you to switch spots with me, so go. Go rest for a bit before I hand her back over."

I nodded, and before I left, I cleared my throat once more. "I apologize."

"For?"

"The way I pushed you away this morning. It was rude, and for that I'm sorry."

Her head tilted and she stared at me with questioning eyes. "Why do I feel like there are a million words floating around in your mind, but you only allow a certain number to escape?"

I didn't reply.

As I stared at her rocking my daughter who was growing more and more upset, Lucy smiled and winked my way. "See? Told you. She's just being a baby. I'll take care of her for a while. You go ahead and take care of yourself."

I thanked her in my mind, and she smiled as if she heard me.

༺♡༻

The moment my head hit the pillow, I was fast asleep. I hadn't known I was so tired until I truly had a moment to rest. It was as if my body melted into my mattress and sleep swallowed me whole. No nightmares or dreams found me, and for that, I was thankful.

It wasn't until I heard Talon screaming that I tossed and turned in my bed.

"Jane, can you get her?" I whispered, half asleep. Then my eyes opened and I glanced at the other side of my bed—it was still completely made, no wrinkles in the sheets. My hand grazed over the empty spot that reminded me I was in this alone.

I climbed out of bed, and as I walked through the hallways, I heard a soft whisper.

"You're okay, you're okay."

The closer I grew to the nursery, the more the gentle voice calmed me. I stood in the doorway, watching Lucy as she held Talon and fed her.

Maybe in many ways, staring at my empty bed was a reminder that Jane was gone, but seeing Lucy before me was a small reminder that I wasn't alone.

"Is she okay?" I asked, making Lucy turn, surprised.

"Oh, yeah. Just hungry, that's all." Her eyes traveled across my body. "I see you don't smell like a sewer anymore."

My hands ran through my still damp hair. "Yeah, I took a quick shower and a quicker nap."

She nodded and walked over to me. "Want to feed her?"

"I—no. She doesn't..."

Lucy nodded me over to the glider chair. "Sit." I started to protest, but she shook her head. *"Now."*

I did as she told me, and when I sat, she placed the baby in my arms. The moment the exchange happened, Talon started to cry, and I tried to quickly give her back to Lucy, but she refused to take her.

"You're not going to break her."

"She doesn't like it when I hold her. She's not comfortable."

"No, *you're* not comfortable, but you can do this, Graham. Just breathe and calm your energy."

I grimaced. "Your hippie weirdo side is showing."

"And your fear is showing," she countered. She bent down, placed Talon's bottle in my hand, and helped me feed her. After a few moments, Talon began to drink and calm down, her tired eyes closing. "You're not going to break her, Graham."

I hated how she could read my mind without my permission. I was terrified that each touch from me would be the one that would end Talon. My father once told me everything I touched, I ruined, and I was certain that would be the case with my baby.

I could hardly even get her to take a bottle, let alone raise her.

Lucy's hand was still wrapped around mine as she helped me feed Talon. Her touch was soft, gentle, and surprisingly welcoming to my unwelcoming soul.

"What's your greatest hope?"

Confusion hit me at her question. "What does that mean?"

"What's your greatest hope for life?" she asked again. "My mother used to always ask us girls that question when we were kids."

"I…I don't hope."

Her lips turned down, but I ignored her disappointment in my reply. I wasn't a man to hope; I was a man who simply existed.

When Talon was finished with her bottle, I handed her to Lucy, who burped her then laid her back in her crib. We both stood over the crib, staring down at the resting child, but the knot that had been in my stomach since Talon was born remained.

She twisted a bit with a tiny grumpy look on her face before she relaxed into a deeper rest. I wondered if she dreamed while her eyes were shut, and if someday she'd have a greatest hope.

"Wow," Lucy said, a tiny smile on her lips. "She definitely has your frown."

I chuckled, making her turn my way.

"I'm sorry, did you just…" She pointed a finger at me and poked me in the arm. "Did Graham Russell just laugh?"

"A lapse in judgment. It won't happen again," I said dryly, standing up straight.

"Oh, how I wish that it would." Our eyes locked as we stood inches away from each other, no words finding either of us. Her blond hair was wild with tight curls, and it seemed to be her natural state; even at the funeral, her hair had been a mess.

A beautiful mess, somehow.

A loose curl fell over her left shoulder and I reached out to move it when I saw something caught in it. The closer my hand got to her, the more I noticed her tensing up. "Graham," she whispered. "What are you doing?"

I combed my fingers through her hair, and she shut her eyes, her nervousness plain to see. "Turn around," I commanded her.

"What? Why?"

"Just do it," I told her. She cocked an eyebrow, and I rolled my eyes before tossing in a "Please." She did as I said, and I grimaced. "Lucille?" I whispered, leaning in closer to her, my mouth inches away from her ear.

"Yes, Graham Cracker?"

"There's vomit all over your back."

"What?!" she exclaimed, twisting around in circles, trying to view the back of her sundress, which was covered in Talon's spit-up. "Oh my God," she groaned.

"It's in your hair, too."

"Oh, fuck me backward." She realized her words and covered her mouth. "Sorry, I mean, oh crap. I was just hoping to not go back into the real world covered in vomit."

I almost laughed again. "You can use my shower, and I can loan you some clothes while I toss this into the washer."

She smiled, something she did quite often. "Is that your sly way of asking me to stay to help with Talon for a few more hours?"

"No," I said harshly, offended by her comment. "That's ridiculous."

Her grin dropped and she laughed. "I'm just kidding, Graham. Don't take everything so seriously. Loosen up a little. But, yes, if it's okay, I'd love to take you up on your offer. This is my lucky dress."

"It can't be that lucky if it has vomit on it. Your definition of luck is off."

"Wow." Lucy whistled, shaking her head. "Your charm is almost sickening," she mocked.

"I didn't mean it in…" My words died off, and even though she kept smiling, I saw the small tremble in her bottom lip. I'd offended her. Of course I'd offended her—not on purpose, but still, it had happened. I shifted around before standing taller. I should've said more, but no words came to mind.

"I think I'll head home to wash it," she said, her voice lowering as she reached for her purse.

I nodded in understanding; I wouldn't want to stay near me either.

As she walked outside, I spoke. "I'm bad with words."

She turned around and shook her head. "No, I've read your books, and you're great with words—almost too good. What you lack are people skills."

"I live in my head a lot. I don't interact with people very often."

"What about my sister?"

"We didn't speak much."

Lucy laughed. "That makes for a hard relationship, I'm sure."

"We were close enough to being content."

Her head shook back and forth, and her eyes narrowed. "No one in love should ever be anything less than content."

"Who ever said anything about love?" I replied. The sadness that flooded her stare made me shift.

When she blinked, the sadness was gone. I appreciated the way she didn't live too long in the emotion. "You know what will help your people skills?" she asked. "Smiling."

"I do smile."

"No." She laughed. "You frown. You scowl. You grimace. That's about it. I haven't seen you smile once."

"When I encounter a valid reason to do so, I'll be sure to notify you. By the way, I am sorry, you know—for offending you. I-I know I can come off as somewhat cold."

"Understatement of the year." She laughed.

"I know I don't say much, and what I do say is normally the wrong thing, so I apologize for offending you. You've been nothing but giving to Talon and me, which is why I'm a bit thrown off. I'm not used to people giving just to… give."

"Graham—"

"Wait, let me finish before I say something else to ruin it all. I just wanted to say thank you for today, and for the hospital visits. I know I'm not easy to deal with, but the fact that you still helped means more to me than you'll ever know."

"You're welcome." She bit her bottom lip and groaned as she muttered the word maktub repeatedly before she spoke to me again. "Listen, I might really, really end up regretting this, but if you want, I can stop by early mornings before work, and I can come help afterward. I know at some point you'll have to get back to writing your next bestseller, and I can watch her as you write."

"I...I can pay you for your services."

"It's not services, Graham, it's help, and I don't need your money."

"I'd feel better if I paid you."

"And I'd feel better if you didn't. Seriously. I wouldn't offer if I didn't mean it."

"Thank you, and, Lucille?"

She raised an eyebrow, waiting for my comment.

"That's a very nice dress."

She slightly twirled on her tiptoes. "Vomit and all?"

"Vomit and all."

Her head lowered for a moment before she looked back toward me. "You're both hot and cold all at once, and I cannot for the life of me figure you out. I don't know how to read you, Graham Russell. I pride myself on being able to read people, but you are different."

"Perhaps I'm one of those novels where you have to keep turning the page until the very end to understand the meaning."

Her smile stretched, and she started walking backward toward my bathroom to clean off the vomit. Her eyes stayed locked with mine. "A part of me wants to skip to the last page to see how it ends, but I hate spoilers, and I love a good suspense." After she finished cleaning up, she headed to the foyer. "I'll text to see if you need me tonight, otherwise I'll stop by early tomorrow morning, and, Graham?"

"Yes?"

"Don't forget to smile."

chapter ten

Lucy

THE NEXT FEW WEEKS REVOLVED AROUND FLOWER ARRANGEMENTS AND TALON. If I wasn't at Monet's Gardens, I was helping Graham out. Whenever I went to his house, we hardly spoke. He'd pass Talon to me then head into his office, where he'd close the door and write. He was a man of very few words, and if I'd learned anything, it was that his few words were harsh. Therefore, his silence didn't bring me any harm.

If anything, it brought me peace.

Sometimes I'd wander by his office, and I'd hear him leaving voice messages for Lyric. Each message was an update on Talon's life, detailing her highs and lows.

One Saturday evening when I pulled up to Graham's house, I was somewhat surprised to see a brown station wagon sitting in the driveway. I parked my car, walked up to the front door, and rang the doorbell.

As I waited, swaying back and forth, my ears perked up when I heard laughter coming from inside.

Laughter?

From Graham Russell's home?

"I want you to have less fat and more muscle next time I come back," a voice said seconds before the door opened. When I saw the man, I smiled wide. "Oh, hello there, young lady," he said cheerfully.

"Professor Oliver, right?"

"Yes, yes, but please, call me Ollie. You must be Lucille." He extended his hand for a shake, and I gave him mine.

"You can call me Lucy," I told him. "Graham just so happens to think Lucy is too informal, but I'm a pretty informal girl." I smiled at Graham, who stood a few feet back, not speaking a word.

"Ah, Graham, the formal gentleman. You know, I've been trying to get him to stop calling me Professor Oliver for years now, but he refuses to call me Ollie. He thinks it's childish."

"It *is* childish," Graham insisted, grabbing Ollie's brown fedora and handing it to him pointedly. "Thank you for stopping by, Professor Oliver."

"Of course, of course. Lucy, it's a pleasure to meet you. Graham speaks very highly of you."

I laughed. "I find that hard to believe."

Ollie wiggled his nose and snickered. "True, true. He hasn't said much about you. He's a bit of a silent asshole in that way, isn't he? But you see, Lucy, if I could let you in on a secret."

"I'd love to hear any secrets and tips I can get."

"Professor Oliver," Graham said sternly. "Didn't you say you have another engagement to be off to?"

"Oh, he's getting testy, isn't he?" Ollie laughed and continued talking. "But here's a clue for dealing with Mr. Russell: he doesn't say much with his mouth, but he tells a full story with his eyes. If you watch closely, his eyes will tell you the complete story of how he's feeling. He's truly an open book if you learn how to read his language, and when I asked him about you, he said you were fine, but his eyes told me he was thankful for you. Lucy, girl with the brown doe eyes, Graham thinks the world of you, even if he doesn't say it."

I looked up at Graham, and there was a frown on his lips, but also a small spark of softness in his eyes that melted my heart. Talon had that same beauty in her gaze.

"All right, old man, I think we've had enough of your mumbo jumbo. It's clear you've overstayed your welcome."

His grin stretched far, and he was completely unmoved by Graham's coldness. "And yet you keep asking me back. I'll see you next week, son, and please, less fat, more muscle. Stop selling yourself short with average writing when you are far above it." Ollie turned to me and bowed slightly. "Lucy, it was a pleasure."

"The pleasure was all mine."

As Ollie walked past me, he tipped his hat, and he whistled the whole way to his car with a bit of a hop in his step.

I smiled at Graham, who didn't smile back. We stood in the foyer for a few moments in silence, simply staring at one another. It was awkward, that was for sure.

"Talon's sleeping," he told me, breaking his stare from mine.

"Oh, okay."

I smiled.

He grimaced.

Our usual.

"Well, I can go do a bit of meditation in your sunroom if that's okay? I'll take the baby monitor with me, and I'll check in on Talon if she wakes up."

He nodded once, and I walked by him before he spoke again. "It's six in the evening."

I turned around and raised an eyebrow. "Yeah, it is."

"I eat dinner at six in my office."

"Yes, I know."

He cleared his throat and shifted around in his shoes. His stare fell to the floor for a few beats before he looked up at me. "Professor Oliver's wife, Mary, sent me two weeks of frozen dinners."

"Oh wow, that was sweet of her."

He nodded once. "Yes. One of the meals is in the oven now, and she made each pan enough for more than one person."

"Oh." He kept staring at me, but didn't say anything. "Graham?"

"Yes, Lucille?"

"Are you asking me to eat dinner with you tonight?"

"If you would like to, there's enough."

A moment of uncertainty hit me as I wondered if I was dreaming or not, but I knew if I didn't reply quickly enough the moment would be gone in a flash. "I'd love to."

"Do you have any food allergies? Vegetarian? Gluten free? Lactose intolerant?"

I laughed, because everything about Graham was so dry and serious. The look on his face when he listed each item was so stern and intense, I couldn't help but giggle to myself. "No, no, whatever it is will be fine."

"It's lasagna," he said, his voice heightening as if it might not be okay.

"That's fine."

"Are you sure?"

I snickered. "Graham Cracker, I'm sure."

He didn't display any emotion, only one nod. "I'll set the table."

His dining room table was ridiculously large, big enough to seat twelve people. He set the plating and silverware at each end of the table, and he motioned for me to take a seat. It was hauntingly quiet as he served the meal, and he took his seat at the other end.

There weren't many lights in Graham's home, and oftentimes the shades were drawn, not letting much sunlight through at all. His furniture was dark too, and sparse. In his whole home, I was certain I was the brightest item to exist with my colorful clothing and outrageous, wild blond hair.

"The weather's nice outside, ya know, for a spring day in Wisconsin," I said after several minutes of uncomfortable silence. Weather talk was the blandest of bland, but it was all I could think of. In the past, that flavor of small talk had always helped ease any situation.

"Is it?" he muttered, uninterested. "I haven't been out."

"Oh. Well, it is."

He didn't comment at all, just kept eating his dinner.

Hmph.

"Have you thought about putting a garden outside?" I asked. "It's the perfect time to start planting stuff, and you have such a beautiful backyard. All it would need is a bit of a trim and you could really brighten the place up."

"I'm not interested in that. It's a waste of money."

"Oh. Well, okay."

Hmph.

"Ollie seems sweet," I mentioned, trying one last time. "He's quite the guy, isn't he?"

"He's fine for what he is," he muttered.

I tilted my head, watching his stare, applying the tip Ollie had shared with me. "You really care for him, don't you?"

"He was my college professor and now serves as my writing coach—nothing more, nothing less."

"I heard you laughing with him. You don't really laugh with a lot of people, but I heard you laughing with him. I didn't know you had a sense of humor."

"I don't."

"Right, of course," I agreed, knowing he was lying. "But it did seem as if you two were close."

He didn't reply, and that was the end of our discussion. We continued dinner in silence, and when the baby monitor alerted us of Talon crying, we both leaped up to go check on her.

"I'll get her," we said in unison.

"No, I—" he started, but I shook my head.

"That's why I'm here, remember? Finish your meal, and thank you for sharing it with me."

He nodded, and I went to check on Talon. Her eyes were wide and she stopped crying, the tears replaced by a small smile on her face. It was what I imagined Graham's grin would look like. As I prepared a bottle for her and began feeding her, Graham entered the room and leaned against the doorframe.

"Is she all right?" he asked.

"Just hungry."

He nodded and cleared his throat. "Professor Oliver has a loud personality. He's forward, talkative, and full of nonsense ninety-nine percent of the time. I have no clue how his wife or his daughter put up with his ridiculousness and wild antics. For a man in his eighties, he acts like a child, and oftentimes appears like a well-educated clown."

"Oh." Well, at least I knew he disliked everyone equally as much as he seemed to dislike me.

Graham's head lowered and he stared at his fingers, which he latched together. "And he's the best man and friend I've ever known."

He turned and walked away without another word, and just like that, for a small fraction of a second, Graham Russell showed me a glimpse of his heart.

Around eleven that night, I finished cleaning up Talon's room and headed to Graham's office where he was writing, his focus completely zoomed in on his words.

"Hey, I'm heading home."

He took a beat, finished typing his sentence, and turned to face me. "Thank you for your time, Lucille."

"Of course. Oh, and just a heads-up, on Friday I don't think I can make it. My boyfriend is having an art show, so I'll have to be there."

"Oh," he said, a small twitch finding his bottom lip. "Okay."

I tossed my purse strap over my shoulder. "You know, if you want, you can bring Talon to the show. It might be nice to get her out and about to places other than the doctor's office."

"I can't. I have to finish these next few chapters by Saturday."

"Oh, okay…well, have a great night."

"What time?" he said right as I stepped into the hallway.

"Hmm?"

"What time is the show?"

A lump of hope formed in my gut. "Eight o'clock, at the art museum."

He nodded once. "I might finish early. Fancy attire?"

I couldn't even hold the smile to myself. "Black tie."

"Noted." He must've noticed my excitement because he narrowed his eyes. "It's not a promise that I'll make it. I just prefer to be informed in case I do attend."

"No, of course. I'll put you on the guest list, just in case."

"Good night, Lucille."

"Good night, Graham Cracker."

As I walked away, I couldn't help but think about the way the evening had progressed. To the average person, his interactions would've seemed normal at best, but I knew for Graham, it had been an extraordinary day.

Sure, he hadn't given me a guarantee that he'd make it to the show, but there was a small chance. If this was the man he became after a visit from Professor Oliver, I secretly prayed he'd stop by each day.

⁂

There were small moments that I sometimes witnessed with Graham as he cared for his daughter. Those moments were what I held onto when he was colder than cold. Oftentimes I'd walk in on him shirtless, lying on the couch with Talon in his arms. Each day he did the kangaroo care, out of fear of not bonding with Talon. But they were bonded more than he could've noticed. She adored him, just as he adored her. Once as I rested in the living room, I overheard him on the baby monitor speaking to his daughter as he tried to soothe her crying.

"You are loved, Talon. I promise to always take care of you. I promise to be better for you."

He would've never showed that side of his heart if he was standing near me. He would've never been seen in such a vulnerable state of mind. Yet the fact that he wasn't afraid to love his daughter so carefully in the quietness of his home, lit me up inside. It turned out the beast wasn't such a monster after all. He was simply a man who'd been hurt in the past and was slowly opening back up due to the love of his daughter.

◦◦◦

I arrived at the museum a little after eight due to a late floral delivery, and when I walked in wearing my sparkly purple dress, I was shocked by the amount of people already there. Richard's display was in the west end of the museum, and the individuals who'd shown up were dressed as if they were at the Met Gala in New York City.

I'd found my dress on sale at Target.

My eyes darted around the room in search of Richard, and when I spotted him, I hurried over. "Hey." I smiled, stepping into the conversation he was having with two women about a piece of his artwork. The women were stunning in their red and gold gowns that traveled to the floor. Their hair was pinned up perfectly and their makeup was flawless.

Richard looked up at me and gave me a half smile. "Hey, hey, you made it. Stacy, Erin, this is Lucy."

The two ladies eyed me up and down as I eased my way closer to Richard and held my hand out to each of them. "His *girlfriend*."

"I didn't know you had a girlfriend, Richie," Erin said, shaking my hand with a look of distaste on her lips.

"Me neither," Stacy replied.

"Of five years," I gritted through my teeth, trying my best to give a fake smile.

"Oh," they said in unison, disbelief dripping from the word.

Richard cleared his throat, placed his hand on my lower back, and started to guide me away. "Ladies, go grab yourselves a drink. I'm going to show Lucy around a bit."

They walked off, and Richard slightly leaned in to me. "What was that about?"

"What are you talking about?" I asked, trying to play off the fact that I had not been completely normal in that interaction.

"Your whole, 'this is my man, back off, bitches' persona back there."

"Sorry," I muttered, standing up straighter. I wasn't a jealous girl, but the feeling those ladies had given me was so uncomfortable; it was as if they were displeased by my whole existence.

"It's fine, really," Richard said, taking off his glasses and cleaning them with a pocket cloth. "Your dress is short," he mentioned, looking around the room.

I spun a bit. "Do you like it?"

"It's short, that's all. Plus, your high heels are bright yellow and *really* tall. You're taller than me."

"And that's an issue?"

"It just makes me feel a bit undermined, is all. When I introduce you, I'll look like the small guy next to his giant girlfriend."

"It's only a few inches."

"But still, it's belittling."

I wasn't sure how to take his words, and before I could reply, he commented on my hair.

"And there are rose petals in your hair."

I smiled and patted the flower crown I'd crafted at the floral shop before I came. It was made up of roses, tulips, and baby's breath, and it sat on top of my hair, which was placed in a big French braid that lay over my left shoulder. "Do you like it?" I asked.

"It just seems a bit childish," he replied, placing his glasses back on. "I just…I thought I told you how important this event is to me, Lucy. To my career."

I narrowed my eyes. "I know. Richard, this is all amazing. What you've done is amazing."

"Yeah, but it just looks a bit odd for you to arrive dressed in such a way."

My lips parted, uncertain what to say, but before I could reply, he excused himself, saying he needed to go say hello to some very important people.

Clearing my throat, I walked off by myself and wandered around the room before eventually making my way to the bar, where a nice gentleman smiled at me. "Hey there, what can I get you?"

"A different dress," I joked. "And maybe a shorter pair of heels."

"You look beautiful," he remarked. "And between you and me, I think you're the best dressed in the room, but what do I know? I'm just a bartender, not an artist."

I smiled. "Thank you. I'll just take a water with a lemon slice for now."

He cocked an eyebrow. "You sure you don't want vodka? This seems like a room that needs serious quantities of vodka."

I laughed, shaking my head. "While I agree, I think I'm already drawing enough attention to myself. No need to allow the drunken version of myself to escape." I thanked him for the ice water, and when I turned around, I saw the back of a man standing in front of one of Richard's paintings. Beside him sat a car seat that held the most beautiful child in the world. A wave of comfort washed through me at seeing them before me. It was hard to explain how seeing those two familiar faces brought me a level of confidence.

"You made it," I exclaimed, going over to Talon and bending down to lightly kiss her forehead.

Graham turned my way just a bit before looking back at the painting. "We did." He stood tall in an all-black suit with a deep gray tie and gray cuffs. His shoes were shiny, as if freshly polished for the gala. His hair was slicked back with a bit of gel, and his beard was nicely groomed.

"Does that mean you finished your chapters?"

He shook his head once. "I'll finish once I get home."

My chest tightened. He hadn't even finished his work, but he'd still made time to make an appearance.

"Lucille?"

"Yes?"

"Why am I staring at a twelve-by-twelve-foot painting of your naked boyfriend?"

I giggled to myself, sipping my water. "It's a self-discovery collection where Richard dived deep to express his inner thoughts, fears, and beliefs through how he sees himself using different mediums, such as clay, charcoal, and pastels."

Graham glanced around the room at the rest of Richard's self-portraits and clay creations. "Is that a six-foot-tall statue of his penis?" he asked.

I nodded uncomfortably. "That is indeed a six-foot-tall statue of his penis."

"Hmph. He's quite confident in his"—he tilted his head slightly and cleared his throat—"manhood."

"I like to believe confidence is my middle name," Richard joked, walking up to our conversation. "I'm sorry, I don't believe we've met."

"Oh yes, right, sorry. Richard, this is Graham. Graham, this is Richard."

"Lucy's *boyfriend*," Richard said with a bit of bite to his words as he reached out to shake Graham's hand. "So you're the one who's been stealing my girlfriend's time day and night, huh?"

"More so Talon than myself," he replied, dry as ever.

"And you're an author?" Richard asked, knowing very well that Graham was indeed G.M. Russell. "I'm sorry, I'm not exactly sure I've heard of your novels. I don't think I've ever read anything you've published." He was being oddly aggressive, making the whole situation uncomfortable.

"That's fine," Graham responded. "Enough other people have, so your lack of awareness doesn't inflict any damage on my success."

Richard laughed obnoxiously loud and slugged Graham in the shoulder. "That's funny." He chuckled awkwardly then slid his hands into his pockets. Richard's eyes traveled to the glass in my hand and he raised an eyebrow. "Vodka?"

I shook my head. "Water."

"Good, good. It's probably best for you to not drink tonight, right, sweetheart?"

I gave him a tight smile, but didn't reply.

Graham grimaced. "Why's that?" he asked.

"Oh, well, when Lucy drinks, she becomes a bit…goofy. Very talkative, if you can believe it. It's like it heightens all of her quirks, and it can be a lot to handle at times."

"She seems grown-up enough to make her own choices," Graham countered.

"And her choice was not to drink tonight," Richard replied, smiling.

"I'm sure she can speak for herself," Graham said, his voice cold. "After all, she was given her own vocal cords."

"Yes, but she would've just said exactly what I have stated."

Graham gave a forced, tight grin. It was the unhappiest smile I'd ever witnessed in my lifetime. "Please excuse me, I must go someplace other than right here," Graham coldly stated, lifting the car seat and walking off.

"Wow." Richard whistled low. "What an asshole."

I lightly pushed his shoulder. "What was that? You were a bit aggressive, don't you think?"

"Well, I'm sorry. I just don't know how comfortable I am with you being at his place all the time."

"I'm there helping taking care of Talon, who is my niece, my family. You know this."

"Yeah, but you seem to have left out the fact that he looks like a freaking Greek god, Lucy. I mean, Jesus Christ, what kind of author has arms the size of the Titanic?" Richard exclaimed, his jealousy loud and clear.

"He works out when he has writer's block."

"There must be a lot blocking that writer. Anyway, come over here. There are some people I need you to meet." He took my arm and started pulling me forward. When I turned around to check on Graham, he was sitting on a bench, holding Talon and staring my way. His stare was intense, as if his mind was running with a million thoughts.

Richard took me around the room, introducing me to a bunch of people who were dressed much fancier than me. Every time, he'd speak about my outfit, mentioning how it was quirky, like my heart. He said it with a smile, but I could sense the frown underneath it.

"Can I take a break?" I asked after speaking to a woman who looked at me as if I were trash.

"Just two more people. This is important—they are *the* couple to talk to tonight."

Apparently my break would have to wait.

"Mr. and Mrs. Peterson," Richard said, reaching his hand out for handshakes. "I'm so happy you could make it."

"Please, don't be so formal, Richard. Just call us Warren and Catherine," the gentleman said as they both greeted us with warm smiles.

"Right, of course. Again, I'm so happy you're here."

Catherine wore a fur shawl around her shoulders, and her body was decked out in expensive jewelry, making her smile shine even more. Her lips were painted fuchsia, and she carried herself as if she were royalty.

"We wouldn't have missed it for the world, Richard. And you must be Lucy." She grinned and took my hand in hers. "I've been asking a lot about the lady in this talented man's life."

"That's me." I laughed unenthusiastically, tugging on the bottom of my dress with my free hand, hoping Richard wouldn't comment on it. "I'm sorry, how do you both know—"

"Mr. Pet—*Warren* is one of the greatest artists in the world, and he's from Milwaukee, Lucy," Richard explained. "I've told you about him many times."

"No," I said softly. "I'm not sure you have."

"Yes, I have. I'm sure you've just forgotten."

Warren chuckled. "Don't worry about it, Lucy. My own wife forgets me about fifty times a day—isn't that right, Catherine?"

"I'm sorry, do I know you?" Catherine joked, winking at her husband. While they were nothing but pleasant, I could tell Richard was somewhat annoyed with me, though I was certain I'd never heard of them.

"So, Richard, what's the next step in your career?" Warren asked.

"Well, I was invited to a showcase in New York City by a friend of mine," he stated.

"Oh?" I asked, surprised to just be hearing about it right then. "I had no clue."

"It just happened this afternoon actually," he said, leaning in and giving me a kiss. "Remember Tyler? He's going to this big art gala in the city and said I could crash at his apartment."

"Oh, the Rosa Art Gala?" Warren asked, nodding. "I spent many years at the Rosa. It's a week of magic. I swear every artist must partake in it at least once. I've found some of my strongest artistic influences during those times."

"And lost plenty of brain cells, too," Catherine joked. "From paint fumes, alcohol, and marijuana."

"It's going to be amazing, that's for sure," Richard agreed.

"Are you going too, Lucy?" Warren asked.

"Oh, no. She's actually running a floral shop," Richard cut in, not even giving me a chance to answer. I hadn't even been invited in the first place. "But I wish she could make it."

"You're a florist?" Warren asked eagerly. "You should consider pairing with an artist for the floral show that the museum hosts here. You make a floral arrangement, and then the artist paints a piece based on your creation. It's quite fun."

"That sounds amazing," I agreed.

"If you need an artist, let me know and I'll see what I can do. I'm sure I can get your name on the program, too." Warren grinned.

"Now's the time for the most important question of the night: what are you drinking, Lucy?" Catherine asked.

"Oh, just water."

She looped her arm with mine and started to walk off with me. "Well, that won't do. Are you a gin lady?" she asked.

Before I could reply, Richard spoke. "Oh, she loves gin. She'll have whatever you're having, I'm sure."

As the four of us started walking to the bar, Catherine paused. "Oh my God, Warren! Warren, *look*!" She nodded in the direction of Graham, who was putting a sleeping Talon back into her car seat. "Is that G.M. Russell?"

Warren reached into his pocket and pulled out his glasses. "I think it is."

"You know his work?" Richard asked, unamused.

"Know it? We're in love with it. He's one of the best authors out there—besides his father, of course. May he rest in peace," Warren said.

"Oh, no. He's much better than Kent was. He writes with so much pain, it's hauntingly beautiful."

"Yes." Warren nodded. "I completely agree. In fact, my Shadows series was inspired by his novel *Bitter*."

"That's one of my favorites," I glowed, remembering the novel that had a permanent spot on my bookcase. "And that twist!"

"Oh my gosh, honey, that twist!" Catherine agreed, her cheeks turning red. "Oh, I'd just love to meet him."

I wasn't certain if it was possible for my boyfriend to be full of any more crap in one night, but he for sure continued to amaze me with his out-of-this-world lies. "He's actually a good friend of Lucy's," he said effortlessly. Graham was far from my friend, even though he was the only thing that felt right in the room that evening. "Lucy, do you think you can introduce him?"

"Um, sure, of course." I smiled at the excited couple and led them over to speak with Graham. "Hey, Graham."

He stood up and smoothed out his suit then placed his hands in front of him, fingers knotted. "Lucille."

"Are you having a good time?" I asked.

He remained silent, awkwardly so. After a moment, I cleared my throat and gestured toward the couple. "This is Warren and Catherine. They are—"

"Two of your biggest fans," Catherine exclaimed, reaching out and grabbing Graham's hand, shaking it rapidly. Graham gave her a big smile, which was fake and forced, also known as his 'author brand' smile, I assumed.

"Thank you, Catherine. It's always a pleasure to meet readers. I've been informed tonight that some have not heard of my work, but the fact that you both have is refreshing," Graham replied.

"Haven't heard of your work? Blasphemy! I can't think of a soul who wouldn't know of you," Warren said. "You're a living legend in a sense."

"Sadly, good ol' Richard seems to disagree," Graham mocked.

"Really, Richard? You don't know Graham's work?" Catherine said, a tinge of disappointment in her voice.

Richard laughed nervously, rubbing the back of his neck. "Oh no, of course I know his work. I was just teasing."

"Your definition of teasing is a bit inaccurate," Graham replied dryly.

Talon started to fuss a bit, and I bent down to pick her up, grinning at her sweet face as Graham and Richard waged their own odd war against one another.

The group could feel the tension building, and Warren broke out a large smile before glancing around the room. "So, Richard, your work is quite unique."

Richard stood up, proud. "Yes. I like to think of it as an awakening to all of my deepest and darkest shadows. It's been a process for me to dig so deep, and for a long time, I had a lot of emotional breakdowns about being so vulnerable and open with myself, let alone the idea of allowing others into my soul. It was a very hard time for me, that's for sure, a lot of tears, but I made it."

Graham huffed, and Richard shot him a stern look.

"I'm sorry, did I say something funny?"

"No, except for every single word that just came out of your mouth," Graham replied.

"You seem to know it all, don't you? Well, go ahead, tell me what you see when you look around," Richard urged.

Don't do it, Richard. Don't awaken the beast.

"Trust me, you don't want to know my thoughts," Graham said, standing tall.

"No, come on, enlighten us, because I'm kind of sick of the attitude," Richard replied. "Your pretentious tone is extremely unwarranted, and frankly, extremely disrespectful."

"Disrespectful? Pretentious?" Graham asked, arching an eyebrow.

Oh no. I took note of the vein popping out of the side of Graham's neck, and even though he kept his voice calm, he was growing more and more irritated as he spoke.

"We're standing in a room full of paintings and sculptures of your penis, which, if I'm honest, seems to be nothing more than a little man trying hard to overcompensate for something he's lacking in his life. Judging by his height and need to force people into a room to stare at his cartoonish, oversized genitals, he's lacking quite a bit."

Everyone's mouths hung open, stunned by Graham's words. My eyes stayed wide, my chest tight as I yanked on Graham's arm. "Can I please have a word in the other room?" I asked, but it was much more a demand than a polite request.

"What was that about?!" I whisper-shouted, carrying Talon into the darkened exhibit where Graham headed.

"What are you talking about?"

"You. That whole act back there."

"I don't know what you're talking about," he replied.

"Come on, Graham! For once in your life can you not be condescending?"

"Me? Condescending? Are you joking? He made portraits, of himself, *naked*, and deemed it as artwork when truly it's just some kind of hipster bullshit that doesn't belong in this museum."

"He's talented."

"Your idea of talent is jaded."

"I know," I replied harshly. "I do, after all, read your books."

"Oh, good one, Lucille. You really told me," he said, rolling his eyes. "Yet unlike your so-called boyfriend, I know my flaws when it comes to my craftsmanship. He believes he's the best of the best."

"What do you mean? What do you mean 'so-called' boyfriend?"

"He doesn't know you," he said assertively, making me raise an eyebrow.

"We've been together for more than five years, Graham."

"And yet he still hasn't a clue who you are, which isn't shocking, because he seems to have his head so far up his own ass he has no time to focus on anyone else."

"Wow," I said, completely baffled by his words. "You don't know him."

"I know his type, the type of people who get the smallest taste of success and feel as if they can toss away the things and people from their past. I don't know how he used to look at you, but he stares at you as if you're nothing now. As if you're below him. I give your relationship two weeks. I bet it's over in a month, tops."

"You're being a jerk."

"I'm telling you the truth. He's a self-righteous piece of shit. Do you know what the nickname for Richard is? It's Dick, which is so fitting. I mean really, Lucille, you sure know how to pick 'em."

He was fuming, his face bright red as he fiddled with his cuffs nonstop. I'd never seen him so mad, so far from his normal unemotional self.

"Why are you so angry? What's wrong with you?"

"Never mind, forget it. Hand Talon over."

"No, you don't get to do that. You don't get to explode and be disrespectful to my boyfriend and then tell me to forget it."

"I can, and I did."

"No. Graham, stop it. For once in your life, just say what you are actually feeling!"

He parted his lips, but no words escaped him.

"Really? Not a word?" I asked.

"Not a word," he softly replied.

"Then I think you're right. I think it's time for you to go."

"I agree." He stood inches away from me, his hot breaths melting against my skin. My heart pounded against my ribcage as I wondered what he was doing, and he took a few seconds before moving in closer. He straightened his tie, lowered his voice, and spoke so sternly. "Just because you smile and act free doesn't mean the cage doesn't exist. It merely means you lowered your standards for how far you'll allow yourself to fly."

Tears burned at the backs of my eyes as he took Talon from my grip and turned to leave. Right before he stepped out of the darkened area, he paused and took a few deep breaths. He turned back my way, locking eyes with mine, and his lips parted slightly as if he were going to speak again, but I held my hand up. "Please, just go," I whispered, my voice shaky. "I don't think I can take any more tonight, Mr. Russell."

The coldness of me using his last name made him stand up straighter, and when he disappeared, my tears began to fall. My fingers wrapped around my necklace, and I took in a few deep breaths. "Air above me, earth below me, fire within me, water surround me..." I repeated the words until my heartbeats returned to a normal pace. I repeated the words until my mind stopped spinning. I repeated the words until I erased the shock Graham had caused to my soul. Then, I headed back to the gala with a fake smile on my lips, and in my head, I repeated my words some more.

chapter eleven

Lucy

"He's still calling you?" Richard asked, cleaning up his paintbrushes in the bathroom sink. I leaned against the wall in the hallway, staring down at Graham's name flashing against the screen.

"Yup." I hadn't seen Graham since he exploded at Richard's gala five days ago, and he hadn't stopped calling me since then.

"And he doesn't leave a message?"

"Nope."

"Block him. He's the definition of a psychopath."

"I can't. What if something happens to Talon?"

Richard glanced my way with an arched brow. "You do know she's not actually your responsibility, right? As in, she's not your kid."

"I know, it's just..." I bit my bottom lip and stared down at the phone. "It's hard to explain."

"No, I get it, LuLu. You're a giving person, but you gotta be careful, because a man like him is just a taker. He'll take all he can from you and treat you like crap."

My mind thought back on the dinner Graham and I had a week before, the night when he showed me a small, softer side of him I'd wondered about. The thing about Graham Russell was he lived almost completely inside his mind. He never really invited a person to see his inner thoughts or feelings. So, the night he exploded at the art show, it was a complete one-eighty from who I'd come to know him to be.

Instead of engaging in more talk about Graham, I shifted the conversation. "Do you really have to be gone for a week?"

Richard walked past me, out to the living room where his suitcases were lying open. "I know, I wish I didn't have to, but now that I hit the museum, I have to keep the momentum going, and when you're invited to a gala in New York City, you go."

I walked up behind him and wrapped my arms around him. "Are you sure girlfriends can't tag along?" I joked.

He turned around with a smile and kissed my nose. "I wish. I'm gonna miss you."

"I'm gonna miss you, too." I grinned, giving him a light kiss. "And if you want, I can show you exactly how much I'm going to miss you."

Richard grimaced and glanced at his watch. "While that sounds ridiculously enticing, I gotta leave for the airport in like twenty minutes, and I'm hardly done packing." He unwrapped our bodies and went back to his suitcases to pack his brushes.

"Okay. Well, are you sure you don't want me to drive you to the airport?"

"No, it's fine, really, I'll just get a Lyft. You're training the new girl at work today, aren't you?" He glanced at his watch one more time before looking up at me. "I think you're already late."

"Yeah, you're right. Well, okay. Text me before your plane takes off, and call when you land." I bent down and kissed him on the lips.

"Okay, sounds good—and, babe?" he called after me as I scooped up my keys to leave.

"Yes?"

"Block that number."

"I'm sorry I'm late," I said, hurrying into Monet's Gardens through the back door.

Mari was going over the weekly orders with Chrissy, our new florist. Chrissy was a beautiful woman in her seventies who'd once owned her own floral shop. Teaching her the ins and outs of the shop was easy—she knew more than both Mari and me when it came to flowers.

When we mentioned that she was over-qualified for the position, she disagreed, saying she'd been a busy florist and shop owner for many years, but it was a lot of work for her to keep up with. She said her friends told her to retire, but her heart knew she needed to be surrounded by flowers for a bit longer and the position at our shop was perfect.

"No worries." Chrissy smiled. "I already started arranging the orders for today."

"Yeah, and she also taught me this new computer organization system—in other words, I think we hired a wizard," Mari joked. "Is Richard off to New York?"

"Yup, sadly enough, but he'll be back soon."

Mari narrowed her eyes. "This is the first time you two have spent a week apart—are you sure you can handle the separation?"

"I'm planning to binge on comfort foods—kale chips and guacamole."

"Sweetheart, no offense, but kale chips are not comfort food," Chrissy sassed.

"That's what I've been telling her for the past million years!" Mari said with a sigh as she walked over to unlock the front door and open the shop. "But okay, I'm going to take Chrissy with me to set up a wedding in Wauwatosa—do you need anything from us?"

I shook my head. "No. Have fun! I'll be here when you get back."

As they walked out of the back door, an older gentleman with a fedora walked in the front and was quick to take off his hat.

My chest tightened seeing him, and when his stare found mine, he smiled wide. "Lucy," he said warmly, tipping his hat my way.

"Hi, Ollie. What are you doing here?"

He walked around a bit, studying the flowers in the shop. "I was hoping to buy a few roses for a special lady." He gave me his charming smile and started whistling as he wandered around the shop. "Though, I'm not certain which ones she'd like. Will you help?"

"Of course. Tell me a little about her."

"Well, she's beautiful. She has these eyes that just pull you in, and when she looks at you, she makes you feel like the most important person in the room."

My heart warmed hearing him talk so endearingly about the woman. As he continued, we walked around the shop, pulling a flower for each facet of her seemingly vibrant personality. "She's gentle and caring. Has a smile that lights up a room. She's smart, too, so smart. She's not afraid to give a helping hand, even when it's tough. And the last word to describe her…" he said, reaching out and picking out a deep red rose. "Is pure. She's pure, untainted by the world's cruelty. Just simply, easily, and beautifully pure."

I took the rose from him, a grin resting on my lips. "She sounds like a wonderful woman."

He nodded. "She is indeed."

I walked to the counter and started to trim the flowers for Ollie as he picked out a red vase. The flowers were an arrangement of different colors and styles—a stunning collection. That was my favorite part of my job: when people came into the store and had no idea what they wanted. Roses were gorgeous, yes, and tulips were pretty, too, but there was something so creatively rewarding about being able to have free range and create a piece that expressed the artistic personality of the customer's loved one.

As I tied a bow around the vase, Ollie narrowed his eyes at me. "You're ignoring his calls."

I grimaced for a second, fumbling with the ribbon. "It's complicated."

"Of course it is," he agreed. "We are, after all, talking about Graham." He lowered his voice and held his fedora to his chest. "Sweetheart, whatever he did, he's sorry."

"He was cruel," I whispered, the bow not quite perfect enough, leading me to untie the ribbon to begin again.

"Of course he was," he agreed. "We are, after all, talking about Graham." He softly snickered. "But then again, he's Graham, which means he didn't mean it."

I didn't say anything else on the subject. "So, the flowers are $44.32, but I'll give you the first-time visit discount, bringing it to $34.32."

"That's very kind of you, Lucy. Thank you." He reached into his wallet and handed me the money. Then he placed his fedora back on his head and turned to leave.

"Ollie, you're forgetting your flowers," I called after him.

He turned back to me and shook his head. "No, ma'am. A friend of mine asked me to stop in to pick out those for you. I asked him some characteristics about you, and that is the creation that came to be."

"Graham said those things about me?" I asked, my chest tightening a bit as I stared down at the arrangement.

"Well, he gave me one of the words, and I just kind of gathered the others on my own, based on the few moments we spent together." He cleared his throat and tilted his head. "Listen, I'm not saying you have to go back, but if you do, you'll prove him wrong."

"Prove him wrong?"

"Graham lives a life where he believes everyone leaves. If his past has taught him anything, it's that. So, a part of him feels relief that you left. After all, he was certain you'd disappear eventually, anyway. That's why he can't for the life of him stand me. No matter what, I keep showing up, and it drives him bonkers. So, if you in any way, shape, or form want to get back at Graham for hurting you, the best revenge is proving to him that he's wrong, that not everyone is going to walk out. I promise you, he'll act like he hates you for it, but remember: the truth lies within his eyes. His eyes will thank you a million times over."

"Ollie?"

"Yes?"

"Which word did he give you? To describe me?"

"Pure, my dear." He tipped his hat one last time and opened the door. "He called you pure."

***

His brow was knitted, and his arms crossed when I approached him. "You came back," Graham stated, sounding surprised as I stood on his front porch. "Honestly, I thought you would've come back days ago."

"Why would you have thought that?" I asked.

"Professor Oliver told me you received the flowers."

"Yes."

He raised an eyebrow. "That was four days ago."

"Uh-huh."

"Well, it took you long enough to come say thank you." His stern, dry words were not shocking, but still, for some reason, they shook me.

"Why would I thank you for the flowers? You didn't even pick them out."

"What does that matter?" he asked, brushing the back of his neck. "You still received them. You seem ungrateful."

"You're right, Graham. *I'm* the rude one here. Anyway, I'm only here because you left a message saying Talon was sick." I walked into the house without being invited and took off my jacket then laid it on his living room chair.

"A small fever, but I wasn't certain that…" He paused. "You came back because she was sick?"

"Of course I came back," I huffed. "I'm not a monster. If Talon needs me, I'm here for her. You just didn't leave a message before today."

"Yes, of course." He nodded. "Listen…"

"Don't apologize, it seems too weak."

"I wasn't going to apologize. I was going to say I forgive you."

"Forgive me?! For what?"

He shifted around, picking up my jacket from the couch and hanging it in the front closet. "For being childish and disappearing for days."

"You're joking, right?"

"I'm not one to joke."

"Graham…" I started to speak then closed my eyes and took a few deep breaths to stop myself from saying something I'd regret. "Can you at least for a second accept some kind of blame for how you acted at the museum?"

"Blame? I meant every word I said to you that night."

"Every word?" I huffed, shocked. "So, you're not sorry?"

He stood taller and placed his hands in his jeans pockets. "Of course not. I only spoke the truth, and it's a pity you're just too emotional to fully accept it."

"Your definition of truth and my definition of truth are wildly different. Nothing you said held any truth to it. You were just stating your opinionated thoughts, which weren't asked for."

"He treated you like—"

"Just stop, Graham. No one asked you how he treated me. No one came to you for your thoughts. I just invited you to the event because I thought it would be nice to get you and Talon away from staring at the same four walls. My mistake."

"I didn't ask for your pity."

"You're right, Graham. Silly me for reaching out a hand to someone, for trying to build a relationship of some sort with the father of my niece."

"Well, that's your fault. Your need to find life in everything and everyone is ridiculous and reveals your childish ways. You let your emotions drive everything you are, which in turn makes you weak."

My lips parted in disbelief, and I slightly shook my head. "Just because I'm not like you doesn't mean I'm weak."

"Don't do that," he said softly.

"Do what?"

"Make me regret my comments."

"I didn't make you do that."

"Then what did?"

"I don't know, maybe your conscience."

His dark eyes narrowed and as Talon started crying, I started in her direction. "Don't," he said. "You can go, Lucille. Your services are no longer needed."

"You're being ridiculous," I told him. "I can get her."

"No. Just go. It's obvious that you want to leave, so leave."

Graham was a monster born from the ugliest of circumstances. He was painfully beautiful in such a dark, tragic way. His words urged me to go while his eyes begged me to stay.

I walked past him, our shoulders brushing against each other, and I stood tall, staring into his dark eyes. "I'm not going anywhere, Graham, so you can stop wasting your breath telling me to go."

Walking into Talon's room, I partly expected Graham to try to stop me, but he never followed. "Hey, honey," I said, reaching down to Talon and taking her in my arms. I knew it had only been about a week since I last saw her, but I swore she was bigger. Her blond hair was growing in, and her chocolate eyes smiled all on their own.

She smiled more, too, even with her tiny cough and somewhat warm forehead. I laid her on the floor to change her diaper and quietly hummed to myself as she smiled brightly at me.

I wondered if her father's smile would look like hers if he ever took part in the expression. I wondered what his full lips would look like if they curved up.

For about thirty minutes, Talon sat in her swing, and I read her books that sat on her small bookcase. She smiled and giggled, and she made the cutest sounds in the world as her tiny nose ran. Eventually, she fell asleep, and I didn't have the nerve to try to move her back into her crib. She looked beyond comfortable as the chair swayed back and forth.

"I'll need to give her medicine in about an hour," Graham said, breaking my stare away from the sleeping baby. I looked up at the doorway, where he stood with a plate in his hand. "I, um…" He shifted his feet around and avoided eye contact. "Mary prepared meatloaf and mashed potatoes. I figured you might be hungry, and that you wouldn't want to eat with me, so…" He placed it on the dresser and nodded once. "There you go."

He hurt my mind with the way he twisted my opinions about the person he truly was compared to the person he presented himself to be. It was hard to keep up.

"Thank you."

"Of course." He still avoided eye contact, and I watched as his hands clenched and released repeatedly. "You asked me what I was feeling that night. Do you remember?" he asked.

"Yes."

"Can I share now?"

"Of course."

When his head rose and our eyes locked, I swore he somehow squeezed my heart with his stare. When his lips moved, I drank in every word that spilled from his tongue. "I felt anger. I felt so much anger at him. He looked at you as if you were unworthy of his attention. He insulted your clothing all night long as he introduced you to people. He discussed you as if you're not good enough, and for the love of God, he gawked at other women whenever you turned your back to him. He was insensitive, rude, and a complete idiot."

He dropped his head for a split second before bringing his eyes back to mine, his once cold stare now soft, gentle, caring as his lips continued to move. "He was a complete idiot for thinking you weren't the most beautiful woman in that room. Yeah, I get it, Lucille—you're a hippie weirdo and everything about you is loud and outlandish, but who is he to demand that you change? You're a prize of a woman, rose petals in your hair and all, and he treated you as if you were nothing more than an unworthy slave."

"Graham—" I started, but he held a hand up.

"I do apologize for hurting you, and for offending your boyfriend. That night just reminded me of a past I once lived, and I am ashamed that I let it get to me in such a way."

"I accept and appreciate your apology."

He gave me a half smile and turned to walk away, leaving me wondering what had happened in his past that upset him so much.

chapter twelve

New Year's Eve

"IT HIT THE NEW YORK TIMES BESTSELLER LIST, ON TODAY OF ALL DAYS. YOU KNOW what that means, Graham?" Rebecca asked, spreading a new tablecloth on the dining room table.

"It means another reason for Dad to get drunk and show off his house to people," he muttered, just loud enough for her to hear.

She snickered and grabbed the fancy table runner, handed him one end, and took the other in her hands. "It won't be that bad this year. He hasn't been drinking as much lately."

Poor, sweet, naïve Rebecca, Graham thought to himself. She must've been blind to the whisky bottles that sat in his father's desk drawer.

As he helped her set the dinner table for the sixteen guests coming over in two hours, his eyes traveled across the room to her. She'd been living with him and his father for two years now, and he'd never known he could be so happy. When his father was angry, Graham had Rebecca's smile to fall back on. She was the flash of light during the dark thunderstorms.

Plus, every year, he had a birthday cake.

She looked beautiful that night in her fancy New Year's Eve dress. When she moved, the gold dress traveled with her, slightly dragging on the floor behind her. She wore high-heeled shoes that stretched out her small body, and still she seemed so tiny.

"You look pretty," Graham told her, making her look up and smile.

"Thank you, Graham. You look quite handsome yourself."

He smiled back, because she always made him smile.

"Do you think any kids are gonna come tonight?" he asked. He hated how the parties always had grown-ups and never any kids.

"I don't think so," she told him. "But maybe tomorrow I can take you to the YMCA to hang out with some of your friends."

That made Graham happy. His father was always too busy to take him places, but Rebecca always made time.

Rebecca glanced at the fancy watch on her hand, one his father had given her after one of their many fights. "Do you think he's still working?" she asked, raising an eyebrow.

He nodded. "Uh-huh."

She bit her bottom lip. "Should I interrupt?"

He shook his head. "Nuh-huh."

Rebecca crossed the room, still glancing at her watch. "He'll be mad if he's late. I'll go check." She walked toward his office, and it was only seconds before Graham heard the shouting.

"I'm working! This next book isn't going to write itself, Rebecca!" Kent hollered right before Rebecca came hurrying back into the dining room, visibly shaken, her lips now twisted in a frown.

She smiled at Graham and shrugged. "You know how he is on deadlines," she said, making up excuses.

Graham nodded. He knew better than most.

His father was nothing more than a monster, especially when he was behind on his word count.

Later that night, right before the guests began arriving, Kent changed into his brand-name suit just in time. "Why didn't you get me earlier?" he shouted to Rebecca as she set up appetizers in the living room. "I would've been late if I hadn't seen the time because I had to use the bathroom."

Graham turned his back to his father and rolled his eyes. He always had to turn his back to mock his father, otherwise his father's backhand would mock him right back.

"I'm sorry," Rebecca replied, not wanting to dig any deeper and upset Kent. It was New Year's Eve, one of her favorite holidays, and she refused to get into an argument.

Kent huffed and puffed, straightening his tie. "You should change," he told Rebecca. "Your outfit is too revealing, and the last thing I need is for my friends to think my wife is a floozy." His voice was short, and he didn't even look at Rebecca as he spat out the words.

How did he miss it? Graham thought to himself. How did his father not notice how beautiful Rebecca looked?

"I think you look beautiful," Graham voiced.

Kent cocked an eyebrow and looked over at his son. "No one asked you for your thoughts."

That night, Rebecca changed into something else, and she still looked beautiful to Graham.

She still looked beautiful, but she smiled less, which simply broke his heart.

During dinner, Graham's role was to sit and be quiet. His father preferred when he blended in, almost as if he weren't in the room. The grown-ups talked about how great Kent was, and Graham internally rolled his eyes repeatedly.

"Rebecca, what a delicious meal," a guest commented.

Rebecca parted her lips to speak, but Kent spoke before her. "The chicken is a bit dry and the salad a little underdressed, but otherwise it's edible," he said with a laugh. "My wife isn't known for her cooking skills, but boy does she try."

"She's better than me," a woman chimed in, winking at Rebecca to ease the sting of Kent's passive aggressive comment. "I hardly make macaroni and cheese from a box."

The meal went on with a few more undercuts from Kent, but he stated his grievances about Rebecca with such humor that most people didn't think he was serious.

Graham knew better, even though he wished he didn't.

When she reached for more wine, Kent placed his hand on top of hers, halting her. "You know how wine affects you, my love."

"Yes, you're right," Rebecca replied, retracting her hand and placing it in her lap. When a woman inquired about it, she grinned. "Oh, it just makes me a bit dizzy, that's all. Kent's just watching out for me." Her smile became more fake as the night went on.

After dinner was served, Graham was sent to his room for the remainder of the evening, where he spent time playing video games and watching the New Year's Eve countdown on ABC. He watched the ball drop first in New York City, and then again when they replayed the clip to celebrate midnight in Milwaukee. He listened to the grown-ups cheering in the other room, and could faintly hear the sounds of the fireworks exploding over Lake Michigan.

If Graham stood on his tiptoes, glanced out of his window to the left, and looked way up high, he could see some of the fireworks painting the sky.

He used to watch them all the time with his mother, but that was so long ago that he sometimes wondered if it was a real memory or one he made up.

As the people began to leave the house, Graham crawled into bed and pushed the palms of his hands over his ears. He was trying his best to drown out the sound of his father drunkenly yelling at Rebecca about all of her mistakes that night.

It was amazing how Kent could hold in his anger until his company left.

Then, it just spilled out of all of his pores.

A toxic amount of anger.

"I'm sorry," Rebecca always ended up saying, even though she never had anything to apologize for.

How could his father not see how lucky he was to have a woman like her? It hurt his heart knowing that Rebecca was hurting.

When Graham's door opened a few minutes later, he pretended to be sleeping, unsure if it was his father or not.

"Graham? Are you awake?" Rebecca whispered, standing in his doorway.

"Yes," he whispered back.

Rebecca walked into the room and wiped at her eyes, removing any evidence that Kent had caused her pain. She wandered over to his bed and combed his curly hair out of his face. "I just wanted to say Happy New Year. I wanted to stop by earlier, but I had to clean up a bit."

Graham's eyes filled with tears as he stared at Rebecca's eyes, which were heavy with exhaustion. She used to smile more.

"What is it, Graham? What's wrong?"

"Please don't..." he whispered. As the tears began to roll down his cheeks and his body began to shake in the bed, he tried his hardest to be a man, but it wasn't working. His heart was still the heart of a young boy, a child who was terrified of what would happen if his father didn't ease up on Rebecca.

"Please don't what, sweetie?"

"Please don't leave," he said, his voice strained with fear. He sat up in his bed and placed his hands in Rebecca's. "Please don't leave, Rebecca. I know he's mean and he makes you cry, but I promise you're good. You're good and he's mean. He pushes people away, he does, and I can tell he makes you so sad. I know he tells you you're not good enough, but you are. You are good enough, and you're pretty, and your dress was beautiful, and your dinner was perfect, and please, please don't leave us. Please don't leave me." He was now crying full-blown tears, his body shaking from the idea that Rebecca was two suitcases away from leaving him forever. He couldn't imagine what his life would be like if she was gone. He couldn't even begin to envision how dark his life would become if she walked away.

When he was only with his father, he was so, so very much alone.

But when Rebecca came, he remembered how it felt to be loved again.

And he couldn't lose that feeling.

He couldn't lose his light.

"Graham." Rebecca smiled, tears falling from her own eyes as she tried to wipe his away. "You're okay, please, it's okay. Calm down."

"You're going to leave me, I know you are." He sobbed, covering his face with his hands. That was what people did—they left. "He's so mean to you. He's too mean to you, and you're going to leave."

"Graham Michael Russell, you stop it right now, okay?" she ordered, holding his hands tightly in hers. She placed his hands against her cheeks and nodded once. "I'm here, all right? I'm here, and I'm not going anywhere."

"You're not leaving?" he asked, hiccupping as he tried to catch his next breath.

She shook her head. "No. I'm not leaving. You're just overthinking everything. It's late, and you need rest, okay?"

"Okay."

She laid him back down and tucked him in, kissing his forehead. As she stood up to leave, he called after her one last time. "And you'll be here tomorrow?"

"Of course, honey."

"Promise?" he whispered, his voice still a bit shaky, but Rebecca's remained strong and sure.

"Promise."

chapter thirteen

Graham

Lucy and I fell back into our normal routine. In the mornings, she'd show up with her yoga mat and do her morning meditation in the sunroom, and whenever she wasn't working a special event, she'd come over to my house at night to help take care of Talon while I worked on my novel. We ate dinner together at the dining room table almost every night, but didn't have much to talk about other than the cold that had found its way into both Talon's body and mine.

"Drink it," Lucy told me, bringing me a mug of tea.

"I don't drink tea." I coughed into my hands. My desk was still scattered with tissues and cough syrup bottles.

"You will drink this twice a day for three days, and it will make you one hundred percent better. I have no clue how you're even functioning with that nasty cough. So, drink," she ordered. I smelled the tea and made a face. She laughed. "Cinnamon, ginger, fresh lemons, hot red peppers, sugar, black pepper, and peppermint extract—plus a secret ingredient I can't tell you about."

"It smells like hell."

She nodded with a small smirk. "A perfect drink for the devil himself."

For the following three days, I drank her tea. She pretty much had to force-feed it to me, but by day four, the coughing had disappeared.

I was almost positive Lucy was a witch, but at least with her tea I was able to clear my head for the first time in weeks.

The following Saturday evening, dinner sat on the table, and when I went to get Lucy to eat, I noticed her in the sunroom on her cell phone.

Instead of interrupting, I waited patiently, until the roasted chicken was cold.

Time passed quickly. She'd been standing in the sunroom on her cell phone for hours now. Her eyes were glued to the rain cascading down from the sky as she moved her lips, speaking to whoever was on the other end of the line.

I wandered past the room every now and then, watching her move her hands to express herself, watching the tears fall from her eyes. They fell heavily, like the rain. After a while, she hung up and lowered herself to the floor, sat with her legs crossed, and stared out the window.

When Talon was down, I stepped into the sunroom to check on her.

"Are you all right?" I asked, concerned about how someone as bright as Lucy could appear so dark that afternoon. It was almost as if she blended into the gray clouds herself.

"How much do I owe you?" she asked, not turning my way.

"Owe me?"

She turned around, sniffling, and allowed the tears to keep falling down her cheeks. "You bet me that my relationship would be over in a month tops, and you win. So, how much do I owe you? You win."

"Lucille…" I started, but she shook her head.

"He, um, he said New York is the place for artists. He said it's the place for him to grow his craft, and there are opportunities there that he wouldn't have in the Midwest." She sniffled some more and wiped her nose on her sleeve. "He said his friend offered him a couch in his apartment, so he's going to stay there for a while. Then he said a long-distance relationship wasn't something he was really interested in having, so my stupid heart tightened, thinking he was inviting me out there to be with him. I know what you're thinking, too." She giggled nervously then shrugged and shook her head. "Silly, immature, naïve Lucille, believing love would be enough, thinking she was worthy of being someone's forever."

"That's…not what I was thinking."

"So, how much?" she asked, standing up. "How much do I owe you? I have some money in my purse. Let me go grab it."

"Lucille, stop."

She walked in my direction and put on a fake smile. "No, it's fine. A bet is a bet and you won, so let me go get the money."

"You don't owe me anything."

"You're good at reading people, you know. That's probably what makes you a fantastic author. You can look at someone for five minutes and know their entire story. It's a gift really. You saw Richard for a moment and knew he'd end up breaking me. So what's my story, huh? I hate spoilers, but I'd love to know. What's going to happen to me?" she asked, her body shaking as the tears kept rolling down her cheeks. "Am I always going to be the girl who feels too much and ends up alone? Because, I…I…" Her words became a blurred mess as her emotions began to overpower her. She covered her face with her hands and broke down right in the middle of the sunroom.

I didn't know what to do.

I wasn't made for these kinds of moments.

I wasn't one to give comfort.

That was true, but when her knees started to tremble and her legs began to look as if they were going to collapse, I did the only thing I could think to do.

I wrapped her in my arms, giving her something to hold on to, giving her something to hold her up before gravity forced her down to the solid ground. She wrapped her fingers in my shirt and cried into me, soaking my shoulder as my hands rested against her back.

She didn't let go, and I figured I shouldn't ask her to pull her emotions together.

It was all right that she and I handled things in a different fashion. She wore her heart on her sleeve, and I kept my heart wrapped in steel chains deep within my soul.

Without thought, I held her closer as her body continued to shake. The woman who felt everything leaned in closer to the man who felt nothing at all.

For a split second in time, I felt a little of her pain while she encountered my coldness, and neither one of us seemed to mind.

"You can't go home," I told her, glancing at my watch, seeing that it was almost midnight. "It's pouring rain, and you rode your bike to my house."

"It's fine. I'll be okay," she told me, trying to grab her jacket from the front closet.

"It's not safe. I'll drive you."

"No way," she argued. "Talon has a cold. She shouldn't be leaving the house, especially in the pouring rain. Plus, you're a bit sick yourself," she told me.

"I can handle a cold," I stated.

"Yes, but your daughter cannot. I'll be okay. Plus, there's whisky back home," she joked, her eyes still swollen from her emotional breakdown over Dick.

I slightly shook my head, disagreeing. "Stay here for a moment." I hurried into my office, picked up three of the five whisky bottles that sat on my desk, and took them back to the foyer where Lucy stood. "Yours for the choosing. You can have all the whisky you want, and one of the spare rooms for the night."

She narrowed her eyes. "You're not going to let me ride my bike home tonight, are you?"

"No, definitely not."

She bit her bottom lip and narrowed her eyes. "Fine, but you cannot judge me for the intense romance Johnnie and I are about to have," she said, taking the bottle of Johnnie Walker whisky from my hand.

"Deal. If you need anything, you can knock on my office door. I'll be up and can assist you."

"Thank you, Graham."

"For what?"

"Catching me before I hit the ground."

Knock, knock, knock.

I glanced over at my closed office door and raised an eyebrow as I typed the final few sentences in chapter twenty of my manuscript. My desk was covered in tissues, and a half bottle of cough syrup sat beside me. My eyes burned a bit from exhaustion, but I knew I still needed another five thousand words before I could call it a night. Plus, Talon would be awake in a few hours for a bottle, therefore it seemed pointless to even consider going to bed.

Knock, knock, knock.

Standing up, I stretched a bit before opening the door. Lucy stood there with a glass of whisky in her hand and a remarkably wide smile on her lips.

"Hi, Graham Cracker," she said, stumbling a bit as she swayed back and forth.

"Do you need something?" I asked, completely aware and alert. "Are you all right?"

"Are you a psychic?" she asked, placing her glass to her lips and taking a sip. "Or a wizard?"

I cocked an eyebrow. "I beg your pardon?"

"I mean, it has to be one of those," she said, dancing down the hallway, back and forth, swirling, twirling, humming. "Because how did you know that Richard—er, *Dick* would break up with me? I've been thinking about that repeatedly with Johnnie tonight, and I've concluded that the only way you could've known is if you are a psychic." She came closer to me and tapped my nose once with her pointer finger. "Or a wizard."

"You're drunk."

"I'm happy."

"No, you're drunk. You're simply covering your sadness with a blanket of whisky."

"Que sera, sera." She giggled before trying to peer into my office. "So, is that where the magic happens?" She giggled again then covered her mouth for a second before leaning in closer and whispering, "I mean, magic as in your stories, not your sex life."

"Yes, I figured, Lucille." I closed my office door, leaving us standing in the hallway. "Would you like some water?"

"Yes, please, the kind that tastes like wine."

We walked past the living room, and I told her to wait on the couch for me to grab the drink.

"Hey, Graham Cracker," she called. "What's your greatest hope?"

"I already told you," I yelled back. "I don't hope."

When I walked back, she was sitting straight up on the couch with a smile on her face.

"Here you go," I said, handing her the glass.

She took a sip of the water and her eyes widened, stunned. "Oh my gosh, I know who you are now. You aren't a psychic, you aren't a wizard—you're Reverse Jesus!" she exclaimed, her doe eyes wide with wonderment.

"Reverse Jesus?"

She nodded quickly. "You turned wine into water." Even I couldn't hold in my smile at that one, and she was quick to notice. "You did it, Graham Cracker. You smiled."

"A mistake."

She tilted her head, studying me. "My favorite mistake thus far. Can I tell you a secret?"

"Sure."

"You may not be a psychic, but sometimes I think I am, and I have this psychic feeling that one day I'm going to grow on you."

"Oh, I doubt that. You're pretty annoying," I joked, making her laugh.

"Yes, but still. I'm like an ingrown toenail. Once someone lets me in, I dig my claws in."

"What a disgusting thing to compare yourself to." I grimaced. "I mean, that's literally the worst comparison I've ever heard before."

She poked me in the chest. "If you end up using that in one of your novels, I want royalties."

"I'll have my lawyer talk to your lawyer." I smirked.

"Oh, you did it again," she said, leaning in toward me in awe. "Smiling looks good on you. I have no clue why you avoid doing it."

"You just think it looks good on me because you're intoxicated."

"I'm not intoxicated," she insisted, slurring her words a bit in the process. "I'm perfectly sober."

"You couldn't walk a straight line if your life depended on it," I told her.

She took it as a challenge and leaped up from the sofa. As she began walking, she stretched out her arms as if she were walking an invisible tight rope. "See!" she said a second before stumbling over, forcing me to lunge to catch her. She lay in my arms, looked up into my eyes, and smiled. "I totally had it."

"I know," I told her.

"This is the second time you've caught me in one day."

"Third time's a charm."

Her hand rested on my cheek and she stared into my eyes, making my heart stop for a few moments. "Sometimes you scare me," she said candidly. "But most of the time your eyes just make me sad."

"I'm sorry, for anything I've done to scare you. It's the last thing I'd want to do."

"It's okay. Every time I walk in on you playing peekaboo with Talon, I see your true aura."

"My aura?"

She nodded once. "To the rest of the world, you seem so dark and grim, but when you look at your daughter, everything shifts. Everything in your energy changes. You become lighter."

"You're drunk," I told her.

"I can walk a straight line!" she argued again, trying to stand but failing. "Oh wait, I couldn't, could I?"

I shook my head. "You definitely couldn't."

She kept touching my face, feeling my beard in her hands. "Talon is very lucky to have you as her father. You're a really shitty human, but a pretty awesome dad." Her voice was soaked in kindness and misplaced trust, which made my heart beat in a way I was certain would kill me.

"Thank you for that," I said, fully accepting both of her comments.

"Of course." She giggled before clearing her throat once. "Graham Cracker?"

"Yes, Lucille?"

"I'm going to vomit."

I scooped her up into my arms and rushed her to the bathroom. The moment I placed her on the floor, she wrapped her arms around the toilet, and I wrapped her wild hair in my hands, holding it out of the way as Lucy appeared to lose everything she'd ever put into her stomach.

"Better?" I asked after she finished.

She sat back a bit and shook her head. "No. Johnnie Walker was supposed to make me feel better, but he lied. He made me feel worse. I hate boys who lie like that and break hearts."

"We should get you to bed."

She nodded and went to stand up, but almost tumbled over.

"I got you," I told her, and she nodded once before allowing me to lift her into my arms.

"Third time's a charm," she whispered. She closed her eyes as she laid her head against my chest, and she kept them shut the whole time I pulled the covers back, laid her down, and pulled the blanket over her small body.

"Thank you," she whispered as I shut off the light.

I doubted she'd remember any of the night's events come morning, which was probably for the best.

"Of course."

"I'm sorry my sister left you," she said, yawning with her eyes still closed. "Because even though you're cold, you're still very warm."

"I'm sorry Dick left you," I replied. "Because even when you're upset, you're still very kind."

"It hurts," she whispered, wrapping her arms around a pillow and pulling it closer to her chest. Her eyes stayed closed, and I watched a few tears slip out. "Being left behind hurts."

Yes.

It did.

I stood still for a few moments, unable to leave her side. As someone who'd been left behind before, I didn't want her to fall asleep being alone. Perhaps she wouldn't remember me standing there in the morning, and maybe she wouldn't have even cared. But I knew what it felt like going to bed alone. I knew the cold chill that loneliness left drifting through a darkened room, and I didn't want her to suffer from that same feeling. Therefore, I stayed. It didn't take long for her to fall asleep. Her breaths were gentle, her tears stopped, and I shut the door. I couldn't for the life of me understand why a person would leave someone as gentle as her behind—with or without her weird sage stick and crystals.

chapter fourteen

Lucy

Ouch, ouch, ouch.

I slowly sat up in bed, realizing quickly it wasn't my bed at all. My eyes examined the room, and I shifted around in the sheets a bit. My hands fell against my forehead.

Ouch!

My mind was spinning as I tried to recall what happened the night before, but everything seemed to be a blur. The most important piece of information came flooding back to me, though—Richard had chosen New York City over me.

I turned to my left and found a small tray sitting on the nightstand with a glass of orange juice, two pieces of toast, a bowl of berries, a bottle of ibuprofen, and a small note.

Sorry for misleading you last night.
I'm a jerk. Here's some medicine and breakfast to make up for me
making you feel like shit this morning.
—Johnnie Walker

I smiled and popped a few berries into my mouth before washing down the ibuprofen. Pulling myself up, I walked to the bathroom and washed my face—my mascara was smeared all over, making me look like a raccoon. Then, I used the toothpaste in the top drawer and my finger as the brush to clean my nasty morning-after-whisky breath.

As I finished washing up, I heard Talon crying and hurriedly went to check on her. I walked into her nursery and paused when I saw an older lady standing over her, changing her diaper.

"Hello?" I asked.

The woman turned for a moment then went back to her task.

"Oh hello, you must be Lucy," the woman exclaimed, lifting Talon into her arms and bouncing the smiling girl. She turned my way with a big grin. "I'm Mary, Ollie's wife."

"Oh, hi! It's nice to meet you."

"You too, darling. I've heard so much about you from Ollie. Not as much from Graham, but, well, you know Graham." She winked. "How's your head?"

"It's somehow still there," I joked. "Last night was rough."

"You kids and your coping mechanisms. I hope you're feeling better soon."

"Thank you." I smiled. "Um, where's Graham exactly?"

"He's in the backyard. He called me early this morning to ask me to come watch Talon while he went to run some errands. As you know, that's a big deal for Graham—asking people for help—so I swooped in to watch her while he left and you rested."

"Did you leave me the breakfast?" I asked. "With the note?"

Her lips stretched farther, but she shook her head. "No, ma'am. That was all Graham. I know—I'm as surprised as you are. I didn't know he had it in him."

"What is he doing in the backyard?" I asked, walking in that direction.

Mary followed me, bouncing Talon the whole way. We walked into the sunroom and stared out the floor-to-ceiling windows at Graham as he cut the grass. Against the small shed lay bags of soil and shovels.

"Well, it seems he's making a garden."

My chest tightened at the idea, and no words came to me.

Mary nodded once. "I told him to wait to cut the grass seeing as how it rained last night, but he seemed eager to get started."

"That's amazing."

She nodded. "I thought so too."

"I can take Talon for you, if you need to get going," I offered.

"Only if you're feeling up to it. I do need to get going if I'm going to make the afternoon church service. Here you go." She handed Talon over and kissed her forehead. "It's amazing, isn't it?" she asked. "How a few months ago, we weren't sure she was going to make it, but now she's more here than ever before."

"So, so amazing."

She placed her hand on my forearm, a gentle touch, and gave me a warm smile, just like her husband. "I'm glad we were finally able to meet."

"Me too, Mary. Me too."

She left the house a few minutes later. Talon and I stayed in the sunroom, watching Graham working hard outside, turning his head every now and then to cough. It had to be freezing out there after the cold rain the night before, and it couldn't have been doing anything great for his cold.

I walked to the back door that led out to the yard and pushed it open, a cold breeze brushing against me. "Graham, what are you doing?"

"Just fixing up the backyard."

"It's freezing out here, and you're making your cold worse. Get inside."

"I'm almost finished, Lucille. Just give me a few more minutes."

I arched an eyebrow, confused as to why he was so determined. "But why? What are you doing?"

"You asked me to make a garden," he said, wiping his brow with the back of his hand. "So I'm making you a garden."

My heart.

It exploded.

"You're making a garden? For me?"

"You've done plenty for me," he replied. "You've done even more for Talon. The least I can do is build you a garden so you can have another place to meditate. I bought a ton of organic fertilizer—they told me it was the best kind, and I figured a hippie weirdo like yourself would enjoy the organic part." He wasn't wrong. "Now please close that door before you make my daughter freeze."

I did as he said, but not for a second did I take my eyes off him. When he finished, he was covered in dirt and sweat. The backyard was beautifully trimmed, and all that was missing was the plants.

"I figure you can pick out the flowers, or seeds, or whatever gardeners garden," he told me as he wiped his brow. "I know nothing about these kinds of things."

"Yeah, of course. Wow, this is just…" I smiled, staring at the yard. "Wow."

"I can hire someone to plant whatever you choose," he told me.

"Oh no, please let me. That's my favorite part of spring—digging my hands into the earth's soil and feeling myself reconnect with the world. It's very grounding."

"And once again, your weird is showing," he said with a small twinkle in his eye, as if he were…teasing me? "If it's all right with you, I'd like to shower. Then I can take Talon so you can start your day."

"Yes, for sure. No rush."

"Thank you."

He started to walk away, and I called after him. "Why did you do this?" I asked. "The garden?"

He lowered his head and shrugged his shoulders before looking into my eyes. "A smart woman once told me I was a shitty human, and I'm trying my best to be a little less shitty."

"Oh no." I pulled the collar of my shirt over my face and scrunched up my nose. "I said that last night, didn't I?"

"You did, but don't worry. Sometimes the truth needs to be voiced. It was much easier to hear it from someone as giggly, drunk, and kind as you."

"I'm sorry, come again?" Mari asked me that afternoon as we walked our bikes to the hiking trail. Spring was always exciting because we could bike a lot more and explore nature. Sure, I loved it more than my sister, but somewhere deep, deep, *deep* inside of her soul, I was sure she was thankful to have me to keep her healthy.

"I know." I nodded. "It's weird."

"It's beyond weird. I cannot believe Richard would break up with you via a phone call," she gasped. Then she grimaced. "Well, on second thought, I'm surprised it took this long for you to break up."

"What?!"

"I mean, I'm just saying. You two were so much alike in the beginning, Lucy. It was kind of annoying how much of a match made in heaven you two were, but over time, you both seemed to...shift."

"What are you talking about?"

She shrugged. "You used to laugh all the time with Richard, but lately...I can't even think of the last time he made you giggle. Plus, tell me the last time he asked how you were doing. Every time I saw him, he was talking about himself."

Hearing that from Mari didn't make it any easier to deal with the fact that Richard had broken up with me. I knew she was right, too. The truth of the matter was, Richard wasn't the same man who fell in love with me all those years ago, and I was far from the girl he knew me to be.

"Maktub," I whispered, looking down at my wrist.

Mari smiled my way and hopped on her bike. "Maktub indeed. You can move in with me, so you're not stuck in his apartment. It will be perfect. I needed more sister time. Look at it this way—at least now you don't have a mustache going down on you."

I laughed. "Richard hasn't gone down on me in what feels like years."

Her mouth dropped open in disbelief. "Then you should've broken up with him years ago, sister. A boy who doesn't go down doesn't have the right to your services once he goes up."

My sister was filled with irrefutable knowledge.

"You don't seem that sad about it at all," Mari mentioned. "I'm a bit surprised."

"Yeah, well, after drinking my weight in whisky last night and spending the rest of the morning meditating today, I'm feeling okay. Plus, Graham made me a garden this morning."

"A garden?" she asked, surprised. "Is that his form of an apology?"

"I think so. He bought a ton of organic fertilizer, too."

"Well, he gets an A for that one. Everyone knows the way to Lucy's forgiveness is through dirt and organic fertilizer."

Amen, sister.

"So, are we still on for going to visit Mama's tree up north for Easter?" I asked as we started biking the trail. Every holiday, Mari and I tried our best to make it up to visit Mama. One of Mama's old friends had a cabin up north that she didn't use often, and that was where we'd planted Mama's tree all those years ago, surrounded by people from all around the country who made up her family.

If I'd learned anything from all my traveling with Mama, it was that family wasn't built by blood—it was built by love.

"So, you're going to hate me, but I'm going to be visiting a friend that weekend," Mari said.

"Oh? Who?"

"I was going to catch the train to Chicago to see Sarah. She's back in the States visiting her parents, and I thought I'd swing by, seeing as how I haven't seen her since I got better. It's been years."

Sarah was one of Mari's closest friends and a world traveler. It was almost impossible to pinpoint where Sarah would be one month from the next, so I completely understood Mari's choice. It just sucked because with Richard gone, it would be the first holiday I'd be spending alone.

Alas, maktub.

chapter fifteen

Graham

Professor Oliver sat across from me at my desk, his eyes roaming over the first draft of chapters seventeen through twenty of my novel. I sat impatiently waiting as he flipped each page slowly, his eyes narrowed, deep in thought.

Every now and then he'd glance my way, make a low hum, and then go back to reading. When he finally finished, he sat the papers back on my desk and remained silent.

I waited, arched an eyebrow, but still, no sound.

"Well?" I asked.

Professor Oliver removed his glasses and crossed his leg over his knee. With a very calm voice, he finally spoke. "It's kind of like a monkey took a big shit and tried to spell their name in it with their tail. Only, the monkey's name is John and he wrote Maria."

"It's not that bad," I argued.

"Oh no." He shook his head. "It's worse."

"What's wrong with it?" I asked.

He shrugged his shoulders. "It's just fluff. All fat, no meat."

"It's the first draft. It's supposed to be shit."

"Yes, but it's supposed to be human shit, not monkey shit. Graham, you're a New York Times bestseller. You're a Wall Street Journal bestseller. You have millions of dollars in your bank account from your craftsmanship in creating stories, and there are numerous fans around the world with your words tattooed on their bodies. So, it's a shame that you had the nerve to hand this complete and utter bullshit to me." He stood up, smoothed out his velvet suit, and shook his head. "Talon can write better than this."

"You're joking. Did you read the part about the lion?" I asked.

He rolled his eyes so hard, I was certain his eyeballs were going to get lost in the back of his head. "Why the hell is there a lion loose in Tampa Bay?! No. Just—no. Find a way to relax, okay? You need to loosen up, break free a bit. Your words read as if you have a stick up your ass, and the stick isn't even teasing you right."

I cleared my throat. "That's a really weird thing to say."

"Yes, well, at least I don't write monkey shit."

"No." I smiled. "You only speak it."

"Listen closely, okay? As the godfather to Talon, I am proud of you, Graham."

"Since when are you her godfather?"

"It's a self-proclaimed title, and don't kill my spirit, son. As I was saying, I am proud of how great of a father you are to your daughter. Every minute of your day is spent caring for her, which is amazing, but, as your writing mentor, I am demanding that you take some time for yourself. Go smoke some crack, hump a stranger, eat some weird mushrooms. Just loosen up a bit. It will help your stories."

"I've never had to loosen up before," I told him.

"Were you getting laid before?" he countered with an eyebrow arched.

Well, fuck.

"Goodbye, Graham, and please, don't call me until you are high or having sex."

"I'm probably not going to call you while I'm having sex."

"That's fine," he said, grabbing his fedora off the desk and placing it on his head. "It probably wouldn't last long enough for you to dial my number anyway," he mocked.

God, I hated that man.

Too bad he was my best friend.

◈

"Hey, Talon's down for a nap. I just wanted to see if you wanted me to order a piz—" Lucy's words faded away as she stepped into my office. "What are you doing?" she asked warily.

I set my phone down on my desk and cleared my throat. "Nothing."

She smirked and shook her head. "You were taking a selfie."

"I was not," I argued. "A pizza is fine. Just cheese on my half."

"No, no, no, you cannot change the subject. Why are you taking selfies while dressed in a suit and tie?"

I straightened my tie and went back to my desk. "Well, if you have to know, I need a picture of myself to upload on this site."

"What site? Are you joining Facebook?"

"No."

"Then which site?" She giggled to herself. "Anything but Tinder and you'll be okay."

My jaw tightened, and she stopped laughing.

"*Oh my God*, you're joining Tinder?!" she hollered.

"Say it a bit louder, Lucille. I'm not certain the neighbors heard you."

"I'm sorry, I just…" She walked into my office and sat on the edge of my desk. "G.M. Russell is joining the world of Tinder…I knew it felt a little cold in the house."

"Huh?"

"I mean, when I first met you, I figured you were the devil, which meant your home was hell, which means with it now being cold that—"

"Hell has finally frozen over. Clever, Lucille."

She reached for my cell phone and started trying to unlock it. "Can I see your photos?"

"What? No."

"Why not? You do know Tinder is like…a hookup site, right?"

"I'm fully aware of what Tinder is."

Her cheeks reddened and she bit her bottom lip. "You're trying to get laid, eh?"

"Professor Oliver is convinced my writing is suffering from the fact that I haven't had sex in a while to loosen myself up. He thinks I'm uptight."

"What?!" she gasped. "You?! Uptight?! No way!"

"Anyway, he's one hundred percent wrong about the manuscript. It's good."

She rubbed her hands together, giddy. "Is it? Can I read it?"

I hesitated, and she rolled her eyes.

"I'm your biggest fan, remember? If I don't love it, you'll know Ollie was right. If I do love it, you'll know you're right."

Well, I did love to be right.

I handed her the chapters, and she sat reading, her eyes darting back and forth over the pages. Every now and then she'd glance at me with a concerned look. Finally, she finished and cleared her throat. "A lion?"

Shit.

I rolled my eyes. "I need to get laid."

"Take off your tie, Graham."

"Excuse me?"

"I need you to unlock your phone and take off your tie and the suit jacket. No girl who is trying to have sex is in search of a man with a freaking suit and tie on. Plus, you buttoned the top button on your shirt."

"It's classy."

"It looks like your neck has a muffin top."

"You're being ridiculous. This is a custom-made designer suit."

"You rich people and your labels. All I hear is that it's not a penis, and therefore it eliminates your opportunities to get laid. Now, unlock your phone and take off the tie."

Annoyed, I followed her orders. "Better?" I asked, crossing my arms.

She grimaced. "A little. Here, unbutton the top three buttons on your shirt."

I did as she said, and she nodded, taking photographs.

"Yes! Chest hair—women who are trying to get it on love some chest hair.

It's like the three little pigs; it has to be the right amount. Not too much, not too little, your hair is justtttt right." She grinned.

"Have you been drinking again?" I asked.

She laughed. "No. This is just me."

"That's what I was afraid of."

After taking some shots, she studied them with the biggest frown I'd ever seen. "Yeah, no. You have to take off your shirt completely."

"What? Don't be ridiculous. I'm not taking off my shirt in front of you."

"Graham," Lucy whined, rolling her eyes. "You have your shirt off every other day doing that kangaroo thing with Talon. Now shut up and take off your shirt."

After some more arguing, I finally gave in. She even had me switch into dark black jeans—to "look more manly." She started snapping photographs, telling me to turn left and right, to smile with my eyes—whatever that meant—and to be moody but sexy.

"Okay, one more. Turn to the side, drop your head a little, and slide your hands into your back pockets. Look as if you hate everything about me taking pictures of you."

Easy enough.

"There," she said, grinning from ear to ear. "Your pictures are now uploaded. Now all that's left to do is perfect your bio."

"No need," I told her, reaching for my cell phone. "I already did that part."

She raised an eyebrow, seeming unsure, and then went to read it. "New York Times bestselling author who has a six-month-old child. Married, but the wife ran away. Looking to hook up. Also, I'm five foot eleven."

"Everyone seems to put their height. I guess it's a thing."

"This is awful. Here, I'll fix it."

I hurried over to her, standing behind to watch what she typed.

Looking for sex. I am a big dick.

"I think you meant I *have* a big dick," I remarked.

She wickedly replied, "No, I meant what I wrote."

I groaned and went to grab my phone.

"Okay, okay, I'll try again!"

Looking for casual sex, no strings attached.

Unless you're into being tied up.

Looking at you, Anastasia.

"Who's Anastasia?" I asked.

Lucy tossed me my phone and laughed to herself. "All that matters is that the women will understand. Now all you have to do is swipe right if you find them attractive, left if you think they're not. Then, just wait for the magic to happen."

"Thank you for your help."

"Well, you gave me a garden, so the least I can do is get you laid. I'm going to order the pizza now. I'm exhausted after all of that."

"Only cheese on my half! Oh, Lucille?"

"Yes?"

"What's Snapchat?"

She narrowed her eyes and shook her head twice. "Nope, not even touching that one. Only one social media adventure a night. We'll save the snapping for another day."

chapter sixteen

Lucy

Graham's first Tinder date was on Saturday, and before he left, I forced him to change out of his suit and tie and into a plain white T-shirt and dark jeans.

"It feels too casual," he complained.

"Um, it's not like your clothes are going to stay on anyway. Now go. Go on and spread some legs, do some pelvic thrusts, and then come back home and write about horror stories and monsters."

He left at eight-thirty that night.

By nine, he'd returned.

I arched an eyebrow. "Um, not to sound totally disrespectful to your manhood and all but…that was legit the fastest round of sex in the history of sex."

"I didn't sleep with her," Graham replied, dropping his keys on the table in the foyer.

"What? Why?"

"She turned out to be a liar."

"Oh no!" I frowned, feeling my chest tighten for him. "Married? Kids? Three hundred pounds bigger than her picture? Did she have a penis? Was her name George?"

"No," he said harshly, plopping down on the living room couch.

"Then what was it?"

"Her hair."

"Huh?"

"Her hair. On the app, she was a brunette, but when I got there, she was a blonde."

I blinked repeatedly. Full-on blank stare. "Come again?"

"I'm just saying, it's obvious that if she'd lie about something like that, she'd lie about gonorrhea and chlamydia." The way he said it with such a straight face made me burst out into a giggling fit.

"Yes, Graham, that's exactly how it works." I laughed, my stomach hurting from laughing so hard.

"This isn't funny, Lucille. It turns out I'm not a person who can just randomly sleep with someone. I'm on a deadline, and I cannot for the life of me figure out how I'm going to loosen up in time to send the book to my editor. It was supposed to be done by the time Talon was born. That was over six months ago."

I smiled widely and bit my bottom lip. "You know what? I think I have an idea, and I'm one hundred and ten percent sure you're going to hate it."

"What is it?" he asked.

"Have you ever heard of hot yoga?"

◈

"I'm the only man in here," Graham whispered as he walked into the yoga studio with me that Sunday morning. He was in a white tank top with gray sweatpants, and he looked terrified.

"Don't be silly, Graham Cracker. The instructor is a guy. Toby. You'll fit right in."

I lied.

He didn't fit right in, but at least watching a grown man with muscles on top of muscles trying to do a sun salutation was the highlight of my life—and of the lives of all the women in class that morning.

"Now travel from cobra to downward dog to pigeon with controlled movement," Toby instructed.

Graham groaned, doing the movements but complaining the whole time. "Cobra, pigeon, camel—why is every move named after a sex position?" he asked.

I giggled. "You know, most people would say those are named after animals, Graham Cracker, not sex positions."

He turned my way and after a second, realization broke through. A tiny smile formed. "Touché."

"You're super tight," the instructor noted to Graham as he walked around to help him.

"Oh, no, you don't have to—" Graham started, but it was too late. Toby was helping adjust his hips.

"Relax," Toby said in his soothing voice. "Relax."

"It's hard to relax when a stranger is touching my—" Graham's eyes widened. "Yup, that's my penis. You are actually touching my penis," Graham muttered as the instructor helped him with one of the positions.

I couldn't stop giggling at how ridiculous and uncomfortable Graham looked. His face was so stern, and when Toby made Graham pop his butt out, I had tears rolling down my cheeks from laughter.

"Okay, class, one final breath. In with the good energies, out with the bad. Namaste." Toby bowed to us all, and Graham just stayed there, lying on the floor in a pile of sweat, tears, and his manhood.

I kept giggling to myself. "Come on, get up." I reached down to him, and he took my hand as I pulled him up. As he stood up, he shook his nasty, sweaty hair all over me. "Ew! That's disgusting."

With a sly smile, he said, "You made me get touched in public, so you get to enjoy the sweat."

"Trust me, you're lucky it's Toby who touched you instead of the women who are currently gawking at you over in the corner right now."

He turned to see the women staring his way, waving. "You women and your sex-driven minds," he joked.

"Says the man who does camel as a sex position. What do you do exactly? Do you just sit on your knees and like"—I thrust my hips—"do this repeatedly?" I kept making the humping motion, which turned Graham's face even redder than it had been during the class.

"Lucille."

"Yes?"

"Stop humping the air."

"I would, but your embarrassment is too rewarding right now." I laughed. He was so easily humiliated, and I knew being around me in public would be awful for him. I'd take every opportunity to make myself look like a fool. "Okay, so needless to say, hot yoga isn't your thing."

"Not at all. If anything, I feel more stressed out, and a pinch violated," he joked.

"Well, let me try a few more things to see if they help you."

He cocked an eyebrow as if he could read my mind. "You're going to sage my house, aren't you? Or put crystals on my windowsills?"

"Oh yeah." I nodded. "I'm going to weird hippie the crap out of your house, and then you're going to help me in the garden."

I spent the next few weeks out in the backyard, teaching Graham the ins and outs of gardening. We planted fruits, vegetables, and beautiful flowers. I made lines of sunflowers that would look so beautiful as they grew tall over time. In one corner of the yard was a stone bench, which would be perfect for morning energy meditations and great as an afternoon reading corner. I surrounded it with beautiful flowers that would light up the area—Peruvian lilies, nepeta faasseniis, coreopsis, forget-me-nots, and gloriosa daisies. The colors would be beautiful mixed together. The pinks, blues, yellows, and purples would add a pop of color to Graham's life, that was for sure.

As the baby monitor started going off, Graham stood up from the dirt. "I'll get her."

Only a few minutes passed before I heard him shouting my name.

"LUCILLE!"

I sat up in the dirt, alarmed by the urgency in Graham's shout.

"LUCILLE, HURRY!"

I shot up to my feet, my heart pounding in my chest, dirt across my face, and I sprinted into the house. "What is it?!" I hollered back.

"In the living room! Hurry!" he shouted once more.

I ran, terrified about what I was about to witness, and when I made it into the space, my heart landed in my throat as I wrapped my hands over my mouth. "Oh my gosh," I said, my eyes watering over as I looked at Talon.

"I know, right?" Graham said, smiling at his daughter. For a long time, he'd tried his best to hold in his grins, but he hadn't been able to lately. The more Talon laughed and smiled, the more she opened Graham's heart.

He was holding Talon in his arms, feeding her.

Well, he wasn't feeding her—she was feeding herself, holding the bottle in her own hands for the first time.

My heart exploded with excitement.

"I was feeding her, and she wrapped her hands around the bottle and started to hold it herself," he told me, his eyes wide with pride.

As we cheered her on, Talon started giggling and spat milk into Graham's face, making us both laugh. I grabbed a cloth and wiped the milk from his cheek.

"She amazes me every day," he said, staring at his daughter. "It's too bad that Jane…" He paused. "That *Lyric* is missing out on it. She has no clue what she left behind."

I nodded in agreement. "She's missing everything. It's just sad."

"What was it like, growing up together?" he asked.

I was a bit surprised—we'd spent months together and he hadn't once asked me any questions about my sister.

I sat on the couch beside him and shrugged. "We moved around a lot. Our mom was a bit of a floater, and when my dad couldn't take any more, he left us. Lyric was older and noticed more issues than Mari and I did. Every day with my mother felt like a new adventure. The lack of a real home never bothered me because we had each other, and whenever we needed something, some kind of miracle would happen.

"But Lyric didn't see it that way. She was very much like our father—grounded. She hated not knowing where our next meal would come from. She hated that sometimes Mama would give what little money we did have to help out a friend in need. She hated the instability of our lives, so when she'd finally had enough, when she could no longer take the person Mama was, she did exactly as our father had—she left."

"She's always been a runner," he stated.

"Yes, and a part of me wants to hate her for how distant and cold she became, but another part understands. She had to grow up fast, and in a way, Lyric wasn't wrong. Our mother was kind of a child herself, which meant we didn't have much parenting growing up. Lyric felt as if she had to take on that role and parent her parent."

"Which is why she probably never wanted kids," he said. "She'd already done the parent role."

"Yeah. I mean, it doesn't forgive her actions at all, but it makes them more understandable."

"I think I could tell when I met her that she was a runner. Also, I'm certain she could tell I was cold, that I'd never once ask her to stay."

"Do you miss her?" I asked, my voice low.

"No," he answered quickly, no hesitation whatsoever. "She and I were never in love. We had an unspoken agreement that if one was ever ready to go, they were free to do so. The marriage arrangement was just something she thought would help her advance in her career.

"We were simply roommates who happened to have sex sometimes. Before Talon, it would've been fine if she left. It would've been completely acceptable. Hell, I was somewhat surprised she stayed as long as she did. I wouldn't have cared, but now…" He smiled down at Talon as she burped for him, and then he laid her on the blanket on the floor. "Now I call her each night, asking her to come back, not for me, but for our daughter. I know what it's like to grow up without a mother, and I'd never want that for Talon."

"I'm so sorry."

He shrugged. "Not your fault. Anyway, how's the garden?"

"Perfect. It's perfect. Thank you again for the gift. It means more to me than you could imagine."

He nodded. "Of course. I'm guessing you're gone this weekend, for the holiday?" He climbed from the couch onto the floor and started playing peekaboo with Talon, which made my heart do cartwheels.

"I was supposed to be, but it turns out I'm spending the holiday alone."

"What? Why?"

I explained that Mari would be out of town, and that I normally made the trip up north but didn't want to do the drive alone.

"You should come to Professor Oliver's house with Talon and me," Graham offered.

"What? No. No, it's really okay."

He pulled out his cell phone and dialed a number. "Hello? Professor Oliver, how are you?"

"Graham, no!" I whisper-shouted, reaching out my arm to stop him, but he stood up and wouldn't allow me to grab the phone.

"Good, I'm good." *Pause.* "No, I'm not trying to back out. I'm calling to see if you could add another chair to your table. It appears Lucille was going to sit in her apartment for Easter and cry into a pint of Ben & Jerry's, and while I think that's a completely normal thing to do, I thought I'd see if you could host her at your place."

Another long pause.

Graham smiled.

"Very well. Thank you, Professor Oliver. We'll see you this weekend." He hung up and turned my way. "They are having a brunch at one. It will be us, Professor Oliver and Mary, and their daughter, Karla, and her fiancée, Susie. You should bring a dish."

"I cannot believe you did that!" I hollered, grabbing a throw pillow from the couch and tossing it at him. He smiled even more.

God, that smile.

If he had smiled more often before, I was certain Lyric would've never been able to leave his side.

He picked up the pillow and threw it back at me, making me fall backward onto the couch. "We can drive over there together. I can pick you up from your house."

"Perfect." I grabbed the pillow and threw it back at him. "Dress code?"

He tossed it at me one last time and bit his bottom lip, allowing the small dimple in his right cheek to appear. "Anything you wear will be good enough for me."

chapter seventeen

Graham

I arrived at Lucy's house to pick her up for Easter brunch, and when she walked down the apartment staircase, I sat in the driver seat of my car. Talon babbled, and I nodded once. "Exactly." Lucy looked beautiful. She was wearing a yellow dress with tulle underneath the skirt that made it flare out. Her makeup was sparse except for the apple red lipstick that matched her high heels. Her hair was braided up with daisies threaded throughout, like a crown.

I stepped out of the car and hurried to the passenger side to open the door for her. She smiled my way with a bouquet of flowers in one hand and a dish to pass in her other.

"Well, aren't you just dapper looking." She smirked.

"Just a suit and tie," I said, taking the dish from her. I walked around to the other side of the car and opened the door, placing the dish on the seat.

As I climbed back into the driver's seat, I closed the door and glanced once at Lucy. "You look beautiful."

She laughed and patted her hair before smoothing out her dress. "You're not wrong, sir."

We drove to Professor Oliver's home, and when we arrived, I introduced Lucy to Ollie's daughter, Karla, and her fiancée, Susie.

"It's lovely to meet you, Lucy," Karla said as we walked into the house. "I would say I've heard a lot about you, but you know Graham—the guy doesn't talk," she joked.

"Really?" Lucy asked sarcastically. "I can't get the guy to ever shut up."

Karla laughed, took Talon from my arms, and kissed her forehead. "Yeah, he's a real loud mouth, that one."

Karla was the closest thing I'd ever had to a sister, and we argued like it, too. As a kid, she had been in and out of the foster program and had found herself in a lot of trouble with drugs and alcohol. I never knew her back then, though. When I came across her, she had already kind of figured out life. She was this beautiful African American woman who was a strong activist for kids who have no place to call home.

Professor Oliver and Mary wouldn't give up on her when she was a teenager, and Karla always said because of that, something changed in her heart. Not many kids would be asked to be adopted at the age of seventeen, yet Oliver and Mary wouldn't let her go.

They had that skill about them—seeing people's scars and calling them beautiful.

"Here, I'll take that dish," Susie offered, taking Lucy's tray from her. Susie was also a stunning person. She was a beautiful Asian woman who fought hard for women's rights. If ever there was a couple destined for a true love story, it was Karla and Susie.

I was never a people person, but these people were good.

Like Lucy.

Just wholeheartedly good people who didn't ask for anything but love.

When we walked into the kitchen, Mary was there, cooking, and she hurried over, giving me a kiss on the cheek and doing the same to Talon and Lucy. "You've been requested to join Ollie in his office, Graham. You were supposed to bring him new chapters of your book to read, and he's waiting," Mary said. I glanced over at Lucy, and Mary laughed. "Don't worry about her, she'll fit right in. We'll take good care of her."

Lucy smiled, my heart expanded, and then I headed to Professor Oliver's office.

⁓

He sat at his desk reading the newest chapters I'd presented to him, and I waited impatiently as his eyes darted back and forth. "I took out the lion," I told him.

"*Shh!*" he ordered, going back to reading. Every now and then he made facial expressions as he flipped the pages, but mostly, nothing. "Well," he said, finishing and placing the papers down. "You didn't have sex?"

"No."

"And no cocaine?"

"Nope."

"Well." He sat back in his chair in disbelief. "That's shocking, because whatever it is that made you step up your game, it's mind-blowing. This…" He shook his head in disbelief. "This is the best work you've ever written."

"Are you shitting me?" I asked with a knot in my stomach.

"I shit you not. Best thing I've read in years. What changed?"

I shrugged my shoulders and stood up from the chair. "I started gardening."

"Ah." He smiled knowingly. "Lucy Palmer happened."

⁓

"So, Karla, I owe you fifty dollars," Oliver stated, coming to the dining room table for brunch after we finished talking shop in his office. He straightened his tie and sat down at the head of the table. "You were right about Graham—he still knows how to write. Turns out he's not a twenty-seven-book wonder."

Lucy chuckled, and it sounded beautiful. "You bet against Graham's words?"

He cocked an eyebrow. "Did you read his last draft?!"

She grimaced. "What was the deal with the lion?"

"I know, right!" he hollered, nodding in agreement. "That freaking lion!"

"Okay, okay, we get it, I suck. Can we move on with the conversation?" I asked.

Lucy nudged me in the arm. "But the lion."

"It was hideous," Professor Oliver agreed.

"Poorly written."

"Weird."

"Odd."

"Complete trash," the two said in unison.

I rolled my eyes. "My God, Lucille, you're like the female version of Oliver—my worst nightmare."

"Or your favorite dream come true," Professor Oliver mocked, wiggling his eyebrows in a knowing way. What he knew—hell if I could tell. He reached across the table for bacon, and Karla slapped his hand.

"Dad, no."

He groaned, and I welcomed the change in subject. "A few pieces of bacon won't kill me, darling. Plus, it's a holiday."

"Yeah, well, your heart doesn't know it's a holiday, so keep to the turkey bacon Mom made for you."

He grimaced. "That's *not* bacon." He smiled over at Lucy and shrugged his shoulders. "You have a mini heart attack once and three minor heart surgeries, and people take that stuff so seriously for the rest of your life," he joked.

Mary smiled over at her husband and patted his hand with hers. "Call us overprotective, but we just want you around forever. If that includes you hating us for forcing you to eat turkey bacon"—she put three strips onto his plate—"so be it."

"Touché, touché." Professor Oliver nodded, biting into the *non-bacon* bacon. "I can't really blame you all. I'd want to be forever surrounded by me, too."

We spent the rest of brunch laughing with one another, exchanging embarrassing stories, and sharing memories. Lucy listened to everyone's words with such grace, asking questions, wanting more details, fully engaging in the conversations. I adored that about her, how she was such a people person. She made every room fill with light whenever she entered the space.

"Lucy, we're so happy you joined us today. Your smile is contagious," Mary said as we finished up the afternoon. We all sat at the dining room table, stuffed and enjoying the good company.

Lucy smiled wide and smoothed out her dress. "This has truly been amazing. I would've just been sitting at home lonely." She laughed.

"You don't normally spend holidays alone, do you?" Karla questioned with a frown.

"Oh, no. I'm always with my sister, but this year an old friend of hers is back in the States for such a short period of time, so she went to visit her. Normally, Mari and I go up to a friend's cabin to visit my mother's tree every holiday."

"Her tree?" Susie asked.

"Yeah. After my mom passed away years ago, we planted a tree to honor her memory, taking a life and making it grow, even after death. So, each holiday, we go, eat licorice—Mama's favorite candy—and sit around the tree, listening to music and breathing in the earth."

"That's so beautiful." Karla sighed. She turned to Susie and slapped her in the arm. "When I die, will you plant a tree in my memory?"

"I'll plant a beer—seems more fitting," Susie replied.

Karla's eyes widened and she leaned in to kiss Susie. "I'm going to marry you so hard in three months, woman."

Lucy's eyes widened with joy. "When are you two getting married?"

"Fourth of July weekend, the weekend we met," Karla said, giddy. "We were going to wait until next year, but I can't wait any longer." She turned to Professor Oliver, smiling wide. "I just need my papa to walk me down the aisle and give me away to my love."

"It's going to be the best day," Oliver replied, taking his daughter's hand and kissing it. "Only second best to the day you officially became my daughter."

My heart expanded even more.

"Well, if you need a florist, it'll be my treat," Lucy offered.

Susie's eyes widened. "Seriously? That would be amazing. Like, beyond amazing."

If it weren't for the love I saw between Professor Oliver and Mary, and the love between Karla and Susie, I would've been certain love was an urban legend, something made only for fairytale books.

But the way those people stared at one another, the way they loved so freely and loudly...

True, romantic love was real.

Even if I'd never been able to feel it for myself.

"You know, Graham still needs a plus one for the ceremony. Hint, hint." Susie smirked widely.

I rolled my eyes, feeling a knot in my stomach. A quick change of subject was needed. "Susie and Karla are amazing singers," I told Lucy, leaning in and nudging her in the side. "That's how they met—at a Fourth of July music showcase. You should ask them to sing something."

"Graham is full of crap," Karla replied, throwing a piece of bread at him.

"No, he's not." Mary smiled. "I might be a bit biased, but they are amazing. Come on, girls, sing something." Right at that moment, Talon's baby monitor started going off, telling us she was up from her nap. "I'll grab her, and you ladies pick out a song," Mary ordered.

"Mom, geez, no pressure, huh?" Karla rolled her eyes, but there was a bit of light in her gaze that revealed how much she loved to perform. "Fine. What do you think, Susie? Andra Day?"

"Perfect," she agreed, standing up. "But I'm not singing at the table. This diva needs a stage."

We all headed to the living room, and I sat on the sofa next to Lucy. Mary walked in with my daughter in her arms, and for a moment I considered that was what a grandmother should've looked like. Happy. Healthy. Whole. Filled with love.

Talon had no clue how lucky she was to have a Mary.

I hadn't a clue how lucky I was to have a Mary, too.

Karla sat down at the piano in the corner, stretched out her fingers, and began to play "Rise Up" by Andra Day. The music floating from the piano was stunning all on its own, but when Susie started to sing, I thought the whole room felt the chills. Lucy's eyes were glued to the performance, while mine stayed glued to her. Her body started to tremble, and her legs shook as she watched the girls perform. It was as if the words were swallowing her whole as tears began to stream down her cheeks.

Her tears fell faster and faster as the lyrics of the song found her heart and planted their seeds. She blushed nervously and tried to wipe her tears away, but when she wiped some away, more came.

The next time she went to wipe them, I took her hand in mine, stopping her. She turned my way, confused, and I squeezed her hand lightly. "It's okay," I whispered.

Her lips parted as if she were going to speak, but then she just nodded once before turning back to the girls and closing her eyes. The tears kept falling as she listened to the beautiful vocals, her body rocking slightly as I held her hand.

For the first time, I began to understand her fully.

The beautiful girl who felt everything.

Her emotions weren't what made her weak.

They were her strength.

When the girls finished performing, Lucy started clapping, the tears still falling. "That was so amazing."

"Are you sure you're not crying because we suck?" Karla laughed.

"No, it was so amazing. My mom would have…" She paused for a moment and took a deep breath. "She would've just loved it."

My eyes fell to our hands, which were still clasped together, and I released my hold, along with the tugging feeling in my chest.

When night came, we packed up our things, thanking everyone for including us.

"It was amazing," Lucy told Mary and Ollie as she hugged them both tightly. "Thank you for keeping me from sitting on my couch eating Ben & Jerry's tonight."

"You're always welcome here, Lucy," Mary said, kissing her cheek.

"I'll go put Talon in her car seat," Lucy said to me, taking Talon from my arms before thanking everyone once more.

Mary gave me a tight smile and pulled me into a hug. "I like her," she whispered as she patted me on the back. "She has a good heart."

She wasn't wrong.

Once she went back inside, Professor Oliver stood on the front porch, grinning wide.

"What?" I asked, my eyebrows knotted.

"Oh, Mr. Russell," he sang, placing his hands in his pockets, rocking back and forth.

"What?!"

He whistled low, shaking his head back and forth. "It's just funny that it's happening to you of all people, and you seem one hundred percent ignorant to it."

"What are you talking about?"

"I guess it's harder to see the plot line when you're the one living the story."

"Did someone forget to take their crazy pills again?" I asked.

"In every story, there's the moment when the characters go from act one, the old world, into act two, the new world. You know this."

"Yes…but what does that have to do with anything?"

Professor Oliver nodded toward Lucy. "It has everything to do with everything."

Realization set in and I cleared my throat, standing up straighter. "No, that's ridiculous. She's just helping with Talon."

"Mhmm," he said, almost mockingly.

"No, really—and, regardless of your batty mind games, she's Jane's sister."

"Mhmm," he replied, driving me crazy. "The thing is, the heart never listens to the brain's logic, Mr. Russell." He nudged me in the side with an all-knowing hitch in his voice. "It just feels."

"You're really starting to annoy me."

He laughed and nodded. "It's just funny, isn't it? How the main characters never know about the adventures they're about to go on."

What bothered me the most about his words was how much truth was contained in them. I knew my feelings for Lucy were growing, and I knew how dangerous it was to allow myself to develop any kind of emotions toward her.

I couldn't remember the last time I felt the way I did when I held her hand or when I saw her caring for Talon, or even when I saw her merely existing.

"What do you think of her, Graham?" Professor Oliver asked.

"What do I think of Lucille?"

"Yes. Maybe if you can't be with her, perhaps you still have room for a friendship."

"She's my complete opposite," I told him. "Lucille is such an odd character, a freak of nature. She's clumsy and always speaks out of turn. Her hair's always wild, and her laughter is at times annoying and too loud. Everything about her is disastrous. She's nothing more than a mess."

"And yet?" he urged me on.

And yet, I wanted to be just like her. I wanted to be an odd character, a freak of nature. I wanted to stumble and laugh out loud. I wanted to find her beautiful disaster and mix it together with my own mess. I wanted the freedom she swam in, and her fearlessness of living in the moment.

I wanted to know what it meant to be a part of her world.

To be a man who felt everything.

I wanted to hold her, but still have her move freely in my arms. I wanted to taste her lips and breathe in a part of her soul as I gave her a glimpse of mine.

I didn't want to be her friend—no.

I wanted to be so much more.

Yet, I knew the possibility of that was impossible. She was the one thing off-limits, and the only thing I'd ever craved. It wasn't fair, the way this story was unfolding for me, yet it wasn't at all shocking. I never wrote happily ever afters, and Lucy would never be featured in my final chapter.

"You're overthinking something right now, Graham, and I urge you to believe in the opposite," he told me. "Jane has been gone for almost a year now, and let's face it—you never looked at her the way you stare at Lucy. Your eyes never lit up the way they do whenever she walks into a room. You spent most of your life struggling to avoid embracing a form of happiness, my son. When in the world will you allow yourself to be free of the chains you placed upon yourself? This life is short, and you never know how many chapters you have left in your novel, Graham. Live each day as if it's the final page. Breathe each moment as if it's the final word. Be brave, my son. Be brave."

I rolled my eyes and started walking down the steps. "Professor Oliver?"

"Yes?"

"Shut up."

chapter eighteen

Lucy

"I have to stop by the store to grab some diapers. I hope that's okay," Graham told me as he pulled the car into the parking lot of a twenty-four-hour grocery store.

"That's fine."

He hurried inside, and when he came out, he tossed a few bags into the trunk and hopped back into the car. "Okay," he said, putting the car in drive. "Which way do we go to get to the cabin?"

"What?"

"I said which way do we go? To visit your mother's tree?"

My chest tightened, and I shook my head. His words replayed in my head as I blankly stared his way. "What? No way, Graham. You're already behind on your book, and I just can't imagine having you drive that far just to—"

"Lucille Hope Palmer."

"Yes, Graham Michael Russell?"

"You've never missed a holiday visiting your mother, right?"

I bit my bottom lip and nodded. "Right."

"Okay then. Which way do we go?"

My eyes closed, and my heart beat faster and faster as I realized Graham wasn't going to let this one go. I hadn't even mentioned how much my heart ached not seeing Mama that day. I hadn't even mentioned how hard it was to watch Susie and Karla love on their mother that evening. A tear rolled down my cheek, and a smile found its way to my lips. "You can take highway 43 north for two hours."

"Perfect," he said as he pulled out of the parking spot. When I opened my eyes, I glanced back at a sleeping Talon, and my hands wrapped around my heart-shaped necklace.

When we arrived, it was pitch-dark out until I plugged the extension cord into the outlet outside the cabin. The plug lit up the area with the white lights Mari and I had hung in December for our Christmas visit. Mama's tree lit up bright, and I walked over to it, standing still as I watched the lights sparkle. I sat down on the ground and clasped my fingers, looking up at the tree. It was bittersweet, staring at the beautiful branches. Each day it grew was a day Mama was gone, but visiting her in the spring was my favorite time to come, because that was when the leaves began to bloom.

"She's beautiful," Graham said, walking over to me with Talon bundled up in his arms.

"Isn't she?"

He nodded. "She takes after her daughter."

I smiled. "And her granddaughter."

He reached into his coat pocket and pulled out a pack of licorice, making my heart skip a beat.

"You picked it up at the grocery store?" I asked.

"I just wanted today to be good for you."

"It is," I replied, overwhelmed by his kindness. "It's a very good day."

As we sat there staring, breathing, existing, Graham pulled out his cell phone and started playing "Rise Up" by Andra Day.

"You said she might like it," he told me.

Once again, I began to cry.

And it was beautiful.

"Are we friends, Lucille?" Graham asked.

I turned to him, my heart feeling tight in my chest. "Yes."

"Then can I tell you a secret?"

"Yes, of course. Anything."

"After I tell you, I need you to pretend I never spoke of it, all right? If I don't say it now, I fear the feeling will only grow, and it will mess with my head even more than it is now. So, after this, I need you to pretend I never said this. After this I need you to go back to being my friend, because being friends with you makes me a better person. You make me a better human."

"Graham—"

He turned and placed sleeping Talon into her car seat. "Wait, just tell me first—do you feel anything? Anything more than friendship when we do this?" He reached out and took my hand in his.

Nerves.

He moved in closer to me, our bodies closer than they'd ever been. "Do you feel anything when I do this?" he whispered, slowly grazing the back of his hand against my cheek. My eyes shut.

Chills.

He moved in even closer, his small exhales hovering over my lips, his exhales becoming my inhales. I couldn't open my eyes because I would see his lips. I couldn't open my eyes because I would crave to be closer. I couldn't open my eyes because I could hardly breathe.

"Do you feel anything when we're this close?" he asked softly.

Excitement.

I opened my eyes and blinked once.

"Yes."

A wave of relief traveled through him and he reached into his back pocket, pulling out two pieces of paper. "I made two lists yesterday," he told me. "I sat at my desk all day listing all the reasons why I shouldn't feel the way I feel about you, and that list is long. It's detailed with bullet points expressing every single reason why this—whatever this is between us—is a bad idea."

"I get it, Graham. You don't have to explain yourself. I know we can't—"

"No, just wait. There's the other list. It's shorter, much shorter, but in that list I tried to not be so logical. I'm trying to be more like you."

"Like me? How so?"

"I'm trying to *feel*. I imagined what it would be like to be happy, and I think you are the definition of happiness." His dark eyes locked with mine, and he cleared his throat twice. "I tried to list the things I find pleasant, outside of Talon of course. It's a short list, really, only two things so far, and oddly enough, it begins and ends with you."

My heart pounded against my chest, my mind spinning faster and faster each second that passed. "Me and me?" I asked, feeling his body's warmth. I felt his words grazing across my skin and seeping so deep into my soul.

His fingers slowly trailed along my neck. "You and you."

"But..." *Lyric*. "We can't."

He nodded. "I know. That's why after I tell you this last thing, I need you to pretend we are only friends. I need you to forget everything I've said tonight, but first, I need to tell you this."

"What is it, Graham?"

His body slowly turned away from me, and he stared at the blinking lights on the tree. My eyes watched as his lips moved so slowly. "Being around you does something strange to me, something that hasn't happened in such a long time."

"What happens?"

He took my hand in his then led it to his chest, and his next words came out as a whisper. "My heart begins to beat again."

chapter nineteen

Lucy

"Are we okay?" Graham asked a few days after Easter as I drove him to the airport to catch his flight. His publisher needed him to fly out to New York City to do interviews and a few book signings around the city. He'd been putting off taking trips ever since Talon was born, but he was being forced to attend the meetings. It was the first time he'd be away from Talon for a weekend, and I could tell he was filled with nerves about the separation. "I mean, after our talk the other night?"

I gave him a smile and nodded. "It's fine, really."

It was a lie.

Ever since he mentioned that feelings for me lived inside of his chest, I hadn't been able to stop thinking about it. But, since he had been brave enough to be more like me by feeling everything that night, I was forcing myself to be more like him by trying to feel a little less.

I wondered if this was what his whole life was like, feeling everything only in the shadows.

"Okay."

As we pulled up to the airport, I climbed out to help him with his suitcases. I grabbed Talon from the back seat, and Graham held her so close to his chest. His eyes glassed over as he looked at his daughter.

"It's only three days," I told him.

He nodded once. "Yes, I know, it's just..." His voice dropped and he kissed Talon's forehead. "She's my world."

Oh, Graham Cracker.

He made it so hard not to fall for him.

"If you need anything, day or night, call me. I mean, I'll be calling you every break I get." He paused and bit his bottom lip. "Do you think I should cancel and stay home? She had a bit of a fever this morning."

I laughed. "Graham, you can't cancel. Go to work, and then come back to us." I paused at my word choice and gave him a tight smile. "Back to your daughter."

He nodded then kissed her forehead once more. "Thank you, Lucille, for everything. I don't trust many people, but I trust you with my world." He touched my arm lightly before handing Talon over to me and leaving.

The moment I placed Talon in her car seat, she started screaming, and

I tried my best to calm her down. "I know, little lady." I buckled her in and kissed her forehead. "I'm gonna miss him, too."

○○○

The next day Mari asked me to take a bike ride with her, but since I had Talon, it became a stroller hike. "She's just beautiful," Mari said, smiling down at Talon. "She has Mama's eyes, just like Lyric, doesn't she?"

"Oh yeah, and Mama's sassiness, too." I laughed as we started walking toward the beginning of the trail. "I'm glad we're finally getting to spend some time together, Mari. I feel like even though we live in the same apartment, I hardly ever see you. I didn't even get to ask how seeing Sarah went."

"I didn't see her," she blurted out, making me pause my steps.

"What?"

"She wasn't even in town," she confessed, her eyes darting around nervously.

"What are you talking about, Mari? You were gone all weekend. Where were you?"

"With Parker," Mari said nonchalantly, as if her words weren't drenched in toxicity.

My eyes stayed narrowed. "I'm sorry, come again?"

"A while back, he stopped by Monet's again when you were out, and I agreed to see him. We've been talking for a few months now."

Months?!

"You're mad." She grimaced.

"You lied to me. Since when do we lie to each other?"

"I knew you wouldn't approve of me seeing him, but he wanted to talk to me about things."

"Talk about things?" I echoed as anger rocketed through me. "What in the world could there be to talk about?" Her head lowered, and she started tracing her shoe in the dirt. "Oh my gosh, he wants to talk about getting back together, doesn't he?"

"It's complicated," she told me.

"How so? He walked out on you during the worst time of your life, and now he wants to walk back in during the best."

"He's my husband."

"*Ex*-husband."

Her head lowered. "I never signed the papers."

My heart shattered.

"You told me—"

"I know!" she cried, running her hands through her hair, pacing back and forth. "I know I told you it ended, and it did. Mentally, I was done with my marriage, but physically…I never signed the papers."

"You have got to be kidding me, Mari. He *abandoned* you, when you had *cancer*."

"But still…"

"No. No 'but still'. He doesn't get a pass, and you lied about being *divorced*! To *me*! You're supposed to be my person, Pea. We're supposed to be able to tell each other everything, and this whole time you've been living a lie with me. You know what Mama always said about lying? If you have to lie about it, you probably shouldn't be doing it anyway."

"Please don't quote Mama to me right now, Lucy."

"You have to leave him, Mari. Physically, emotionally, mentally. He's toxic for you. No good is going to come from this."

"You have no clue what it's like to be married!" Her voice heightened. Mari never raised her voice.

"But I do have a clue what it's like to be respected! Jesus, I cannot believe you've been lying this whole time."

"I'm sorry I lied, but if we're honest, you haven't been the most honest person lately."

"What?"

"This," she said, gesturing toward Talon. "This whole Graham thing is weird. Why are you taking care of his kid? She's obviously old enough for him to take care of himself, or hell, he could hire a nanny. Tell me the truth, why are you still there?"

My gut tightened. "Mari, that's not the same thing…"

"It's exactly the same thing! You say I'm staying in a loveless marriage because I'm weak and you're pissed that I lied to you, but you've been lying to me, and to yourself. You're staying with him because you're falling for him."

"Stop it."

"You are."

My jaw dropped open. "Mari…this, right now, this isn't about me, or Graham, or anything other than you. You're making a huge mistake talking to him. It's not healthy and—"

"I'm moving back home."

"What?!" I exclaimed, shock reverberating through me. I stood up straighter. "That's not your home. I'm your home. We are each other's home."

"Parker thinks it will be best for us, to work on our marriage."

What marriage?! "Mari, he called you after you were in remission for two years. He waited it out to see if the cancer would come back. He's a snake."

"Stop it!" she screamed, shaking her hands back and forth in annoyance. "Just stop. He's my husband, Lucy, and I'm going home to him." Her head lowered and her voice cracked. "I don't want to end up like her."

"Like who?"

"Mama. She died alone, because she never let any man get close enough to love her. I don't want to die without being loved."

"He doesn't love you, Pea…"

"But he can. I think if I just change a little, if I just become a better wife…"

"You were the best wife out there, Mari. You were everything to him."

Tears fell from her eyes. "Then why wasn't I enough back then? He's giving me another chance, and I can do better this time."

It was crazy how fast it happened, how quickly my anger transformed into pure sadness for my sister. "Mari," I said softly.

"Maktub," she said, looking down at the tattoo on her wrist.

"Don't do that." I shook my head, hurting more than she'd ever know. "Don't take our word and give it some kind of dirty meaning."

"It means all is written, Lucy. It means everything that happens was meant to be, not only what you believe to be destined. You can't only accept the positive in life. You must accept it all."

"No. That's not true. If a bullet is coming toward you and you have enough time to move, you don't just stand there and wait for it to hit. You step sideways, Mari. You dodge the bullet."

"My marriage is not a bullet. It's not my death. It's my life."

"You're making a huge mistake," I whispered, tears falling down my cheeks.

She nodded. "Maybe, but it's my mistake to make, just like it's yours to make with Graham." She crossed her arms and shivered as if a chill had found her. "Listen, I didn't want to tell you like this but…I'm glad you know. My lease is up soon, so you'll have to find a place. Look…we can still go on the hike if you want, to clear our heads."

"You know what, Mari?" I grimaced and shook my head. "I'd rather not."

The hardest part of life was watching a loved one walk straight into fire when all you could do was sit and watch them as they burned.

~

"You'll stay with us," Graham said over FaceTime from his hotel room in New York.

"No, don't be ridiculous. I'll find something. I'll start searching the minute you get back in two days."

"Until then you'll stay with us, no ifs, ands, or buts. It's fine. My house is big enough. I'm sorry, though, about Mari."

I shivered at the thought of it all, at the idea of her going back to Parker. "I just don't get it. How can she just forgive him?"

"Loneliness is a liar," Graham told me, sitting down on the edge of his bed as he spoke. "It's toxic and deadly most of the time. It forces people to believe they are better off with the devil himself than being alone, because somehow being alone means a person failed. Somehow being alone means a person isn't good enough. So, more often than not, the poison of loneliness seeps in and makes a person believe that any kind of attention must stand for love. Fake love that is built on a bed of loneliness will fail—I should know. I've been alone all my life."

"I hate that you just did that." I sighed. "I hate that you just took my annoyance with my sister and made me want to go hug her."

He chuckled. "Sorry. I can call her names if you'd…" His eyes narrowed as he stared at his phone. I noticed the panic in his stare instantly. "Lucille, I have to call you back."

"Is everything okay?"

He hung up before I received a response.

chapter twenty

Graham

I WAS A MASTER OF STORIES.

I knew how a great novel came to exist.

A great novel didn't involve tossing together words that didn't interconnect. In a great novel, each sentence mattered, each word had a meaning to the overall story arc. There was always forewarning to the plot twists and the different paths the novel would travel down, too. If a reader looked closely enough, they could always witness the warning signs. They could taste the heart of every word that bled on the page, and by the end, their palate would be satisfied.

A great story always had structure.

But life wasn't a great story.

Real life was a mess of words that sometimes worked, and other times didn't. Real life was an array of emotions that hardly made sense. Real life was a first draft novel with scribbles and crossed out sentences, all written in crayon.

It wasn't beautiful. It came without warning. It came without ease.

And when the novel of real life came to fuck you up, it made sure to knock the air from your lungs and leave your bleeding heart for the wolves.

―

The message was from Karla.

She tried to call me, but I sent her to voicemail.

I was looking at Talon.

She left a voice message, but I ignored it.

I was staring into Lucille's eyes.

She then sent me a text message that made a part of me die.

Dad's in the hospital.

He had another heart attack.

Please come home.

―

I took the next flight home, my hands clenched the whole time, too nervous to take a full breath. When the plane landed, I grabbed the first taxi I could find and rushed to the hospital. Hurrying inside, I felt like my chest was on fire. The burning sensation shook me as I tried to blink away the emotion racing through my veins.

He must be okay.

He has to be okay...

If Professor Oliver didn't make it through this, I wasn't certain I'd survive. I wasn't certain I'd survive if he wasn't going to always be there for me. When I made it to the waiting room, my eyes fell to Mary and Karla first. Then, I noticed Lucy sitting with Talon sleeping in her lap. How long had she been there? How had she even known? I hadn't mentioned I was coming back. Every time I'd tried to type out the words, I'd deleted them instantly. If I sent out the words that Professor Oliver had had a heart attack, it would be real. If I'd thought it was real, I would've died on the flight home for sure.

It couldn't be real.

He couldn't die.

Talon wouldn't even remember him.

She needed to remember the greatest man in the world.

She needed to know my father.

"How did you know?" I asked Lucy, walking over and gently kissing Talon's forehead.

Lucy nodded over to Karla. "She called me. I came right away."

"Are you all right?" I asked.

"I'm okay." Lucy grimaced, took my hand in hers, and lightly squeezed it. "Are you?"

I narrowed my eyes and swallowed hard, speaking so low that I wasn't certain the word actually left my lips. "No."

My eyes darted over to Mary and I told Lucy I'd be back. She told me to take all the time I needed. I was thankful for that, for her watching over Talon, for her being there for my daughter and for me while I needed to be there for others.

"Mary," I said, calling after her. She looked up and my heart cracked seeing the pain in her stare. Karla's broken stare cracked my heart once more.

"Graham," Mary cried, hurrying over to me.

I wrapped my arms around her, holding her so close to me. She parted her mouth to say more, but no words came out. She began sobbing uncontrollably, as did her daughter, who I pulled into the tight hug. I held them both against me, trying to convince their shaky bodies that everything would be okay.

I stood tall like a tree, not shaking because they needed me as their foundation. They needed strength, and I played the role.

Because that was what he would've wanted me to be.

Brave.

"What happened?" I asked Mary once she could calm down. I led her to the waiting room chairs, and we sat down.

Her back was curved as she clasped her fingers together, a little tremble still in her soul. "He was in his office reading, and when I went to check on him…" Her bottom lip started to tremble. "I have no clue how long he was down. If I could've gotten there faster…if…"

"No ifs, just now," I told her. "You did everything you could. This isn't your fault, Mary."

She nodded. "I know, I know. We've been preparing for this day, but I just didn't think it would come so soon. I thought we had more time."

"Preparing?" I asked, confused.

She grimaced and tried to wipe away her tears, but more continued to fall. "He didn't want me to tell you…"

"Tell me what?"

"He's been sick for a while, Graham. A few months ago, he was told if he didn't have surgery, he'd only have a few months before his heart gave out. The surgery was very risky, too, and he didn't want to do it. Not after all the surgeries he had beforehand. I fought long and hard to get him to do it, but he was too afraid he'd go in that day and not come back, instead of spending each and every day he had left surrounded by love."

He knew?

"Why didn't he tell me?" I asked, a bit of anger rising in my chest.

She took my hands in hers and lowered her voice. "He didn't want you to push him away. He thought if you learned about his sickness, you'd become cold, to protect yourself from feeling too much. He knew you'd go deeper into your mind, and that idea broke his heart, Graham. He was so terrified of losing you, because you were his son. You are our son, and if you left during his final days…he would've left this world brokenhearted."

My chest was tight and it took everything inside of me to not cry. I lowered my head a bit and shook it back and forth. "He's my best friend," I told her.

"And you are his," she replied.

We waited and waited for the doctors to come tell us what was happening. When one finally returned, he cleared his throat. "Mrs. Evans?" he asked. We all shot up from our chairs, our nerves shot.

"Yes, I'm right here," Mary replied as I took her trembling hand in mine.

Be brave.

"Your husband suffered from heart failure. He's in the ICU on breathing machines, and the truth of the matter is that if those came off, there's a significant chance he wouldn't make it. I'm so sorry. I know this is a lot to take in. I can arrange for you to meet with a specialist to help you decide what the best choice is for moving forward."

"You mean we have to decide to either unplug the machines or keep him in his current state?" Mary asked.

"Yes, but please understand, he's not in a good state. There's not much we can do for him except keep him comfortable. I'm so sorry."

"Oh my God," Karla cried as she fell into Susie's arms.

"Can we see him?" Mary asked, her voice trembling.

"Yes, but only family for now," the doctor said. "And maybe only one person at a time."

"You go first," Mary said, turning to me, as if the idea that I wasn't family was ridiculous.

I shook my head. "No. You should, really. I'm good."

"I can't," she cried. "I can't be the first to see him. Please, Graham? Please go first so you can tell me how he is. Please."

"Okay," I told her, still a little worried about not being there to hold her up. Before I could say anything else, Lucy was standing on the other side of Mary, holding her hand tight and promising me with her gentle eyes that she wouldn't let go.

"I'll take you to the room," the doctor told me.

As we walked down the hallway, I tried my best to keep it together. I tried my best to not show how much my heart was hurting, but the moment I was left alone with Professor Oliver in that room, I lost it.

He looked so broken.

So many machines beeping, so many tubes and IVs.

I took a deep breath, pulled a chair up to his bed, and then cleared my throat. "You're a selfish asshole," I stated, stern, angry. "You're a selfish asshole for doing this to Mary. You're a selfish asshole for doing this to Karla weeks before her wedding. You're a selfish asshole for doing this to me. I hate you for thinking if I knew, I'd run. I hate you for being right about it, too, but please, Professor Oliver..." My voice cracked and my eyes watered over. They burned, the way my heart was burning from the pain. "Don't go. You can't go, you selfish fucking asshole, okay? You can't leave Mary, you can't leave Karla, and you absolutely, one hundred percent, cannot leave *me*."

I fell apart, taking his hand in mine, and I prayed to a god I didn't believe in as my cold heart that had only recently thawed began to shatter.

"Please, Ollie. Please don't go. Please, I'll do anything...just...just..."

Please don't go.

chapter twenty-one

Christmas Day

H E HADN'T LIKED HER GIFT, SO HE ALLOWED HIMSELF A DRINK. KENT NEVER ONLY HAD one drink, though. One led to two, two led to three, and three led to a number that brought out his shadows. When Kent lived in his shadows, there was nothing able to bring him back.

Even though Rebecca was beautiful.

Even though Rebecca was kind.

Even though Rebecca tried hard each day to be enough.

She was more than enough, Graham thought.

For the past five birthdays, she'd watched him blow out his candles.

She was his best friend, the proof that good existed, but that wouldn't last, because Kent had had a drink—or ten.

"You are shit!" he screamed at her, throwing his glass of whisky at the wall, where it shattered into a million pieces. He was more than a monster, he was darkness, the worst kind of man that ever existed. Kent didn't even know why he was so angry, but he took it all out on Rebecca.

"Please," she whispered, shaken as she sat on the couch. "Just rest, Kent. You haven't taken a break since you started writing."

"Don't tell me what to do. You ruined Christmas," he slurred, stumbling over to her. "You ruined it all, because you are shit." He raised his hand to take his anger out on her, but before he could slap her, his palm slammed against Graham's forehead as he stepped in the way to protect Rebecca. "Move!" Kent ordered, wrapping his hands around his son and tossing him to the side of the room.

Graham's eyes filled with tears as he watched his father hit her.

How?

How could he hit someone so good?

"Stop!" Graham cried, rushing over and hitting his father repeatedly. Each time Kent would push him away, but Graham didn't stop. He kept rising from the floor and going back for more, unafraid of how his father would hurt him. All he knew was that Rebecca was being hurt, and he knew he had to protect her.

What lasted for minutes felt like hours. The room spun as Graham got hit, and Rebecca got hurt, and it wasn't until both lay there still, not trying to fight back, that it finally stopped. They took the hits and punches, and stayed quiet until Kent grew tired of it all. He wandered off to his office where he slammed his door and probably found some more whisky.

Rebecca wrapped her arms around Graham the second Kent was gone, and she let him fall apart in her arms. "It's okay," she told him.

He knew better than to believe such a thing.

Late into that night, Rebecca stopped by Graham's room. He was still awake, sitting in the darkness of his room, staring at the ceiling.

When he turned her way, he saw her in her winter coat and boots.

Behind her was a suitcase.

"No," he said, sitting up. He shook his head. "No."

Tears rolled down her cheeks, which were bruised from the hands of darkness. "I'm so sorry, Graham."

"Please," he cried, running over to her and wrapping his arms around her waist. "Please don't go."

"I can't stay here," she told him, her voice shaking. "My sister is waiting outside, and I just wanted to tell you face to face."

"Take me with you!" he begged, tears falling faster and faster as the panic of her leaving him with the darkness set in. "I'll be good, I swear. I'll be good enough for you."

"Graham." She took a deep breath. "I can't take you…you're not mine."

Those words.

Those few and hurtful words cracked his heart in half.

"Please, Rebecca, please…" He sobbed into her shirt.

She pulled him back a few inches and bent herself down so they were eye level. "He told me if I take you, he'll send his lawyers. He told me he'd fight. I have nothing, Graham. He had me quit my job years ago. I signed a prenup. I have nothing."

"You have me," he told her.

The way she blinked and stood up told him he wasn't enough.

In that moment, the young boy's heart began to freeze.

She walked away that evening and never looked back. That night Graham sat at his window, staring out at where Rebecca had driven off, and he felt sick to his stomach as he tried to understand. How could someone be there for so long and then just let go?

He stared at the road covered in snow. The tire tracks were still on the ground, and Graham didn't take his eyes off them once.

Over and over again in his head, three words repeated.

Please don't go.

chapter twenty-two

Lucy

His eyes were swollen when he walked back into the waiting room. Karla and Susie wandered off to find coffee, and Graham gave Mary a fake smile and a quick hug before she went to visit Ollie.

"Hey." I stood up and walked over to him. "Are you okay?"

He grimaced, his stance strong, but his eyes so heartbroken. "If anything happens to him…" He swallowed hard and lowered his head. "If I lose him…"

I didn't give him a chance to say another word. I wrapped my arms around him as his body started to shake. For the first time, he let himself feel, let himself hurt, and I was there to hold him close.

"What can I do?" I asked, holding him closer. "Tell me what I can do."

He placed his forehead against mine and closed his eyes. "Just don't let go. If you let go, I'll run. I'll let it overtake me. Please, Lucille, just don't let go."

I held him for minutes, but it felt like hours. Against his ear, I softly spoke. "Air above me, earth below me, fire within me, water surround me, spirit becomes me…" I kept repeating the words, and I felt his emotions overtake him. Each time he felt himself slipping, he held my body closer, and I refused to let him go.

It wasn't long until Talon woke up in her car seat and started fussing. Graham slowly let go of me and walked over to his daughter. When her eyes met his, she stopped her fussing and she lit up as if she'd just met the greatest man alive. There was complete love in her eyes, and I saw it happen—the moment of relief she had delivered to her father. He lifted her up into his arms and held her close. She placed her hands on his cheeks and started babbling, making noises with that same beautiful smile that matched her father's.

For that one moment in time, for that small second, Graham stopped hurting.

Talon filled his heart with love, the same love he had once believed didn't even exist.

For that one moment in time, he seemed okay.

Mary decided to wait to see if things changed. She lived those weeks with a knot in her stomach, and Graham stayed by her side throughout it all. He showed up at her house with food, forcing her to eat, and forcing her to sleep when all she wanted to do was stay in the waiting room at the hospital.

Waiting for a change.

Waiting for a miracle.

Waiting for her husband to come back to her.

Karla called me when it came time to make the toughest decision of her family's life. When we arrived at the hospital, the light in the hallway flickered repeatedly, as if it were going to die any moment.

The chaplain walked into the room and we all stood around Ollie, our hands joined together as we prepared for our final goodbyes. I wasn't certain how anyone would come back from a loss like this. I'd only known Ollie for such a short period of time, but I knew he'd already changed my life for the better.

His heart was one that was always filled with love, and he'd be missed forever.

After the chaplain's prayer, he asked if anyone had any final words to say. Mary couldn't speak as the tears flowed down her cheeks. Karla's face was wrapped in Susie's shoulder, and my lips refused to move.

Graham held us all up. He became our strength. As words flowed from his soul, I felt the squeezing of my heart. "Air above me, earth below me, fire within me, water surround me, spirit becomes me."

In that moment, we all began to crumble into the realm of nothingness.

In that moment, a part of each of us left with Ollie's soul.

chapter twenty-three

Graham

Everyone was gone. Mary, Karla, and Susie had left to deal with the next steps, and I knew I should've gone with them, but I couldn't force myself to move. I stood still in the hospital hallway with the flickering light. His room had been emptied, and there wasn't anything else that could be done. He was gone. My professor. My hero. My best friend. My father.

Gone.

I hadn't cried. I hadn't processed it at all.

How was it possible for this to be the outcome? How could he fade so fast? How could he be gone?

Footsteps were walking in my direction, nurses moving on to their next patients, doctors checking in on those who still had a pulse, as if the world hadn't just stopped spinning.

"Graham."

Her voice was deep, drenched in pain and sorrow. I didn't look up to see her; my head wouldn't turn away from the room where I had just said my final goodbye.

"He was right," I whispered, my voice shaky. "He thought if I knew about his heart, if I knew he was about to die at any moment, I would've run. I would've been selfish, and I would've left him, because I would've closed myself off. I wouldn't have been able to mentally deal with him dying. I would've been a coward."

"You were here," she said. "You were always here. There was nothing cowardly about you, Graham."

"I could've talked him into the surgery, though," I argued. "I could've convinced him to fight."

I stopped speaking. For a moment, it felt as if I were floating, as if I were in the world, but no longer a part of it, floating high in disbelief, denial, guilt.

Lucy parted her lips as if she were going to offer some kind of comfort, but then no words came out. I was certain there weren't any words that could make this better.

We stayed still, staring at the room as the world kept moving on around us.

My body started to tremble. My hands shook uncontrollably at my sides as my heart caved into my chest. *He's gone. He's really gone.*

Lucy lowered her voice and whispered, "If you need to fall, fall into me."

Within seconds, gravity found me. Every sense of floating was gone, every sense of strength no longer mine. I began to descend, faster and faster, crashing down, waiting for the impact to hit, but she was there.

She was right beside me.

She caught me before I hit the ground.

She became my strength when I could no longer be brave.

"She's finally sleeping, though she put up quite the fight." Lucy's eyes were heavy, as if she were exhausted but forcing her eyes to stay open. "How are you feeling?" she asked, leaning against my office doorframe.

I'd been sitting at my desk, staring at my blinking cursor for the past hour. I wanted to write, wanted to escape, but for the first time in my life, there were truly no words to be found. She grew closer to me and placed her hands on my shoulders. Her fingers started kneading into my tense shoulder blades, and I welcomed her touch.

"It's been a long day," I whispered.

"It's been a very long day."

My eyes moved over to the windows, watching the rain falling outside. Sheets of water pounded against the exterior of my home. Professor Oliver would've rolled his eyes at the coincidence of rain on the day he passed away. *What a cliché.*

I shut off my computer.

No words were going to come that night.

"You need to sleep," Lucy told me. I didn't even disagree. She reached out for my hands, and I allowed her to take them. She pulled me up and walked me to my room so I could try to shut my eyes for some rest.

"Do you need water? Food? Anything?" she asked, her eyes filled with concern.

"There is one thing."

"Yeah? What can I do for you?" she asked.

"Stay with me. Tonight, I just..." My voice cracked, and I bit the inside of my cheek to hold back the emotion. "I don't think I can be alone tonight. I know it's a weird thing to ask, and you are free to go, of course, it's just..." I took a deep breath and slid my hands into the pockets of my slacks. "I don't think I can be alone tonight."

She didn't say another word. She simply walked over to the bed, turned down the blanket, and lay down. Lucy's hand patted the spot beside her and I walked over, lying down beside her. It started slow, our fingers moving closer to one another. I shut my eyes and tears started falling down my cheeks. Then, somehow our fingers locked, Lucy's warmth slowly filling up my cold heart.

Then, her body inched closer and closer. My arms somehow found their way around her, and as I lay there holding her close, I allowed sleep to find its way to me.

Oh, how badly I needed someone to stay that night.

I was so thankful it was her.

chapter
twenty-four

Lucy

When the day came for Ollie's funeral, there were not nearly as many people as there'd been at the last funeral I'd attended; it was nothing like Kent's service. We stood in an open field, surrounded by nature, in the place where he'd proposed to Mary many moons ago. She said it was the day her life began, and it only seemed right to go back there to absorb that same love she'd felt years ago.

And oh, there was love. So, so much love showed up for Ollie, including former students, colleagues, and friends. Although the space wasn't packed with reporters, fans, or cameras, it was filled with the only important thing in the world: love.

Everyone made sure to comfort Karla and Mary to the best of their ability, and the two were never alone. As the service went on, there were tears, laughter, and stories filled with light and love.

The perfect tribute to a perfect man.

When the pastor asked if anyone would like to share words, it only took Graham a second to rise from his seat. My eyes locked with him as he handed Talon over to me.

"A eulogy?" I whispered, my heart racing fast. I knew how hard something like this would be for Graham.

"Yes." He nodded. "It might not be any good."

I shook my head slowly and took his hand, squeezing it lightly. "It will be perfect." Each step he took to the podium was slow, controlled. Everything about Graham had always been controlled. He almost always stood tall, never wavering back and forth. As my eyes stayed glued to him, my stomach tightened when I saw him stumble a bit. He grabbed the podium and refocused his stance.

The space was silent and all eyes were on him. I could smell the lilacs and jasmine surrounding us as the wind blew through them. The earth was still wet from all the rain we'd received over the past few days, and whenever the air brushed past, I could almost taste the moisture. My eyes didn't move from Graham. I studied the man I had learned to quietly love as he prepared to say goodbye to the first man who ever taught me what love was meant to look like.

Graham cleared his throat and loosened his slim black tie. He parted his lips, looking down at his sheets of paper, which were filled with words front and back. Once more, his throat was cleared. Then, he tried to speak. "Professor

Oliver was a…" His voice cracked, and he lowered his head. "Professor Oliver…" His hands formed fists on the podium. "This isn't right. You see, I wrote this long speech about Oliver. I spent hours upon hours crafting it, but let's be honest, if I turned this paper in to him, he would call it complete shit." The room filled with laughter. "I'm certain many of the people here have been his students, and one thing we all know is that Professor Oliver was a hard-ass when it came to grading papers. I received my first F on a paper from him, and when I challenged him about it in his office, he looked at me, lowered his voice, and said, 'Heart.' I didn't have a clue what he was talking about, but he gave me a tiny smile and repeated, 'Heart.' I later realized he meant that was what was missing from my paper.

"Before his classes, I had no clue how to put heart into a story, but he took the time to teach me what it looked like—heart, passion, love. He was the greatest teacher of those three subjects." Graham picked up his pieces of paper and ripped them in half. "And if he were to grade this speech of mine, he'd fail me. My words speak on his achievements in his career. He was an amazing scholar and received numerous awards that recognized his talents, but that's just fluff." Graham chuckled, along with other students who'd had Ollie as a professor. "We all know how Oliver hated when people added extra fluff to their papers to reach the required word counts. 'Add muscle, not fat, students.' So now, I'll just add the strongest muscle—I'll add the heart. I'll tell you the core of who Professor Oliver was.

"Oliver was a man who loved unapologetically. He loved his wife and his daughter. He loved his work, his students, and their minds. Oliver loved the world. He loved the world's flaws, he loved the world's mistakes, he loved the world's scars. He believed in the beauty of pain and the glory of better tomorrows. He was the definition of love, and he spent his life trying to spread that love to as many people as he could. I remember my sophomore year, I was so mad at him. He gave me my second F, and I was so pissed off. I marched straight to his office, barged in uninvited, and right as I was about to shout at him for this outrageous issue, I paused. There he was, sitting at his desk crying with his face in the palms of his hands."

My stomach tightened as I listened to Graham's story. His shoulders drooped, and he tried his best to hold himself together as he continued speaking. "I'm the worst person in those situations. I don't know how to comfort people. I don't know how to say the right things—that was normally his job. So, I just sat. I sat across from him as he sobbed uncontrollably. I sat and allowed him to feel his world falling apart until he could voice what was hurting him so deeply. It was the day one of his former students committed suicide. He hadn't seen the student in years, but he remembered him—his smile, his sadness, his strength—and when he learned that the student passed away, Ollie's heart broke. He looked at me and said, 'The world's a little darker tonight, Graham.'

Then he wiped away his tears and said, 'But still, I must believe that the sun will rise tomorrow.'"

Tears flooded Graham's eyes, and he took a beat to catch his breath before continuing, speaking directly to Ollie's family. "Mary, Karla, Susie, I tell stories for a living, but I'm not very good with words," he said softly. "I don't know what I can say to make any sense of this. I don't know what the meaning of life is or why death interrupts it. I don't know why he was taken away, and I don't know how to lie to you and tell you everything happens for a reason. What I do know for a fact is that you loved him, and he loved you with every ounce of heart that he possessed.

"Maybe someday that fact will be enough to help you through each day. Maybe someday that fact will bring you peace, but it's okay if that day's not today, because it's not that day for me. I don't feel peace. I feel cheated, sad, hurt, and alone. All my life I never had a man to look up to. I never knew what it meant to be a true man until I met Professor Oliver. He was the best man I've ever known, the best friend I've ever had, and the world's a lot darker tonight because he's gone. Ollie was my father," Graham said, tears freely falling down his cheeks as he took one final deep breath. "And I will forever be his son."

For the past few nights, I'd been sharing a bed with Graham. He seemed to be more at peace when he wasn't alone, and all I wanted was for him to find a little bit of peace. The May rain showers had been coming down heavily, and it was our background music as we fell asleep.

One Sunday morning, I woke up in the middle of the night due to the sound of thunder, and I rolled over in the bed to see that Graham was missing. Climbing out of bed, I went to see if he was with Talon, but once I reached her nursery, I saw she was sleeping calmly.

I walked throughout the house searching for him, and it wasn't until I stepped into the sunroom that I saw a shadow in the garden. I quickly tossed on my rain boots and grabbed an umbrella, walking outside to see him. He was soaked from head to toe with a shovel in his hands.

"Graham," I called after him, wondering what it was he was doing until I glanced over at the shed where a large tree was leaning, waiting to be planted.

Ollie's tree.

He didn't turn back to look toward me. I wasn't even certain he heard my voice. He just kept shoveling into the ground, digging a hole that would hold the tree. It was heartbreaking watching him soaking wet, digging deeper and deeper. I walked over to him, still holding my umbrella, and lightly tapped him on his shoulders.

He turned to me, surprised to see me standing there, and that was when I saw his eyes.

The truth lies in his eyes, Ollie had told me.

That night I saw it, and I saw that Graham was breaking. His heart was breaking minute by minute, second by second, so I did the only thing I could think to do.

I placed the umbrella on the ground, picked up another shovel, and started to dig right there beside him.

No words were exchanged—none were needed. Each time we tossed the earth's soil to the side, we took a breath in honor of Ollie's life. Once the hole was large enough, I helped him carry the tree over, and we placed it down, covering the base back up with mud.

Graham lowered himself down to the ground, sitting in the mess of nature while the rain continued to hammer down on us. I sat down beside him. He bent his knees and rested his hands on top of them with his fingers laced. I sat with my legs crossed and my hands in my lap.

"Lucille?" he whispered.

"Yes?"

"Thank you."

"Always."

chapter twenty-five

Graham

"Lucille?" I called from my office late one afternoon. Over the past few weeks, I'd forced myself to sit at my desk and write. I knew that was what Professor Oliver would've wanted me to do. He would've wanted me to not give up.

"Yes?" she questioned, stepping into the room.

My heart skipped. She looked exhausted—no makeup, messy hair, and absolutely everything I'd ever wanted.

"I, um, I have to send a few chapters to my editor, and normally, Professor Oliver would read them, but…" I grimaced. "Do you think you could read them for me?"

Her eyes widened and her smile stretched wide. "Are you kidding? Of course. Let me see."

I handed her the papers, and she sat down across from me. She crossed her legs and began to read, taking in all my words. As her eyes stayed glued to the paper, my stare was stuck on her. Some nights I wondered what would've happened without her. I wondered how I would've survived without the hippie weirdo in my life.

I wondered how I'd gone so long without telling her she was one of my favorite people in the whole wide world.

Lucy Palmer had saved me from the darkness, and I'd never be able to thank her enough.

After some time, her eyes watered over and she bit her bottom lip. "Wow," she whispered to herself as she kept flipping the pages. She was deeply focused as she read my words, taking her time. "Wow," she muttered again. When she finished, she placed all of the pages in her lap and shook her head slightly before looking at me, and then she said, "Wow."

"You hate it?" I asked, crossing my arms.

"It's perfect. It's absolutely perfect."

"Would you change anything?"

"Not a single word. Ollie would be proud."

A small sigh left my lips. "Okay. Thank you." She stood up and started walking toward the door, and I called after her once. "Do you think you'd want to be my plus one for Karla and Susie's wedding?"

A gentle smile landed on her lips and she shrugged her left shoulder. "I've been waiting for you to ask me."

"I wasn't certain you'd want to come. I mean…it seems weird to take a friend to a wedding."

Her voice lowered and her chocolate eyes showed a touch of sadness as she stared my way. "Oh, Graham Cracker," she said softly. Her voice was so low that for a moment, I wondered if I imagined the words. "What I wouldn't give to be more than your friend."

The day of the wedding, I waited in the living room as Lucy finished getting ready in her bedroom. My chest was tight waiting to see her, and when she appeared, it was better than I could've ever imagined. She came out like a spark of perfection. She wore a floor-length baby blue gown and had baby's breath twisted into her hair.

Her lips were painted pink, and her beauty was louder than ever.

Each second I saw her, I fell a little more.

Plus, she held Talon in her arms, and the way my daughter, my heart, snuggled into this woman made me fall even more.

We weren't supposed to feel this way.

We weren't supposed to fall for one another, she and I.

Yet it seemed gravity had a way of pulling us closer.

"You look beautiful," I told her, standing up from the couch and smoothing out my suit.

"You don't look half bad yourself." She smiled as she walked over to me.

"Dada," Talon said, babbling and reaching out to me. Every time she spoke, my heart grew in size. "Dadadada."

I'd never known love could be so real.

I took her into my arms and kissed her forehead as she kissed mine back. Lucy stepped forward, straightening out my bow tie, which she had picked out. She'd picked out my whole outfit. She was convinced my closet contained too much black, so she had forced me out of my comfort zone with a light gray suit and a baby blue polka dot bow tie.

We drove to Lucy's employee, Chrissy's, house before heading to the ceremony. Chrissy had said she'd take care of Talon for the evening, and a part of me worried. Talon had never spent time with anyone other than Lucy or me, but Lucy told me she trusted Chrissy, and in turn, I trusted Lucy.

"If you need anything, you have our numbers," I told Chrissy as I handed her Talon, who seemed timid at first.

"Ah, don't you worry, we're going to have a great time. All you two have to worry about is having a great time tonight. Embrace each moment."

I gave her a tight smile before leaning in to kiss Talon's forehead one last time.

"Oh, and, Graham? I'm sorry about your father. Professor Oliver seemed like a great man," Chrissy told me.

I thanked her as Lucy took my hand and squeezed it lightly.

As we walked to the car, I turned her way. "You told her he was my father?" I asked.

"Of course. He was your father, and you were his son."

I swallowed hard and opened her car door to help her in. As she climbed inside, I waited a second before shutting the door. "Lucille?"

"Yes?"

"You make the world a lot less dark."

We arrived at the ceremony about ten minutes before it was going to begin and sat in a middle row on the edge of the aisle. The space was surrounded by beautiful flowers, which Lucy herself had arranged for the event and set up earlier that morning. She was the best at making every moment beautiful.

When it was time, everyone in attendance stood up as Susie walked down the aisle first with her arm looped through her father's. She was smiling wide and looked breathtaking in her white gown. Once she made it to the front, her father kissed her cheek and took his seat. Then, the music shifted and it was Karla's turn. She looked like an angel, holding her beautiful bouquet of pink and white roses. Her dress flowed effortlessly, but her steps seemed to be a struggle. With each one she took, I could tell what was weighing on her heart—she was missing her father, the man who was supposed to be walking her down the aisle on the happiest day of her life.

Halfway down the aisle, her steps stopped, she covered her mouth with her hand, and she began sobbing, the overwhelming pain of the situation swallowing her whole.

Within seconds, I was there. My arm wrapped around hers, I leaned in closer to her, and I whispered, "I have you, Karla. You're not alone."

She turned to me, her eyes filled with broken pieces of her soul, and she wrapped her arms around me. She took a few seconds to fall apart, and I held her each second that passed. When she was strong enough, I kept her arm linked with mine and walked her down the aisle.

The officiant smiled wide when we reached the end of the aisle. Susie's eyes locked with mine for a moment and she silently thanked me. I simply nodded once.

"Who gives this beautiful bride away?" the officiant asked.

I stood tall, staring straight at Karla. "I do." I wiped a few of her tears away and smiled. "With every ounce of my being, I do."

Karla turned and hugged me so tight, and I held her close to me as she softly spoke. "Thank you, brother."

"Forever, sister."

I walked back to my seat and sat beside Lucy, who had tears streaming down her face. She turned to me and gave me the greatest smile I'd ever seen. Her lips parted and she whispered, "I am in love with you," and then she turned to face the ceremony.

Within seconds, my heart filled with more love than I had thought possible.

Because that was the thing about hearts—when you thought they were completely full, you somehow found room to add a little more love.

Loving Lucy Hope Palmer wasn't a choice; it was my destiny.

※

The rest of the ceremony ran smoothly. The evening was filled with love, laughter, and light—and dancing. So much dancing.

When a slow song came on, Mary walked over to me and held her hand out, asking me for a dance. I stood up and walked her to the dance floor. As she placed her hand on my shoulder, we started to sway.

"What you did for Karla...I'll never be able to thank you enough for that," Mary said, a tear rolling down her cheek.

I leaned in and kissed her tear away before it could hit the floor. "Anything you ladies need, I am here for you. Always, Mary. Always."

She smiled and nodded. "I always wanted a son."

"I always wanted a mom."

We danced, and she laid her head against my shoulder, allowing me to guide our moves. "The way you look at her," she said, speaking of Lucy. "The way she looks at you..."

"I know."

"Let her in, my dear. She makes you feel the way Ollie made me feel—whole—and a love like that isn't something one should ever pass up. There might be a million reasons why you think it couldn't work, but all you need is one reason why it could. That reason is love."

I knew she was right about Lucy and love.

If love were a person, it would be her.

When our dance finished, Mary kissed my cheek and said, "Tell her. Tell her everything that scares you, everything that excites you, everything that moves you. Tell her all of it and let her in. I promise every moment will be worth it."

I thanked her and took a breath as I turned around to see Lucy finishing up a dance with one of the older gentlemen in his seventies. I could hear Professor Oliver in my head, and I could feel him in my heart as it beat.

Be brave, Graham.

I met her at our table, and she sat down, beaming with happiness. It was as if happiness was the only mode she knew.

"Thank you for bringing me, Graham. This has been—"

I cut her off. There wasn't a chance that I could wait one more minute. I couldn't waste another second of time where my lips weren't against hers. My mouth crashed into hers, making my mind swirl as I felt her lips on mine. I felt her entire being wrapping around my soul, soaking me in, changing me into a better man than I'd ever thought I could be. I'd died a million deaths before I gave living a chance, and my first breath of life was taken from her lips.

As I pulled away a bit, my hands stayed resting around her neck as my fingers slightly massaged her neck. "It's you," I whispered, our lips still slightly touching. "My greatest hope is, and always will be, you."

And then, she kissed me back.

chapter twenty-six

Lucy

WE DIDN'T KNOW HOW TO ACT WITH ONE ANOTHER AFTER OUR FIRST KISS. Our situation wasn't the norm when it came to building a relationship. We did everything backward. I fell in love with a boy before our first kiss, and he fell for a girl who he wasn't allowed to have. Our connection, our heartbeats, matched one another in our fairytale world, but in reality, society deemed us as an awful accident.

Maybe we were an accident—a mistake.

Maybe we were never supposed to cross each other's paths.

Maybe he was only meant to be a lesson in life and not a permanent mark.

But still, the way he kissed me…

Our kiss was as if heaven and hell collided together, and each choice was right and wrong at the same exact time. We kissed as if we were making a mistake and the best decision all at once. His lips made me float higher, yet somehow descend. His breaths somehow made my heart beat faster as it came to a complete halt.

Our love was everything good and bad wrapped in one kiss.

A part of me knew I should've regretted it, but the way his lips warmed up the cold shadows of my soul…the way he left his mark on me…

I'd never regret finding him, holding him, even if we only had those few seconds as one.

He'd always be worth those tiny seconds we shared.

He'd always be worth that soul-connecting feeling we created when our lips touched.

He'd always be the one I spent my nights dreaming of being near.

He'd always be worth it to me.

Sometimes when your heart wanted a full-length novel, the world only gave you a novella, and sometimes when you wanted forever you only had those few seconds of now.

And all I could do, all anyone could ever do, was make each moment count.

After we went home that night, we didn't talk about it at all. Not the following week, either. I focused on Talon. Graham worked on his novel. I believed both of us were waiting for the right time to come up for us to speak about it, but that was the tricky thing about timing: it was never right.

Sometimes you just had to leap and hope you didn't fall.

Luckily, on a warm Saturday afternoon, Graham jumped.

"It was good, right?" he asked, surprising me as I was changing Talon's diaper in the nursery.

I turned slightly to see him standing in the doorway, looking my way. "What was good?" I asked, finishing up fastening the diaper.

"The kiss. Did you think it was good?"

My chest tightened as I lifted Talon into my arms. I cleared my throat. "Yeah, it was good. It was amazing."

He nodded, walking in closer. Each step he took made my heart ache with anticipation. "What else? What else did you think?"

"Truth?" I whispered.

"Truth."

"I thought I'd been in love before. I thought I knew what love was. I thought I understood its curves, its angles, its shape. But then, I kissed you."

"And?"

I swallowed hard. "And I realized you were the first and only thing that ever made my heartbeats come to life."

He studied me, uncertain. "But?" he asked, moving in closer. He slid his hands into his pockets and bit his bottom lip before speaking again. "I know there's a 'but'. I see it in your eyes."

"But...she's my sister."

He grimaced knowingly. "Jane."

I nodded. "Lyric."

"So, you think never? You and I?" The hurt in his eyes from his question broke my heart.

"I think society would have a lot to say about it. That's my biggest worry."

He was even closer than before, close enough to kiss me again. "And since when do we care what society thinks, my hippie weirdo?"

I blushed, and he moved my hair behind my ear.

"It's not going to be easy. It might be very hard, and weird, and out of the norm, but I promise you, if you give me a chance, if you give us a few moments, I'll make it worth all of your time. Say okay?"

I lived in the moment, and my lips parted. "Okay."

"I want to take you out on a date. Tomorrow. I want you to wear your favorite outfit and allow me to take you out."

I laughed. "Are you sure? My favorite outfit involves stripes, polka dots, and a million colors."

"I wouldn't expect anything else." He smiled.

God. That smile. That smile did things to me. I placed Talon on the floor so she could crawl around as Graham kept speaking.

"And, Lucille?"

"Yes?"

"There's poop on your cheek."

My eyes widened in horror as I moved to a mirror and grabbed a baby wipe to clean my face. I looked at Graham who was snickering to himself, and my cheeks didn't stop turning red. I crossed my arms and narrowed my stare. "Did you just ask me on a date even though there was poop on my face?"

He nodded without hesitation. "Of course. It's just a little poop. That wouldn't change the fact that I'm in love with you and want to take you out on a date."

"What? Wait. *What*? Say that again…" My heart was racing, my mind spinning.

"I want to take you out a date?"

"No. Before that."

"That it's just a little poop?"

I waved my hands. "No, no. The part after that. The part about—"

"Me loving you?"

There it was again. The racing heart and the spinning mind. "You're in love with me?"

"With every piece of my soul."

Before I could reply, before any words left my mouth, a little girl walked past me. My eyes widened at the same exact moment Graham's did as he stared at his daughter.

"Did she…?" he asked.

"I think…" I replied.

Graham scooped Talon into his arms, and I swore his excitement lit up the whole house. "She just took her first steps!" he exclaimed, swirling Talon in his arms as she giggled at the kisses he was giving to her cheeks. "You just took your first steps!"

We both began jumping up and down, cheering Talon on, who just kept giggling and clapping her hands together. We spent the rest of the evening on the floor, trying to get Talon to take more steps. Every time she did, we cheered as if she were an Olympic Gold Medalist. In our eyes, she was exactly that.

It was the best night of my life, watching the man who loved me love his baby girl so freely. When Talon finally fell asleep that night, Graham and I headed to his bedroom and held each other before sleep overtook us.

"Lucille?" he whispered against my neck as I snuggled myself closer to his warmth.

"Yes?"

"I don't want it to be true, but I want to prepare you. There's going to come a time that I let you down. I don't want to, but I think when people love each other, they sometimes let each other down."

"Yes," I nodded, knowingly. "But I am strong enough to lift myself back up. There will be a day that I let you down, too."

"Yes," he yawned before pulling my body closer to his. "But I'm certain on those days I'll somehow love you more."

The next morning, I was still on my high from Graham and Talon. That was until I went into work. Mari sat in the office at Monet's Gardens with her fingers laced together as she examined the bookkeeping binders. Normally she handled the paperwork side of the business while I handled the front of the house. She was good at what she did, too, but when I walked into the office that afternoon, I could almost see the heavy cloud sitting over her.

I knew exactly what Mama would've said if she saw her baby girl in that moment.

Overthinking, again, my Mari Joy?

"What is it?" I asked, leaning against the doorframe.

She looked up at me, her brow knitted, and leaned back in her chair.

"Those are pretty much the most words you've said to me since I—"

"Moved back in with your ex?"

"My husband," she corrected.

We hadn't really spoken since the Parker situation exploded and she moved back in with him. I avoided all conversation about it, because I knew she'd made a choice. That was one thing about Mari—she overthought everything, but when she made her final decision, she followed through. There was nothing I could say to make her leave the monster she was currently sharing a bed with.

All I could do was patiently wait to piece her heart back together when he destroyed her—again.

"What is it?" I asked, nodding toward the paperwork.

She shook her head. "Nothing. I'm just trying to figure out numbers."

"It's not nothing," I disagreed, walking over to the desk and sitting across from her. "You have that look about you."

"That look?" she asked.

"You know, your worried look."

"What are you talking about? I don't have a worried look."

I gave her an are-you-seriously-trying-to-say-you-don't-have-a-worried-look look.

She sighed. "I don't think we can keep Chrissy on staff."

"What? She's great. She's actually way *too* good—better than both of us. We need her. I was actually going to talk to you about giving her a raise."

"That's the thing, Lucy, we don't have the money to give her a raise. We hardly have enough to keep her here. I think it's best if we let her go."

I narrowed my eyes, confused by her words and certain they had been tainted. "Is this you or Parker talking?"

"I'm my own person, Lucy, with a college degree. This is me."

"She loves her job," I told her.

Mari slightly shrugged. "I like her, too, but this is business, nothing personal."

"Now you sound like Lyric," I huffed. "All business, no heart."

"She has heart, Lucy. The two of you together just never really worked."

I cocked an eyebrow, flabbergasted by Mari backing up Lyric. "She left her child, Mari."

"We all make mistakes."

"Yes." I nodded slowly, still confused. "But a mistake is spilling milk, burning a pizza, missing an anniversary. Walking out on your newborn child who was in the NICU for weeks? Staying gone when the child is fully okay? That's not a mistake—that's a choice."

She grimaced. "I just think it's odd how involved you are with it all. I mean, you didn't even know Graham, and it's clear that you and Lyric have your issues. Why make things worse? It just doesn't make sense. It's not normal."

"You could get to know her more too, you know. She's your niece, our niece. We are throwing her a first birthday party next weekend…maybe if you come, you'll understand."

"*We* are throwing her a party? We? Don't you see how that's weird? Lucy, she's not your daughter."

"I know that. I'm just helping Graham—"

"You're living with him."

"You kicked me out!"

She shook her head. "I didn't kick you out exactly, and I definitely didn't push you into his home. Your heart did that."

"Stop," I said, my voice growing low as a knot formed in my stomach.

Mari gave me her knowing stare. "Lucy, I know you're falling for him."

I blinked away some tears that were trying to fall. "You don't know what you're talking about. You have no clue what you're talking about."

"You're making a mistake. He was with Lyric. She's your sister," Mari exclaimed. "I know you live by your emotions, but this isn't right."

I bit my bottom lip, feeling my anger building. "Oh, right, because you are the world's most knowledgeable on what a relationship should look like."

"A *relationship*?" she hissed. "Lucy, you're not in a relationship with Graham Russell. I know this will hurt to hear, but I get Lyric when it comes to you. You're too much like Mama. You're too free, and freedom can be suffocating. If you settle down, don't settle for him. He's not yours to love."

I didn't know what to do. The burning in my chest was so painful. I parted my lips to speak, but no sound came out. I couldn't think of the words I needed to say, so I turned around and left.

It didn't take long for me to find myself in nature. I headed to my favorite running trail, took a deep breath in, and let a heavy breath out before I started to run. I ran through the trees, allowing the air to slap against my skin as I ran faster and faster, trying to rid myself of the hurt and confusion.

Part of me hated Mari for the words she spoke, but another part wondered how right she was.

In my mind, I played out the fairy tale of what Graham and I would be. Selfishly, I thought how it could be if maybe someday our love led to forever. Selfishly, I allowed myself to feel completely.

I was a dreamer, like my mother, and while I'd always adored that fact, I was slowly beginning to see her flaws. She floated more than she walked, skipped more than she stood, and no matter what, she never faced reality.

So, whenever reality came for her, she was always alone.

That terrified me—being alone.

But not being with Graham and Talon terrified me more than anything.

When I arrived at Graham's house, I didn't have the nerve to walk inside. Even the run hadn't cleared my mind, so instead, I went and sat in the backyard near Ollie's tree. I sat with my legs crossed, staring at the tiny tree that had so many years of growth to go. I stayed there for seconds, minutes, hours. It wasn't until the sun started setting that Graham joined me outside. He was dressed in a perfectly fitted suit and looked out of this world amazing. I felt awful missing our date, but I knew due to my emotions I wouldn't have been ready to go out with him. Mari put more guilt in my heart than I knew I could hold. Maybe I was being naïve about the way Graham made me feel…maybe I was being foolish.

"Hi," he said.

"Hi," I replied.

He sat.

He stared.

He spoke.

"You're sad."

I nodded. "Yes."

"You've been here for four hours."

"I know."

"I wanted to give you space."

"Thank you."

He nodded. "I think you've had enough space, though. You can only be alone for so long before you start convincing yourself you deserve to be that way—trust me, I know—and you, Lucille Hope Palmer, do not deserve to be alone."

No more words were exchanged, but the feeling of wholeness was loud and clear. If only the world could feel the way our hearts beat as one, then maybe they wouldn't be so harsh to judge our connection.

"This is a terrible first date." I laughed, nerves shaking my vocals.

He reached into his suit pocket, pulled out a pack of licorice, and handed it to me. "Better?" he asked.

I sighed and nodded once before opening the package. "Better." Being beside him always felt right to me. Like home.

In that way, I was different than Mama. While she always wanted to float away, my heart craved to stay beside Graham Russell.

For the first time in my life, I desperately wanted to stand on solid ground.

chapter twenty-seven

Graham

"YOU SHOULD CALL HER," I TOLD LUCY AS SHE WENT AROUND THE HOUSE, making up reasons to keep distracted. For months, she and her sister Mari hadn't talked about anything but work-related issues, but apparently they'd had a big falling out over something a few days before. I could tell the issues were eating her alive, but she tried her best not to talk about it.

"It's fine. We're fine," she replied.

"Liar."

She turned to me and cocked an eyebrow. "Don't you have a book to finish or something?"

I smiled at her sassiness.

I loved that side of her.

I loved all sides of her.

"I'm just saying, you miss her."

"I don't," she said, her poker face communicating the complete opposite of her words. She bit her bottom lip. "Do you think she's happy? I don't think she's happy. Never mind. I don't want to talk about it."

"Lucil—"

"I mean, he literally left her during the worst days of her life. Who does that?! Whatever, it's her life. I'm done talking about it."

"Okay," I agreed.

"I mean, he's a monster! And he's not even a cute monster! I just hate him, and I'm so angry with her for choosing him over me, over us. And now this afternoon is Talon's first birthday party, and Mari won't even be here for it! I can't believe—oh crap!" she screamed, running into the kitchen. I followed right behind her to witness her pulling out Talon's chocolate cake, which was badly burned. "No, no, no," she said, placing it on the countertop.

"Breathe," I told her, walking behind her and placing my hands on her shoulders. Her eyes watered over and I laughed. "It's just a cake, Lucille. It's okay."

"No! No, it's not okay," she said, turning her body around to face me. "We were going to backpack across Europe. We started saving up when she got sick. We started a 'Negative Thoughts' jar and every time we thought something negative about her diagnosis or fear took over our minds, we had to put a coin in the jar. After the first week, the jar was filled to the brim, and we had to get another jar. She wanted to go right after she was in remission, but I was too scared. I was afraid she might not be strong enough, that it might be too soon, so I kept her home. I kept her locked away, because I wasn't strong enough to get on a plane with her." I swallowed hard. "And now she's not talking to me, and I'm not talking to her. She's my best friend."

"She'll come around."

"I invited her today, for Talon's party. That's what started the argument."

"Why was that an issue?"

"She..." Lucy's voice cracked and she took a deep breath as we stood just inches apart. "She thinks this is all wrong, you and me, Talon. She thinks it's weird."

"It is weird," I told her. "But that doesn't mean it's not right."

"She told me you're not mine. She said you're not mine to love."

Before I could reply, the doorbell rang, and she tore herself away from me, finding a fake smile to plaster on her face. "It's fine, really. I'm just upset that I burned the cake. I'll get the door."

I stood there, staring at the cake, and then I pulled out a knife to see if perhaps I could somehow save it by scraping off some of the inedible parts. Lucy needed a win that day. She needed something to make her smile.

"Oh my God," I heard from the other room. Lucy's voice sounded terrified, and when I walked into the living room, I knew exactly why.

"Jane," I muttered, staring at her standing in my doorway with a teddy bear and a gift in her other hand. "What the hell are you doing here?"

She parted her lips to speak, but then her eyes traveled back to Lucy. "What are you doing here?" she asked her, a bit of a sting lacing her words. "Why on earth would you be here?"

"I..." Lucy started, but I could tell her nerves were too shaken for words to come out.

"Jane, what are you doing here?" I asked her once more.

"I..." Her voice shook the same way Lucy's had a moment before. "I wanted to see my daughter."

"Your daughter?" I huffed, stunned by the nerve she had to walk into my home and use those words.

"I...can we talk, Graham?" Jane asked. Her eyes darted to Lucy, and she narrowed them. "Alone?"

"Anything you say can be said in front of Lucille," I told her.

Lucy's already bruised heart was taking another beating. "No, it's okay. I'll go. I should probably get some work done at the floral shop, anyway. I'll just grab my coat."

As she walked past me, I lightly grabbed her arm and whispered, "You do not have to go."

She nodded her head slowly. "I just think it's best if you two talk. I don't want to cause any more issues."

She gave my hand a light squeeze then let go. When she grabbed her coat, she walked straight out of the house without another word, and the room somehow filled with darkness.

"What is it you want, Jane?"

"It's been a year, Graham. I just want to see her."

"What makes you think you have any right to see her? You abandoned her."

"I was scared."

"You were selfish."

She grimaced and shifted around in her shoes. "Still, you need to let me see her. As her mother, I deserve that much. It's my right."

"Mother?" I hissed, my gut filled with disgust. Being a mother didn't simply mean giving birth. Being a mother meant late-night feedings. Being a mother meant sleeping next to a crib because your child was sick and you needed to watch their breaths. Being a mother meant knowing Talon hated teddy bears. Being a mother meant you stayed.

Jane was not a mother, not for a minute.

She was a stranger to my child. A stranger in my house.

A stranger to me.

"You need to leave," I told her, uneasy about the fact that she apparently believed she could walk back into our lives after all this time.

"Are you sleeping with Lucy?" she questioned, throwing me for a complete loop.

"Excuse me?" I felt it form in my gut and start rising to my throat—my anger. "You abandoned your daughter months ago. You left without more than a bullshit note. You didn't take a second to look back once. Yet now, you think you have the right to ask me something like that? No, Jane. You don't get to ask me questions."

She pushed her shoulders back. Although she stood tall in her high heels, there was a tremble in her voice. "I don't want her near my child."

I walked over to the front door and opened it. "Goodbye, Jane."

"I'm your wife, Graham. Talon shouldn't be around someone like Lucy. She's a toxic person. I deserve—"

"*Nothing!*" I hollered, my voice hitting a new height of anger, panic, and disgust. "You deserve nothing." She'd crossed a line by using the word wife. She'd crossed a bigger line by speaking ill of Lucy, the one who had stayed. She'd crossed the biggest line by saying how Talon should be raised. "*Leave!*" I shouted once more. The second I hollered, Talon started crying and I swallowed hard.

I had grown up in a home with screaming, and it was the last thing I ever wanted my daughter to witness.

My voice dropped low. "Please, Jane. Just go."

She stepped outside, her head still held high. "Think about what you're about to do, Graham. If you slam this door, it means we must fight. If you slam this door, it means there's going to be a war."

With no thought needed, I replied, "I'll have my lawyers call yours."

With that, I slammed the door.

chapter twenty-eight

Lucy

"Lyric's back in town," I said, hurrying into Monet's Gardens where Mari was putting together a new window display.

She glanced over at me and gave me a small nod. "Yeah, I know."

"What?" I asked, surprised. "When did you find out?"

"I saw her two days ago. She stopped by Parker's place to talk." The way the words rolled off her tongue so effortlessly and carelessly confused me. Who had taken my sister, my favorite person in the world, and changed her?

What had happened to my Mari?

"Why didn't you tell me?" I asked, my chest hurting as my heart began to crack. "You saw me yesterday."

"I was going to mention it, but our last conversation didn't lead to the best place. You stormed off," she told me, picking up the vase and moving it over to the windows. "And what does it matter if she's back? Her family is here, Lucy."

"She abandoned them for months. She left her newborn in the NICU because she was selfish. Don't you think it's terrible for her to just walk back into Graham's life? Into Talon's life?"

"We don't really get a say in that, Lucy. It's none of our business."

More pieces of my heart shattered, and Mari acted as if she didn't even care.

"But..." Mari took a deep breath and crossed her arms, looking my way. "We do have to talk about the business. I thought I could hold out for a while longer, but since we're here now, we might as well talk."

"About what?" I asked, confusion filling me up.

"Lyric is a bit worried about how some of the things in the bookkeeping are adding up, and I mean, I think she's right. I think we jumped the gun hiring Chrissy. We aren't bringing in enough profit."

"Why in the world are you talking to Lyric about the store?" Mari grimaced, and I cocked an eyebrow. "What aren't you telling me?"

"Don't freak out," she said, which of course made me freak out even more. "Remember when we were starting out and we couldn't get a loan to cover the rest of our needs?"

"Mari...you said you got another loan from the bank. You said after months of trying, it finally went through."

She continued, breaking her stare from mine. "I didn't know what to do. You were so happy and excited to move forward after me getting sick, and I didn't have the guts to tell you the truth. You gave up so much of your life for me, and all I wanted was to give you our shop."

"You lied to me about the loan?" I asked Mari, my chest tight. "You asked Lyric for a loan?"

"I'm sorry, Lucy, I really am. With the medical bills and everything piling up, I knew I'd never be able to get a bank to help me—"

"So you went behind my back and asked Lyric for the money."

"You would've never let me take it if I told you."

"Of course I wouldn't have! Do you think she gave it to you out of the goodness of her heart? Mari, everything is leverage with Lyric. She only does things that will benefit her."

"No," Mari swore. "She did this for us, to help us get back on our feet. There were no strings attached."

"Until now," I huffed, my hands falling to my waist. "If it weren't for you taking money from her, letting her hold something so big over us, this wouldn't even be a problem, Mari. Now she's trying to tell you how to run our shop. We could've worked harder to get the loan ourselves. We could've done it, but now she wants to ruin everything we've built, all because you trusted the snake. We need to destroy the deal."

"I won't," she said sternly. "I was talking to Parker about everything, and he thinks—"

I huffed. "Why would I care what he thinks? It's none of his business."

"He's my husband. His opinion matters to me."

"I don't understand why. He abandoned you when you needed him the most. I was there, remember? I was the one who picked up your pieces after he destroyed you."

"So what?" she asked.

"*So what?*" I replied, flabbergasted. "That means you should at least trust my opinion over his."

She nodded slowly. "He said you'd say that."

"Excuse me?"

"He said you'd play the cancer card on me, reminding me that you were there for me when no one else was. Parker made a mistake, okay? And based on the past few months of your life, you know what it's like to make a mistake."

"That's not fair, Mari."

"No, you know what's not fair? Holding it over my head every day that you stayed. Reminding me whenever I have any kind of feelings that you were the one who stuck around to help me during the cancer. So, what, am I now forever indebted to you? I can't move on and live my life?"

"You think working under Lyric is going to be you living your life? All of this is happening because of Lyric's need to control everything."

"No, all of this is happening because you slept with your sister's husband."

"What?" I whispered, shocked by my sister's words, by the way they fell from her lips so effortlessly, and I stood there for a second, stunned, waiting for her to apologize, waiting for her cold stare to soften, waiting for my sister, my best friend, my Pea to come back to me.

"Take it back," I said softly, but she wouldn't.

She'd been poisoned with love—the same love that had once destroyed her.

It amazed me how love could hurt so much.

"Look, Parker thinks..." She paused and swallowed hard. "Parker and I both think that Lyric helping take control wouldn't hurt things. She's a businesswoman. She knows the laws and how to help build up the shop. She wants the best for us. She's our sister."

"She's *your* sister," I corrected. "She's your sister, and this store now belongs to you and her. I want nothing to do with it. I want nothing to do with either of you. Don't even bother firing Chrissy. I quit."

I walked around to the back, gathered all my belongings, and tossed them into a cardboard box. When I walked to the front of the store, I took the shop's keys off my keychain and placed them on the front counter.

Mari's eyes were still cold, and I could tell she wasn't going to change her mind. I knew I wasn't going to change mine either, but before I could leave, I had to speak my final truths—even though she'd think they were lies.

"They're going to let you down, Mari. They are going to use your trust and let you down and hurt you. This time, though, it's your choice. You have the free will to deal with the devils or not, and just don't come crying to me when you get burned."

"I know what I'm doing, Lucy. I'm not stupid."

"No," I agreed. "You're not stupid. You're just too trusting, which is a million times worse." I swallowed hard and blinked back the tears that wanted to fall. "For the record, I never slept with him. I love him with every ounce of my heart. I love the way he loves me so quietly, but we never slept together, not once, because I could never get past the idea of doing something like that to my sister. Now, though, I see the truth—being a sister isn't just defined by blood. It's defined by unconditional love. Lyric was never my sister, and she never will be." I took the heart-shaped necklace from around my neck and placed it in Mari's hands. "But, you are my heart, Mari, and I know I'm yours. So, when they hurt you, find me. Find me and I'll put your heart back together, and then maybe you can help me fix the cracks in my own."

"Hey, where have you been? I've been calling you, but your phone went straight to voicemail," Graham said as I stood on his front porch, exhausted. His eyes were filled with concern and a heavy dose of guilt as he held Talon in his arms. "Are you okay?"

I nodded slowly and stepped into his foyer. "Yeah. I stopped by Monet's and got into another big fight with Mari. Then I went for a run to clear my head, and when my phone died, I realized my charger was here, so I just came to pick it up. I hope that's okay." I brushed past him and blinked my eyes a few times, trying to hide the emotion that was seeping from my spirit.

"Of course it's okay, I was just worried." His eyes stayed glued to me, his concern never easing up, but I tried my best not to notice as I walked into Talon's room to grab my charger.

My heart was beating uncontrollably as I tried my best not to fall apart. My mind was spinning, thinking about everything that had just unspun with Mari in the shop. It was as if my favorite person in the whole world had been drugged and was being controlled by the hands of hate and confusion, yet was being told it was love driving her decisions.

It was heartbreaking to watch your best friend set herself up for heartache.

"Lucille," Graham said, following after me.

I blinked.

Oh, Graham...

The comfort of his smooth voice went right to my soul.

"I'm okay," I told him, walking past him with my charger. I avoided eye contact, because I knew eye contact would make me melt, and I couldn't melt into him. Maybe Mari was right—maybe every feeling I had for the man before me was wrong.

If only love came with a timeline and instructions.

If it had, I would've fallen in love with him when our timing was right. If love came with a timeline, Graham Russell would've always held my heart.

"I think I'm going to just stay at a hotel for a few nights. I think it's too messy to stay here knowing Lyric is back. I'm going to grab some of my things."

"That's ridiculous," he told me. "You're staying here. This is your home."

Home.

If he knew me, he'd know that all my life, home was always shifting. I never planted my roots anywhere, and when it was time to move, it was time to move.

Even if going meant leaving my heartbeats behind.

"No, really, it's okay," I said, still avoiding eye contact. I didn't want to fall apart, not in front of Graham. I'd wait until I got to the hotel to lose myself. *Feel less, Lucy. Feel less.*

That was almost impossible when I felt a tiny hand reach out to me and tug on my shirt. "LuLu," Talon said, making me turn toward her. She had the brightest smile and the widest beautiful eyes, which were staring my way. Oh, how her smile made my heart beat. "LuLu," she repeated, reaching out for me to lift her up.

It cracked my heart, which I was trying so hard to keep intact.

"Hey, honey," I said, taking her from Graham's arms. I knew it wasn't right, knew she wasn't mine to have, but that little girl had changed me in more ways than I could've ever imagined. She never looked at me with judgment for my mistakes. She never turned her back on me. She only loved unconditionally, fully, honestly.

As I held her so tight in my arms, my body started to shake. The idea that I wouldn't wake up to her sounds every day was weighing on my soul. The idea that the past year with Talon and Graham would be the last year we all spent together was soul-crushing.

Yes, Talon wasn't mine, but I was hers. All of me loved that child. All of me would give my world for her and her father.

I couldn't stop shaking, couldn't fight the tears that started flooding my eyes. I couldn't change the person I'd always been.

I was the girl who felt everything, and in that moment, my whole world began to crumble.

I held Talon against me and cried into her shirt as she kept speaking her random words. My eyes shut tight as I sobbed against the beautiful soul.

This was where I had felt it for the first time.

What it felt like to be happy.

What it felt like to be loved.

What it felt like to be part of something bigger than myself.

And now, I was being forced to leave.

A hand fell against my lower back, and I curved into Graham's touch. He stood behind me, tall like the oak trees in the forest, and lowered his lips against my ear. As the words danced from his mouth and into my spirit, I remembered exactly why he was the man I chose to love fully. When he spoke, his words forever marked my soul as his. "If you need to fall, fall into me."

chapter twenty-nine

Graham

Jane came back the following day, as if she had a right to stop by whenever she pleased. I hated the fact that I didn't know what she had up her sleeve. I hated the unease I felt about the idea of her being back in town.

I knew she was capable of anything, but my biggest fear was that she'd try to take Talon away from me. If I knew anything about Jane, it was that she was intelligent—and sneaky. One never really knew what she was up to, and that made my skin crawl.

"Is she here?" Jane asked, stepping into the foyer of the house. Her eyes darted around the space, and I rolled my eyes in response.

"She's not."

"Good." She nodded.

"She's taking Talon for a walk."

"What?!" Jane exclaimed, shocked. "I told you I didn't want her around my child."

"And I told you that you didn't have a say in the matter. What exactly are you doing back here, Jane? What do you want?"

There was a moment where her eyes locked with mine. She looked nothing like her sister. There was no light in her eyes, only her dark irises that didn't contain much heart within them, but her voice contained more gentleness than I'd ever witnessed before. "I want my family back," she whispered. "I want you and Talon in my life."

I couldn't believe the nerve of her—to think she could just walk back into our lives as if she hadn't taken a year-long vacation.

"That's not happening," I told her.

She tightened her fists. "Yes, it is. I know I made a mistake leaving, but I want to make it right. I want to be here for the rest of her years. I deserve that right."

"You deserve nothing. *Nothing*. I was hoping we wouldn't have to go to court, but if that's the way it's going to be, that's the way it's going to be. I'm not afraid to fight for my daughter."

"Don't do this, Graham. You really don't want to," she warned, but I didn't care. "I'm a lawyer."

"I'll fight you."

"I'll win," she told me. "And I'll take her from you. I'll take her away from this place if it means Lucy won't be anywhere near her."

"Why do you hate her so much?" I blurted out. "She's the best person I've ever met."

"Then you need to meet more people."

My chest was on fire at the idea of this monster taking my child from me. "You cannot come back and just decide you're ready to be a mother. That's not how it works, and I would never in my life let you do that. You have no right to her, Jane. You are nothing to that child. You mean nothing to her. You're merely a human who abandoned a child because of your own selfish needs. You are not equipped to take my child away from me, even if you are a lawyer."

"I can do it," she said confidently, but I noticed the vein popping out of her head from her anger building. "I won't stand around and see my daughter be transformed into the person Lucy is." Her words made my skin crawl. I hated the way she spoke as if Lucy was the monster in our lives. As if Lucy hadn't saved me from myself. As if Lucy was anything less than a miracle.

"And who are you to say who Talon can and cannot be around?" I asked, my chest aching as my heart beat rapidly.

"I'm her mother!"

"And I'm her father!"

"*No, you're not!*" she screamed, the back of her throat burning from anger as her words bounced off the walls and slammed into my soul.

It was as if a bomb went off in the living room and shook the entire foundation of my life. "What?" I asked, my eyes narrow and low. "What did you just say to me?"

"*What?*" a voice questioned from behind us. Lucy stood there with Talon in the stroller, stunned.

Jane's body was still, except for her shaky hands. When her eyes met Talon's, her shoulders rounded, and I saw it happen—her heart started to break, but I didn't care. Not for a moment did I care about her pained expression. All I cared about was the fact that she was trying to tear my family away from me.

"I said, you're..." She swallowed hard, looking at the floor.

"Look at me," I ordered, my voice stern and loud. Her head rose and she blinked once before releasing a heavy sigh. "Now repeat yourself."

"You're not her father."

She was lying.

She was evil.

She was dirty.

She was the monster I always thought I would be.

"How dare you walk in here with your lies to try to take her," I whispered low, trying my best not to let them overtake me—my shadows, my ghosts, my fears.

"It's not…" She grimaced and shook her head back. "I, um…"

"It's time for you to leave," I said, sounding strong, hiding my fear. A part of me believed her. A part of me felt as if there was always that feeling somewhere deep in the back of my mind and I just did my best to hide it, but a bigger part of me looked at Talon and saw pieces of me in her stare. I saw myself in her smile. I saw the best parts of me in her soul. She was mine, and I was hers.

"You were on a book tour," she whispered, her voice shaky. "I, um, I was sick for weeks around that time, and I remember being annoyed that you went a week without even checking on me while you were on the road."

My mind started racing back to that time period, trying to grasp any memories, trying to pick up any kind of clues. Talon had been early. When I'd thought she was thirty-one weeks, she was twenty-eight, but I hadn't let that idea simmer. Talon was my daughter. My baby. My heart. I couldn't imagine that being anything less than true. "You had the flu, and you kept calling me."

"I just wanted…" She paused, unsure what else to say. "He stopped by to check on me."

Lucy's voice was low. "Who's he?" she asked.

Jane didn't reply, but I knew exactly who Jane was speaking of. She'd told me the story many times. How caring he was, while I was cold. How he was gentle to all people. How he was always there for strangers, and truly there for those he loved.

"My father," I said, my voice cracking. Kent Theodore Russell, a man, a father, a hero.

My personal hell.

There *were* parts of me that I saw in Talon's eyes, but a bigger part of me looked at Talon and saw pieces of him in her stare. I saw him in her smile. I saw parts of him in her soul—and yet, she was not his, and he was not hers.

Even so, it was enough to break my soul.

"You should go," Lucy told Jane.

Jane stood up straight and shook her head. "If anyone should go, it's you."

"No," I scolded, uncertain how my heart was still beating. "If anyone should go, it is you. Right now."

Jane went to argue, but she saw it—the fire inside me. She knew if she got one step closer, I would burn her to the ground. She gathered her things and left after stating that she'd be back.

When she was gone, I hurried over to Talon and lifted her in my arms. How could she not be my world?

She was mine, and I was hers.

I was hers, and she was mine.

She'd saved me.

She'd given me something worth living for, and now Jane had come back to try to rip that away from me.

"Can you watch her?" I asked Lucy, feeling the world crashing against me. She walked over and took her from my hold. Lucy's hand landed on my arm and I pulled away slightly.

"Talk to me," she said.

I shook my head and walked away, not speaking a word. I went to my office, closed the door behind me, and sat staring at the blinking cursor on my computer screen.

I hated him. I hated how he controlled me. I hated that even after death, he had still somehow destroyed my life.

chapter thirty

Thanksgiving

"You must be the woman who's inspiring my son's writing," Kent said, walking into Graham's home seconds before he was about to leave with Jane to go introduce her to Professor Oliver for the first time.

"What are you doing here?" Graham asked his father, coldness in his voice, harshness in his stare.

"It's Thanksgiving, son. I was hoping we could catch up. I saw your last book hit number one, and we haven't celebrated the success of it yet." Kent smiled over at Jane, who was staring his way with wide eyes, as if it were a legend standing before her instead of a monster. "He takes after his father."

"I'm nothing like you," Graham barked.

Kent snickered. "No, you're a bit grumpier."

Jane giggled, and the sound drove Graham insane. He despised how everyone laughed when they were around Kent.

"We're leaving for a dinner," Graham told Kent, wanting nothing more than for him to leave.

"Then I'll be quick. Listen, my publicist was wondering if you'd do an interview for ABC News with me. He thinks it will be great for both of our careers."

"I don't do interviews, especially with you."

Kent bit his lip and his mouth slightly twitched. It was a warning sign that he was growing upset, but over the years, he'd learned how to control it around strangers. Graham, however, knew the look well, and he knew the anger that simmered under his father's surface.

"Just think about it," he said, a bit of bark in his tone that Jane missed. Kent turned to her and gave her the smile that made all people fall for him. "What's your name, sweetheart?"

"Jane, and I have to say I am your biggest fan," she gushed.

Kent smiled wider. "Bigger fan than you are of my son?"

Graham grimaced. "We're leaving."

"Okay, okay. Just email me if you change your mind, and, Jane," Kent said, taking her hand and kissing it. "It was a pleasure to meet such a beauty. My son is a lucky man."

Jane's cheeks reddened and she thanked him for his kind words.

As he turned to leave, he allowed his eyes to dance across Jane's figure one last time before he spoke to Graham. "I know we've had some tough times, Graham. I know things haven't always been easy for us, but I want to fix that. I think this interview is a step in that direction. Hopefully soon you'll let me back into your life. Happy Thanksgiving, son."

Kent drove off, leaving Graham and Jane standing on the porch. Jane shifted her feet around. "He seems lovely," she commented.

Graham lowered his brows and stuffed his hands into his slacks, walking toward his car. "You do not know anything about the monster you speak of. You're merely falling into his trap."

She hurried behind him, trying to keep up in her high heels. "But still," she argued. "He was kind."

She didn't say anything else, but Graham knew what she was thinking—that Kent was kind, funny, charming, and the opposite of the man Graham presented himself to be.

Kent radiated light while Graham lived in the shadows.

chapter thirty-one

Lucy

SHE HAD SET HIM UP. SHE HAD GIVEN HIM NO REAL CHOICE IN HIS FUTURE BY controlling his heart. Graham didn't settle into the idea of not being Talon's father. He fought it the best he could, and when he took the paternity test, I believed his heart hoped Lyric was wrong. When the results came in, I saw the light inside of him die away.

Lyric presented him with the biggest choice of his life that wasn't even a choice, really: invite her back into his life so he could keep his daughter, or stay with me and she'd take Talon.

The day she told him, I was there. I stood by his side as she threatened to rip his world apart. She had all the control over every part of Graham, and I knew there was only one thing for me to do.

I had to pack my bags and go. I was certain I had to do it before he came back, too. He'd been speaking with a lawyer all afternoon, and I knew if I didn't leave now, I'd only make things harder for him. He couldn't lose his daughter; he couldn't lose his soul.

And so, I began to pack my bags.

"What are you doing?" he asked, his voice dripping with confusion.

"Graham." I sighed when I saw him standing in the doorway of the bathroom. His heavy-lidded mocha eyes stared at me as I reached for a towel and wrapped it around my body. "I didn't know you were home."

"I saw your things in the front lobby."

"Yes."

"You're leaving," he said breathlessly. He had shaved the day before, and yet his five o'clock shadow was already back. His lips were tight, and I knew for a fact he was clenching his teeth. His chiseled, square jawline was always more evident when he clenched his teeth.

"I think it's for the best."

"You really think so?" He stepped into the bathroom, shutting the door behind him. The sound of the running water was the only noise for a few seconds as we stared at one another.

"Yes, I do," I replied as the pit of my stomach fell and my heart drummed. I followed his hand as he reached for the doorknob and locked it. His steps toward me were slow as heat curled down my spine. "Graham, please," I begged, although I didn't know if I was begging for him to stay or go.

"I need you," he whispered. He was in front of me, his stare locked with mine, and even though he hadn't touched me yet, I felt his entire being. "Please," he begged back, his thumb tilting my chin up as he bit his bottom lip. "Don't leave me." His hands grasped my behind through the towel and my breath hitched. His mouth grazed down my neck and he whispered between kisses as he lifted me up, forcing me to drop my towel to the floor. "Stay with me. Please, Lucy, just stay."

I knew how hard that was for him—to ask for someone to stay—but I also knew the reasons why I couldn't.

My mind sizzled as he held my body against his and stepped over the edge of the tub, forcing the shower to rain over us. His lips bit against my breast before he took my nipple into his mouth, sucking it hard. My mind fogged as he shoved my back against the shower wall, his clothes getting soaked and clinging to his skin.

"Gra…" I felt dizzy, faint, happy, high. *So high…*

His fingers moved down my chest, down my stomach, and he slid them inside me with need, with want, with ache. "Don't leave me, Lucille, please. I can't lose you," he whispered against my lips before discovering my mouth with his tongue. "I need you more than you know. *I need you.*"

Everything quickened—his motions, his grips, his fingers, his tongue. I hurriedly unbuckled his jeans, sending them to the bottom of the tub, and stroked his hardness through his soaked boxers. When those were removed, he pulled his fingers from my core and locked eyes with me.

We made a choice that we added to our list of mistakes. We used each other's bodies to get high. We soared as we touched, moaned, and begged. I ascended as he lifted my butt cheeks and slammed me against the tiled wall. I cried out as he slid his hardness into me, inch by inch, filling me with indescribable warmth. He kissed like heaven and made love like sin. As the water fell around us, I silently prayed for this to be mine, Graham and me, forever and always. My heart told me I'd love him for all time. My brain told me I only had a few more moments and that I should enjoy each one, but my gut…

My gut told me I had to let go.

As he continued making love to every inch of my body, he moved his lips to the edge of my ear. His warm breaths brushed against me as he spoke. "Air above me…" He grasped one of my breasts in his hand and lightly pinched my nipple. "Earth below me…"

"Graham," I muttered, dazed, confused, in guilt, in love.

He wrapped his fingers in my hair and slightly pulled it, putting a curve in my neck. A spark shot down my spine as he began sucking my skin. "Fire within me…" He continued sliding his hardness deeper and harder into me, taking control of his speed, taking control of his desires, taking control of our love. He moved me to the other wall, and the steaming water slapped against us as I moaned his name and he moaned his words against my neck. "Water surround me..."

"Please," I begged, floating on the edge of make-believe, feeling the final buildup of our final mistake as he placed one hand against the wall and one hand around my waist. His arms were tight, each muscle defined with tight, sharp lines. We locked eyes and my body began to shake. I was so close...so close to pure ecstasy, so close to our final goodbye. "Please, Graham," I muttered, unsure if I was begging for him to let me go or to hold me forever.

His mouth slammed against mine, kissing me harder than we'd ever kissed before, and I could tell as his tongue danced with mine, as he sucked me with his hurts and his love, that he also knew how close we were to goodbye. He, too, was trying to hold on to the high that was already slipping to the ground.

He kissed me to say goodbye, and I kissed him to pray for more seconds. He kissed me to give me his love, and I kissed him to give him mine. He kissed me with his always, and I kissed him with my forever.

Right after we soared to our highest heights, we descended and crashed to our lowest lows—but not before his air became my breaths, not before his earth became my ground. His flames were my fire, his thirst was my water, and his spirit?

His spirit became my soul.

Then, we prepared ourselves for goodbye.

⁓⁓

"I didn't think it would be this hard," I whispered, hearing Graham's footsteps behind me as I stood in Talon's bedroom, where she slept peacefully. The idea that I wouldn't be there to watch her grow up made my chest ache more than ever.

"You can wake her," Graham told me as he leaned against the doorframe.

"No." I shook my head. "If I see those eyes of hers, I'll never be able to leave." I wiped away the tears that fell from my eyes and took a deep breath, trying to face Graham. As we looked at one another, we both wanted nothing more than to stay together, to be a family, to be one.

But sometimes what one wanted wasn't what one received.

"Your taxi is here, but I can still take you to the airport," he offered.

I had finally taken the leap and cashed in all the coins from the negative jars I'd collected over the years. I was taking the trip to Europe that Mari and I had always dreamed of. I had to get away, as far away as I could, because I knew if my heart was still on the same continent as Graham, I'd find my way back to him.

"No, it's okay, really. It's easier this way." I placed my fingers against my lips, kissed them, and then placed them on Talon's forehead. "I love you more than the wind loves the trees, sweet girl, and I'm always here for you, even when you don't see me."

As I took steps toward Graham, he moved in closer as if he were going to hug me, to try to take away my grief, but I wouldn't allow it. I knew if I fell into his arms again, I'd beg him to never let me go. He helped me carry my luggage out of the house and loaded it into the car.

"I won't say goodbye," he told me, taking my hands in his. He brought the palms of my hands to his lips and kissed them gently. "I refuse to say goodbye to you." He released his grasp and walked back to the porch, and right as I went to open the door to the taxi, he called my way. When his lips parted, he said, "What's the secret, Lucille?"

"The secret?"

"To your tea—what's the secret ingredient?"

I narrowed my eyebrows and bit my bottom lip. My feet started walking in his direction. The closer I got, the more steps he took toward me. When we stood in front of one another, I studied the caramel color of his eyes, a color I might never see again, and I held that sight close to my heart. I'd remember those eyes as long as I could.

"Tell me what ingredients you think are in it, and then I'll tell you the final one."

"Promise me?"

"Promise you."

He shut his eyes and began to speak. "Cinnamon, ginger, fresh lemons."

"Yes, yes, yes."

"Hot red peppers, sugar, black pepper."

"Uh-huh." I breathed out, chills running up and down my spine.

"And peppermint extract." When his eyes opened, he stared at me as if he could see a part of me that I'd yet to discover.

"That's all correct," I said.

He smiled, and I almost cried, because when he smiled, I always felt at home.

"So, what is it?" he asked.

I glanced around the area, making sure no one was within earshot, and I leaned in closer to him, my lips slightly grazing his ear. "Thyme," I told him. I stepped backward and gave him the kind of smile that forced him to frown. "Just give it a bit of thyme."

"Thyme." He nodded slowly, stepping farther away from me.

"Sorry, ma'am, but I can't wait here all day," the taxi driver called after me.

I turned to him and nodded before looking back at Graham, who was still staring at me. "Any final words?" I joked, nerves rocking my stomach.

He narrowed his eyes at me and combed my hair behind my ears. "You're the best human being of all human beings."

I swallowed hard. I missed him. I missed him so much, even though he was standing right there in front of me. I could still reach out and touch him, but for some reason, he felt farther and farther away. "One day you'll be happy we didn't work out," I promised him. "One day you'll wake with Talon on your left side and someone else on your right, and you'll realize how happy you are that you and I didn't work out."

"One day I'm going to wake up," he replied, his mood somber, "and it will be you lying beside me."

My hand went to his cheek, and I placed my lips against his. "You're the best human being of all human beings." A tear rolled down my cheek, and I kissed him slowly, lingering against his lips for a moment before finally letting him go. "I love you, Graham Cracker."

"I love you, Lucille."

As I opened the taxi door and stepped inside, Graham called out to me one last time.

"Yes?"

"Time," he softly said.

"Time?"

He shrugged his left shoulder and allowed it to drop quickly. "Just give it a bit of time."

chapter thirty-two

Graham

That night I awoke from a dream only to find myself in a waking nightmare.

The left side of my bed was empty, and Lucy was on a flight, traveling far away from me. It had taken everything inside of me to not beg her to stay when that taxi pulled up in front of the house. It had taken every ounce of me to not allow gravity to force me to my knees. If she'd stayed, I would've never let her go again. If she'd stayed, I would've started all over from day one, learning how to love her even more than I already had. If she'd stayed, I would've always flown, but I knew she wouldn't—she couldn't. With my current situation, there was no way I could've kept her and given her the love she deserved.

She was my freedom, yet I was her cage.

I lay in bed, my chest tight from the longing my heart felt, and I almost fell apart right then and there. I almost let my heart harden back to the way it was before Lucy walked into my life, but then a beautiful little girl started crying in the nursery, and I hurried to go get her. When I arrived, she reached for me and instantly stopped her crying.

"Hey, love," I whispered as she curled in against me, lying her head on my chest.

We headed back to my bedroom, lay down, and within minutes she was sleeping. Her breaths rose and fell, and she lightly snored as she curled up against me.

It was in that moment I remembered why falling apart wasn't an option. I remembered why I couldn't allow myself to fall into a pit of loneliness—because I wasn't alone. I had the most beautiful reason to keep moving forward.

Talon was my savior, and I'd promised myself to be a dad to her, not merely a father. Any person could be a father. It took a real man to step up to the role of being a dad. And I owed that to her. She deserved to have me fully.

As she clung to my shirt and found dreams that brought her comfort, I allowed myself to rest, too.

It amazed me how love worked.

It amazed me how my heart could be so broken and yet so full all at once.

That night my greatest nightmares and most beautiful dreams intermixed, and I held my daughter closer, as a reminder of why I'd have to rise in the morning, just like the sun.

Jane moved her things into the house the following week. She made herself comfortable in a home that held no love for her. She went about doing things as if she knew what she was doing, and every time she picked Talon up, I cringed.

"I was hoping the three of us could go out to dinner, Graham," she told me as she unpacked her suitcases in my bedroom. I didn't care enough to tell her not to sleep in my room. I'd sleep in the nursery with my daughter. "It might be good for us to start reconnecting."

"No."

She looked up, bewildered. "What?"

"I said no."

"Graham—"

"I just want to make something really clear to you, Jane. I didn't choose you. I want nothing to do with you. You can live in my house, you can hold my daughter, but you need to understand that there's not an ounce of me that wants *you*." My hands formed fists and my brow knitted. "I chose her. I chose my daughter. I'll choose her every second of every day for the rest of my life because she is my everything. So, let's stop pretending that we are ever going to live happily ever after. You are not my final sentence, you are not my last word. You are simply a chapter I wish I could delete."

I turned and walked away from her, leaving her standing stunned, but I didn't care. Every moment I could, would be spent with my daughter in my arms.

One day, somehow, Lucy would come back to us both.

Because she was always meant to be my last word.

"You shouldn't be here," Mari told me as I walked into Monet's Gardens.

I took off my hat and nodded. "I know."

She stood tall and shifted her feet around. "You really should go. I don't feel comfortable with you being here."

I nodded once more. "I know." But, I stayed, because sometimes the bravest thing a person can do is stay. "Does he love you?"

"Excuse me?"

I held my hat against my chest. "I said does he love you? Do you love him?"

"Listen—"

"Does he make you laugh so hard you have to toss your head backward? How many inside jokes do you share? Does he try to change you or inspire you? Are you good enough for him? Does he make you feel worthy? Is he good enough for you? Do you sometimes lie in bed beside him and wonder why you're still there?" I paused. "Do you miss her? Did she make you laugh so hard you had to toss your head backward? How many inside jokes did you share? Did she try to change you or inspire you? Were you good enough for her? Did she make you feel worthy? Was she good enough for you? Do you sometimes lie in bed and wonder why she's gone?"

Mari's small frame started to shake as I asked the questions. She parted her lips, but no words left her tongue.

So, I continued speaking. "Being with someone you aren't meant to be with out of fear of being alone isn't worth it. I promise you, you'll spend your life being lonelier with him than you would being without him. Love doesn't push things away. Love doesn't suffocate. It makes the world bloom. She taught me that. She taught me how love works, and I'm certain she taught you the same."

"Graham," Mari said softly, tears falling down her cheeks.

"I've never loved your oldest sister. I've been numb for years, and Jane was just another form of numbness. She never loved me either, but Lucille…she's my world. She's everything I needed, and so much more than I deserve. I know you might not understand that, but I'd go to war for her heart for the rest of my life if it meant she'd find her smile again. So, I'm standing in your shop right now, Mari, asking if you love him. If he is everything you know love to be, stay. If he is your Lucille, then don't for a second leave his side. But, if he isn't…if there is even a sliver of your soul that doubts that he's the one—*run*. I need you to run to your sister. I need you to go to war with me for the one person who always stayed, even when she owed us nothing. I can't be there for her right now, and her heart is broken halfway across the world. So, this is me, going to war for her by coming to you. This is me, begging you to choose her. She needs you, Mari, and I am going to assume that your heart needs her, too."

"I…" She started to fall apart, shaking as she covered her mouth with her hands. "The things I've said to her…the way I've treated her…"

"It's okay."

"It's not," she said, her head shaking. "She was my best friend, and I tossed her and her feelings to the side. I chose them over her."

"It was a mistake."

"It was a choice, and she'd never forgive me."

I grimaced and narrowed my eyes. "Mari, we're talking about Lucille here. Forgiveness is all she knows. I know where she is right now. I'll help you get there so you can do whatever you need to do to get your best friend back. I'll handle all of the details. All you have to do is run."

chapter
thirty-three

Lucy

Monet's gardens at Giverny were everything and more. I spent time walking around the land, breathing in the flowers, taking in the sights day after day. In those gardens, I almost felt like myself. Being surrounded by that much beauty reminded me of Talon's eyes, of Graham's crooked smile, of home.

As I walked a stone path, I smiled at all the passersby who were taking in the experience of the gardens. Oftentimes I wondered where they came from. What had brought them to the point they were at in that very moment? What was their story? Had they ever loved? Did it consume them? Had they left?

"Pod."

My chest tightened at the word, and the recognition of the voice that produced it. I turned around and my heart landed in my throat when I saw Mari standing there. I wanted to step closer, but my feet wouldn't move. My body wouldn't budge. I stood still, as she had.

"I…" she started as her voice cracked. She held an envelope tight to her chest and tried again. "He told me you'd be here. He said you visit every day. I just didn't know what time." No words from me. Tears formed in Mari's eyes and she tried her best to keep it together. "I'm so sorry, Lucy. I'm sorry for losing my way. I'm sorry for settling. I'm sorry for pushing you away. I just want you to know, I left Parker. The other night I was lying beside him in bed, and his arms were wrapped tightly around me. He was holding me so close, but I felt as if I was falling apart. Every time he told me he loved me, I felt less and less like myself. I've been so blind to the truth that I let my fear of being alone drive me back into the arms of a man who didn't deserve me. I was so worried about being loved, that I didn't even care if I loved back. And then, I pushed you away. You've been the only constant in my life, and I can't believe I hurt you the way I did. You're my best friend, Lucy, you're my heartbeats, and I'm sorry, I'm sorry, I'm—"

She didn't have time to say anything else before my arms wrapped around her body and I pulled her closer to me. She sobbed into my shoulder, and I held her tighter.

"I'm so sorry, Lucy. I'm so sorry for everything."

"Shh," I whispered, pulling her closer to me. "You have no clue how good it is to see you, Pea."

She sighed, relief racing through her. "You have no clue how good it is to see you, Pod."

After some time of settling down, we walked across one of the many bridges in the gardens and sat down, cross-legged. She handed me the envelope and shrugged. "He told me to give this to you, and he told me to not let you leave the gardens until each page is read."

"What is it?"

"I don't know," she said, standing up. "But I was instructed to give you time to read it by yourself. I'll be exploring and I'll meet you here when you're done."

"Okay. Sounds good." I opened the package, and there was a manuscript titled *The Story of G.M. Russell*. I inhaled hard—his autobiography.

"Oh, and, Lucy?" Mari called out, making me turn to look her way. "I was wrong about him. The way he loves you is inspiring. The way you love him is breathtaking. If I am ever lucky enough to feel even a fourth of what you two have, then I'll die happy."

As she walked away, I took a deep breath and started chapter one.

Each chapter flowed effortlessly. Each sentence was important. Each word was required.

I read the story about a boy who became a monster who slowly learned to love again.

And then, I reached the final chapter.

The Wedding

His palms were sweaty as his sister, Karla, straightened his tie. He hadn't known he could be so nervous about making the best decision of his life. Throughout his whole life, he'd never imagined falling in love with her.

A woman who felt everything.

A woman who showed him what it meant to live, to breathe, to love.

A woman who became his strength during the dark days.

There was something romantic about the way she moved throughout the world, the way she danced on her tiptoes and laughed without any regard for appearing ridiculous. There was something so true about how she held one's eye contact, and the way she smiled.

Those eyes.

Oh, how he could've stared into those eyes for the rest of his life.

Those lips.

Oh, how he could've kissed those lips for the rest of his days.

"Are you happy, Graham?" asked Mary, his mother, as she walked into the room to see her son's eyes glowing with excitement.

For the first time in forever, the answer came so effortlessly. "Yes."

"Are you ready?" she questioned.

"Yes."

She linked her arm with his, and Karla took his other. "Then let's go get the girl."

He stood at the end of the aisle, waiting for his forever to join him—but first, his daughter.

Talon walked down the aisle, dropping flower petals and twirling in her beautiful white gown. His angel, his light, his savior. When she reached the end of the aisle, she ran to her father and hugged him tight. He lifted her up into his arms and the two of them waited. They waited for her to join them. They waited for those eyes to meet their stare, and when they did, Graham's breath was stolen from his soul.

She was beautiful, but that wasn't a surprise. Everything about her was stunning, and real, and strong, and kind. Seeing her walking toward him, toward their new life, changed him in that moment. In that moment, he promised her all of him, even the cracks—they were, after all, where the light shined through.

When they stood together, they locked their hands as one. His lips parted when it was time, and he spoke words he'd dreamed of speaking. "I, Graham Michael Russell, take you, Lucille Hope Palmer, to be my wife. I promise it all to you—my broken past, my scarred present, and my complete future. I am yours before I am my own. You are my light, my love, my destiny. Air above me, earth below me, fire within me, water surround me. I give you all of my soul. I give you all of me."

Then, in every cliché way possible, in every facet of their lives, they lived happily ever after.

The End

I stared at his words, my hands shaking as tears rolled down my cheeks. "It has a happily ever after," I whispered to myself, stunned. Graham had never in his life written a happily ever after ending.

Until me.

Until us.

Until now.

I stood up from the bridge and hurriedly found my sister. "Mari, we have to go back."

She smiled wide and nodded knowingly. "I was hoping you would say that." She took off the heart-shaped necklace Mama gave to me and placed it back around my neck. "Now come on," she softly said. "Let's go home."

chapter thirty-four

Lucy

I STOOD ON GRAHAM'S PORCH, MY HEART POUNDING IN MY CHEST. I WASN'T certain what was on the other side of that door, but I knew whatever it was wouldn't make me run. I was going to stay. Forever and always, I was staying.

I knocked a few times and rang the doorbell, and then I waited.

And waited.

And waited some more.

When I turned the doorknob, I was surprised to find it open. "Hello?" I called.

The room was dark, and it was clear that Graham wasn't home. When I heard footsteps, I tensed up. Lyric came from the bedroom hurriedly, two suitcases in her hands. She didn't see me right away, and when she looked up, there was a look of panic in her eyes.

"Lucy," she said breathlessly. Her hair was wild, like how Mama's had always looked, and her eyes were bloodshot. I knew I owed her nothing. I knew I didn't have a word to say to her, or comfort to give her way.

But the way her eyes looked, the heaviness of her shoulders...

Sometimes the ugliest people were the ones who were the most broken.

"Are you okay?" I asked.

She snickered, and a few tears fell from her eyes. "As if you care."

"Why do you think I hate you?" I blurted out. "Why in the world do you hate me?"

She shifted her feet and stood tall. "I don't know what you're talking about."

"Sure you do, Lyric. I don't know why, but it seems you've always had a problem with me, especially after Mama passed away. I just never understood why. I always looked up to you." She huffed, not believing me. "Seriously."

She parted her lips and at first, no words came out, but then she tried again. "She loved you more, okay? She always loved you more."

"What? That's ridiculous. She loved all three of us girls the same."

"No, that's just not true. You were her heart. She was always talking about you, how free you were, how smart you were, how amazing you were. You were her light."

"Lyric, she loved you."

"I resented you. I resented how she loved you, and then, I come back here and he loves you too. Everyone has always loved you, Lucy, and I was left unlovable."

"I always loved you, Lyric," I said, my chest hurting from the pain in her voice.

She snickered in disbelief as her body shook and tears rolled down her cheeks. "You know the last thing Mama said to me as she was lying on her death bed and I was holding her hand?"

"What's that?"

"*Go get your sister*," she said, her voice cracking. "*I want Lucy.*"

I felt it, too, the way those words cracked my sister's heart, how ever since she'd never been able to put the pieces back together.

"Lyric…" I started, but she shook her head.

"No. I'm done. I'm just done. Don't worry, you can have your life. I don't belong here. Nothing about this house is home to me."

"You're leaving?" I asked, confused. "Does Graham know you're leaving?"

"No."

"Lyric, you can't just walk out on them, not again."

"Why? I did it before. Besides, he doesn't want me here, and I don't want to be here."

"But you could've at least left a note like you did last time," Graham said, making us turn to face him. When his eyes locked with mine, I felt my heart remember how to beat.

"I didn't think it was necessary," Lyric said, grabbing the handles on her suitcases.

"Okay, but before you go, wait here," Graham said, walking over to me with Talon in his hands. "Lucille," he whispered, his voice low, his eyes filled with that same gentleness I'd seen a few months back.

"Graham Cracker," I replied.

"Can you hold her?" he asked.

"Always," I replied.

He wandered off to his office, and when he came back, he was holding paperwork and a pen.

"What is this?" Lyric asked as he held the sheets of paper out to her.

"Divorce papers, and legal paperwork granting me full custody of Talon. You don't get to run again without making this right, Jane. You don't get to walk away and then leave the possibility of you taking my daughter away hanging over my head."

His voice was stern, but not mean, straightforward, yet not cold.

She parted her lips as if she were going to argue, but when she stared at Graham she probably took strong note of his stare. His eyes always told a person all they ever needed to know. It was clear that he'd never be hers, and it finally clicked in Lyric's head that she'd never truly wanted him. She slowly nodded in agreement. "I'll sign them at your desk," she said, walking into his office.

When she was out of view, I watched the heavy sigh leave Graham's body.

"Are you okay?" I asked him.

He kissed me to say yes.

"You came back to me," he whispered, his lips against mine.

"I'll always come back."

"No," he said sternly. "Just never leave again."

When Lyric walked back into the room, she told us the paperwork was signed and she'd be no more trouble. As she stepped out of the front door, I called after her.

"Mama's last words to me were, 'Take care of Lyric and Mari. Take care of your sisters. Take care of my Lyric. Take care of my favorite song.' You were her final thought. You were her final breath, her final word."

Tears rolled down her cheeks and she nodded, thanking me for a level of peace only I could give her soul. If I had known how heavy it weighed on her heart, I would've told her years ago.

"I left Talon a gift," she said. "I figured it was better for her than it was for me. It's sitting on her nightstand." Without another word, Lyric disappeared.

As we headed to the nursery, my hand fell to my chest as I saw the gift Lyric had left for her daughter—the small music box with a dancing ballerina that Mama had given her. It sat there with a note on top, and tears fell down my cheeks as I read the words on the paper.

Always dance, Talon

chapter thirty-five

Lucy

When Christmas came around, Graham, Talon, and I had three celebrations. The day started with us being bundled up and drinking coffee in the backyard with Ollie's tree. Each day Graham visited that tree and he'd sit and talk to his best friend, his father, telling him every story of Talon's growth, of his growth, of us. I was glad he had that connection—it was almost as if Ollie would live on forever in a way.

It was beautiful to see his tree standing tall every morning and night.

That afternoon, we headed to Mary's home to celebrate the day with their family. Mari joined us, and we all stayed close, laughing, crying, and remembering. The first Christmas without a loved one was always the toughest one, but when you were surrounded by love, the hurts hurt a little less.

That evening Graham, Talon, and I packed up the car to go spend the remainder of the holiday with Mama's tree. Mari told us she'd meet us up there a few hours later. On the whole trip to the cabin, I stared at my hand that was linked with Graham's. My air, my fire, my water, my earth, my soul.

I hadn't known a love could be so true.

"We're doing this, aren't we?" I whispered, glancing back at Talon, who was sleeping in the back seat. "Staying forever in love?"

"Forever," he promised, kissing my palm. "Forever."

As we pulled up to the cabin, everything was lightly dusted with snow. Graham climbed out of the car and hurried over to the tree, carrying Talon's car seat in his hand. "Graham, we should head inside. It's cold."

"We should at least say hi," he told me, looking at the tree. "Can you plug in the lights? I worry if I put Talon's car seat down, she'll cry."

"Of course," I said, hurrying over in the chilly air. When I plugged them in, I turned to Mama's tree, and my chest tightened as I saw the lights spelling out words that forever changed my life.

Will you marry us?

"Graham," I whispered, shaking as I slowly turned around to face him. When I did, he was down on one knee, holding a ring in his hand.

"I love you, Lucy," he said, not calling me Lucille for the first time ever. "I love the way you give, the way you care, the way you laugh, the way you smile. I love your heart and how it beats for the world. Before you, I was lost, and because of you, I found my way home. You're the reason I believe in tomorrow.

You're the reason I believe in love, and I plan to never let you go. Marry me. Marry Talon. Marry us."

Tears formed in my eyes as I stood in front of them. I lowered myself down so I was kneeling beside him. I wrapped my body around his, and he held me close as I whispered yes repeatedly, the word traveling from my lips and straight into his soul.

He slid the ring onto my finger, and as he held me close, my heart pounded more and more, knowing that my greatest hope had finally come true.

I was finally planting my roots in a home so warm.

"So this is our happily ever after?" I asked softly against his lips.

"No, my love, this is merely our chapter one."

When he kissed me, I swore, in the darkness of the night, I felt the warmth of the sun.

epilogue

Graham
Six Years Later

"And he was your best friend, Daddy?" Talon asked as she helped me dig around in the garden. The summer sun touched our faces as we picked green peppers and tomatoes for dinner that night.

"My very best friend," I told her, knee deep in dirt. The sunflowers we planted a few months ago were as tall as Talon. Whenever the wind blew past us, the flowers Lucy picked out lit up our senses.

"Can you tell me his story again?" she asked, placing her shovel into the ground. She then picked up a green pepper and bit into it as if it were an apple—just like her mama. If I were inside and couldn't find the two, they were normally in the backyard eating cucumbers, peppers, and rhubarb.

"The dirt is good for the soul," Lucy always joked.

"Again?" I asked, arching an eyebrow. "Didn't I just tell the story last night before bed?"

"Maktub," she replied with a sly grin. "It means all is written, which means you were supposed to tell the story again."

I laughed. "Is that so?" I asked, walking over to her and scooping her into my arms.

She giggled. "Yes!"

"Well, okay, since all is written after all," I joked. I walked her over to Professor Oliver's tree where three chairs were lined up. Two full-sized chairs and one child's plastic chair. I placed Talon in her chair, and I took mine beside her. "So, it all began when I was in college and failed my first paper."

I told her the story of how Professor Oliver came into my life and how he planted a seed into my heart that grew into love. He was my best friend, my father, my family. Talon always loved the story, too. The way she smiled as she listened closely always filled me up with love. She listened like Lucy—wholeheartedly with a sparkle in her eyes.

When I finished the story, Talon stood up as she did every time, walked over to the tree, and hugged it tight. "I love you, Grandpa Ollie," she whispered, giving the bark a kiss.

"Again?" Lucy asked, speaking of Professor Oliver's story, as she walked outside. She waddled over to Talon and me, with her full-grown pregnant stomach, and when she lowered herself to her chair, she sighed heavily as if she'd just run a full 5k.

"Again." I smiled before I bent over to her and kissed her lips, and then her stomach.

"How was your nap, Mama?" Talon asked, filled to the brim with energy. It was amazing to watch her run around and grow excited. Years ago she fit in the palm of my hand. Years ago it wasn't certain that she'd survive, and today, she was the definition of life.

"Nap was good," Lucy replied, yawning, still tired.

Any day now, we'd be losing even more sleep each night.

I'd never been more excited and ready in my life.

"You need anything?" I asked. "Water? Juice? Five pizzas?"

She grinned and closed her eyes. "Just the sun for a little bit."

The three of us sat outside for hours, soaking in the sunlight. It felt amazing, being surrounded by my family.

Family.

I somehow ended up with a family. Never in my life had I thought my life would end up like this—happy. The two girls who sat beside me were my world, and the little boy who would be here soon was already controlling my heartbeats.

When it was time to go prepare dinner, I helped Lucy out of her chair, and the minute she stood, we both paused for a moment.

"Mama, why did you pee your pants?" Talon asked, looking over at Lucy.

I cocked an eyebrow, realizing what had just happened. "Hospital?" I asked.

"Hospital," she replied.

Everything was different than when Talon was born. My son was welcomed into the world at eight pounds and three ounces. He came into the world screaming, allowing us all to be aware of his strong lungs.

I often looked back on the happiest seconds of my life and wondered how a man like me became so blessed. There was the moment Talon was released from the NICU. The first time Professor Oliver called me son. The time Lucy first told me she loved me. The second when the adoption papers went through for Talon to officially become Lucy's and my daughter. My wedding day. And now, as I held my handsome son for the first time in my arms.

Oliver James Russell.

Ollie for short.

We headed home one day after Ollie was born, and before Talon was off to bed that night, she walked over to her brother, who was sleeping in Lucy's arms, and kissed his forehead. "I love you, baby Ollie," she whispered, and my heart expanded more. It grew each day, being surrounded by my loves.

I carried Talon to her bed, knowing in the middle of the night she'd find herself sleeping between her mother and me. I welcomed her each night with a hug and a kiss, because I knew there would come a day when she wouldn't be lying beside Lucy and me. I knew there would come a day when she was too old, and too cool to be near her parents. So whenever she wandered into our room, I held her tight and thanked the universe for having my daughter to show me what true love looked like.

After Talon was tucked in, I headed back to the nursery where Lucy was falling asleep in the gliding chair with Ollie still resting. I took him from her arms and laid him in his crib, gently kissing his forehead.

"Bedtime," I whispered to my wife, gently kissing her cheek and helping her stand.

"Bedtime," she muttered back, yawning as I helped her to our room. After I pulled back the covers on the bed and laid her down, I crawled into bed beside her and held her close to me.

Her lips brushed against my neck as she moved in closer. "Happy?" she yawned.

I kissed her forehead. "Happy," I replied.

"I love you, my Graham Cracker," she said softly seconds before she fell asleep.

"I love you, my Lucille," I said, kissing her forehead.

As we lay there that night, I thought about our story. How she found me when I was lost, how she saved me when I needed her the most. How she forced me to stop pushing people away and proved to me that real love wasn't something from fairytale books. She taught me that real love took time. Real love took work. Real love took communication. Real love only grew if those involved took the time to nurture it, to water it, to give it light.

Lucille Hope Russell was my love story, and I promised myself I'd spend the rest of my life being hers.

After all, maktub—it was already written.

We were destined to live happily ever after as our hearts floated near the stars and our feet remained on solid ground.

The End

about the author

Brittainy C. Cherry is an Amazon #1 Bestselling Author who has always been in love with words. She graduated from Carroll University with a Bachelor's degree in Theatre Arts and a minor in Creative Writing. Brittainy lives in Brookfield, Wisconsin with her family. When she's not running a million errands and crafting stories, she's probably playing with her adorable pets or traveling to new places.

The Elements Series (All Complete Standalones)

The Air He Breathes

The Fire Between High & Lo

The Silent Waters

The Gravity of Us

Other Books by Brittainy C. Cherry

Loving Mr. Daniels

Art & Soul

The Space in Between

Our Totally, Ridiculous, Made-Up Christmas Relationship

forever right now

EMMA SCOTT

playlist

Sex and Candy, Marcy Playground
Down, Marian Hill
One More Light, Linkin Park
Tightrope, LP
Open Your Heart, Madonna
You and Me and the Bottle Makes Three Tonight, Big Bad Voodoo Daddy
Cheek to Cheek, Ella Fitzgerald
In the Mood, The Glenn Miller Band
To Wish Impossible Things, The Cure
Muddy Waters, LP
Cell Block Tango: Chicago the Musical, Kander and Ebb
Only Hope, Mandy Moore

dedication

To those fighting secret battles, don't let your light go out. This one is for you.

act one

Coincidence of Opposites (philosophy): a revelation of the oneness of things previously believed to be different.

prologue

Sawyer
August 15, 10 months ago

I BARELY HEARD THE DOORBELL UNDER THE POUNDING MUSIC AND THE LAUGHING conversations of a hundred of my closest friends. Jackson Smith jerked his head at me from across the room, a shit-eating grin on his face. He was dressed as Idris Elba's Roland the Gunslinger, to my Man in Black. Across the crowd of costumed guests—each dressed as a villain from movies or comics—he mouthed the words, *Your turn.*

I widened my eyes and inclined my head at the beautiful redhead in the Poison Ivy costume beside me. She was a second year at Hastings, asking me for advice about which professors were the hardest in Year Three, my year, but I don't think she was listening. Her gaze kept drifting down to my mouth.

Jackson shook his head and made eyes at the pretty Nurse Ratchet beside him, then held up his hands in an exaggerated shrug.

I sighed at my best friend and scratched my eye with my middle finger.

"I gotta get that," I told Poison Ivy. I think she said her name was Carly or Marly. Not that it mattered. Her name wasn't what I wanted from her. I flashed her what my friends called my trademark panty-dropping smile. "Save my spot?"

Carly-or-Marly nodded and tilted her own approving smile back. "Not going anywhere."

"Good," I said, and the way our eyes met and held was like a pact being sealed.

I'm going to get laid tonight.

I shot Jackson a triumphant smile, which he answered with a two-finger-gun salute. I laughed and wound my way through our place.

Jackson, myself and two other guys lived in a rented Victorian in the Upper Haight neighborhood. There were no frats at UC Hastings College of the Law, so our three-story house had become the next best thing. Our parties were infamous, and I was happy to see this one was no exception. Guests swayed to "Sex and Candy" playing on Jackson's state-of-the-art sound system. They smiled at me, thumped me on the back, or leaned in to shout drunkenly above the music that this Evil-Doer party was "The Best Party Ever." I just smiled back and nodded.

Every party of ours was "The Best Party Ever."

I opened the door; a charming smile and an excuse on my lips should it be one of my neighbors complaining about the noise. My smile dropped off my face like a mask and I stared.

A young woman with dark hair tied in a messy ponytail, strands falling loose to frame her narrow face, stared back at me. Her eyes were shadowed and bloodshot. She wore faded jeans, a stained shirt, and she struggled under the weight of an enormous bag on her shoulder. Old alcohol oozed out of her pores—the stench of someone who'd got plastered the night before.

The vision before me warred with a hazy memory of this same girl, wild and laughing next to me at a bar; tossing down drinks like they were water; kissing me in a cab. The taste of vodka and cranberry came to my lips, and then her name.

"Molly…Abbott?"

"Hi, Sawyer," she said, and shifted a baby in her arms.

A baby.

My stomach tightened and my balls tried to crawl back into my guts. The hazy memory became stark and vibrant, with brutal clarity.

A little more than a year ago. A summer trip to Vegas. A kiss in the cab had led to a drunken night of lustful tumbling on Molly's bed in her tiny apartment and a half-heard assurance that she was on the pill. And then I was inside her without a fucking care in the world.

The words fell out of my mouth. "Oh shit."

Molly barked a nervous laugh and shifted the huge, overstuffed nylon bag on her other arm. "Yeah, well, here we are," she said, and stood on tiptoe to peek over my shoulder. "Having a party? Looks epic. Sorry to just show up like this but…"

I stepped into the hallway and closed the door behind me. The music and laughter cut in half, became distant. My eyes darted to the baby bundled in a faded blanket with yellow teddy bears on it, stained and grimy. My heart panged against my chest like a heavy drum.

"What…What are you doing here?"

"I was in the city," Molly said, swallowing hard, her eyes not meeting mine. "I wanted to introduce you."

"Introduce me…"

Molly swallowed again and looked up at me as if it took effort. "Can I come in? Can we…talk? Just for a minute. I don't want to ruin your party."

"Talk."

Shock had turned me stupid. I'd been valedictorian of my class at UCSF, now a straight-A law student at Hastings, reduced to repeating the last thing I heard like a parrot. My glance darting to the baby whose face was bundled out of sight.

Introduce me. Holy fuck.

I blinked, shook my head. "Yeah, uh, sure. Come in."

I took the bag off Molly's shoulder and my own arm dropped at its weight. I hefted it over mine and hustled Molly through the evil-doers, into my bedroom off the kitchen. The room was dim, and I flipped on a light. Molly blinked, glanced around.

"This is a nice room," she said. She had dirt on her jeans and one of her jacket pockets was inside out. Her costume wasn't evil nurse or witch, but homeless girl with a baby.

"The house is great. Huge." She sat on the edge of the bed, hefted the baby in her arms. "You look good too, Sawyer. And you're going to law school, right? You're going to be a lawyer?"

I nodded. "Yeah."

"I read on your Facebook page you're going to work for a federal judge when you graduate. That's a big deal, right? That sounds like a really good job."

"I hope so," I said. "I don't have the job yet. I still have to graduate. Pass the bar exam and then he has to choose me."

I had a mountain of pressure already. My glance darted to the baby again and my throat went dry.

"That sounds good, Sawyer," Molly said. "You seem like you're really doing well."

"I'm doing okay." I heaved a breath. "Molly…?"

"Her name is Olivia," she said, shifting the baby. "That's a good name, right? I wanted one that sounded…smart. Like you."

My stomach was tied in the tightest of knots and my legs were itching to run out the door and not look back… Instead, I sank down on the bed beside Molly, like a magnet, drawn to the bundle in her arms.

"Olivia," I murmured.

"Yes. And she *is* smart. Advanced. She can already hold her head up and everything."

Molly pulled the blanket from the baby's face and my damn breath caught in my throat. I saw a rounded cheek, tiny, pouty little lips, and eyes squeezed shut. Molly's breath was tinged with booze, same as mine from the 'special punch' one of my roommates had made. But Olivia smelled clean, like talcum powder and some unidentifiable sweet smell that was probably reserved for babies.

"She's pretty, right?" Molly said, glancing at me nervously. "She looks just like you."

"Just like me…"

Outside my door, the party was blaring but muted. Young people laughing and drinking and probably hooking up…just as I had thirteen months ago.

"Are you sure she's…?" I couldn't say the word.

Molly's head jerked in a fast nod. "She's yours. One hundred percent." She bit her lip. "Do you want to hold her?"

Fuck no!

My arms fell open and Molly put the baby in them.

I stared down at Olivia, willing her little features to become recognizable. A clue or hereditary whisper that she really was mine. But she looked nothing like Molly or me. She was just a baby.

My baby?

Molly sniffed and I looked up to see her smiling at Olivia and me. "You're a natural," she said softly. "I knew you would be."

I stared down at the baby and swallowed a jagged lump of every emotion known to man.

"H-how old is she?"

"Three months," Molly said. She nudged my arm with her elbow. "Remember that night? Pretty wild, right?"

My head shot up. "You told me you were on the pill."

She flinched and tucked a lock of hair behind her ear. "I was. It didn't work. That happens sometimes."

I stared, incredulous, and then my gaze dropped back down to the baby in my arms. She stirred in her sleep, her little fist brushing her own chin. One half of the impenetrable confines of my heart battened down like a storm was coming, shoring up defenses, building walls because this *can't be happening*. The other half marveled at this baby's tiny movements like they were minor miracles. I felt like laughing, crying, or screaming all at once.

"I almost didn't come here," Molly was saying. "I just wanted you to meet her and so...here we are."

"Are you in the city? Do you have a place...?"

I wondered if Molly needed to move in with me, and the reality of the situation was like a bucket of ice water. I still had another nine months of law school. I had the bar exam to take and pass—the *first* time—if I had any prayer of getting the clerkship with Judge Miller. The clerkship was my ticket to my dream career as a federal prosecutor.

"What the hell, Molly. I can't...I can't have a *baby*," I said, my voice rising. "I'm twenty-three fucking years old."

Molly sniffed. "Oh really?" She crossed her arms over her chest. "You *can* have a baby, Sawyer. If you can fuck, you can have a baby. So that's what we did and that's what we have."

I gritted my teeth and spat each word slowly. "You told me you were on the pill..."

She stared back and I knew it was useless. Saying those words over and over wasn't going to make the baby in my arms magically evaporate. The pill may have failed or Molly may have been lying about taking them, but in the bleary, booze-soaked memories of that night, there had been one second where I told myself to put on a condom like I always did, and that time I didn't.

"Fuck," I whispered, and a terrible sadness gripped me as I stared into

Olivia's little face. Sadness for all of the fear and anxiety wrapped up with her in one tight bundle. I took a deep breath. "Okay, what happens now?"

"I don't know," Molly said, her fingers twitching in her lap. "I just…wanted to see you. To see how you were and let you know that she's yours. I've made a lot of mistakes in my life. I'm still making them." She smiled wanly. "But you… You're a good guy, Sawyer. I know you are."

I frowned, shook my head. "I'm not. Jesus, Molly—"

"Can I use your restroom?" she asked. "It was a long drive up."

"Yeah, sure," I said. "Down the hall, first door on your left."

She sucked in a breath and bent to kiss the baby on her forehead, then quickly rose and went out.

I held Olivia and watched as she woke up. Her eyes fluttered open and met mine for the first time. They were blue like Molly's, not brown like mine, but I felt something shift in me. One tiny tear in my fabric, the first of many that would eventually lead to a complete unraveling and remaking of me into someone I'd hardly recognize.

"Hi," I whispered to my daughter.

My daughter. Oh Christ…

Sudden panic tore through the shock and fear. I jerked my head up and glanced frantically around my empty room, to the huge bag on the floor, to the empty space where Molly had been sitting. My breath caught in my chest at my brain's slow realization of what had happened.

I tore off the bed with the baby in my arms, and hurried to the living area where the party was going on full blast. The noise frightened Olivia and her cries spread through the party like a fire hose, dousing everything until the music shut off. All talk and laughter dampened down to nothing. I glanced around the room, searching for Molly and found only slack-jawed stares and snickers. Jackson gaped with a million questions in his eyes. My other roommates stared. Carly-or-Marly's sexy smile had turned into one of bemused pity. I barely registered any of it as my eyes found the front door, left slightly ajar.

Oh my God…

In between Olivia's growing cries, someone snorted a small laugh. "This party is *so* over."

chapter one

Darlene
June 15, present day

THE MUSIC BEGAN WITH A LONE PIANO. A FEW HAUNTING NOTES, THEN A YOUNG woman's soft, clear voice.

I began on the floor, barefoot in leggings and a T-shirt. Nothing professional. No choreography. I hadn't meant to come here, but I was passing by on the street. The space happened to be free and I'd rented it for thirty minutes before I could talk myself out of it. I'd paid with shaking hands.

I shut out thoughts; let my body listen to the music. I was rusty; out of practice. My muscles were shy, my limbs hesitant, until the beat dropped—a tinny high-hat and uncomplicated techno beat—and then I let go.

Are you down…?
Are you down…?
Are you down, down, down…?

My back arched into a back bend, then collapsed. I writhed in controlled movements—my body a series of flowing shapes and arches and undulating flesh and sinew, swaying to the rhythm that simmered back to the piano and the singer's voice—haunting and lonely.

Are you down…?

The pulse increased again and I was up, crisscrossing the studio, leaping and dragging, spinning three turns, my head whipping, arms reaching up and then out, grasping at something to hold onto and finding only air.

Are you down…?

Muscles woke up to the dance, aching, complaining at the sudden demands. My breath was heavy in my chest like a stone, sweat streaking between my shoulder blades.

Are you…?
Are you…?
Are you…?

It dripped off my chin as I collapsed to my knees like a beggar.
…down?

I sucked in a breath, the faintest of smiles pulling my lips. "Maybe not."

On the subway back to the dinky studio apartment in Brooklyn I shared with my boyfriend, my pulse wouldn't slow down. Sweat was sticking to my back under my gray old man sweater. I had just danced. For the first time in more than a year. A tiny little step that was a mile wide; it covered so much empty distance.

Today, I stepped into the humid June of New York City. Three years ago, I'd stepped off the bus at Brooklyn Metropolitan Detention Center after a three-month stint for misdemeanor drug possession. A year and a half after that, I OD'd at a New Year's Eve party. Rock bottom.

I hadn't danced in all that time—it felt wrong to allow myself to do something I loved when I'd been polluting my body and mind. But Roy Goodwin—the best parole officer in the world—had helped me take the steps necessary to shorten my parole. I'd have mandatory NA meetings for another year, but otherwise a clean slate. And I was nearly finished getting an esthetician's license and massage therapist certificate.

And today, I danced.

Things were getting better. I was getting my shit together. And Kyle…I could fix things with Kyle. We were going through a rough patch, that's all. A rough patch that had been going on for two months.

My hopes deflated with a sigh. Just this morning, it took three tries to get him to answer to his name. Lately, his smiles were full of apologies, and he had a detached fade in his eyes. I'd seen it before. There'd be no big drama. No epic fight. Just a disappearing act. Maybe with a note or a text.

Despite the heat, I shivered and walked faster, as if I could outrun my thoughts. I wondered—for the millionth time—if I were trying to hold on to Kyle because I cared about him, or because I couldn't stand the thought of letting another relationship slip through my fingers.

"It's not over. Not yet," I said as my combat boots clomped down our block.

This time I wasn't going to fail. Not again. This time I could do something right. I'd been clean for more than a year, and with Kyle for longer than that. My longest relationship. I wasn't a fuck up. Not anymore. I'd hold on tighter, if that's what it took.

On the third floor of the shabby walk-up, I opened the door on 3C, and stepped inside…and nearly tripped on the duffel bag. Kyle's duffel bag. It was stuffed so full, the zipper looked ready to burst. I shut the door behind me and looked up, squinting, as if I could minimize the pain of what I was seeing.

Kyle was at the small kitchen counter writing a note. He set down the pen when he saw me. Slowly.

A note, not a text.

"Hey, babe," he said, hardly looking at me. "I'm sorry, but I…."

"Don't," I said. "Just don't." I hugged myself at the elbows. "You weren't even going to tell me?"

"I…I didn't want a scene." He sighed and ran a hand through his shaggy blond hair. "I'm sorry, Darlene. I really am. But I can't do this anymore."

"Can't do what?" I shook my head. "No, never mind. I don't want to hear it. Not again."

Again, I'm not enough. Not good enough. Not funny or pretty or something *enough.*

"Didn't hold on tight enough." I murmured.

"Darlene, I do care about you, but…"

"You're sorry, *but.* You care about me, *but.*" I shook my head, tears choking my throat. "Go if you're going to go, but don't say anything else. You're just making it worse."

He sighed and looked at me imploringly. "Come on, Dar. I know I'm not alone in this. You feel it too. There's just…nothing left in the tank, right? The engine's grinding and grinding, and we're hoping something will catch and spark back up again. But we both know it's not going to happen." He sighed and shook his head. "It's not you. It's not me. It's us."

I opened my mouth to speak. To deny. To scream and curse and rage.

I said, "Yeah, I guess."

Kyle sighed again, but this time with relief. He came to me and I hugged him tight; tried to absorb the feeling of his arms around me one more time. I inhaled him, to hold on. Then exhaled, and he slipped away.

He moved to the door and I stepped back toward our tiny kitchen.

Kyle hefted his bag onto his shoulders. "See you around, Dar."

I kept my eyes averted and then squeezed them shut at the sound of the door closing. The click was as loud as a slap.

"See you around," I murmured.

"Are you sure you want to do this?" Zelda asked. The screech of an incoming bus lurching into the depot nearly drowned her words, and a light summer shower sprinkled diamonds in my friend's long, dark hair.

Beckett, her fiancé and my best friend, towered over her. Instinctively, he leaned in slightly, to shield her from the elements. I don't even think he realized he was doing it. A frown pulled his mouth down. Worry made his blue eyes sharp.

"I'm sure," I answered Zelda, hefting my heavy-as-shit backpack higher on my shoulder. A porter came and took my green army duffel to stow it under the bus. "Whether or not I'm *ready* to do this, is another question."

"Are you ready to do this?" Beckett asked with a small smile.

Zelda nudged him. "Smart ass."

My gaze went between them fondly…and with envy. Zelda and Beckett were living their happily-ever-after, publishing their comic books, and busy being madly in love. Jealousy bit at me for what they had; a kind of love that seemed impossible for someone with my history. But I wasn't leaving the city to find someone, I was leaving someone behind. The old me.

Leaving Zelda and Beckett was scary, but because they were my best friends, I knew they would not fade away to the background of my life as I left New York.

"Holy shit, I'm leaving New York."

"Yes, you are," Zelda said. "Not just leaving the city, but going clear across the country." She pursed her lips and fixed me a look with her large green eyes. "Tell me again what San Francisco has that Brooklyn doesn't?"

The chance to start over where no one knows me as a former drug addict.

"A job, an NA sponsor, and a six-month sublet," I said, mustering a smile. "No fear; if my new city chews me up and spits me out, I'll be back in NYC by Christmas."

"You're going to do great," Beckett said, pulling me into a hug.

I clung tight. "Thank you."

"But call if you need anything. Any time."

I hid my fallen smile against his jacket. I was never the person someone called when they needed help. I was the call-er, never the call-ee.

But I can change that.

Zelda took her turn with a hug that smelled like cinnamon and ink. "Love you, Dar."

"Love you, Zel. And you too, Becks."

"Take care," Beckett said. The rain became more insistent. Beckett shielded Zelda with his jacket.

"Get out of here before I cry," I said, shooing them.

They started away and when they were out of sight, I stepped into the rain and turned my face to the sky.

There was nothing like New York rain. I let it baptize me a final time before I stepped on the bus, praying I would step off in San Francisco, clean and new.

༺༻

Turns out, there's nothing cleansing about a three-day bus ride.

Three thousand miles of road later—most of which was spent with a little old lady snoring on my shoulder—I stepped off the Greyhound into sharp, early morning San Francisco sunlight. It was more gold and metallic than New York's hazy yellow, and I stretched in it, welcoming it. I let it infuse me, imagining it was a beam of golden light that was going to fill me with mental fortitude and the willpower to be a better version of myself. The sun's warmth didn't magically turn me into one of Zelda's comic book superheroes, but it felt good anyway.

After the porter emptied the underbelly of the bus, I found my huge army duffel and slung it over my shoulder to join the weight of my purple backpack. I walked out to the bus plaza and searched for a transit map to show me the way to my new neighborhood. My eyes landed on a young guy leaning against a cement pillar, scanning the crowd. He was Hollywood-handsome; an actor playing a greaser from the 50's with his gelled, dark brown hair and chiseled jaw. He wore a white T-shirt, jeans, and black boots. All he needed was a cigarette tucked behind one ear and a pack rolled up his sleeve. He caught sight of me and pushed himself off the pillar with his shoulder.

"Darlene Montgomery?"

I stopped. "Yeah? Who…? Are you Max Kaufman?"

"That's me," he said, and offered his hand.

"Aren't you a little young to be a sponsor?" I asked, my gaze roaming over his broad, muscled chest, then up to his handsome face and piercing brown eyes.

He's way too hot to be my sponsor. Lord, have mercy.

"The powers-that-be seemed to feel I have experience enough to be of some help," Max said. "I started down the path of turpitude early."

I grinned. "Advanced for your age?"

Max grinned back. "First in my class at juvie."

I laughed, then heaved a sigh. "Dammit, you're adorable."

"Say again?"

I planted one hand on my hip and wagged a finger at him with the other. "Let me just tell you straight off the bat that I have sworn off men for a year. So no matter what, nothing is going to happen between us, got it? If I call you up crying and desperate some night, you have to stay strong, okay?"

Max gave an incredulous laugh.

"I'm only half kidding," I said. "I'm not presuming you want to jump in the sack with me, but I can guarantee you I will have at least one lonely night, and you're ridiculously good-looking. A bad combination."

Max laughed harder. "I can tell I'm going to love this assignment already. But your chastity is safe, Darlene, I promise. I'm gay."

I narrowed my eyes. "A likely story."

"Scout's honor."

"Fine. That's a good place to start," I said, "but that doesn't mean you're not going to get that phone call, that's all I'm saying."

Max chuckled, shaking his head. "I think I can handle it." He offered me his arm and I hooked mine in it. "Let's see your new digs."

"You're my official San Francisco welcome wagon?"

"Brought to you by Narcotics Anonymous and the Justice Department."

I harrumphed. "Three meetings a week is excessive, isn't it? I've been clean for a year and a half."

"Not up to me," Max said. He glanced down at me. "You know you can't skip any, right?"

"I won't," I said. "And while I might have a lonely night or *ten*, that doesn't mean I'm going back to using. I won't. Not ever."

Max smiled thinly. "Good to know."

"I know, I know," I said. "You've heard it all before."

"Yep, but it's a good place to start."

We stepped out into San Francisco and I turned my gaze all around, taking in my new city. The street sign on the corner read Folsom and Beale. The letters were black on white, instead of New York's white on green.

"Brand new," I murmured.

"What's that?" Max asked.

"Nothing."

From the bus depot, Max led me underground and we took a Muni train—San Francisco's public transit system—deeper into the city. Compared to New York's subway system; the red, green, and yellow snakes on the transit map looked simple.

"This doesn't look too bad."

"The city is only about seven by seven miles," Max said, holding on to the overhead bar, as the Muni train screeched underground to my sublet in a neighborhood called the Duboce Triangle. "Big enough to feel like a real city, not so big as to get lost in."

"That's good," I said. "I didn't come here to get lost."

"On the contrary," Max said. "You came here to find yourself."

"Ooh, that's deep."

He shrugged one shoulder. "It's the truth, isn't it?"

I nudged his arm. "Are you on the clock already?"

"Twenty-four, seven. I'm here for you whenever you need me. I know how hard it is to start over." Max scratched his chin. "Or even just to keep going, come to think of it."

I smiled as warmth spread through my chest. "Did you have someone like you as a sponsor when you were recovering? I hope you did."

Max's dark eyes clouded up a bit, and his smile tightened. "Yes and no." The train screeched to a stop. We were above ground again and the day was brilliant. "This is you."

We exited the train, and Max tossed my army duffel over one shoulder as if it were nothing, while my overstuffed backpack felt like it weighed a thousand pounds.

"I hope it's not a far walk," I said.

"What's the address again?"

I told him and he led me west along Duboce Street.

"This is a nice neighborhood," Max said. "You found a place here?"

"My friend said it was the last rent-controlled Victorian in all of San Francisco."

"Your friend is probably right," Max said. "In most parts of the city, the words 'rent-control' bring about fits of disbelieving laughter." He grinned. "And then crying."

"Then I won't tell you what my rent is."

"Bless you."

"So when you're not spending every waking hour being my sponsor, what do you do?" I asked.

"I'm an ER nurse at UCSF."

"Really? You weren't kidding. You are an around-the-clock lifesaver."

He shrugged nonchalantly, but his smile told me he liked hearing that. "And what about you? Do you have a job lined up?"

"Indeed," I said. "Massage therapist by day…"

"Yes?" Max said into my silence. "Usually there's another half of the sentence."

"I used to dance," I said slowly. "In my old life, if you know what I mean."

"I do," he said. "Old life, drug life, new life. The life cycle of recovery. So did dance survive the drug life to re-emerge in the new life?"

"That remains to be seen," I said with a small smile. "But I have hope."

Max nodded. "Sometimes that's all you need."

We walked along a row of Victorian houses, each tucked between another, in a variety of colors. I glanced down at the address on my hand, then up to a cream-colored three-story wedged between a smaller, beige house, and one the color of old brick.

"That's the one," I said, pointing to the cream-colored.

"You're kidding." Max stared. "You're going to live *there*? By yourself?"

"The studio on the third floor," I said, hefting my backpack. "It's really pretty, isn't it?"

"*Really pretty*?" Max gaped. "That house is *rent-controlled*?"

"There's that word again. Are you going to laugh or cry?"

"Cry." He whistled through his teeth. "What you have here is a unicorn eating four-leaf clovers while shitting rainbow turds in the shape of winning lottery numbers."

I laughed. "Well, it's only for six months, and then I have to give it back and find a new place."

"That'll suck," Max said. "After this Shangri-La, you're going to be shell-shocked at how the rest of us plebes make it in SF."

"That's easy, I'll just shack up with you."

He laughed. "Maybe. But I could be outta here in a few months. Maybe sooner."

I sagged. "What? Noooo. Don't say that. I like you too much already."

"Nothing set in stone, but I have a potential job transfer to Seattle in the works." Max smiled down at me with warmth in his eyes. "I like you a lot, too. I don't think I've ever made a friend faster."

"I don't like to waste time," I said with a grin. "Want to come check out my unicorn?"

"So I can be more jealous? Some other time. In fact…" He pulled his phone from the back pocket of his jeans and checked the time. "Oh shit, I gotta run. My shift starts in twenty," he said. "But I'll take your bag up."

"Nope, I got it." I took it off his shoulder and dumped it on the sidewalk.

"You sure?"

"I carry my own weight, bub."

"Okay, then." Max offered his hand. "Good to meet you, Darlene."

I scoffed at his hand and gave him a hug. His arms went around me and I felt his broad chest reverberate with a chuckle.

"Mmmm, you smell like bus."

"Eau de Greyhound."

He pulled away, still grinning. "I'll see you Friday night. At the Y on Buchanan Street. Room 14. Nine o'clock, sharp."

I pursed my lips. "Friday night? Ugh."

"Disappointed?" He held his hands out and started walking backwards to the bus stop. "Cry it out in your rent-controlled penthouse."

I laughed and hefted my army bag with a grunt, and stepped up to the house. The Victorian really was beautiful, and perfectly maintained. My key turned in the lock and I stepped inside a tiny entry.

I was no architect, but I could tell the house had once been a *house* and was now cut up into separate flats. I peeked around a wall that no sane homeowner would put in the entry, to see a tiny laundry room with one coin-op washer and dryer. On the other side of the hallway was a door with #1 on it. A potted plant and welcome mat with bright colors adorned the threshold. Faintly, I could hear what sounded like Spanish music and the sound of children's laughter.

I dragged my army duffel up the one flight of stairs to an awkward landing—also a new construction to give the second floor some separation. The door on this floor was marked #2 and had no welcome mat or plant or décor of any kind. Silence on the other side.

I continued up one more flight. The ceiling was lower and angled, and door #3 opened on a tiny studio. Bed, table, chair, kitchen and postage-stamp bathroom. My friend in NYC who had arranged this sublet for me said the owner—a gal named Rachel who worked for Greenpeace—had cleaned the place out of everything but sheets, towels, pots and pans. It could not have been more perfect; I didn't need much.

A slow smile spread over my lips, and I shut the door behind me. I headed to the window where I had to duck my head a little at the sloped ceiling. The view stole my breath. Rows of Victorians lined up on the hill, and over their roofs, the city spread out before me. It was a different kind of city than New York. A quieter city; with colorful old buildings, hills, a green rectangle of a park, all cradled in the blue of a bay.

I sucked in a breath and blew it out my cheeks.

"I can do this."

But after a three-day bus ride, I was too tired and overwhelmed to think about conquering a new city just then. I turned to my borrowed bed and collapsed face down.

Sleep reached for me at once, and music drifted into my scattered thoughts. I danced.

Are you down...?

Are you d-d-d-down...?

I smiled against my borrowed pillow. It smelled like laundry soap and the person who actually lived here. A stranger.

Soon it would smell like me.

Are you down, down, down...?

"Not yet," I murmured, and slipped into sleep.

chapter two

Sawyer

Study Room #2 at UC Hastings College of the Law was silent but for the turning of pages and keyboards clacking. Students sat together in stuffed chairs, barricaded behind laptops and headphones.

My study partners, Beth, Andrew and Sanaa were on couches and chairs in our circle, bent over their work, nary a joke or smartass remark among them. I missed Jackson, but the bastard had the nerve to graduate one quarter ahead of me.

The relentless overhead fluorescents seared my tired eyes and made the text on the page in front of me blur. I blinked, focused, and took a mental snapshot of a paragraph of California Family Law Code. With the image firmly in mind, I put pen to a page in my notebook and wrote what I saw in my own words. To lock them down.

When I finished my notes, I leaned back in my chair and let my eyes fall shut.

"Hey, Haas," Andrew said, a millisecond later. I could hear the smug smile color his words. "You going to sleep through the rest of the hour?"

"If you'd shut up, I might," I said without opening my eyes.

He *hmphed* and sniffed but didn't rejoin. Jackson would have given me a smart-ass remark back and we'd be off to races to see who could out-insult the other. Andrew was no Jackson.

"This Family Law exam is going to kill me," Andrew groused. "Someone quiz me."

"Section 7602?" Beth asked.

"Uh…shit." I heard Andrew tap his pen on the table. "It's right there…"

I smiled to myself. My focus was Criminal Justice, but since a certain Evil-Doer party ten months ago, Family Law had become my unofficial minor.

I mentally scrolled through my Family Law code photo album to section 7602, and recited, *"The parent and child relationship extends equally to every child and to every parent, regardless of the marital status of the parents."*

Silence. I peeked one eye open. "Sorry. It's one of my favorites."

"I'll bet." Andrew snorted and took up his laptop. "Okay, let's see what else you got, Haas."

The others leaned forward with interest. It was a novelty, what I could do. Very little escaped the mental darkroom in my mind; names and faces, years-old memories down to the smallest detail; even whole pages of text—word for word—if I read them enough times. I don't know how I ended up with a photographic memory, but thank God I did, or I'd never have made it through these last ten months. Not on three or four hours of sleep every night.

"What other section is applicable to Section 7603?" Andrew asked smugly. He was kind of an asshole. I think he thought he'd feel better about the incredible stress of law school if he stumped me. I never tried to make him feel better.

"Section 3140," I said. I was kind of an asshole too.

"In 7604, a court may order *pendente lite* relief consisting of a custody or visitation if…?"

"A parent and child relationship exists pursuant to Section 7540 and the custody or visitation order would be in the best interest of the child."

"Why do you even bother coming here?" Andrew groused and shut his Mac.

"To give you the answers," I said.

The women snickered while Andrew shook his head and muttered under his breath, "Arrogant prick."

"You're wasting your time, anyway," Sanaa said to him. "Sawyer's memory is infallible." She shot me with a knowing smile. "I'm sure he could go for days."

I didn't miss the double meaning behind her words, and the invitation behind her eyes. My body went warm all over, begging me to reconsider my rule. Sanaa was beautiful and smart; a new addition to our group when Jackson and another friend graduated last quarter. But I could've told her the same thing she told Andrew. She was wasting her time. My days of hooking up with random women were over with a capital O.

Beth didn't miss Sanaa's approving smile at me. She rolled her eyes at all of us. "We should name this group Dysfunction Junction." She checked her watch. "Come on. It's time to go."

We gathered our shit, stuffing notebooks and laptops back into bags, and chucking our empty coffee cups. I shuffled out of the room after my study group. Beth was right. Even in my mind, these people weren't my friends. I didn't have too many of those anymore, but I looked at Beth with her severe hair and Andrew with his shirt buttoned up to his ears and tried to imagine them at one of our epic Evil-Doer parties. I tried to imagine *me* at another Evil-Doer party and couldn't do it.

"Something smell bad, Haas?" Andrew asked.

"Nah," I said, blinking as we stepped into the sharp June sunlight. "Just remembering some ancient history."

"You probably have the Classics memorized too. Got some *Odyssey* up in that steel trap of yours?"

I met his gaze steadily.

"*Speak, Memory—*
Of the cunning hero,
The wanderer, blown off course time and again…Sounds like you, Andy."

"Shut up. And don't call me Andy."

Sanaa hid a smile in her coat collar. "See you all Monday," she said to the others, then moved to stand beside me. "You're so mean to poor Andrew."

I shrugged. "I've never met a guy with zero interest in hiding his short-comings."

"He's just jealous. He struggles to get this stuff down and it's all so easy for you."

I could've laughed at that if I wasn't so damn tired.

"So." Sanaa tossed a lock of silky black hair over her shoulder. "Any weekend plans? I have an extra ticket to The Revivalists at the Warfield tomorrow night."

A couple of mild excuses came to me, but I was too tired to bullshit too. "I'm out of commission. No social engagements for me until graduation and the bar exam."

"That doesn't sound healthy."

I shrugged and tried a smile. "Thanks for the offer, though."

"Okay," she said, with her own smile that barely contained her disappointment. "See you Monday, then."

"Yep."

I watched her walk away and the weariness hit me.

It did that sometimes, like being punched in the gut. The late nights and sleeplessness, stress and anxiety; it all bowled right into me. No beers with the guys. No dates with hot study partners. No sex, no parties…

"Suck it up, Haas," I muttered into the wind as I began to walk. "This is what you signed up for."

At the Civic Center Muni station, I got onto the J line for Duboce Triangle, and slumped against my seat. The train wasn't crowded with rush hour commuters yet. Friday was my one early day; no late classes. I was usually home by four, instead of five or six.

The rumble of the train beneath me lulled my tired eyes closed. The Family Law code seemed projected onto the back of my eyelids—an unpleasant side effect of eidetic memory. The more I committed something to memory, the greater the chance it would stick with me forever.

…when one parent has left the child in the care and custody of another person for a period of one year without any provision for the child's support, or without communication, that parent is presumed to have abandoned the child…

Those words I would never forget, and the gentle gyrations of the train took me back to last August. Ancient history. I wasn't tired, then. Not yet.

The drab building with the Department of Family and Child Services sign loomed across the street. The sky was overcast; a chilly wind swept over me as I held the bundle in my arms more tightly. It didn't feel like summer, but like a cold winter was about to set in.

"Tell me again what happens when I turn her in?" I asked.

Jackson gave me a wary, side-eyed glance. "They'll try to track Molly down."

"I tried that and got nowhere."

"Then the baby goes into foster care."

"Foster care." I glanced down at the sleeping face tucked in the blankets. My arms were getting tired. Olivia was small, but holding her on the Muni, then the three-block walk was rougher on me than any workout at the Hastings gym. I would have taken an Uber but I didn't have a car seat.

I had nothing.

"It's the best thing," Jackson said for the hundredth time since the party, six days ago.

"Yeah," I murmured. "The best thing."

He gave me a dimmer, sympathetic version of his mega-watt smile. "C'mon. The light's green."

He nudged my arm to walk but I didn't move. My feet were rooted to the corner.

I cast my gaze over the busy city streets. The wind whistled through the cement buildings that rose up all around us, cold and flat and gray. I tried to imagine walking into the CPS building and handing the baby over to some stranger. It would be so easy. She felt so heavy with the weight of the years that lay ahead, and all I had to do was set her down and walk away.

But already Olivia felt melded to my arms; to myself.

"I can't."

My friend's smile stiffened then crumbled away. "Christ, Sawyer."

"Molly entrusted her to me, Jax. Olivia's mine."

He stood, gaping at me. Then he shook his head, and turned in a circle on the street corner, arms out. "I knew it! Give me a prize, folks, I fucking knew it."

He stopped and faced me.

"I knew six nights ago. After the party. Everyone was gone and you were sitting on the couch, sitting in a mess of beer cans and Solo cups, feeding her a bottle like there was no one else in the world. So is that what you're going to do? Raise her? You're going to raise a baby, Sawyer?"

"I don't know what I'm doing, Jackson," I said. "But this feels wrong. Being here feels fucking wrong."

Jackson pressed his lips together. "So you keep her? How? With what money?"

"My scholarship fund is—"

"Just enough so you can go to school and pay rent," Jackson finished. "It's not enough to pay for childcare. And that shit is expensive."

"I'll figure it out. I'll get a job."

"You're going to upheave your life. For what?"

"For what? For her," I snapped, inclining my head at the baby.

"She's not—"

"Shut up, Jax," I said harshly. "Molly abandoned her, and in one year from now, the law will say she did too. I looked it up. I can put my name on her birth certificate. Molly should have done it, but a year from now, it won't matter."

Jackson stared at me for a long moment.

"You have to graduate, Sawyer, and you have to pass the bar—the first time—or your clerkship with Judge Miller? You can kiss it goodbye. You'll lose that job and everything you've worked for."

I clenched my jaw. He was right about that too. I'd laid out the stepping-stones of my life so clearly and concretely. Graduate Hastings, pass the bar, earn a clerkship with Judge Miller, then begin my own career in criminal prosecution, maybe a run for district attorney. Who knew where I could go from there? I glanced down at Olivia and realized I wanted those things just as badly as ever.

But I wanted her too.

More than that, my goals would mean exactly shit if I achieved them with the mystery of her life trailing me wherever I went.

Jackson read it all in my eyes. He ran a hand over his close-cropped hair. "Sawyer, I love you, man, and I get that you think you're doing what's best. But as hard as you think it might be? It's going to be a million times harder than that."

"I know."

"No, I don't think you do. My mother had to work three jobs, one for each of me and my two brothers. Three jobs just to keep food on the table for us, and a roof over our heads, and never mind doing something like law school."

"But she did it, and now her youngest son is finishing law school," I said. "She's proud of you. I'd like to think my mom would be proud of me too."

"She would be, man," he said quietly. "I know she would be."

I clenched my teeth against the old pain, locked it down deep. A drunk driver had killed my mother when I was eight years old. If I tallied all of the things I thought she might be proud of me for, my full-boat scholarship to Hastings was pretty much it.

Jackson sighed, shook his head. "I don't know."

"Olivia's mine," I said. "That's what I know. I have a responsibility to take care of her."

Jackson's stiffened expression softened, and the faintest smile tugged the corners of his mouth. "I must be living in bizarro world."

"I'm right there with you," I said. I felt a tightness around my heart unclench, and a swamp of unfamiliar, strong emotion nearly drowned me.

My daughter.

"So you going to help or what?" I said, gruffly. "Someone once told me this single-parenting shit is hard."

"There's that exceptional memory of yours again." Jackson grinned, then his face fell. "You'll have to move out, you know that, right? The other guys aren't going to do any Three Men and a Baby. Kevin's already panicked that we're losing street cred."

"I'll find a new place."

Jackson stared at me a few moments more, then blew air out his cheeks and laughed. He lifted the baby bag off my shoulder and slung it over his. "Christ, this is heavy. You are one crazy bastard."

I eased a sigh of relief. "Thanks, Jax."

"Yeah, yeah, just don't call me at two in the morning asking me about whooping cough or... what are they called? Fontanels?"

I laughed but a gust of cold, SF wind tore it away.

I hefted the baby in my aching arms, held her tighter to me. "Come on," I told her. "Let's go home."

∽∘∾

I woke with a start when my chin touched my chest, and blinked blearily. The Muni was screeching to a stop at Duboce. I shouldered my bag and got off, and walked the block and a half to the cream-colored Victorian in which I rented the second-story flat.

I passed the first floor door where Elena Melendez lived, and shot it a small smile, then dragged my tired ass up to the second. In my place, I took off my jacket, hung it on the stand and tossed my bag under it. I veered left, straight to the kitchen to put on a pot of coffee, then to the living area, to my desk by the window. The clock read 4:42 pm. Technically, I still had eighteen minutes to myself.

I slumped in the chair and closed my eyes... then opened them again.

I didn't want those minutes, I wanted my girl.

I headed downstairs, taking them two at a time and knocked on #1. Hector, Elena's five-year old, opened the door.

"Hey, Hector," I said. "Can you tell your mom I'm here?"

He nodded his dark-haired head and retreated. I heard from inside, "Sawyer? Come on in, querido. She's ready."

I stepped inside Elena's flat that smelled like warmth, spices, and laundry soap. It was a tad cluttered, but not messy. Homey. A family lived here. Elena—a plump, forty-five-year-old woman with thick dark hair in a braid down her back and large, soft eyes—was bending to pick Olivia out of the playpen.

I smiled like a dope when Olivia's little face lit up to see me. Her blue eyes were bright and clear, and her wispy dark curls framed her cheeks that were rounded with thirteen-month old baby chub.

She reached for me. "Daddy!"

Not Dada or Dah-yee, but Daddy. All syllables. My stupid heart clenched.

Elena handed her over with a soft smile, and Olivia wrapped her little arms around my neck.

"She had a good day. Ate all of her peas."

"You did? Were you a good girl?" I kissed Olivia's cheek and then fished in my pocket and pulled out my wallet. Olivia made a grab for it, and I gave it to her after I pulled out a check. "Thank you, Elena."

"Always my pleasure, Sawyer," she said, pocketing this week's pay. She reached out and gave Olivia's little wrist a tug. "See you Monday, little love."

I took my wallet out of Olivia's hands—and mouth—and shouldered the diaper bag. "Say bye-bye."

"Bye-bye," Olivia said.

Elena clasped her hands over her heart. "Already so smart, this one. Like her daddy."

I smiled. "Come on, Livvie," I said. "Let's go home."

chapter three

Darlene

The alarm went off at the ungodly hour of 5:30 a.m. I dragged my ass out of bed, started the coffee pot in my little kitchen, then swayed with my eyes closed under the shower spray in my tiny bathroom. I had never been much of an early-riser, but a friend of a friend in NYC had pulled a gazillion strings to get me a job at a posh spa in the Financial District. The pay was worth getting up for, but *God*.

"Is this what being responsible feels like?" I muttered as I dropped the shampoo bottle for the second time.

After showering, I sipped coffee in the kitchen, wrapped in my towel with another turban'ed around my hair, marveling that the sky outside my window was still dark.

Being responsible, I decided, sucked ass.

But after the initial sluggishness passed, I felt more awake than I had in a long time. Ready. The day was dawning on my new life, I decided, and I didn't even care if that sounded cheesy. It felt good.

I dressed in beige skirt, men's button-down shirt, thigh-high maroon socks, and my black combat boots. In the bathroom mirror, I put on the usual dark shadow and heavy liner around my blue eyes, gold hoops in my ears, and tied my long brown hair in a ponytail. I still looked like my New York self.

I couldn't decide if that was good or bad.

Outside, I pulled on my favorite old man sweater and shouldered my purple backpack. The sun was finally climbing out of the sky, and the sheer early-ness of the day was palpable. The street was quiet. Asleep.

An app on my phone told me I needed the J train to take me to the Embarcadero Muni station. Twenty minutes later, I emerged in a neighborhood of condos, modern loft space, and shops with a view of the Bay. My map said the Wharf, and all the fun touristy stuff was just around the corner so to speak, another ten minutes by train. This neighborhood felt quiet, and I wondered if I'd have enough clients to keep me afloat, or if I'd need a second job.

If you get a second job, you won't have time to start dancing again.

I couldn't decide if that was good or bad, either.

Turns out, I needn't have worried. Serenity Spa was a pretty, sleek storefront that screamed *expensive*, and was bustling with clients inside, even at 6:45 a.m.

My supervisor, Whitney Sellers, looked to be in her mid-thirties, with strawberry blonde hair and hard blue eyes. She eyed me up and down with a furrowed brow.

"*Darlene*, right?" she asked, as if my name didn't taste right in her mouth.

I nodded. "Yes, hi. Nice to meet you."

She reached a hand for me to shake, hard and short.

"I wouldn't get attached to this place," she said. "Turnover is high. I'm up to my neck in hires and fires every week. You start in ten minutes and you need a uniform." She appraised my outfit. "Badly."

She gave me a pair of white yoga pants and a soft, white button-down shirt with short sleeves. I changed in the employee bathroom and checked myself out in the mirror

"I look like a nurse," I told Whitney when I came out for her inspection.

"That's the idea," Whitney said. "You work in healthcare now, massaging for the therapeutic well-being of our clients." She arched a brow. It seemed eyebrows did most of the talking around here. "Well? Go. Your first client is waiting."

It took me all of three minutes to determine that the serenity of Serenity Spa was reserved for the clients. For a place that catered to luxury and relaxation, every employee there looked like they were stressed to the max.

"Do you like working here?" I asked one of my coworkers in the break room after my first appointment was done. The gal gave me a strange look.

"You must be new." She sighed and rubbed her shoulder. "It's like kneading dough all day, but what other job can you say you can make this much per hour?"

Selling X at a rave, I thought but did not say.

Serenity Spa was the elegant business of my new life, and I vowed to never go back to the old. I was going to keep myself as clean and pristine as my new uniform. But by the time my shift was over, my arms felt like they weighed a hundred pounds each, and my shoulders and forearms were screaming.

"I just have to get used to it," I muttered to myself on the street. It was like a new dance routine. At first, your body was sore as the same muscles were worked over and over again, but I'd adjust. No, more than adjust. I'd conquer.

The clang of a cable car sounded, and I watched a sailboat glide across the Bay. A smile spread over my lips. "I did good today."

And then my gaze landed on a post on the corner beside me, covered in bills and flyers; someone offering guitar lessons, a lost cat sign…and flyers for an independent, modern dance troupe that was having a showcase at a theatre in the Mission District in a few weeks. They were holding auditions. One spot. A female dancer for the ensemble.

I bit my lip. The cable car was rounding the corner, going the opposite direction from where I needed to be. If I jumped on, I might get lost, but I was feeling brave that day.

The car made its stop and I went for it. As I did, my hand snaked out to grab a phone number tag from the bottom of the dance flyer. I stuffed the scrap of paper in my pocket and jumped on the car to who-knew-where.

After a late afternoon doing touristy stuff at Pier 39 along the Wharf—and eating chocolate from Ghirardelli Square to celebrate me in my new city—I navigated the buses and trains to get back home.

Duboce Street was bathed in twilight copper, and the beautiful houses, fronted with trees and flowers, looked idyllic. Like a postcard for San Francisco. I grinned and pulled out my phone and took a photo of the cream-colored Victorian.

I live here! I typed in a message to Carla, my sister, and attached the photo.

No response.

I told myself she was busy with family stuff or having dinner. It was seven o'clock in New York, after all.

On the first floor in the Victorian I heard voices. The door to #1 was open, and a middle-aged Hispanic woman stood in it, talking to a young man. The guy looked to be about my age. He cradled a toddler on his hip with one hand, held a briefcase in the other, and wore a diaper bag slung over his shoulder. He had short, dark blond hair with soft, loose curls, sharp brown eyes fringed with long lashes, a square jaw, and a broad mouth that was currently turned down in a stiff frown…

I could have kept mentally appraising his attributes for days, but in the space of a second, my brain had tallied up the sum of his parts and came to the very definitive conclusion that he was fucking gorgeous.

Seriously? Do not tell me Mr. Mom is my neighbor.

He and the Hispanic woman both stopped talking when they saw me. The woman's face broke out into a warm, welcoming smile. The guy stared at me with a mixture of alarm and disdain.

"Who are you?" he demanded rudely, shifting the diaper bag higher on his shoulder while hoisting his little girl in his other arm. Six feet of hotness in a rumpled suit, glaring at me with suspicion in his dark eyes.

The woman swatted his arm lightly. "Sawyer, be a good boy."

"I…I'm your new neighbor?" I said. It sounded more like a question; as if I needed this guy's permission to *live.* I straightened to my full height. "I'm Darlene. I just moved in upstairs. I'm a dancer. Well, I was. Had to take some time off but I'm going to get back into it soon…ish." I put on my friendliest smile. "I'm a massage therapist now. Just got my license and…"

My words died under Sawyer's withering stare.

"A dancer. Fantastic," he said bitterly. "Just what I always wanted. Someone leaping and thumping above me, waking my kid up and disturbing my studies at all hours of the night."

I planted my hands on my hips. "I can't dance in a dinky apartment, and besides…"

Words failed me again as the sharp planes and hard angles of Sawyer's face melted when his daughter—I guessed her to be about a year old—clapped her small hand over his chin. Sawyer's gaze softened, and his broad mouth turned up in a smile—a beautiful smile I was sure he saved only for his little girl, and one so full of love that, for a moment, I could hardly breathe.

"It is *very* nice to meet you, Darlene," the woman interjected. "I'm Elena Melendez. This is Sawyer, and his little angel is Olivia. They live upstairs."

"Me too," I said. "Third floor, I mean. Obviously," I added with a weak laugh. "The studio?"

"You're subletting for Rachel, yes?" Elena smiled. "She's such a nice girl."

"And *quiet*," Sawyer added, earning himself another swat from Elena.

"Yes, I'm subletting for six months," I said. "Rachel's doing a Green Peace tour."

Elena beamed. "Welcome to the building."

Sawyer took his little girl's hand off his chin, gave it a kiss, then grunted something unintelligible as he brushed past me to go upstairs. I got a whiff of cologne and baby powder, and the strangest sensation ripped through me. It was as if every sexual and maternal molecule in my body ignited in response to Sawyer's masculinity and the sheer *babyness* of his little girl at the same time.

Oh my God, cool your jets, girl. He's probably married and is definitely kind of an asshole.

Except to his daughter. Over Sawyer's shoulder, Olivia watched me and smiled.

I waved at her.

She waved back.

"He's really a very nice young man," Elena said with a sigh, watching Sawyer round the corner.

"I'll take your word for it," I said, easing a sigh of relief that Sawyer had taken the strange tension—and his arsenal of potent pheromones—upstairs with him. "His death-glare could cut diamonds. His daughter's a cutie, though. How old?"

"Thirteen months," Elena said. "I've been babysitting her since she was an infant, and I love every minute. I'd do it for free but Sawyer insists on paying the 'going rate.'" She leaned in conspiratorially and whispered, "I tell him *my* going rate because it's much less. My pleasure to help him. He works so hard. Every day, all night."

"What does he do?"

"He's studying to be a lawyer," she said proudly. "Very close to being done too."

I scuffed my combat boot on the thinly carpeted floor. "What…um, what does Olivia's mom do?"

Tell me he's happily married. Have mercy.

"She is not in the picture," Elena said quietly.

"Oh? That's…too bad."

"Sawyer has never mentioned her and I don't ask. I figure if he wants to tell, he'll tell but he's sealed up tight. Like a drum. He has a heart of gold, that one, but so serious. All the time, so much stress. I worry about him." She smiled warmly. "I tell him his handsome face was meant for smiling, but he saves those for Livvie."

"I noticed."

Elena gave my hand a pat. "And what do you do for work, Darlene? Massage therapist, you say?"

"Yes," I said. "I started today."

"A massage therapist. Isn't that something?" Elena's smile widened and her glance darted upward, to the heavens or Sawyer's apartment. "Dios trabaja de maneras misteriosas."

"What's that?"

"A guess. I tell you later."

A little dark-haired girl with large eyes appeared at Elena's hip. She put her hand on the girl's head. "This is Laura. She's two and I have a son, Hector, who is five. My husband works late but you'll meet him someday."

I smiled and waved at the little girl. "You really have your hands full."

"I do," Elena said, "or else I'd invite you in like a proper neighbor and make you dinner. But I have to get these two in the bath."

"That's so sweet of you. Another time, maybe?" I said, and I meant it. Elena was like a prototype for the ideal mother, and a wave of homesick with a side of lonely washed over me. I had a sudden urge to sit on her couch, rest my head on her shoulder, and pour my guts out to her.

You are being extra ridiculous right now. No one needs to know anything. Not here, in your new life.

"Speaking of dinner," I said brightly, "I should get going. I haven't done any shopping since I got here except for the essentials: coffee and tampons. Where's the closest grocery?"

"There's a Safeway and a Whole Foods. Both are a short walk up 14th, then cross over to Market."

"Perfect. Thank you so much, Elena."

"Of course, querida. I'm very happy you're here, and I believe Sawyer will soon come to feel the same."

I blinked and laughed. "I'm pretty sure he'll forget all about me. In New York you can go months without talking to anyone else in your apartment building."

"Ah, but this is not an apartment building, is it? It's a house. A home." Elena's smile was like warm bread. "You'll see."

chapter four

Darlene

Back in my place, I changed out of my clothes and put on some yoga pants, and a black, dance camisole. I figured my best bet for keeping ahead of massage-soreness was to stretch out every night.

I sat on the floor in my little living area, between the couch and TV stand, and began a mini-routine, but I didn't get very far. My cupboards were bare and I was hungrier than I realized. I threw on my gray sweater, my boots; shouldered my purple backpack, and headed out.

On the landing in front of #2, I hesitated. Did Sawyer need anything? It couldn't have been easy to get to the store often with a toddler.

My hand rose to knock but I mentally reiterated how I'd sworn off men for an entire year. No need to torture myself in the meanwhile.

Or you could be mature about it and be helpful. Grown-ups do that.

I knocked softly on the door. No answer.

"Welp, can't say I didn't try."

I turned on my heel and hurried down the rest of the stairs.

Outside, the twilight was golden and perfect, and the air felt warmer than I expected. Before I'd left New York, Becks had told me there was a famous saying about my new city—that the coldest winter ever spent was a summer in San Francisco. But it was the middle of June and no hint of the chill wind I'd been warned about. I added the warm night to my mental tally of all the things that were good about being here. It was a small thing, but if I thought for longer than a second about Beckett or Zelda, or my family, the loneliness would seep in. And if it got too bad, I was apt to do something stupid.

I'm done with that shit, I told myself. *I'm brand new.*

I concentrated on the city as I walked. My neighborhood of Victorians quickly gave way to commercial towers and shops along Market Street, which I'd deduced was a major vein in the network of the city. Whole Foods appealed to my will to eat healthy, but Safeway appealed to my scrawny bank account. But as I perused the aisles with a basket on my arm, I decided I was better off finding a bodega. Supermarkets, like everything else in SF, were expensive as hell.

I rounded an aisle and crashed basket-first into my new neighbor, Sawyer.

"It's you," I said softly before I could regain control of my brain that had become momentarily paralyzed at the sight of him.

He'd changed from his suit to jeans, a hooded sweatshirt over a green T-shirt, and a baseball cap. He was pushing Olivia in a stroller, and the carry-space underneath was filled with fresh fruit and vegetables.

Up close, he was even more ridiculously handsome but tired. So, so tired.

"Oh," he said. "Hey."

"I don't think we were *properly* introduced." I stuck out my hand. "Darlene Montgomery. Your new upstairs neighbor who will *not* be—how did you say it? *Prancing and jumping* at all hours of the night?"

"Leaping and thumping," he said, not smiling. He gave my hand a brief shake. "Sawyer Haas."

For a moment, I became lost in the deep brown of his eyes and my words tangled on my tongue. I sought refuge with the toddler between us and knelt in front of the stroller.

"And this is Olivia? Hi, cutie."

The little dark-haired girl watched me with wide, blue eyes, then arched her back and pushed at her tray with a squawk.

"She doesn't like being cooped up for too long," Sawyer said. "I try to get through this quick. On that note…" he added pointedly.

I stood up quickly. "Oh, sure, of course. See you back at the house."

His brows came together and he frowned.

"That sounded weird, right?" I said with a short laugh. "We're virtual strangers but also practically roommates. Isn't it funny how two things can be so opposite and yet completely true at the same time?"

"Yeah. Weird," he said tonelessly. "I have to go. Nice meeting you. Again."

He pushed off, wheeling Olivia away, the sounds of her frustration trailing after. I heaved a sigh and watched him go.

"Nice talking to you."

No, that's good. Let him go. You're working on you.

I perused a few aisles, filling my cart with cottage cheese, lettuce, ravioli and pasta sauce. I was reaching for a packet of coffee filters which happened to share space with the baby food when I heard a child's fussing growing louder one aisle over. Olivia was on the verge of a full-blown meltdown. Below her screeching came Sawyer's low admonitions asking her gently to hold on, they were almost done.

I bit my lip and scanned the colorful rows of brightly-colored baby food packaging. With a *woot* of triumph, I found a box of zwieback toast biscuits, and hurried around the corner.

"Hi, again," I said. "I think maybe she could use a food diversion."

"We're fine, thanks."

Olivia squawked loudly, as if to say, *No, father of mine, I am distinctly not 'fine.'*

I bit back a smile. "Can I help?"

Sawyer took off his baseball cap, ran a hand through his loose, dark blond curls, then put it back on with a tired sigh. "She finished all of her strawberries and I don't want to feed her a bunch of crap baby snacks."

"How about one good one?" I held up the box of biscuits. "Talk about old school. I can't believe they still make these. They're like dog bones for babies."

"*Dog* bones?" Sawyer took the box out of my hands and scanned the ingredients. Or at least I think he did—it took only a second before he handed it back. "Yeah, looks okay but…"

"Great." I opened the box and tore apart the plastic bag inside.

"What are you doing? I haven't paid for those," Sawyer said, then muttered, "Guess I am now…"

"You won't regret it." I offered Olivia an oblong piece of the toast and she reached for it with one chubby little hand. "My mom gave my sister and me these things when we were little," I said. "They take some serious slobbering to turn into mush, and that'll give you time to shop."

Sawyer peered into the stroller, which had gone quiet as Olivia happily worked on the biscuit.

"Oh. Okay. Thanks," Sawyer said slowly. He took the box from me and tried to make room under the stroller amid the avocado, turkey slices, pineapple, peas and squash.

"Are you on a raw food diet?" I asked.

"That's all for her," Sawyer said.

"What about you?"

"What about me?"

"Do you eat food?"

"In theory," he said. "I have a date with aisle twelve, actually, so if you'll excuse me…"

I scanned the aisle markers. I found twelve and wrinkled my nose. "Frozen dinners? That doesn't sound healthy. You prepare all this fresh food for her but none for yourself?"

"I don't have room to carry a whole lot more," he said. "I'll be okay, thanks for your concern…"

"I'll help," I said. "What do you want? I'll carry it for you."

Sawyer sighed. "Listen…Darlene? That's nice of you to offer, and thanks for the crackers, but I'm good. After she goes to bed, I'll throw something in the microwave and hit the books." He stopped, shook his head, perplexed. "Why am I explaining this? I have to go."

He started to walk away and I was tempted to let him. He was kind of a jerk, but that was probably the exhaustion. I tried to imagine what it would be like taking care of an entire little human being all by myself. It was hard enough taking care of one adult me. I decided to set aside Sawyer's gruffness (and his ridiculous attractiveness) and help the guy out. Be neighborly.

"You're being so silly right now," I called after him.

He stopped, turned. "Silly?"

"Yes! I'm right here. Let me help you." I crossed my arms. "How long has it been since you've had a really nice meal for yourself?" He didn't say anything but stared back at me.

"That's what I thought," I said. "Come on. I'll make you something."

"Now you're going to cook for me? We met eight seconds ago."

"So?"

Sawyer blinked. "So…you don't have to cook for me."

"Of course I don't *have* to. I want to. We're neighbors." I peered at the aisle markers again to get my bearings. "I was going to make tuna casserole. Mostly because it's the only thing I know how to make. How does that sound?" I squatted beside the stroller. "Do you like casserole, sweet pea?"

Olivia smiled at me over her biscuit and kicked her foot with spastic baby joy. I smiled back and straightened.

"Olivia said she would love some casserole."

Sawyer looked at me with a strange expression on his face. I gave the sleeve of his hoodie a tug.

"Come on. Looks like fish is this way."

Sawyer hesitated. "I'm not going to get out of this, am I?"

I cocked my head, frowning. "Why would you want to?"

He was still frowning, but he pushed the stroller after me. "I'm just not used to people doing things for me. Elena does enough already. I feel like a charity case."

"You're not a charity case," I said. "One dinner isn't going to kill you."

"I know, but I'm juggling a hundred balls in the air and if someone reaches in and grabs one, it's going to throw me off." He covered his mouth with the back of his hand as a jaw-cracking yawn came over him. "Shit, I don't know why I just said that. I don't even know you."

"That's the benefit to talking," I said. "Getting to know someone. A revolutionary concept, I know."

He rolled his eyes and yawned again.

"You really do burn the midnight oil, don't you?" I said. "Elena told me you're studying law."

"Oh yeah?" he said. We'd arrived at the meat section. He picked up a package of rib eye steak, then tossed it back with a sigh. "What else did she tell you?"

I selected some fresh tuna and put it in my basket. "That you have a heart of gold, but you're stressed out all the time."

His head came up, alarmed. "What? Why…why did she say that?"

"Maybe she thinks it's true. The second part looks like it, for sure. As for the first?" I shrugged, then gave him a dry smile. "The jury is still out."

"Ha ha," he said dully. He glanced at me, then looked away. "Are you always this blunt?"

"I wish I could say honesty is the best policy, but it's more of a lack-of-filter situation."

"I noticed."

"Says the guy who began our acquaintance with *Who are you?*" I said, with a laugh.

Sawyer stopped and stared at me like I was a puzzle he couldn't figure out. My pulse thumped a little harder while under his sharp, dark-eyed scrutiny. I cleared my throat and cocked an eyebrow.

"Take a picture, it'll last longer," I said with a nervous laugh.

Sawyer's eyes widened in surprise and he shook his head. "Sorry, I…I'm just really tired."

He moved ahead of me and I watched a pretty young woman check out Sawyer, then Olivia, then Sawyer and Olivia together. I could practically see the hearts in her eyes. Sawyer was oblivious.

"So you're in law school," I said, catching up to him.

"Yeah," he said. "At UC Hastings."

"Oh, is that a good school?" I asked, then froze. "Wait. It just hit me. You're going to be a lawyer?"

"Yeah?"

"Sawyer the Lawyer?"

He groaned. "Please don't call me that."

"Why not? It's cute."

"It's childish and stupid."

"Oh, come on." I scoffed. "Surely you can see how cute it is. Such a funny coincidence."

"Yeah, one I haven't heard a million times," he muttered. "Anyway, I'm going to be an attorney, not a lawyer."

"What's the difference?"

"If you finish law school, you're a lawyer. If you pass the bar and are licensed to practice, you're an attorney. I'm going to be an attorney."

"Sawyer the Attorney doesn't have the same ring to it." I fished my phone out of my backpack. "Wikipedia says the terms are practically interchangeable." I shot him a grin.

He sighed, and a tired chuckle escaped him, one that seemed to surprise him. He gave me another perplexed look.

"I've never met anyone like you," he said. "You're like a…"

"I'm like a, what?"

Our eyes met and held, and despite the perpetual supermarket cold, I felt warm in Sawyer's gaze. His stiff expression loosened, the tension he carried on him eased slightly. He was locked up tight, this guy; but for that handful of heartbeats, I saw him. A thought slipped into the crevices of my mind.

He's lonely.

Then Sawyer blinked, shook his head and looked away. "Nothing," he said. The tension came back—I could feel it like a prickly force field around him—and I was locked out again. "Let's get out of here before your magic baby biscuit wears off."

I smiled and followed after silently, while internally I was dying to know what he'd been about to say.

Maybe nothing good, I thought. That was likely; I didn't know when to stop talking and got all up in people's business.

But that warm feeling in my chest—in the general vicinity of my heart—didn't go away. Sawyer had been about to pay me a compliment, I was sure of it. Nothing boring or bland—he was too smart for that. But something extraordinary, maybe.

A compliment that didn't sound like a compliment but it was, because it was made only for me.

You're the one being silly now, I thought, and walked with him to the checkout. But it seemed that I'd traveled three thousand miles, and the deep longing to have someone see *me* trailed after like a shadow I would never shake.

chapter five

Sawyer

We walked home together, Olivia and I...and my new neighbor.
How in the hell did this happen?
Mere hours ago, it had been a typical Friday. While the rest of my friends and fellow law students were out drinking or partying to blow off the stress of Third Year, I was going to make dinner for my daughter, play and read with her before bath time, then put her to bed and study until my eyes gave out.

And now...

Now, Darlene Montgomery was going to cook dinner for me.

Mental alarms and whistles were going off, telling me this was a bad idea. I didn't bring women home anymore, and yet I'd caved so easily. I chalked it up to my fatigue and her energy. Darlene must be a flexible dancer, I thought, because she slipped past all of my usual barricades and defenses, bending and contorting herself through a field of red laser beams like a ninja in a spy movie.

One dinner. That's it.

Twilight had fallen, coppery and warm, as we walked. Darlene talked non-stop about the differences between New York and San Francisco. I thought it would drive me crazy but I liked listening to her. She had a pretty voice, and my conversations these days consisted mostly of cajoling my kid to eat her peas, or listening to law students bitch about finals.

My eyes kept stealing glances at her.

In the grocery store, my photographic memory had taken an entire reel of just her face. She was a collage of striking features—a wide mouth, large eyes, full lips, high cheekbones, dark eyebrows—not one aspect insignificant.

Here, under the yellow of the streetlights, her eyes were deeper blue and full of light. Over her lithe frame, she wore a bulky sweater, but it didn't conceal what she was. She *looked* like a dancer—slender but with lean muscle, and she walked with an easy grace, despite the heavy black combat boots on her feet.

"So what's with the boots?" I asked. It was the most harmless part of what she was wearing.

"Protection."

"From what?"

"Not from. For. For my feet," she said. "I'm a dancer—or will be again soon, and my feet are a precious commodity."

"What kind of dance do you do? Ballet?"

"When I was little," she said. "But I'm into modern dances and capoeira. Have you heard of capoeira?"

"An Afro-Brazilian martial art that combines elements of dance, acrobatics, and music, developed in Brazil at the beginning of the 16th century."

Darlene stopped. "Well, look at you, Encyclopedia Brown. Are you a fan?"

"I read something about it once."

"Once? Do you always remember something you read once so precisely?"

"Yes."

I felt her gaze on me and glanced over to see an expectant look on her face—the kind women wear when the guy has said or done something that obviously requires further explanation.

"I have an eidetic memory," I said.

"A what?"

"Eidetic—photographic memory."

"Get out!" Darlene swatted my arm. "For real?"

I nodded.

"So you can remember long strings of numbers, or… what you were wearing on January 24th, 2005."

I shrugged. "It's pretty strong."

"Well…how strong is it?" Darlene demanded. "On a scale of one to you-should-be-on-*The Ellen DeGeneres Show*?"

"Not sure what Ellen's requirements are. Eight?"

Darlene was staring at me with wide eyes. "Wow. You've got a mega-mind. That must help with law school, yeah?"

"Yeah, it does," I said. "I probably wouldn't be graduating on time otherwise."

"Very cool," Darlene said.

I could feel her gearing up to quiz me like Andrew from my study group and cut her off at the pass.

"Anyway, you're getting back into dancing?" I asked. "Just in time to be my upstairs neighbor? Lucky me."

She grinned but it wilted quickly. "Not sure yet." Her fingers toyed with a tiny scrap of paper from her sweater pocket. "I've nearly thrown this away a hundred times since this afternoon."

"Is that your fortune?"

"It does look like that, doesn't it?" she said. "Who knows? Maybe it is. It's a phone number for a dance troupe, but I'm not sure if I'm going to call it."

"Why not?"

She shoved the paper back into her pocket. "I've only been here a few days. I have a great place, a job. I'm not sure what I'm doing yet. I sort of came here to start over again."

"Why? Are you on the run from the law?"

It was a joke, but Darlene's eyes flared and she looked away.

"No, nothing like that," she said quickly. Her smile looked forced. "I kind of like how no one knows me here. It's like the proverbial blank slate and I can write whatever I want on it."

I nodded, at a loss. The conversation had taken a turn for the personal and that was forbidden territory. I didn't have the time to dive deep into anyone; I was barely keeping my head above water as it was. I was heavy and anchored down, dragging myself through the days until one year was up and Olivia was safely all mine. The exhaustion was like a suit of armor, but Darlene…She seemed weightless—as if she wore combat boots to keep her from floating away. She smiled constantly, laughed easily, and she swept into my life at a grocery store like it were nothing.

She's the exact opposite of me in every way.

A short silence fell, that lasted all of three seconds.

"Anyway, tonight, I'm your chef," Darlene said.

"You don't have to…"

She stopped and planted her hands on her hips. "I've seen *Law and Order*. Are we going to, what's the word? Where you argue over the same thing a second time?"

"Relitigate."

"Yes, that. Are we going to relitigate dinner tonight?"

"I'm just not used to—"

"Overruled, Sawyer the Lawyer," she said. "I'm going to make dinner and you're going to let me or I'm going to tell Elena on you."

"Jesus, you're a pain in the ass, you know that?"

Darlene grinned. "That's just another way of saying *persistent*."

I rolled my eyes and bent to check on Olivia. She was still happily munching on the little biscuit and babbling. She grinned over a mouthful of mush at me. I grinned back.

Holy hell, I love that face.

I straightened to see Darlene watching me, her eyes soft, and I realized I was still smiling like a moron. I reverted back to neutral, took the stroller handle and started pushing.

"You're so sweet with her," Darlene said. "How long has it been just the two of you?"

"Ten months," I said. My jaw stiffened. I never talked about Molly if I could help it. I had an irrational fear that even saying her name would call her back from wherever she was, to try to take Olivia away from me.

My shoulders hunched in anticipation of the next questions; more personal questions that I hated. But Darlene must've gotten the memo since she didn't say anything else about it.

At the Victorian, I carried the stroller with Olivia in it up the three steps while Darlene unlocked the front door. In the foyer, she glanced at the flight of stairs leading up with a frown.

"Do you carry the baby and the stroller up a whole flight of stairs?" she asked.

"No, I take Olivia up, then come back for it." I shot her a dry look. "Hence, the-not-buying-a crap-ton-of-stuff to carry."

"Such a man." Darlene sighed. "I'll help. Stroller or baby?"

I hesitated. The stroller was heavier and bulkier but the alternative was Darlene carried Olivia. I scrubbed my chin.

Darlene gave me a tilted smile. "I won't break her, I promise. Or I can take the stroller," she added quickly. "Whatever you're comfortable with."

"Oh, *now* you're concerned about what I'm comfortable with?" I asked with laugh. "That's a first."

She grinned and rolled her eyes. "Such a crank. Pick."

"The stroller is heavy," I said slowly. "If you don't mind taking her?"

"Mind? Not in a million years."

She knelt in front of Olivia and moved the tray aside, undid the mini-seatbelt.

"Hey, sweet pea. Can I hold you?" Olivia's little face split open with a smile as Darlene lifted her up and cradled her easily on her hip. "Is that a yummy cracker? I bet it is. Can I have some?"

She pretended to bite at the biscuit and Olivia squealed with laughter.

The alarm bells were screaming now as I folded up the stroller and carried it up the stairs, Darlene following after. At my door, I fumbled for my key, acutely conscious of Darlene's presence behind me, like a low heat against my back. A sliver of something electric slipped down my spine. I hadn't brought a woman back here since I moved in.

Darlene isn't a woman by your usual definition, she's a neighbor. And you didn't bring her back; she somehow finagled her way in.

My body didn't give a damn how she got there, only that she was.

I opened the door and set the stroller against the wall just inside, then shut the door behind us. Us. Three of us.

Don't get soft now. One dinner, strictly neighborly.

"She's precious." Darlene handed Olivia back to me, and then slipped out of her backpack to set it on the kitchen counter. "And this is a nice place. Much bigger than mine. Two bedroom?"

"Yeah."

"I've never seen a baby-proofed bachelor pad." Darlene tilted her chin at the coffee table that had a protective slab of rubber on each corner. "Super cute."

I started to tell her my place was the furthest from a bachelor pad as you could get, but my words died.

Darlene had taken off her ratty old sweater and tied it around her slender waist, then rummaged in my cupboards. She was wearing a black dancer's top with straps that crisscrossed her back. I became mesmerized by her lean muscles that moved under her pale skin, the elegant line of her neck, and the sleek cut of her arms as she reached up on a high shelf for a pan.

I suddenly had the urge to see her dance. To see her move the way the lines of her body hinted she could.

And just like that, ten months of celibacy came crashing into me. The blood rushed to my groin, and *going soft* was suddenly the least of my worries. I coughed to conceal a sudden groan that nearly erupted out of me.

"You okay?" Darlene asked over her shoulder.

"Sure. Fine."

This is a bad idea.

I started to put Olivia in her playpen but she fussed and squirmed out of my arms once she saw where she was headed. I set her on the floor instead, and watched her toddle straight to the kitchen, to Darlene.

"What are you doing down there?" Darlene cooed. "You want to come up here and help?" She scooped Olivia up and set her on her hip again, holding her one-armed. "Now, tell me, where does your daddy keep the baking pans?"

I watched a beautiful woman hold my daughter in my kitchen, talking easily to her, making her laugh. An ache—a thousand times more potent than any sexual frustration—rose up from a deep place in my heart. It felt like hundreds of emotions I'd been keeping locked down were suddenly erupting out all at once: what I wanted for me, for Olivia, what she had lost and what I was working for to keep her. They were all spilling out of me like a bag of marbles, and now I had to scramble to put them all back before I fell on my ass.

"This wasn't a good idea," I said.

Darlene was making a silly face at Olivia. "Hmmm?"

"I can't do this."

"Do what? Eat dinner?"

"Yes," I snapped. "I can't eat dinner. With you. And I can't have you over here all the time, helping me out or playing with Livvie. I can't."

Darlene's expression folded and I hated myself for stealing the light out of her eyes.

"Oh."

She carefully set Olivia down and Olivia immediately squawked to be picked up again.

"Shit," I said, running a hand through my hair. "This is exactly why I didn't want any help. Because one thing leads to the next and before you know it…"

"Before you know it you're eating a decent meal?" Darlene said with a weak smile.

"It's not that." I ground my teeth in frustration.

Darlene waved her hands. "No, you're right. I'm sorry. It's your place. Your privacy. I do this a lot. I get *involved*. I moved here to work on me." She shouldered her backpack and took Olivia by the hand to walk her to me. "I have a lot of work left to do."

"Darlene…"

She bent down to Olivia. "Bye-bye, sweet pea." She raised her head and flashed me the tattered remains of her brilliant smile. "Have a nice night."

The sound of the door shutting made me flinch. The room suddenly seemed a little dimmer. Quieter.

Olivia was tugging on my jeans. "Up," she said "Up, Daddy."

I picked her up and held her. She smiled at me and I bottled up my spilled emotions but for one. My love for her. She was the only thing that mattered.

"Come on," I told her. "Let's have some dinner."

Darlene had the tuna in her bag, which she'd taken with her in her hurry to escape. I gave Olivia avocado, cubes of turkey, a hard-boiled egg, and another one of those biscuits Darlene had introduced me to. After, I bathed Olivia, and read *Freight Train* to her about ten times until she was yawning instead of saying, "Again!"

After I put her to bed in her small bedroom, I set up my study materials at the desk in the living room. The clock on the wall said it was eight-fifteen. I went to the fridge to find a frozen dinner. My stomach growled for damn tuna casserole.

Now that Livvie was in bed, guilt churned my empty stomach.

You didn't have to kick her out.

I had a thousand good reasons for keeping my private business private, and yet being an ass to Darlene was like saying 'fuck off' to someone after they said they hoped you have a nice day.

I leaned my head against the freezer. Now I'd have to apologize.

I hated apologizing.

A soft knock came at the door. I whispered a prayer to any god that would listen it wasn't Elena coming to tell me she had a conflict sometime next week and couldn't babysit.

I opened the door to Darlene. She had a plate of food in one hand covered in aluminum foil. Steam wafted up in little tendrils, carrying with it the scents of warm noodles, mushrooms and tuna.

Dammit, she's beautiful.

The images stored in my perfect memory were dull copies compared to the real thing. I crossed my arms over my chest as if I could put a barricade between us.

"Hi, again," Darlene said. "I am not here to make you feel bad, or barge in again, I promise." She thrust the plate of food toward me. "This is a peace offering *and* a parting gift. A promise that I won't get up in your business."

I took the plate. "This is a lot of casserole."

"You insisted on paying for it back at the store, and I know you'd never cook it yourself." Her radiant smile was back. "You can eat what you want now and have leftovers tomorrow."

I stared down at the food in her hand. A simple apology and a thank you was all it would take, and then I could close the door and get back to my life. My stressed out, anxiety-ridden life.

Darlene tilted her head. "Okay, so…I'm going to go. Good ni—"

"Olivia's mom abandoned her ten months ago," I heard myself say. "My buddies and I were having a party and she showed up and just…left her. She left Olivia without a mom."

"Oh no," Darlene said softly. She wilted against the doorjamb. "I'm so sorry."

"Yeah, so, it is what it is, but…that's why I don't bring anyone here. I don't have time for a relationship with anyone, and I don't bring anyone over casually. Not even friends, really. I hate the idea of Livvie having strange women in her house. It's hard enough for her without a mom. I don't want to confuse her."

"I get it," Darlene said.

"It's probably stupid or overprotective but… She's starting to call Elena 'mama.' She hears her kids call her that and I…I don't know what to do."

Darlene's smile was soft and she reached her hand to pat my hand awkwardly for a moment, then pulled it away.

"I think you're great with her. And she's obviously very happy with you."

"Yeah, well…" I ran a hand through my hair. "So listen, this is dumb. Olivia's sleeping. Come in and help me eat this."

Darlene grinned and shook her head before I finished my sentence. "Nope. I have my rules too. I'm working on me, remember? Trying to, anyway."

Her cell phone chimed a text and she pulled it out of her sweater pocket. Her face went pale.

"Shit. I have to go," she said. "Um, I have a meeting. It's a…a work meeting in, oh hell, thirty minutes. I totally forgot."

I frowned. "A work meeting at nine on a Friday night?"

"Yeah, bummer, right?" Darlene laughed loosely. "So I can't stay to eat anyway. I'd be neglecting my obligations. I'm trying to be responsible to myself. No distractions."

"Right," I said, my chest feeling heavy. "No distractions. Well, thanks again for the casserole."

"No problem," Darlene said. She chucked me on the arm. "See? Not so bad, right? We don't have to be BFF's but we don't need to be strangers, either. Neighbors."

"Yeah, I guess that could work."

"Good," Darlene said, her smile widening, as she walked backward down the hall. "Okay. Bye." She flashed me a little wave, spun on her heels and raced downstairs.

"Bye."

I shut the door, and leaned against it for a few seconds, more tired than before. The entire night I'd been swept up in Darlene's energy. I'd felt more awake than I had in a long time, and now I was sagging again.

Friend or stranger.

Aside from Jackson, I didn't have a ton of friends anymore, and didn't have time for them anyway. I didn't have time for anything. 'Neighbor' fit somewhere in between 'friend' and 'stranger.' Darlene could be there.

I couldn't put her anywhere else.

chapter six

Darlene

"Oh my God, this is going to *suck*," I moaned.

I was hanging on to Max's arm as we made our way into the YMCA. My heart was racing after my mad dash from the parking lot. Praise be to Uber, I'd made it on time to my first NA meeting.

Praise be to Max's reminder text, I added but didn't say aloud.

"What's going to suck?" he asked, frowning. "The meeting?"

That too.

"No," I said. "My new living situation. It's going to be a true test of my sexual willpower."

"Sexual willpower," Max mused. "That's one I haven't heard before."

He looked exceptionally handsome in jeans and a black T-shirt under a black leather jacket, but I noticed my observation of him had changed. He was gorgeous, no question, but his eyes were the wrong shade of brown, and his hair was perfectly straight with no soft curls.

He's not as attractive in the same way because you know he's gay. That's all.

I gave my head a shake. "I'm a warm-blooded American woman," I said. "I have needs. Urges. Like, a lot of them, and yet I've relegated myself to a year's worth of celibacy. A *year*."

"Unrealistic expectations are failures waiting to happen," Max said.

"Is that in your Sponsor's Manual?"

"It's the title," he said, shooting me a small smile. "Anyway, I thought your plan was to stay out of a relationship for a year. Not to go full chastity."

"I can't do one without the other," I said. "It's my addiction, too. Not sex, but filling the emptiness with something that makes me feel good. And being with a man…that makes me feel good. The sex and the touching and the mornings afters. God, I love the morning afters."

I glanced up to see Max smiling at me with amusement. I flapped my hand. "But then I get attached and try to make something out of nothing, and it all slips through my fingers. I'm back to square one, only with another failure under my belt."

"Mmmkay," Max said. We stepped inside the linoleum and fluorescent hallway of the Y where our footsteps joined the soft clopping of other people headed toward their respective groups. "So what brought this sudden revelation on?"

"The unbearable hotness of my new neighbor."

"Oh…? Do tell."

"He lives below me. And he has a little girl, and I don't even care. I thought that would be a total turnoff but it's not. The way he cares for her only adds to his ridiculous sex appeal."

A small voice in my head whispered that Sawyer was attractive in a hundred different ways, but his extreme good looks was the only one I'd let myself admit.

We stepped inside the meeting room. It looked to be a small group, only fifteen chairs sat facing a podium. I glanced around at my fellow recovering addicts. They ranged from young like Max and myself, to the oldest, who looked to be in his mid-sixties. In a corner was a table with coffee and donuts, and a woman, with dark hair and a tired but warm smile, who was setting out napkins and paper cups. Angela, the program director, I guessed.

We headed for the snack table. Max gave Angela a nod and a smile of greeting and leaned in to me. "I think you need to be careful."

"Of what?" I asked, perusing the donuts. "Aside from the hundred million other things I'm trying to be careful of…?"

"This guy—your neighbor—has a kid?" Max said. "If you start anything with him, that's two relationships you'd be having, not one. And the one he has with his daughter is always going to be the most sacred."

"I told you, there will be no relationship, sexual or otherwise, for one whole year," I declared. I chose a bear claw and poured a Styrofoam cup of black coffee.

A year. God, that felt like a prison sentence too. The image of Sawyer's handsome face, smiling at his little girl, rose unbidden in my mind.

"And even if I wanted to pursue something, it couldn't be with Sawyer," I said quickly, as if I were casting a spell to banish him from my thoughts. "He's got too much going on with Olivia and his studies to be with anyone."

"This Sawyer is a student? Please tell me he's not in high school."

I swatted Max's arm with a laugh. "Don't be gross. He's at UC Hastings," I said proudly. "He's going to be a lawyer."

"Sawyer the Lawyer?"

"This is why I love you, Max."

"So he has no time for relationships."

"Correct! So that's good, right?" I said, taking a huge bite of donut. "He has no time, and I have to get my shit together." Crumbs spilled down the front of my shirt. I brushed them off irritably. "It would just be easier if he weren't so damn hot. And smart. And funny. He's grouchy as hell too, but only on the surface. It's like he turns this certain face to the world, but when it's just him and Olivia…"

"Whoa, whoa, whoa," Max said. "How do you know all that about him?"

He gave me a stern look. "Are you hanging out with the guy who already said he has no time for you?"

"Jeez, when you put it that way." I rolled my eyes. "Yes, we hung out. Once. Tonight. I ran into him at the grocery store. The poor guy is living in frozen dinner hell. So I cooked for him."

"You *cooked* for him?"

"Tuna casserole. It wasn't as sinister as it sounds."

We took seats toward the back of the group. Max wrinkled his lips.

"I'm serious, Dar. If you want to succeed at being sober, or at finding your own self, or whatever it was you came out here for, then you have to give yourself a chance."

"I am."

"You moved in two days ago and you're already having dinner with the guy."

"I did *not* have dinner *with* him," I said, and busied myself smoothing my napkin on my lap. "I cooked for him, true, but we…decided it was better if we kept things strictly neighborly."

I glanced up quickly to see Max watching me. I suddenly felt naked, as if my stupid little half-truth was tattooed all over my skin. I thrust my chin out.

"I'd never have told you about him if I knew you were going to freak out."

Max frowned. "I just don't think it's a good idea to put yourself in a situation that is only going to get more intense."

"We're not even *friends*, Sawyer and me. Not really."

"And you're okay with that?"

"Of course. Sure. Why wouldn't I be? I'm not going to be the same idiot I was in New York who gets attached to the first guy who's nice to me. I'm *not*."

Max inclined his chin to the podium where Angela was standing, bringing the meeting to order. "Tell it to them."

"We have someone new with us tonight," the program director said. "Will everyone please give a warm welcome to Darlene."

The group turned in their seats and gave me a smattering of applause.

Max nudged my elbow. He'd finally exchanged his gloomy grimace for an encouraging smile. "You're on. Let's see what you got."

I moved to the front of the room. I hated this part. Getting up and telling my story to a bunch of strangers. I know it was supposed to make me feel a sense of solidarity, and to keep confronting what I had done and what I was; to speak it out loud so I couldn't pretend like it never happened. But it just felt like telling the story of my weakness all over again.

"Hi, I'm Darlene."

The chorus returned with, "Hi, Darlene."

Ugh. So stupid.

Briefly, I sketched my history. Three months in jail for possession, parole, an overdose at a New Year's Eve party, more parole, and finally freedom but for mandatory meetings three times a week.

"And how do you feel being here?" Angela asked when I moved to take my seat.

"Good. Great. Happy to be here in a new city. Starting over where everything is new. Except, for here. NA meetings are the same no matter where you go, right?"

I laughed weakly. No one else did.

When I'd slunk back into my seat, Max's frown looked etched in stone.

"Didn't your mom ever tell you if you keep making that face, it'll freeze that way?" I whispered as another gal, Kelly, was taking the podium to continue a story she'd begun last session.

"Later," Max said and nudged his chin at Kelly. "Listen."

After the meeting, a few other group members introduced themselves and shook my hand. Two younger gals and one nervous-looking guy offered to hang out some time and grab coffee. I declined politely, blaming work. I'd already decided that the only time I was a recovering addict was when I was in this room. The old Darlene was here. Everywhere else, I was brand new.

I gathered my backpack as Angela and Max talked near the podium. They both glanced at me at the same time, like parents trying to figure out what to do with their problem child.

Let them, I thought. *The past stays inside these walls. That's what anonymous means. No one has to know. Sawyer doesn't have to know...*

Why he should pop into my thoughts—again—irritated me. Being here irritated me. I stood up and headed for the door, feeling as if I were being chased by the ghosts of everything I was trying not to be anymore.

Outside, Max still hadn't shaken his frown.

"I take it you were not impressed with my debut?" I said, trying to keep my tone light.

"You sounded like you were reading a grocery list," he said.

"What you mean? I told my story."

"That was more of a plot summary. Point one: I did drugs. Point two: I got caught. Point three: I did more drugs."

"Yeah? And?" I snapped. "Look, to be honest, I don't really feel as if there's much more to tell. I got clean and have been clean for a long time." I squared my shoulders to him. "I'm never going back. I hit my rock bottom and I came out the other side. End of story."

"You hit rock bottom?"

"Yes."

"When?"

"Weren't you listening? When I OD'd at a New Year's party a year and a half ago."

"You said that happened but you didn't talk about what rock bottom meant for you. Or what it felt like."

"How do you think it felt? It sucked! But right now I feel good. Why should I talk about all the bad crap when I've gotten past all that?"

Max crossed his arms over his broad chest. "So you're just here because the court has ordered you to be?"

I sighed. "I'm not going to fail, Max. That's what my family is expecting. But I'm better than I have been. I have my massage license, a good job, a fresh start. I have to hope my worst days are behind me, right?" I grinned weakly and slugged him in the shoulder. "I'm going to prove my parents wrong, you'll see."

Max's expression softened. "I can't tell you how to recover, Dar. That's a long dark road that each addict takes on their own. As your sponsor, all I can do is point out the road signs you don't want to miss, ones that I've passed myself."

"And?"

"And from my pseudo-professional opinion, I don't think you've passed as many as you think you have."

I started to argue, but then snapped my mouth shut. That's what addicts do. They *talk* about how they're not addicts anymore. But I was recovered. Actions mattered more than words.

"Then I'll prove you wrong, too."

chapter seven

Sawyer

"Let me get this straight," Jackson said, pressing the bar up and holding it. Sweat ran down his temples to the bench beneath him. I stood over him as a spotter.

"This new neighbor of yours…" He eased the bar down to his chest. "She's hot, funny, great with Olivia, so—*naturally*,"—he grimaced and pushed the weight up—"you kicked her out."

I helped him set the bar on the rack, and he sat up, sucking in air.

"It wasn't quite like that," I said.

My best friend fixed me a look. Hastings gym was never crowded this early in the morning on a Monday, he had nearly the entire place to himself in which to lecture me uninterrupted.

"I love you, bro, but you have lost your ever-loving mind."

"Come on, Jax, you know my deal." I went to the tricep rope machine. "What the hell was I supposed to do?"

"Is this a trick question?" Jackson moved to a rack of hand weights. He hefted a forty-pounder in each hand and faced the wall mirror. "Forget your deal, and ask her out. Or take her to bed. Or take her out and *then* take her to bed."

Take Darlene to bed.

Instantly, there she was in my mind's eye; naked and curled against me, her dark hair spilled over my pillow, her brilliant smile muted in the soft light of morning.

I shook my head, irritated.

"You can't have a one-night stand with a person who lives in the same building as you. That's madness."

"And something beyond a one-night stand is impossible?" Jackson said, his eyebrows raised.

"Yes. If it goes south—which it will—I'll have to move."

He chuckled, then narrowed his eyes. "Hold up. If the whole situation with the lovely Darlene is hopeless, why tell me about it? Because you want me to talk sense into that thick skull of yours, am I right?"

Shit.

"Wrong," I said. "I told you because it was newsworthy. She's a new person in my building." I heard how stupid that sounded and kept talking as if I could bury the words with more words. "And we're not compatible anyway. We're too different. She's..."

Weightless.

"She's not serious," I said. "And I am."

"Understatement of the century," Jackson muttered. "So she's fun? You need fun. You're in desperate need of fun."

"What I need is to graduate, then pass the bar. Besides," I added in-between reps, "she's not interested in dating. She said she moved here to *work on herself*, which is code for, 'I'm a young, hot girl who doesn't want to hang out with a guy and his toddler.'" I pressed the ropes down, hard as I could, my muscles screaming. "She's going to go out. Party. Have dates. I don't have the time or funds for either one, never mind the mental energy to put toward a girlfriend."

"Hold the phone." Jackson's triumphant smile was blinding. "In all the *five years* I've known you, you have *never* used the word 'girlfriend' in my presence."

"Because I've never wanted one."

"*Wanted*? Past tense? But now you do?" Jackson said through the strain of bicep curls. "The plot thickens."

I rolled my eyes. "I don't have girlfriends and I'm not doing casual hookups around Livvie. And I can't ask Elena to babysit more than she does already so I can take someone out. I don't see Olivia enough as it is."

"That's noble, my friend. And stupid," Jackson said. "You need to blow off steam before you have a mental breakdown. Remember Frank? In our second year? All the guy did was study. Got busted snorting rails of coke between classes to stay awake."

"I'm not going to do drugs, for fuck's sake. I have a kid."

"Not saying you are, but the pressure of law school breaks people down. And you're buried."

"I've got it under control."

Jackson looked like he was going to pursue it, but he stared at me for a moment, then went back to his reps. "So what does this Darlene do?"

"She's a dancer."

"Ooh, so she's flexible. Bonus."

I shot him a dirty look. "The dancing's a side thing. She's a massage therapist."

Jackson dropped his arms and glared at me through the mirror.

I stared back. "What?"

"She's a *massage therapist*?"

"Yeah? So?"

"Jesus, man, have you lost your game entirely? Tell her you're stressed out—not a lie—and that she can practice on you. Do you need me to think of everything? Hell, if you won't date her, maybe I will."

The sudden rush of blood to my face shocked me, and the rope slipped out of my hands. The weights *clanged* on the rack.

"Wow, easy there, tiger," Jackson said. "I was kidding. Possessive, are we?"

"What? No...fuck, I'm just tired. I've got a few more weeks of law school, the bar, and in two months, I can petition to get my name on Olivia's birth certificate. Until then..." I shrugged and grabbed the ropes again.

"Nada," Jackson said. He heaved a sigh. "Okay, then. But don't blame me if your dick shrivels up and falls off from lack of use."

"I'll keep that in mind."

Jackson grinned. "How's everything else? How's your scholarship fund holding up?"

"It's going to run out just in time for my first clerkship paycheck to come in," I said. "Of course, I have to actually *get* the job."

"A minor detail," Jackson said. "And Olivia?"

"She's perfect."

"No sign of Molly?"

"No." I pressed down as hard as I could. My triceps burned. "How's the job at Nelson and Murdoch?" I asked before he could ask me anything else. "It's been two months. Have they made you partner yet?"

"It's only a matter of time," Jackson said, resuming his reps.

He'd been hired straight out of Hastings, before the notice came in the mail he'd passed the bar. I was only half-kidding about his new firm making him partner so fast; Jackson was a genius tax attorney, but I'd never say it out loud.

"But for real, tell me about your shot at the clerkship with Miller," Jackson said. "Has your competition cracked yet?"

"No, but I got this," I said after one last pull. I let the weights crash down and leaned against the machine, sipped from my water bottle. "We have a progress report this afternoon. Judge wants to make sure we're both on track for finals and the bar."

"Are you?"

I snorted. "Of course. I can see the damn finish line. The last thing I need is to get sidetracked by—"

"A beautiful massage therapist with dancer-flexibility who's great with your kid and lives ten feet away from you?" Jackson batted his eyes at me. "Solid plan, Haas."

I laughed despite myself. "Shut up, Smith, or I'll remind Hastings you haven't returned your gym card."

I showered, changed, and went to two classes—Advanced Legal Research and Analysis, and American Legal History, then took the Muni home. I'd enough time to grab a fast lunch, change into a suit and tie, say hi to Livvie at Elena's, then head to the Superior Courthouse for the progress meeting with Judge Miller.

I'd just opened the front door of the Victorian when I heard a commotion by Elena's place. She was coming out with her phone in one hand, Olivia cradled in her other arm, all the while gently guiding a sniffling Hector into the hallway. The little boy was holding his elbow and tears streaked his face. His little sister, Laura, followed behind looking nervous.

I rushed over and took Olivia out of Elena's arms. "What happened?"

"I was just going to call you on the way to the ER," Elena said with a sigh of relief. "I think Hector broke his elbow." She gave him a stern look overlaid with worry. "He jumped off the couch—again, though I told him a million times no—and landed funny."

"Oh damn." I knelt in front of Hector. "You okay, buddy?"

He sniffed and nodded, his little mouth stiff with repressed tears.

"Brave man." I ruffled his hair and straightened. "Let's go."

"No, no, we'll be fine. The Uber car is coming," Elena said, then put a hand to her mouth. "Oh, and you have your special meeting today…"

"Don't even think about it."

I walked them to the front door, and held it open for them so that Elena could help cradle Hector's arm as they walked. The car was already pulling up to the front of the house. I helped Hector into his seat and buckled him in while Elena took care of Laura.

"We're fine," Elena said from the backseat. "You stay. Maybe a friend can watch the baby?"

"I'll figure it out. Shoot me a text when you know he's okay."

"I will."

I stood on the sidewalk with Olivia patting the top of my head and giggling as they drove away.

The prospects of making my meeting vanished down the street along with that car, and I wondered if I'd blown my chance at the clerkship. Roger Harris, the other candidate was probably camped outside Judge Miller's chambers with a box of cigars at that moment, the little ass-kisser.

My mind scrolled through a mental rolodex of people I could call, last minute, but even if one were available, getting to me in time was impossible.

"Shit," I muttered.

"Shih," Olivia said.

"Is that Sesame Street's word of the day?" asked a voice behind me.

I turned and blinked. Darlene was practically glowing under the blazing afternoon sun in her white spa uniform.

"What happened?" she asked. "Where was Elena running off to?"

"Hector broke his elbow," I said.

Darlene put a hand over her mouth. "Oh, no, the poor little guy. I hope he's okay." She bent toward Olivia. "And what are you doing, sweet pea? Just hanging with Daddy?"

Olivia cooed laughter, and Darlene started to touch her hand but pulled it back and straightened quickly.

"Sorry," she said. "I know you'd prefer I...*not*. But I can't help it. She's too cute for words." She cocked her head at me. "Are you usually home this early?"

"No, I'm not," I said, carving a hand through my hair. "I came home to change for a meeting with Judge Miller. I'm a clerkship candidate. If I miss it, I could be sincerely screwed."

"Scrooo," Olivia said and kicked her foot for emphasis.

"And I've just taught my one-year-old daughter two curse words in the space of a minute."

Darlene laughed. "You won't miss your meeting. I got her." She gave me a look when I hesitated. "*Really?*"

"Darlene..."

"Look, I know the score, but you need help and I just happened to have a cancellation that brought me home early." She grinned. "I'll teach her the word 'babysitter', I promise."

I rubbed my chin. "Are you sure?"

"Of course. Happy to." Her eyebrows rose. "Are *you* sure?"

No, I was not sure. Not by any stretch. Darlene was a natural with Olivia—I didn't doubt her babysitting abilities. But already, I was having a hard time keeping my eyes off of her and my thoughts in line around her. It was only going to get worse the more we came in contact.

My inner alarms blared.

Judge Miller! Because of Darlene, you aren't going to miss this meeting after all. Do not fuck this up!

I shook my head. "Yeah, yes, of course. Thanks." A sigh of relief that began in my feet gusted out of me. "Yeah, thank you."

In the Victorian, Darlene ran up to her place to change out of her uniform, while I put Olivia in her playpen and threw on gray suit pants and white dress shirt. Darlene knocked, then peeked her head in while I was tying my tie in the living room mirror.

"You decent?"

"Yeah, come in." I glanced at her through the mirror, then quickly away.

Darlene had changed into leggings and an oversize white shirt that came down to mid-thigh. It wasn't anything fancy, but it draped over her lithe body, somehow highlighting her elegant lines and soft curves just as perfectly as if she were wearing skin-tight clothing.

You haven't been laid in ten months. She could be wearing a bag and you'd get hard.

I cleared my throat and sought sanctuary behind my desk. "So...emergency numbers are on the fridge," I said, pawing through papers and throwing those I needed into my briefcase. "But honestly, if anything happens, call 911 first, me second."

"Got it," she said. Olivia was squawking to be picked up. Darlene lifted her and set her on her hip. "Oh, but I don't have your phone number."

I scribbled my number on a piece of paper and moved to hand it to her. "Write yours down," I said, and shrugged into my suit coat I'd set out on the desk chair.

Darlene put pen to paper as Olivia played with her hair, then she frowned. "Wait. You can't take my number with you; I need to keep your number. Let me get my cell; I'll punch yours in."

"No need," I said. I picked up the paper and took a mental snapshot of Darlene's phone number, then handed it back. "Got it."

Darlene's smile was ridiculously beautiful. "Mega-mind strikes again."

I leaned in to kiss Olivia on the cheek, and caught a whiff of Darlene's perfume and the faint scent of massage oil.

"Call for any reason," I told her and hurried to the door. "I'll be back in an hour and a half. Two, tops."

"No problem," Darlene said. "We're good, aren't we, sweet pea? Say bye-bye to Daddy."

"Bye-bye, Daddy," Olivia said from where she was securely fastened to Darlene's slender hip, both of them smiling at me and waving.

My stupid perfect memory took a snapshot of that too.

chapter eight

Sawyer

My competition, Roger Harris, stood at attention outside the judge's office at the Superior Courthouse, looking impeccable and put-together while I flew in with sweat slipping between my shoulder blades and my tie flying over my shoulder. I'd made it with a minute to spare. Roger glanced at his watch and gave me a smug nod in greeting.

In his office, Judge Miller went over our Hastings curriculum progress, results from latest finals, and read the mock briefings he'd assigned us since the last meeting a month ago.

Judge Jared Miller was a kind man but he never gave compliments or reprimands; his poker face was legendary in and out of the courtroom. He nodded with equal fervor—hardly any—at both Roger's and my progress.

"Your final assignment before I make my decision," Judge Miller said, regarding us both. "Write a brief regarding a personal incident in your lives and how you would handle it as prosecutors. That's it. Until next month."

I blinked then eased a breath. I'd been expecting something difficult, but this was easy. I knew already what I'd write about and what I'd say.

My mother. I'll write about my mother.

"Mr. Haas, may I speak to you a moment?"

Roger's eyes flare in panic before he recovered himself. I returned his smug smile earlier with my own. "Of course, Your Honor."

Judge Miller sat behind his desk without his black robe looking less like an acclaimed federal judge and more like a grandfather. Framed photos of his family lined his desk and hung on the walls beside degrees and honors from various universities. An 8x10 of what looked to be a granddaughter the same age as Olivia, shared wall space with a certificate of appreciation from the San Francisco Police Officers Union. He'd removed his tie and loosened his collar, then sat back in his seat, regarding me.

"Your finals are in the next two weeks," he said.

"Yes, Your Honor."

"No real chance you won't pass with flying colors."

"I hope not, Your Honor."

"And you're registered for the bar in Sacramento next month."

I nodded. It had cost me a small fortune and I'd had to tutor other law students after Livvie had gone to bed for two weeks but I did it.

"All set."

He nodded. "I like you, Mr. Haas. I think you're a brilliant lawyer."

I fought to keep my face neutral. "Thank you, Your Honor."

He's made a decision. He's going to give it to me. Holy shit, all that work and struggle and long nights.

"On paper," he said.

My body stiffened. "Thank you." It almost came out sounding like a question.

"Your brief today was impeccable; not a precedent missed, every argument meticulously researched. It was better than Mr. Harris's in that regard. But do you know what his briefing had that yours lacked?"

"No, Your Honor."

"Life."

I frowned. "I don't understand…"

"You have a little girl, do you not?"

"Yes. Thirteen months old."

Judge Miller smiled and inclined his chin at the photo on the wall. "My granddaughter, Abigail, is about that age. She's a joy." His smile tightened. "I want to give you the clerkship, Mr. Haas, but if I had to choose today, I would pick Mr. Harris."

My galloping heart stopped and plummeted to my knees. I straightened my shoulders, determined to take this like a man, but my mouth had gone dry.

"I'm sorry, Your Honor," I managed. "I don't understand."

"As I said your brief was impeccable. Scholarly and purely academic. Which is understandable as you are an academic at this stage." He leaned his arms on his desk, fingers laced. "In the course of preparing this brief, did you consider *Johnson v. McKenzie?*"

I scanned my mental catalog and pulled up the case.

"That was…an appeal," I said, mentally reading. "The defendant's sentence was reduced due to good behavior and programs completed during prison time. I don't see how that's relevant…"

"It's relevant," Judge Miller said, "to a brief concerned with the overcrowding of prison populations. You argued, strongly I might add, for the strict use of mandatory sentencing and unequivocal upholding of the Three Strikes law."

"Yes, Your Honor," I said. "Those are the laws."

Judge Miller nodded. "Nowhere in your brief did you make any stipulation for the defendant's rehabilitation or his continued education in the prison system."

"I wasn't aware that you were asking for me to take a position on such things," I said. "I was merely providing the appropriate laws pertinent to the matter at hand."

"Yes, and you did it brilliantly. You *are* brilliant, Mr. Haas. I have no question or doubt that you would make an exceptional prosecutor. And to be perfectly frank, I'd rather *not* work with Mr. Harris." He pursed his lip. "He's a bit of a bore. But I'm concerned that you see only the law; the words on paper, and not the lives behind them."

I straightened to my full height. "I don't understand, Your Honor. The law is the law. Isn't our duty to uphold it as it is written?"

He held my gaze, lips pursed. "Why do you want to be a federal prosecutor?"

For my mother.

"Justice," I said. "The punishment should fit the crime, and the criminal *should* be punished."

"And leniency?"

"I…I don't know," I said. "I don't know that personal feelings should interfere with this kind of work."

Judge Miller sighed. "I've seen your type before. Full of piss and vinegar, as my father would've said. More concerned with being right than with being fair. You are not a coldhearted man. I can see that in you. But feelings, Mr. Haas, are what make us human. And humanity should be the beating heart of justice." He leaned back in his seat and reached for some papers on his desk. "That is all."

I left Judge Miller's chambers feeling as if I had just been sucker punched and then doused in ice water. I had no idea what he was asking of me. In the deep catalog of California law codes I had committed to memory, there wasn't one mention of emotions or feelings. That's why I liked law. It was black and white, right and wrong.

On the Muni home, I racked my brain for a way to give the Judge what he wanted.

Life.

But my mother was dead. Killed by a drunk driver when I was eight years old.

I gripped the Muni bar hard as the train screeched into a tunnel and the windows went black, as if it were taking me into the dark heart of my worst memories.

Blue and red flashing lights fill the foyer with garish color. Clown colors, from a nightmarish carnival. A knock at the door. I step into the hallway behind my dad. Emmett tugs on my pants. He's only four, but my little brother's smart. He knows something's very, very wrong, and he's scared.

Like me.

I'm so scared I can't breathe.

"Mr. Haas?"

My dad's head bobs. "Yes?"

"I'm very sorry but there's been an accident."

Dad staggers back a step then clutches the doorjamb. His knuckles are white. The red and blue lights spin around and around. Their sirens are off, but the sound is deafening. Screaming. Ripping the black of the night, tearing through my father and brother and me like a banshee; shrieking with sinister glee that nothing will ever be the same again.

The Muni train surged into daylight and I blinked the horrible reverie away. The memory retreated slowly, never far from sight and always crystal clear in my perfect memory.

The defendant—my mother's murderer—had been jailed for alcohol-related incidents twice before, and was driving with a suspended license. But it didn't matter. The judge used discretion. *Discretion.* I fucking hated that word. The driver was released and three weeks later, he killed my mother. He was sentenced to twenty-five years but what the fuck did that matter? He'd already put my mother to death and given my father, brother, and I life sentences.

And none of it needed to happen.

My hand on the Muni rail tightened again until my joints ached. The senselessness of it gnawed at my guts whenever I thought of it for too long. I turned my focus on what I could do as a prosecutor, instead. Sought sanctuary, as I always did, in the law.

But Miller's lecture in his office had me scared shitless. If I didn't give him what he wanted—life, in a briefing about senseless death—I'd lose everything.

I was still pondering these questions when I walked up to the Victorian. In my flat, Darlene was at the kitchen table, sitting next to Olivia in her high chair, feeding her a snack of cubed cheese and grapes that Darlene had cut in half.

"Hey," she said brightly. Her beautiful face like a ray of sun I basked in for a moment. "Elena came by. She said Hector did break a bone but it was a clean break, no surgery needed."

"Good, good," I said. "Glad to hear it."

"How was your meeting?"

Catastrophic.

"Fine."

I leaned over Olivia's high chair from behind. "Hey, baby. Having a snack?" I plucked a piece of Jack cheese from her tray and ate it.

"Cheece, cheece," she said, and I watched her tiny fingers pick up the white cube and bring it to her mouth.

I looked up to see Darlene watching me. She quickly averted her eyes.

"She's got a great vocab," she said, brushing a curl of Olivia's hair out of her eyes. "She's a smarty, aren't you, sweet pea?"

"Would you mind hanging out for one more minute?" I asked. "I want to change out of this suit."

"Knock yourself out."

In my bedroom, I changed into my evening uniform of flannel sleep pants and a white, V-neck undershirt. I grabbed my wallet from my suit on the bed, and pulled out a twenty dollar bill. In the kitchen, Darlene was wiping Olivia's face with a cloth, and saying something to make my daughter laugh.

Jackson's words from this morning came back to haunt me. Darlene was beautiful, fun, and great with Olivia.

Why not ask her out?

It seemed like such a simple thing, but I was on the verge of losing my clerkship. Aside from studying and classes, I was going to have to devote even more time to Judge Miller's final assignment to ensure I gave him what he wanted.

The tiredness fell over me like a heavy coat.

I have nothing to offer her.

Darlene removed the tray from Olivia's highchair, and set her down on the floor where my daughter made a bee-line for the wooden blocks scattered on the carpet by my desk.

"We were making towers," Darlene said. "I'll clean those up."

"No, it's fine. Here." I held out the twenty. "I don't know what your going rate is but…"

She was already shaking her head. "Nope. I owe you from the other night. I was so pushy, and I still feel bad about it."

"What? No. Take it."

Darlene ignored my money and knelt beside Olivia. "Bye-bye, sweet pea."

"Bye-bye," Olivia said. She stacked a wooden block with letters on each side on top of another that was covered in numbers.

"So smart, this girl." Darlene popped back up with a breathy exhilaration. Her eyes were impossibly blue. "I should go."

"Darlene…"

Her phone chimed a text. She fished it out of her bag. "Oh, that's Max. He's a friend. I told him I'd meet him later, so yeah." She shouldered her bag and headed for the door.

Max. Okay.

I followed Darlene to the door to open it.

Max is the guy who's going to ask her out if he hasn't already because you won't.

"Such a gentleman," Darlene said as I held the door for her.

"You should take the money," I said stiffly. Almost harshly. "You saved my ass today so…"

I held out the cash again but Darlene pushed my hand away and held on for a moment. Her fingers were soft and warm on mine.

"Your money's no good here. We're even."

A short silence fell, and my mind—so full of every goddamn thing I'd ever seen and read—had no words.

"Goodbye, Sawyer the Lawyer."

She let go of my hand, her smile softer now, and turned to go. Half a second later, she stopped and spun back around.

"I changed my mind. I know how you can pay me for today."

A small laugh erupted out of me, despite myself. *God, this girl.*

"How?"

"Last Friday, at the grocery store? You said that I was a…" She held her hands out.

I blinked. "A what?"

"That's just it. I don't know. You never finished your sentence."

I thought back to that night, that moment. "Oh, yeah."

"You remember, right? Your mega-mind has it?"

"Yeah, I have it but I'm not sure you want to hear it."

"Try me."

"Well, I was going to say you're like a human tornado."

"Oh," Darlene said. Her face fell, the light in her eyes dimmed slightly. "I'm like a twisty windstorm that destroys everything I touch?"

"No, not at all." I rubbed the back of my neck. "I didn't say it then because I thought you'd take it as an insult. And saying it now, it *sounds* like an insult. But it's actually—"

"A compliment?"

Her light was back and she was standing so close to me.

"Yes. I meant, you're like this whirling ball of energy that sweeps people up so they…can't help getting caught up in you."

"Oh," she breathed. "They can't?"

I can't.

I was leaning over her, my shoulder against the doorjamb, and she was right there, her breath on my chin and her eyes so blue with light and life.

Darlene is full of the life Judge Miller wants. I'm the machine that has to keep going and going until there's nothing left of me.

I straightened and smiled faintly. "Thanks for taking good care of Olivia, Darlene."

Darlene's smile was brilliant and her words, seemingly innocuous, hit me right in the chest and sank in.

"Thank you, Sawyer, for the lovely compliment."

chapter nine

Darlene

I WENT BACK TO MY LITTLE PLACE WITH A SMILE ON MY FACE THAT MADE MY CHEEKS hurt, and a warmth in my chest that wouldn't quit. Max's text said he wanted to grab dinner before the NA meeting tonight, so I jumped in the shower. After, I did my makeup in the mirror.

Can't help getting caught up in you.

My cheeks turned pink without blush, and my eyes looked bluer than I'd ever seen them.

I pointed my mascara wand at my reflection. "Stop right there. You are doing great at this responsibility stuff. Don't mess it up now."

But visions of Sawyer Haas looking devastatingly handsome in his suit, tangled with those of him looking deliciously sexy in his pajamas. And his compliment, like a song stuck in my head, played over and over, except I didn't want it to stop.

It was only going to get harder to mind my own business, I thought, as I put on my usual smoky eyeshadow. My attraction to Sawyer was bad enough, but his little girl was an angel too. Watching her smile and hearing her talk or build block towers or even eat her 'cheece' were like special little gifts, the kind of mini-joys you never knew you wanted in your life until you had them.

My reflection's smile slipped.

Back off, girl. He's got too much going on and you...

"I'm working on me."

Another tiny thought whispered that maybe part of who I was here in SF might have something to do with Sawyer and Olivia, but I bottled it up quick.

I grabbed my old gray sweater and headed out.

◦◦◦

Mel's Drive-In on Geary Blvd was a hopping, 1950's style hamburger joint that pleasantly assaulted the senses with its red and white décor, chrome details, and posters of the movie *American Graffiti* on every wall. The air smelt of French fries and milkshakes. On the jukebox, Chuck Berry sang about a country boy named Johnny B. Goode.

"I'm in love already," I said, plopping down across from Max in a red-upholstered booth.

"With Sawyer the Lawyer?"

The question shocked me so much I nearly knocked my silverware into my lap.

"What? *No*. With this diner! It's super cute." I shot Max a dirty look. "Why on earth was that your first thought?"

Max held up his hands. He looked like he'd stepped out of one of the *American Graffiti* posters himself, with his gelled hair and black leather jacket. "You wear your heart on your sleeve, Dar," he said with a grin. "I took a shot."

I wrinkled my nose at him. "Well, I'm not. I've been in love hundreds of times. I know what it feels like. It's not like that with Sawyer. It's…not the same."

Max raised his eyebrows.

"Never mind." I flapped my hands at him. "There is no 'with Sawyer' anyway. I babysat for him earlier today, and left his place without making a fool of myself." I held up my hands. "And here I am."

"Here you are, looking radiant," Max said, a dry grin on his lips. "Hence, my supposition that it was Mr. 'the Lawyer' who was responsible."

I rolled my eyes. "Oh, stop. I met the guy a few days ago. Even I don't fall that fast."

"Right. You need a week, minimum."

I chucked a sugar packet at him, as a waitress wearing a 50's uniform with a cap on her head appeared. Her nametag read *Betty*.

Betty put a pen to her pad. "You ready, hon?"

"I'll have a jack cheeseburger—extra pickles—fries, and a Coke with three cherries in it," I said, and gave Max a scolding look. "And bring him something to put in his mouth before I get mad."

Max laughed, and ordered a bacon cheeseburger, fries and a root beer.

"I thought you were all for me *not* getting involved with someone," I said when Betty had gone.

"I don't know," Max said with a wistful smile. "I have my own good days and bad. Today wasn't great. Your happiness seems more like something to boost up instead of tear down with a bunch of warnings."

My heart ached a little, and I reached my hand across the table to hold his. "What happened?"

"Nah, it's nothing," Max said, smiling thinly. "I'm the sponsor. I'm supposed to have my shit together."

"The meeting's not until nine," I said. "You're not on the clock yet."

"I'm always on the clock."

"I just smashed the clock."

He chuckled, then heaved a sigh and sat back in the booth. I put my hand in my lap and listened.

"My parents caught me with a guy when I was sixteen. So nine years ago. They didn't take it well, especially considering they hadn't known I was gay.

They disowned me, kicked me out." He shook his head, his brown eyes heavy. "God, my life is such a cliché."

"It's not," I said. "It's what happened to you. Go on."

Max toyed with his fork and waited while Betty set down our drinks and hurried off again.

"I'd met this guy. Travis. He was a little bit older than me, in college at the University of Washington."

"Seattle?" I asked. I popped a cherry into my mouth. "Is that where you're from?"

Max nodded. "Travis was a good guy, too. He was good to *me*. Never tried anything; was willing to wait until I got older. We were both new to actually living as ourselves. We weren't in a hurry to experience everything all at once. We just wanted to be together."

"What happened?" I asked softly.

"My parents freaked out. They told Travis if he came near me they'd have him arrested for statutory rape, even though we hadn't come close to actual sex. But it scared him. His first relationship with a guy and he's being threatened with jail. He broke it off with me and I was devastated."

Max wrenched himself from his story to look at me.

"I don't know if I should be telling you this."

"Why not?" I asked. "We're friends, aren't we?"

His smile flickered over his lips. "Yeah, we are." He took a sip of root beer, wiped his mouth on a napkin. "Not much left to tell, actually. My parents' concern about me being 'violated' by Travis was utter bullshit. They just wanted to punish him. And me." He managed a grin. "My parents were trapped in another era. *This* era," he said, indicating the restaurant. "You walked into their bedroom half-expecting to find twin beds, instead of one."

I smiled for him, while inside I braced myself for something terrible.

"They forced me to break up with Travis, and then kicked me out of the house anyway."

My eyes widened. "You were sixteen?"

He nodded. "I had no job, no place to live and a shit-ton of anger." He lowered his voice, toyed with his straw. "I hooked up with some other homeless guys and they got me into selling drugs. Selling quickly became doing. I felt like I was carving up my soul into little pieces. I got caught a bunch of times, went to juvie a bunch of times, ran away from any foster home they tried to stick me in. It's so movie-of-the-week."

"How did you survive?"

"I don't know, to be honest. I hitchhiked down here and fell in with a new set of bad guys. They sold more than drugs and convinced me I could make a lot of money if I did the same."

"You mean... prostitution?"

He nodded. "That's drugs for you. They make you think fucking terrible ideas are really good ideas."

"Or even better, not think at all."

Max lifted his soda in mock toast. "Anyway, I was seventeen, and got busted one night. The cop was a good guy. Instead of taking me to the station, he took me home, let me crash on his couch. I thought he was a perv with ulterior motives but I was too high to care."

"But he wasn't a perv," I said.

"No. He got me cleaned up, got me in the program, helped me get my GED, then nursing school after that. All of it. I'd be dead without him." He shook his head, his blue eyes cloudy with heavy storms of memory. "It's funny how someone can be a better dad to you than the one who shares your blood."

"Where is he now?" I asked.

"He died a couple years back," Max said. "Myocardial infarction."

"A what?"

"Heart attack." He smiled a little. "Sorry, I take refuge in medical terminology. Easier to take sometimes."

"I'm so sorry. But I'll bet he was really proud of you," I said with a gentle smile. "Is that why the shitty day? Were you missing him?"

Max shrugged. "No, no reason. It just happens sometimes, doesn't it? Like the weight of your personal pain is hiding in your psyche, and something will trigger it to jump with claws out."

"What triggered yours?"

"A lamppost," Max said with a rueful smile. "This morning on the way to work, my bus broke down. I got off to walk the rest of the way and took a street I hadn't been on in a long time. And there's a lamppost there, papered up in flyers and graffiti. When I first came to SF, that was the street where I sold myself for the first time. That night was black, except for under that light, and I held on to that lamppost so tight. I can still feel the rough cement under my palm. The first car pulled up. The window rolled down, and I remembered thinking, *Don't let go of this lamppost. If you hold on, you'll be safe.*"

I nodded, a lump thick in my throat. "I know how that feels."

"But I let go and I got in the car," Max said. He twisted his soda around and around, leaving wet rings on the table. "This morning, I saw that lamppost and the rest of my day's been half here, half in the past." He smiled faintly. "Seeing you so happy did not suck."

I tucked a lock of hair behind my ear. "I planned it that way."

Max chuckled and the sadness hanging over him lifted. By the time we'd finished our food, it had dissipated completely, and he was laughing again.

After dinner, we headed out to catch a cab for the Y, arm in arm. On Geary, near the diner, was an AMC movie theater. I sighed loudly.

Max looked down at me, in full sponsor mode again. "What's that for?"

I nodded my chin at the theater. "Don't you wish we could blow the meeting and go see a flick? Eat popcorn and forget everything for a little while?"

"Of course," Max said. "But forgetting is the first step down the road toward relapse. You lull yourself into thinking the pain of addiction is asleep forever, then something wakes it up and you're fucked."

"I don't get it," I said as a cab pulled up. "Isn't forgetting a good thing? Like, why do I want to relive the shitty past, instead of all the good stuff now?"

"Forgetting is pretending it never happened," Max said. "You need to remember and remember and remember, until it has no power over you anymore. Someday, I'm going to walk up to that lamppost and all of the memories will still be there, but they'll be a part of who I am. Instead of having a shitty day, I'll smile and think of how it was a piece of my past, but not the sum of it."

We climbed into the cab and on the entire ride to the YMCA, I tried to imagine my overdose at the New Year's party as something I would ever smile about. Or how I'd tell someone—*Sawyer*, my heart whispered—what I was, and it wouldn't make me feel like curling up and dying inside for shame.

Impossible.

At the Y, we headed up the lamp-lit stairs with a thin crowd of people. I hunched deeper into my sweater and my hand curled around the dance troupe's phone number in the pocket. Calling it sort of felt impossible, too.

Inside, the meeting began, and I chose not to share that night. My brain was too full of thoughts and words and feelings; Max's story and Sawyer's compliment for me, all tangled together.

Afterward, Max and I walked out into a warmer-than-usual San Francisco night.

"You didn't talk tonight," he said.

I shrugged. "Didn't feel like it."

Silence.

I sighed. "I'm doing really good, Max. Working, paying rent…"

"Are you dancing?"

"I'm still…limbering up."

Max glanced down at me. "Lonely?"

I bit my lip. "Maybe. A little. But I sometimes wonder if that's my default setting."

He nodded, a soft smile on his lips. "The loneliness of the recovering addict. I get it. I have it too." He jerked his thumb to the Y behind us. "You should talk about it in group."

"I want to talk about it with you."

"I'm here."

I heaved a breath. "I used to think I was needy or clingy, the way I stuck like glue to the men in my life. But I just want to love someone. It's so simple and yet feels so impossible at the same time. And yes, I know, I'm supposed to be focusing on me, but isn't that the whole point of working on myself? To become worthy of love?"

"Everyone is worthy of love," Max said. "But it starts with loving yourself first. That sounds like cheesy, clichéd shit, but it's true. You have to know you can be good for someone else. Not just to fill up that hole in yourself, but to give."

"I know, but it seems like, in the past, I've done all the giving. I'm the one who holds on and they don't."

"Are you holding on because you love them, or holding on because the alternative is being alone?"

I frowned, opened my mouth to speak, then shut it again. Finally, I huffed a sigh. "You're wise in the way of life, O Max."

"I know," he said, puffing his chest out. "That's why I'm the sponsor."

I laughed and tucked my arm in his as he walked me to my bus stop.

"Have you told him?" Max asked after a minute.

"Told who, what?"

Max gave me a look. "Have you told *your neighbor* where you are tonight? Where you're court-ordered to go three times a week?"

"No," I said. "Why would I?"

"Are you ashamed? I know it's hard, but don't be. Or don't let it rule you, it'll just cause more problems in the end."

But if I never tell, there will be no end. Only beginnings.

Max gave my arm a squeeze.

"We're all made up of strengths and weaknesses, every one of us. You have strengths. Plenty. Getting clean is a strength. Picking yourself back up again after you fall, that's a strength."

"I don't feel strong. Not yet. I feel like…"

"What?"

I sniffed and wiped my eyes with my sleeve. For some stupid, unknowable reason I was on the verge of tears. "He'll hate me, Max."

"I'm more concerned about *you* hating you."

"I don't…"

"Addicts lie, Dar," Max said gently. "That's one of our defining characteristics. You'll always be an addict. You'll always fight that battle. But fight it with your best, most honest self, if you want a chance to win." His smile was sad and knowing at the same time. "It's too easy to slip if you don't."

☙

At the Victorian, I crept up the stairs past Sawyer's place like a burglar, sure that his door would swing open and he'd loudly demand where I'd been, or that he'd see right through me without having to ask. The evidence was all over me, inside me, and coming out through my pores—the scent of cheap YMCA coffee and shame.

I flinched and hurried into my studio.

Inside, I dumped my bag on the floor, and stretched out on my tiny couch under the window. It was a loveseat, hardly big enough for two; beige with reddish swirls of flowers. Gerber daisies—my favorite—and roses.

Outside the window, the night sky deepened. San Francisco was a quieter city than New York, and the silence felt thick and stifling, like a blanket on a hot night. I felt restless.

I had to keep myself busy. I jumped off the couch to make chocolate chip cookies for Hector. While I stirred the batter, everything Max and I had talked about floated in and out of my thoughts. All of his warnings and advice sounded so wonderful and smart and helpful, but as if they were meant for someone else. Someone far worse off than me. Things were fine as they were without anyone here knowing, especially Sawyer. He might need me again, for Livvie, and hell would freeze up before I *ever* brought anything bad near that little angel, so why worry him?

A twinge of something unpleasant settled in my stomach. The same uneasy feeling I'd had as a kid, where I'd done something wrong and it was only a matter of time until I got caught.

I put the cookies in the oven and let the door slam shut.

"It was too damn hot in here, that's all," I muttered. I started to take off my sweater and my hand found the phone number in my pocket again. I sat up and contemplated the ten digits.

Actions, not words.

I picked up my phone, then hesitated at the time. Ten-thirty on a weeknight. But I'd already wasted four days.

"They probably already found someone," I said as I punched in the numbers.

"Hello?" a man's voice answered.

"Yeah, hi, sorry it's so late. I'm calling about your dance troupe?" I twirled a lock of hair around my finger. "I was wondering if you still needed someone?"

"*Yes*," the guy said, then lowered his voice. "Yes, we are still auditioning dancers. Are you available tomorrow?"

I pulled my sweater sleeve over my hand and bit the cuff.

This is really happening, if you have the guts.

I squeezed my eyes shut.

"Yeah, I am."

chapter ten

Darlene

In the break room at Serenity Spa the next day, I changed out of my uniform and slipped a black leotard and spandex dance shorts on under my sundress. My stomach was twisted in knots and my arms felt heavy from the day's massages.

This is stupid, I thought for the hundredth time as I left the spa. I was ridiculously unprepared for this dance audition, and certain to fail.

Is that why you agreed to audition in the first place? A voice in my head sounding suspiciously like Max wondered. *So you can say you tried without really trying?*

"Oh, hush," I murmured, and gnawed on the cuff of my sweater the entire bus ride to the studio.

I arrived at the San Francisco Dance Academy with thirty minutes to spare. The woman at the front desk told me a space had been reserved for the audition but was open now if I wanted it. I paid $15 to jump in early and warm up.

The dance room had a mirror covering one entire wall, with a barre running along its length. Golden sunlight streamed in from the high windows, and spilled across the wooden floors. A sound system with a tangle of cords sat against the wall under the windows beside a couple of simple wooden chairs and a few wooden rifles. I picked up a rifle and gave it a spin. Maybe someone was rehearsing the finale to *Chicago,* one of my favorite musicals.

If I let myself envision my perfect show, it was *Chicago.* I wasn't the strongest singer, but I could hold a key. I wanted to play Liz, the inmate who killed her husband because he wouldn't stop popping his gum. "The Cell Block Tango" was my dream performance, but instead of preparing and training for a major role, I was winging an audition for a tiny, independent dance troupe that advertised on a lamppost.

You aren't even prepared to dance for a tiny, independent dance troupe that advertises on a lamppost.

"Stupid." I put the prop down and sat on the floor.

My eyes kept glancing at the door as I stretched. Any second now, it would open. The director I'd spoken to on the phone would walk in and I'd make a ginormous fool of myself. But I kept stretching and breathing, waking my body from its hibernation. I wanted to get up and run, but at four-fifteen, the door opened and I was still there.

Greg Spanos was a tall, dark-haired guy; early thirties, dressed all in black.

He was followed by an artsy-looking gal in glasses and streaks of blue in her hair.

"I'm the director and choreographer of *Iris and Ivy*," he said, shaking my hand. "This is Paula Lee, the stage manager."

"Hi," I said with breathy nervousness. "Hi. Nice to meet you. I'm Darlene."

I watched them size me up, certain that the fact I was utterly unprepared was written all over my face.

"A moment, please," Greg said.

He and Paula carried two chairs from the side of the room, and set them up on one end, their backs to the wall mirror. With no table, they rested their folders on their laps and endeavored to look professional.

"Whenever you're ready."

At the sound system against the wall, I plugged my phone in and hurried back to the middle of the room. I'd barely taken my position on the floor—lying on my back as I had in New York—when the music started.

"The music is the language and your body speaks the words."

My first dance teacher told me that when I was eight years old, scowling in a pink tutu. I hated the tutu and the ballet flats on my feet. I wanted to be barefoot and raw. Even then, the *something* inside me that wanted to dance was a fierce energy that I loved to feed. I'd given it everything—my sweat and tears; aching muscles and sprained ligaments. It was there, that urge to sing for the world with my entire self.

Until I'd ruined it with drugs. Dirtied it. Soiled myself so that dancing while the X or the coke surged through my veins felt like a violation of that pure energy.

But I'm here now.

I closed my eyes and let the first notes of the music seep into my bones and muscles and sinew; I listened with my body. When Marian Hill sang the first lines, my back arched up off the wooden floor, and then I was gone; lifted up by the soft words and gentle piano, then sparking to life when the techno beat dropped.

I forgot everything else and lived between each note, moment to moment, feeling everything I wanted to feel without thinking or stopping myself. I let my body speak for the music and there was no shame, in these words. No loneliness.

Only myself, and I was alive.

I collapsed to my knees, arched back, and lifted one arm—grasping at air—as the last note on the last word faded away to silence.

One heartbeat. Two.

I looked through a few tendrils of hair that had come loose from my ponytail. Greg and Paula were staring at me, then bent their heads to confer. A bead of sweat slipped down my temple, and I realized the twisting feeling in my stomach was gone. My pulse pounded from the dance, not nerves, and I suddenly didn't care if they wanted me or not.

But they did.

"You have..." Greg exchanged a look with Paula, "quite a lot of natural talent."

"Pure, raw talent," Paula said, nodding.

"Thank you," I said, breathlessly. "Thanks so much for saying so."

Somehow, I wasn't crying.

"Have you, auditioned anywhere else?" Greg asked slowly.

"I just moved here last week," I said. "I saw your flyer and took a shot."

They exchanged knowing looks again, laced with relief.

"Opening night is closing in," Paula said "We'd prefer not to have to recast so late in the game. We need full commitment to rehearsal, which is every night, six to nine p.m. and some afternoons on the weekend."

I bobbed my head. "Of course, absolutely. But I'll have to cut out early Monday, Wednesday, and Friday. There's a place I have to be at nine. But it's not far from here. Fifteen minutes?"

"I suppose," Greg said. "If it can't be avoided."

"It can't," I said.

"Fine," he said. "There's no pay," he added stiffly. "This is a labor of love. An independent piece of art, not a commercialized package of glitz and sequins."

"It's raw," Paula said. I guessed she must like using that word. "Stripped down and real. No pretense."

"Sounds great, really," I said. "Perfect."

"Good," Greg said, offering his hand. "Welcome to the show, Darlene."

Outside on the street, I sucked in air. "Holy shit."

It had been almost four years since I'd danced in front of an audience. Four years. I tried to tell myself it wasn't a big deal; *Iris and Ivy* was a far cry from a big dance company. But it was a huge fucking deal. I'd begun to wonder if the dancer version of myself was gone forever, still locked up behind bars even after the drug-addict had been released.

But it's still there. Me. I'm still here.

I dug my phone out of my purse and stared at it, my thumb hovering over the contacts. I called up my parents at their house in Queens. The answering machine picked up but I didn't leave a message. I needed voices. A live person. I scrolled down to my sister.

She picked up on the sixth ring, sounding harried and distracted with just one, "Hello?"

"Hey, Carla, it's Dar."

"Oh hey, hon. How are you? How's Frisco treating you?"

"It's going great here. In fact, I have the best news—"

"Are you keeping your nose clean? Staying out of trouble?"

I winced. "Yes. I'm doing really great, actually. I auditioned for a dance company—a little one—and you'll never believe it, but they hired me. There's going to be a show in a few weeks—"

Carla's voice became muffled. "Sammy! Sammy, get off the couch!" She turned her mouth back to the phone. "That dumb dog, I swear…" Her breath hissed a sigh. "Sorry, what? A show? Good for you. Are they paying you?"

I hunched my shoulders, as if I could contain the excitement that was fast draining out of me. "I'm not doing it for the pay. It's mostly for the experience. It's been four years—"

"Uh huh. Well, just don't go and do something crazy and quit your spa job over it."

I frowned. "No, no, of course not."

"Good, because you know how these things go."

I slumped against the wall. "How do these things go, Carla?"

"Sammy! I swear to God…" She huffed a sigh. "Sorry, what?"

"Nothing. So I called Mom and Dad but no answer."

"It's Bridge night. They're at the Antolini's."

"Oh yeah. Bridge night. I forgot."

"So listen, hon. I've got a roast in the oven for tomorrow. The cousins are coming over for Aunt Lois' birthday and I've got a million things left to do."

"Oh, okay. That sounds fun."

I imagined my sister's house bustling with my loud family; kids bumping into adult legs as they chased each other around the living room, while Grandma Bea screeched at them to stop "rough-housing like monkeys at the zoo."

I smiled against the phone. "I wish I could be there."

"Listen, you got a good thing going with that spa job. Keep it up. I'll talk to you soon, yeah?"

"Yeah, sure," I said. "Bye, Carla. Love you."

"Love you too, hon."

The phone went quiet.

My thumb hovered over Beckett's number but I didn't feel like talking on the phone anymore. I thought about shooting Max a text to ask him to meet me somewhere, but he was working a double shift at UCSF Medical Center and wouldn't be home until dawn. People passed me on the street and I had a crazy urge to reach out and grab one by the sleeve and tell them I was going to dance again.

The faces were all strangers.

I went home.

At the Victorian, Elena's place was bustling with muffled talk and laughter. It was six o'clock; they were probably getting ready to sit down to dinner. On the second floor, Sawyer's place was quiet. He was probably heating up some crappy food for himself while taking care to make sure Olivia ate the good stuff.

In my place, the silence was stifling.

I threw open the window in the living area but the neighborhood was quiet too; sleepy under the falling twilight. I tried the TV, but it was too loud, talking at me. I shut it off and contemplated the rest of my night. Hours stretched before me.

I had the makings of another tuna casserole in my cabinets and fridge; the only thing I could cook.

My stomach voiced its approval of the plan but a terrible claustrophobia was sneaking up on me, sucking the air out of the room. I needed someone. People. A face and a voice and a kind smile when I shared my news.

I stripped out of my dress and took a shower, keeping the water lukewarm.

As the water fell over me, I replayed my conversation with Carla. I didn't expect my sister to go into hysterics of joy at my news. But in the eyes of those who knew my past, my accomplishments were always going to be tempered by how close I might be to fucking them all up.

The loneliness of an addict, Max had said.

I stepped out of the shower with my heart beating like a heavy metronome in my chest, counting out the seconds. The exhilaration of my dance morphed into fear. The kind that whispered that I wasn't good enough to dance anyway, and how much easier would it be to lose myself for a few hours in manufactured happiness? Wouldn't it be better to feel pretend-good than to feel like this?

"No." My voice was like a croak.

Wrapped in my towel, I went to the living area and grabbed my phone. I opened my music and hit shuffle. LP's "Tightrope" came on, like some sort of gift.

I stood in the middle of my little studio, listening to her achingly beautiful voice that said, with every soaring syllable, that she knew exactly what longing was.

Just look out into forever.

My hands balled into fists and tears stung my eyes.

Don't look down, not ever.

"Don't look down," I said. "Just keep going."

I sucked in deep breaths. My hands unclenched.

And when the song ended, I put on some clothes and went into the kitchen to make a tuna casserole.

chapter eleven

Sawyer

I SET DOWN MY PEN AND BENT MY FINGERS BACK TO STRETCH THE STIFFNESS OUT OF them. My latest notebook was nearly full, every page covered in my 'translations' of California Family Law code. I felt pretty confident about the final next week. Not so confident about Judge Miller's latest assignment.

Beside me, my trashcan was brimming with snowballs of paper. Rough drafts of the brief I'd started and stopped a dozen times when the pain threatened to bubble up and spill out onto the page. He wanted life and I saw only death.

Red and blue flashing lights colored my memory and I blinked them away.

I stretched and rubbed my aching neck. The clock read eleven-thirty. Above me, a floorboard creaked.

Darlene.

I wondered what she was doing tonight. Earlier, I'd heard the faint sounds of a song she was listening to. Did she dance to it? Was she wearing that tight black dance top with the crisscrossing straps? The top that accentuated the lean muscle of her arms and shoulders in the back, and highlighted the small perfection of her breasts in the front. Was she smiling that smile of hers that made it seem like nothing in the entire fucking world could possibly be bad?

You're getting loopy. Time to call it.

I started to pack up my materials into my briefcase. A soft knock came at the door.

I opened it to Darlene.

She wasn't wearing that dance top, but a peach-colored sundress, no shoes. The dress skimmed her breasts and flared out at her narrow waist. Her hair fell over shoulders, dark with dampness from a recent shower. Oven mitts covered her hands to protect them from the glass pan she held. The delicious scent of tuna casserole wafted up from underneath the tinfoil. It smelled warm and good in a way my TV dinners never did.

"I know it's late, but I took a chance that you were up," she said. "I made another casserole. Mostly because it's the only thing I know how to make. And to keep myself out of trouble."

She seemed on the verge of tears for a second, but blinked them away to smile brightly. "Anyway this is for you. Can I just drop it off? Then I'll go."

"Uh, sure," I said, opening the door for her. "Thanks."

"I don't want it to go to waste." She breezed past me and set it on the kitchen counter. "You can return the pan whenever."

"Are you okay?" I asked.

"Sure. Great. I don't want to bother you. I should go back…" She headed for the door, head down and her voice thick. "Livvie's asleep? Of course, it's late…"

"Darlene, what's wrong?"

"It's nothing. Stupid, really." At my door, she took off the oven mitts and tucked them under her arm. "I just had some kind of good news today and I wanted to tell somebody. At 11:30 at night," she said with a small laugh. "Sorry, never mind. I don't want to bother you."

She turned to leave and I knew I'd never sleep that night if I let her.

"Don't go," I said. "I could really use some good news right about now."

"Oh, did you have a bad day?" Darlene said softly. Her beautiful face that had been wrought with inward pain, instantly opened with outward concern. For me. "You can talk about it. If you want."

Talk to her. Such a simple concept, but I didn't do this. I didn't let women into my place. I didn't talk about my day. Except with Olivia, I was on auto-pilot, slogging through the hours to get to the finish line. But Darlene kept slipping in and I couldn't keep her out.

Maybe I don't want to keep her out.

I cleared my throat. "You were going to tell me *your* good news."

She put one bare foot on top of the other, her smile tentative. With her face scrubbed free of makeup, she was impossibly beautiful. I crossed my arms over my chest, a flimsy shield against her.

"It's so weird, but I feel like I need to tell someone or I'll burst or cry, or I don't know what."

"Tell me."

"Okay, well…" She heaved a breath. "I auditioned for this little dance company earlier today and they gave me a small part. It's the first time I've danced in a while so it's kind of a big deal to me. And my place is so quiet…" She tucked a lock of hair behind her ear. "My friends and family are all asleep on the East Coast now. I called my sister earlier but it's not the same thing, talking on the phone. Silly, I know."

"It's not," I said, moving to the kitchen, grateful for an excuse to put some space between us. For a second, she looked so small and vulnerable, my arms wanted to go around her. "That's awesome. We need a celebratory piece of tuna casserole."

I pulled two plates from the cabinet, and two forks, and a serving spoon I'd never used, from a drawer.

"I don't want to keep you up."

I turned with a small smile. "But I'm already up."

"Thank you," Darlene said softly. She joined me at the kitchen table. "I'm not used to living alone. The quiet gets to me and I'm not a fan of TV."

I cut two squares of the casserole, and ladled one onto her plate, one onto mine. I took a bite.

"Holy shit, this is better than the first one."

"Yeah?" Darlene's smile brightened. Her light was always on but now her internal dimmer switch was turned up higher.

"I put peas in it. I thought you might want to give Livvie some tomorrow." She took a taste. "Not bad, eh?"

"Not bad at all." I watched her mouth as the tip of her tongue touched her lower lip. "It's fucking perfect."

She raised her eyes to meet mine. I went back to my food.

"So, what's the show?" I asked. "Anything I would've heard of?"

"God, no," she said. "It's a tiny little dance troupe doing a revue. Independent. But even so, it's the first time I've danced in about four years."

"Really? Why the long break?"

She shifted in her seat and poked her food with the fork. "I got distracted by… other things. And it's really easy to let something go if you don't let yourself *be* that something. Do you know what I mean?"

I did, but I shook my head no. I wanted to hear Darlene talk. Now that she was here, I realized my place had been damn quiet too.

"I always danced but I didn't call myself a *dancer*," Darlene said. "I still don't. I feel like I haven't earned the title, but maybe this little show is a good step towards something bigger."

"I think it's fucking awesome that you took a shot and it paid off," I said.

Darlene looked at me through lowered lashes. "You do?"

"Yeah. You put yourself out there. You faced rejection."

The bitterness of my meeting with Judge Miller crept into my voice. I could hear it and Darlene did too.

"Did something happen today?" she asked.

"Nah, nothing," I said. "We don't need to talk about it."

"We don't *need* to, but you can if you want. I'm here."

You sure as hell are.

I shifted in my chair. Talking about myself was like trying to get a rusted engine to turn over.

"I'm trying to win a clerkship with a federal judge after I graduate. It's between me and another guy, and I'm just stressed out that the judge is going to choose my competition. If he does, I'm fucked. And on that note…" I went to the fridge. "I need a beer. You want one?"

"No, thanks," she said. "What's a clerkship?"

"It's a job in which you act as a sort of assistant to a judge." I popped the cap off an IPA and rejoined her at the table. "A Clerk of the Court advises them on codes and precedents and procedures during a trial."

I took a pull off my beer. The cold ale went beautifully with Darlene's casserole.

"Sounds like an important job," Darlene said.

"It's a vital stepping-stone on a path to a career as a federal prosecutor. To have a clerkship on your résumé, especially for a judge like Miller, is a big deal." I took my last bite of casserole and pushed the plate away. "Moreover, I need the salary. I'm on a scholarship that's going to run out right about the same minute I'm handed my law degree. If I don't have this job waiting for me, I'll have to find something else."

"So what makes you think you're not going to get this job?" Darlene asked. "Doesn't this judge know about your mega-mind?"

"Maybe. But the competition isn't just about academics."

"No? Is there a talent portion, too?" Darlene speared the last pea on her plate with a grin. "Does your opponent look better in a bathing suit?"

My thin smile morphed into a full-blown laugh. "Probably."

"I find that impossible to believe," she said. Darlene's cheeks turned pink and her eyes widened. "Why yes, I did say that out loud…"

She shook her head at herself. The nervous sadness was gone from her now that she'd shared her news

I did that. I made her happy.

I took another sip of cold beer. A long one.

"But for real," Darlene said, "why on earth wouldn't he pick you?"

"He's eccentric," I said. "Hard to know how to please him sometimes."

I took another sip of beer to wash the lie from my tongue. But talking about Miller's assignment would lead to talk of my mother, and that wasn't going to happen.

A short silence fell that lasted as long as Darlene could tolerate—all of three seconds.

"So Elena says you're about ready to graduate."

"Yeah, I have finals over the next two weeks, then the bar exam. I think I'm good with the finals, but the bar," I shook my head. "The pass rate is only 33% right now, which is pretty fucking scary."

"What does that mean?"

"Only 33% of everyone taking the test will pass. The state puts a cap on how many lawyers will get a license per year. The cut score is 1440 out of 2000, which is insanely high. So I could answer all the multiple choice questions correctly and write essays that show I know my shit and still not 'pass' the exam on paper. If my work isn't first rate, it'll get tossed in the fail bin."

Darlene's eyes widened. "So it's not even a matter of your mega-mind getting most of the answers right?"

"It's a matter of getting *all* of the answers right and writing the most exceptional essays. And that," I said, leaning back in my chair, "is what keeps me up at night."

"Wow, I've never heard of a test where you could be good enough to pass and still fail."

"Well, it's technically a fail if you score below the cut, but the cut score has never been this high. The standards have risen. Which is a good thing—no one wants a bunch of shitty lawyers running around—but it's still fucking scary. My buddy, Jackson, took the exam last quarter and barely passed with a 1530. And he was top of his class."

Darlene toyed with her fork, scraping it lightly on her empty plate. "So you have Judge Miller's decision, finals, and a bar exam with a crazy low pass rate, all the while taking care of a one-year-old."

I nodded with a small smile. "When you put it that way…"

"And yet, you still find time to comfort your neurotic neighbor over her dance audition news." She rested her cheek on her hand. "Elena was right about you after all."

Another flood of warmth suffused my chest, and I knew it was Darlene, slipping past the defenses I'd built around my heart. The moment held, wavered, and then broke when the baby monitor on my desk lit up. Olivia began to stir.

Darlene straightened. "Shit, did we wake her up?"

"No," I said. "She wakes up once or twice a night, like clockwork."

We both listened for a moment. Olivia fussed sleepily and then the baby monitor went quiet.

"She went back to sleep," I said. "Sometimes that happens too, but around three a.m. she'll wake up and I'll have to hold her for a bit. Most of the baby books I've read said to stop indulging her in it, but I'm not going to just let her *cry*." I shrugged, rubbed my neck. "So I'm a big pushover, I guess."

"No, it's sweet," Darlene said. She had a soft smile on her face that I didn't like because I liked it too much. "You take good care of her."

"I try. She probably doesn't even remember her mom. But what if she does?" I glanced over at the monitor, quiet now. "Those baby books don't cover what to do if your kid's mom abandons her. Livvie might know that deep down. She might not. But I sometimes think she wakes up just to make sure she's not alone."

I blinked and tore my gaze from the monitor to Darlene. She was watching me, her eyes soft and shining, and I realized what I'd said. How much I'd said.

"Shit, sorry. I don't… I'm so tired, I just started rambling."

"You weren't rambling," Darlene said, then added in a brighter tone, "But you do look really tired. And stressed. And I happen to be a certified massage therapist." She held up her hands. "It's like, fate, or something."

"No, no, I'm fine, thanks."

"Are you sure? Because your shoulders look like they're growing out of your ears."

"I'm used to it."

"You can get used to a lot of things," Darlene said. "Doesn't mean they're good for you."

I hesitated. I hadn't had a beautiful woman's hands on me in ten months.

This is bad. Or really fucking good, which is also bad.

"Aren't you tired after massaging people all day?"

Darlene grinned, seeing victory at hand. "I think I have one more left in me. My shoulders hurt just looking at you. Five minutes and then I'll leave you in peace."

Without a word, I sat ramrod straight while Darlene rose from her chair to move behind me. I could feel her all up and down my spine. I was in the soft cloud of her space, and the scent of her—shower soap and her warm skin—fell over me. The light weight of her hands on my shoulders sent little shocks coursing straight down to my groin.

See? Bad idea.

Then Darlene's thumbs dug into my shoulders with an exquisite pain, and all rational thought fled. A small groan of relief was pushed out of me with her digging fingers.

"Holy crap," Darlene murmured. "Your knots have knots. I have never, in all my weeks of professional massage, had anyone as tense as you."

I murmured something intelligible. My words were turning to mush in my brain. Darlene's hands were merciless and my eyes fell shut. Tight fists of muscle unclenched in me, and sleepy warmth flooded in.

"You're going to knock me out," I said.

"You should be lying down," she said. "I can work much better that way."

"If I fall out of the chair, does that count?"

She murmured a small laugh, and then her fingers sunk into my hair, grazing my scalp, and sending gentle currents down my back. I felt drunk.

"Darlene," I said, my chin sinking to my chest. "You're really good at this."

"Thank you."

Her small hands were stronger than I expected, and she slid them down over my shoulders, to press into my solar plexus. Stiff knots loosened, and as the relief flooded me, the dormant physical needs I'd been denying myself began to wake up under her hands. Blood flowed and as muscles loosened, my own hands clenched to keep from reaching up to touch her.

The air between us felt thick and charged, and I knew Darlene felt it too. Her hands stilled. I felt her stiffen behind me.

"Darlene," I said, my voice gruff and thick.

"I should go," she said, her own voice hardly more than a whisper. She gave my shoulders a final, stiff little pat, and moved to the door.

I moved sluggishly, like an animal coming out of warm hibernation into cold, harsh light, to open the door for her, but she was already there.

"You should get some sleep," she said. "I have to be up super early for the spa, then rehearsal. Thank you for listening to my news. You're a good neighbor, Sawyer. Good night."

And then the tornado that was her, swept out of my place just as fast as she'd swept in, and I was alone.

chapter twelve

Darlene

I PRACTICALLY RAN UPSTAIRS TO MY STUDIO, AND SHUT THE DOOR HARD, AS IF I COULD barricade my feelings and aching want on the other side.

I'd massaged male clients—handsome ones, even—at Serenity, and it was nothing to me. Part of the job. I'd never felt like this.

I leaned with my back to the door and looked down at my hands. They were warm and I could still feel Sawyer's hard muscle under them; the impossible softness of his hair; the warmth of his skin through his undershirt. I'd wanted to pull that shirt off of him, touch his skin with mine, and then…

"No, no, no, you do this *every* time," I hissed.

I let physical attraction pull me under and the next thing I knew, I wouldn't be working on me; I'd be losing myself in the touch of a man, the pleasure, the attention that came from feeling wanted.

And with Sawyer, it felt a hundred times more dangerous, because he wasn't like any other guy I usually associated with. He was a law student with a real career ahead of him, and a little girl.

I shut my eyes. *This is bad. So bad.*

Except it didn't feel bad.

"It will, if he finds out where you go three nights a week," I said aloud, and my words were like a cold bucket of water, dousing the pleasant warmth and washing away the memory of his skin under my hands.

Tears stung my eyes but I blinked them away.

∽

For the next two weeks, my days became a sameness of work at the spa, NA meetings, and rehearsal. The dance troupe paired me up with a guy named Ryan Denning who, I could only guess, made the cut because he looked ridiculously hot in guy's dance shorts and no shirt. Hot, but a total klutz; I spent most of every rehearsal sidestepping his crushing feet, and subtly correcting for his bad positions and holds.

"Sorry about that," Ryan said one day, after he mistimed his cue and we smacked heads on a close turn. "Paula's my cousin, so here I am. I'm not a professional, that's for sure."

You've got that right.

I rubbed my head where a lump was forming and forced a smile. "No problem. The show must go on, right?"

Ryan wasn't the only one. The whole troupe was barely professional—I felt like I'd joined an after-school club in high school doing black-box theatre. Greg, the director, was overly pompous about his 'vision', and aside from flyers on lampposts, there was no marketing of any kind.

But I showed up to every rehearsal and gave it my all, even though the other dancers—especially the other three women—hardly spoke to me. The lead, Anne-Marie, wouldn't even look my way, unless giving me the stink-eye counted. When rehearsal was over they hustled out to drinks without me.

"*Darlene,*" I once heard her whisper. "Sounds like a truck-stop waitress."

I fled the tiny theater with their tittering laughter chasing me.

Saturday morning, and I woke up with the dawn. My work schedule had drilled it into me and now I couldn't sleep in. An uncommon heat wave made my third-floor studio feel stifling. I lay on my loveseat in my underwear and watched the sun fill the sky with white, gauzy light as it rose. A mug of coffee cooled on the table beside me as I wondered just what in the hell was supposed to come next.

I hadn't missed a single NA meeting. Granted, I wasn't talking as much or as deeply as Max wanted me too. But talking felt like giving a eulogy, over and over again, for someone who had died a long time ago. I didn't want to resurrect that addict-self. That girl was gone and I wanted her to stay gone.

I was working hard—my arms and back ached after every day of work, only to be worked harder at rehearsal.

I was doing everything right.

And still, the other ache was there. The emptiness.

I watched the sun rise from my loveseat, and remembered my favorite poem by Sylvia Plath, "Mad Girl's Love Song." I wasn't much of a book-reader; the long blocks of text couldn't hold my attention. I loved songs. Lyrics. Poems. Where a writer has the entirety of the English language to choose from and she picks only a handful of words.

I was the Mad Girl. Lying on my couch that morning, I closed my eyes and made the world vanish.

I haven't seen Sawyer in two weeks.

"I think I made you up inside my head," I murmured.

My hands tried to remember his skin, and crept down my thighs, brushing the edges of my underwear. A tingle of electricity shot through me, and I bolted off the couch.

"No, that's cheating."

I balled my hands into fists and sucked in several deep breaths. I couldn't cool my heated blood, I always ran hot. My only cure was to set fire to the passion, to feed it until it burnt out. But I still had hours until rehearsal where I could channel my restless want into dance.

I threw on jogging shorts—green with white stripes along the edges—a white T, and my running shoes, socks pulled to my knees. I grabbed my phone, ear buds, water bottle, and headed out.

Two blocks north of the Victorian was a park with large expanses of green grass, surrounded by more beautiful old houses. A path ran around the perimeter and I set out to do laps.

At only nine in the morning, it was already warm. From all I'd heard of San Francisco, this heat wave wasn't just rare, it was unheard of. The city dwellers were taking advantage. There were already couples and families gathered, enjoying the sun. Some people were alone, stretched out on the grass, an open book acting as a sun shield while they read.

I did a loop around the perimeter of the park, Madonna's "Open Your Heart" playing in my ears. On my second pass, I saw Sawyer.

He stood about twenty yards away from the jogging path in jeans, a dark blue t-shirt and a Giants baseball cap on backwards. Olivia's stroller was beside him; I could just see her little feet kicking to get out.

I slowed to watch Sawyer lay out a blanket, then extricate his daughter from her stroller. She immediately started to toddle away. My heart felt too big for my chest as Sawyer laughingly scooped her up and planted her on the blanket, then gave her a snack to keep her occupied while he finished setting up. A zwieback biscuit.

My feet wanted to turn in their direction, as if my inner compass was pulling to Sawyer's magnetic north. I kept on the path, running faster.

On my next loop, Sawyer was playing catch with Olivia as best as one could play catch with a one-year-old. Olivia, dressed in pink overalls, held her biscuit in one hand and spastically chucked a small yellow ball in Sawyer's general vicinity. He laughed and bent to retrieve it, then rolled it across the grass toward her.

My head was craning to keep watching, and I turned my attention forward before I crashed headfirst into someone. I felt like a stalker, spying on them, and had to remind myself I was there first, taking a jog and minding my own business.

Working on me.

On my third lap, two young women were with Sawyer. One was laughing way too hard at something he said, while the other was kneeling at eye-level with Olivia, smiling and talking to her. A crazed urge to run straight at the women and tackle them both to the grass came over me.

I wrenched my gaze away just as a stitch in my side stopped me short and bent me double. I wheezed for breath, hands on my knees. I hadn't realized how fast I'd been running but my face was covered with sweat and the pain in my side was like a little knife stabbing me.

When I was able to stand straight I sucked in deep breaths, and glanced over at Sawyer. My breath stuck all over again.

Sawyer was looking right at me, his expression unreadable from this distance, though I thought I caught a glimpse of a small smile on his lips.

I watched, rooted to the spot, as he picked up Olivia and headed toward me without so much as a word to the two women. They watched him walk away, twin expressions of confusion and disappointment morphing to disdain on their faces before they gave up.

"Are you being chased?" Sawyer asked with a small smile. On his hip, Olivia beamed and bounced to see me.

"Ha ha, no," I huffed. God, I must've looked like a mess. My face felt red and puffy from running so hard and sweat made my shirt stick to my skin. "I got confused for a second and thought I was Usain Bolt."

Olivia reached her little hand out to me.

"Hi, sweet pea," I said, giving her hand a gentle squeeze. "Are you being good?"

"Always," Sawyer said with that smile he reserved just for her. He plucked a blade of grass off her overalls, not looking at me. "So, haven't seen you in a while."

"Yeah, I've been busy. Job, rehearsals." I dug my toe into the dirt. I'd caught my breath but my heart was still pounding loudly. "How are your finals going?"

"Good. Finished two. Two more to go."

"And then the bar exam?"

"Yeah, in Sacramento in a few weeks. Three days of motel living." He made a face. "Can't wait."

"Three days? Will Elena be watching Olivia?" I asked. "Because I can help. If you need it."

"Maybe," Sawyer said. His dark brown eyes were soft as they met mine. "Thanks."

"Anytime."

A silence fell and then Olivia squirmed. "Down. Down."

"Well, we'd better get back before someone steals our wheels." Sawyer nodded his chin at the bulky, second-hand stroller. "It's such a beaut."

I smiled and tried to think of something witty to say but my brain was addled by the V of Sawyer's tanned chest revealed by his shirt, and the flexing muscles in his arms as he set Olivia down.

"Yeah, I'd better get back...to...more running."

More running? Seriously?

I felt a tug on my hand. "Ball, Dar-een?" Olivia pulled me toward their blanket. "Ball?"

A joyful laugh burst out of me, erasing my nerves. "Oh my God, she just said my name." I knelt down beside her. "Did you just say Darlene?"

"Dar-een," Olivia said, and pointed toward her yellow ball sitting on the green grass. "Play?"

"Well, if it's okay with your daddy?"

I looked up to see Sawyer watching his daughter.

"I didn't know she knew your name," he said quietly.

"I didn't either," I said. I got to my feet. "I'll play with her if you want. Or if you'd rather I not…"

"No, that'd be great. If you don't mind."

"Not at all."

I joined Sawyer and Olivia on their patch of grass and played three-way catch—Sawyer threw to me, I rolled the ball to Olivia, and she threw it to Sawyer who inevitably had to go chasing it down or pick it up when she torpedoed it straight into the grass.

Olivia's thirteen-month-old attention span wore out five minutes later, and she dropped the ball, game over.

"Snag? Snag, Daddy."

He scooped Olivia up. "Do you want a snack? What about a swing first?"

"Swing!"

Sawyer swung her down and then tossed her up in the air in the way that guys did that made babies squeal with laughter, and made every human with ovaries in a twenty-yard radius inwardly panic.

"Oh jeez," I whispered.

I peeked at them through my fingers, but Sawyer caught his little girl smoothly and planted her on his hip.

"Okay, snack time." He looked to me and laughed. "It's safe to come out now. Do you want to join us?"

"I don't want to interrupt your private time…"

"Nah, we do this every Saturday," Sawyer said. He set Olivia down on the blanket—where she found her half-chewed biscuit—and rummaged in the stroller. He held up two pieces of fruit. "Apple or banana?"

"Apple," I said.

He tossed it to me and I caught it and sat with them on the blanket. We ate and talked, and Olivia helped to give us something to focus on when the air between us seemed to thicken. It had been too long since Sawyer and I had been in the same space. Since his skin had been under my hands. My face felt perpetually hot, and I turned my eyes to Olivia whenever I found myself staring at Sawyer for too long. Twice I thought I caught him staring at me before doing the same.

An elderly couple, strolling arm in arm, veered our way.

"We just had to tell you, that you are such a beautiful young family," the woman said. "Just beautiful."

I glanced at Sawyer. "Oh, um…we're not…"

"Thank you," he said. "Thanks very much."

The couple beamed and moved on.

"It's easier than explaining," Sawyer told me.

"Oh. It's happened to you before?" I asked lightly.

"Yeah, with my friend, Jackson," he said. "He joined us one Saturday and an entire bachelorette party surrounded us, thinking that we were a couple and that Olivia was our adopted daughter."

I took a long pull from my water bottle. "That's too cute."

"I didn't bother to tell them the truth, though Jax hitting on the Maid of Honor the entire time must've been confusing."

Sawyer was good at making me laugh, and I vowed to relax and enjoy the day, instead of crowding it with silly, impossible thoughts. I leaned back on my hands, let the sunshine spill over me.

"Jackson's a lawyer, too? I think you mentioned that."

"Yeah, practicing. So he's an *attorney*," Sawyer said with a grin. He smiled fondly at Olivia who was eating bits of strawberry, alternating with bites of biscuit. "He does tax law at a big firm in the Financial District."

"Tax law. God, I'm getting sleepy just thinking about it." I started to take a bite of apple, then froze. "Oh shit. I just realized I never asked you what kind of law you're studying."

"Tax law," Sawyer deadpanned, but the glint in his eye gave him away.

"Liar," I laughed, and crunched my apple. "What is it, for real?"

"Criminal justice. I want to be a federal prosecutor."

"Oh," I said, and it seemed as if a cloud had crossed the path of the sun. My skin broke out in gooseflesh and I swallowed my lump of apple like it was a rock. "That's the kind of attorney who works to put people in jail, isn't it?"

I knew perfectly well that's what it was, because I'd had one standing across from me in a courtroom three years ago. He helped get me sentenced to three months in jail for misdemeanor drug possession.

"There's more to it than that," Sawyer said. "A federal prosecutor represents the state or federal government in criminal cases, argues before grand juries…"

"But is that why you want to be a lawyer? To punish those who have broken the law?"

He frowned as if the question didn't make any sense. "It's not only about punishment, it's about justice." A smile softened his face. "It's not like the Pirate Code. The laws aren't there to serve as *guidelines*. They're meant to be followed."

I nodded faintly. "Yeah, they are."

A short silence descended. Livvie was turning the heavy cardboard pages of a book about a hungry caterpillar. The sunlight made her brown hair gold at the edges.

I cleared my throat, determined to keep my spirits up. "What made you decide to practice?"

He gave me a smile but it faded as he spoke. "I like the law. I like how black and white it can be. Words on paper that last and have power." He plucked a few blades of grass, tearing them from their roots. "I want that power to protect people from what happened to my family."

"What happened?"

Sawyer seemed to be struggling to find the words, or whether to speak them at all.

"No, you don't have to tell me," I said gently. "I do that. I pry."

"You're not prying," Sawyer said. "You're making conversation. Something I'm not very good at lately."

I smiled. "You're doing fine."

He smiled back but it was flimsy and faded quickly. "I don't talk about this very much. Or ever, actually."

I itched to touch him. "You don't have to."

"No, I should, I guess. For her sake. My mom died in a car accident when I was a kid," he said all at once, then swallowed. "She was killed by a drunk driver."

My hand flew to my throat. "Oh my God, Sawyer. I'm so sorry. How old were you?"

"Eight," he said. "My little brother, Emmett, was four. Worst fucking day of our lives."

My eyes stung with tears at the sudden image of two little boys learning they no longer had a mother. "I don't know what to say. I'm so sorry."

He shrugged, as if he could minimize the whole thing, but I could see the pain behind his deep brown eyes. A muscle in his jaw ticked.

"Anyway, the guy who killed her had been arrested twice before," he said, his voice hardening. "And both times he pled before a judge he wouldn't do it again, that he'd cleaned up his act. The prosecutor was weak. He didn't push hard enough. Three weeks after his latest release from jail for DUI, the guy drove his truck—on a suspended license—into my mom's car as she was coming home from work."

I shook my head. "That's so awful."

"I don't like talking about it, and I don't want to write it about it, either, but I don't know what else to do."

"What do you mean?"

"Judge Miller has asked us to write a brief about a personal incident in our lives and how we'd handle it as prosecutors."

"Judge Miller, this is the guy you're trying to have a clerkship with?"

Sawyer nodded. "And I plan to write about my mother, but it makes me so fucking angry and…"

"Hurt?" I offered gently.

Sawyer shrugged. "I don't have time to hurt. Maybe that's my problem. Miller told me I lack feeling." He scoffed. "I have no idea what that means. Law doesn't have feelings. It has direction. It tells you where to go and what comes next."

"But that's not how life is," I said.

Sawyer's head shot up. "What did you say?"

"Life has no guide map. Things happen and people react, and no two people will do the same thing." Now I plucked at the grass at the edge of the blanket. "Some people are beyond saving, like that asshole who…killed your mom. But not everyone is like that."

"He was given plenty of chances," Sawyer said darkly. "He threw them away."

"So you don't believe in second chances anymore?" I asked, my voice sounding high and tight in my own ears.

Sawyer watched me for a minute, his dark eyes full of thoughts. Then he shook his head. "I don't know. It shouldn't be about what I *believe*. It should be about what I can do. The law failed my mom. I'm going to make sure it doesn't fail anyone else."

"He sounds nice, this Judge Miller," I said after a moment. I plucked another blade of grass.

Sawyer nodded. "He is. Sometimes I wonder why I'm in the running for a clerkship with him in the first place."

"Because you have plenty of feelings," I said, shocked at my old boldness but it was too late now. The words had come flying out and there was no taking them back. "And he probably sees it."

Sawyer looked at me from across the blanket. Between us, Olivia dozed. He covered her eyes with a little sunhat. "I do believe in second chances. For her, I do. For criminals like the guy who killed my mom?" He shook his head. "Once a person crosses over the line, it's too easy do it again and again."

"What line?"

"Breaking the law," Sawyer said. "Falling back into drugs and alcohol, or stealing or murder or…any criminal act."

I nodded and looked away, into the gulf of sadness that opened between us. The idea of telling him about my past felt even more impossible.

He won't see me anymore, only my record. A criminal.

I cleared my throat. "Tell me about your brother, Emmett. Where is he now?"

"Good question. Last I heard he was heading toward Tibet. He travels all over. Doesn't have a permanent address. After our mom died, he ran away a lot. He always came back but when he got older, he stayed away longer. Dropped out of school, even though he has a genius IQ. Or maybe because of it."

A quiet, proud smile touched Sawyer's lips. Then it faded.

"I've always felt like the world can't contain Emmett. Or he's too smart to deal with it. Like he can see all of its moving parts, and it's too much for him. He has to keep going. To outrun it, maybe."

"Do you miss him?"

"Yeah, I do. I don't have much family left. Dad remarried and now they live in Idaho. Patty—his wife—has her family there, so I never see my dad. Birthday cards and the occasional phone call."

He glanced at me, took in my darkened expression. "Hey, sorry for dumping all that about my mom on you. I don't normally talk about my shit. Not to anyone."

"I'm glad you told me," I said, smiling faintly. "I'm glad you feel like you can."

"It's not a pretty story."

"Not many people's are, I think."

"What about you?" he asked. "I don't mean you have to tell me your not-so-pretty story, if you have one. I meant, you mentioned you had a sister?"

"One sister, back in Queens," I said. "She's older. And married. Perfect husband, perfect house, perfect everything."

"And you didn't get the perfect gene?" Sawyer asked lightly.

"Oh no, I'm the fuck-up," I said.

Sawyer frowned. "You don't seem like a fuck-up to me."

If you only knew.

"My sister went to college, I didn't. She pursued a 'real career' in interior design. I didn't. I wanted to be a dancer, which everyone knows is no way to make a living. So speaketh my parents, away."

"Is that why you moved out here? To do your own thing?"

"Yes," I said. "A fresh start."

He nodded. Smiled. "Fresh starts are good. Emmett makes one every day," he said. "Once I get this clerkship, *if* I get this clerkship, I'll have one too."

"You will get it," I said. "You'll pass the bar. Your brother isn't the only one with the genius IQ."

Sawyer waved a hand. "Nah. He's the real deal."

"But you have a photographic memory, right?" I blew air out my cheeks with a laugh. "I can hardly remember what I wore yesterday."

"You wore jean shorts over ripped black tights, and a black, satiny-type blouse with gold flowers and skulls on it," Sawyer said. "And combat boots."

I stared, a blush creeping up my cheeks. "How do you know that?"

"I was getting off the Muni last night when you were getting on. You didn't see me."

"I was on my way to rehearsal," I said automatically.

And an NA meeting after that.

But that part I kept to myself. I wanted to put as much distance between myself and the kind of person he imagined an addict could be. I cleared my throat.

"Okay, Mega-mind, what did I wear when I babysat for Olivia on the fly?"

"You wore black leggings, a long white shirt. And combat boots."

"What was I wearing the day we met?"

"A beige skirt—linen, maybe—with a men's jean button down shirt, and maroon socks pulled up to your knees." He grinned. "And combat boots."

"God, hearing it like that, I sound like a slob."

"You don't look like a slob," he said quickly, his gaze intent. "You look like you. I've never met anyone who looks and acts and dresses one hundred percent like themselves."

My blush deepened. "Thanks."

The moment caught and held, and the entire city went silent. I could hardly blink, I wanted to hold on to every second of that moment. The way the sun glinted off the burnished gold of his hair, and how his dark brown eyes were looking at me.

Olivia stirred in her sleep.

"She got up super early this morning," Sawyer said, "which means I got up super early this morning. I should get back."

"Yeah, me too. I have rehearsal."

We packed up the mini-picnic, and Sawyer gently laid his daughter in the stroller. We walked back to the Victorian in silence, and for once I wasn't tempted to fill it with talk. I didn't know what to say anyway. Half of me felt devastated by Sawyer's ideas about addicts being beyond redemption, and the other half was floating over the rest of the morning, and how he looked at me in that one, perfect moment in the sun.

"So this rehearsal," Sawyer said as we entered the Victorian. "It's for the dance show you auditioned for?"

He unlatched Olivia from her stroller and lifted her gently in his arms. I folded the stroller and followed him up the stairs as if we'd been doing it like this for ages.

"Yeah, at the American Dance Academy, until five."

He unlocked the door to his place and I followed him in, and left the stroller by the door. He went to put Olivia down in her bed, and came back with his hands jammed in the pockets of his jeans.

The silence that fell was different now. Olivia wasn't here to act as a buffer between us. It was just Sawyer and me. I didn't know what to say, so I blurted the first thing that came to mind.

"Is it hard having a memory that doesn't let you forget anything?"

"Sometimes," he said, and the word felt loaded.

"I'd think it would be annoying, remembering things that have no meaning. Like what your neighbor wears every time you see her."

His gaze held mine. "It's not all bad." He glanced away for a moment. "I remember what you were wearing the night you came over to tell me about your audition."

"What was I wearing?" I asked softly.

"A dress. You were wearing a pink-ish, orange dress that looked like a slip."

He glanced at me and there was something in his eyes that hadn't been there before. "And nothing else."

"You remember that?"

"I remember everything about that night, Darlene."

"Oh." I swallowed hard. "That's nice."

That's nice?

I winced. "Well, okay, I should go."

"Let me get the door."

He moved to me, leaned over me to reach for the handle, but somehow we ended up face to face, my back to the door. My heart clanged madly and my eyes felt fixated on his, unable to tear away.

Sawyer's expression was anguished, unsure. "Darlene…"

"Yes?"

Oh my God, he's going to kiss me.

The need tore me in half again; to run away before we did something we couldn't undo, and to let him kiss me until I could hardly remember my own name.

Sawyer's gaze moved from my eyes, to my lips, to my forehead, and for a crazy second, I thought he looked straight into my mind where all my secrets were laid bare. His brows furrowed.

"What is it?" I asked.

He frowned and his hand came up to brush a wisp of hair from my temple. "You have a bruise there." His eyes dropped to mine. His fingertips were still resting on my cheek.

"Oh, that," I said, with a nervous, whispery laugh. My heart was now pounding so loud I could hardly hear myself. "My dance partner in the show? He clobbered me."

Sawyer's expression hardened. "What does that mean?"

"Oh, no, it was an accident," I said. "We bonked heads. He's kind of a klutz."

Sawyer lifted his chin and took a step back. "Tell him he'd better be more careful."

I nodded. "I will. Okay…bye."

I reached behind me for the door and slipped out, into the empty hallway where the only sounds were my shallow breaths and the blood rushing in my ears.

chapter thirteen

Sawyer

"Holy shit, I almost kissed her."

My discipline had nearly gotten away from me, but Darlene was so beautiful and full of light and life, who the hell could blame me? Her tornado-like ability to sweep people up was so potent, it drew me in so that I wanted to kiss her and touch her and tell her everything.

I told her about my mother.

It had been years. And while I hated to see the story cloud Darlene's light, I felt better for sharing it with her. My mother was gone, but instead of turning that horrible memory over and over in my mind, like a bad song stuck on repeat, she'd become a real person again with Darlene.

I wanted to kiss Darlene for that, too. When she was at my doorway with her chin tilted up, it was almost impossible not to. Until I saw the bruise on her forehead. Anger that some careless asshole hurt her—accident or not—surged through me with a different kind of heat. I was glad that my anger had pulled me out of the moment because it reminded me that I couldn't start something with her. Not now.

I was so close to the end. A few more weeks and I would be done with law school and the bar exam.

Maybe then?

I had a purely selfish moment where I felt as if maybe, if I kept my head down and worked my ass off, I'd have this beautiful, vibrant woman waiting for me on the other side.

I went to my bathroom and took a very long, cold shower.

I spent the rest of the day without my studies, focusing only on Olivia as I did every Saturday. We read books and ate lunch and I let her watch Sesame Street. As usual, when it was over, she asked for more.

"Elmo?"

"You want more Elmo?" I asked, and tickled her until she was squealing. I was paranoid about too much TV, but it was hard to resist her baby voice and wide blue eyes. She was smart and I loved watching her blow past the milestones like a champ.

A month and a half left to go to the biggest milestone.

I'd had Jackson, acting as my attorney, draw up the petition for a Voluntary Declaration of Paternity. As soon as it had been a year since Molly left us, I could petition to have my name put on Olivia's birth certificate.

"She should have done that before she gave her to me," I muttered, watching my daughter watch her show. But instead of the thought irritating me, the tension I perpetually carried around with me on my shoulders relaxed a little bit and I was almost surprised to find I was in a really good mood. It was easy to do around Olivia but now that I had Darlene my life too…

"Settle down, Haas. Go take another cold shower."

Around six, I was putting Olivia's and my dinner dishes in the sink when there came a knock at the door. My heart stuttered to think it might be Darlene, maybe this time with a chicken pot pie, or some other concoction she wanted to share.

I opened the door to Jackson and his mother, Henrietta.

"Sawyer, my man," Jackson said. He was dressed to go out in a dark blazer, white button down, and black pants. We clasped hands and he pulled me in for a half-hug. "Are you ready?"

"For what?" I moved to hug his mom. "Hi, Henrietta. Are you dropping him off? Because I don't want him either."

Henrietta Smith looked like a younger version of Toni Morrison; heavyset with graying dreads down to her shoulders. She always dressed in billowy, silky clothes and large jewelry that Olivia loved to play with whenever she babysat.

She chuckled and took my face in her hands to kiss my cheek. "Hey, baby boy. How've you been? You look tired."

"I'm well," I said, pulling away from her embrace with a small ache in my chest. With my own mother gone, my brother trekking around God-knew-where, and my dad in Idaho with his wife's family, Henrietta and Jackson were the closest I had to family.

"What are you guys doing here?" I asked, shutting the door behind them.

Olivia bounced and squawked from her highchair, her arms reaching. Henrietta freed her from the highchair and gave her a squeeze. Olivia hugged her back and immediately reached for the bulky necklace around Henrietta's neck.

"This," Jackson said, "is an intervention. Get dressed, you're going out." He held his arms out and did a Michael Jackson-esque turn in my living room. "Dancing."

"Say again?"

Jackson pointed one finger to the ceiling. "Is the lovely Darlene home?"

"I have no idea. I think she had rehearsal until five so yeah, she should be… hey, where are you going?"

Jackson had made an about-face, and strode out the door.

I looked to Henrietta who laughed heartily, Olivia secure in her arms, and I chased Jackson upstairs.

I caught up to him just as he knocked on Darlene's door. He jerked his jacket down to straighten it and smoothed his short hair that didn't need smoothing.

"What are you doing?" I hissed.

"I told you," Jackson said. "It's an intervention. You're off your game and what kind of wingman would I be if I—why, hellooo," he said smoothly as the door opened.

A cloud of clean scents, daisies, soap and warmth, billowed out with Darlene. She was fresh from the shower and wrapped in a silky robe. Her hair fell around her shoulders in damp, dark waves. Her brilliant blue eyes took in Jackson and me and lit up from within. She crossed her arms, a laughing smile on her lips, and leaned against the doorframe.

"If you're here to sell me a set of encyclopedias, you're too late."

Jackson threw his head back and bellowed a laugh.

I rolled my eyes. "Sorry, about him, but—"

"You must be the lovely Darlene," my friend cut me off, holding his hand out. "Jackson Smith, Esquire."

Darlene's grin widened and she gave me a raised-eyebrow-look as she shook Jackson's hand. "Nice to meet you, Jackson. Sawyer has told me so much about you."

"Has he? What a coincidence. Sawyer has told me quite a lot about you, as well."

I shot my friend a death glare, which he completely ignored.

"One of the *many* things Mr. Haas has told me about you, Darlene, is that you are dancer. Therefore, I am here to extend an invitation for you to come dancing."

Darlene's arms dropped. "Really? Oh my God, yes, please. I just moved here a few weeks ago and I don't know anyone. I'm dying to go out."

Jackson shot me a dirty look and whacked me in the chest. "Are you hearing this? This beautiful woman—who lives right above you—is new to the city and you haven't even taken her out to show her the town?"

The blood rushed to my face on a heated current of embarrassment that left me tongue-tied. "I don't...I..."

"There's a bunch of us going to Café du Nord on Market Street. Have you been?"

"Never heard of it," Darlene said.

"It's a throwback, speakeasy kind of scene," Jackson said. "Is swing dancing part of your repertoire?"

Darlene's grin widened. "It's been a while, but yes."

Jackson clapped his hands together once. "Great. We're meeting some friends at Flore for dinner and then walking up to the club. You're officially invited to come with us."

Her glance darted to me. "I'm trying to imagine Sawyer the Lawyer dancing."

Jackson laughed again. "Sawyer the Lawyer? Holy hell, I love this woman already." He clapped me on the shoulder and gave me a fond look while I glared daggers. "He can't dance for shit but I'm convinced it's only because he doesn't have the right instructor."

I rolled my eyes as if his comments were no big deal, but the blood was leaving my face, heading due south at the idea of dancing with Darlene.

"It sounds awesome," she said. "Thank you so much for inviting me. Give me half an hour?"

"Of course," Jackson said. "Head down to Sawyer's place when you're ready."

"Thank you," Darlene said. She glanced at me almost shyly, her cheeks pink, before shutting the door.

Jackson turned to me with a triumphant look on his face that morphed into confusion at my hard stare.

"What?"

"What the hell, man?" I dragged him away from Darlene's door.

"I'm just being a good friend," Jackson said as we took the stairs down. He stopped at the bottom and turned, put his hand on my shoulder. "I appreciate your dedication to your work, but I cannot let you turn down the chance to see that woman—" he pointed a finger at Darlene's door—"dressed up to go out and dance. You going to say no to that? And Ma's been dying to see Olivia again." His eyes widened with mock alarm. "You going to say no to *Henrietta*?"

I laughed despite myself. "I can't dance for shit, remember? Not exactly the best way to impress a woman."

"Details, details." He waved a hand. "You'll thank me when a slow song comes on."

In my place, Henrietta was sitting on the floor with Olivia, playing with blocks. She looked up when we came in, the same conspiratorial smile on her face as her son's. "Well?"

"It's on," Jackson said.

Henrietta laughed and clapped her hands together. "Oh baby, you should see your face," she said to me. "Go on now, get ready. This little angel and I have some catching up to do."

It was useless to argue, and part of me realized I had no intention of arguing at all. I took a quick shower and then dressed in black slacks, a dark gray dress shirt I hadn't worn in a year, and a jacket.

Twenty minutes later, Darlene knocked on the door. Jackson opened it and a low whistle issued from between his teeth. "Darlene, you're a vision," he said "Don't you agree, Haas?"

He stepped aside to let Darlene in, and closed the door behind her. My heart nearly fucking stopped beating in my chest; I don't think I'd ever been so glad for my photographic memory in my entire life.

I took her all in, every detail. Her sleeveless dress hugged her slender body in black silk, then flared out at the waist. Instead of her usual combat boots, her shoes were the black, low-heeled, strappy kind dancers wore, and she carried a black coat in her arms. Her dark hair was pulled back from her face on the sides and curled softly down over her shoulders. She'd done her eyes in smoky shadow; and the dark of her clothing and makeup left me transfixed by her translucent skin and fire-engine red lips that stood out, like white and red slashes of paint in a dark masterpiece.

I blinked from staring at her to realize she was staring at me.

"Hi," she said, a nervous little smile. "You clean up good, Sawyer the Lawyer."

"Ha!" Henrietta cackled and slapped her thigh. "Haven't heard that one in a while." She got up and came over to Darlene and took both her hands in hers.

"Why, aren't you an angel?" she said. "I'm Henrietta, Jackson's mother."

"So nice to meet you. Your son is quite a charmer," Darlene said warmly.

"That's one word for him," I muttered.

"Dareen!" Olivia said, reaching a hand up.

Darlene knelt beside her. "Hi, sweet pea. Are you playing with your blocks?"

"Bocks."

I wrenched my gaze from her and my daughter to see Jackson watching me with a shit-eating grin on his face. He held his hands up like a circus ringmaster for whom everything was going precisely as planned.

"Shall we?"

⁓⁓

We met some friends of ours I hadn't seen in a long time at Flore restaurant. Twelve of us crowded around the long table by the window that afforded a perfect view of bustling Market Street.

Jackson sat next to Darlene and directed me to sit across from her. For a split second, I wondered at my friend's actual motives, but Jackson wasn't a dick. As soon as I sat down, I understood his plan; I had a full view of Darlene sitting across from me, looking stunningly gorgeous in the amber light of the restaurant.

Our friends took to her immediately. Even the most outgoing women among them seemed reserved compared to Darlene. She wasn't loud or obnoxious but laughed and talked easily with no self-consciousness about being amongst a group of new people. Now and again, her eyes stole glances at me, and as the dinner plates were being served, she leaned over the table.

"How am I doing?" she asked. "It's been a while."

"You're fucking perfect," I said, but the noise and clatter of silverware on dishes was so loud, she didn't hear me.

"What? Say again?"

I shook my head with a smile, and we both were pulled toward other conversations.

After dinner, the group of us walked down Market Street. I'd forgotten what it was like to hang out with friends, to be part of the city's energy. Darlene linked her arm in mine as we set out.

"Is that okay?" she asked, when I stiffened.

"Yeah, sure," I said. Her sudden touch on my arm had sent a current shooting through me and I cursed myself. Jackson was right; I was completely off my game. I'd forgotten what it was like to flirt with a girl.

Because you always flirted with an agenda, a voice whispered. With Darlene, just being with her, having her hand on my arm, was enough.

Café Du Nord was a small, former speakeasy underneath an actual restaurant. We walked down the short stairs into the windowless, oval-shaped room. At the far end was a place for a band, but tonight the red curtains were closed and swing music came in from the sound system. We passed pool tables on the left, and Jackson led us immediately to the bar on the right.

"The first one's on me," he told Darlene, and clapped his hand on my shoulder. "The rest are on him."

She laughed. "I'll take a Coke with three cherries."

The music was loud. Jackson craned in. "A what? Rum and Coke?"

"No, a Coke with three cherries in it." Her smile tightened. "I don't drink… when I dance."

"Fair enough." Jackson turned to me. "What will it be, slugger? The usual?"

"Just one," I said. "I don't want you taking advantage of me later."

Jackson ordered Darlene's soda, and two Moscow mules for him and me. Big Bad Voodoo Daddy blared overhead, and dozens of dancers were swinging on the dance floor, ringed by onlookers. Old-fashioned lamps on the walls cast a golden light.

The bartender set down Darlene's soda and two copper mugs, brimming with vodka, ginger beer, and ice—each with a lime perched on the rim.

Jackson tossed down a twenty, and then lifted his drink in a toast. "To interventions."

"To interventions," Darlene echoed, her voice low.

We clinked classes and I watched, mesmerized as Darlene plucked a cherry from her drink and put it to her lips that were painted just as red. She held the cherry with her teeth to pull it free from the stem, and then it vanished into her mouth.

"My God," Jackson murmured to me under his breath. "Did you see that?"

"Hell yes, I did."

"She's the hottest woman in this joint."

"I know," I said, watching as Darlene struck up a conversation with Penny, one of our friends from Hastings. "And she has no idea."

That's part of what makes her so damn beautiful.

Jackson nudged my arm. "What the hell are you waiting for? Ask her to dance."

"I can't fucking dance," I said. "You know that."

Jackson heaved a sigh. "You leave me no choice. Hold this for me?"

I gritted my teeth as Jackson handed me his cocktail like I was a freshman at a hazing, compelled to do his bidding. Jackson took Darlene's hand and gave an exaggerated bow.

"Care to dance?"

She shot me a glance and a smile, then nodded her head. "I'd love to."

He led her to the dance floor with a parting glance at me. Jackson, that smooth bastard, had taken a ballroom dance class as an undergrad. I watched him spin Darlene expertly across the floor, and goddamn, watching her dance…

Her dress whirled over legs that seemed to go on forever, and her body moved through complex steps effortlessly. She was better than Jackson, but they looked good together. Watching them, I suddenly felt ravenously hungry. I took a long pull of my cocktail.

It had been ages since I'd drunk anything—the vodka went straight to my head. I started to order another and drank Jackson's instead. By the time the second copper mug was drained, the room's muted light had taken on a pleasantly fuzzy glow, and I watched my best friend dance with Darlene with a small smile over my lips.

He met my eye several times, eyebrows raised to his hairline, and inclined his head at his dance partner as if to say, *What are you waiting for?*

I only grinned back. I was content now to wait. I'd been off my game, true, but I realized with Darlene I didn't need one.

The song ended and Jackson bent Darlene over his knee in a deep dip. Her back arched as if she had no bones, and when he hauled her up, her face was radiant.

A slow song began, "Cheek to Cheek" sung by Ella Fitzgerald, and I pushed myself off the bar, through the crowds.

"May I?" I asked, cutting in before Jackson could answer.

"It's about damn time," he muttered under his breath.

"You're going to need a new drink," I told him as he slipped away, and then I was holding Darlene.

I slipped an arm around her slender waist, and held her other against my chest. Her body radiated soft warmth through the silky material of her dress, and I imagined her lean muscles moving under my hands. Her face was flushed from the dancing, and her eyes were crystalline blue over her red lips.

"I wondered if you were ever going to come over here," she said.

"I don't dance," I said. The vodka had stripped my words down to the bare bones. "I liked watching you."

"Jackson is very good."

"You're better."

"Mmm, now I know what you were doing instead of dancing," she said with a small smile. "Are you having a good time?"

"I am now." I couldn't take my eyes off of her.

She held my gaze for a moment, then laid her head against my chest. "I'm having a good time too," she said. "Maybe a better time than I should."

"I know."

"I'm supposed to be working on me."

"I know," I said again. "I can see my finish line from here. I should keep going but…"

"But what?" she asked against my heart.

"I don't want to kiss you drunk, but I want to kiss you."

Her breath caught and she raised her head to look at me, her lips parted. It took everything I had not to kiss her anyway, but it felt wrong; with vodka on my breath and my thoughts clouded and dizzy. I'd kissed a hundred women drunk or tipsy, but something stopped me with this woman.

She deserves more.

"You want to kiss me?" she asked.

I tilted her chin up with a loose fist, and my thumb brushed the skin just beneath her lower lip. My mouth was clumsy with the alcohol, but the booze had freed my emotions that I'd kept on lockdown, always, and I was helpless against her beauty to keep them in.

"I think about you," I said. "A lot."

"I think about you, too," she whispered, and I smelled the sweetness of Maraschino cherries on her breath. "And Olivia."

Instantly, my arms held her tighter at those words. "You do?"

She nodded. "And I know it's fast, but I feel like," she swallowed. "I don't know what I feel. Like I'm supposed to be getting myself together and not getting swept up in all the things I usually get swept up in. I keep saying I need to work on me, but I'm doing everything right and I still feel like something's missing." Her eyes were impossibly blue as they gazed up at mine. "Is it you?"

"I don't know," I said. *But maybe it could be.*

I held her and turned a slow circle, possibilities whispering in my ear.

"What do you want, Darlene?"

"I think I want you to kiss me, too. No, I know I do. More than anything, actually."

Hearing her say the words conjured something deep in me. Not sex or lust. What I wanted with her went beyond that. And deeper, somehow.

"But Sawyer, there's something I have to tell you."

"Anything."

"I wish it were that simple."

Her beautiful face morphed into anguish, and then the song ended. "In the Mood"—the quintessential swing song—came on and the crowd filled the floor in a mad rush.

The heat and depth between us vanished and it felt like I'd been thrust up from somewhere hot and dark, into bright, cold light.

Darlene was asked to dance by some other guy but she declined and walked with me back to the bar where Jackson was watching us, a new Moscow mule in his hand.

He opened his mouth to make a joke, but snapped it shut again.

"Are you having a good time?" he asked.

"I'm having a great time," Darlene said, not looking at me. "I'm so happy to have gotten out into the city."

"Glad to hear it," Jackson said, his gaze landing on mine. "I thought it was about overdue."

The three of us said goodbye to our friends and Darlene exchanged phone numbers with Penny. I hoped a friendship would come out of it.

Anything, if it makes Darlene happy.

Jackson, Darlene and I, took an Uber back to the Victorian. There, Darlene gave Jackson a peck on the cheek.

"Thank you so much. I had such a good time." Her glance landed on me then darted away. "It was a lovely night."

Then she hurried upstairs in a cloud of soft perfume and cherries.

Maybe it was the vodka, but a sense of certainty and peace settled over me.

Jackson was staring at me. "Well? What the hell happened?"

I smiled like an idiot but I wasn't trying to be smooth; I didn't have game, or moves, or an agenda anymore. I pulled my bewildered friend in for a sloppy hug.

"Thanks, man," I said.

"For what?"

"For tonight."

For her.

chapter fourteen

Sawyer

TUESDAY AFTERNOON, IN STUDY GROUP, I STARED ABSENTLY AT THE NOTEBOOK IN my lap. Andrew's voice droned in the background of my thoughts like a mosquito as he pestered Beth and Sanaa to quiz him. He monopolized the group, in a panic over the American Legal History final this week. Our last final, and, as with the others, I was confident I was going to pass. My eidetic memory had gotten my tired ass through so many late nights, not only would I graduate, but I'd do it with honors. But three days of grueling testing in Sacramento loomed ahead for the bar exam, and I was no closer to finding an angle for my brief to Judge Miller.

I can't get distracted now.

But I was. I tapped my pen on my knee, determined to focus, as visions of red lips and a cherry; a black dress and long legs; a heated body pressed to mine wafted into my thoughts like a delicious scent to a starving man.

I was hungry for Darlene, in every way.

Henrietta once told me that it was hard for a person to imagine a better life than the one he had; to really know and feel that it was possible. It was the reason, she said, so many people worked so hard just to stay where they were. They never reached out for what they really wanted because they believed what they wanted was out of reach. But it wasn't. Like words written on a mirror: *Objects may be closer than they appear.*

I still had so much work left to do, and even if I passed the bar and Judge Miller hired me, I'd have to work my ass off just as hard to keep that job, to keep providing for Olivia on my own. There would always be another finish line to cross. Was it stupid of me to not reach a little more for what I wanted? To imagine a life with something more than what I had?

My pen rattled against the denim on my knee.

The law that I had taken such refuge in for being black and white, was cold compared to Darlene's smile. The sanctuary I had found in the codes and sections was an empty place. She was life, and maybe, if I didn't screw it up, I had something to offer her too.

How about you start with a first date?

A slow smile spread over my lips. I shut my notebook with a snap, startling the others, and packed up my stuff.

"Where are you going?" Andrew demanded.

"Home."

"We're one final away from graduation."

I clapped him on the shoulder. "I have no doubt you will pass with adequate colors."

Andrew shook me off. "Asshole."

I grinned. "Ladies. It's been real."

Outside, I fished out my cell phone and called Serenity Spa. The snobby sounding woman at reception told me that Darlene had already left for the day.

"Early," she added with a sniff.

I had Darlene's phone number programmed into my photographic memory, but I didn't want to call or text her. I wanted to see her, to talk to her in person when I took the monumental, earth shattering, life changing step of actually asking a woman out on a date.

Jackson will shit his pants.

I laughed at myself, and called Elena. After asking about Olivia, I tried my best to sound casual as fuck. "Has Darlene come home by any chance?"

"She did," Elena said. "She dropped off more chocolate chip cookies for the kids on her way out. Such a sweet girl."

"Do you know where she was going?"

"No, but she looked dressed to practice her dance."

"Right. Okay, thanks, Elena. I'll be home on time tonight."

"No rush, querido. No rush at all."

Quickly, I recalled Darlene and my conversation at the park. She'd said she rehearsed at the American Dance Academy. I looked up the address on my phone for directions and headed to the Muni.

⚜

There was no one manning the front desk at the Academy, but a layout of the building on the wall guided me to the practice rooms. I headed down the pristine white hallway, passing open doors of ballet dancers at a barre, a jazz class for older couples. I expected to find Darlene with her dance troupe.

She was alone.

My breath caught. My heart stopped. Every part of me froze as I watched her from the doorway. She was wearing that damn black top with the crisscrossing straps along her back that made it hard for me to think. Her long legs were bare but for tight spandex short-shorts. Her dark hair spilled out of a high ponytail. A New Age-sounding instrumental played over the sound system, and Darlene folded and unfolded herself across the wooden floor in a series of flowing movements.

I was mesmerized, my eyes tracking her and when she stopped short, I flinched.

She tossed her head from side to side, as if her neck was stiff and rubbed one hand, then shook out her arms. She listened to some internal count in the music for a moment, then continued the dance.

Twenty seconds later, she stopped again, and she shook her arms, frustrated, and crossed to a small sound system against one wall. The music went quiet, and that was my cue; I'd lurked long enough.

"Hey," I said, stepping into the room.

She turned around and the surprised smile that flitted across her face was like a gift.

"What are you doing here?" she asked.

"I needed to talk to you," I said, "but I got side tracked watching you. Sorry, I don't mean to come off like a creepy stalker. You're really good, Darlene. Incredible, actually."

She shook her head, her cheeks turning pink as she walked to meet me in the center of the room. "It's not a good show," she said. "Or maybe it could be but…" She sighed and rubbed her fingers.

"What's going on here?" I asked, indicating her hands.

"God, it's my job at the spa," she said. "My supervisor told me turnover was high when I first started working there. Now I know why. My hands hurt all the time."

"You need a massage for yourself," I said. "Don't they give employees a discount?"

"They do, but I don't like being there," Darlene said. "No one is friendly. It's not my scene. And all of the employees are stressed out and sore. The last thing we want to do is give a discount massage to one of our own."

I reached out and took her hand in both of mine before I could talk myself out of it. Her hand was soft skin and delicate bone, and I gently rubbed circles into her palm with my thumbs.

"How is your show going?" I asked. "Has your partner learned to watch himself?"

"No," she said, with a small laugh. "He's a menace, as always, but I think I've learned to dance around him. Some added choreography. That's why I'm here, rehearsing alone. Safer that way." She glanced down at her hand in mine, then back to me. "That feels nice," she said softly.

I nodded, and let go of her hand to take the other one, gently massaging and squeezing the tension out.

"I had a really good time the other night," she said.

"You were an incredible dancer then, too," I said. "With Jackson."

"I wanted to dance with you."

"I'm no good."

"I'll bet that's not true."

I smiled, concentrating on her hand. If I looked up at her beautiful face this close to mine, I wouldn't do what I came here to do. "I'm pretty sure the only move I could pull off is the dip."

"A dip is easy," Darlene said. "All you have to do is be there for the woman. Hold her. Make sure she doesn't fall."

Slowly, I raised my eyes to meet hers. "I want to try."

Our gazes held for a moment, the air thick between us. Darlene moved close into my space, and my senses were overwhelmed by the heat of her body and the perfume of her skin; daisies tinged with the salt of her sweat.

Her mouth was inches from mine, as she ringed her arms around my neck. Her breasts pressed against my chest.

"Hold your right arm out at an angle," she said. Her breath was sweet against my cheek.

I did as she said and, effortlessly, she hooked her leg over so that my arm held her under the crook of her knee.

"Make a right angle out of your other arm," she said.

I did, creating a stiff-armed frame around her.

"You got me?" she asked.

"Yeah," I said, daring a glance at her eyes. "I got you."

A smile spread over her lips, and slowly, with precise yet fluid movements, she bent herself back over my arm, her hands reaching for the floor, while her leg, hooked on my other arm, anchored her. I watched her bend, watched her breasts strain against the black material of her shirt as she flowed backward like water. She stretched her other leg behind her in a split, and her reaching fingertips grazed her foot.

Instinctively, I bent my knee to dip her lower, keeping my arms stiff like scaffolding while she flowed and ebbed around me.

I held her securely for a long moment, then slowly straightened. She came up with me, graceful in my arms, our gazes locked. Her leg came down but her arms were still around my neck. Mine slipped around her waist.

"How was that?" I whispered my mouth inches from hers.

"Perfect," she said.

I watched her form the word. Her teeth grazed her lower lip over the 'f' and then I had to have her. Without thought or hesitation, I laid my mouth to hers.

She gave a little gasp and her lips parted for me. I deepened the kiss, while wondering how I'd lived twenty-four years without having kissed her before.

Kissing Darlene was kissing all of her. I tasted the sweetness of her, the energy she put into her art. Her breath suffused my mouth and I inhaled her.

This is life.

My tongue slid against hers, and the taste of her went straight to my head like a shot of whiskey. She moaned—not quietly—and I swallowed that, too.

Our gentle kissing turned harder and needier. I wanted to devour her, every breath, every touch…my hands skimmed down her back, to her ass, to fill my hands with her. Her fingers slid down my chest, then back up around my neck and into my hair, to pull me closer. Her leg hooked around my waist this time, and cinched tight, pressing herself against the erection that strained against my jeans. In every electric inch of her body, I felt how badly she wanted me too.

I kissed her until I was nearly biting her, and my fevered imagination wanted to know what it would be like to have her—this woman—in my bed, under me and naked. I wanted all of her skin on mine, and the soft little moans she was making now would turn to screams under my hands, my mouth, every part of me touching all of her.

"God, Darlene," I ground out between kisses. My hands tangled in her hair, to angle her head, to kiss her more. "I want you, right now."

She nodded against my lips. "Yes, me too. So much," she breathed.

Voices sounded in the hallway outside the open door, prying the moment apart. With effort, I broke from her but stayed close, feeling her breath on my lips that were wet with her kiss.

"We should stop," I said, striving to catch my breath. "This is not why I'm here. To hook up. I don't want to just hook up with you. I want you. Fucking hell, I've never wanted anyone more. But I want to take you out. A real date. It sounds insane, but I've never done that."

Her eyes were glassy and bright with desire. "Neither have I. Not at first, I mean. It always starts with this. But Sawyer—"

"I want you to have more," I said. I pulled away, and sucked in a breath. "Will you have dinner with me? Tonight, if you can. Or tomorrow?"

"I can't tomorrow," she said, and the brilliant light in her eyes sparked with something like fear. "But tonight is short notice. What about Olivia?"

"I'll take care of her," I said.

The urge to touch her again was like a hunger in my entire body. But if I did, we wouldn't make it out of this room.

"I'll make reservations," I said. "Someplace nice."

"Not too nice," she said quickly. "I don't want you to spend a lot of money on me."

"I do. I want to take you to a place nice enough where you can wear another dress like the one you wore on Saturday," I said. "Something that will make every man in the room seethe with jealousy."

Darlene's smile was tremulous. She opened her mouth to speak and I dared to take her face and kiss her again.

"Tonight. Seven o'clock? A real date. Okay?"

She nodded, and with supreme effort, I pulled myself away and went home, toward something more.

chapter fifteen

Darlene

On the way home from the Dance Academy, I opened the contacts in my phone a hundred times to call Max. Each time, my thumb hovered over the call button, and each time I chickened out.

You know what he'll tell you to do. He'll say you have to tell Sawyer the truth.

I squeezed my eyes shut as the Muni train rumbled and swayed beneath me.

With every passing block, my resolve waxed and waned. Yes, Sawyer deserved the truth, and I started to call Max for moral support in that endeavor. The next instant, the thought that Sawyer would hate me filtered in, and I shoved the phone away.

Instead, I let my fingers touch my lips, where I could still feel Sawyer's kiss. Our first kiss. My heart crashed against my chest at the sense memory.

Sawyer's mouth on mine was exactly as I had imagined it and nothing I had ever prepared for. Soft and hard. Sweet and masculine. Demanding and generous at the same time. I wanted more of his kisses, his body holding mine tightly to him. I thought of how he looked at me…

He won't look at me the same way if I tell him.

By the time I'd arrived at the Victorian, my stomach was a knot of nerves, worry mixed with butterflies of excitement. I dashed up the two flights of stairs to my place, hoping the exertion would burn off the anxiety and I'd know what to do.

"Why do I have to tell him at all?" I asked my empty studio. "There's no reason! It's in the past and that's where it should stay."

I took a hot shower, scrubbing my skin with a loofah, as if I could scrub out the whispers of memory imbedded there; of nights spent on a jail cell cot, or on a hospital bed with an IV drip in my arm to flush out the heroin…

Even though the drugs were long gone, the shame they left behind hurt in so many ways.

I stepped out on a cloud of steam, wrapped myself in a towel, and grabbed the phone. Before I could stop myself, I jabbed Max's number.

"Hello, Max speaking."

"Hi, it's me."

"Hey, Me. What's up?"

"Sawyer kissed me," I blurted. "And we have a date tonight. I just thought… as my sponsor, you should know that."

A silence.

"Are you there?"

"I'm here," he said slowly. "Processing. Is there anything else you want to tell me?"

"Nope. That's it." I wrapped a lock of dripping hair around my finger. "He's taking me out to dinner. Oh, and we went dancing on Saturday night too. It was fun. No big deal."

See how well I'm handling this? I wanted to shout.

"Okay."

Max hadn't been able to get out of a shift on Monday night and had missed the NA meeting with me. I'd considered that lucky at the time, but now I wished he'd been there. I wished I'd talked.

I wish I could talk.

A small sob tore out of me, and the pretend bravado gusted out with it. I sank onto my little loveseat. "Fucking hell, Max, this sucks."

"I know," he said. "Tell me."

"I want to. I want to be honest. I do. That's why my stomach is in knots, isn't it? Sawyer isn't like any other man I've ever been with. I'm not just attracted to him, Max. I like him. A lot. In a different way than I've ever… *liked* a man. And his little girl…" Tears sprang to my eyes. "I like her, too. So much. And I want…"

"What, Dar?" Max asked gently. "What do you want?"

Everything.

"I don't know," I said. I wiped my eyes irritably. "I hate that no matter what I do, I'll always be *that girl*. The girl who was weak and sad. Who had this big yawning hole of *want* in her and filled it up with terrible shit. And you know what? The drugs are gone but the *want* is still there, and the good things I want to fill it with are right in front of me but I'm scared to grab for them." My voice turned small and watery. "I'm scared, Max, that he'll hate me."

"If he's any kind of a good guy, he won't hate you. But you have to tell him. Not just so he lives with your truth, but so that you do too. That's fair to him and it's fair to you. You deserved to be loved as you are, Darlene. Not in bits and pieces."

I sniffed. "How come you're not telling me to cancel the date? To forget about all of this and stick to my year-long men boycott?"

"Unreasonable expectations…" he said gently. "Besides, telling you not to love is like depriving a flower of sunlight. You aren't meant to be contained, Darlene. It would be a crime against humanity. Just do it honestly, okay? And then tell me all about it. Then tell the *group* all about it at tomorrow night's meeting."

I nodded against the phone, my tears burning hotly down my cheek. "God, this is so hard." I huffed a sigh. "Can't I sleep with him first?"

Max laughed. "You're going to be fine, I promise. Okay?"

"Okay. I should go. I have to get ready for this dinner. What does one wear to tell a future criminal prosecutor that you're a former criminal?"

"Something with bold patterns. Maybe ruffles…"

I sniffed a laugh.

"Call me later, Dar."

"I will."

I hung up and stared at the phone. Then I got dressed for my first—and probably last—date with Sawyer Haas.

I chose ruffles after all. I put on a soft, prairie style blouse-dress in light beige with tiny pink and green flowers. It had puffy sleeves and a high collar, but barely skimmed the tops of my thighs. I paired it with white ankle boots and piled my hair on my head in a loose, messy bun with tendrils falling down, to frame my face and show off my lucky gold hoop earrings.

I glanced at myself a final time in the mirror as the clock read seven.

"You can do this," I told my reflection and heaved a sigh. I plastered on a wide smile. "Hi, Sawyer! Guess what? I spent three months in jail for misdemeanor drug possession. I just wanted to do the responsible thing and tell you that before you let me *babysit your daughter again.*"

I covered my eyes with my hand.

"He's going to hate me."

The doorbell rang.

"Oh, God."

I sucked in deep breaths and smoothed my dress.

"Okay, here we go."

I mustered a pitiful amount of mental fortitude, and it all fled the exact second I opened the door.

Sweet Jesus, no fair. No fair at all.

I forgot how to breathe and my heart sent rushes of heated blood throughout my entire body. Sawyer was dressed up as he had been on Saturday night, only this time he was dressed up just for me. He wore a black jacket, white dress shirt—unbuttoned at the top—black slacks and a stylish leather belt with a sleek silver buckle around his slender waist. He looked casually elegant—like a Best Man at a wedding after the ceremony was over; where every bridesmaid was ready to drop her panties for a stolen moment with him in a closet during the reception.

"I…oh my God," I stammered, my eyes drinking him in. "You are…so hot."

I cringed at my clumsy words but Sawyer didn't seem to have heard.

"Darlene…" he said. "You're…" His words tapered to nothing as his gaze swept over me unabashedly.

"Take a picture, it'll last longer," I joked weakly.

"Oh, I did," he said, and gave his head a little shake. He withdrew a bouquet of three white roses from behind his back. "It's the best I could do on short notice."

"They're beautiful," I said.

"You're beautiful," he said. "You're stunningly beautiful, Darlene."

"Thank you, Sawyer," I said, and my cheeks warmed at the lovely compliment even as my anxiety deepened into a deep blue of sadness for how I was going to ruin the perfection of this night. "I'll just put them in some water."

He waited by the door as I scrounged for a vase. A tall drinking glass was all I could find. I put the flowers in it with shaking hands and grabbed my black coat. Sawyer helped me into it.

"Where are we going?" I asked in a small voice, as we headed down the stairs.

"A restaurant called Nopa," he said, his own voice sounding thick. "Jackson said it's a good one."

At the bottom of the stairs, in the entry of the house, Sawyer's hand snaked out to grab mine. He pulled me close, and his hands slipped around my waist. I melted against him as he hauled me in for a deep kiss. His tongue slid against mine, then swept through my mouth. I clung to him, the clean taste of him, the scent of his masculine cologne, the softness of his lips, the intense want that coiled in his muscles under my hands…they all bombarded my senses and threatened to melt me into a puddle at his feet.

"The kiss is supposed to come at the end of the date, but I can't help myself," he said, his voice gruff, his eyes dark and so beautiful in the dim light.

"You don't have to stop," I whispered, kissing him again. "We don't have to go out. We can stay here. Go upstairs and…"

Not say a word.

"God, you have no idea how badly I want that." He kissed my neck, my cheek, just under my ear. He pinned me to the wall with his body and my hips adjusted to him on their own so that he fit so perfectly against me. His erection brushed me between my legs.

"Or maybe you have some idea…" he said hoarsely.

I pressed my body into his as his hand slid up my thigh, to the lacy thong I wore beneath the dress. One more moment, one more touch and he would take me upstairs, and it would be too late to tell him. I wouldn't have to. It would be so easy…

"Jesus," Sawyer whispered. He backed off so that the only place we touched was his forehead pressed to mine, and his hands on my hips, bracing himself. "Okay, wait," he said. "I want to take you out. I'm *going* to take you out." He grinned sheepishly. "Just give me a minute."

My heart ached at that grin, one that I don't think many people saw. He was so serious, so stressed, all the time. But with me he smiled and made jokes and let himself be a little bit vulnerable.

And once I told him what I'd done, it would all go away.

I took his handsome face in my hands. "Do you ever wish you could take a moment and keep it forever? Like right now…how you taste on my mouth, and your hands on me, and your eyes…God, Sawyer, the way you're looking at me… If I could have just one moment, one feeling, and live in it forever, I would choose this one."

Sawyer's brows came together, his smile tilting. "No one's ever said anything to me like that before." His hands came up to take mine. "But you look… sad. Is everything okay?"

The words came to my lips and I nearly let them out. I drew in a breath… and let that out instead.

"Yes, sure. Sorry, I don't know what came over me. I'm hungry, I guess. We can go. We should go."

Sawyer held the door for me, and I walked down to the street, wishing for San Francisco's allegedly famous cold wind to slap some sense into me. But the heat wave was lingering long enough that I hardly needed my coat.

"The restaurant isn't far," he said. "We could walk or Uber. Up to you."

"Let's walk," I said. Maybe, I thought, if I kept moving my body, I could work out the nerves and be able to talk. "So…where is Olivia tonight?"

"Jackson took her over to Henrietta's," Sawyer said. "Olivia knows her. Before I moved to the old Vic and was blessed with the miracle of Elena, Henrietta did all my babysitting."

"Have you lived in the Victorian long?"

"Almost a year now. When Olivia's mom left her with me, I had to move there."

"Why?"

"Jackson and I, and some buddies of ours, had a killer place on Stanyon Street. Big parties every month. Not a place to raise a baby."

"No, I guess not," I said.

His expression took on a tint of faint wistfulness, as if he were talking about something he'd had that was gone forever.

"All of UC Hastings showed up at our parties. They all had costume themes, like Marvel heroes, favorite musicians, evil-doers. No costume, no admittance."

"Evil-doers?"

"Yeah, you had to dress as a villain. From anything; movies, comics, TV, books…It was awesome." He chuckled. "One time, a chick showed up dressed as Lizzie Borden and brought her own axe."

"A real axe?"

"We confiscated that pretty quickly. Axes and tequila do not mix." The wistful look came over his face again. "Yeah, those were fun times. Seems like a lifetime ago. *Olivia's* lifetime ago."

"Do you miss it?" I asked.

"Yeah, I do," he said. "But she's worth it. No more parties for me."

"Yeah, me too," I said, keeping my gaze firmly on the sidewalk sliding under my boots. "I used to party pretty hard."

There. That was the truth. Ish.

"Yeah?" Sawyer asked. "If I had an Evil-Doer party next weekend, who would you come as?"

A convict.

"I don't know," I said. "Catwoman, I think. Michelle Pfeiffer's version."

Sawyer's grin turned sly. "I wouldn't mind seeing you in that costume."

I managed a smile.

"She's not truly evil though," I said. "She's vulnerable too, which is why I like her. But I think it would be nice to maybe not care so much about everything all the time. It's not always easy being the good guy, especially when being good or nice is so often mistaken for being weak."

"What do you mean?"

I shook my head. "I'm nice at the spa, I'm nice with the dance troupe, but I can't seem to do anything right with either group."

Sawyer scowled. "Why not? Are they being assholes to you?"

"No, just…indifferent."

His scowl deepened. "I find it hard to believe that anyone could be indifferent where you're concerned."

His hand closed around mine, holding on to me just as tightly as I held on to him, and maybe I was weak and cowardly, but it felt too good to let go.

The street around us had changed from rows of old houses to a bustling city. The restaurant, Nopa, was a squat building that looked somewhat plain on the outside, but I could tell even before I saw the menu on the outer wall that it was a 'nice place,' as my Grandma Bea would say. The kind where your food didn't come with a side of vegetables; you had to order them separately.

I turned to Sawyer.

"Hey, how about pizza and a walk along the Pier? And ice cream sundaes after?"

Sawyer's smile tilted again. "You don't like the menu…?"

"It looks amazing. But…I don't want you to spend a lot of money on me."

"The reservations are made," he said. "And I told you, I want to. I don't want to be cheap or…tacky. I want to take you out and have a nice dinner. I want to talk and then maybe take a walk somewhere, and kiss you goodnight at your door, and leave it at that." He brushed the backs of his fingers down my cheek. "You're not like any other girl, Darlene. I'm not…indifferent about you."

I swallowed and blinked hard. "You don't have to prove anything to me, Sawyer."

"Maybe not, but this is for me too. I've never been on a real date, remember?" His charming grin reappeared. "You going to deprive me of the experience?"

I managed a smile. "How could I do that?"

He held the door open for me. "After you."

The interior of Nopa was industrial chic, with cement floors and elegant booths in gray leather. Amber lights cast a golden hue over the crowds that talked and laughed over pork chops or roasted salmon.

A host ushered us to a table for two, and I sat across from Sawyer, a candle flickering between us. We opened our menus and my stomach dropped. The prices weren't outrageous but this was definitely a 'nice' restaurant. Even the beers were expensive and had eccentric names.

A waiter in a black apron approached us. "Something to drink?"

Sawyer looked to me. "Would you like wine?"

My gaze darted to the wine list and the double-digit—and triple digit—numbers beside the bottles.

"No, thank you," I said and smiled weakly. "Not a fan."

Sawyer smiled back. "A Coke with three cherries, maybe?"

"I'll just have water for now."

"I'll have a Death and Taxes Lager," Sawyer told the waiter. "I don't think I have a choice."

"Inevitable," the waiter agreed, and the two men chuckled at the joke.

Inevitable, I thought. *What a horrible word.*

It was inevitable that Sawyer would have to know about my past. If we continued seeing each other he'd have to know where I went three nights a week. If he needed me to babysit on a Monday, Wednesday or Friday, I couldn't do it, and he'd want to know why.

And then there's the whole 'being your honest self' thing. You might want to try that.

I looked over at Sawyer, devastating in black and white, and the inevitable felt impossible.

"God, you look…so handsome right now," I said.

"Thank you…"

"I'm not kidding. Your mouth…God. You have the most beautiful mouth."

Sawyer shook his head, laughing. "Okay, wow. Every time I think I'm used to how direct you are…"

"I'm not always direct. Not when it counts. But I'm very serious about your mouth. And when you kissed me…I've never been kissed like that before. I've never been smiled at by a man the way you're smiling at me now. It's almost too much."

Sawyer's smile froze on his face then wilted as tears filled my eyes.

"Darlene, what's wrong?"

"It *is* too much." I set my menu down. "This place. It's too nice. Too much for you to spend on me."

"It's not…"

"It is, because…" The words choked my throat. "It's not fair to you."

Sawyer frowned. "What are you talking about? I want to be here with you. I want to spend money on you and—"

I shook my head vigorously, my tears falling faster now. "No. No, you shouldn't. You work so hard and you take such good care of Livvie, and I'm just…I'm not what you think, and I'm sorry. This was a mistake. I'm so sorry, but I have to go. I have to…"

The waiter returned. "Are you ready to order?"

"No, I have to go."

I rose to my feet, and my chair scraped loudly. Diners at other tables were looking at us. The waiter's eyebrows rose.

"Darlene…" Sawyer leaned over the table. "What's going on?"

"I can't do this. It's not right and I just… *can't.*"

I grabbed for my purse on the back of the chair but the damn thing was snagged.

The nearby diners were snickering and murmuring now.

"No, no, it's not him," I said loudly. "It's not him. He's wonderful. He is…" I looked to Sawyer who was staring at me in a kind of mild shock. "You are, Sawyer. You're wonderful, and I'm so sorry."

I yanked my purse off, knocking my chair over, and stumbled out of the restaurant.

"Darlene, *wait.*"

Outside, I walked faster, my boots clopping on the cement, and then a hand closed around my arm.

"Darlene, come on." Sawyer pulled me to a stop and turned me to look at him. "You're scaring me. What just happened?"

"Nothing," I said, and that was so obviously a lie, I cringed at my own cowardice. "I can't tell you. I can't. Please…I need to go."

"No," he said, his dark eyes hardening. "You need to tell me what the hell is going on." His expression softened slightly. "Are you okay? Tell me."

"I…I can't…" I whispered. "I don't want to…"

Sawyer's jaw clenched and he looked away for a moment. "Is there…another guy?" he asked tightly.

I froze, the absurdity of it shocking me. "What? *No…*"

"Is it what's his name? Max?"

"No, nothing like that."

"Are you sure? You mentioned him a couple of times and he's always texting you…"

Sawyer bit off his words and carved his hand through his hair.

"Dammit, Darlene, I don't want to be *that guy.* The jealous asshole. So I never asked about Max or where you go some nights. It wasn't my place, but then our moment in the dance studio happened, and now it feels like it *is* my place. I mean...I'm not saying you can't see other people. We haven't figured anything out. But I have to be honest, if you are seeing other people, it would fucking suck, okay? And I think you should tell me, so I know the score." He held his hands out, a hard, joyless smile playing over his lips. "So there. I guess I'm a jealous asshole after all."

The tears blurred my eyes so I almost couldn't see him. "You...you would be jealous if I were seeing someone else?"

"Jesus, do I have to say it again?" Sawyer gave an incredulous shake of his head. "What the hell, Darlene, just *tell me*."

"I'm scared," I whispered. "I'm scared that if I tell you what I need to tell you, you'll never look at me like you looked at me tonight." My lips trembled over a teary smile. "I just wanted that for a little bit longer, you know? That feeling...?"

Sawyer held my gaze a moment, and then swallowed hard. "Darlene," he said gruffly. "I haven't so much as touched a woman in almost a year. You're the first. Because I care about...I think about you..."

He clenched his teeth and carved his hand through his hair again.

"Fucking hell, I can't talk about what I feel. I don't. I never do. My life has been Olivia and law school and keeping my goddamn head above water. And that's it. And then you came along and now everything's different. It's better. It's *better*, Darlene, when I'd sort of given up on being happy."

"Oh, God, don't say that," I whispered. "Or no, I want you to. Part of me wants you to keep talking because it's incredible to me that I could...*be* that for someone. For you. But it makes this so much harder."

He looked to the ground and planted his hands on his hips, bracing himself. "Just tell me the truth. Are you seeing someone else?"

"No," I said. "I—"

A text came in on my phone, and I knew without looking it was Max. He'd gotten the news about his transfer. I froze and Sawyer's expression hardened to stone. The rare vulnerability in his eyes vanished. He was walling himself up, second by ticking second. Another chime came, and then my phone rang.

"It's him, isn't it?" Sawyer said.

"Yes. But he's not... I'm not dating him. I'm not dating anyone."

"Then who is he?"

"A friend, I promise. He's... not what you think."

Sawyer held up his hands as he walked backward a few steps. "I don't know what to think." My phone rang on and on. "You should get that," he said, then turned and strode away.

I watched him go, the words to call him back stuck in my throat. My phone went quiet, then started ringing again. I fished it out of my bag.

"Hi, Max," I said softly.

"Hey, Dar." He sounded breathless and exhilarated. "I'm calling you first.

Before my other friends or anyone…I had to tell you. It doesn't feel real until I tell you."

"You got the job."

"I got the job. They say I might have to leave at any time. Whenever the paperwork is finalized and something about a contact in Seattle, but holy shit, I got it."

I sagged against Nopa's wall, my shoulders hunched against the world. "I'm so happy for you. I'm so happy and yet completely crushed at the same time."

"I know," he said. "I'm sorry and yet I have to thank you."

"Thank *me*? Why—?"

"Oh *shit*, wait. You're on your date with Sawyer the Lawyer, aren't you? Oh my God, I'm such an idiot. I got so excited and completely forgot everything else. Fuck, I'm so sorry…"

I shook my head. "It's okay. It's over now."

It's all over.

"What's wrong? What happened?"

"I can't tell him, Max," I whispered. "I can't. I try and the words stick. He'll look at me like everyone else in my family does, and I'll die a little inside." I huffed a breath, wiped my nose on the back of my hand. "He thinks you and I are dating."

"You *wish*," Max said, coaxing a small laugh out of me. His voice softened. "Dar, you have to tell him the truth. You know you do."

"I know," I said. "You're right. You were right about everything."

"Of course I was, but it's so hard to keep track. What else was I right about?"

"You know that emotional rock bottom you keep talking about?"

"Yeah."

"I'm standing at the edge of it, staring right down into it. Teetering," I said, my voice hardly a whisper. "It'll just take one push and…"

"And?"

"I'm going to fall in."

chapter sixteen

Sawyer

I WALKED BACK TO THE VICTORIAN ALONE, CURSING MYSELF FOR LETTING THE WHOLE night fall apart; the ruination of what had the makings of a perfect night was a bitter pill I couldn't swallow. I'd never let myself care about a woman before. My mother's death made caring too much seem like a dangerous proposition. I already lived with the constant fear Molly would show up any minute and try to fight me for Olivia. That kind of strain on my heart was already too much, but Darlene…

"Fuck," I muttered.

She'd gotten past every one of my usual defenses so now the mere idea of her with another man felt like a goddamn knife in my chest.

She was upset and you walked away.

Like an instinct, the steely cage around my heart was resurrecting itself, reforming minute by minute. I'd been stupidly optimistic, I told myself. Taken my eye off the prize and got knocked on my ass for it.

Henrietta had planned to keep Olivia all night, but I went and got her, muttering some excuse about Darlene being under the weather and having to cancel.

I took my daughter home, fed her dinner, and put her to bed.

"Just you and me," I told her, brushing the brown curls from her eyes as she drifted to sleep. "I'm going to take care of you, Livvie. We're almost at the finish line, aren't we?"

I put on sleep pants and a T-shirt, and sat at my desk, my study materials arrayed in front of me. I had one last final, Judge Miller's assignment, and the damn bar exam. I didn't need any more distractions.

I tried to focus on my studies, but my stupid heart felt bruised, and when I heard her footsteps on the stairs going up, I fought the urge to bolt out of my chair and confront Darlene. Or comfort her. I didn't know which.

I did neither.

"Fuck me," I muttered.

I opened my laptop to the document I'd begun for Judge Miller's assignment when writing by hand wasn't working. Typing didn't work either.

He wanted life. The brightest burst of life I knew was right above me, and I was down here, afraid of how much I wanted to be with her, knowing all too well how the things—and people—we care about most can vanish right before our eyes.

I went to bed and tossed all night.

The next morning, I dragged myself through the motions of getting Olivia and myself ready for the day.

"Everything all right, querido?" Elena asked when I dropped Livvie off.

"Fine," I said. I kissed my daughter. "Be good. I love you."

"Wuv, Daddy," Olivia said. From Elena's arms she pressed her palm to her mouth and then flung her arm spastically to blow me a kiss.

My eyes stung as I turned to go.

She's the most important thing in the world. Focus on her.

The idea of having more happiness than that would have to wait.

I stepped outside the front of the Victorian and started down the stairs. A silver sedan was parked at the curb in front. Before I took one step, the door opened and a man looking to be in his early fifties stepped out. He straightened his pale blue, seersucker suit jacket. He looked like he just stepped off a yacht.

"Sawyer Haas?"

I froze. "Yes."

"A moment."

The man opened the back door of the sedan and an older couple, both looking to be in their mid-sixties stepped out. The man wore khaki pants and a white button-down shirt, the woman in a lavender dress. The June sunshine glinted off his gold Rolex and sparkled in diamond studs in her ears. They stood hand in hand on the sidewalk, nervous smiles on their faces.

"Hello," the man said. "My name is Gerald Abbott and this is my wife, Alice. We're Molly's parents."

The blood drained from my face.

Molly's parents. Molly. She's here. She's back and now—

"This is our attorney, Mr. Holloway," the woman, Alice said, indicating the man in the dark suit.

"Mr. Haas." Mr. Holloway extended his hand to me.

They stood at the bottom of the three stairs, me at the top. I stared back without taking it.

"What do you want?"

Gerald and Alice exchanged grief-stricken looks, a shared pain that only they knew. They couldn't speak, so their attorney spoke for them.

"Molly has unfortunately passed way," Holloway said.

I went cold all over while breaking into a sweat at the same time, as my body tried to process the thousand conflicting emotions that shot through me at those words.

"She's...dead?"

He nodded. "Yes. A car accident."

Alice slipped her hand into Gerald's and they exchanged a pained look that was brief but went miles deep.

"What happened?"

"Car accident."

"When?" I choked out.

"Six months ago."

My eyes darted between Gerald and Alice Abbott, and I felt like I couldn't move; *shouldn't* move, from the front stoop of the house. I had to guard it. Because Olivia was inside and they were here.

"We're here," Holloway said, each word like a knife in my chest, "to talk about the custody arrangements for Molly's daughter—my clients' *granddaughter*—Olivia Abbott."

chapter seventeen

Sawyer

Jackson hung up the phone and tossed it on the coffee table. "Not the best news. The officer said since Molly is an adult and left of her own free will, she's not technically 'missing.'"

I looked up from the baby in my arms taking a bottle Molly had left in the gigantic diaper bag. "She abandoned Olivia," I said. "That has to be illegal. You've finished the Family Law section. Tell me. They'll track her down for child abandonment, right?"

Jackson rubbed his chin. "Safe Haven laws protect her. She can't be arrested. If she leaves the baby with a parent—you—it's considered legal abandonment after six months. If she leaves her with a non-parent—maybe also you—it's one year."

"I can't do this alone."

"You might not have to do it at all," Jackson said, his Mac open on his lap. "They sell paternity tests at the Walgreens. It's non-legal for any official capacity, but accurate. You'll at least know if Molly was telling the truth. And if she was lying, you take the baby to CPS and go back to your life."

I glanced down at Olivia. *Go back to my life*, I thought. *Like nothing happened.* I swallowed the sudden lump in my throat.

"How long does the test take?"

"Three days from the time you mail it to the lab," Jackson said. "Simple enough."

"The test won't hurt her, right?" I asked. "If I have to draw her blood or prick her finger, forget it."

"Nah, man, cotton swab to the cheek."

I nodded. The baby stirred, made a little sound as she ate. I settled her better in my arms. Around me—us—the detritus of the party lay scattered across the coffee table and on the floor. Olivia's bottle from this morning stood next to an empty pilsner.

I was still in my Man in Black costume. I'd had to sleep with Olivia on my chest, propped on my bed and surrounded by pillows, paranoid she'd roll out of my arms, and woke up every time she moved. I had no place to put her down.

I didn't want to put her down.

Jackson shut his laptop. "I'll go get the test. There's no point in panicking until we know for sure what the deal is."

"Three days until results?" I said. "What the hell do I do in the meanwhile? I have nothing."

"We'll take her to my mom," Jackson said with a grin. "Henrietta will set you up." He clapped a hand on my shoulder. "Everything's going to be okay."

I stared at the people in front of my house.

Everything's going to be okay.

Except at that precise moment, the words felt laughably weak. I tightened my grip on my briefcase.

"Mr. Haas," the lawyer, Holloway, said. "We'd like to have a sit-down with you. The four of us."

My gaze darted to the Abbotts, who were watching me with a strange mixture of sadness, fear and hope in their eyes and painted over their features.

"I have a final this morning," I said. "My last final for law school. It's kind of important."

The Abbotts stiffened at my sarcasm. Holloway was unperturbed. "Perhaps, after?"

"After, I have a meeting with my advisor to sign off on my graduation requirements. My schedule is full."

"Please," Alice said. "We only need a little time. An hour?" Her glance darted to the house behind me. "Is she there? We'd like to see her…"

"Not going to happen," I said, making her flinch, and despite my bone-numbing fear, I felt a little sorry for her.

Fuck that, they want to take her away from me.

I straightened my shoulders. "How do I even know you're who you say you are?"

Gerald reached into pocket for his wallet to show ID, while Alice pulled a small stack of photos from her purse.

"Mr. Holloway said to bring these. Here's Molly as a little girl, and one as a teenager." Her voice thickened with tears. "Here she is at her Sweet Sixteen birthday party…"

She held the photos to me while Gerald flashed his driver's license. I barely glanced at them and I didn't move any closer. They exchanged troubled looks again, their arms slowly lowering. Holloway cleared his throat.

"We need to sit down, Mr. Haas. Today. I advised the Abbotts to limit all contact with you for the hearing before the court, but they insist on speaking to you first."

A hearing. There's going to be a hearing…

My heart dropped to my stomach, but outwardly my armor was on, my face impassive. "Three o'clock," I said stiffly. "At the Starbucks on Market and 8th. One hour. I'll be bringing my attorney."

I said all this as if I were calling the shots, while inside I felt like I was disintegrating.

"Very good," Holloway said. He opened the back of the sedan, and indicated for the Abbotts to get in.

They did so, reluctantly, both of them looking like they wanted to say more. Both of them giving the Victorian a final, longing glance. After his wife was in the car, Gerald Abbott fixed me with a stern look.

"Good luck with your test," he said, then climbed in.

I watched the sedan drive away. The instant it rounded the corner, out of sight, I sank to the steps, my briefcase scraping along the cement beside me as I dropped it to cover my face with my hands. I sucked in deep breaths, grasping for calm when panic was tossing me like a tiny ship on a vast ocean.

Holy fuck, it's happening. And I was so close. A few more weeks…

Defeat tried to drown me, but I shrugged it off. I had rights. If the Abbotts were here for a fight, I'd give it to them. I'd give everything until there was nothing left of me.

Livvie…

I fished my phone out of my jacket pocket. "Jackson," I said, my voice hoarse. "I need you."

I'd never been more grateful for my eidetic memory in my life. The American Legal History exam was all names and dates, statutes and by-laws, ground-breaking precedents and Founding Fathers. I scanned my mental database for the answers, and finished the exam in record time.

At the meeting in my advisor's office, she asked me twice if I needed a glass of water and once if I wanted to reschedule when I was 'feeling better.' I pushed through, pushed my emotions aside where they sunk their claws in my back and shoulders. Under the conference table, my leg wouldn't stop bouncing.

The day crawled and yet flew by, and at a quarter to three, I met Jackson at the Starbucks.

"Jesus, will you calm down?" he said while waiting in line to order. "I'm getting an ulcer just looking at you."

"I have a bad feeling about this," I said. "A fucking horrible feeling. I have *rights*," I spat. "They can't just take her from me…"

"Whoa, whoa, slow down," Jackson said. "We have no idea what they want yet."

"They want a hearing, Jax," I said, glancing over my shoulder at the front entrance. "It's already set up."

"We'll see," he said.

"Do you know what you're doing? It's a far cry from tax law…"

Jackson fixed me with a raised-eyebrow stare. "You have the money to retain someone else? 'Cause if you do, I'll give you my phone to call him right now. I'm taking time out of my work to be here."

"I'm sorry," I said, sucking in a breath. I clasped his hand. "God, I'm sorry, man, really. I trust you. I'm just scared shitless."

"I know you are. Go ahead and be an asshole to me if it helps, but as your attorney, I'm officially advising you to *not* be an asshole to these people, okay?

They're Olivia's family, for one thing. For another, you catch more bees with honey, or some shit."

I nodded absently. My mind was reeling, going in a thousand different directions. One thought stuck out from the rest, in bold type.

Molly is dead.

I'd spent the last ten months praying she wouldn't come back to try to take Olivia from me. She'd obviously been a mess the night she gave her to me; drunk and disheveled, and looking as though she lived out of her car. Maybe that wasn't the real her, or she'd had a bad night, but that was the mental snapshot she'd left me of her as a mother.

But she *had* been Olivia's mother, and in the back of my mind, I'd always assumed she'd be in our daughter's life somehow. Now that was over. I would never have to explain to Olivia that her mother had left her. Instead, I would have to tell her she died.

She has no mother, either.

A deep pain for my little girl that I added to the noxious concoction of emotions swirling in my guts.

It was my turn to order. "I'll take a tall coffee."

"*Decaf,*" Jackson told the barista, and shot me a wink. His reassuring smile faded as he looked over his shoulder. "This must be them."

I looked to the front where the Abbotts were coming in, Holloway holding the door for open.

"That's them," I said.

"They look like money," Jackson said.

The knot of fear twisted tighter. The Abbotts had money. Enough to fight me. Enough to tell a judge they had the means to provide Olivia with a life I couldn't afford.

Jackson sighed and elbowed me in the arm. "Hey. You're jumping to conclusions in that big brain of yours. Cut it out. Nothing's happened yet."

"*Yet.*"

We took our coffees to a table in the corner that was big enough for five and waited for the Abbotts to join us. My leg bounced under that table too.

"Mr. Haas," Holloway said, extended his hand.

This time I shook it, and gave the Abbotts a small nod in greeting.

"This is Jackson Smith, my attorney," I said.

Jackson offered his hand and a bright smile. Introductions were made all around and then the five of us sat with drinks in front of us that only the attorneys touched. The Abbotts studied me with that same mix of hope and fear in their eyes. They had nice faces. Kind. They weren't monsters, but a grandma and a grandpa. *Olivia's* grandma and grandpa.

I tried to loosen my clenched-jaw and unfurrow my brow to look less like an asshole next to Jackson's friendly smile.

"I'll get straight to the point," Holloway said. "Mr. and Mrs. Abbott were only recently made aware of their daughter's passing six weeks ago."

"She'd always been on the run," Alice said in a shaky voice. "We tried to give her everything but it wasn't enough."

Gerald covered his wife's hand. "We hadn't seen her in so long. We had no idea she'd been in an accident. Nor did we know that she'd had a baby."

"We knew nothing," Alice said. "So much joy and sadness all at once…"

Jackson nodded sympathetically. "And when, exactly, were you made aware that you had a granddaughter?"

"Two weeks ago," Holloway answered. "Through a friend of the late Miss Abbott's."

Alice sat straighter, imploring me with her eyes as she spoke. "As soon as we knew, we wanted to see Olivia. To be a part of her life."

"In what capacity?" Jackson asked. He looked to Holloway. "What's this I hear about a hearing?"

Holloway folded his hands on the table, his gold watch glinting in the sun in tandem with his gold pinky ring.

"The friend of Molly's informed us that Olivia's birth certificate is most likely in your possession. Is that true, Mr. Haas?"

My heart did a slow roll in my chest. I nodded.

"And is your name listed as the father?"

"No, it is not," I said slowly. "There is no name there. It's blank."

Holloway nodded. "I presume you have taken a paternity test?"

I glanced at Jackson. He nodded his head. Once.

"Yes. A few days after Molly left Olivia with me. She's my daughter. And I'm not saying another word until you tell me what you want."

Holloway opened his mouth to speak, but Alice put her hand on his arm.

"Wait, please. This is not going at all as I'd hoped. Perhaps it was a mistake to bring our attorneys into this so quickly." She looked to me. "Can we see her? We'd like to see her." Her voiced teetered on the edge of breaking. "Our daughter is gone. Our only daughter. All we have left of her is Olivia. We'd like to spend some time with her and maybe…get to know each other better. And you, but in a warmer setting."

She looked to Jackson when my hard stare shut her out. "Is this possible?"

"Let me confer with my client."

Jackson ushered me onto the sidewalk outside.

"You're not making a great impression."

I gritted my teeth. "Jackson…"

"I know. We'll deal with that later. For now, let them see Olivia. Do what she said; get to know them. They don't seem like bad people." He cocked his head. "Don't you want a family for Olivia?"

"Yeah, I do, but on *my* terms," I said. I took my friend's arm and gripped it tight. "She stays with me, Jax. You do whatever you feel is right. If they want to come see her, fine. But I want full custody. I'm *keeping* full custody. They can visit, they can have a weekend, maybe a week in the summer, but they're *not taking her from me.*"

Jackson's expression showed no trace of his usual cheerful self. He gripped my shoulder and met my eyes with an unwavering, intense stare.

"I'll do my best, Sawyer, but it might not be up to us," he said. "And you know it."

The Abbotts took the sedan, and Jackson and I took an Uber back to the Victorian. Four o'clock on a Wednesday. Where was Darlene, I wondered as I climbed out of the car. Rehearsal? I would've given my right arm to see her smile just then. Her smile that made all the bad shit in the world seem far away.

But I fucked up. The thought of her with someone else hurt more than I was prepared for. Instead of talking to her, I renamed that pain *jealousy*, and shut down. Walked away.

Maybe I've lost her too.

I gave myself a shake.

Get a grip, you haven't lost Olivia. This isn't over. It hasn't even started.

But unlocking the front door of the Vic for the Abbotts and their lawyer felt like inviting the dragon straight into the damn castle.

"This is quite a lovely old house," Alice said in the entry. "I just love San Francisco architecture."

"Are you not from this area?" Jackson asked.

"Huntington Beach, in southern California."

The night Molly and I hooked up in Vegas whispered in my memory; Molly in a pale dress in the dimly lit bar. *I'm from So Cal, originally. My folks are still there in their huge, white bread mega mansion…*

"Jackson can take you to my place," I said, my voice wooden in my ears. "I'll get Olivia from her sitter and bring her up."

I waited until they were upstairs, then knocked on Elena's door.

"You're early today," she said with a smile. It faded at once. "But you're so pale, my dear. Is everything okay?"

Everything is going to be okay…

I nodded. "I got finished early."

Elena's mouth turned down in concern. "Come in. I'll just get her bag."

I stepped inside Elena's place. Olivia was on the floor in the living room with Laura, Elena's two-year-old, playing blocks. Olivia looked up and her little face broke into a smile.

"Daddy!"

Oh Christ…

My chest constricted and goddamn tears stung my eyes. With trembling arms, I picked her up and held her tightly, my hand behind her little head. Her arms went around my neck. I closed my eyes and fought to contain the maelstrom of emotions, to push them down, lock them up. If there was a battle to be fought, I needed to be strong.

Elena's hand on my arm and her voice gentle. "Sawyer."

I sucked in deep breaths, still holding Olivia tight to me. When my exhales were no longer shaky and I opened my eyes.

"Thanks for watching her," I said, shouldering the bag Elena handed me. "I'll see you tomorrow."

"Bye-bye," Olivia said to Elena. "Bye bye bye bye…"

I took Olivia upstairs on leaden legs.

In my place, the Abbotts were seated at the small kitchen table with Jackson, glasses of water before them. Mr. Holloway was standing with his hands clasped behind his back in front of the wall near my desk, eyeing my degree from UCSF with Honors; my Valedictorian certificate; my award for a full scholarship at Hastings that had been like winning the lottery.

He turned and all conversations ceased as I stepped inside and set my daughter down at my feet.

"This is Olivia."

Alice's hand flew to her heart, and Gerald's jaw clenched as if fighting back some strong emotion.

"Oh my heavens, she's beautiful." Alice rose slowly and approached Olivia who stood clinging to my pant leg. "Hi, sweetheart. I'm your Grandma Alice."

"Hey, there, angel," Gerald said gruffly, joining his wife. "I'm your Grandpa Gerry."

My own jaw tightened. *I want this for her.* I felt like I was in a dream and I didn't know if it was going to turn out to be everything I wanted or a nightmare.

Olivia pressed herself closer to my pants.

"She likes blocks," I said, indicating the pile on the floor. "Can't get enough of them."

Alice clapped her hands on her thighs. "Would you like to show us your blocks, Olivia?"

Alice and Gerald sat down on the floor with no aching or complaining about joints or bad knees. They were fit, strong, good people, with a lot of money, and their DNA in Olivia's veins. My little girl babbled in a baby talk/English hybrid, and plopped down beside them.

I moved to the kitchen for a glass of water and Jackson joined me.

"Not so bad, right?" he said in a low voice.

I poured a tall glass with a shaking hand. "I'm going to puke."

Jackson chuckled. "Be cool. I have a good feeling about this."

Jackson and I joined the others in the living room, sitting on my small couch while Holloway took the chair. The Abbotts stayed on the floor with Livvie, playing and chatting and making her smile.

"She looks just like Molly, doesn't she?" Alice said, and her smile wavered. I reached for the tissue box beside me and handed it over. "I'm sorry," she said, dabbing her eyes. "It's still so new, losing her."

"What happened?" I asked in a low voice.

Alice smiled sadly.

"Molly was always the rebellious girl but when she turned eighteen, she began to drink pretty heavily. It was like she'd been stricken with a disease. That's what they say it is, don't they? A disease."

I shifted in my seat, blue and red lights dancing across my vision.

"She had a happy childhood, or so we thought," Gerald said.

Alice smiled weakly. She handed Olivia a block and Olivia stacked it on top of another. "Did she mention us at all?"

I shook my head slowly. "I did not know Molly very well."

She and Gerald nodded in silent understanding.

"We did our best," Gerald said, "but whatever was driving her away from us got worse. She called and texted us occasionally, but we didn't see her for two years. She never said anything about a baby or even being pregnant."

"A friend of hers got in touch with us," Alice said. "She told us about Olivia and gave us your name. I guess Molly had told her about you."

My cold silence created another look between them, and then Gerald continued.

"We're renting a condo by the Marina. We've talked about retiring to the Bay Area."

"We've always loved San Francisco," Alice said, "and when we found out you were here it seems like the right thing to do."

I swallowed hard. "What was the right thing to do?" My voice sounded cold and hard but I couldn't help it. The fear had tightened me up inside so I could hardly breathe.

"To be a part of Olivia's life. An important part."

There was pity in Alice's eyes, which scared me more than anything else.

"We want to make sure she's provided for," Gerald said. "And ensure she has everything she needs for a happy and healthy life."

"Well, she does," I snapped. "I'm giving her that."

Jackson put a hand on my arm. I fought for calm, and tried to see these people as something other than the enemy. "I'm sorry, but I've been raising Olivia on my own for the last ten months and I'd begun to believe it was always going to be just her and me."

"But it's not," Gerald said, in a low voice. He stood up and put his hands in his pocket and looked at Holloway. "We have rights. And some information…"

My gaze jumped to Holloway who was making a negating motion with his hand.

"What kind of information?" Jackson asked.

Holloway reached into his jacket and pulled out an envelope. Now we were all on our feet but Alice who clapped hands with Olivia, tears in her eyes.

The Abbotts attorney handed Jackson the envelope. "Now, I really must insist we depart," he said to his clients. "Everything will be elucidated at the Family Court in two days' time."

Gerald helped Alice to her feet.

"Bye-bye, sweetheart," Alice said to Olivia. "We'll see you again."

"Bye-bye," Olivia said and babbled in a sing-song voice. "Bye-bye-bye-bye…"

"She's darling," Alice said to me, and that pitying look was there again. She opened her mouth to say something more, and her husband gently took her by the shoulders and guided her toward the door.

I shut it after them while Jackson opened the envelope.

"What is it?" I asked. I could hardly hear my own words for the blood rushing in my ears.

"A hearing notice. For Friday." He raised his eyes to mine. "They've filed an Order to Show Cause for custody of Olivia."

"Based on what?" I asked. "What cause?"

But of course, I already knew. The Abbotts had plenty of cause and if they didn't know it yet, soon they would.

I turned the letter over and over in my hand, the Sensaya Genetic Lab address disappearing then reappearing with every rotation. Beside me, Olivia slept in the middle of my bed. I had barricaded the three-month-old in a ring of pillows to keep her safe but I was still paranoid she'd roll off. I sat beside her, watched her sleep. Watched the shallow rise and fall of her chest, and her rapid pulse beat in her neck.

Was it my blood that flowed in her veins?

Slowly, so as not to wake her, I tore the envelope open. Inside were the test results that would tell me probabilities. The probability that my life would change forever, or that I would turn this baby over to the proper authorities and my life would continue on, as planned. But a whisper in the back of my mind told me my life was already changed—probability 100%—no matter what the test said.

I unfolded the paper with shaking hands and scanned the columns of numbers; they meant nothing to me. It was the conclusion at the end that mattered.

DNA Test Report
For Personal Knowledge Only

Case 8197346 Name Test No.	CHILD Olivia A 8197346-20	Alleged FATHER Sawyer Haas 8197346-30
Locus / PI	Allele Sizes	Allele Sizes
D3S1358 1.91	16	15 16
vWA 0.00	18	16 17
D16S539 3.86	10 11	10 11
CSF1PO 0.00	10	12
TPOX 0.96	8 11	9 11
D8S1179 0.00	11 12	13 15
D21S11 0.00	28 29	30 32.2
D18S51 0.00	14 18	12 20
D2S441 1.02	12 14	14 15
D19S433 0.00	12 14	13 16.2
TH01 0.97	8 9.3	6 9.3
FGA 2.67	19 25	22 25
D22S1045 0.70	15 16	12 15
D5S818 1.43	12	10 12
D13S317 0.00	11	10 12
D7S820 0.91	10 12	9 10
SE33 0.00	20 22.2	13 17
D10S1248 0.00	15 16	14
D1S1656 0.00	12 17.3	16 18.3
D2S1338 0.00	21	17 23
Amelogenin		

Interpretation:
Combined Paternity Index: 0   Probability of Paternity: 0%

0% probability.

A burden had just been lifted. Eighteen years and more. My life could carry on as it had. On track. Law school, clerkship, federal prosecutor, District Attorney...

I waited for the relief to hit me.

It never did.

I shook myself from the memory. It felt like a bad dream that had been on hold for ten months, and now was picking up where it left off.

Jackson was shaking his head, and his gaze dropped to Olivia. Mine followed. To my little girl, because why did I need a piece of paper to tell me what I felt in my heart? In my goddamn soul?

Olivia looked up at me from her pile of blocks on the floor and smiled. "Bye-bye!"

act two

Forever (adv.): for all future time

Now (adv.): at present time

chapter eighteen

Darlene

I WIPED A RIVULET OF SWEAT OFF MY BROW, AND THEN PLANTED MY HANDS ON MY hips to catch my breath. Ryan, my partner, was bellowing beside me, and I fought a wave of irritation. He had mistimed three cues during the run-through—nearly head-butting me, *again*—and with the show a week away, his clumsiness wasn't just annoying, it was going to make the rest of us look bad.

We already look bad.

I hated to even think it, but the show completely lacked inspiration and in my humble opinion, Anne-Marie, the lead dancer, was wooden and mechanical. Worse, she was the kind of person who thought she no longer had anything left to learn in dance, or life in general. The kind of person who began almost every sentence with "I know."

Greg and Paula had watched from foldout chairs at the head of the practice room at the Dance Academy. They shifted in their seats like they were sitting on splinters. There should have been a palpable air of excitement this close to opening night. Instead, the six of us dancers were like humming electrical posts, filling the room with nervous tension.

The director and stage manager put their heads together for a moment. Anne-Marie tossed her blonde ponytail over her shoulder.

"Well?" she demanded. "Are you going to give us notes, or what?"

Greg and Paula murmured and nodded, having come to some sort of agreement.

"It's…good," the director said. "It's coming together well. But it's short, even for a showcase."

"We timed it at twenty-seven minutes," Paula said. "Thirty would be better."

"We need one more act to fill out the time," Greg said. "Darlene."

My head shot up. "What?"

"We'd like you to perform your audition piece. As a solo."

My glance immediately shot to Anne-Marie who audibly gasped.

"We're a week out," she said. "You can't just change the whole show."

"We're not changing the whole show," Greg said. "We need one more act. A time filler, really."

Oh, is that what I am? I wanted to say. Truthfully, between the menace that was my partner, and the cold shoulders from the rest of the troupe, the words

I quit, were teetering from my lips. But I was trying to be professional and not quit something just because it wasn't what I'd hoped. And I wasn't about to leave them in a lurch so close to opening night.

"Darlene?" Greg asked. "Can you?"

"Umm," I glanced at Anne-Marie who was glaring poison-tipped daggers at me. "Are you sure?"

"We'll put it between *Entendre* and *Autumn Leaves.*"

"Okay, I guess I could do that."

"This is ridiculous," Anne-Marie said. "Who cares if we're three minutes short?"

Greg pretended not to have heard her. "Take your positions for the finale of *Entendre,* and then Darlene—"

"Rehearsal is over," Anne-Marie said. "I have somewhere else to be."

She flounced to the wall to grab her stuff and headed out. The other dancers shuffled their feet until Greg dismissed them too.

"Right, time's up. We'll have the music cues set up for tomorrow's rehearsal then," Greg said stiffly, trying to hold on to his authority. "Will you be ready?" he asked me, and I saw the spark of nerves dancing behind his eyes.

"Sure, no problem," I said. "I'll just stay here for a little bit and put in some extra time."

And try to turn my improv into a routine.

Greg eased a sigh. "Good. That's fine then."

He left and Paula sidled up to me. "Anne-Marie *really* wanted to be the only soloist."

"I noticed."

"Thank you for stepping up."

I smiled. "Doesn't suck to have a solo on a résumé."

"Yeah, well, we need it. The show needs it. A spark. Having just watched the whole run-through." She bit off her words with a sigh. "Anyway, thanks."

"No problem."

After everyone had gone, I stood in the center of the room, and stared at the girl in the wall of mirrors.

"Persistence," I murmured.

I didn't quit, and I got a solo out of it.

If I told Sawyer the truth.

What would I get out of that? I wondered. Recriminations or acceptance?

I hit 'play' on my music app and Marian Hill asked her question. But I couldn't answer. I wasn't down or up. I was in limbo, unable to move. My body suddenly stiffened by all the words I needed to say, and I began to see why I'd quit dancing when the drugs started; when I'd begun to lie to my family and friends about what I was doing and where I was going. Dancing was my honest self. My body speaking the truth of the music, and I couldn't *be* that while stuffed with lies.

I was probably just as stiff and mechanical in the run-through as Anne-Marie.

I took the Muni home, showered, made dinner. Always doing something, never letting myself stop and think. While doing the dinner dishes, a text came in on my phone from Max.

Well?

I bit my lip and typed, **Not yet.**

When?

Tonight. After his daughter goes to bed.

Shit. There it was, in black and white.

There was a short pause and then Max wrote back, **"Don't ever regret being honest. Period."—Taylor Swift**

I laughed, and it was like a sigh of relief.

You can't argue with T-Swift, I typed.

No you cannot. Max wrote back. **Call me any time if you need to.**

I smiled at my friend, who was going to move to Seattle any minute and leave me alone. **I will. <3 you**

Love you, D.

I held the phone to my chest. It wasn't a hug, but it was the next best thing.

At eleven-thirty, dressed in soft shorts and a white T-shirt, I headed down to Sawyer's. I was going to bring some food for him and Livvie, but changed my mind. I wanted no pretense; there was no other reason for me being there than to tell him the truth.

My pulse was jittery as I tapped lightly on his door. It opened after an agonizing thirty seconds in which I almost ran away. Twice.

Sawyer was there in what I called his jammies—V-necked T-shirt and plaid flannel pants—though it didn't look as if he'd done any sleeping in them. Dark circles ringed his eyes that were bloodshot. For a split second, the dark pools of them lit up to see me, then faded again.

"Hey," he said.

"Hey. Is this a bad time?"

"You can come in." He shoved the door open and then turned his back to walk inside. "You want anything? Something to drink?"

"No, I'm fine." I shut the door behind me. "I came here to tell you what I should have told you the other night." I heaved a calming breath and started with the easy part. "I'm not seeing anyone else, I promise. Max is only a friend."

"Okay," he said. Sawyer moved slowly to his desk. He slumped in the chair, and covered his eyes with his hand.

Is he this torn up about our failed date?

A selfish part of me would like to think he cared that much about me, but no, it had to be something big, like he failed a final or that judge picked someone else for the clerkship he needed. It suddenly seemed horribly out of place to talk about myself when he was so obviously upset.

Not just upset. Devastated.

My fear for myself reshaped itself into fear for him.

"Sawyer, are you okay?" I moved to stand on the other side of his desk. "What happened?"

Sawyer dropped his hand from his eyes like it was too heavy, then reached over his desk to take a folded piece of paper. He tossed it closer to my side of the desk and slumped back in his chair.

I snatched it up and read it, my heart clanging harder with every word, then stared at him, incredulous.

"A hearing? For custody of Livvie?" The paper trembled like a leaf in my hands. "Who…who are these people?"

"Olivia's grandparents." Each sentence came out dull and staccato. "They were here with their lawyer. They have money. Lots of it. They met Olivia and they want custody."

I let the notice of the hearing fall back to the desk. "But they can't do that," I said. "You're her father. They can't just…take her from you."

Sawyer covered his eyes again and I rushed to him, behind his chair and wrapped my arms around him. He didn't move but let me hold him and I fought not to burst into tears.

"It's going to be okay," I whispered. "It has to be. You're so good for her."

I straightened and without thinking—my body charged with panic I needed to channel—I rubbed his back, talking and kneading his muscles that felt like rocks under my hands. "There has to be a law, right? They can't just barge in here and take her away from you."

"It's not that simple," Sawyer said, his voice gruff.

"But it doesn't make any sense—"

"There are circumstances, Darlene."

"What kind of circumstances let the grandparents take a baby away from her father?"

"I'm not her father."

I reeled, his words pushing me back a step from his chair. It felt as if the air had been sucked out of the room.

"What…what are you saying? Of course you are."

Sawyer looked around at me, shaking his head miserably.

"I'm not. I took a paternity test when Molly first left her with me. I'm not a match, but it doesn't matter. Even after only a few days of having her in my life, she was mine. I tried to take her to CPS with Jackson. He tried to convince me it was the best thing, that I was crazy to try to raise her on my own. But I couldn't do it. Molly told me she was mine and that's how I thought of her. I still do. In my heart and fucking soul, she's mine and I love her."

He bit off the words, fighting for control.

"It doesn't matter to me what some stupid fucking test says. It only matters what I feel." He shook his head, a harsh, bitter laugh breaking free. "But turns out, that doesn't matter either. The court is going to order another paternity test. The Abbotts will demand one, and when the results come out, I'm going to lose her."

I put my hands back on his shoulders, shaking my head. "No. They can't do that. Not after so long. She calls you Daddy," I bit back my own tears. "Because you *are* her daddy and they have to see that. They *have* to."

He shook his head and a small silence fell. I pulled myself together and Sawyer's shoulders rose and fell under my hands as he took deep breaths to compose himself.

"Do you have help? A lawyer?"

"Jackson."

I bit my lip. "He does taxes…"

"I can't afford anyone else. And I trust him."

"Okay. Okay good."

I kept massaging Sawyer, working at his shoulders; the coiled knots of worry that his deepest fear was coming true. His entire body hummed with tension and I felt so helpless to do anything for him but this. I dug my thumbs into the hard muscles of his back, working circles over his shoulder blades, then back up, over his collar bone.

For long moments, there was silence. I didn't know what else to do or what to say. I could only try to ease his pain somehow, because I had nothing else.

Sawyer didn't move and I wondered if he'd fallen asleep, chin to his chest. Then his hand rose to take one of mine. He pressed my palm to his lips and I sucked in a breath as the kiss slipped up my arm, raising goosebumps, then spread over my shoulder and chest like a flame.

Sawyer turned my hand over and kissed the back, then held it to his cheek, still saying nothing. My heart thumped hard as he pulled me around in front of him, and then sideways onto his lap.

Face to face, and so close, he was breathtaking, but his eyes were so heavy. I lifted my hands and continued the massage, pressing circles on either side of his face, at the hinge of his jaw, below his eyes, his forehead. Then I grazed my fingernails along the sides of his head, just above his ears, over and over.

Our gazes never broke, we shared a breath, and then his hand was on my thigh. The other slipped up to hold my cheek, and even that small touch I felt everywhere. It scared me how much I wanted him.

"Did it help?" I asked. "I want to help."

He nodded. "You're the best thing in my life right now, Darlene," he said hoarsely. "The only good thing."

And then he kissed me. Like a drowning man needing a breath, he kissed me hard and desperately, his brows furrowed as if he were in pain. His hand found the back of my head, and he made a fist in my hair, gently but urgently, pressing me closer, deeper; holding me to him when I felt weightless. My mouth opened for him; Sawyer holding me to his kiss was the only reason I didn't float away.

A little moan of want fell out of my mouth and he took it in his. The kiss deepened as I came back to myself, wanting to feel every second, every sensation. His tongue ventured into my mouth and another little sound escaped me. My arms went around his neck, my fingers slid into his hair, nails grazing as our kiss intensified.

Sawyer's breath rasped in his nose as he kissed me harder, his arms wrapped around me now, both hands in my hair now, angling my head to take him deeper. The bite of his teeth on my lower lip made me dizzy and the chair was suddenly too small to contain us.

But Sawyer wrenched himself away from me, shocking me with the sudden break. He gently but quickly moved me off his lap and strode to the kitchen where he stood with his back to me, head bowed, hands resting on the counter.

"I'm sorry," he said. "Shit, I'm sorry, Darlene, I shouldn't have done that. Everything is so fucked up right now, and kissing you is like stepping outside of a nightmare."

I nodded quickly, thinking of my original reason for coming here tonight. "Me too. I'm sorry. I didn't mean…"

"We can't do this. *I* can't. I can't do this to you." He turned to face me, carved his hand through his hair. "Goddamn, Darlene, *now*? Why is this, why are *we* happening now? My whole life is about to implode. I have *nothing* to give you. Nothing."

"That's not true."

"It is," he said tiredly. "You deserve someone who's not stretched to the goddamn breaking point every second of his life." His jaw clenched and his dark eyes shone. "I was close to being done and now this hearing…"

"I know," I said in a small voice.

"I have to fight for her," he said, his tone hardening. "I have to put everything I have into that. No, not just that. I have to pass the bar, and get the goddamn clerkship so that I can prove I can provide for her. *Fuck*."

He rubbed his eyes and my heart broke for him, for the weight that was pressing down on him, trying to crush him.

"I know it's so hard for you right now…"

"Too hard. I feel like my fucking heart is being torn in half. I'm scared shitless about losing Olivia, and yet when I'm with you, I see something real. For the first time in my life, I want whatever we have to be real."

Real. But I'm a liar. A fraud. He doesn't know me, I haven't told him anything.

He shook his head. "But I can't give you anything right now but stress and pain. When all this shit blows over…" he said hoarsely. "If I still have her when it's done…"

"You will. You will, Sawyer."

His jaw worked and for a moment he said nothing. "I don't know, Darlene. I've never been so terrified in my life. But when it's all done and if I have Olivia," he swallowed hard. "Then I can really be with you, if you still want that. Or at least we can try. Until then…" He let his hands drop to his sides. "I have nothing."

"That's not true," I said. "But I understand. I do. And I'm supposed to be working on myself, and God knows there's still so much left to do. To say to you."

I wiped my eyes with the heel of my hand.

"But I can be here for you," I said. "As a friend. Or to babysit Olivia if you need me to. Whatever you want, okay?"

He nodded. "Thank you."

I moved to the door, feeling like I was running away, but God, how could I tell him anything when he was about to face the fight of his life? Keeping Olivia was the most important thing right now, but it still felt like a cop out.

"Tell me how the hearing goes," I said, opening the door. "Tell me if you need anything. Anything at all. Tell me…"

Tell me you'll forgive me when you know the truth.

The words stuck in my throat, and I flew out of his place, tears spilling over.

I guessed not being so much of a coward was something I still needed to work on.

chapter nineteen

Sawyer

I didn't want to—seeing her was too painful now—but I needed Darlene sooner than I'd expected. The day before the hearing, Elena told me she had a family emergency in the East Bay, and couldn't babysit. Henrietta was out of town for a wedding so I had no choice but to ask Darlene.

She agreed readily, even though it meant taking the day off her work. I added her lost wages to the tally of things I owed all the people who helped me during these last ten months.

And maybe it was all for nothing.

Friday morning, Darlene came downstairs to watch Olivia in my place. Her eyes were heavy and warm, and she hugged me tight.

"We're just friends right now," she said. "This is a friendly hug, but I'm putting every bit of my positive energy and best thoughts into it that this hearing goes how it's supposed to. For you."

I held her tightly, feeling her dancer's body mold to mine. I closed my eyes, my cheek against her hair, and inhaled her so I could keep some of the light and life she was giving me.

God, you're turning into a sap.

But I needed all the damn help I could get.

Jackson met me at the Duboce Muni, and we took a train to the Civic Center at eight a.m. Outside the Superior Courthouse, my friend stopped me with a hand to my arm.

"You ready?" Jackson asked.

"No."

"That's the spirit!" He chucked me on the arm. "Come on. Let's do this."

I smoothed down the lapel of my best suit—a slate gray jacket and pants with a white shirt, and ruby-colored tie. Jackson looked impeccable in blue and beige, a briefcase in his hand. We climbed the steps—me on wooden legs—and into the courthouse where we followed the signs for the Family Court. Jackson spoke in a low voice as we walked.

"This might be a bit of a battle but I've done my homework and I'm sure you've got the entire Family Law Code memorized."

"Section 7611, subsection D," I said.

"Exactly. Additionally, we can show removing Olivia from your custody would be detrimental to her. You're providing for her in a safe environment and have been for months. Courts don't like taking children out of good homes."

"They're her family, Jax." I rubbed my tired eyes. "Fuck me, I was so close. A few more weeks and the year would have been up."

"We can't worry about that now. Fight the fight in front of us, okay?"

I nodded. We'd arrived at the designated room on the hearing notice. "Breathe. Stay calm. Think positive."

"Thank you doing this," I told him. "For taking time off work..."

"Forget it," he said. "You're my family, too. And so is she."

"Jesus, don't say shit like that," I said with small laugh. I blinked my eyes hard.

"I'm trying to wipe that serial-killer look off your face," he said.

I tried to loosen the stiff expression, but I was fighting for my kid. My life. I left the smiling to Jackson.

Inside, the Abbotts were on their side of the courtroom, at a table with Holloway. They turned to watch me come in and the small smiles on their faces faded at my glare. I tore my eyes away. Instinctively, I liked them. Down deep, somewhere beneath the fear, I wanted to know them.

That's just your shitty childhood talking. They're here to take Olivia away from you.

I sat down stiffly at the table with Jackson, eyes forward, and didn't look their way again.

"All rise."

We got to our feet as the bailiff announced Judge Allen Chen, a stern-looking man, with dark hair that was graying along the sides. He put on glasses as he inspected the paperwork in front of him.

"In the matter of Olivia Abbott, a minor child, there is an order before the Court to show cause for custody filed by Gerald and Alice Abbott, maternal grandparents." He glanced up at Jackson. "I've read the preliminary facts of the case and I'm familiar with the position of Mr. and Mrs. Abbott. I'd like to hear from Mr. Haas, please."

Jackson got to his feet. "Your Honor, my client has been raising Olivia since her mother disappeared ten months and two weeks ago. At that time, she made it clear that Sawyer was the father of their child. Pursuant to 7611 of the Family Law Code, section one, subsection D, Sawyer received Olivia into his home and openly held out that she was his natural child. He has provided a home, food, safety; healthcare via his university, and has been a devoted and loving father. The law clearly grants therefore, in black and white, that he is her natural father and should retain full custody." Jackson held out his hands. "Honestly, I don't even know why we're here."

Mr. Holloway rose to his feet. "That is a very narrow reading of the law," he began. "Molly Abbott did leave Olivia with Mr. Haas, though what she told him with regards to his paternity is a matter of hearsay. The birth certificate, of which we have retained a copy, lists no father. Additionally, neither Mr. Haas, nor his attorney, have provided us with a copy of the results of any paternity test."

Jackson was back on his feet. "Uniform Parentage Act, Your Honor?"

Judge Chen nodded. "Quite so." He turned to Holloway. "The State of California is not in the habit of tearing children from a secure home environment without cause. The Court will determine whether a paternity test is warranted based on the evidence presented."

"I understand, Your Honor, and to that end, we would like to read a notarized statement from Karen Simmons—friend to the deceased Molly Abbott—and to enter said statement into the record of proceedings here."

"Objection, Your Honor," Jackson said, but the judge held up a hand.

"This is not a trial, but an evidentiary hearing. I'll allow it." He nodded at Holloway. "Proceed."

Holloway set a pair of glasses on his nose.

"'I, Karen Jane Simmons, do swear under penalty of perjury that the following is true and correct: Molly Abbott was a close friend of mine since we were thirteen years old. After high school, Molly began to drink pretty heavily, and traveled place to place, hooking up with different boyfriends. But we always managed to stay in touch. She told me when she got pregnant, and I met up with her in Bakersfield after the baby was born. She told me the baby's father was a guy named Ross Mathis but that he wanted nothing to do with Olivia. Molly said she'd hooked up with another guy around the same time named Sawyer. He was studying to be a lawyer and that meant he was going to be well off. She said that her current boyfriend wouldn't stay with her if she kept the baby so she was going to drive to San Francisco where Sawyer lived, and tell him it was his baby. I didn't see her or hear from her again after that and was saddened to learn of her death. She was my best friend and I miss her.'

"Signed," Holloway concluded, "Karen Simmons." He took off his glasses. "Miss Simmons has provided text exchanges between her and Miss Abbott around the time in question that verify her statement, and has agreed to testify, either in deposition or in open court, should the Court desire it."

Ross Mathis. Olivia's natural father. Hearing the name brought bile to my mouth. He didn't want his own child, but I did. I would fucking die for that girl, but instead I was, fighting to keep her. Under the table, my hands clenched into fists.

"Your Honor," Holloway said in a closing-statement kind of tone, "Alice and Gerald Abbott are loving, devoted people who lost their daughter to the terrible disease of alcoholism. They had no idea they had a granddaughter, and the instant they learned of her existence, they set about taking the steps to see her, to be with her, and to provide for her the kind of life she needs and deserves.

At this time, they request weekend visitation rights, and that a paternity test be administered, to either establish or refute Mr. Haas's claim that he is Olivia's father, before any further steps are taken toward granting permanent custody. Thank you."

I couldn't move. Couldn't breathe. Even my pounding heart slowed to a heavy clang.

The judge nodded. "Supervised weekend visitation is hereby granted, and a paternity test shall be administered at the Health and Human Services department on Monday of next week."

Jackson was on his feet again. "Your Honor, my client has just completed the requirements for graduating UC Hastings law school, and is set to take the bar exam in Sacramento the week after next. We request a postponement of all proceedings until the completion of the exam, to give him time to focus and prepare without the threat of this outrageous and callous attempt to separate a loving father from his daughter hanging over his head."

The Abbotts visibly flinched at this. Judge Chen fixed me with a scrutinizing look. I probably looked like nothing like a 'loving' father, but I remained still as stone, afraid I'd shatter if I moved.

"There is one other issue we feel is of interest to the Court," Holloway said.

"Jesus, now what?" I whispered to Jackson.

He made a silencing motion with his hand.

"Mr. Smith has stipulated that his client has provided safe and adequate care for Olivia, yet a rudimentary investigation reveals that his childcare provider, Elena Melendez, is not licensed to run a daycare. She is merely a neighbor who babysits Olivia for eight hours a day while also taking care of her own two small children."

Jackson shot to his feet.

"I believe the obvious health and happiness of Olivia speaks for itself. This is irrelevant, Your Honor, and frankly, it's insulting to the good work and kindness of Ms. Melendez whom Mr. Haas pays appropriately for her excellent care."

"I am merely speaking to the general environment in which the child is raised," Mr. Holloway said. "Mr. Haas relies on unlicensed childcare from Ms. Melendez and occasionally from Darlene Montgomery, his upstairs neighbor."

Jackson held up his hands. "Again. Relevance?"

"It's relevant," Mr. Holloway said, "as Ms. Montgomery was incarcerated for drug possession three years ago and spent three months in a New York County jail."

It felt as is the air in the room had dropped twenty degrees, as I went cold all over.

"What'd he say?" I blurted stupidly. The words fell out of my mouth. I had to have misheard...

"Is this true, Mr. Haas?" the judge asked.

Jackson looked to me, eyes full of questions.

I shook my head. "I don't…I never…"

Darlene. Jail. Drug possession.

The words went around and around in my head individually but I couldn't get them to make sense all together.

"This was three years ago, Your Honor?" Jackson asked, still looking at me. He tore his gaze to stand and face the Court. "Do we punish people for the rest of their lives for mistakes that are years old?"

Mr. Holloway smiled placidly. "We wanted to ensure the Court had all of the information before making any rulings. In light of these revelations, we feel a speedy resolution to this matter is in the best interest of the child."

Judge Chen pursed his lips at me. "Agreed. We will reconvene next Thursday to read the DNA test results, and to make a further determination as to custody of Olivia Abbott. This hearing is adjourned."

Alice and Gerald should have been victorious, but both wore concerned expressions on their faces when they looked in my direction. I stared back in a daze. Jackson had to haul me to my feet when the judge left the room.

I loosened my tie but it wasn't what was strangling me.

"You didn't know about Darlene?" Jackson asked.

"I had no clue," I said. "She told me she had something she wanted to tell me." I gripped my friend's arm as the enormity of what had happened hit me like a punch in the chest. "Jesus, Jax. What do I do now? It's over. Isn't it?"

"Don't think that way," Jackson said, though his pre-hearing optimism had all but vanished. "The Abbotts did their homework, I'll give them that, but the stuff about Elena and Darlene is bullshit. They're throwing anything at the wall to see what sticks."

"It doesn't feel like bullshit," I said.

But truthfully, I didn't feel anything at all. Numb. Like how I felt when that cop told us my mother was dead. I had to feel nothing or else I'd feel fucking everything and collapse under the weight of it.

"It's the test results that we need to deal with," Jackson said, walking us out of the courtroom. "But it's not over. You have rights. Molly left her with you. She wanted you to be Olivia's dad. We'll make a game plan. We'll prove how well you've taken care of Olivia, we'll get character witnesses…"

Jackson kept talking as we stepped outside into the overly warm Indian summer heat. The bright sun was muted now. Thick storm clouds were brewing overhead, turning the sky gray. My entire world had caved in, and everything was gray, as if all the color and light had been drained out until there was nothing left.

chapter twenty

Darlene

"DAREEN!" Olivia kicked her feet in her high chair and pushed at the tray.

"All done, sweet pea?" I wiped her mouth of the strawberry residue, then *booped* her nose with the cloth. She laughed. "You want to get down?"

"Down," she agreed. "Bocks."

"Jeez Louise, girl. You're all about the blocks, aren't you?"

I took off the tray and set Olivia down on the floor. She immediately toddled to her pile of wooden blocks with the letters and numbers on the sides, and started stacking.

I watched her for a moment, my smile fading, my heart aching. What was happening at the hearing? Surely, a judge wouldn't just rip a child from the man who'd been taking care of her as his own just because the grandparents had more money. There had to be some rule or law that protected Sawyer.

"There is, and he and Jackson know about it," I murmured.

But worry laced the blood in my veins and wouldn't leave. I sat down with Livvie on the floor and played blocks with her, then read her a story. When she began to yawn and rub her eyes, I put her down for a nap in her little room and left the door open a crack.

The house felt quiet. Waiting. Outside, thunder boomed distantly, ominously. As if something terrible were on the horizon, rolling this way.

"Oh stop. It's just weather."

I paced around a bit, shaking out my stiff arms from yesterday's spa work. I couldn't afford to miss any more shifts, I was glad I took the day off to babysit for Sawyer. It wasn't the same as being with him, but taking care of Livvie made me feel good about myself in a way I hadn't felt in a while.

And maybe, after all is said and done, the three of us…

I shut that thought up quick. In my experience, holding on too tightly to something I wanted was the surest way to lose it.

I wandered around Sawyer's living area, taking him in through his degrees and awards; his messy desk covered in his study materials he worked so hard on. I missed him. He wasn't really gone, but I missed him anyway.

And you still have to tell him…

"I should've told him at the beginning," I muttered, my fingers trailing over his pen lying on a stack of notebooks.

But if I had told him, maybe nothing would have happened between us. The Small Something we had was better than Nothing, wasn't it?

I could practically see Max roll his eyes at that one.

"I know, I know, I'm supposed to be working on being honest and responsible," I said. "On that note."

I plopped on the couch and fished my phone out of my purse, to make the call I'd been putting off for days. I opened my contacts and scrolled down to the H's.

Home.

I breathed out and hit 'call.'

My mother picked up on the second ring. "Montgomery residence, Gina speaking." Her Queens accent was pronounced, so it came out 'Geen-er speakin'.'

"Hi, Mom, it's me."

"Hello, baby, what's wrong? Is everything okay?"

I flinched at her standard opener. "Everything is fine. Really good, in fact. Did Carla tell you I got a spot with a dance troupe? I didn't even have a planned routine, I just winged it and got in."

"She didn't mention it, but that's wonderful, honey. But how's the spa job? You keeping up over there? You need money?"

"What? No, I'm fine."

"Keeping your nose clean?"

"Yes."

"Good girl."

"So listen, Ma," I said, my own accent coming back as if she were drawing it out of me from across the country. "The dance show isn't a huge deal. It's in a small space in the city, but they just gave me a solo, and I'd love for you guys to see it."

"I don't know, Dar," Mom said. "That's a lot of travel for a show that's what? An hour?"

Thirty minutes. I thought. *She's right. This was a dumb idea.* But persistence had paid off for me before, and hearing my mom's voice awakened in me how much I missed her.

"Not to mention, Grandma Bea's hip is acting up," she said. "She can't travel so good anymore."

"I know, Ma, but I haven't danced at all in four years. And anyway, the show would only be one part of it. You could come visit me, and see where I live—in this really cool, old Victorian house. And I could show you around San Francisco. It's such a beautiful city."

"When is this show?"

"Next weekend."

"Oh honey, I can't wrangle your father into something like that in a week."

I nodded, trying to ignore the relief in her voice.

"You know how he is," she said. "Work, work, work."

I knew how he was. My dad owned a successful auto body shop. He made good money and could take time off whenever he needed to. Or wanted to.

"No, you're right," I said softly. "It's a huge expense to fly all this way, and the show isn't a big deal. Next time."

"Absolutely."

"Give Daddy a kiss for me," I said.

"I will, baby. Take care, now, and call if you need anything."

I just did.

"Sure, Mom." I wiped my cheek with the heel of my hand. "I'll talk to you soon. Love you."

"Love you too. Bye, now."

I let my hand fall in my lap.

"Stop feeling sorry for yourself," I muttered, but the ache in my heart wouldn't go away.

A text came in on the phone in my lap from Max.

I need to see you. Work, home, or dance?

Home. Second floor, I typed back, and my heart sank even lower. **You'd better not be coming over here to tell me what I think you're coming over here to tell me.**

I'll tell you when I get there.

Smartass, I tapped, but the ache in my chest deepened.

Twenty minutes later, a soft knock came at the door.

I opened it to Max, and stepped into the hallway, leaving the door ajar.

"The baby's sleeping," I said. "And you're leaving, aren't you?"

He nodded. "I got the call. My flight leaves in a few hours."

"I'm so proud of you, Max."

"Are you?" The softness in his voice and the tears in his eyes shocked me. "I may have been your sponsor, but you've also been a friend. It means a lot to me, what you think."

"Thank you," I said. "No one's said anything like that to me in a long time."

I put my arms around him and held him tight. He held me tighter.

"You're going to do great," I said. "Going back to Seattle's going to be the best thing for you. You can maybe reconcile with your parents, and you'll definitely meet some hot doctor who is going to love you. How could he not?"

Max kept hugging me. "You're going to be okay, too. I know it."

"I don't. I feel like everyone I care about is moving farther and farther away and I can't hold on to anyone. My family, Sawyer, you. And I feel that other rock bottom coming. I wish you could be here when it does."

He pulled away to look at me, concern heavy in his dark eyes.

"I hate that I'm leaving right now. Maybe I should postpone…"

"Don't you dare," I said. "I need to deal with this on my own, I think. Maybe that's why you got the transfer now. Everything happens for a reason, right?"

"It does," he said. "And you're so much stronger than you know. You've come far, Darlene. Hold on to *that*. And call me. Any time." He gave me a stern look. "And don't skip any meetings. Not one, or I'll have to fly back, away from my hot doctor boyfriend."

I laughed. "I'm going to miss you."

"Miss you too."

I hugged him until I heard footfalls on the stairs. Sawyer stood at the end of the hallway. He stared at me in Max's arms, and his hand resting on his shoulder bag dropped to his side.

I took a step back from Max. "Hi, Sawyer."

Max whipped his head around and the action prompted Sawyer to stride up to us, eyes forward, his face unreadable. Blank. And that worried me more than anything else.

"Hey, man," Max said, offering his hand. "Max Kaufman. Good to meet you."

Sawyer stopped in the door. He stared down at Max's offered hand, then met my eye for one blood-curdling second before pushing past us into his apartment.

"He had a very important hearing," I whispered. "I don't think it went well. God, I'm so scared for him."

"I hate that I have to leave you like this," Max said. "I'll call you when I land."

He kissed my cheek and I watched him until he was down the stairs and out of sight. I suddenly felt like a tightrope walker strung up between two high-rises.

And my safety net just left to get on a plane to Seattle.

Inside Sawyer's place, he was shaking off his suit coat that was smattered with rain. He tossed it on the back of his chair, then loosened his tie.

"Where is Olivia?" he asked. No, demanded.

"Sleeping. She's fine. She's…sleeping."

"You can't just bring strangers into my place. With my kid. You know that, right?"

"I know, I'm sorry," I said. "He didn't come in, I promise. He's—"

"He's what?" Sawyer asked. "Your drug dealer?"

The blood drained from my head, leaving me dizzy. I reeled. "My…what?" I breathed.

"Were you ever going to tell me?" Sawyer demanded.

"Tell you…?"

"About your criminal record?"

There they were, those three words in all their ugly glory. My criminal record. But how was it coming up *now*?

"Yes, I was going to tell you," I said, my voice weak and watery. "I wanted to, so many times but I was scared. But how…how did you find out?"

"I found out at the *preliminary custody hearing* for my child," Sawyer spat. "The Abbotts investigated this entire fucking building. Now, in the eyes of that judge, I'm the kind of guy who leaves his kid either with unlicensed childcare all day or drug addicts."

I stiffened all over. "I'm not a drug addict," I said, my voice quavering. "Not anymore. I'm recovering. I don't even drink. Max isn't a *drug dealer*, for God's sake. He was my NA sponsor. That means—"

"I know what it means," Sawyer said. "I just have no fucking clue what I should think about it. Jesus, Darlene."

He shook his head and the stony exterior started to shatter; I could feel the tension radiating off of him as he tried to hold himself together.

"Did you lose her?" I asked, my voice hardly a whisper. "Because of me?"

"It doesn't matter. It's over." He shook his head, then planted one hand on the wall as if it were the only thing keeping him standing. "It's all over."

And I knew he meant me, too. Whatever we had had, it was gone now. I'd tried, once again, to hold on by not telling him, and it all was wrenched out of my fingers.

"I'm sorry," I whispered. "For so much. For everything."

Sawyer raised his eyes to mine and for a split second the hard, stony exterior cracked and the pain flooded out. He opened his mouth to speak, and at that moment, lightning flashed and a booming thunder followed after. Rain lashed the windows in a sudden deluge, as if the sky had cracked open.

The sound woke up Olivia; the baby monitor chirped with her fussing. Neither of us moved and that ugly feeling of wanting to escape everything I was and all I had done came over me. I hurried to Olivia's room.

She was standing in her crib, and her sleepy little face broke into a smile to see me.

"Dareen."

She held her arms to me and I picked her up; held her close for a moment, breathing in her sweet, baby powder smell. Her arms went around my neck, squeezing tears from my eyes in her little hug.

It felt like goodbye.

Back in the living room, Sawyer stood with his arms crossed, his gaze cast down and his expression hard again.

"Look who's awake," I said weakly.

"Daddy," Olivia said, her voice still cloudy with sleep.

Sawyer looked up at Olivia and me, his face a blank mask. And then he strode forward and took the baby out of my arms.

My skin went cold all over; I felt where Olivia's warmth had been, and a goose bumps raised on my skin. Sawyer took his child a few steps away and turned his back on me.

"Okay," I said, my voice barely a whisper. A thousand more words rose up behind that one: how I'd been clean for almost two years, the progress I'd made, how proud Max was...

Max. He was gone. That pain hit me in the chest to join that of Sawyer's silent rejection. Tears drowned every other word I had, and I grabbed my bag off the kitchen chair.

"Okay," I managed again. "Okay."

It was all I could say and yet nothing was okay. Not one thing.

I went to the door and opened it. Sawyer stood in profile to me, his gaze over Olivia's head, full of thoughts but none for me. His silence was worse than a thousand condemning words.

"Goodbye."

My voice broke and Sawyer's head whipped toward me, his hard features morphing into pain and regret, and his mouth opened as if he might finally have something more to say, but I shut the door between us.

Outside in the hallway, I leaned my forehead against the cool wood. Rain smattered the small window in the hallway, and lightning lit up the night sky. I pushed off the door, and headed out instead of up. Out into the cold wind and rain that had doused the summer heat. It tore through my clothing. I was drenched immediately and shivered hard enough to rattle my teeth.

There's a bar two blocks down. Someone there will know someone. Know where I can score. Whiskey sour and a pill, and who gives a shit what Sawyer thinks of me.

"Max," I whispered, like a cry for help. The wind tore the word and drowned it in rain. I looked up and down the street to see if I could still catch him, but there was no Max. No help, save what I gave myself.

The bar was two blocks away.

The Y with tonight's NA meeting was six.

Backward or forward.

I stood on the empty street, and the rain came down.

I pulled my phone from my purse with shaking fingers and shielded it from the downpour. My finger hit the Uber app and I waited. I'd had no words in Sawyer's apartment but they were coming back to me now. So many of them, filling me up, filling that emptiness that lived within me that I'd tried to fill with drugs. Filling me with the truth, that I was not the sum of my criminal record; I was not words on paper, black and white.

I was everywhere in between.

At the Y, there was an NA meeting already in progress. It wasn't my group, but it didn't matter. It was my community.

A woman stood at the podium, but she fell silent when she saw me come in. The rest of the group turned in their seats to follow her jaw-dropped stare, to me, dripping rainwater and shivering.

I strode to the front of the group and the woman wordlessly gave up the podium. I met the gazes of those assembled. My lips trembled with cold. All the words I'd wanted to tell Sawyer but couldn't were boiling up now, and I wished, more than anything, that Max was here one final time, to hear them. Because if he could have, he'd be getting on that plane knowing he had done his job. And that he didn't have to worry about me. Not anymore.

I faced the assembled group, my hands clutched the side of the podium.

"Hi," I said. "My name is Darlene and I'm an addict."

My voice was strong despite my trembling jaw, and the voices that answered were just as strong, lifting me up and carrying me on a simple, two-word current of acceptance.

"Hi, Darlene."

chapter twenty-one

Sawyer

I soothed Olivia back to sleep. The thunder quieted so that she was nodding off on my shoulder within minutes. I held her for a long time, my eyes closed, feeling her little weight and warmth against my chest.

Is this one of the last times?

I fortified myself against the thought, but hope was draining out of me, minute by minute. It didn't matter how much I loved her and that I thought of her as my own. The paternity test would read **0% probability**, in black and white, and the judge's ruling would be final.

The impassivity of the law I'd taken such great comfort in was now a faceless stranger turning its back on me, uncaring that my heart was breaking.

I set Olivia gently down in her bed and went out. Outside the living room window, rain was still falling in sheets and Darlene was out in it.

Her heart was broken too, and I'd broken it. Shattered it into tiny pieces when I'd taken Olivia out of her arms.

"Fucking asshole," I muttered, but my voice cracked at the end, my throat thick.

I'd been holding on to anger at the revelation of her past; using it to keep the pain at bay, but it hit me hard like a heavy fist to the chest. Darlene wasn't why I was going to lose Olivia, but—Jesus Christ—my life was infused with addictions. My mother, Molly, and now Darlene? Was I destined to lose her too?

The fear, anger, confusion all swirled in me like a tornado, and at its center, in the calm eye, was what I felt for her.

"What the fuck do I do now?"

I sank into the chair at my desk and pulled out my phone for the hundredth time. No messages or texts, but why would there be?

"There won't be. Because I broke her heart," I muttered and felt each syllable stab me.

I typed a text.

Tell me you're okay.

I backspaced it away. She didn't owe it to me to make me feel better.

Are you okay?

I deleted that too. Of course she wasn't okay. I'd seen to that.

I'm sorry.

My thumb hovered over the send button but I was too chickenshit to push it. And too ashamed.

Another voice whispered in my ear, like the proverbial devil on my shoulder. *What if she was doing hard stuff? What if she associated with felons or owed money? Maybe she moved clear across the country to escape bad people? You want that kind of stuff around Olivia?*

My excuses about what I didn't know about Darlene fell apart under the sheer weight of all that I did know about her.

And what I felt about her.

I hit 'send.'

I sat at the desk, listening to the rainfall and waiting to see if she'd read the message. Waiting for her to answer. Waiting for her to tell me that she was okay. The thought flitted into my head that she might be doing something to herself that she shouldn't, but I swatted it dead.

You know nothing about her situation because you didn't ask. You shut down on her.

That was one truth. The other was that the image of Darlene, standing in a doorway, being held by another man, was an added layer of misery. Another crack in my stony heart that was already on the verge of shattering, and the emotions that seeped out weren't any I recognized.

"That's because you're a fucking asshole," I said, dully.

I tossed the phone on the desk and rubbed my face with both hands. The clock ticked the hours away. Olivia woke up from her nap. I fed her, played with her, read to her, cherishing each second with her and trying not to imagine the internal countdown in which she'd be taken from me.

Every other moment, I felt something different; the mind-numbing pain that I'd already lost her, followed by the red-hot anger that I'd fight for her until I didn't have a breath left in my body.

And when I put her down for bed that night, I was wrung out, and my anguish turned back to Darlene.

"Jesus Christ," I muttered, staring at my haggard reflection in the mirror after I changed into sleep clothes and brushed my teeth. "You're a fucking mess. Pull your shit together, Haas."

I made a pathetic attempt to study for the bar, and gave up after a minute. What was the fucking point?

I sat and stared at nothing. I was so exhausted I could hardly move, but my phone was still silent. My agonized mind wanted to know which would come home first: the blue and red silent sirens? Or Darlene, safe and well?

The rain kept falling but the wind quieted enough for me to hear the door shut below and footsteps on the stairs.

Panic and relief sent a jolt through my bones, and I bolted out of my chair for the front door. I threw it open just as Darlene went past.

"Darlene."

She stopped and turned to me, and I hated myself even more for taking note of her eyes, that were clear and sharp. Rainwater dripped off the end of her nose, and her clothes clung to her lithe body as she looked at me, waiting.

"Come in," I said. "Please."

She shook her head, her damp hair falling over her face. "I don't think that's a good idea."

"Please, come in. Please," I said again, and the word was the start to every thought in my head.

Please don't hate me.

Please forgive me.

Please.

"Please," I said. "Stay. Talk to me."

"No, I shouldn't," she said. "I'm cold and tired and it's been a really long day. For both of us. I'm going to take a hot bath and get some sleep." Her smile was gentle, sad. "You should try to, too."

"Darlene," I said, my voice thick and frayed at the ends. "It's the paternity test that's going to ruin me. Not you. I just…My mother…Molly. I don't know what to do. Or what to think."

"I know," she said. "But the idea that I could, in some way, jeopardize your situation with Livvie makes me sick inside, and it was stupid to try to hide the truth. There is no hiding it. Not from you, the court, or myself. It's on my record."

"In black and white," I muttered.

She nodded. "I thought about going to a bar to get drunk or high tonight, because if people are going to look at me like a drug addict, I might as well act like one. But the truth is, people will always look at me like that, no matter if I've been clean for one year, or two, or ten. It's a part of my past and a part of who I am. Sliding backwards because I got hurt doesn't solve anything. But being proud of what I've accomplished does."

Tears filled her eyes, but there was a blue flame burning behind them I hadn't seen before, and her tears didn't douse it.

"I will always be an addict even if you put the word 'recovering' in front of it. I will always have to work ten times as hard to be trusted, to be trustworthy but that's the price I have to pay for my mistakes."

I clenched my teeth; tossed on a sea of emotions I had no idea how to navigate.

"I'm sorry I took Olivia away from you," I said. "That was…a shitty, shitty thing to do."

Darlene leaned against the doorframe. "I get it. I really do," she said and even then, shivering with cold, she found a smile for me. "I totally understand, and it totally sucks. It's amazing how two opposite things can be completely true at the same time, isn't it?"

"I don't know what to say," I said. "Or what to feel. I don't feel…anything. To keep myself safe. And when I saw you with Max…"

She drew her old man's sweater, damp with rain, around her shoulders.

"He's my friend. My best friend. And I'm sorry he showed up at your apartment. He jumped on a plane tonight to Seattle, which is too bad because everything I told you is what I said at my NA meeting tonight. I think he would've been happy to hear it, and know that I'm going to be okay. Because I am. I'm going to be okay for me."

Darlene reached out and cupped my cheek in her hand. "If there is anything you need, tell me. I don't know what I can do, but I'm here."

I couldn't speak; I only nodded, and it sent a tear sliding down my cheek, to her hand.

"See?" she said with a quavering smile. "You feel so much, Sawyer. So much." She wiped the tear into her palm. "I'm going to keep this," she said, then turned and walked away.

chapter twenty-two

Darlene

The hours of the weekend dragged me behind them. I didn't see Sawyer at all, at least not up close. I watched from my upstairs window as the Abbotts came to pick up Olivia. Elena had told me they'd won supervised weekend visitation at the condo they were renting in the Marina.

I watched, my heart in my throat, as Sawyer helped them put Olivia in a sleek, white BMW SUV and drive off. He sat down on the front steps and was still sitting there long after they'd gone.

Every part of me ached to go to him, but after the other night, my mind felt as if it had been scrubbed free of the nagging whispers and doubts that always plagued me. I could think clearly. Sawyer had so much to contend with already. He didn't need me adding to the storm of his turbulent emotions. If he wanted to talk to me, he knew to call or visit, and I'd be there for him.

He didn't.

After work on Monday, I rehearsed with the dance troupe, dodging both Anne-Marie's stink-eye and Ryan's clumsy feet the entire time. But Greg loved my solo, even if he wouldn't say it out loud.

"Saturday night, we open," he said, as if we didn't know that. "Take some of these flyers to pass out to your friends and family. "It'd be good if each of you brought at least two people to the show as your guests."

"How many tickets have been sold?" Anne-Marie asked.

"We're doing okay," Greg said. "We could use a few more."

Glances were exchanged among us. That was code for "hardly any" and my heart sank a little. I wasn't doing the show for fame or fortune, that's for sure, but it would be nice if someone other than Anne-Marie's bitchy friends witnessed my first dance in four years. I took a handful of the Xeroxed papers and posted a few of them on my way home.

My phone rang after dinner, while I was curled up on my loveseat. I picked it up and a smile burst over my face.

"Maximilian," I said. "Just the person I wanted to talk to."

He told me about his new job at a Seattle hospital, and I told him about my emotional rock bottom and the NA meeting after.

"It was like taking a *Silkwood* shower," I said.

"What does that even mean?" he asked with a chuckle.

"You haven't seen *Silkwood*? That old movie where Meryl Streep works at a nuclear plant or something, and she gets irradiated? So these guys in Hazmat suits blast her with water hoses—in her eyeballs, gums, and everywhere—to decontaminate her?"

"That's what your NA meeting felt like?"

"Yes. Being brutally honest in front of God and everyone feels like a *Silkwood* shower." I smiled against the phone. "Put that in your Sponsor's Manual."

"Maybe, I will." Max laughed. "Or you could put it in yours."

I snorted. "Ha. I'm a long way from that."

"Maybe. Maybe not," Max said. "I'm so fucking proud of you."

"Thank you. Me too. And I'm proud of you. Seen your folks yet?"

"Not yet. I have tentative dinner plans with Mom on Saturday. I'll see how that goes before I tackle The Dad Situation."

"Let me know how it goes. I'm always here for you."

"Ah, and the student has become the master," Max said.

I laughed. "Oh, stop." My smile faded, and Max read my silence.

"How is Sawyer?" he asked gently.

I curled up on my loveseat, making myself into a ball. "Not good. He's fighting for custody of Olivia and I'm scared he's not going to win."

"God, that's awful. And what about you two?"

"There isn't much to say," I said. "I don't want to add to his problems."

"Darlene…"

"No, I mean that honestly. He has so much to contend with right now. I don't want to pressure him and I told him if he needed me, I'd be there."

"Sawyer the Lawyer, in the brief moments of our acquaintance, didn't strike me as the kind of guy who goes around asking for help or comfort when he needs it."

"Maybe not," I said softly. "And he definitely doesn't want it from me."

∽

The week felt as slow as the weekend, and yet was rushing up to meet me at the same time. Saturday was opening night. On Thursday, we rehearsed in the actual theater space for the first time. My heart sank a little at the shabby little place—the Brown Bag Theatre—with black walls and floors that needed paint, and fifty seats facing a tiny stage.

But my fellow dance troupers were getting excited. Anne-Marie was bringing a bunch of people, apparently.

"Who's coming to see you?" Paula asked as we cleared out after dress rehearsal.

"Oh, it's bad timing for me all around," I said with a small laugh. "My family is in New York and can't get over here, and my best friend upped and moved to Seattle on me, the bastard."

I realized then, that my other best friends, Zelda and Beckett, would've dropped everything to fly out and see me, but I never asked. It had felt like too much. Now that I had begun to grow some semblance of a backbone, it was too late.

Paula gave me a gentle smile. "That's too bad," she said, and leaned in to whisper, "You're the best part of this thing."

I watched her go and stood in the black box, alone.

"If a dancer dances for the first time in four years and no one sees it, did she actually dance?" I murmured under my breath.

I wiped a tear away. I should've called Zelda and Becks, but I was too scared of coming off as weak and needy. Again. But I *did* need them, and I realized—too late—that being with the people who love you isn't weak. It's how you stay strong.

"See, Max?" I sniffed. "I still have a long way to go."

Back home, I showered, changed, and set about to make another tuna casserole. It was the only thing I could think to do and I had to do something. Sawyer's hearing was tomorrow, and Max's words about him never asking for help wouldn't leave my head. I could drop off the casserole and let him decide if he wanted my company.

A knock came at the door just as I was pulling the finished casserole from the oven. My pulse fluttered, and I took the oven mitts off my shaking hands.

But it was Jackson at my door, looking casually elegant as usual, in slacks and a dark sweater over a blue dress shirt. His handsome features were drawn together with worry and his dark eyes were heavy.

"What happened?" I blurted, my pulse hammering in my chest.

"Nothing yet," Jackson said. "Can I come in? I told him I was stepping out to make a phone call."

I blinked, shook my head. "Sorry, yes. Come in."

Jackson was at least six-feet-three and seemed like a towering presence in my small space. I was suddenly glad Sawyer had this imposing and charismatic guy on his side.

"Would you like anything? Something to drink?"

Jackson shook his head.

I braced myself. "The paternity test…?"

"He and Olivia took it on Monday. The results are sealed until tomorrow at the hearing. Unless there's been a miracle of science since he took the first test, it's not going to go well."

I sagged against the counter. "I don't know what to do. I feel so helpless." I waved a hand at the pan. "I made a casserole…"

"Come with us to the hearing."

I jerked my eyes up. "What? No…I'm the drug addict neighbor, remember? I didn't help his cause at all."

"That was a low blow by their attorney," Jackson said. "If the judge sees the real you and not the image Holloway tried to plant in his mind, it'll help. And frankly, we need all the help we can get."

"Can they really just take Olivia away?"

Jackson rubbed the back of his neck. "The system's improved for fathers' rights in the last ten years, and courts never want to pull children out of good homes. There's a statute about Sawyer acting and providing for Olivia as if she were his own, which gives him some claim to her, but it's all we have. I don't know that it's going to be enough. Especially since Molly gave the baby to Sawyer but never bothered to put his name on the birth certificate," he added bitterly. "If she had just done that…"

He broke off and shook his head.

"I'll go if you think it will help," I said, slowly. "Of course, I will. But are you sure that's what he needs?"

Jackson nodded. "Yeah, I do. Sawyer needs you. He needs…" He blew air out his cheeks. "God, he needs something and I don't know what to do for him. He's like a robot these last few days. Hardly talks except to Olivia and even then it's like…"

"Like what?" I whispered.

"He looks at her like, inside his mind, he's already saying goodbye."

My hand flew to my mouth. "Oh no."

"I know he'd fight for her with everything he has, but that's just it. We don't have much to fight with. At least not as far as the law goes." Jackson put his hands on my shoulders. "Sawyer needs you. You do something for him I've never seen before. You make him happy."

Tears filled my eyes. "I don't know, Jackson."

"I do. The judge needs to see Sawyer as something other than cold and stiff. I think you're the only person who can bring that out of him."

"I'll try," I said. "But what if Sawyer doesn't want me there? What if…"

"He doesn't have a choice," Jackson said, his old smile coming back. "He has to take the advice of his attorney—me—and I say I want you there."

I smiled and hugged Jackson. "Okay, I will."

"Thank you, Darlene." Jackson gave me a final squeeze and let me go. "I'll have a car out front at nine o'clock."

"I'll be there. Oh, wait! Come here."

Jackson followed me to the kitchen area and I put the oven mitts on his hands.

"Take the casserole to him. It has peas in it. For Livvie."

Jackson smiled. "He *might* guess that I didn't step out to make a phone call."

I grinned. "Your cover is blown."

I opened my front door and craned up on tiptoe to give Jackson a peck on the cheek. "Thank you for helping him."

"Right back at you, Dar," he said, and went out.

The next morning, I put on my best I'm Not A Junkie outfit—a flowing, white dress with colorful flowers that brushed my knees. I usually paired it with my combat boots to give it some edge, but today I wore my low-heeled dance shoes, and toned my usually heavy eye-makeup down. I piled my hair on my head in a loose bun and put on my lucky gold hoop earrings.

I was downstairs at ten minutes to nine, my stomach twisting itself in knots. Sawyer and Jackson were at Elena's, giving Olivia over to babysit. I slipped past them to wait outside. If I talked to Olivia for even a second I was going to burst into tears.

The front door opened behind me a few minutes later. Sawyer stopped short. He was devastating in a dark blue suit and paler blue tie. I could swear I saw the stoniness of his eyes melt a little as he took me in.

"There she is," Jackson said, his smile brilliant. "Our secret weapon." He kissed my cheek. "You're a vision. Everyone in that courtroom will be helpless not to fall in love with you."

My face flushed red up to my ears. "Oh my God, stop." I looked to Sawyer. "Jackson said I should come. That it might help…"

"Don't you have to work?" Sawyer asked dully.

It was going to put a dent in my bank account to miss another day, but what was that to what Sawyer was facing? I'd worry about it later.

"This is much more important," I said.

Sawyer held my gaze a moment more, then nodded and moved to the sedan idling at the curb.

"See?" Jackson murmured in my ear as we followed him down. "He's shut down."

"No," I said, my heart heavy. "He's just scared to death."

In the car, I sat wedged between Sawyer and Jackson in the backseat. Sawyer propped his chin on his hand, his gaze on the streets outside. His other hand was in his lap. Without giving myself a chance to outthink it, I reached over and took it in mine. Sawyer stiffened and didn't pull his gaze from the window. But after a moment, he sighed; a little tension left his body and he laced his fingers with mine.

I eased a sigh of relief too and glanced over at Jackson. He gave me a surreptitious a-okay sign. But as the car rolled up in front of the Superior Court, Sawyer's body tensed all over again. He let go of my hand and got out of the car without a word.

Inside the courtroom, the Abbotts were already there. My immediate reaction was confusion; I'd imagined them as heartless monsters, but they looked put together and wealthy with their pastel clothing and silver hair.

They look like nice people.

Both of them turned in their seats when we came in, their eyes searching to meet Sawyer's, both wearing hopeful smiles. But he refused to look at them, and their gazes landed on me.

I smiled brightly at them, almost like a reflex. I couldn't help myself, and besides, I figured it couldn't hurt if someone on Sawyer's side acted as a goodwill ambassador.

The Abbotts' attorney frowned at me, whispered something to his clients. They turned back to me as I took a seat in the audience, directly behind Sawyer and Jackson's table, wary now.

Yes, that's me. I'm the recovering drug addict, I thought. But I kept my chin up and smile friendly. A few minutes later, the bailiff told us to rise and the judge came in.

He settled his glasses on his nose and took up an envelope in his hand. "In the matter of the custody provisions for Olivia Abbott, a minor child, the Court has received Mr. Haas' paternity results." He fixed his stern gaze on Sawyer. "Mr. Smith, does your client have anything to enter into the record at this time?"

Jackson rose to his feet. "Your Honor, we'd like the Court to recognize Darlene Montgomery." He turned to gesture to me. "The last time we met, Mr. Holloway tried to cast aspersions on those who have helped Sawyer take care of Olivia, and we would like the Abbotts, and the Court, to hear a few words from Ms. Montgomery herself."

My eyes widened and I shot Jackson a panicked look.

No one said anything about talking!

But I sucked in a breath to calm down. Hell, I'd already taken the *Silkwood* shower. What was saying nice things about Sawyer compared to that?

But the judge shook his head.

"There will be time enough after the test results are read for any character statements, though if Mr. Haas himself has anything he'd like to say, he is free to do so."

From my vantage behind them, I saw Jackson nudge Sawyer under the table, but Sawyer remained still as stone. My gaze darted to the Abbotts. Both looked on the edge of their seats, craning in with hopeful expressions on their faces.

The judge sighed. "Very well. The Clerk of the Court shall now read and enter the DNA test results into the record."

He handed the envelope to a young woman in a sharp navy suit. The courtroom went silent but for the soft tearing of paper. My imagination told me that was the sound of Sawyer's heart tearing in two.

He lifted his head, and the sudden movement drew everyone's attention.

"Please don't."

The words hung in the air and it took me a second to realize Sawyer had said them. A collective gasp whipped through the courtroom. My own breath stuck in my throat to hear the pain that saturated every syllable; he sounded exhausted down to his soul.

"Please don't read that," he said.

Sawyer rose to his feet. His shoulders were rounded, as if he carried the weight of the universe in every pore and sinew of his body. But I watched him unfold, stand straighter, his voice strengthening but still soft with pain and hope and love.

"Olivia is my daughter," he told the courtroom. "She is, no matter what that test says. And in a few weeks, none of this would have mattered. I would have crossed that arbitrary finish line the law has drawn in the sand, and petitioned to have my name put on her birth certificate. And it would've been done, no matter the test results. But there *is* a line, and simply because we're on this side of it, I could lose her."

I was riveted to Sawyer, but out of the corner of my eyes, Holloway whispered frantically to the Abbotts. They shushed him with shakes of their head. Everyone in that room hung on Sawyer's every word.

"I have raised Olivia since she was three months old. She calls me Daddy." His voice cracked and my heart cracked right along with him. "That test? It doesn't mean anything to me. I don't need it to tell me how I feel, or how much I should love that little girl. I love her with every molecule in my body, and it doesn't matter that none of mine match any of hers. I don't care that they don't. I never did."

He heaved a steadying breath. "I took a paternity test before. Ten months ago, after Molly left the baby with me. That test didn't matter, either. It had only been a few days but it was still too late. Since the minute Molly put Olivia in my arms and said she was mine, she was."

I bit the inside of my cheek, but tears streamed down my face anyway. Mrs. Abbott dabbed her eyes with a tissue and her husband pressed his fist to his mouth, listening.

Sawyer turned to them, his eyes full. "I know you don't know me, but Olivia does. Please don't take her from me. Please. She's my daughter. She's my little girl. Thanks…thank you."

He slumped back down and it took everything I had not to jump out of my chair and go to him, to hold him. Jackson gripped his shoulder and said something but Sawyer only shook his head, covered his eyes with his hand.

Judge Chen looked to the Abbotts who were talking in hushed, urgent voices at their attorney, who whispered and gestured back in a mess of confusion.

"Mr. Holloway," the judge said, "is there something your clients would like to say?"

Reluctantly, the lawyer got to his feet. "Your Honor, we'd like a conference in chambers."

Judge Chen's face remained impassive, but I could swear I saw relief touch his features. He nodded.

"Granted."

I watched as the bailiff led the court reporter, and both parties to the judge's chambers at the rear of the courtroom. Jackson put his arm around Sawyer, who moved like a sleepwalker carrying a thousand pounds on his back. Just before he stepped into the chambers, he turned and our eyes met. His beautiful face was painted with anguish and hope. I smiled through tears and gave him two thumbs up.

The smallest twitch of a smile touched his lips, and stepped inside. The bailiff followed him and shut the door behind him.

I let my hands drop and my tears fell with them. I felt like fool for giving him such a silly gesture but it's all I had. That and hope, because it was so apparent that if he lost Olivia, nothing would ever be okay ever again. And I realized with a horrible pang that added to the already heavy anguish in my heart, that losing Olivia would hurt me too. More than I realized.

Minutes ticked by. I was the only person in the gallery besides the Clerk who sat at her desk, shuffling papers. She had the results of the DNA test. I wanted to hurdle the rows of benches, tear it from her hands, and rip it to pieces so no one could ever know what it said.

Finally, the chambers' door opened and a jolt of panic and hope jerked me ramrod straight. The judge emerged first, his face impassive as ever, followed by the Abbotts, who exchanged nervous smiles with each other. I craned my head, practically jumping out of my seat, until I saw Jackson's wide smile and Sawyer…

I love him.

The thought tore through me with heat and electricity both.

Oh my God, I love him. I'm in love with him.

I was in love with Sawyer, because in that moment, his happiness—the wholeness of his heart—was the only thing that was important to me. And I realized too, that all times I'd thought I'd been in love before were nothing. Infatuations of my lonely heart. I had no thought for myself in that courtroom. Only love for Sawyer and the fervent hope that nothing would ever hurt him.

I drank him in, searching for a sign of what happened in that meeting. His eyes were red-rimmed but and he looked shell-shocked; heaving a sigh—of relief?—and answered Jackson's smile with a wan one of his own. As he crossed the courtroom, his eyes found mine. His smile widened a little, and then he turned to take his seat.

I sucked in a breath. The judge cleared his throat.

"The Petitioners have requested a motion to delay reading of the order for paternal DNA results until the Respondent has completed his bar exam for the State of California, scheduled to begin on Monday of next week. The motion is granted. The test results will remain sealed until that time as this Court reconvenes on the following Friday. Plaintiffs, in addition to their prearranged weekend custody, are granted temporary, supervised custody of Olivia Abbott, the minor child, for the three-day duration of Mr. Haas's bar examination. Hearing adjourned."

He banged his gavel and Sawyer slumped in his chair. The Abbotts approached and words were exchanged. Jackson shook Mr. Abbott's hand. Alice Abbott moved to Sawyer and it looked to me like she was trying not to touch him or hug him. She looked like a mother regarding her son, and hope took flight in my chest. A few more words were passed between them, and then the Abbotts left, both giving me a nod as they did.

I hurried around the partition to Sawyer and Jackson.

"What does this all mean?"

"It means the Abbotts didn't want to tank Sawyer's bar exam with bad results," Jackson said. "We haven't won, but this delay gives me hope that no matter what happens, the Abbotts are flexible." He elbowed his friend. "Either that, or susceptible to your manly displays of emotion."

Sawyer heaved a ragged breath. "Now what do I do?"

"They take Olivia tomorrow morning through Wednesday," Jackson said. "You have this weekend to study, and then the Big Test, which you are going to kill."

Sawyer nodded. "So we can go? Right now I just want to get back to Olivia."

We left the courthouse. The sun was high and golden, and almost as bright as Jackson's smile as we walked to the sedan he said his company had given him to use. It seemed the entire world was different from the one we woke up in this morning.

"So, Darlene, what's going on with you?" Jackson asked as we walked to the parking lot. "Have any fun plans this weekend?"

I gave a small laugh at his infallible humor and optimism.

"Uh, yeah, I have a dance thing Saturday night."

In my peripheral, Sawyer raised his head. With effort, I kept my eyes on Jackson. "It's totally no big deal, though. Tiny little show in a nothing theatre. Like, fifty capacity." I laughed nervously. "If we fill ten seats I'd consider it a success."

"Damn, my brother's got a graduation party tomorrow night in Oakland, or I'd totally show up," Jackson said. "I didn't know you were part of a dance company."

"I wouldn't call it a company," I said. "It's super small. I just auditioned to dip my foot back in the waters, you know?"

We arrived at the sedan and the driver opened the door for us. "Well, break a leg," Jackson said. "Wait, am I supposed to say that for dancers, or just actors?"

"If you're wishing me luck, I'll take it."

We climbed in and once again, I was wedged between Sawyer and Jackson. My thigh pressed against Sawyer's and I felt every place where we touched, just the same as we had on the way over.

Except now I know I'm in love with him.

The car dropped us off first. Jackson climbed out to say goodbye. He pulled Sawyer into a hug.

"I'll drive you to Sac on Sunday, but just know you're going to kill it. You're ready."

"Thank you," Sawyer said. "For everything."

"You did all the heavy lifting." Jackson turned his smile to me. "And you go bring that fifty-seat house down with your dance, okay?" He raised his eyebrows meaningfully. "Where is it again? And what time? Just in case I can sneak out of the party early."

"Um, eight o'clock at the Brown Bag Theatre, off Capp Street? But really, it's cool. You don't have to. It'll take longer to find parking than to watch the actual show."

"That's what these babies are for," Jackson said and tapped the roof of the car. "Or Ubers. Or cabs. Or trains. Or buses," he said at Sawyer, then grinned. "Take care, you two."

Outside our house, Sawyer carved a hand through his hair.

"Thank you for coming today."

"I didn't do anything…"

"You did," Sawyer said. "It was good to have you there. I think it helped me to find the words when I needed them most."

A warmth spread through my chest. "I'm glad I could help," I said in a small voice.

Sawyer turned his gaze to the Victorian. "I don't want to go to Sacramento," he said. "I feel like I'm losing whatever time I have left with her. I'm too scared to let myself think today was anything but a stay of execution."

I touched his hand. "The Abbotts are good people. Even if they get custody, I feel like they won't cut you out. You'll have partial custody, or visitation…"

"I don't want that," Sawyer said, his eyes hard. "I want full custody. All the time."

"I know you do. But I think, somehow, it will be all right. In a way that we can't see yet."

He nodded. "I can't fall apart right now. Or at all, I guess. Not until after the exam." He looked up at me suddenly, the anguish pulling at him again. "Five days, Darlene. Jesus, I wish…"

"What?" I asked softly. "Tell me."

His jaw clenched and anger hardened his features in a way I recognized; when he was overcome with emotions and didn't know what to do with them. The anger was directed inward, as if he thought he was a failure for having them.

His dark eyes caught and held mine. "I wish Olivia was staying with you."

I reeled at the words. Words that meant he trusted me. That my past didn't scare him. It was like a gift of hope, that maybe there was still a future for us too, even if we couldn't see that yet either. Hot tears sprung to my eyes.

"Me too," I said.

chapter twenty-three

Sawyer

The front door buzzed promptly at eight a.m. I had Olivia bathed and dressed, and her bag packed until the zipper looked ready to burst.

Like the bag Molly gave me the day she left.

"I'm not giving her up," I muttered, jamming her sippy cup into a side pocket. "It's just for five days and then…"

I couldn't see anything after that. All the prepping and studying and planning ahead wasn't going to get me out of the unknown. I was that kid again, standing in the foyer of my house, blue and red lights flashing, waiting with a horrible anticipation for what was to come.

The buzzer sounded again. I picked Olivia off the floor. "Come on, baby. Time to see Grandma and Grandpa."

I took Olivia down to the Abbotts, into September's amber light. The smiles on Gerald and Alice's faces were genuine and it felt impossible to hate them.

But if they take Olivia from me, how could I help it?

The court-appointed supervisor, a kind-faced woman named Jill, waited by the BMW, as the Abbotts and I stood in a tense silence.

"Good morning," Alice said as I came down the steps with Olivia in my arms. "How are you, little one?" Olivia rested her head on my shoulder. "Tired, honey?"

She wasn't tired. Olivia wasn't a complainer; she was resting her head on me to stay close. I tightened my hold on her.

"And how are you, Sawyer?" Alice asked quietly.

"Fine. Why did you ask for a delay on the DNA results?"

She and Gerald exchanged glances.

"As we stated at the hearing, you have your big exam," Alice said. "We… didn't want you to be distracted any more than you probably are."

"We didn't realize you had so much going on right now," Gerald added.

Newsflash, folks: there is no good time to rip apart a guy's life and take his kid away.

The words were on my lips but I swallowed them down. Animosity wasn't going to get me anywhere, and I didn't want Olivia to feel it and be wrapped up in it.

And you like them, a voice sounding like Jackson spoke up.

"Thank you for that," I said grudgingly.

Alice smiled nervously. "We hope you do well on your test, and when you get back, maybe we can all have lunch?"

"Alice," Gerald said in a mild tone of warning.

"Just a thought." Alice smiled.

"Sure. Lunch," I said, trying not to sound like a complete asshole, but goddammit, they were going to take my daughter and drive off with her and the pain was squeezing my heart so I could hardly breathe.

It's just five days…isn't it? Please, God, I can't do more than that.

Jill approached. "Can I help put her in her car seat?"

I nodded slowly. It was time to go. I wanted to hold Olivia forever; or grab her and make a run for it… I kissed my girl on the cheek.

"I love you. I'll see you soon." I put Olivia in Jill's arms. "Be good, honey."

"Be goo, Daddy."

My chest tightened and I busied myself with fishing a piece of paper out of my pocket while I pulled myself together.

"This is the name of the hotel I'll be staying at in Sacramento," I told the Abbotts. "This is my cell phone number. This is Darlene's number—my upstairs neighbor, and this is Elena, my sitter's number."

You remember them? My unlicensed, irresponsible babysitter and my drug addict neighbor?

I bit back those words too, hid them behind a stiff, expressionless mask.

"If you need anything and can't get a hold of me, call one of them," I said.

"Will do," Gerald said.

They both seemed to be waiting for me to do or say something more.

"Okay, so…that's it, I guess," I muttered.

Apparently that was the wrong answer. Gerald pressed his lips together, and ushered his wife to the car.

Alice gave me a final, small smile. "Good luck."

I watched them climb in and the engine roared to life.

"God help me walk away," I whispered.

I couldn't move. As with last weekend, I stayed rooted to the curb until their SUV, with Livvie safely buckled inside, drove down the street and around the corner. It wasn't possible to walk away, but if the court gave full custody to the Abbotts, I'd chase their car down until I hadn't breath left in my body. A dumb notion. It wouldn't do me any good if the law sided with them.

Fuck the law.

I couldn't help but feel it had betrayed me when I was trying so hard to be its agent and advocate. And now I had to devote three full days to proving I had what it took to do just that.

I dragged myself up to my place.

Inside, it was quiet; the silence amplified my aloneness. No sound of Olivia or her baby babble that was fast growing into language; no wooden *clunk* of her blocks coming together as she stacked them. The baby monitor was silent; her crib empty. I refused to believe this was a preview of my future, but it was hard. So damn hard.

I put on a pot of coffee and while it brewed, I slumped at my desk and pulled my study materials around me. But they blended together in a mash of words that were already familiar to me. I knew this stuff, forwards and back. All those endless nights hadn't been for nothing. I was as ready as I ever could be for this exam.

I shut my books and sat in the quiet of my place. My stomach growled loudly in that quiet, and I shuffled to the kitchen for something microwavable. I found Darlene's latest tuna casserole in the refrigerator.

I pulled it from the fridge and set it on the counter, staring at the tinfoil-covered pan. My stomach was still complaining, but another hunger grew and spread, upward and out, like a strange fire that had nothing to do with food.

I needed to see Darlene; my hands wanted to touch her, my overworked brain needed to laugh with her, and my stony heart wanted to be with her, and give whatever we had between us an honest chance.

How? How can I be with her when my heart could be shattered with one bang of a judge's gavel?

"Fuck," I said, shoving the tray away.

Above was quiet too. No creaks. Darlene might still be sleeping or maybe she was out taking a run, or getting ready for her dance that night.

Jackson, with all the subtlety of an elephant on roller skates, had gotten the theater address from Darlene and now it was in my brain forever. She'd tried hard—too hard—to minimize it, but I knew the truth. She hadn't danced in four years. This was a big deal to her.

My phone rang, and I looked at the number.

Speak of the devil…

"What's up, Jax?"

"Just calling to make sure you didn't beat up two nice old people, and were now racing toward Mexico in their white Bronco with Livvie."

"It's a white Beemer," I said dully. "And the thought crossed my mind."

A bunch of clicking and shuffling sounds came over the line.

"What are you doing?" I asked.

"Driving to my bro's grad party in Oak-town," Jackson said. "I put you on speaker. So listen. Darlene's show."

"What about it?"

"You're going, right?"

I glanced at the tuna casserole. "I don't know."

"Goddammit, Haas," Jackson said, nearly shouting. "What the fuck is wrong with you?"

I blinked, shook my head at the sudden volley, then fired back. "What is wrong with *me*? Where should I fucking start? You think it's easy sitting down here when she's up there, ten steps away?"

"Then get your ass up there."

"And do what? Sleep with her? Start a relationship with her? And what happens after the hearing next Thursday? If I lose, I'm not going to be good for anyone, Jax. It's going to fuck me up. Hard."

"You're so sure you're going to lose…?"

"I'm not super optimistic," I said snidely. "I don't know what else I can do."

"You can start but not being a colossal asshole to the Abbotts. They *want* to like you, Sawyer, but you are making it so easy for them not to. And furthermore, they want *you* to like *them*. The delay in the test results? That was a gift. Did you even thank them for it?"

"Yes," I spat. "I did. But what the fuck, Jackson? Should I send them a gift basket too? 'Thanks for not ripping my daughter away from me… *yet?*' Like that's some kind of huge favor and I should be kissing their ass? If they want me to like them so fucking much, they can leave Olivia and me alone. I'd let them see her. Be a part of her life. I want that for her, but I want it on *my* terms."

"You might not get that, but you could get *something*, but not if you throw it all away by shutting them out. Stop fucking shutting people out."

I gaped. "Who have I been shutting out?"

"How about every single one of our friends? When was the last time you spoke to any of the guys from our old group?"

"I've been a little bit fucking busy taking care of Livvie and trying to get through law school," I said through gritted teeth. "This isn't exactly news."

"Mmkay, how about Darlene?"

I rubbed my eyes with my free hand. "What about her?"

"You shouldn't throw away a chance at happiness with an awesome chick because everything else is shitty. Or is it her drug history freaking you out? Because I know that's not easy for you. I get that, but—"

"But what? Suddenly you're an expert at this shit because you've had *how many* long-term relationships? Oh that's right, *none*. Get off my back, Jackson. I don't care about her past. I trust Darlene, and I know she deserves a lot better than me."

"That's a fucking cop-out. She cares about you. She might even love your dumb ass, and you're just going to let her go?"

The fire in me died at his words, at the possibilities behind them.

I sank into my desk chair.

"Got your attention, did I?" Jackson said with a small laugh, the warmth returning to his voice immediately.

"I don't want to hurt her, Jax," I said quietly. "I don't know what I'm doing, and all this custody shit just makes everything a million times harder. It's not a cop-out to want everything good for her. She deserves to be happy."

"So do you, man," Jackson said in a low voice. "That's all I'm saying. You do too." There was a pause. "And Henrietta agrees with me. Hold on, she wants to say something."

I jerked up straight. "What?"

More shuffling sounds and then I heard Jackson's mother's muffled voice. "I want to talk to him off the speaker. Is it this button? Hello?" Then loudly, *"Hello?"*

I winced and held the phone away from my ear, a smile I couldn't keep back spreading over my lips. "Hi, Henrietta."

"Hello, Sawyer," she said. "How are you doing, baby?"

"I've been better."

"I know it, but listen to Mama. I know what you're trying to do, and it's sweet. You're trying to protect that girl because you're going through some hard times, and they might get harder, right?"

"I don't have anything to offer her, Henrietta."

"That's where you're wrong, honey. No one expects you to be okay through this situation. It could get rough, no lie. But when things get rough, that's when you draw people to you. You don't push them away. And the lovely Darlene? She can take all your rough times. She's been through rough times of her own, I've heard. She's not expecting you to get it all right the first time because she won't either. But reach out, baby. Reach out and hold on to those you need, because they need you too more than you think. And that's how you get through the rough stuff. You hold on and don't let go. Okay?"

I nodded, my jaw clenched. "Okay."

"Good," Henrietta said. "Now you go be with your woman. Don't worry about what to give or not give. Just be with her. Sometimes that's more than good enough."

"Thank you, Henrietta."

"Any time, baby. I'm going to give you back to Jackson and you two had better watch your language this time. You sound like a pair of fools with all that swearing."

I grinned. "I didn't know there was a lady present."

"Well, now you know."

"Yes, ma'am."

More scuffling and muffled talk, then Jackson put me back on speakerphone. "Hello? Who's this? Sawyer? Are you still there?"

I laughed. I didn't think it was possible, but I laughed. "I'm going."

"Good."

"Hey, Jax…" My damn throat closed up. "I…"

"I know," he said. "Love you too, bro."

I hung up and heaved a sigh that felt miles deep. And though it felt a little bit like lowering my guard, I decided to do something I hadn't done in almost a year. I crawled into my bed without setting an alarm, and tried to take a nap.

But as exhausted as I was, sleep eluded me. I tossed and turned on cold sheets. My bed had always been empty. Even in the past, when I'd had a woman in it, it was only for a few hours. No sleep, just sex and then the woman left. I made sure of that.

I closed my eyes and used my infallible memory to recall Darlene, in perfect detail. A few tricks of mental Photoshop, and she was lying next to me, her dark hair splayed across my pillow, her mouth inches from mine—laughing and smiling…

I slipped into the twilight world between sleep and awake, and the image of her wavered like a mirage, just out of reach.

When I finally did fall asleep, it was fitful, skimming above the surface of deep rest, and when I awoke, the bed was still empty.

chapter twenty-four

Sawyer

The afternoon sun was high when I climbed out of bed, and I was hungry as hell. I heated up a huge portion of Darlene's casserole and ate every bite. After, I took my best gray suit to the dry cleaners and told them to rush it. While it was being cleaned, I wandered into Macy's on Union Square and bought a new tie.

After, I picked up my dry cleaning, showered, changed, and at a quarter to seven, I headed out. At the florist on 14th, I started toward the red roses, but a stand of daisies in brilliant yellow and orange caught my eye.

"Gerber daisies," said the florist with a smile. "In Egyptian times, the *gerbera* daisy represented light and sun. In the Victorian era, they came to represent happiness."

"In the *Victorian* era…" At the word, my photographic memory conjured my house; Darlene's house too.

The florist smiled. "They're my favorite."

I touched one of the soft, bright petals. "Mine too."

With a bouquet of two-dozen Gerber daisies wrapped in green tissue paper under my arm, I jumped on the Muni for the Mission District; an artsy, bohemian part of the city.

I walked along a busy street lined with shops and cafés, and one too many new condo complexes. The tech industry was sucking some of the life out of the old San Francisco. The Brown Bag Theater was a hole in the wall; a holdover from before the tech boom, and that still existed by the city's sheer force of will, though I wondered for how much longer.

I paid a $10 ticket at the rickety box office and stepped into the shabby interior. The wallpaper was faded and covered in posters from previous shows. The lobby was nonexistent; a small space where one wall was heavy with black curtains. A handful of people loitered in the space, talking and drinking wine from a tiny bar stand. I was the only one wearing a suit.

At ten to eight, a nervous-looking guy in black passed out programs and told us to take our seats. I filed in to the fifty-capacity space with the rest of the audience; we filled maybe twenty seats.

I laid the flowers across my knee and watched the stage—a small rectangle of scuffed black illuminated by a single light in the center. My stomach twisted as if I were the one about to perform, and I scanned the program—a smudgy Xerox folded in half.

Most of the dances were as a group, but Darlene had a solo, halfway into the show.

She never told me.

Then the house lights dimmed and the show began.

It wasn't good.

I was no dance connoisseur but every number felt amateurish and overly dramatic. Trying to make a statement, somehow. Except for Darlene. My considerable bias aside, she was riveting. Stunning. I couldn't take my eyes off of her. The dumbass director shoved her in the back of every ensemble dance, and still she shone brighter than the lead dancer we were supposed to be watching.

Three routines later, and Darlene took the stage. She moved gracefully into a cone of light in a simple black dancer's dress with billowy material that floated around her long legs. Her hair was tied up on her head in a loose ponytail, revealing the long lines of her neck and shoulders. Like my favorite shirt of hers, the back of her dress crisscrossed her shoulder blades—highlighting the lines and lean muscle. The sleeves were long but sheer, also giving elegant definition to her arms.

God, she's so beautiful.

The program said she'd be dancing to a song called "Down." I'd never heard it before, the first notes—a lone piano—descended like downward steps. Darlene remained frozen until a woman began to sing. A lonely voice, yet bright and clear.

I stared at Darlene, watched the play of her muscles under her skin as she moved, filled the small space with her presence, flowing like shadows and light; slow with the piano, fast and precise with the techno beat.

As the song came to an end, Darlene collapsed onto her back, braced on one elbow; the other arm reached for the unlit space above her, her hand grasping at nothing. On that final note and last haunting lyric, her back arched and her head fell back, as if she were being pulled upward by an unseen force, and then left there, suspended in the silence.

The moment hung and then the meager crowd caught their breath. I broke free from her spell and my hands slammed together over and over. A few other audience members whistled or whooped where they had only politely applauded every act that had come before.

My chest swelled with pride. She was the best and they all knew it.

Then the next and final dance came, and Darlene was once again relegated to the back of the stage. I didn't know what kind of hierarchy this dance troupe had but it was painfully obvious Darlene deserved to be the lead.

I watched her make-do in the back with her partner—the clumsy schmuck who'd bruised her head in rehearsal a few weeks ago. She struggled with him now. I saw her correct mistakes, or cover for him when he was off-time. A sneer curled my lips, and I tried to focus on her. Just her.

And then it happened.

The pairs of dancers in the back came apart and then flew together, and Darlene's klutzy partner stomped on her foot with his heel. I shot halfway out of my seat as Darlene's face contorted in sudden pain. No one else seemed to have noticed—the lead dancer had executed some sort of gymnastic feat to capture their attention.

Darlene put on a stage face and I sank down slowly, watching in awe as she powered through the rest of her dance—about ten more seconds. She favored her right foot, but subtly, and the only real sign of her pain was the sweat the glistened across her chest.

As soon as the dance ended, the dancers bowed, and Darlene's partner shot her an apologetic look. She stared straight ahead, into the lights that blinded her to the audience, but I saw the tears in her eyes and the clench of her jaw. She kept her right foot behind her left as she bowed to the smattering of applause, but as soon as the black curtain began to drop, she limped off.

The lights came up and while everyone else filed toward the exit, I raced down the small aisle with the flowers and jumped onto the stage. I had to paw at the heavy material for a moment but I found the split and stepped through it.

It was dim, but backstage lights guided me to a small anteroom where the dancers were laughing with post-show nerves and being congratulated by their director.

"Where's Darlene?" I demanded.

They all stopped and exchanged glances. Her asshole partner had the good graces to look chagrined but said nothing.

"Probably in the dressing room," the lead dancer said in a bitchy tone I didn't like. "She kind of...does her own thing."

I remembered how Darlene had told me they didn't welcome her with open arms, but made her feel like an outcast.

Even though she's the best of them. Because *she's the best of them.*

I snorted in disgust and turned back the way I'd come. I found the tiny dressing room. Empty. A short corridor led behind the stage. I heard the muffled crying first, and followed it to her, picking my way carefully through the dimness.

Darlene sat on the floor, her back against one of the movable backdrops that had been used in show. Her right foot was propped up on a coil of rope and even in the dark, I could see the swelling and bruising around the last two toes.

"Darlene."

She lifted her tear-stained face, taking in me and my suit, and the flowers in my hand. And in one glance, I felt how she appreciated all of it more than she had words for. More than I deserved. Because her every emotion lived in her body, in her eyes, and beautiful face that couldn't keep anything a secret.

She smiled through her tears, her voice whispery and tremulous. "You came."

I knelt beside her, examined her foot to conceal the sudden rush of emotions that swept through me. I had too many and didn't have the first clue what to do with them all.

I've never felt this way about a woman before…

And she was hurt. That clumsy asshole hurt her. I channeled my feelings into anger at him and felt more in control.

I set the flowers down, and carefully pulled her foot onto my lap. Her last two toes were swollen, and the bruising was spreading down the outside edge of her foot and across the top in purple splotches. "This isn't my specialty, but it looks broken."

"I think so. It's hurts. A lot." She sniffed and shook her head. "So much for my dance comeback."

"For now," I said fiercely. "You'll heal and get out there again. You have to. You were the best damn part of that show."

Darlene smiled, or tried to, for me. But it crumpled under the weight of her tears.

"I try so hard…and it all just slips out of my grasp. My best friend…now this job…" She tilted her head up to look up at me, her blue eyes brimming and her cheeks stained with the trails of dark makeup. "I can't hold on to anything…"

I swallowed hard, Henrietta's words filtering into my thoughts. I put my arms around her.

"Not this time." I said, gruffly. "Hold on to me."

She raised her eyes to mine, uncertain. "Sawyer…"

"And I'll hold on to you, okay?" I said. "Just as tightly."

A little sob escaped her and she wrapped her arms around my neck. I held her for a long, selfish moment, until her body in my arms tensed with pain, pushing a little whimper from her. I set the flowers in her lap, and lifted her off the ground carefully, holding her around the back and under her knees.

"The daisies are beautiful," she said, with a sniff. "They're so bright and cheerful."

I nodded. In the dark, and in pain, Darlene was still giving, still generous and vibrant. I held her closer, and carried her through the theatre, her head tucked under my chin and her hand on my chest. We passed through the green room, and the troupe stopped their small celebrations.

"You broke her damn foot," I snapped at her partner.

"It was an accident," Darlene said, clinging to me tighter.

"Accident or not, he should have known better. *Been* better to her," I said, still pinning the guy with a hard stare, then sweeping it over the room. "You all should have. You should have taken care of her."

I should have taken care of her.

I gritted my teeth. "Whoever you find to replace her won't be one tenth the dancer she is." I looked down at Darlene. "You have stuff here?"

She nodded. "In the locker."

"I got it." A small woman in glasses brought Darlene's bag and her ratty old gray sweater. Darlene added them to her lap, beside the flowers.

"You were great tonight," the woman said, her eyes darting to mine and back. "He's right. I hope you get better quick. Some other company's going to be lucky to have you."

"Thanks, Paula," Darlene whispered.

I carried her out of the theatre, onto the street, where the night was cold and the wind made Darlene's black dance dress slide up her legs. She shivered, and then let out a little cry.

"God, it hurts," she whispered.

"Do you mind calling me an Uber or a cab?" I said, trying to take her mind off of it. "I'd do it, but my hands are tied."

She smiled and fished her phone from her purse. "You can put me down. I must be heavy."

"You're not," I said.

I'm not letting you go.

An Uber arrived within minutes, and I was glad the driver had the heat turned up. In the backseat, I kept her against me, holding her. And the way she molded herself to me, I felt like she was mine, and never in my life had I known such happiness. A bruised happiness, given what I faced with the Abbotts, but a happiness I hadn't ever experienced. It felt like too much to ask for more, but in my mind's eye, I tentatively reached for a future that had both her and Olivia. A real life.

A family?

"Thank you for coming to the show," Darlene said, pulling me from my thoughts. "It meant so much to me, I can't even tell you."

Shame ripped through me at how I almost hadn't. At how close I came to letting my own fear keep me home. I wouldn't have been there to witness her dance, or be there for her when she got hurt.

I said nothing but held her tighter.

"I called my parents a few days ago," Darlene said against my chest. "I waited so long to tell them about the show because what if I gave them plenty of notice, and they still said no? I thought it would hurt less if I told them at the last minute. Then they could say no, and it would make sense. Kind of like insurance, you know?"

"Yeah, I know."

"And I didn't even tell my best friends back home at all. But I wished I had. I wish I'd been braver."

"You are brave, Darlene," I said. "You're braver than anyone I know."

"My best friend Beckett told me that once, too. I don't know if I believe it but I feel like I'm getting closer. This may not be the best show, but it was my first since I started using. My first since I'd been clean."

She craned her head to look up at me. "Tonight was a disaster, but it was also better than anything I could have imagined. I needed someone there." Her eyes shone. "You were there."

"It wasn't a disaster. You were incredible." I swallowed hard. "And I showed up, yeah, but I should've been there for you a hell of a lot sooner."

She shrugged and smiled, her fingertips touching my cheek. "You're here now, Sawyer. That's all that matters."

chapter twenty-five

Darlene

SAWYER DIRECTED THE UBER DRIVER TO TAKE US TO THE ER ENTRANCE AT UCSF medical center. A team approached with a gurney. Sawyer helped me out of the car, and held me gently, reverently, as if he were reluctant to let me out of his arms. He set me down on the gurney and I bit back a cry at the pain when my heel touched down. But I couldn't hold the next little moan in as we went over a bump. Sawyer grabbed my hand and I squeezed. He squeezed back.

The ER was bustling with nurses, doctors and people in pain; the air a sterile cold. They wheeled me into a space and closed a curtain around me. A nurse tucked a pillow under my foot, and then laid an ice pack on it. I clenched my teeth as the pain turned icy and bit deep. Under the bright glare of the hospital lights my foot looked awful; swollen and wearing a bouquet of purple, red, and blue bruises. My last two toes throbbed dully; a terrible just-stubbed-my-toe pain that wouldn't fade.

Sawyer pulled up one of the two chairs in the little space, and took my hand, wrapping his warm fingers around my cold ones.

"A doctor will be in shortly to examine you," the nurse said. "It looks like you've broken a toe or two. He'll want x-rays to confirm. In the meanwhile, I can give you something for the pain."

"Advil," I said.

"Are you sure you don't want something stronger?"

"No, just your strongest Advil, please."

She smiled. "My strongest Advil is called Percocet, honey, but you're the boss."

I took the little pills and the glass of water, not looking at Sawyer.

"I try to stay away from anything that alters my mental state," I said in a quiet voice when the nurse had gone.

"You don't have to explain," Sawyer said.

"I feel like I do," I said. I forced my eyes to find his. "I hate how you learned about my past. I'm sorry it came out like that—at the worst time and place for you."

"It's not what's going to hurt my chances with Olivia."

"I would never, ever bring anything bad near her." Tears stung my eyes again. "I promise you that. I never would."

"I know you wouldn't," he said. "I freaked out about your record because of what happened to my mom. And Molly, too. And because I had my own ideas about what justice means. But what I believe has been turned up on its ass, and the only thing that matters right now is you."

I sniffed and wiped my eyes. "It's a good feeling."

"What's that?"

"Being trusted."

Sawyer took my hand and pressed it to his lips just as a young doctor with a bald head and warm smile stepped into the space and examined my foot.

"Looks like a few breaks, judging by the swelling and bruising," he said. "Let's get you to x-ray and see what's what."

They wheeled me to the radiology department where it was determined I had hairline fractures of the fourth and fifth middle phalanges. I breathed a sigh of relief. As far as breaks went, I could do worse than hairlines.

Back in the ER space the doctor was all smiles. "You'll live to dance another day,"

"Are you sure?"

"If you rest well, you should be ready to roll in six weeks."

"Six weeks," I said. "What about work? I have to stand for my job."

The doc wrinkled his lips. "Better if you didn't. We'll get you a walking boot but the more you can stay off it, the faster it'll heal. A nurse will be in soon to wrap you up, and give aftercare instructions."

He went out, but no nurse made an appearance. I was obviously a low priority in an ER filled with more serious injuries and illnesses. I shivered in the cold, sterile air, and sharp pain shot up my foot at the movement, making me wince.

"Will you hand me my sweater?" I asked.

"There's something I've been meaning to tell you," Sawyer said, reaching at his feet. He came up with the old, ratty thing with holes at the cuffs. "This is the ugliest sweater I have ever seen in my life."

I giggled then winced again. "Don't make me laugh. It hurts."

Sawyer tucked the sweater around my shoulders. My eyes closed and wanted to stay closed. The exhaustion of the dance performance and the pain were dragging me down.

Sawyer brushed a lock of hair from my forehead. "You should try to get some sleep, if you can. We might be here awhile."

"What about you? You should go. It's so late and you have studying to do…"

He shook his head, his chin rocking on the back of his hand. "You've been taking care of me for ages," he said. "It's my turn."

I smiled and my eyes started to close against the bright lights glaring down over us. No sooner had I begun to drift, then the nurse came back. She wrapped my foot, put a heavy walking boot on it, and gave me a cane.

"A cane to go with your granny sweater," Sawyer said, pushing me to the front of the hospital in a wheelchair.

"Ha ha. Sawyer the Comedian."

"I'm here all night, folks."

I hoped that was true.

We took a cab home and Sawyer carried me up the two flights of stairs like it was nothing. He set me down in my place, and I gave a cry as I tried to put weight on my foot. "They said I can walk in this," I said, holding on to his shoulder. "Do you think they lied to get me out of there?"

Without hesitation, Sawyer picked me up again, cradling me. He carried me to my bed in a corner alcove between the kitchen and the loveseat under the window, and gently set me down.

"Do you want anything?"

"Maybe some water? And then you can go and study. I don't want to keep you."

He shot me a small grin. "What if I want to be kept?"

"Then stay," I said. "I *do* want to keep you. And I don't want to sleep alone."

"Me neither. I'm tired of it. And I'm just…tired."

"Come here," I said. "Actually, take off your suit and then come here."

"If I take off my suit will you take off that sweater?"

"Will you stop? I love this sweater. I wear it all the time."

"I know," he said, bringing me the glass of water.

"Your mega-mind remembers everything I wear, doesn't it?"

"I remember more than what you wear, Darlene," he said, loosening his tie enough to take off. "I remember many things about you."

"Like what?"

He removed his jacket and tossed it on the loveseat. "I remember you in the grocery store the day we met, and how you smirked at me like I was an idiot for not wanting you to cook dinner for me."

I grinned. "Stubborn man-pride."

Sawyer took off his pants and dress shirt, leaving him in his boxers and undershirt.

"I remember how your hands felt on my shoulders the first time you massaged me. I remember how red the cherry was that you ate at the club that night. I wanted to kiss you so badly; more than I'd ever wanted to kiss anyone. I remember how you tasted the first time I did kiss you, and secretly wondered if you'd ruined me for all other women."

He climbed into bed beside me. Instantly, I curled into him and he wrapped his arms around me. We held each other close, my face nestled in the crook of his neck, and his chin on my head. My heart pounded to be this close to him. In bed with him, even if all we did was this.

"Why are you telling me all this?" I whispered.

"I'm trying to be romantic. How am I doing so far?"

I smiled. "Not bad. But you'll have to continue for me to know for sure."

Sawyer chuckled and pulled back to look at me. His eyes softened as they swept over me, like he was memorizing me over and over again, only because he wanted to. His fingers drew my face as he spoke.

"I remember every time you made me laugh when it felt like it had been ages since I'd even smiled," Sawyer said, and his voice turned gruff over his next words. "And I remember how you held my daughter like you'd been doing it forever, and that was the first time I imagined having something more than what I had."

Tears filled my eyes. "Sawyer…"

"Darlene, I don't know what I'm doing. I don't know what's coming around the corner and I'm fucking scared to death. But the half of my heart that isn't banged up from this fight for Olivia is all yours. It's not much but it's all I got right now."

"I'll take it."

"Are you sure? Because I'm scared I can't give you what you deserve. I'm living partially in the real world, and partially in a future that's a handful of days away. Jackson—and his mother—think otherwise, but dammit, Darlene, it's not fair to subject you to the shit storm that might be coming."

"I can take it, Sawyer," I said. "I want to take it. I'd rather be here for you, if it helps at all."

"It does," he said. "So much."

I snuggled closer to him, ignoring the throbbing of my foot. That pain was a much weaker echo of the one that lived in my heart, for him.

He stroked my hair. "I've never slept with a woman before. Just sleep, I mean."

"Neither have I," I murmured against his neck. "I've never just…been held. It's nice."

I felt him melt around me, the tension seeping out, at least for now. For a few precious hours, we slept deeply, tangled together. I held on to him, and he held on to me, just like he promised.

The following morning, I woke to sunlight streaming in from the window above the loveseat and Sawyer standing, looking out, his eyes full of thoughts.

"Hey," I said softly. "Sleep well?"

He nodded. "It's nearly ten o'clock. I haven't slept this late since the summer before I started Hastings." He turned to me, and I could see the weight of his exam, and the fight for Olivia were back, pushing him down again. "How's the foot?"

"Hurts, but I'll live."

"I wish I didn't have to leave you," he said, coming to sit with me on the bed.

I turned him so I could rub his back, keep the tension from digging deep, but I was too late. "What time is your bus to Sacramento?"

"One o'clock," he said. "I'll get you some groceries or…anything else you need before I go."

I turned him to me and cupped his cheek. "You're good at taking care of people."

His smile wilted a little and I knew he was thinking of Olivia. He patted my arm and rose quickly. "I'll make you some coffee."

Sawyer made the coffee, then left to shower, change and pack. He came back afterward and sat with me, hardly saying anything. I let him have his silence, and just held him, our fingers laced together.

At noon, Jackson arrived to take him to the bus depot. His suit looked slept in, and he kept sunglasses over his eyes, even indoors. He propped one hand against my doorway.

"I am…so hungover." He craned his neck forward, then took his sunglasses off to blink blearily at me. "I was going to ask how your dance show went. Judging by that boot on your foot, I'd say either really badly, or you slayed so hard, you up and hurt yourself."

"The first one," I said, with a smile.

"The second," Sawyer said.

"Thatta girl." Jackson shuffled into my place, and clapped Sawyer on the shoulder.

"You ready?"

"As I'll ever be."

"My man. Let's roll."

I got to my feet and hobbled on my cane. The pain wasn't as bad though the notion of a six-hour shift at the spa the next day made me vaguely nauseated.

"Are you sure you want to come?" Sawyer asked. "Maybe you should rest."

"Shush, I'm coming."

"Shush, she's coming," Jackson said. He jerked a thumb at Sawyer. "This guy, am I right?"

The guys helped me down the stairs and into the car Jackson had waiting. I guessed he was doing really well at his firm. I wanted that for Sawyer; to get his clerkship and the career he dreamed of. But he needed to pass the bar first, and in the car ride to the bus depot, he was silent. Preoccupied. His eyes were full of thoughts he didn't share with Jackson or me.

I held his hand the entire time and he held mine, but he hardly spoke. I hoped Jackson would get him talking with his usual jovial humor, but Jackson was nursing a hangover and when I looked over at him, he was snoozing against the window.

At the bus depot, we roused Jackson, and Sawyer got his bag from the trunk. We stepped outside into the brilliant sun, and I recognized this spot as the place where I got off the bus after my trek from New York.

"Jesus, the sun hates me," Jackson muttered, shielding his eyes even though his sunglasses were back on. He clapped his hands together once, winced at the sound, and then turned to Sawyer. "This is it. The big one. How you feeling, champ?"

Sawyer shook his head. "I don't know. My head's not in the game."

"Get your head off the bench and onto the field," Jackson said. "It's fourth-and-one. Ten seconds left on the buzzer. Hail Mary pass. Slap shot from center line, and other assorted sports metaphors."

Sawyer rolled his eyes. "You watch too much ESPN."

"No such thing."

The two men clasped hands, then pulled each other in for a hug.

"You got this," I heard Jackson say in a low voice. "I know you do."

"Thanks, Jax," Sawyer replied.

He turned to me, his eyes still so heavy. Jackson shot us a small smile, and took a few steps back to give us privacy.

"I gave the Abbotts your number in case Livvie needed anything," Sawyer said. "I didn't think to ask you. I hope that's okay."

"It is," I said. "You're going to do great."

"We'll see."

"I'd tell you to break a leg, but the last time someone said that to me I wound up in the ER."

He smiled thinly and I didn't know what else to say or do to make this easier for him. The pressure was sitting on his shoulders, pressing him down.

What would Max say to make me feel better?

Max. He was like a guardian angel, watching over me. From Seattle.

I smiled to myself.

"You see that pillar over there?" I said, jerking my chin to the white column of cement. "When I first got off the bus from New York, Max was standing right there. I'd just left my home and traveled three thousand miles away from friends and family to a brand new city. But he was there, waiting for me. We didn't know each other, but it didn't matter. Just the fact he was there for me...that made all the difference in the world."

I put my hands on Sawyer's shoulders and kissed him softly on the cheek. "I'm going to be waiting for you right there when you get back. Okay?"

Sawyer nodded, his eyes sweeping over my face. Then he abruptly took my face in his hands and kissed me. Hard. A kiss I felt in every part of me, like a sudden rush of electricity, surging through me and leaving me breathless.

He kept his forehead to mine after he broke apart, his own breath coming hard.

"A tornado, Darlene," he whispered. "I'm swept up."

Then he pulled away, shouldered his bag, and got on the bus.

○○○

Jackson drove me back home, and helped me inside. He gave me a hug and one of his trademark, brilliant smiles.

"You call if you need anything," he said. "I'm at your beck and call."

"Thank you, Jackson."

"Anything for you, Darlene."

He turned to for the door.

"What are his chances?" I asked before he could turn the handle.

Jackson stopped, shrugged. "He's got that freakish memory. That'll get him through the multiple choice—"

"No, I meant what are the chances he's going to keep Olivia?"

He blew air out his cheeks, and ran a hand over his close-cropped hair. "I don't know, Dar. We just have to hope for the best."

I shook my head incredulous. "Jackson, how do you stay so positive? My stomach feels like it's going to turn itself inside out."

"Well, according to Henrietta, the universe is listening."

"What's that mean?"

"You get back what you put in. Negative shit gets you negative shit. Positive energy begets positive energy. Whatever you put out there in the universe…it listens. And then it answers. So when I talk, I try to give it something it wants to hear and hope it answers with something *I* want to hear." He shot me a wink. "Now if you'll excuse me, I'm going to go lay down. I put in too much vodka last night and my body has answered." He rubbed his temple. "Loudly."

I watched him go, and heard voices on the stairs after he shut the door. A knock came, and Elena peeked her head in.

"I saw you come in with the boot and the cane," she said. "Poor dear, is it broken?"

"Just two toes. The little ones. I'll be fine."

She nodded, her hands turning over and over in front of her. "Henrietta tells me the hearing was hard on Sawyer." She leaned in, as if she were afraid the universe was listening too. "They can't take her from him, can they?"

"I don't know," I said. "There's a law. A deadline, of sorts. If he'd had Olivia for a year, with no help, he'd have been able to put his name on her birth certificate."

Elena scoffed. "A year? That's weeks away! What difference does a few weeks make?"

I shrugged helplessly. "That's the law."

Elena shook her head and then reached to pat my cheek. "We will tell the judge. I'll come to the next hearing too. Character witnesses. Whatever he needs."

Acting on pure instinct, I threw my arms around her. She hugged me back in a motherly embrace I was loathe to leave, and I smelled cumin and a light perfume, and over that, the clean baby scent of Olivia. She was still there, in Elena's clothes and in her skin.

When I pulled back, the woman had tears her in eyes.

"I love that little girl. And I love him, the sweet boy."

"I do too," I said. "Both of them."

Elena's face burst into a smile like a sun from behind dark clouds. "See? What did I tell you," she said, moving toward the door. "This is no house. It's a home."

Elena left and the quiet of my place descended, leaving me with a thought that sunk its claws into me and wouldn't let go; if Sawyer lost Olivia, I'd lose them both, and this home would be empty.

chapter twenty-six

Darlene

The next day, Monday, I struggled through my shift at Serenity. My foot throbbed with a second heartbeat and by three o'clock, I was fighting back tears. Whitney, my supervisor, was more concerned that my boot was 'unsightly.'

"If it's too much, maybe you should stay home tomorrow," she said in the break room as I readied to head out.

I took up my cane and limped past her, my chin up. "I've dealt with worse."

The Muni home was blessedly empty. I put my aching foot up on the seat beside me and fantasized about three Advil, my bed, and maybe a Sylvia Plath poem or two.

As I was making the arduous block-and-a-half trek to the Victorian, my phone rang with a number I didn't recognize. I rested on someone else's front stoop and answered.

"Hello?"

"Darlene Montgomery?" an older woman's voice asked.

"Yes…?"

"This is Alice Abbott."

I froze, a bolt of anger-laced fear ripping through me. "Yes? What is it? Is Livvie okay?"

"She's…upset. She didn't sleep well last night. Or at all, really."

"Why not?"

A pause.

"She misses Sawyer. I wondered if we might come over to his place for a bit? So that she can play with her toys there and maybe sleep in her own bed."

I pressed my lips together. The poor woman sounded tired and more than a little sad, though she tried to hide it. I was caught between wanting to comfort her and wanting to chew her out.

"Come over," I said. "I think I can get a key from Elena."

"Thank you, Darlene," Alice said, and I heard Olivia's plaintive cry in the background. "Thank you so much."

Elena gave me Sawyer's spare key, and I waited in his place. I scattered a few of Olivia's blocks out on the floor in case she wanted to play with them.

Twenty minutes later, the door buzzed and I limped over to let them up. I left the door ajar, then started the journey back to the sofa. Footsteps, voices, and Olivia's little cries stopped me. She pushed the door open first and my heart broke at her distraught expression and tear-stained cheeks.

"Where Daddy?" she cried, looking around her home. Her blue eyes, shining with tears, found mine. "Dareen. Where Daddy? Where Daddy?"

"Oh, honey, come here."

She hurried to me, bypassing the blocks on the floor, and I picked her up and held her close. Her little body shuddered with sobs, and I glared daggers at the Abbotts coming in the door behind her.

But my anger burnt out with one glance at their kind faces. They both looked exhausted and worn out; identical defeated expressions of the best intentions gone awry.

"We didn't know what else to do," Alice said, and Gerald put his arm around her.

"She's very…astute for such a young child," Gerald said. "None of the diversions our supervisor told us to try have worked."

"She doesn't want a diversion," I said in a low voice. "She wants her daddy."

I limped to Sawyer's chair at his desk and sat with Olivia against my chest.

"Where Daddy?" she sniffled against my neck. "Wan' Daddy."

"I know you do. He'll be home soon, sweat pea. Soon."

I rubbed her back and rocked her as best I could. The Abbotts sat at the kitchen table, watching me as if I were a lion-tamer or magician. Olivia's crying tapered away to hiccupping sobs, and then she fell asleep.

"Should I put her down in her bed?" Alice whispered, rising from her chair.

"No, I want to hold her," I said. "I don't know how much longer I'll be able to."

Gerald and Alice both stiffened, looking both chagrined and defensive at the same time. Alice sat back down.

"I'm just being honest," I said. "I know you're doing what you think is right, but it's hurting people I love."

"I know," Alice said tiredly. "We're the bad guys, aren't we? But Molly… she was our only daughter. And Olivia is our last tie to her. She's our family."

"She's Sawyer's family too," I said.

"Are you sure about that?" Gerald asked.

I didn't answer. I held and comforted Olivia for long moments in the strange silence between the four of us, until my arm—already sore from massaging all day, began to complain.

"My arm's getting numb," I said. "I'm going to put her down after all."

With effort, I hauled myself out of the chair and carried Olivia to her bed. I set her down and she whimpered and stirred like she was going to wake up. But within moments, her little chest rose and fell, and the splotchy red of her cheeks from crying had faded.

I limped back to the kitchen and sat down at Sawyer's table, with the Abbotts. The air between us was thin and tight, and I, who usually burst out the first words that came to mind, knew that I had to choose them carefully. To help Sawyer if I could.

Don't fuck this up, don't fuck this up, don't fuck this up…

"How did you injure your foot?" Alice asked.

"It wasn't from chasing my next high," I said, and inwardly winced.

Good start, Dar. That should do the trick.

Gerald bristled. "Our attorney suggested we find out precisely who is living in the same house as our only granddaughter."

"You have to understand," Alice said. "We hadn't seen her in two years. Her calls and texts became more sporadic and then stopped altogether. We lived in fear of one of those visits from the highway patrol, or the phone call in the middle of the night."

"And then we got one," Gerald said. "Our baby was gone, but her friend told us she'd had one of her own."

Alice's eyes filled with tears. "I've never been so scared and…lost. Our only child was gone and her baby—a helpless, little baby—was in the hands of a complete stranger." She composed herself and met my gaze steadily. "We had to act. To find her and protect her."

"We thought Sawyer would be happy to see us," Gerald said. "Or at least friendly enough that we could get to know each other. To work together and… maybe build something."

"But he thought you were coming to tear everything down," I said softly. "Aren't you?"

Alice's hands twisted on the table, her brows drawn together. "I hate that I feel this way. That we're trying to do the right thing for Olivia, as we should, and yet it feels wrong too."

Gerald covered her hand with his.

"We were prepared to let the judge read the paternity test results," he said. "In fact, we were fairly certain, even before Sawyer spoke, what the outcome would be."

"But then Sawyer spoke," Alice said, picking up where her husband's thought left off with the ease of two people who have been married for decades. "He spoke and I had hope that he was the sort of man who would let two strangers—family and strangers both—share Olivia's life. But after the hearing, he was cold again. So cold."

"He's not cold," I said. "If he's an asshole it's because he's scared you're going to take Olivia from him. Doesn't he have every right to fear that?"

"Is he her father?" Gerald asked, with a directness that said whatever his occupation had been, he was used to being in charge.

I lifted my chin. "Yes," I said. "He is. By every standard that matters."

They exchanged pained looks. "I just wish we'd seen more of him as he was at the hearing. If we had assurance that he…was loving and kind, that Olivia felt cherished by him…"

"She is," I said softly. "God, she is. I wish you could see them together when he thinks no one is looking. How he smiles at her, or makes her laugh; how he cooks her healthy food and makes sure she eats her peas, while he heats up a frozen dinner for himself because he's working so damn hard to create a beautiful life for her."

I wiped my cheek, and shook my head. "How you saw him at the hearing is who he really is. Underneath the prickly armor, he's full of love and humor and goodness, and he would never let anything hurt that little girl." I inhaled a ragged breath. "He wants to protect her because he knows what it's like to not have a mom."

Gerald sat up straighter, and Alice's hand went to her throat. "He does?"

"He got the same visit from the highway patrol that you did. A drunk driver killed his mother when he and his brother were little. His entire world fell apart. His family fell apart, and I know that he wants Olivia to have more than he did." I leaned my arms over the table toward them. "He wants you in her life, I swear it. He won't shut you out, but… he wants full custody too."

They bristled at this and I ventured to touch Alice's hand. "Isn't that a good thing? He doesn't want to be a part-time dad. But that doesn't mean he wants to do this alone, either."

"Olivia seems quite fond of you," Alice said. "Will you be a part of her life too?"

"I'd like that," I said. "I'm quite fond of her too. And I know what you must be thinking about me. What Holloway dug up on me is true. I was arrested and did time in jail. But what his investigation didn't show you was how hard I've worked to get past that. I've been clean for a really long time, and I'm never going back. Not only for the people I love, but for me too. Especially for me."

The Abbotts were quiet, though it seemed as if they exchanged a thousand thoughts with one look.

"Does that couch fold out?" Gerald asked after a moment, nodding at the sofa.

Hope bloomed in my chest. "Only one way to find out."

The couch did fold out and Gerald went back to the condo to pack a few things for Olivia and Alice to stay through until Wednesday.

"Do you think Sawyer will mind?" Alice asked. "We're invading his space…"

"He won't mind," I said, "because Olivia is home."

Alice met my eye. "I think it's important you know that our being here doesn't mean we're giving up our petition, necessarily."

"I know," I said. "But I'm glad you're here."

Her eyes widened and a small smile lit up her face for a fleeting moment. "Are you? I've been feeling like the evil witch in a story."

Her pain was there, just beneath the surface of her coiffed and elegant exterior and I realized that on top of everything, she was mourning her child.

"I'm sorry about Molly," I said.

Tears filled her eyes at the name; the name that she'd said a million times over her child's life, and was now imbedded in her soul. It had meaning and conjured memories only she could know.

"Where did we go wrong?" she whispered, more to herself than me. "We did everything right. Good schools, opportunities, and we loved her. God, we loved her."

In my mind, I saw Max leaning against a pillar, arms crossed, smiling at me expectantly. I drew in a breath.

"When I was sixteen, I was in the running for a dance scholarship to an academy in New York. My parents weren't one hundred percent on board, but a scholarship meant something to them. They were proud of me, in their own way. And my teachers and friends were sure I'd get it. But I was petrified. I felt like I was so close to catching something I'd wanted even before I had a name for it."

I toyed with the cuff of my ratty gray sweater.

"The night before the audition, I went to a party. Some guy offered me Ecstasy and I took it, even knowing it would keep me up all night and wreck me for the audition in the morning. I took it because that euphoria was right there and I didn't have to do anything but take a pill. I wasn't scared any more. I didn't have to care so hard about...*everything*. The desire I had in me to be, and do, and dance...I filled it up with that drug. Of course, I blew the audition, and once the X wore off, the pain of that failure swooped in. So I did the only thing I could think to do to make it go away." I shrugged my shoulders. "I took more."

I looked up to see Alice watching me with a mother's eyes; full of concern and care, and I wished, just then, she'd had the chance to talk to her own daughter like this.

"I can't speak for Molly, but maybe she was chasing something too. Something in her she couldn't catch and she filled that emptiness the best she could."

"We could have done more," she said. "We should have tried harder to find her."

"Addicts don't always like to be found," I said. "Sometimes it's just as simple and awful as that."

Alice stared at me a moment, then wiped her eyes. "Darlene, I'd like to hug you right now. May I?"

A sudden warmth spread through every part of me. My head bobbed. "Sure, yeah," I whispered.

She pulled me into a warm embrace full of her expensive perfume, but beneath that her arms were soft and I held her tight.

She hugged me for long moments, then pulled away, laughing sheepishly. "Well. I'm suddenly very hungry. Shall we have dinner?"

I grinned. "How do you feel about tuna casserole?"

chapter
twenty-seven

Sawyer

I TYPED THE FINAL SENTENCE ON MY SECOND OF TWO PERFORMANCE TESTS. I WAS instructed to research, analyze, and support a solution to the case as if I were a practicing attorney. Earlier that day, I had written three essays, each requiring a demonstrated knowledge of law and relevant precedents. The day before that I had written three others. Monday, I had answered two hundred Multistate Bar Exam questions over the course of six hours. My brain was fried, but I was done.

I read over the final draft of the PT, my eyes burning. I made a few changes, and then, with aching fingers and my stomach twisting in knots, I hit 'save.'

Done. There's no going back now.

A red light on the specialized testing computer lit up. In another room, the test proctor's computer lit up with the same light, and the guy arrived at my closet-sized test space a few moments later.

"Finished?"

"That's the exact right word," I said.

"Yeah, you look pretty done," he said. He checked my area one last time for any contraband items—especially those of the digital persuasion—but all my stuff was locked away in another room, including my cell phone, wallet, and even my watch.

I shuffled out of the testing center in the Sacramento Hilton, and through the lobby. Other potential attorneys had gathered in the bar for drinks at three in the afternoon. Their laughter was loud; years of study, stress, and long hours were over, for better or worse. 33% of us would pass. The rest would put in more study and stress to come back next year and try again. Or quit. I prayed to whatever god would listen that I was not one of them.

I veered away from the bar, and headed to the elevator bank. An attractive young woman in a black skirt and white blouse got into the elevator with me. Her blonde hair was up in a twist and her perfume filled the small space.

"Bar exam?" she asked.

"Yep."

"Me too."

I was facing forward, but I felt her eyes rake me up and down. She shifted an inch closer to me.

"Why don't sharks eat lawyers?" she asked.

I smiled faintly. "I think I've heard this one before."

"I'm sure you've heard a million of them," she said. "So? Why don't sharks eat lawyers?"

"Professional courtesy," I said.

She laughed. "Indeed. Your turn."

I scrolled through my mental database. "How do you save a drowning lawyer?"

"How?"

"Take your foot off his head."

The woman laughed again, and the elevator *dinged* her floor. She stood with her back against the door to hold it open, affording me a full view of her slender body and her breasts pushing against the silk of her blouse.

"So listen, that exam was a monster," she said. "Want to have a drink with me? To celebrate? I may have already started a little bit at the bar," she said with a small laugh, "but you can catch up."

God, here it was; one of my oldest fantasies since I decided to become a lawyer come to life. A previous version of myself, the kind that had parties and never went on dates—only hookups—would've taken this woman up on her offer without a second thought. Hell, I would have *made* the offer.

And now…

I smiled thinly. "No, thanks. I'm with…someone."

"Someone?" the woman said. "Girlfriend?"

I tried the thought on for size.

Darlene's my girlfriend.

It didn't fit. One failed date and a few kisses did not a girlfriend make. We hadn't even slept together, yet I felt closer to her than I'd ever had to a woman; my feelings for her ran so deep they scared me. But she wasn't my girlfriend. The word was both too strong and not enough at the same time.

"Darlene is someone special," I said.

"Oh God, say no more," the woman said. "I was hoping I'd caught you early, but the way your entire face changed when you said her name…" She shook her head with a rueful sigh. "I'm too late."

She shouldered her purse and let the doors close, giving me a little knowing smirk and a small wiggle of her fingers goodbye.

The shiny silver doors shut, leaving me to stare at my own reflection. A blurred face of exhaustion, and a smile that I hadn't realized I'd been wearing.

I'd planned to take the bus back in the morning in the event the test ran late, but as I got back to my hotel room, I was torn. My exhausted brain cried out for sleep, while my heart demanded I jump on the next bus back to Olivia and Darlene.

I picked up my phone and punched in Darlene's number.

"Hi," she said softly when she picked up. "Done?"

"Yeah, I'm done," I said. I hadn't called her or Jackson while in Sacramento in an effort to stay focused. In two syllables, how much I missed her came roaring back.

"How do you think it went?" she asked.

"I did my best," I said, and a ragged breath gusted out of me. I lay back against the pillows on the bed as one part of the tremendous pressure I'd been carrying, lifted off. "Yeah," I said, wiping my eyes in the crook of my elbow. "I did my best for Olivia. And for you. For us. Whatever we are after the hearing on Friday."

"Oh, Sawyer," she said, her own voice tremulous. "I'm proud of you. And I know someone else who is proud of you too. Want to say hello to Olivia?"

I sat up. "She's there? Where are you?"

"I'm at your place. I've been staying here the past couple of days with Olivia. And the Abbotts."

"You have?" I shook my head. "What...why? What's happening?"

"Olivia missed you too much. Being here in her home has helped. And being with me has helped too," she added in a small voice. "It's kind of amazing, but this little human likes being with me. I feel...honored, if that makes any sense."

I had to clench my jaw for a moment. "It makes perfect sense," I said, gruffly. I swallowed hard, and took a breath. "But...the Abbotts? They're there?"

"They've been camping out on your sofa, and that lady, Jill, from CPS, pops in and out to make sure everything's kosher. I hope that's okay."

"I...don't know what to think," I said. "But it feels like that's a good thing. Is it?" A sudden, genuine laugh of happiness burst out of me. "Holy shit, Darlene, what have you done?"

She laughed too with happy tears. "I don't know, Sawyer, but I'm just trying to be as positive about this whole situation as I can. Because the universe is listening."

"And it will answer," I murmured. "Jackson told me that once. Or maybe it was Henrietta."

"Yep. He told me the same the other day, and I think he's right." Darlene's sigh gusted over the line and when she spoke again, her voice was cheerful and strong. "Olivia wants to say hi to you now."

"Okay," I whispered, and heard Darlene calling Olivia to her.

"You want to say hi to Daddy?"

A muffled sound came and then I heard little breaths. I could see it so clearly; Darlene holding the phone to Olivia and my little girl not having any idea what to do.

"Hi, honey," I said, my voice thick. "It's Daddy."

"Daddy?" Olivia said, and my goddamn heart cracked in two. "Where Daddy?"

"I'm right here, honey, and I'll be home soon."

Olivia babbled a little. She sounded good. Happy and safe.

"Say, 'love you, Daddy,'" I heard Darlene say. "Say, 'see you soon.'"

"Wuv, Daddy," Olivia said, and then there was more breathing and babbling. Darlene came back on.

"We haven't yet grasped the concept of the phone but she heard you," Darlene said. "She's back to playing blocks. And Alice and Gerald want me to tell you that they hope your test went well. They—"

"Darlene?"

"Yes?"

The words bubbled up from my heart, scraping and bumbling their way up my throat where they got stuck.

"I…I…Jesus, I can't speak."

"I hate the phone, don't you?" Darlene said, quickly. "It's so lame. Even babies don't like it." She heaved a tremulous breath. "Come home, Sawyer. Tomorrow? Your bus arrives at eight?"

I nodded. "Yeah," I managed. "Yes. Eight."

"Okay, get some sleep. You need it. And I'll see you then, Sawyer the Lawyer."

"See you then, Darlene." *My tornado.*

I hung up with her, and sat with the phone in my lap. She'd swept me up, then Olivia and Jackson, and now the Abbotts too.

And now, thanks to her, I might have a chance.

I ordered some dinner through room service, then crashed at nine o'clock. I slept almost as deeply as I had when wrapped in Darlene's arms, in her bed.

Almost.

The hour and a half bus ride took me from the dark of dawn to a rising sun. I got off at the depot and, just as promised, Darlene was there, at the white pillar. Standing beside her were the Abbotts, looking as nervous and hopeful as I probably did. Olivia was in Darlene's arms, and she squirmed to get down as soon as she saw me.

I set down my bag, willing myself not to cry like a baby in front of God and everyone at the bus depot as Olivia toddled her little legs as fast as she could straight for me. I scooped her up and held her tight, my face pressed against her hair.

"Hi, honey," I whispered. "I'm back."

"Daddy back!" Olivia said, and jounced up and down in my arms. She pulled away and her blue eyes—sharp and clear—studied my face. She put her little hand on my chin, and I struggled mightily to hold it together.

"Wuv, Daddy," she said, almost solemnly, and I could feel that my absence perplexed her.

"I love you too, Livvie." I hugged her again, as Darlene hobbled over with her cane. She was wearing that ugly old sweater that I loved so much. Because I loved her.

Oh Christ, I do...

Her smile was brilliant as she joined Olivia and me. "The conquering hero returns," she said. "We missed you, didn't we, Livvie?" She gave my daughter's hand a little tug, then raised her eyes to mine. "I missed you. A lot. And Sawyer—"

"I love you," I said. Still holding Olivia in one arm, I reached over and cupped Darlene's cheek, and kissed her softly. "I love you, Darlene. No matter what happens, I know that's true."

She stared at me in shock, then her entire being seemed to grow brighter, blinding in her beauty. "I love you, too," she whispered, kissing me again. "I do. No matter what happens, I love you." She turned her face to Olivia. "And you too, sweet pea. I love you, Livvie."

I held them both tightly, and this time I couldn't keep a damn tear from escaping. But through my blurred vision, I saw the Abbotts, standing in front of that cement pillar, hands clasped together. And they were smiling.

≈

"All rise."

The courtroom got to its feet, as Judge Chen entered from his chambers to take a seat at his desk.

My heart thundered in my chest, and Jackson gripped my arm under the table, reassuring. I glanced behind me at Darlene. Her smile was shaky but she gave me two thumbs up, and that little gesture sent a small flash of warmth through me. Then the judge cleared his throat and I was stiffened by fear all over again.

"This hearing, in the matter of custody and establishment of paternity for Olivia Abbott, a minor child, the Clerk of the Court will now read the DNA results as subscribed in our last hearing that was since delayed."

He nodded his head at the clerk, and she started to rise.

Mr. Holloway, sitting beside his clients on the other side of the courtroom got to his feet first.

"Your Honor, before we begin the Abbotts have requested I read a statement to the Court."

Judge Chen frowned and peered over his glasses. "I hope this isn't yet another delay in proceedings, Mr. Holloway?"

"No, Your Honor."

I nudged Jackson. He shrugged back.

"Very well," the judge said. "Proceed."

Holloway cleared his throat. "It is the wish of my clients, Gerald and Alice Abbott, that they hereby rescind their petition for custody of Olivia Abbott. With this statement, they do intend to terminate their Order to Show Cause, and request that the paternity test results remain sealed in perpetuity and/or destroyed. Furthermore, they, as the parents of the deceased Molly Abbott, wish to sign on her behalf a Voluntary Declaration of Paternity, naming Sawyer Haas the natural father of Olivia Abbott and inscribing his name on her birth certificate as required by law."

The words rolled over me like an avalanche. I'd hardly grasped one revelation of what the Abbotts had done before Holloway read another. Dazed, I glanced up at Jackson who looked like he was trying his best not to jump out of his chair. I turned to Darlene, sitting beside Henrietta. She had her fingers pressed to her mouth, tears streaming. Lastly, my robotic movements brought my gaze to the Abbotts. Alice's kind face was tear streaked and Gerald's lips were pressed tight. Their hands were clasped on the table, tightly.

I opened my mouth to speak, not quite sure what would come out, but Holloway wasn't finished.

"It is the Abbotts' further wish to pay child support in the amount of five thousand dollars per month until such time as Mr. Haas's bar exam results are known and his employment secured. This support comes with no conditions or caveats." Holloway flashed a pleased smile my way. "That is all."

The judge's eyebrows came together. "Are your clients aware, Mr. Holloway, that rescinding all claims to custody—permanent or partial—means that any visitation or contact with Olivia Abbott will be left to the sole discretion of Mr. Haas?"

"They are aware, Your Honor. But they have hope that Mr. Haas will honor the faith the Abbotts have in him as Olivia's father, and do what is best for all parties."

I nudged Jackson but he needed no prompting. He shot to his feet.

"He will, Your Honor," Jackson said, and I was shocked to hear my friend's voice crack a little. "In the eyes of the law, a judge's ruling carries more weight than one's word, but in this situation, I know that this man's honor and duty to his daughter run deeper than any order…or blood test." He turned to the Abbotts. "And on a personal note, thank you. Thank you very much, on his behalf and mine."

"And mine too," Darlene said in a small voice from her seat in the gallery.

"Amen," Henrietta intoned, as if we were at church.

The judge sighed, though the hint of a smile pulled at the corners of his mouth. "Well, this is the most unorthodox custody hearing I've ever presided over, but if the Abbotts are withdrawing their petition, I have no reason to deny their request. The paternity test results will be destroyed and Mr. Haas, you are free to file a Voluntary Declaration of Paternity. That is all."

He banged his gavel, and it was like a door slamming shut on one terrible future and opening on another. I stood on shaking legs as the Abbotts approached.

"I...don't know what to say," I said. "Thank you doesn't seem strong enough."

Alice tentatively reached out and touched my cheek. "Olivia loves you, and more than anything, that's what we want. What we've always wanted. For her to be happy. She wouldn't be, without you."

I nodded, my teeth clenched. "I love her," I said. "So much. I promise I'll do right by her for the rest of my life."

"We've finalized the purchase of the condo in the Marina," Gerald said gruffly. "It has a spare room that we will keep for her. For when she visits Grandma and Grandpa?"

It was like a question and I wanted to erase all doubt in their minds. "Just make sure it has blocks. You know how she is about her blocks."

Gerald held my gaze a moment, then burst out laughing. He shook my hand and then pulled me in for a hug. Alice joined, and I felt like some huge, empty space in my life I didn't know was there, was filling up with everything I'd ever wanted.

My eyes found Darlene over Alice's shoulder, and she gave me two thumbs up, tears streaming.

She's everything I've ever wanted.

I made a motion with my hand to wave her over. She started to hobble, but Jackson was quicker. He scooped her up and carried her to our little group. Our family, and the last piece fell into place.

chapter
twenty-eight

Darlene

We picked Olivia up from Elena's, and then she and her children, Jackson and Henrietta, the Abbotts, Sawyer and I went to brunch at Nopa. We gathered in the front, Olivia squealing with laughter as she was passed around from hand to hand, to keep her occupied while we waited for our giant group to be seated.

"I hope we get the same waiter as our first non-date," I told Sawyer. "He'd go crazy trying to figure out how we went from that to the Partridge Family."

Sawyer smiled but his eyes were dark as they gazed down at me. He bent to kiss my cheek and whispered in my ear. "I need to be alone with you. Badly."

A flush of heat swept through me, and I tightened my hold on his arm. "Me too," I whispered back. "Do you think they'd notice if we ducked out?"

"Not me," Sawyer said, "but you, mostly definitely."

"That's sweet but—"

Sawyer silenced me with a kiss that I felt down in the deepest part of me. I kissed him back as much as was appropriate in a restaurant, and then swatted his arm. "You can't kiss me like that in public," I teased. "I have to stay away from mind-altering substances, remember?"

He chuckled but over the course of the meal—as we sat beside each other at one long table—our eyes kept finding one another, and our hands were clasped under the table. Mostly to keep the other from exploring, as I longed to touch him and be touched.

I looked around at the table full of faces we loved and thought of what was to come after, and it was almost too much.

Oh my God, this is happening. All of this…

Jackson noticed me surreptitiously dabbing my eyes with a napkin, and leaned in. "The universe listened," he said, "and then it answered."

"Big time," I said with a laugh. "Huge."

"It listened to you, Dar," he said. "What you did? With the Abbotts? You saved him."

I shook my head. "Noooo…They were right there. They just needed a little push."

"And you gave it to them," he said. He inclined his head at Sawyer who was talking animatedly with Gerald about Gerald's former profession as a broker for a large accounting firm. "We might be in a world of hurt had it not been for you."

"That's giving me too much credit," I said. "But this, right now? This is a good feeling. The best."

And I want it to last forever.

We ate and talked, and then said goodbye to everyone. Sawyer made plans with the Abbotts for them to come over tomorrow, Saturday, and play with Olivia at the park.

"It's our Saturday ritual," Sawyer said.

"We'll be there," Alice said, her smile beautiful. She pulled me in for a hug. "And will you be there, my dear?"

"Wouldn't miss it."

We said our goodbyes and headed back to the Victorian with Elena, her kids, and the Smiths. Everyone stayed and chatted and played with Olivia. Sawyer's hungry expression when his eyes met mine never left, and he pulled me into the short hallway between the living area and bedrooms.

His kiss sent currents of electricity shooting through me, and I had to cling to his shirt to keep upright. My need to be with him was a physical ache in my body, but I caught my breath and pushed gently back.

"If Henrietta catches us now, we'll be in big trouble," I said.

"The second everyone leaves..." Sawyer said, pulling me close again. "You're mine."

"I want that," I said. "So badly, but...I have to go out for awhile."

Sawyer frowned. "Go? Where?"

I dropped my gaze to his shirt, smoothed out a wrinkle I'd made, clutching him during our kiss. "I have an NA meeting. I have one every Monday, Wednesday and Friday."

It still felt a little bit strange to say it out loud, but then I mustered my courage and raised my eyes to meet his head-on. My breath caught to see Sawyer looking down at with me with such a potent mix of love and pride, it brought tears to my eyes.

Acceptance, I thought, *is a kind of love too.*

"Dammit, Sawyer, I've cried all my makeup away today because of you."

He smiled and cupped my cheek in his hand. "Go to your meeting," he said, his lips brushing mine. "I'll be here for you when you get back."

I pressed myself into his touch. "You might not believe this, but that's the sexiest thing I've ever heard in my life."

He chuckled and kissed me again. "I think I can do better...tonight."

※

At my meeting, I told the group everything. I watched, with joy in my heart, as the faces of the attendees—who looked tired in a way that had nothing to do with sleep and everything to do with internal battles that never ended—filled with hope.

Afterward, Angela, the program director, approached as I was making plans to have coffee with some of the group members sometime next week.

"Wonderful share tonight, Darlene," she said.

"Thanks," I said. "It felt good. But I'm Max-less. Any word on a new sponsor for me?"

"I've been talking with Max by phone, as a matter of fact," she said. "And we feel that, given your two years' sobriety, and your amazing progress, that you would be an ideal candidate to sponsor someone yourself."

I scrunched up my eyes. "Come again? You want *me* to sponsor someone?"

"You'd still be required to attend the meetings, but you'd be doing it in a more supportive capacity to one of our own." She smiled a gentle smile. "Do you think you'd be up for that?"

I tried to envision it. Me, as a sponsor, helping someone else. The call-ee, not the call-er.

"Yes," I said. "I'd love to help. Any way I can."

The warm fuzzy feeling in my stomach was burnt away on the way back to the Victorian, as I thought about Sawyer, waiting for me.

I snuck past his place, and went up to mine to take a shower. It took me forever, since I had to move so slowly with my broken foot. The swelling had gone down and the bruising had faded from purple to ugly green, but it still didn't look pretty.

"Suck it up, foot," I murmured as I dressed in a thong, sleep shorts, and t-shirt; no bra. "If all goes as planned, it's going to be a rough night for you," I said and laughed nervously.

I'd never been nervous before. I'd never waited this long to consummate an attraction.

"I'm in love with him," I told my reflection. "This is sort of a big deal."

It was also sort of crazy to talk to an empty studio, but I was so nervous, words popped into my brain and out of my mouth before I could stop them.

I put the boot back on my foot.

"Oh yeah, that's sexy," I muttered. Then heaved a breath and headed down.

I knocked on the door softly, but I heard Olivia's little voice crowing excitedly on the other side. Sawyer answered the door with a smirk on his face, looking sexy as hell in his pajama pants and V-neck undershirt.

"Parenthood," he said. "Destroyer of evening plans." His eyes softened as he looked down at me. "God, you're beautiful."

His hands slipped around my head, to bury themselves in my hair as he kissed me deeply, with intention. I melted into his kiss, until Olivia surrounded by blocks on the floor, saw me.

"Dareen!"

I smiled against Sawyer's lips. "To be continued."

We stacked blocks with her, Sawyer and I lying on our sides with Olivia in the middle. I watched him smile and laugh with her easily, none of the terrible tension weighing him down. She was his and the joy of it was practically radiating out of his skin.

When Olivia started to fuss, Sawyer took her into her room to read her a story and put her to bed. My nervousness had long vanished, leaving me with a pleasant, heady anticipation of what was to come.

Sawyer emerged from Olivia's room and smiled at me from across the living area where I was sitting on the sofa with my foot propped, flipping through an issue of *The Harvard Law Review* I'd found on his desk.

"She's asleep," he said. "Finally."

I shook the magazine at him. "Have you been rethinking actual causation in tort law? Because according to this article, you really need to."

He grinned and sat with me on the couch. "I'll keep that in mind. How was your meeting?"

"Fine," I said. "Really fine, actually. They want to make me a sponsor for someone, but I'm not sure..."

"I'm sure," he said. "You should. You'd be amazing at it."

"You think?"

"You saved my life, Darlene," he said. "In more ways than one."

He leaned in and kissed me then. A sweet, deep kiss that asked for nothing in return. But it woke that hunger in me for him, and I kissed him back, with tingles of anticipation shooting down my spine.

"Sawyer," I breathed.

He nodded and I saw that same need darkening his eyes. I kissed him again, hard, opening my mouth for him, my tongue sliding against his. We fell into each other on the couch, hands roaming, getting acquainted, until I moaned when his hand found my breast over my shirt.

"We should move this to the bedroom," Sawyer said, breathing hard. "If she wakes up right now, I'm going to fucking die."

Sawyer stood up and gently pulled me to my feet, then lifted me under my arms and knees. He maneuvered carefully down the hallway so as not to crash my boot into the wall.

"That's some sexy footwear right there," I said.

"I love your sexy boot," he said. He set me down in front of his bed. "I love you, Darlene. All of you."

"I love you too, Sawyer," I said, kissing him between words. "And it feels so...real. So unlike anything I've ever felt before. And it's making me crazy to have you right now."

He nodded. "Me too." He kissed me hard, his hands in my hair again, angling my mouth to take him deeper. "I want you so fucking bad," he whispered. "But your foot… I don't want to hurt you."

"You won't or…God, I don't even care. Touch me, Sawyer. Please…"

He didn't need more than that. He kissed me again, his tongue sweeping into my mouth, his hands in my hair, gripping. I tasted him, felt the soft, warm wetness of his tongue, the sharp bite of his teeth, the sucking of his lips. And then the sweetness of his breath, like resuscitation, breathed into me and I came alive. More alive than I'd ever felt before. My arms came around his neck and I kissed him back, touched him and pulled him to me.

"Sawyer." My hands clasped his face, then I snaked my fingers through his hair at the back of his head. "Is this happening?"

He nodded, breathing heavily, then kissed me again, kissed me like it hurt him to stop. "I need you," he whispered against my lips, then plunged in again, talking and kissing between words. "Wanted you… for so long…"

"You have?"

He pulled back then to look at me, his dark eyes searching and full of want and gentle reverence. "Haven't you?"

I nodded, pressed my cheek into his hand that touched my face. "No man's ever looked at me the way you are right now."

His brows came together for a moment and then he said fiercely, "Good."

"Good?"

"Yeah, good. I'm the first to see you, Darlene," he said, the intensity of his words, his look, making my heart pound. "I'm the first to have you like this. All of you. As you are, and you are…so fucking beautiful."

His eyes glistened in the dimness and mine blurred and stung with tears.

"Sawyer…"

"I'm glad it was me, Darlene," he said, his voice gruff. "Me. And no one else."

I nodded, blinked hard. "No one else," I whispered back. "I don't want anyone else but you, Sawyer. Only you…"

His jaw clenched for a moment and he held my face in his hands, then kissed me with hard sweeps of his tongue. "You're mine. Let me have you…"

God, the possessiveness in his voice and the hunger in his eyes. I'd never felt so wanted, in every way, in my life.

"Yes," I whispered. "Sawyer…."

His mouth on mine was everything, an ecstasy of taste and sensation. But then his hands slipped from my face, needing my body. He stripped off my shirt, and my hair fell down around my shoulders, above my naked breasts.

"Beautiful," he said, trailing kisses down my neck as he took one small breast in each hand. "So beautiful."

I fit perfectly in his palms, and my eyes fell shut when his mouth went to one nipple, sucking and teasing. His hair on my bare skin sent shivers up my shoulders, and I raked my hand through his blond curls. His mouth worked over the other nipple. Electric currents fanned across my chest and down my back, over my spine.

I lifted his shirt off the moment he came up for air, and gaped at his body.

"Jesus, Sawyer," I said, trailing my fingers across the smooth planes of his pecs, down to the hard lines of his abdomen. "Hastings has a gym, I see."

I didn't wait for an answer, but took my turn putting my mouth on one small nipple, biting and nipping, and reveling in the masculine sounds I elicited from him, while my hands slid up and down the hard muscles in his back.

My mouth trailed its way up his chest, his throat, to kiss him again.

"I'm obsessed with your mouth," I told him, taking his lower lip in my teeth and grazing it softly.

"Darlene," he said, his voice rough with need. "Turn around. Want to kiss you everywhere."

I heard the restraint in his voice. If I weren't hurt, he would have manhandled me into any position, and I would have let him; would have let his hands mold me however he wanted, because what he wanted was all of me.

I turned around, and he sat down on the edge of the bed and pulled me on to his lap, my back to his chest. I gasped at his first touch at the nape of my neck. His mouth was soft and wet, his breath hot, and I couldn't contain the little moans that escaped me as he kissed and caressed me until I was writhing.

"Sawyer…" My head fell back. "What are you doing to me?"

"Exploring."

"God…"

This wasn't just sex or lust. It was him touching and tasting me, becoming acquainted with my body. Sawyer knew me—my heart that beat for him and my soul that understood him—and now he wanted to know my body. In the past, it had always been the sex I'd given first, never thinking a man would want me for much more, not right away, if ever. Sawyer took it last, and his every touch and kiss and desperate groan to have me was the completion of us, not the beginning.

"God, right here," he whispered, his mouth trailing wetly between my shoulder blades while his hands came around my breasts, squeezing and pinching until I was half out of my mind. "I've had fantasies about kissing you here."

"You have?" I breathed. My ass ground against his thighs, my body pressing itself into every place he touched me; a contortion of my dancer's sinews and ligaments to be everywhere at once—on his lap, in his hands, against his mouth.

"Fuck, yes," he groaned, and everything tightened; his hands squeezed, and his teeth grazed my flesh. "I have to have you. Now. Are you ready for me?"

I nodded mutely, and bit back a cry as his hand slipped down, below my navel, and then under the hem of my thong. His fingers found me, rubbing a slow circle. I gasped and arched into his hand, and he went inside, two fingers delving into me.

"God, Darlene," he hissed, scraping his teeth along my back. My hips bucked into his hand again and again. "So wet. I want you to come…"

He withdrew his hand and I gave a little cry at the loss. He stood me up and stripped my panties off, careful around my injured foot. He gently laid me on the bed, and then wasn't careful at all as he put his mouth between my thighs. Ravenous.

"Ah, God," I cried, one hand snaking into his hair, the other up and onto the headboard, holding on as his tongue swirled and then plunged, his groans adding vibrations of sensation. My hips undulated; I made a fist in his soft curls and pressed him harder as my legs fell apart, wide and open.

"Yes, yes, *yes*…"

The word came out of me in hissing whispers, then moans, then screams I had to bite back, as Sawyer drew from deep inside me, a heavy ache of ecstasy so strong I became lost in my own body. I felt only that searing, beautiful agony and Sawyer's mouth, his tongue and lips, and his hand on my thigh, squeezing and pressing me open to him, not stopping until my cries filled the room and then tapered to whimpers as the orgasm swept through me.

I sank back against the headboard, after the currents of that first orgasm streaked through me. My legs were boneless. My arms dropped to my sides, my head lolled.

Sawyer wiped his chin with the back of his hand and went crawling back up my body.

"Not done with you yet," he growled in my ear, and then I gasped and sat up straight as his mouth on my neck sent reviving currents through me. The desire for him—to have all of him, naked and inside me—surged through every part of my body.

I reached to pull the drawstring on his pants as my mouth found his. I kissed him hard, with gnashing teeth and a tongue that explored every inch of his luscious mouth that had just unraveled me. My hand slipped inside his pants to find him huge and hard.

"Oh my God," I hissed against his mouth, stroking him. "This. You…I need you."

He nodded, and bent to reach for the nightstand drawer.

I scooted back against the headboard to watch Sawyer strip out of his pants, then his boxer briefs. Another flush of heat swept between my legs at the magnificent sight of his nakedness; defined arms, pecs, abs, under smooth, tanned skin, and then the V that led down to his pure masculine beauty. My hand went to my own wet desire, needing the touch until he finished rolling on a condom.

"Yes," I whispered, as Sawyer knelt over me, kissed me, then lifted me so he could kneel under me, sitting on his heels. I rested on his thighs for a moment, my back against the headboard and Sawyer in front of me, his beautiful dark eyes full of hard want and reverence; gentle care and heated need all at once.

"I don't want to hurt you," he said again with a soft voice, even as his hands gripped my hips painfully. "But Darlene…"

"You won't," I said. "I don't care if you do. I need you…God, Sawyer, please. Please…" I craned my mouth to him and his lips met mine just as he lifted me over him and slipped inside me as I sank down.

"Oh God," I hissed, as the huge, heavy pressure of him filled me, stretched me.

"Jesus," he groaned, his forehead on mine. "You feel…fuck, you feel so good…So…"

"Perfect," I whispered, tears stinging my eyes and then burning away. "This is perfect."

Sawyer lifted his head to look at me in the dimness, and I saw everything I'd ever wanted to see in a man staring back at me.

The moment of stillness caught and held, and then the need in our bodies became ravenous and couldn't wait one second more. His hands on my hips gripped harder, lifting me and then bringing me down on him. I wrapped my arms and legs around him, kissing him at first as the heaviness of him pushed into me, touching deep, and I undulated my hips to bring him deeper, to take his every thrust harder.

Kissing became impossible, and Sawyer reached above me to grip the headboard with both hands, caging me in his arms. I reached up too, held on and lifted into his thrusts, to meet his every movement. My soft breasts brushed against the hard muscles of his chest, while the intense pressure of him inside me grew and tightened, coiled into something ready to explode. I couldn't get enough of him. His warm scent, the taste of his kiss when our mouths clashed frantically, the feel of his powerful body pinning mine against the headboard.

"More," I whispered. "Sawyer… I want more." I could barely speak, barely comprehended the words that fell from my mouth. "Take me…"

Though it didn't seem possible, Sawyer's hips moved faster and harder at my words. He reached one hand down to hook my leg onto the crook of his elbow, to cradle my injured foot, while taking him somehow deeper into me with every thrust.

I could barely hold on as the tight coil he'd been brushing and coaxing and touching inside me came apart like an explosion. My entire body stiffened; I arched into him, opened my body to him, a scream wrenched out of me as the orgasm rocketed up from where we were joined.

"Yes," he groaned, his thrusts slower now, hard and deep. "Come for me, Darlene. Just like that…Christ, you're so beautiful."

And in my ecstatic delirium, I realized I was going to be his first orgasm in almost a year.

He waited until me.

I held his face in my hands reverently, kissed his broad mouth deeply. "Now you," I whispered against his lips. "Come for *me*, Sawyer. Come inside me."

I felt his own body tense, every one of his taut muscles drawing tighter. His hipbones ground against mine, he was so deep in me. I pressed myself into his last thrusts, nails digging into his ass to hold him tight. He let go of my leg to brace himself on the bed, his other hand gripping my hip to push into me. His mouth found my neck, and he bit down, danced the line between pleasure and pain, and came against me, inside me, the masculine sounds of his release breathing hotly against my throat.

I wrapped my arms around him as he shuddered, wound my fingers in his hair, and held him as the tension in him ebbed and our chests met and retreated, over and over, like a tide, as we caught our breaths together.

"Holy hell," Sawyer groaned into my neck.

"I know," I said. My fingers curled in his hair. The aftershocks of the orgasm made me shudder against him. "Oh my God, feel that?"

He nodded against my shoulder. "Everywhere. I feel you everywhere."

I held him tighter, his beautiful body that was warm, soft skin, over hard muscle and power he had unleashed against me so magnificently.

After a time, Sawyer lifted his head to look at me blearily, drunk with the pleasure and utterly spent. I was sure I looked the same—my hair a tangled mess with strands falling over my face and billowing with my breath. Sawyer's eyes sharpened as his hand came up to brush them away.

"Darlene…"

He fought for more words but found none.

"Just kiss me," I said, and he did.

And in that kiss, I felt his emotions he still hadn't found the words for, but knew that he would. We had time now, and the freedom to be happy. His heart that he had kept locked away for so long was mine. He gave it to me in every soft look, and touch, and in the trust he placed in me to care for his little girl.

And in return, I gave him my entire self; I didn't know how to give less. I loved him with all of me, even the tarnished parts that would always bear the bruises of my past.

"I love you, Sawyer." I stroked his cheek. "Always. I won't ever stop loving you."

"I love you," he whispered. "I love you, Darlene. God, I love you. I don't want to stop saying it. I can't say it enough."

His eyes were dark and beautiful in the dimness, and I loved how I look reflected there. And it was real, his love; not something my lonely heart had manufactured to hold on to, and I knew I'd feel this way, like I did in that moment, forever.

chapter twenty-nine

Sawyer

Again and again, I had her.

We spent the night making love, ravenous like wild animals, and everything in between. We stopped to catch our breath; I brought us water, we talked a little and laughed a lot, but inevitably, the gentle touches of Darlene's hand in my hair, or mine gliding down the softness of her skin would make us greedy. Like a flare sparking to life, we'd fall back in a sweaty tangle of arms and legs, grasping at skin, her nails raking down my back, my mouth kissing her everywhere. I couldn't get enough of touching her body or listening to her come undone beneath me, over and over again. It was a celebration of our victories that lasted long into the night, and finally ceased when dawn's first light filtered in through the window.

And, miracle of miracles, Olivia slept through the whole thing.

As we lay in the drowsy silence of the morning, my body heavy and spent, I heard Olivia make a little sound in her sleep, through the baby monitor, but she didn't wake.

"She usually wakes up at least once per night," I said. "This is a first. Not to mention," I added with a grin, "you were loud as hell. We probably woke up *Elena's* kids."

Darlene swatted my arm. She lay curled against me, her leg slung over my hip and her booted foot resting on my thigh.

"That's all your fault, not mine." She nestled closer to me. "You told me you thought Olivia woke up because she was afraid she was alone," she said after a moment. Her fingers trailed over my chest. "Maybe she senses the tension has been lifted and she gets to stay where she belongs. And with whom she belongs."

"Maybe so," I said. "But there's still a little tension. One last hurdle."

"Your meeting with Judge Miller?"

I nodded. "Monday. I have not written a word of that essay he wants."

Darlene propped her chin on my chest. "Are you worried?"

"I should be, but I don't know. So much has happened, I feel like what I need to say to him will come to me."

"It will," Darlene said. "I know it will."

"Well, it had better get here quick. It only has two days."

The baby monitor lit up with Olivia stirring.

"She's so cute when she wakes up," Darlene said.

"I'll get her."

Darlene pushed me back. "Let me."

She drew on her underwear and found one of my dress shirts on the floor. It came down to her thighs, and made her legs look like they went on forever. Her hair was tousled—my hands had been buried in it all night—and her lips were swollen from my kisses.

"God, you're sexy," I murmured as she buttoned up the shirt, leaving the top three undone.

She grinned. "You're only saying that because we just had sex for six hours straight."

"I don't think it's subjective," I said. "But I'm willing to put in more time. Just to be sure."

She laughed as she limped to Olivia's room. I slipped on my boxers, then sat against the headboard, listening over the monitor as my daughter crowed 'Dareen!' and Darlene answered with sweet words and silly noises to make her laugh.

They came back into the bedroom, Olivia on Darlene's hip. My little girl blinked sleep out of her eyes; a lock of Darlene's hair was curled around her fingers.

"Look who's awake," Darlene said, bouncing her lightly. "Say, 'good morning, Daddy.'"

"Daddy," Olivia said, and something caught her eye. "Birr. Birr…" She reached her hand and Darlene moved to the window.

"What do you see? Is that a bird?"

"Birr."

The light streamed in, slanted over Darlene holding my baby, and I drank in every detail. The blue of her shirt against Olivia's pale yellow jammies; the sunlight turning strands of Darlene's brown hair gold with hints of red; Olivia's blue eyes as she pointed and babbled at only something she and Darlene could see.

I saw only them; filled my eyes with them and my photographic memory captured every nuance of that moment, and saved it forever.

Monday morning, I arrived at Judge Miller's office promptly at eight a.m. Roger was already there, naturally. He gave me a short glance.

"How did your brief turn out?" he asked.

"It didn't," I said.

His eyes widened slightly, and a small smile tugged the corners of his lips. "What does that mean, exactly?"

It means I'm taking a colossal chance, and possibly throwing away my dream job.

I shrugged. "We'll see."

Roger pressed a smile between his lips and his fingers smoothed the cover of a sleek portfolio that no doubt held his perfectly collated and annotated brief inside.

My hands were empty.

Judge Miller arrived. "Gentlemen."

We followed him into his office and waited at attention until he sat behind his desk.

"You may sit. So. The bar exam," he said, without preamble. "I know results are weeks away, but how do you feel it went?"

"Very well, Your Honor," Roger said. "I feel good about it."

The judge turned to me. "Mr. Haas?"

"I don't know, Your Honor," I said. "I did my best. I'm proud of my work." I shrugged. "That's all I can say at this point."

Miller nodded. "Indeed. Your briefs, please?"

Roger perked up and handed his portfolio to the judge, who flipped through it to give a cursory glance, then looked to me.

"I don't have a brief written."

Judge Miller's thick white eyebrows shot up. "I see."

Beside me, Roger shifted in his chair, sensing victory.

"And for what reason were you unable to complete the assignment?"

"In part, I'm not prepared because I became locked in a custody battle for my daughter."

The judge sat back in his chair. "And did you prevail?"

"I did," I said, "but I shouldn't have. Not under the law."

The words that had been tangled in knots and locked in my heart, unraveled. Finally. Not on paper, in black and white ink, but in words spoken from one man to another.

"I won custody of my daughter, except she isn't technically my daughter. Under the law as prescribed, I came up just short of the year deadline under which she would have been mine. And without my blood in her veins, I was going to lose her to her grandparents who can provide her with everything she could ever want."

I could feel Roger's eyes darting back and forth between us, watching intently to see how my words landed on Judge Miller's face.

"I did try to write your brief," I said. "About my mother. She was killed by a drunk driver, and I was going to write how I wanted to do a better job than the prosecutor who plea bargained, and put her killer back out on the street. He let him go, my mother died, and my family was ripped apart. My father, brother and I were flung far away from one another because of an addict, and that addict became the standard by which I judged all other addicts."

Judge Miller laced his fingers together and rested his chin on them, listening intently.

"I had facts and figures memorized; recidivism rates, and the statistics that painted a bleak picture for drug-and-alcohol-related crimes. Had I written that brief with those facts and figures, you would have given the job to Roger. But I met a woman who is fighting the same battle as the man who killed my mother. The only difference is that she never gave in, even when no one believed in her. When *I* didn't believe in her. This woman…she showed me life. Not the rules and the laws, but everything in between."

Judge Miller's eyes never left mine, and I drew in a shuddering breath, endeavoring to be professional.

But this is life. Sometimes it's messy.

"I made a promise to my daughter's grandparents that wasn't sealed by law," I said. "They accepted knowing they had no legal recourse should I renege. But they trusted me because Darlene showed them—and me—what a second chance truly means. Thanks to her, my daughter has a father and grandparents, both. Family. I have a family for the first time in fifteen years."

I fought for control, as the enormity of what Darlene had done for me swept through me. I blinked hard, and swallowed harder.

"As a federal prosecutor, I'm going to fight to uphold the law one case at a time. One individual at a time. I want justice for victims, no question; but I will have the evidence in front of me, instead of my anger and rage behind me. That's gone now, and I have one amazing, strong, brave woman to thank for that. My career will be forever aimed at making her proud and doing right by her. All else, including this job, will come second. Thank you."

I slumped in my chair feeling as if I had just purged myself of something heavy and black that had been weighing me down. I wondered if Darlene felt like that, standing in front of her meeting group, telling the absolute truths of her heart, and a wave of pride swept over me. It didn't even matter what the judge decided. I could go home to Darlene and Olivia and be the kind of man they both deserved, with or without this job.

The room grew quiet. Judge Miller was looking at me the way my father once did when I'd come home from school with all A's or after I'd hit a home run in Little League. Before my mother was gone and he was still able to be Dad without it hurting so damn much.

Roger glanced at me, then at Judge Miller's expression. A small smile flitted over his face and he rose to his feet. He straightened his jacket, picked up his briefcase and offered his hand to the judge.

"Your Honor, it's been a pleasure," he said. Then he turned to me and offered his hand. "Congratulations."

Roger walked out the door and closed it behind him. Judge Miller did not call him back.

At the Victorian, I stepped inside my place. Darlene was at the kitchen counter, nervously flipping through a magazine. She stopped when she saw me; searched my face for clues. I fought to keep my expression neutral.

"Olivia's taking a nap," she said in a low voice. "So?"

"Well…" I rubbed the back of my head, keeping my gaze cast down.

"Holy hell, Sawyer Haas, I love you, but I'm going to kill you if you don't tell me right now. Did you get it?"

A smile spread over my face in tandem with love for this woman spreading in my heart. "I got it."

Darlene squealed then covered her mouth. She hobbled over to me and threw her arms around my neck and I lifted her up, holding her tight to me.

"It's not official; I have to have passed the bar. But now that I can look at it without being scared to death with custody hearings, I think I passed that bastard."

"I'm so proud of you," she said kissing me over and over. "But I'm not surprised. Not in the least." She held my face in her hands. "My Sawyer the Lawyer."

"Sawyer the Clerk of the Court."

She pretended to think about that a moment. "Doesn't have the same ring to it, but I'll take it."

"I'll take *you*," I said, carrying her to the bedroom. "Again and again and again…"

"Until the baby wakes up," she said, kissing me hotly.

I set her down and she reached for me, but I held her hands in mine. "Everything good in my life is because of you. How do I thank you for that?"

She smiled and traced the line of my jaw with her finger. "You don't. Just love me, Sawyer."

I nodded wordlessly and kissed her. Of course that's all she wanted. Only love, because that's who she was, and as I took her to bed, touching her gently and slow, I vowed to always be worthy of her, right now and forever.

epilogue

Darlene
One year later...

"How many in your party?" the hostess at Nopa asked us.

I glanced at Sawyer with Olivia on his hip. "Oh gosh, there are... sixteen of us?" I said. "We have a reservation for brunch. Under Montgomery?"

The hostess smiled and checked her book. "We're setting that up now. When your entire party is here, we can seat you."

"She might want to rethink that," I said to Sawyer. "We're going to clog up the works in the front here."

"Probably," he said absently, hoisting Olivia higher. She looked like a cream puff in a ruffled yellow dress. Sawyer looked devastatingly handsome, as always, in a dark gray suit and ruby red tie.

"Every time we come here, our crowd is bigger," I said, smoothing the front of my own black dress. "They're going to have to build an addition for next time."

Sawyer smiled but didn't reply.

I smiled reassuringly. "Hey, if you're nervous about meeting my parents, don't be. They're going to love you. All of my friends are going to love you." My eyes widened over his shoulder. "Speaking of friends..."

I let out a little squeal as Beckett held Nopa's front door open for Zelda.

"Oh my God, you're here!" I hugged them both at the same time. "You smell like New York."

"Like urine and cement?" Zelda asked with her usual sarcasm.

"Like a thousand lights and warm rain," I said, pulling her in for another hug. "I missed you."

"Missed you too, Dar," she whispered. "So much."

"Ten bucks, please," Beckett said, holding his hand to Zelda, which she swatted away. "I bet her ten bucks she'd be tearing up within the first five minutes," he said to Sawyer, and offered his hand. "I'm Beckett and this is my emotional fiancée, Zelda."

"Oh shut up," she said, but I saw something warm and deep pass between them.

"Good to meet you both," Sawyer said. "Darlene's told me a lot about you."

Zelda's green eyes stared at Sawyer, and I could tell the sketch she'd made of my boyfriend in her mind didn't match the one standing in front of her.

"Sawyer, hi," she said, shaking his hand. "Nice to meet you." She turned her head to me so a curtain of her long black hair shielded her from Sawyer, and mouthed, *Are you kidding me?*

I mouthed back. *I know, right?*

They both cooed over Olivia, who immediately grabbed for Zelda's hair.

"Are you nervous about the show?" Zelda asked, gently extracting Olivia's little fist. "*Chicago*…I mean, that's huge, Dar. I'm so excited for you."

"Thanks, yeah, I was nervous at first, but now that we're settling into the run, it's easier."

The San Francisco Repertory was doing six weeks of Kander and Ebb's *Chicago* at the Orpheum Theater. I auditioned for one of the Merry Murderesses—the prison inmate who shot her husband for popping his gum. It was my dream role, though I would have been happy just to be ensemble in such a big, elaborate production.

But I got the part and had done a week's worth of shows to find my groove, and now my friends and my parents had flown from New York to see a Sunday matinee.

They filtered in, in pairs: Henrietta and Jackson, Elena and her husband, Alice and Gerald, my sister Carla and her husband, and my mom and dad. A tingle of nerves shot through me when my family arrived that was more potent than the nervousness I'd felt on opening night.

"Darlene, my God, girl! You look like a million bucks." My sister enveloped me in a perfume and hairspray cloud as she hugged me. "Look at you, I can't get over it. And you must be Sawyer," she said, staring. "Wow. Dar. Just wow. And this peach…this must be Olivia."

Carla introduced her husband, Stan, and then Mom and Dad were there, hugging me.

"She's right," my dad said. "You look like a million bucks, kiddo."

"Thanks, Daddy." I heaved a breath. "Mom and Dad, this is Sawyer and Olivia."

The men shook hands and I thought I saw a glimpse of nervousness dance over Sawyer's brown eyes. Then my mother smacked a kiss on his cheek, and the entire front area dissolved into laughter and loud talk.

The hostess came back and offered to take us to our table. I lingered behind, looking to the front entrance that was crowded with brunch customers. And then I saw him—tall and with the summer sun glinting off the gel in his hair.

I pushed my way through the crowd, and threw my arms around my friend.

"Max," I said against his leather jacket.

"Hey, Dar," he said, holding me tight. "Sorry I'm late."

"You're not late, you're right on time. And I don't even care; you're here, and that's all that matters."

He glanced down at me. "Look at you. A Merry Murderess. Holy shit. Did you know *Chicago* is one of my all-time favorite musicals?"

I made a gun with my index and thumb, and sneered, "If you pop that gum one more time…"

"Jesus, Dar, you gave me the chills." He held out his shaking hands. "Look at this shit? Christ, I can't wait to see you in this."

My murderous expression vanished. "Thank you, Max. Now come on, I need to share the awesomeness that is you with the rest of my people."

I brought Max to our table that was already seated and embarrassed him by making a show of introducing him to everyone. I sat him down with Beckett and Zelda at one end of the table. Sawyer sat across from me. I was beside Olivia, who was scribbling with crayon on a sheet of coloring paper. On the other side of her highchair was my sister, Carla and her husband who was on his phone watching baseball, until she smacked his wrist and told him to put it away.

The waiter came to take our drink order, offering mimosas. Most of our party took her up on that but I abstained, as did Max.

"None for me," Sawyer said, giving me a smile.

"None for me either," Zelda said.

"And I'll abstain too, out of solidarity," Beckett said, and they shared another look over the table.

"Solidarity for what?" I asked.

They exchanged another glance. "Nothing," Zelda said quickly, and they both looked like they were biting back smiles.

My eyes widened and my heart felt like it would burst. "Oh my God… Zelda? Are you…?"

Zelda flapped a hand. "No, hush, this is your day."

I ignored her and turned to Beckett. "Well?"

His proud grin told me everything. "Yes. She is. We're going to have a baby."

"Holy shit!" I screamed and nearly toppled my chair to get to her as the table raised their glasses in cheers. I hugged her and tears were shed all around.

"How far along?" I asked.

"Ten weeks," Zelda said. "We weren't going to say anything until after your show, but this one—" she tossed her napkin at Beckett—"can't keep a secret to save his life."

Beckett held out his hands. "What can I say? I'm too damn happy to keep it quiet."

"You should be," I said. "I'm so happy for you both."

I chatted with them for a while, then sat back down in my seat, flushed with happiness and found Sawyer looking at me from across the table with an expression I couldn't identify.

"It's such great news, isn't it?"

He nodded. "Absolutely."

The food orders were taken, and talk and laughter rolled over the table in waves and swells. Olivia entertained everyone with her ability to count to twenty and recite her ABCs. At one point, Sawyer moved to sit at an empty chair near my dad, and I heard them talking about my dad's business and Sawyer's job as Clerk of the Court for Judge Miller. Of course, Sawyer had passed the bar with an outrageous score of 1990 out of a possible 2000. He was modest as all heck about it, but he'd worked so hard for so long and I was so proud of him. And proud of myself, for being here. For making it to this moment, with these people I loved best.

I bent my head to find Max and met his eye. I didn't have to say a word. He nodded once, and smiled, and I knew he understood.

After we ate, dessert was offered and Sawyer was back in his chair across from me.

"You're so quiet today," I said, leaning toward him and taking his hand. "Everything all right?"

He nodded. "It's perfect."

The desserts were served but I abstained from them too. The last thing I needed before the show was a sugar rush.

"Ma! Hey, Mama," Carla called to our mother over a table of talk. "You have to split this tiramisu with me. I can't do it alone."

"Where Mama?" Olivia asked.

"What's that, hon?" Carla said, leaning sideways to Olivia while she prepped her coffee.

"Where Mama?"

"Oh, she's my mama." Carla pointed at our mother with her spoon. "That's my mama, right there,"

"Ohhh," Olivia said. "Das my mama righ' dare!" she said, and she pointed straight to me.

The whole table stopped, conversations ceased. I felt warm all over, as if a ray of sunlight suddenly fell over me, turning everything gold and soft.

My gaze jumped to Sawyer. He gave a short, disbelieving laugh, his mouth open in shock but wanting to smile.

"What did you say, honey?" he asked Olivia.

"Mama," Olivia said, hooking a little chocolate-covered finger my way again. "Darlene my mama." She said as if this were common knowledge and went back to eating her cake, completely unaware of the knowing laughs and teasing that swept through the rest of the table.

The Abbotts stared in surprise, and a pang of fear shot through me, certain they must be saddened for Molly, that she wasn't here to share in this happiness, and that Olivia had given her title to someone else. To me.

"I didn't tell her…" I said. "I mean, she's never called me that before…"

I held my breath until they both smiled, Alice with her hand over her heart. "It's okay," she told me. "It hurts and yet it's perfectly right. Does that make sense?"

I nodded, tears in my eyes. "Yeah, it does."

"Oh jeez, Dar," my sister said, breaking the solemn moment. She spooned sugar into her coffee. "A mama. You ready for that?"

Jackson was less subtle. He bellowed a great laugh and clapped his hands. "Thatta girl, Livvie! Up top."

He reached across the table to high five the two-year old. Henrietta swatted his arm down.

"You hush. This is personal between them, and you have no cause to say a word."

Henrietta's word was law, and everyone went back to their conversations.

Jackson chuckled and shot me a wink, but I didn't feel like laughing. I leaned over the table to Sawyer.

"I didn't say a word, I promise. She only ever calls me Darlene. I—"

"It's okay," he said, a strange smile on his lips. "We live together. It was inevitable that she'd bond with you even more than she had already.'"

"I know, but I know you don't want to confuse her…"

"Darlene," Sawyer said. "It's fine."

I nodded and sat straight in my chair, the beautiful happiness I'd felt at Olivia's words fading to leave my stomach twisting in knots.

The last few days Sawyer had been acting funny. He was in his head a lot, and not talking as much as usual. And today, he'd been so quiet and subdued. As the others ate their dessert and drank their coffee, I found myself going back over the last few days trying to find something that could be amiss. But I had to keep going, back and back, as this year had been the most incredible of my life.

I'd been able to find big parts in small shows so that my massage work was mostly freelance to make extra income. And now I'd had a small-ish role in a really big show. And the day I told Sawyer, his eyes had widened and the pure joy and happiness for me felt as good as getting the part.

Rachel had returned from her Greenpeace tour wanting her apartment back. After many long talks, I moved in with Sawyer and Olivia. We both wanted to protect Olivia, but we were so much in love, the idea of something going wrong between us seemed impossible. We were happy. I wondered sometimes how it was possible to feel so happy with Sawyer and Olivia, and building a life with a man and his little girl was something I'd never imagined I wanted, and now couldn't imagine living without.

I glanced at Sawyer across the table. Jackson leaned in to tell him a joke but Sawyer only smiled, a far-off expression on his face. My stomach twisted a little more. Was this the slow fade I'd seen before? No big drama, no blow up fights…

You're being ridiculous, I told myself, but I'd seen it too many times. And that impossible happiness…maybe it was just that. Too impossible to last.

I got up from my seat and moved down the table to where Max was talking with Beckett.

"Excuse me," I said, "but I need to borrow this guy for minute."

I tugged Max to his feet and drew him away from the table, to the bathroom alcove.

"Help! How do you shut down overthinking?"

Max looked dashing in a suit he wore with a black leather jacket instead of a coat. "That's the secret to life," he said with a grin. "If I knew that, I'd have written it down and I'd be on Oprah right now."

I bit my lip.

His teasing smile fled. "What is it?"

"It's nothing. I'm jumping to conclusions…or, not even that. I don't know what to think." I looked up at him, tears coming to my eyes. "I've been so happy and that stupid little voice is back. You know the one? It whispers in your ear that everything good is going to go away soon."

He nodded. "I know the voice. That little fucker talks to me. Frequently." He smiled gently at me. "But don't talk back. Don't feed it. That'll get you nowhere. If you're concerned about something with Sawyer, talk to Sawyer."

I nodded. "You're right. I know you're right." I sucked in a breath. I was stronger than this. I'd come so far, and I couldn't let nagging doubt get the best of me. I wasn't the girl who thought a man being upset with her meant the end.

"You're still as wise as ever," I said, as we walked back to the table. "I just…got scared."

"That'll happen. Just don't let it stay."

I kissed his cheek and sat back down. Sawyer was watching me.

"You okay?" he asked.

"I wanted to ask you the same," I said. Jackson laughed loudly at something Gerald said, and I flinched. "But not here. After lunch?"

He smiled warmly and nodded, and I felt a little better.

At the Orpheum theatre, outside the back entrance, I hugged and kissed everyone and they all told me to break a leg.

"Hey, Dar," Jackson said. "You know that's just a figure of speech, right?"

"Such a comedian," I said with a laugh and a roll of my eyes.

I hugged Alice who was holding Olivia. "I'm going to keep her occupied until your big number," she said, "then come out and watch."

"Thank you," I said. "Just cover her eyes over the naughty bits." I bent to kiss Olivia's cheek. "Bye-bye, sweet pea."

"Bye-bye, Mama."

My heart clenched again.

"She's a smart cookie, this one," Alice said with a knowing smile. "Once she gets a notion in her head, it's hard to get it out. Just like her daddy."

She inclined her head at Sawyer who was last to wish me luck before the show. The rest of our people moved away and we were alone.

"She did it again with the Mama, thing," I said. "Sawyer…"

Without a word, he slipped his arms around my waist and kissed me, the kind of kiss that never failed to steal the strength form my legs so that I melted against him. I did then, my arms ringing his neck to keep upright as his hands slid up into my hair, and then down to my cheek. He held my face and broke the kiss, his eyes so beautiful and dark as they bored into mine.

"I love you, Darlene," he said.

"I love you too," I whispered. "And I'm so happy with you. And with Olivia."

"Are you?" he asked, a ragged breath chasing his words. "Truly? I know it's a lot to take…living with a kid…"

"No, I love her to pieces, and I love you so damn much, I feel like my heart's going to burst. But I get scared sometimes."

"I do too," he said, his brows furrowed. "I worry that it's all going to go away…this happiness."

"Yes! Me too," I said, clutching the lapels of his jacket. "What do we do?"

He smiled, his thumb running over my bottom lip. "We make sure it doesn't. We hold on, right?"

I nodded through tears. "Yes. We do."

"*We* do," he said. "Together." Sawyer kissed me again, then inclined his head at the stage entrance door. "I don't want you to be late. You're amazing, and I'm so damn happy your friends and family are here to see this. You deserve it all, Darlene. All of it."

I threw my arms around him and kissed him hard, then swept into the theater, my heart full, and a huge grin on my face.

There is no slow fade. What we have is real.

I went to the dressing area, where the rest of the cast greeted me with cheerful smiles and high fives. The other Merry Murderesses—six of us who performed the Cell Block Tango to tell the story of how we ended up in jail for murdering our husbands—were like sisters to me. I belonged here, just as much as I did in my NA meetings where I was attendee and sponsor, both.

I changed into my costume—tight black dance shorts, black nylons, black knee boots, and a black halter top that left my midriff bare. I put on my dark eye make up and red lips; then a hairdresser brushed out my hair and tousled it so it looked like a man's hands had just been in it.

The show began and I waited for my number. The Cell Block Tango. I had the first line, "Pop", that began a series of key words from each of the Merry Murderesses, and if I didn't hit my cue every time, the entire song would be off tempo.

But everyone I knew and loved was watching me. I didn't want to disappoint them, and as the emcee announced the song, I felt a glowing well of strength in me. Not stiff and unbending, but molten and hot so that I could dance. So that I could tell the story with my body, and give everything that I had to it. Because I had a lot to give, and I'd finally found it.

The energy was running high for a matinee, and we danced the hell out of Cell Block Tango, and after the sound effect of a prison door slamming shut boomed across the stage, the crowd erupted into cheers that carried me on a tide of joy to the end of the musical.

As the last number ended, the crowd grew thunderous—a rolling swell of appreciation and excitement that barreled through the theatre with whistles and applause and hollering.

I stood just offstage with my other Merry Murderesses, waiting for our cue for the curtain call. "Standing O," one said. "Not bad for a matinee."

When it came time for our curtain call, we slunk onto the stage languidly; long-legged steps in our high heels. I slung my arm on my co-inmate's shoulder and tried to look sexy and tough in our curtain-call pose, but the lights had come down and I found my people in the audience.

They were all there, and I wished I had Sawyer's photographic memory; I'd have taken a thousand photos of my parents looking proud of me; my mother dabbing her eye.

Of Max clapping his hands so hard, I was afraid he'd hurt himself.

Of Beckett trying to be stoic as he fought back strong emotion, but the shine in his eyes gave him away.

And Zelda who didn't bother to hide her tears.

And Sawyer…

Sawyer's seat was empty.

My heart dropped but before I could contemplate it, the Merry Murderesses had to relinquish the stage to Mama Morton, and the rest of the *Chicago* cast that had become a second family to me.

After Velma and Roxie took their bows, the entire cast stormed the front of the stage with clasped hands to bow. The energy surged through us, hand to hand, and now we were free to break character and smile. But Sawyer still wasn't there.

Maybe he had to use the bathroom, or Alice needed help with Olivia.

Ushers passed out bouquets of flowers to the dancers from audience members, as the emcee strolled onto the stage. He held a microphone in one hand and a bouquet of Gerber daisies in another, all white.

"Now, hold on folks," the emcee said. "Before we wrap this up, we have a very special little guest who wants to say something to one of our Merry Murderesses. Darlene…? Would you step forward, love?"

I stared for a moment, unable to breathe or move until one of the dancers nudged my elbow. I came forward and the emcee put the bouquet in my hand.

"You have a fan, Darlene," he said, then looked stage right. "Come on out here, little sweetheart."

Olivia toddled out from stage right with Sawyer holding her hand as she raced toward me. The audience cooed at the cuteness before them, Olivia in her puffy yellow dress, her little legs working.

"Here," Olivia said, holding a black velvet box in her hand. "Is for you."

I had no words. The crowd reacted for me, gasps and murmurs and a few *ohhhs*.

"That was supposed to come last," Sawyer said, moving to stand before me. "I was freaking out that doing this here was a bad idea," he said and glanced nervously at the crowd. "Now I'm sure of it. How do you do this every night?"

I shrugged and laughed. My heart was pounding in my chest, I could hardly hear myself talk.

"Here go, Mama," Olivia said, still trying to give me the box.

I bent to touch her cheek, then stood to face Sawyer. "She keeps calling me her Mama."

"Would you...?" His voice cracked and he tried again. "Would you want to be her mom? Because what I'm about to ask...I'm asking for her, too. For both of us."

I nodded, tears spilling down and the audience took a collective intake of breath.

"I would be honored to be her mommy," I whispered.

Sawyer's jaw clenched and he got down on one knee, next to Olivia. The audience *oooohed* and *awwwwed,* but I hardly heard them.

Sawyer put one arm around his daughter. "Give it to her now, honey."

"Here go!" Olivia said, and offered me the velvet box.

"Thank you, baby," I managed. I took the box, but couldn't open it. "My hands are shaking," I whispered to Sawyer.

"Mine too." He took the box from my hand and opened it on a small, square-cut diamond solitaire in a ring of white gold.

My hands flew to my mouth and I felt the energy of the audience wrap around us in joyful anticipation.

"Darlene Montgomery," Sawyer said, his voice ringing out into the auditorium, clear and loud. "Will you marry me?"

I could only nod at first, my voice silenced by happiness and tears, and the future that was waiting on the other side of this question.

"Yes," I whispered, and got to my knees too. "Yes," I said, louder. "Yes, I'll marry you. Of course, I will."

The audience went crazy. Underneath the noise and lights, I kissed Sawyer, and tasted his tears that mingled with mine. Then I turned to Olivia and held her close.

"Can I be your Mommy, sweet pea?"

Olivia gave me a perplexed baby look that said, *I believe we have already established this, silly woman.* Aloud, she said. "You my Mama."

Sawyer looked about ready to fall apart, and I knew that the last thing my stoic man wanted was to burst into tears in front of fifteen hundred people. I hugged Olivia, and we got to our feet. Sawyer slipped the ring on my finger, and held my hand tight as he kissed me again. The crowd swelled with applause and cheers.

In that perfect moment, Olivia slipped one of her little hands into mine, the other into his, and she held on. And we held on to her—and each other—just as tightly.

the end

acknowledgments

The writing of a book is a solitary endeavor, until the moment you send it to the first person to read the words. Then it suddenly becomes too unwieldy for the author to carry alone. I am forever grateful to the following people who helped me haul this book over the mountain and into the world. I could not have done it without them: Angela Shockley, Joy Kriebel-Sadowski, Kathleen Ripley, Jeannine Allison, Sarah Torpey, Suanne Laqueur, Jennifer Balogh-Ghosh, and William Hairston.

To Tom Ripley for his legal expertise, I thank you so very much. And while I stand by my research and his advice, I did take some liberties and exerted creative license over certain aspects of California custody law. Don't kill me.

To the bloggers, readers, and amazing people of this community who make it possible for me to do this job. Thank you.

To Grey, who literally saved me from disaster. Thank you for your kindness, your time, for being there for me at one a.m., and *especially* for that last read-through. With love.

To Melissa Panio-Petersen, who keeps me sane while I write the words, then she wraps the words inside a beautiful cover. Thank you for sharing your time, talent, and artistry, and for being the winner of World's Most Thoughtful and Hilarious Human, six years running.

To Robin Renee Hill for all the reasons, and a thousand more I can't remember but I'm sure we talked about them in an email somewhere, and it probably ended with you sending me an eyeroll emoji. <3 you more than all the babka.

And to every single member of Emma's Entourage. Words cannot express how much you mean to me, how I'm so grateful to all of you each and every day. Thank you for being there, my Blue Ribbon Stalkers. I cry more tears of joy than you know for what you do for me. Thank you. <3

also by EMMA SCOTT

How to Save a Life (Dreamcatcher #1)
Let's do something really crazy and trust each other.

"You're in for a roller coaster of emotions and a story that will grip you from the beginning to the very end. This is a MUST READ…"—Book Boyfriend Blog

Full Tilt
I would love you forever, if I only had the chance…

"Full of life, love and glorious feels."—*New York Daily News*, Top Ten Hottest Reads of 2016

All In (Full Tilt #2)
Love has no limits…

"A masterpiece!"—AC Book Blog

after we fall

MELANIE HARLOW

For J & C

Your love and courage inspired me.

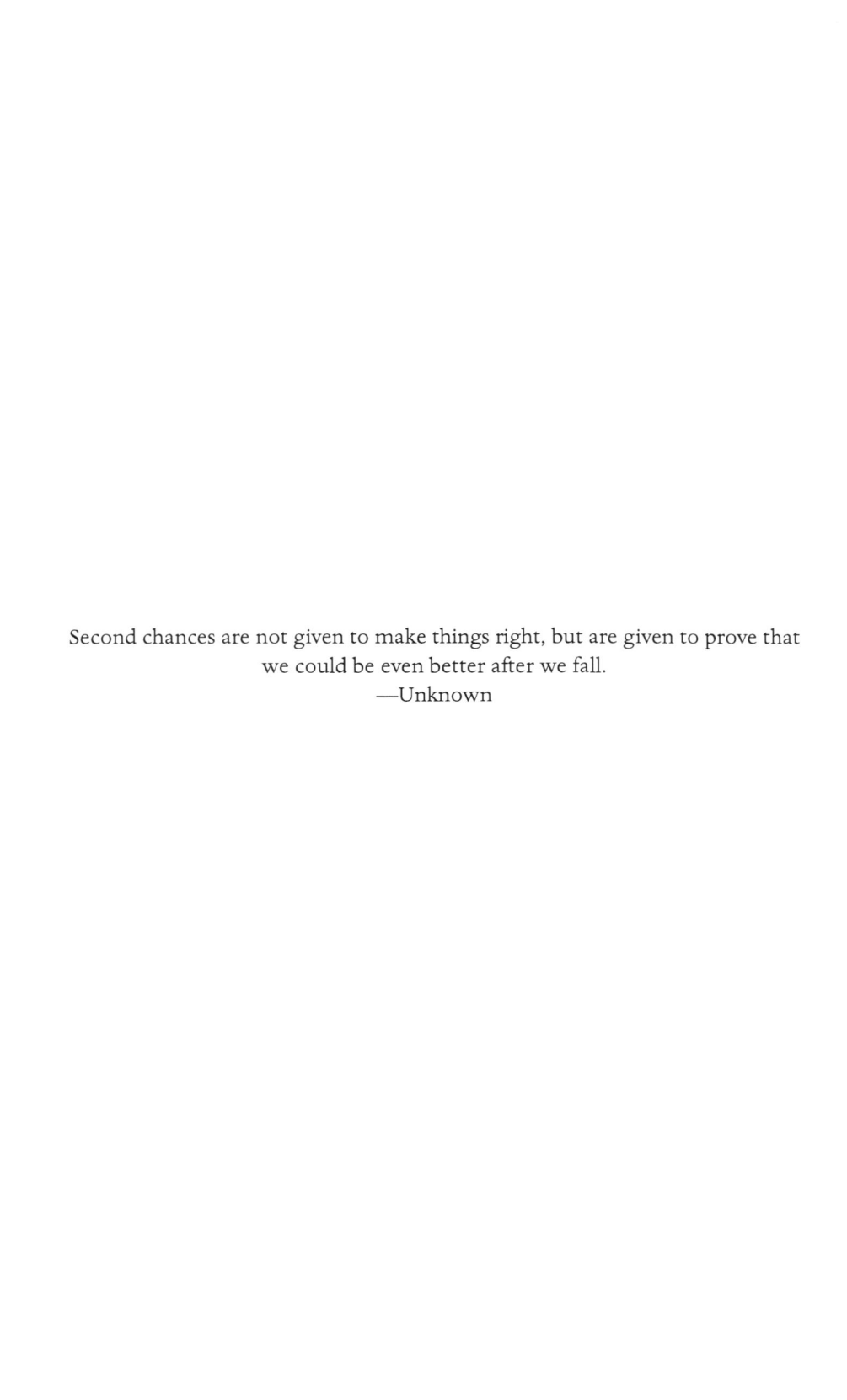

Second chances are not given to make things right, but are given to prove that we could be even better after we fall.
—Unknown

chapter
one

Margot

I DIDN'T THROW THE PIE.

And really, I think that's what everyone should be focused on: the supreme restraint, the Buddhist-like control, the fucking *regal* nature with which I glanced at the award-winning Cheery Cherry Delight and decided against it. (Just so you know, that was only because of the shirt he wore. Furious as I was, even I could not bring myself to desecrate a snowy white, crisply starched Brooks Brothers button-down. I'm not a monster.)

Not that hurling a tray full of scones—one at a time, with admittedly poor aim—at your ex-boyfriend is behavior to be commended. I completely understand that. And anyone who knows me will tell you it was *utterly* out of character. I, Margot Thurber Lewiston, pride myself on my ability to control my emotions. Maintain grace under pressure. Keep calm and carry the fuck on. My composure rarely slips, and it certainly doesn't slip in a room full of donors to my father's Senatorial campaign.

Honestly, I've never thrown food in my life. I've never thrown much of anything, which is probably why I had a bit of trouble hitting the target (I have apologized profusely to Mrs. Biltmore about the singed linen. Also the Belleek vase), and I certainly don't throw things indoors.

Because I was raised with manners. Good old-fashioned, old-money manners. We believe in modesty, courtesy, and—above all—discretion.

No matter what, we do not Cause a Scene.

According to my mother, Margaret Whitney Thurber Lewiston (known to all as Muffy), nothing says *poor taste*—or worse, *new money*—like Causing a Scene.

She tells me I have caused one that people will be talking about for years to come.

This is probably true.

I can explain.

⁓

It was a text no one wants from an ex-boyfriend at one in the morning on a Tuesday night. Or any night, really.

Tripp: I need to see you. I'm outside.
Me: It's so late. Can we talk tomorrow?

Tripp: No, it has to be tonight. Please. I need you.

Frowning at my phone in the dark, I wondered what this could be about. We'd broken up well over a year ago, and though we'd maintained a cordial if stiff relationship since then, we hadn't had a private, in-person conversation since the night we split. While I was considering how to politely handle this request, he texted again.

Tripp: Please, Gogo. It's important.

I softened slightly at the nickname, not because I liked it that much, but because it reminded me of better days. We'd known each other a long time, our families were close, and once upon a time, I'd thought we'd spend the rest of our lives together. I could be gracious.

Me: OK. Give me a minute. Front door.

I used the minute to yank out my ponytail, put on a bra under the Vassar t-shirt I'd been sleeping in, and slip into a pair of pink silk pajama pants. A heavy summer rain drummed against the roof of my townhouse, so I hurried down the stairs to open the front door, but of course, Tripp was perfectly dry.

"Hey," I said, standing back as he closed his dripping umbrella and entered the foyer. Hot, humid air followed him in, and I quickly shut the door against the heat, then snapped on the light.

"Hey." He set the umbrella in the stand near the door and ran a hand through his neatly trimmed dark blond hair. He wore a pink button-down shirt with the sleeves rolled up, and it was tucked in to a pair of white shorts with kelly green whales embroidered on them. He had pants with little embroidered whales on them too, in multiple colors. My eyes lingered on his familiar Sperry deck shoes. No socks.

"Thanks for letting me in," he said.

"What's going on?" I twisted my long hair over one shoulder and crossed my arms over my chest.

"Can we sit down? I need to talk to you." On his breath, I detected a whiff of scotch, and upon closer inspection of his face, I noticed his eyes were bloodshot.

"Can't we talk right here?"

He fidgeted. "Look, I know the way things happened with us wasn't cool."

"That was last year. I'm over it, Tripp." It was mostly true. Sometimes I still felt a tug of sadness when I thought about the three years we'd spent together and the hopes I'd had we'd be engaged or even married by now, but my therapist had me mostly convinced it wasn't so much about the loss of *him* as it was the loss of the dream life I'd envisioned for us. Secretly, I still wasn't sure what the difference was.

"Well—what if I'm not?"

I shook my head, taken aback. "What?"

"What if I'm not over it, or over us?"

"What do you mean? That makes no sense, Tripp. You were over us before I was. It was *you* who said you didn't want to marry me. I was ready."

"I never said that. It wasn't personal like that." His thick slab of a chin jutted forward. "I just said I wasn't sure I wanted to get married."

"Well, I was sure. And I wasn't going to wait around for you to decide once and for all. I moved on, Tripp. And so did you." *Moving on* was a bit of a stretch for me, since I hadn't dated anyone seriously since the split. But he'd been seen around town with a whole slew of sorority girls. Lately he'd been dating someone my friends called Margot 2.0, since she was basically a younger, blonder, bigger-breasted version of me. (But according to Muffy, none of that mattered because she was *new money*; i.e., completely unsuitable in the eyes of Tripp's parents, Mimi and Deuce.) "What about your girlfriend? Does she know you're here?"

"Amber?" He frowned. "No, she doesn't. She thinks I'm with my father, and I *was* with him earlier. He…" The frown deepened, and Tripp swallowed hard.

"He what?" For the first time, I started to get a little worried. Deuce was over seventy, with high blood pressure and a penchant for thick steaks and stiff drinks. He'd had his third heart attack at the end of last year. "Is your father OK?"

"Yes. He's fine. But—" He shifted his weight from one foot to the other, his wet shoes squeaking on the wood floor. It occurred to me I had never seen Tripp this nervous or uncomfortable. On any other day, he was Mr. Confident, especially after some good scotch—brimming with all the entitled self-assurance of a handsome, wealthy, Ivy League-educated white man.

"Spit it out, Tripp," I said, stifling a yawn. "Otherwise we can talk about this tomorrow. I'm tired, and I have to work in the morning. I'll call you a car if you can't drive home, because it smells a little like you've been—"

"Marry me, Margot!" He threw himself down on his knees in front of me. "I want to get married. To you."

"What?" My heart was thundering in my chest. Was this for real?

"Marry me. Please. I'm so sorry for everything." Wrapping his arms around my legs, he buried his face in my knees.

I thumped on his shoulders. "For God's sake, Tripp. You're drunk. Get up."

"I'm not drunk. I know what I'm saying. I have to marry you."

I stopped hitting him and stared down at the top of his head. "What do you mean, you have to marry me? Why?"

He froze for a moment, then recovered. "I have to marry you because I've realized you're the only one for me. We're perfect for each other. You've always been the one, Margot. Always."

OK, it was a fairly pathetic display, what with the squeaky deck shoes and the bloodshot eyes and the whale shorts, but I sort of felt for him. Tripp had never been great at declaring his feelings. I wasn't particularly a champ at it, either. "Tripp, please. Stand up. Let's talk about this."

"First say you'll marry me. Look, I have a ring," he said, as if he'd just remembered he'd brought one. From his pocket he pulled out a small black box, his fingers fumbling a bit as he opened it.

I gasped and covered my mouth with my hands. The huge, brilliant cut stone winked at me from its slender diamond band. It had to be at least two carats, with gorgeous color and clarity.

"Put it on," he urged, taking it from its velvet cushion.

I wanted to. God, I wanted to. But I didn't want to marry Tripp. It would be wrong to put the ring on when I knew I was going to turn him down, right?

Because I had to turn him down. Despite what he said, we weren't right for each other anymore, were we? I didn't love him anymore.

Maybe I should try it on just to be sure, I told myself. I mean, what if I put it on and suddenly the hall was filled with music and rainbows and sunshine? What if I still loved him and just didn't know it? Biting my lip, I held out my left hand and let him slide the ring onto my finger. Perfect fit. I shivered as he got to his feet.

But there was no music. No rainbows. No sunshine. Just the rain outside, the sound of those squeaky deck shoes, the puddle they were leaving on my nice wood floor, and those infernal whale shorts.

Sighing, I looked at it on my hand one last time before starting to pull it off. "It's beautiful, Tripp, but I can't—"

He covered my hands with his, preventing me from removing the ring. "Don't say that. Please don't say that. You have to marry me."

Annoyed, I yanked my hands away and slipped the ring from my finger. "I don't have to do anything."

"I'm begging you, Margot. Please." His voice cracked, and in his eyes I saw real desperation. I hadn't seen that in him since—

"Tripp," I said slowly. "Is something going on with you?" Years ago, Tripp had struggled with a gambling addiction, racking up hundreds of thousands of dollars in debt his father eventually had to pay off. But as far as I knew, he'd stopped the compulsive betting by the time we were together. And why would that prompt him to propose to me, anyway?

He swallowed hard, his Adam's apple bobbing. "No. Honestly, Margot. It's just that I've been so miserable and lonely since we broke up."

"You didn't look miserable or lonely."

"I was. Really, I was. And I was a total asshole to you."

"Well, we can agree on that, at least."

"I'm sorry." He pulled me into an awkward hug, but I kept my arms at my sides, the ring caught in one fist. "We're so right for each other, you know we are. We make sense together. And we're both going to be thirty soon, so we should stop dicking around."

Pushing him away, I stood back and crossed my arms again. "That is not romantic. At all. And you're the only one who's been dicking around."

"I'm sorry. I'm bad at this stuff, you know I am. But...but..." He looked inspired for a second. "You complete me, Margot."

Battling the urge to call him out on his blatant pilfering of Jerry Maguire, I grabbed the ring box and (somewhat reluctantly) tucked the ring back inside. "Listen, this is crazy. We've been broken up for over a year. You can't just show up out of the blue and propose."

"But I want to marry you," he whined, his eyes darting to the left.

"Then maybe you should take me to dinner first." I held out the ring box, feeling a surge of pleasure at how well I was handling this situation. A year ago, I'd have been texting Jaime and Claire pictures of my engagement ring already.

He nodded glumly as he stuck the box back in his pocket. "Sure. OK."

At the door, I handed him his umbrella and gave him an impulsive hug. I could appreciate how hard this had been for him—it wasn't easy for a guy like Tripp to admit he was wrong and ask forgiveness. It showed maturity and growth, didn't it? "Let's talk again in a day or so, OK? I need to think."

I opened the door and he left without saying anything else, opening his umbrella against the punishing rain. After snapping off the light, I moved into the living room and watched him get into his car from the big picture window. Rain cascaded in sheets down the pane, blurring his form. When I saw the headlights come on and then disappear into the rainy dark, I went back upstairs to bed.

Holy shit, I thought, sliding beneath the covers again. What a crazy turn of events. Never in a million years had I thought Tripp would come to my doorstep in the middle of the night, with a diamond ring, begging me to marry him. It was such a complete reversal of his mindset a year ago.

Part of me was mad that *now* he'd decided we were right for each other, but another part wondered if he'd just needed more time all along. Had I been wrong to pressure him when he wasn't ready? Had I been too hasty to issue a "now or never" ultimatum? Had I been too insistent that we do things according to my timeline?

But dammit, we'd talked about everything! For three years, we'd fantasized together about the country club wedding, the center-entrance Colonial, the two kids, the sailboat, the King Charles Spaniel...it wasn't just me who'd wanted all that. He had too.

And didn't I still want it? Should I consider his offer? Annoying as it had been when he brought up my thirtieth birthday, he sort of had a point. My social circle was small, and I hadn't met anyone I was even attracted to in a year—how much longer did I want to wait to start the next phase of my life? As Muffy was fond of telling me, *Thurber women marry and have children by thirty, Gogo. Even the lesbians.*

It wasn't that I was unhappy. I had great friends, close family, a new job I loved, a beautiful place to live. So why did I feel like something was missing?

I was tired, but I lay awake for a while, playing with the fourth finger of my left hand.

chapter two

Margot

"You're kidding me." Jaime paused with her dirty martini halfway to her mouth. Claire seemed just as shocked, but took an extra gulp of her cocktail.

"Not kidding." I shook my head and smiled.

"Why didn't you say something earlier?" Jaime demanded. "I saw you this morning at the office and you didn't say anything about it!"

Jaime and I worked together at Shine PR, the marketing and public relations company we'd started together last year. Her degrees in psychology and marketing and her experience in advertising paired well with my experience in PR and social connections, and our little startup was a big success so far. We'd already hired an assistant to manage social media for several clients and planned to hire another by next year. "Because we were busy this morning, and you were with clients all afternoon. I figured I'd tell you both here tonight."

"Well, I'm glad you waited," Claire said from the other side of Jaime. It was our weekly Wednesday Girls Night Out, and we were at the Buhl Bar, a little earlier than usual since I had to attend a fundraiser for my father later on. "Now that you guys work together and see each other every day," Claire went on, "I fear I'm missing half the life gossip. So he actually *proposed*?"

I nodded. "On bended knee, with an exquisite diamond ring."

"What a surprise!" squealed Claire.

"What a dipshit," said Jaime. "I hope you told him to stick that ring where the sun don't shine."

I sipped my gin martini and replied with careful consideration. "I did nothing of the sort. I was kind and understanding, and I let him down easy."

"Why?" Jaime continued to gape at me with wide blue eyes. "He was such an asshole in the end."

"Because I have manners. Yes, he was an asshole," I admitted, "but he copped to it. Said he was sorry and basically begged to have me back. He said a lot of nice things, actually."

Jaime's stare made me uncomfortable, and I focused on my drink. She knew me too well. That's the problem when you've been best friends with someone since the ninth grade—even for someone like me, usually an expert at concealing how I feel, that friend sees through you.

"Well, it's nice that he finally realized what he had," offered Claire, eternal optimist. "Even if it is a little too late."

"Is it too late?" I braved, giving voice to the question that had been on my mind all day.

It was silent as they both registered what I'd said. "What do you mean?" Jaime's tone said *I know what you mean but you can't actually mean that.*

"I mean, do you think it's too late for us?"

"Fuck yes, I do." She banged a fist on the bar, and the surface of my drink rippled.

"Well, hold on. Maybe not," Claire said wistfully. "I love a good second chance romance."

"This isn't a movie," Jaime insisted, turning to Claire. "This is real life, and he was a real dick to her."

"But people can change," Claire countered. "Look at you and Quinn. You swore you'd never have a boyfriend, least of all him, but you gave Quinn a chance."

"That's different," Jaime said testily. "Plus Quinn is insanely good in bed. Tripp was a disaster, wasn't he Margot?"

I winced. "I don't know if I'd say *disaster*. The sex was just a bit…uninspired. Maybe that's not the most important thing, though. Maybe there are more important elements in a relationship than good sex."

Jaime looked at me incredulously. Blinked. "Like what?"

"Like common interests," I said, sitting up a little taller. "And family ties. And a shared history. Shared values."

Jaime rolled her eyes. "So your families both sailed here on the Mayflower or whatever. Big fucking deal. If you didn't want to tear his clothes off when he walked into your house last night, you don't have any chemistry."

I thought about that for a minute. Then I started to laugh at the idea of tearing off those whale shorts and the pink shirt. "We're just not like that," I said. "We've never been like that. We're both more…reserved. Conservative, maybe. Would I like better sex? Sure." I shrugged. "But I'm almost thirty. And maybe I need to worry less about that kind of thing."

"Thirty isn't old," Jaime scoffed. "And I don't want to see you go backward, Margot. A year ago you were so unhappy. You've made so much progress."

"I agree," I said. "But underneath it all, I'm still the same person. I still want the things I wanted then. I'm traditional, OK? I want a traditional life, the life I grew up with. Husband, house, family."

"And that's OK," Claire soothed, reaching over Jaime's lap to pat my hand. "We're not judging you for wanting those things."

"And Tripp *gets* me," I said, annoyed because it was true. "The ring he picked out was perfect. He knows my style, my taste. He's got a good education, a good job, a good family. Those things matter to me more than sex."

Jaime refused to give up. "But what about passion? What about that mind-blowing physical connection? Don't you want those butterflies in your stomach when he walks in the room? That racing pulse when he gets close?"

"But what if I'm not cut out for that?" I asked, voicing a fear that usually lurked silently in the back of my mind. "What if I'm just not that passionate a person? What if I'm not the type to blow anyone's mind? Does that mean I have to be alone?"

"No," Claire said firmly, shooting Jaime a look. "And if you want to give Tripp another chance, that is completely your choice. We stand by you no matter what."

I looked at Jaime. "Will you?"

"Of course I will." Her face softened, and she tipped her head onto my shoulder. "I'm sorry. You know I love you, Gogo. I just want you to be happy. If you think Tripp is the one, then go for it. I'll always be here for you."

"Thanks. I'm still thinking it over." I checked my phone and noticed the time. "Oh, shoot. I better get over to that thing for my father."

"A dinner thing?" Jaime picked up her drink.

"No, just drinks and dessert with some donors who've written fat checks to the campaign."

"How's the campaign going?" Claire asked.

"Fine, I think. I haven't been involved much since my politics are a bit different than my father's, but we don't talk about that."

Jaime shook her head. "God, I love your family. Have fun tonight. Will Tripp be there?"

I put a twenty on the bar and finished off my drink. "Not sure. But I know Deuce is a major donor, so it's possible. How do I look?"

They glanced at my sleeveless navy blue sheath, which I wore with nude heels and my favorite pearl necklace. My blowout was smooth, my nails were manicured, my legs were shaved. My lipstick would be reapplied in the car, since my grandmother had taught me never to apply cosmetics in public.

"Perfect," said Claire. "Very Grace Kelly."

Jaime nodded. "Classic Margot."

"Thanks. I'll see you tomorrow." After giving them each a kiss on the cheek, I walked out the back to the parking lot.

As I drove to the large private home on a gated street in Grosse Pointe where the fundraiser was being held, I had a strange feeling in my stomach. I can't say it was butterflies exactly, more like a gut instinct that something in my life was about to change. I get a similar feeling when I cut more than an inch off my hair at the salon, like I'm sort of scared but also sort of exhilarated.

After pulling into the drive and handing my keys to the valet—who gazed longingly at the pristine, powder blue 1972 Mercedes my grandmother had given me last year when she finally decided to stop driving—I entered the house.

The strange feeling intensified when I saw Tripp standing to my right in the cavernous living room. It was so large, even the nine foot Steinway in one corner didn't seem out of place. Sofas, chaises, and love seats were arranged in several conversational groupings, and the furniture, drapery, and even the rug had that faded, slightly shabby look that old money homes have. The look that says, *We're terribly wealthy but we don't get rid of anything with a day's use left in it, and we don't like things that are shiny and new.*

I saw my father shaking hands with someone near the fireplace and my mother nursing a G & T, probably her third, on one of the sofas, but I headed toward Tripp, doing my best to will that edgy feeling into butterflies. He was chatting with a group of women near the window, and they were clearly enthralled by whatever he was saying. As I got closer, he took a step back, and I saw that he wasn't alone. Amber was there too, wearing a dress that nearly fit, and she was holding out her left hand toward the little group, as if she were showing off a—

Oh no.

Oh no, he didn't.

He couldn't have.

He wouldn't even.

But he had.

And the ring on her finger was the exact same one Tripp had proposed to me with *last night*.

"It was, like, *so* romantic," she was gushing. "He came over in the middle of the night. Said he just couldn't wait any longer because he knew for sure I was the one."

I nearly gagged. Backing away unseen and shaking with rage, I found the bar and ordered a martini. (One good thing about people with old money, there's never a shortage of good gin.)

In a daze, I took my drink out onto the terrace, where my older brother, Buck, spotted me and roped me into schmoozing with a bunch of men in suits whose names I forgot immediately. All I could think of as I stood there, drinking and half-listening to them banter about politics and boats, was what an asshole Tripp was. *He must have gone right from me to her last night.* What the fuck was wrong with him?

Eventually the men wandered off to refill their scotch glasses, and Buck turned to me. "What's with you? You were totally mute during that conversation, and your expression makes Muffy's Resting Bitch Face look downright pleasant."

"Sorry. I was thinking about something."

He grinned cockily before tipping back his whiskey on the rocks. "Let me guess. Tripp's engagement? Don't let it bother you."

"Why not? It sort of makes a fool of me, doesn't it? Everyone knew we broke up because I wanted to get married and he didn't." I wasn't sure if I wanted to tell him about last night yet.

He took another swallow and shook his head. "He still doesn't. But Deuce changed the conditions of his inheritance because he's such a fuck-up with the gambling. He owes like three hundred grand or something. And if he wants the money, Deuce said he has to quit dicking around, get married and settle down."

My jaw dropped. Quit dicking around and get married? That sounded way too familiar. "You're kidding me."

"Nope. I heard it today from some guy who works for Deuce and heard *him* talking to the lawyers about it." He laughed. "What an asshole. You dodged a bullet, as far as I'm concerned." He clinked his glass to mine. "Cheers."

Fuming, I tipped back the rest of my drink. "Excuse me."

I set the empty martini glass on a passing server's tray and went directly to the bar to order another. Locking myself inside the first floor powder room, I took a gulp of my drink, set it down, and leaned on the marble vanity. I breathed heavily, staring at my reflection in the mirror. Scolding myself. Hating myself.

You fucking idiot! Of course he didn't want you! He told you last year he didn't! He just wanted his money and you were the ticket. You ridiculous, stupid, gullible woman, thinking of giving him another chance.

But I hadn't. Thank God I hadn't. Except now I was filled with gin and frustration and rage—with Tripp, with myself, and even with Amber, for being so blind to his deceit. For once, I wished I was the kind of person to unleash my feelings in public, to go out there and publicly shame him for what he'd done, call him out on his slimy desperation and his lies, expose him for what he was. I wished it so hard I was shaking.

But I couldn't.

That is, I couldn't until I discovered Tripp and Amber holding court in the dining room, regaling yet another crowd of bystanders with the romantic story of their surprise engagement.

"He didn't even want to get married before me," she bragged. "Did you, honey?"

"I sure didn't, baby doll."

Baby doll. What an asshole. I set my third empty glass down on the floor—at least, I think it was the floor. Levels of things were a bit hazy at this point.

"I guess it just took finding the perfect woman to make me change my mind." He gazed at Amber with wretchedly fake adoration. "And when you find her, you know."

Perfect woman. I think I snorted at that, because a few people turned around and looked at me. But I ignored them, looking over the desserts laid out on the table and sideboards, pretending to search for the perfect after-dinner treat.

"The ring's gorgeous," someone said.

"Isn't it?" Amber said delightedly. "He had it custom made for me."

Custom made for her. My hands started to shake as my eyes alighted on a silver tray of scones. I wrapped my fingers around one and eyeballed the possible trajectory.

"That's right." Tripp kissed the back of her hand. "Just for you."

A second later, I hurled the first scone, which missed its target—his smug face—and hit him in the chest.

Startled, he looked up just about the time the second scone pinged off the chandelier and landed at his feet. "What the hell?"

People started looking around, some getting out of the way. Good thing, because the third scone knocked a vase off the table, and it crashed to the floor at Tripp's feet.

He finally made eye contact with me. "Margot, what the hell are you doing?"

I wound up and launched another. "Three years!" I exploded as it beaned him on the forehead. *Finally!* I tried again, but that one curved toward Amber, who ducked out of the way. "*Three years* I put up with your boring golf stories and your pants with the little whales on them and your tiny clueless dick!"

A titter went through the crowd. Tripp was stunned motionless, and I took the opportunity to pelt his chest with another scone.

"Ouch!" he said, which I found hilarious. "Stop throwing things! And my dick isn't tiny! Or clueless!"

"Yes, it is!" I flung another one at him, but he was moving now, so I missed him completely and it bounced off the wall. "You don't know the first thing about a woman's orgasm! I used to have to get myself off after you took me home, asshole!"

I heard muffled laughter as I threw the next scone, which tipped over a skinny pillar candle that, unfortunately, happened to be lit. It burned a hole in the white tablecloth before someone nearby blew it out.

"Margot, have you lost your fucking mind?" Tripp yelled from across the table, hands in front of his face like I was throwing grenades, not scones.

"Maybe," I seethed, reaching for another one but feeling nothing but an empty tray. "Maybe I have, because I was going to tell you tonight that I'd decided to think about your shitty proposal."

Tripp's face went white.

"What proposal?" Amber asked, looking from him to me.

I opened my mouth. Watched him squirm. It felt fantastic.

"Margot, please. Don't do this." His eyes begged me for mercy. "You'll embarrass us both. Let's talk in private. I have a good reason for everything."

I had no desire to talk to him in private ever again, and I already knew about his fucked-up "good reason". But he was right—if I told the truth about last night, I'd be embarrassed too. I'd just announced that I'd come here willing to consider his proposal, which had been a sham anyway.

Glancing down, I spied the cherry pie, slipped my palm beneath it, and briefly considered one final, humiliating heave. Someone in the crowd gasped.

But I looked at Tripp again and felt a surge of power, which prompted a return of my self-control. My dignity. My manners.

I was Margot fucking Thurber Lewiston, and I had class. No one could take that away from me.

Gathering my tipsy wits, I assumed a cool expression and stood tall. "Actually, I never want to talk to you again. Enjoy your evening, everyone. Lewiston for Senate."

As I walked out, I heard him say. "Jesus. Crazy bitch."

I know what you're thinking.

I should have fucking thrown the pie.

chapter three

Jack

I couldn't sleep.
Not like it was a surprise. I didn't sleep well in general, but August was always the worst. I was lucky to get a couple hours a night.

"It's the heat," my sister-in-law Georgia had said last week. "Why don't you come sleep at our place for a few nights?"

"Better yet, put air conditioning in that old cabin," my younger brother Pete had put in. "Wouldn't cost much to get a window unit."

It wasn't the heat.

"Maybe it's the light," Georgia had said last year. "Maybe if you tried going to sleep with the light off, you'd relax more."

But I needed the light. Sometimes I felt like I couldn't even breathe until the sun came up.

I tried not to get mad when my family members told me what to do or tried to solve my problems with simple solutions when the real issue was something so complicated, they'd never understand. But I wasn't always good at thinking before speaking or controlling my temper.

Just yesterday I'd let loose on Pete for sneaking up on me from behind while I was repairing a fence along the property line in the woods. In hindsight, throwing him to the ground while screaming at him for being a "cocksucking motherfucking asshole with shit for brains" was probably a little out of line, but damn it—he knows better than to tap me on the shoulder when I don't know he's there. The whole reason I don't listen to music while I work is so that I can stay aware of my surroundings. I don't like to be taken by surprise.

The only person who ever understood that about me was Steph. A few years ago, my family planned a surprise party for my thirtieth birthday, probably because they knew I'd say fuck no to any kind of social event that required talking to people, and Steph made sure to tell me every detail ahead of time. She'd tried and tried to convince my brothers and parents it was a terrible idea, but they'd insisted that "getting out of the house" and "celebrating my life" would be good for me.

I only went because Steph begged me to. At first, I'd been furious and refused to consider it, but then she told me how my mother and aunt had flown up from Florida, and my sister-in-law had made cassata cake, and my niece Olivia had learned how to play "Happy Birthday" on the piano just for me. It was hard to resist Steph when she really had her heart set on something, plus she'd given me this really amazing blowjob in bed that morning.

She knew all my weaknesses.

Lying there in the dark, I twisted my wedding ring around my finger.

Three years.

It seemed impossible it had been that long. Her glasses were still on her nightstand, her clothes still in the closet, and I still expected her to be there when I rolled over in our squeaky-springed old bed wanting to tuck her little frame against mine.

And then, in other ways, it seemed like forever since I'd heard her singing in the shower, or watched her get ready for bed, or lost myself inside her body. She'd always made me go slow at first, claiming she was worried about my size, even after we'd been together for years. Probably she said that just to flatter me (it worked every time), although she'd been a tiny little thing, with curves in all the right places. I'd never minded the fifteen extra pounds she insisted she had to lose—in fact, I loved them, loved the way her body was soft and mine was hard, the way those curves felt beneath my hands and lips and tongue, the way she'd wrapped herself around me. It had felt so good to take care of her.

Fuck, I missed sex. I missed everything.

"You need to get out there again," said my oldest brother, Brad, because he knew everything. "Let me introduce you to April, the new realtor at the agency. She's hot, and I think you'd have a good time. Or at least get laid."

I told him to piss off.

"Come on, man," he'd said again last week as we jogged together down one of the dirt roads that bordered our forty-six acre farm. "It's been three years. You're not even trying to move on. When are you going to get over her?"

"Fuck you, Brad," I'd replied, taking off with long, fast strides that left him in the dust. Not trying to move on? Every fucking day I got through meant I was moving on. Every morning I got out of bed meant I was moving on. Every goddamn time I took another breath meant I was moving on.

And as for getting over her, it would never happen, so he could parade an endless supply of hot women in front of me, but it would just be a waste of time.

I'd already met the love of my life; I'd known her since we were kids.

I'd married her, and I'd lost her.

There was no reprieve from that. There was no redemption. There was no second chance.

I didn't even want one.

chapter four

Margot

"Are you sure you want to take this on right now?" Jaime reached across my desk and handed me the client file, her expression doubtful. I'd just volunteered to take over a new account that involved a few days of travel, a lot of research, and not much money. The client was a small family farm focused on sustainable agriculture. The perfect place to get the hell out of town and not bump into anyone I knew. "A farm doesn't really seem like your thing."

"Why not?" I asked, stuffing the file into my bag. "I used to ride horses, remember? I think I even have a pair of boots laying around."

"You kept your horse at a hunt club. This is a *farm*."

"How different can it be?" I flipped a hand in the air. "I'm sure I can handle a farm. And like I told you, Muffy says it's best if I leave town for a while anyway, at least until the gossip dies down."

"Until the gossip dies down?" Jaime grinned as she crossed her arms. "That's going to take a while, Sconewall Jackson."

She wasn't kidding. It had been almost a week, but Sconehenge was still a wildly popular tale among the country club set, who hadn't witnessed a good Scene in months. ("All this good behavior is so tiresome," my grandmother had complained at dinner last week.) The story had been embellished to include Tripp taking a scone right in the nuts (a change I liked) and Amber throwing a plate of beignets at my head (one I didn't). Scones were selling out at local bakeries, the shop that made the ones I threw started calling them Jilted Heiresses (I turned down the endorsement deal), and people were fond of quipping, "Revenge is just a scone's throw away" at cocktail parties all over town.

My mother was beside herself ("Really, Margot, who on earth is going to want to be seen with you now?") although my grandmother had cackled with glee when she heard the story. My father seemed rather confused by the whole affair, and Buck was only sorry he'd missed it.

But we'd agreed that after a sincere apology to Mrs. Biltmore (made the following day when I'd had to go back and pick up my Mercedes since I'd been too drunk to drive it home), I should probably make myself scarce for the rest of the summer. "Or at least until someone else behaves badly," Gran whispered. "I'll keep an eye out. Nobody pays any attention to old ladies, and we see everything."

"So tell me what you know about this client," I said to Jaime, packing up the rest of what I'd need from my office over the next two weeks. Valentini Brothers Farm was in the thumb area of Michigan, about two hours north of Detroit. I'd rented a little cottage on Lake Huron that was less than a mile from it, and I figured I'd use the time I wasn't working to relax in a beach chair, read a book, rethink a few things about the direction of my life.

"Not much," admitted Jaime, perching on my desk. "It's owned by three brothers. Quinn met one of the brothers, Pete, and his wife, Georgia, at a local farmers market and they got to talking. You know how Quinn is, he makes friends with everybody." She rolled her eyes, but I saw the blush in her cheeks, which always appeared when she talked about him. Jaime didn't like to believe she was a romantic, but she was head over heels for Quinn. "Anyway, the guy mentioned that they were struggling to grow their brand awareness and increase customer engagement—although he didn't put it like that—and Quinn, of course, was like, 'Oh, my girlfriend can help you. That's exactly what she does!' He gave them my card, and Georgia called me last week."

"But they know it's me coming and not you, right?" I stuck some pens and highlighters into my bag along with a stack of post-it notes.

"Yes. They were fine with that. I think they're just anxious to get some advice."

"Are they farmers too?" In my head I imagined a couple that looked like Auntie Em and Uncle Henry from the Wizard of Oz.

"No. I mean, I think Pete *does* work on the farm but there's another brother who runs things. Georgia and Pete are both chefs, actually." She cocked her head. "Or they were. But a lot of this I'm getting second-hand through Quinn, so you'll definitely want to read the New Client form they filled out, which I just emailed to you this afternoon. That has more info."

"Will do." I closed up my laptop and tucked it into the case, then switched off the lamp behind me. "I'll keep in touch with you while I'm there, and I'll definitely be calling to consult with you."

"Sounds good." She stood up, a mischievous grin on her face. "I'll be trying to picture you on a farm. Milking a cow. Riding a tractor. Maybe a cowboy."

Rolling my eyes, I breezed past her. "The only thing I'm interested in riding is maybe a horse. I have zero interest in tractors or cowboys."

"You never know," Jaime said following me out of my office. "Maybe a roll in the hay with a strapping young cowboy, all big burly muscles and country drawl, is just what you need to get out of that dry spell."

Halfway down the hall, I turned around and parked my hands on my hips. "I'm going up there to get a job done, Jaime. Then I'm going to hide out and just breathe for a while, and I don't need any man, muscled or otherwise, to help me do it."

She clucked her tongue, a glint in her eye. "You're a scone cold bitch, you know that?"

I turned for the door so she couldn't see the smile on my face.

※

I made it to Lexington shortly after seven that night, having made only one wrong turn on my way there, which I saw as a victory. Like all Thurber women before me, I have zero sense of direction. I seriously don't know how any of them got around before GPS. "It was called a chauffeur," says my grandmother.

The property manager had said to call her when I arrived and she'd come over with the key. While I waited for her, I wandered around the side of the quaint shingled cottage down to the beach. It was warm and windy, waves rolling in briskly over the rocky shoreline. Holding my hair off my face, I slipped off my sandals and wandered to the water's edge. The water felt icy cold on my bare feet.

I breathed in the damp air, smelling lake and seaweed and something being grilled nearby. My stomach growled. Had I eaten lunch? I couldn't even remember. But whatever that was smelled delicious.

"Hello?" called a voice behind me. "Ms. Lewiston?"

I turned and saw a stocky, middle-aged woman wearing a hat and sunglasses waving at me, keys dangling from her hand. Heading up the beach toward her, I decided I'd ask if there was a grill at the cottage. I'd never actually used one, but I was sure I could figure it out with a little help from Google. It was time to step out of my comfort zone, anyway.

Without throwing things.

※

The manager, Ann, gave me the key and showed me around the cottage—not that there was much to show. Bedroom and bathroom at the back, one big living room with a kitchen over to one side, and windows along the front with a view of the lake. But it was clean and bright, newly decorated with a beach theme, and almost had a little Cape Cod vibe to it. I felt at home there.

After settling in, I went to the little market I'd seen passing through town and picked up some groceries. There was indeed a small grill on the cottage's patio, but Ann said she had no idea if there were instructions anywhere. "But it's just a standard charcoal grill," she remarked, as if that made any sense to me. "There might even be some charcoal and lighter fluid in the utility closet."

Lighter fluid? Good God, for cooking? Sounds dangerous. I thanked her and said I'd look around, but figured I'd better stick to what I knew how to do in the kitchen, which was basically hit buttons on the microwave, boil water, and spread peanut butter and jelly on bread.

I ended up eating the prepared chicken salad I'd bought, but I did manage to cook some green beans, which I'd picked up on a whim because the sign said they were local, and they were delicious. Same with the peach I ate for dessert with some vanilla ice cream. I wondered if the vegetables or fruit—or even the chicken—had come from Valentini Brothers Farm, and thought how strange it was that I'd never, not once in my life, considered where the food on my plate had been grown.

But then, that would be part of my challenge, wouldn't it? To make people like myself more aware of where the foods I ate came from? Convince them it matters?

I thought about it as I ate, and then later I went through the file and learned as much as I could about the farm and the family that owned it. I read the New Client info sheet Jaime had forwarded, researched terms like "certified organic" and "sustainable agriculture," and googled Valentini Brothers Farm.

Right away, I saw problems.

They had no social media accounts, and the website definitely needed to be updated, if not completely redone. It was cluttered and outdated, difficult to navigate, and had minimal engaging content. Zero personality whatsoever.

But there *was* a family photo.

Zooming in, I studied each person and wondered who was who. The oldest brother was already losing some hair, but he was tall and handsome, in decent shape with only the beginnings of paunch around the middle. He had his hand on the shoulder of a gap-toothed girl who looked to be about seven or eight. Next to them was the couple I assumed Quinn had met at the farm stand, Pete and Georgia. He was definitely the shortest of the three brothers, but had an adorable smile and thick dark hair. His fair-skinned wife, the only blond in the picture, was pretty and slightly taller than he was. Both her hands rested on her huge, pregnant belly, and I wondered how old the baby was now. On the end was the third brother, the only member of the family who wasn't smiling. I zoomed in a little closer.

Well, damn. Maybe I would ride a cowboy.

He was tall, thick through the chest and trim at the waist. His jeans were tight, and because of the way he angled his body in the picture, almost like he was trying to back away from the camera, I could see the roundness of his butt. The sleeves of his plaid button-down were rolled up, revealing muscular forearms, and he had the same thick dark hair as the short brother, although he wore it slightly longer. His full mouth was framed by a good amount of stubble, and the set of his jaw was stubborn. Two vertical little frowny lines appeared between his brows. (Muffy would say he needed a "beauty treatment," which was code for any number of expensive things her dermatologist injected into her face every few months.)

Was he as sullen as he looked, or had the camera just caught him at a bad moment? Maybe the sun had been in his eyes or something.

Still thinking about his ass, I fell asleep to the sound of the waves and dreamt about picking lush, ripe peaches off a tree, biting into them with ravenous delight.

chapter five

Jack

"WAIT A MINUTE. STOP RIGHT THERE." My brothers and I were sitting at Pete and Georgia's kitchen table going over expenses, when Pete said something about a marketing budget. "Why the hell do we need a marketing budget?"

"Well, for one thing, the PR consultant is coming tomorrow, and I'm pretty sure she expects to be paid for her time," Brad said.

I stared at both of them. "What PR consultant?"

"The one we hired last week to help us promote what we're doing," said Pete. "And can you please keep your voice down? Cooper is finally quiet."

"I have no idea what you're talking about," I snapped, although I tried to lower my voice. My one-year-old nephew, Cooper, had a hard time falling asleep on the nights when Georgia worked. I adored him—and I sympathized. "I never agreed to any fucking consultant."

"That's correct, you didn't." Brad was maddeningly calm. "But we outvoted you. The three of us own this business together, and we each have an equal say in how it's run."

"So you didn't even tell me you went ahead with it?" I was yelling again, but I couldn't fucking help it. I hated it when they sprung shit on me.

"Hey, it was *you* that stormed out after you didn't get your way," Pete said. "We sat here and discussed it for a while. And we decided that it would be worth the added expense to hire someone to help us promote."

I crossed my arms. "We can't afford it."

"We can't afford to do nothing, either," Brad said. "Dad was a good farmer with ideas ahead of his time, but he was a terrible businessman, so we inherited a huge amount of debt when we took over. Then we had to buy Mom out when she moved to Florida."

"I'm not a fucking idiot," I snapped. "I know all this."

"We also have families and our own bills to pay."

They had families. I didn't, and the reminder didn't help. "Hey, it's not my problem you've got an ex-wife who sued for alimony. Maybe you should have thought of that before you fucked around."

"Hey." A warning note from Pete. "Don't be a dick about this. We're doing good things here, Jack, but organic farming isn't cheap. And what good will our principles and hard work do us if we can't keep the lights on?"

"And competition is stronger now," said Brad. "The market is getting saturated. We need to do what we can to stand out."

I sank deeper into my chair, a scowl on my face. I didn't need any reminders about competition or market saturation or debt or mortgages or anything else on the list of Reasons Why Farmers Have the Highest Suicide Rate of Any Profession.

Pete put a hand on his chest. "Listen. I'm a chef, not a businessman, Jack. You're an ex-Army Sergeant with farming in your blood and a commitment to doing it responsibly. But if we want to keep this place going, we've got to start thinking of it as a business too." His voice softened. "I know it was always a dream of yours and Steph's. But it's more than a dream now, Jack. It's reality. For *all* of us. And if you want to keep it, we have to invest in it."

"Look, we know you," Brad said. "We are well aware that you prefer to keep to yourself and do things on your own, your way. And we've let you make every major decision so far, supported your vision even though we knew how expensive it was going to be. Fuck, I was ready to sell this entire place when that soybean guy expressed interest. I never wanted to be a farmer."

"Me neither," said Pete. "I saw the ups and downs Mom and Dad dealt with year after year and wanted something more stable for my family. But you had a vision, a good one. It was enough to convince me to move back and help out. And we have history here. We want this place to thrive. That won't happen unless people know about it."

From the monitor on the counter came the sound of Cooper crying, and Pete sighed. "Dammit." He started to get up, but I stood faster.

"It's my fault. Let me." Grateful for a break from the discussion, I switched off the monitor on the kitchen counter and headed up to Cooper's bedroom. My bad mood lifted as soon as I saw him, and I scooped him up from his crib. "Hey, buddy."

He continued to cry as I reached into the crib for the soft little blanket I'd given to him when he was born. It was about six inches square, pale blue, and it had a bunny head on one corner. "Bunny" was one of the only words Cooper said, and he was rarely without it in his little grasp.

I spread Bunny over my shoulder and cuddled Cooper close, and he rested his cheek on the blanket, stuck his thumb in his mouth, and quieted down. Lowering myself into the rocker in his room, I held his warm little body against mine, rubbed his back, and hummed softly. He was a little restless at first, but after a few minutes, I felt his body relax as his breathing became slower and deeper. I kissed his soft brown curls and inhaled the sweet scent of baby shampoo, torn between feeling lucky to be an uncle and heartbroken I'd never be a father.

I'd been close to my own, and his death had been tough.

It had happened suddenly, not even six months after I'd left the Army. I'd been a fucking mess at the time, still struggling to process the things I'd seen and done after deployments to Iraq and Afghanistan. Still trying to fit in again at home when all I wanted to do was isolate myself. Still feeling so on edge that every time I saw so much as a plastic bag in the road, I panicked. I was drinking too much, lost my temper too easily, battled nightmares and constant anxiety. Then in the middle of that, my father had a heart attack.

I'd felt powerless. And I'd wanted to give up.

It was Steph who pulled me back from the edge. God knows why, since I was an emotional fuck-up, and I'd never treated her right when we were young. She'd always been there for me, though, claimed she'd loved me since she was six years old and wasn't about to stop now just because I was going through something. "I'm not letting you wreck yourself, Jack Valentini," she'd said in her toughest voice, all five foot two inches of her. "You promised me you'd come back, and you did. I promised you I'd be here, and I am." Her voice had softened. "Stay with me."

With her support, I saw a doctor about my sleeping problems, a therapist for my PTSD, and stopped abusing alcohol. I thought more about what I was putting in my body and read up on the benefits of organic foods—both eating them and growing them. I remembered my father's beliefs about responsible farming, and researched modern approaches to small-scale, sustainable agriculture. It gave me a purpose. It felt like a way to honor my dad, and I felt a connection to nature that I didn't feel with people.

It took a while, but I got better. Not cured, but better. And Steph was there for me the whole way.

We got married the following year and worked our asses off on the farm, with a plan in place to buy out my brothers within five years.

Less than two years later, she was gone.

God, I fucking miss you, Steph. You should be here with me. I always felt better with you by my side.

Now I'd be stuck with some stranger here telling me what to do, butting in, wanting to make changes so we could *stand out*. She'd probably cook up some bullshit publicity stunt and expect me to participate. Well, I didn't want to stand out. I just wanted to do what I did and lead a quiet life. And it wasn't like we were poor. We weren't rich, but we were doing OK. Certainly better than our parents had done. Frowning, I rose to my feet and carefully laid Cooper on his belly in his crib. Kissing my fingertips, I touched his forehead one last time and slipped out of the room.

"He asleep?" Pete looked at me hopefully when I entered the kitchen.

"Yes." I switched the monitor back on.

"Thanks. You're so good with him."

I shrugged, although secretly it pleased me I was good with Cooper. I was crap with the adults in my family. What did that say about me?

"Did you have a chance to think about what we said?" Brad asked.

I remained standing, hands shoved in my pockets. "I just don't think it's necessary, and I bet it's expensive. What the hell will some city girl know about how to help us here anyway?"

"Maybe nothing," Pete admitted. "But we're going to find out. She'll be here tomorrow at one for a lunch meeting. You coming?"

I scowled. I didn't want to go to their damn meeting, because that would imply giving in, but if I skipped it, I might end up with no say whatsoever, and no clue what they agreed to do or how much they offered to pay her. Which was worse?

I'd decide tomorrow, but I didn't want to show any chinks in the armor. "Whatever. You guys can deal with her. I want nothing to do with this." I strode angrily through the kitchen and out the back door, but I was careful not to let it slam so that it wouldn't wake Cooper.

The sun was setting behind the trees as I walked across the yard. I lived in an old hunting cabin tucked into the woods, which suited me perfectly. It had been on the property when my grandparents bought the land, and my parents had lived in it when they first got married; after that they'd used it as a guest house. When I'd moved back, its privacy and simplicity appealed to me, and I'd asked if I could live there and pay rent.

I'd made some structural improvements, and when Steph moved in, she spent every spare moment making it beautiful—paint and pillows and pictures in frames. Our little hideaway from the world, she called it. Not that she ever wanted to hide away, social butterfly that she was, but she knew I sometimes needed to, and that was OK with her. She never tried to make me into someone I wasn't, unlike the rest of my family.

As soon as I let myself into the cabin, Steph's cat leaped down from the windowsill and twined around my feet. "Hi, Bridget. You happy to see me?" The moment I knelt down and pet her, I felt my anger abate somewhat. I'd always been a dog person, but Steph had been allergic to them. When she came home with a kitten a few months after we were married, I'd groaned, but damn if that cat hadn't grown on me. Whenever I had nightmares, she'd jump up on the bed and crawl over me, purring softly. It reminded me of the way Steph used to whisper to me during those long, arduous, sweat-soaked nights, her hands rubbing slow, soothing circles on my back.

When Bridget had gotten enough attention, she wandered into the kitchen, and I looked around, hoping to see something left undone, some task to distract me from going to bed.

But there was nothing. I always did the dishes right after I ate, and I never let laundry pile up. I'd just cleaned the bathroom two days ago, and I'd washed the kitchen floor over the weekend. The shelves were organized, the furniture dusted, the windowpanes clear. Georgia was always amazed at how clean I kept the cabin. "Your brother could take some lessons from you," she'd say. "He's such a slob."

There was only one chore I refused to do, and that was cleaning Steph's clothing out of the closet. Georgia had offered to do it. Steph's sister Suzanne had offered to do it. Even my mother had said she'd be glad to fly up if I wanted someone else to take care of her things.

But I always said no. What would be the point? To make it easier on myself to live there without her? I didn't want it to be easier. And if my family couldn't understand that, well fuck them.

It was *my* pain. I'd earned it.

I guarded it closely.

chapter six

Margot

I KNOCKED ON THE WOODEN SCREEN DOOR OF PETE AND GEORGIA VALENTINI'S picturesque white farmhouse at one in the afternoon for our business lunch. While I waited on the porch, I looked around. The house sat about a hundred feet back from the highway, on the west side but facing east toward the lake, and although I'd driven, I could easily have walked. The house itself appeared old but well-maintained—fresh white paint on the exterior, hanging baskets of flowers on the porch, comfy chairs on both sides of the center entrance.

To the left of the house were some birch trees, a baby swing, and some other toys scattered on the lawn. A giant red barn sat just beyond the trees, and another white one behind that. To the right of the house was a garage, and on the other side of that were smaller trees planted in neat rows. Apple, maybe? Beyond those was a dirt road, and just across it sat a massive old Victorian, abandoned by the looks of the peeling paint and overgrown gardens.

I was about to knock again when the blond woman I'd seen in the picture answered the door, a pudgy little boy on her hip. Her hair was much shorter, about chin-length, and her body much slimmer. "Hi. Georgia?"

She greeted me with a smile. "You must be Margot. Come on in."

I entered the front hall and held out my hand. "Margot Lewiston."

After giving it a firm shake, she shut the door and switched her son to her other hip. "Georgia Valentini. And this is Cooper. I'm just about to put him down for a nap."

I smiled at the chubby-cheeked boy. "Sweet dreams, Cooper."

"Go on back to the kitchen," Georgia said, gesturing down the hall. "Pete's just making us some lunch. Have you eaten?"

"No, actually. Not even breakfast."

"Perfect. I'll join you in five minutes." She headed up the creaky stairs behind her and I walked back to the kitchen, where Pete stood at the counter, wearing an apron and slicing tomatoes at an alarming speed.

"Hi there." I smiled when he looked up. "I'm Margot. Your wife said to come on back."

"Of course. Welcome." He set down the knife, wiped his hands on a towel, and came around the counter to shake my hand. "Pete Valentini, nice to meet you. Have a seat."

"Thanks." I slid onto one of the stools at the counter and looked around. "Nice big kitchen. Was this original to the house?"

Pete shook his head and returned to his vegetable platter. "No, my parents added this part about twenty years ago. And as you can see, it hasn't been touched since."

I laughed. "It's not so bad." The decor was a little dated, but I was used to houses where nothing changed for long periods of time. "When was the house built?"

"It's about a hundred years old. How was your drive up?"

"Not bad at all. Less than two hours."

"And you're staying nearby?"

"Right across the street and down a couple blocks toward the lake. I got lucky. Someone had booked the cottage for the entire month of August and ended up canceling at the last minute."

"That *is* lucky. This is our high season up here."

I admired the confident way he moved around the kitchen. "Did I hear that both you and Georgia were chefs?"

"We were when we met in New York, but right now Georgia is managing a restaurant in town and I'm only cooking there two days a week because of the work here at the farm, plus taking care of Cooper. When we moved here three years ago, we were hoping to start a farm-to-table restaurant, but…" He sighed as Georgia came into the kitchen. "We haven't gotten there yet."

"We'll get there, babe," she said. "One thing at a time."

I liked the way she smiled at him, which seemed to communicate more than just words.

While Georgia set the kitchen table, we chatted a little about the area, what shops and restaurants they recommended, and how they'd met Quinn. We were joined shortly by the oldest Valentini brother, Brad, who greeted me kindly but seemed more businesslike than his younger brother and sister-in-law. He wore a suit whereas they were both dressed in jeans and t-shirts. I kept glancing at the back door, wondering when the third brother was going to make an appearance, but he still hadn't shown up when Pete suggested we sit down to eat.

"Should we wait for Jack?" Georgia asked, glancing out the window toward the backyard.

Pete and Brad exchanged a look, and neither of them spoke right away. "I'm not sure he's coming," Pete finally said.

"And I have showings this afternoon, so it's better for me if we don't wait around." Brad took off his jacket and hung it on the back of a chair before sitting down.

"Oh. OK." Looking slightly defeated for a second, Georgia indicated a chair for me and filled four plates with slices of quiche and bacon and fresh vegetables. "Everything on the plate in front of you is from this farm," she said proudly. "Eggs from our chickens, bacon from our pigs, veggies from the gardens."

"Wow." I smiled as I unfolded my napkin and laid it across my lap. "That's really—"

Bang!

The sound of the kitchen door slamming shut made me jump. I glanced up, and there he was. Jack Valentini. He appeared even taller and more imposing than he had in the photograph online. Maybe it was because I was sitting. Maybe it was the sweaty t-shirt that said ARMY (was he a Veteran?), which hugged his narrow waist, broad chest, and bulging biceps. Or maybe it was his stance—feet apart, chest out, fists clenched at his sides. If I didn't know better, I'd have sworn he came here looking for a fight.

And from the way he was eyeballing me, I had a pretty good idea who the opponent might be. (Had I known, I'd have brought a tray of scones.)

"Jack, glad you could make it," said Georgia brightly. "Come sit down, I'll get you a plate."

"I'm not staying."

"At least say hello to Margot Lewiston." Pete tried hard to sound casual, but I could sense the tension. "She's the woman we talked about last night."

"I figured." Jack stared at me, crossed his arms over his bulky chest, but offered no hello. His expression was shadowed by the brim of a black cap, but the clenched jaw was plainly visible.

Was he an asshole or was he just having a bad day? *Either way, he's a client.* Rising to my feet, I turned on the charm, flipped my hand in a little wave. "It's nice to meet you. I'm looking forward to working with your family. You've got a beautiful place."

"I was just telling Margot that everything on her plate was grown or raised right here," Georgia said, obviously trying to engage him.

I smiled at him. "That's so impressive. I was thinking as I ate dinner last night that it's never even occurred to me at a restaurant or in the grocery store to wonder about where or how my food was grown."

"You're not alone in that," said Pete, pouring four glasses of wine. "But I think if more people knew about the hazards of large-scale industrial agriculture—to humans, to animals, to the environment—they'd definitely care more about where their food comes from."

"And the food they feed their children," added Georgia as she seated herself next to me. "Jack's taught me so much about the harmful effects of things like pesticides, antibiotics, food additives."

A plaintive cry from the monitor on the counter made everyone look in that direction. Georgia sighed and stood up again. "I knew it was too good to be true when he barely fussed. I'll be right back."

"I'll do it." Jack flipped a switch on the monitor and took off toward the now-distant sound of the crying child. As he passed me, our eyes met. He immediately looked away, but not before I saw up close how handsome he was—or would be if he took the scowl off his face. It left me a little breathless, and I needed a moment to regain my composure.

"Works for me." Georgia sat down and picked up her fork. "Jack's so good with Cooper, especially when it comes to getting him to sleep."

"We have no idea what he does up there." Pete laughed. "I think he drugs him."

"Oh, hush," Georgia said. "He's just gentle and patient. He sings to him."

He sings to him? I couldn't picture it. "Does Jack have kids?" I glanced in the direction of the stairs, curious about the handsome, broody farmer who appeared to have a soft side.

"No." Something in Georgia's voice made me pause. It was a one-word answer, but I felt like there was a story there somehow.

"Come on, let's eat," Brad said impatiently.

We dug in, and a few minutes later, Jack returned, heading through the kitchen toward the back door without stopping. I didn't miss the glance he sent in my direction, though. It made my heart beat a tiny bit faster.

Georgia spoke up. "Why don't you sit with us for just a minute?"

"Because I'm busy," he snapped, his hand on the door handle. "I'm the only one working out there today."

"We're working in here, too, Jack," Brad said.

Jack made a noise, something between a snort and a grunt. "I told you last night I don't want anything to do with this." And by *this*, it was clear he meant *me*, since he looked at me right as he said it. I felt it like a slap in the face, and my cheeks burned.

"Then go on back out." Brad's tone was sharp.

"Gladly." Jack was through the door without another word, and as soon as it slammed behind him, Pete sighed.

"Sorry about that. Jack has…some issues."

I was still reeling, but I tried to find my balance. "I think I can guess what one of them is. He doesn't want to hire me?"

"It's not you," Georgia said quickly. "Jack's just really protective of the farm. He gets prickly when he thinks people are going to tell him what to do."

"Especially if those people are not from around here, I bet." I understood his reluctance to take advice from an outsider, but it didn't excuse his rudeness. *What a waste of a handsome face.*

"Jack doesn't understand that we're not just running a farm, we're running a business," said Brad with more than a trace of annoyance. "And a business needs marketing."

"We don't have a lot of extra money." Pete met my eyes with genuine concern. "But if you think you can help us, we'll find a way to pay for it. Jack would be content to work in the dirt, tend to the animals, and never talk to anyone, but Georgia and I have dreams of our own."

"The farm-to-table restaurant." I smiled at him, vowing to put Jack out of my head. This was my favorite part about what I did—helping people grow their businesses and achieve their goals. And I could help this family, I was sure of it. *Or at least those members who want my help.* "I want to hear about it. And I'm positive we can work something out that fits your budget. Although before we get to that, I'd like to learn more about you, your family, the history here, what your hopes are for the future. That will help me a lot."

I savored every bite of lunch as the three of them told me about how they'd come to own the farm. It was clear that Brad was the least enthusiastic about it but willing to give his brothers a chance to succeed. He mentioned that he hoped they'd be able to buy him out eventually.

"The plan was five years, but after Steph died, no one wanted to hound Jack about it."

For the first time, there was an awkward silence at the table.

"Who was Steph?" I asked.

"Jack's wife." Georgia's voice was so hushed I could hear the tick of a clock on the wall behind me. "She died three years ago."

My breath caught. "How?"

"She was hit by a car. Drunk driver."

"Oh my God. That's awful." Some of my antipathy for him let up.

Brad cleared his throat. "We've been patient with him. And as you'll see, he needs it. Don't take it to heart if he's short with you, or silent altogether at first. But Jack's not dumb. He knows if he wants to keep his farm, he's going to have to take some advice. He just doesn't like it."

I nodded, hoping I was up to this challenge, wanting to prove myself. "Well, I'm going to do my best. Let me ask you some questions and jot some things down."

As I reached into my bag for my notebook, Georgia stood and began stacking plates. "I'll get this stuff out of the way, and then I'll join you."

"Sounds good. Thank you so much for lunch. It was delicious, and I loved hearing about this place. I'm excited to get started." I uncapped my pen. "Let's talk about your brand."

"What brand?" Pete blinked at me.

I smiled. "Exactly."

༄

Later, Georgia walked me out to my car. "Thanks for coming up here," she said. "We really appreciate it."

"My pleasure. You have a gorgeous setting, and I'm looking forward to seeing more of it. Learning more about it. Think I could maybe get a tour of the entire place?"

"Of course. Pete could show you around tomorrow." She frowned. "Jack would be even better, but…" A sigh escaped her. "He can be so difficult."

"That's OK." I didn't want to stir up any more trouble where the middle Valentini brother was concerned. He wasn't happy about my being here to begin with—he certainly wouldn't want to take time out of his work day to show me around.

Georgia shook her head. "It's not. I'm sorry he was rude today. He's such a sweet guy underneath, but he hides it. The last few years have been so rough on him."

Since it was just us women and I was curious, I decided to ask more about him. "I noticed he wore an Army shirt. Is he in the military?"

"He was," she said, tucking her blond bob behind her ears. "He's been out about six years. But he served in Iraq and Afghanistan, and when he got back, he—" She grappled for words. "Well, it was hard for him to adjust."

"Hard how?"

"He had a lot of anxiety. My dad was in the Army too, served in Vietnam when he was really young. It affected him his whole life. Sometimes Jack reminds me of my dad." Her voice was wistful. "Moody, sullen, defensive. It's hard for them to connect with people. And they keep their feelings locked up inside. My dad had my mom, at least, but Jack has no one, and his brothers can be hard on him. They don't understand. So I try really hard to be someone he can turn to."

Something squeezed my heart. "How sad that he lost his wife."

"Devastating. They were so in love. But anyway." She waved a hand in the air. "That doesn't give him the right to be mean to you."

"No, but at least I can better understand where he's coming from. Thanks for telling me. I'll keep it confidential."

She smiled. "Thanks."

We said goodbye, and I told her I'd be in touch tomorrow.

As I drove the short distance back to the cottage, I thought about what she'd said. *They were so in love.* What was that like? Tripp and I had been together for three years, but never once had I felt "so in love" with him, nor could I imagine him thinking that way about me. "So in love" sounded so passionate. And it must have been visible to other people. *Maybe they couldn't keep their hands off each other.*

For a moment, I let myself wonder what Jack was like in bed. Rough or sweet? Selfish or generous? Fast or slow? That hard, muscular body…what would it look like naked? What would it be like to feel his weight on me? Was he a good kisser? Did he use his hands? Did he have a big dick?

My stomach whooshed, and suddenly I realized I'd gone from imagining Jack with his wife to picturing him with *me*. What the hell was wrong with me? The man hadn't even offered me a smile today! In fact, he'd been downright rude! Muscles were nice, but manners were better, and Jack's were sorely lacking.

Still, what Georgia had told me about him made me think there was more to him than boorish bluster.

Someone who'd loved like that had to have a big heart, even if it was buried beneath prickly layers of grief and bitterness.

I'd give him another chance.

chapter seven

Jack

I STAYED AWAY FROM THE HOUSE ALL AFTERNOON, EVEN THOUGH IT DROVE ME CRAZY to think that they were in there talking about *my* farm, making plans that would affect its well-being. Plans that would affect me. Sure, I technically owned only one third of it, but neither of my brothers had invested their heart and soul here like I had. Pete just cared about his restaurant idea, and Brad would be happy to chop the land into bits and sell it.

So go in there and stand up for yourself. Put your boot down. Say no.

But I couldn't do that. It was two against one, and I wouldn't win.

And now they had that fucking Barbie on their side too. How the hell could they think that woman knew anything about farming? She looked like she wouldn't know the difference between a cock and a hen. Maybe I'd ask her.

The thought actually made me crack a smile as I left the barn after checking on one of the older horses who seemed to be struggling with the heat more than the others. *You ever seen a cock before, Barbie?*

I chuckled as I imagined the expression on her face. Her cheeks going pink. Her eyes going wide. She had pretty eyes, I'd give her that. Huge and bright blue. A pretty smile, too.

But she wasn't my type. I liked natural. Down to earth. No makeup. Steph had lived in jeans and boots, her nose freckled in the sun, and I don't even think she owned a hair dryer. She always let her dark, curly hair dry on its own.

Barbie had been wearing some kind of business suit, probably with high heels. Her skin looked like she never left the house, and her lips had been artificially pink. Her hair was nice, though, smooth and gold and shiny. What would it feel like slipping through my fingers? Wrapped around my fist? Brushing over my bare chest?

When my dick answered the question by twitching in my pants, I forced myself to quit thinking about her and move on to the next task.

She was nothing to me.

༺༻

Around five, Pete came out to the little greenhouse I'd built with our dad and found me prepping some kale seedlings for planting. I needed to rotate some beds this weekend.

"Hey. Want help?"

"I'm about done in here. But I could use help repairing some fence along the western property line if you have time."

"I do."

We took a four-wheeler and drove in silence, me dying to know what had been discussed at the meeting but too stubborn to ask, Pete probably trying to figure out how to broach the subject without my taking his head off. I caved first.

"How'd it go with Marketing Barbie?"

Pete sighed. "She's very nice, Jack. And she's smart too. I think she's going to help us a lot."

"For how much? Did you see what she drives? A classic Mercedes in mint condition. Do you have any idea what those cost?"

"No."

"Me neither. But I bet it's a fuck ton of money."

"You know, you don't have to be such an asshole about this. No one is conspiring against you or wants to take anything away from you."

"What the fuck would they take, anyway? Like you said, I don't own this farm, I don't own my house, I don't even have a family." I threw his words back at him as I pulled up at the fence that needed work and parked.

Pete stared at me for a few seconds, then shook his head. "I refuse to argue with you anymore. And I'm done trying to bring you in on this. You want to know what her ideas are, you can ask her."

"I don't," I lied.

"Fine." He jumped to the ground. "Let's just get this done."

⁂

I finished working for the day, cleaned up, and made myself some dinner. But I felt so tense sitting around the cabin by myself that I decided to go into town and grab a beer. I chose a little pub called The Anchor, sat at the end of the bar, and hoped I wouldn't see anybody I knew. Nothing worse than wanting to nurse a beer and some self-loathing and being constantly interrupted by people who wanted to chat. They'd ask how I was doing with that sympathetic look in their eye, but they didn't want the truth. They wanted to hear I was doing fine and then move on to small-town gossip, or better yet, get some to spread.

It was Friday night and the place was busy, but thankfully the last couple seats at the end of the bar were free, and the baseball game was on the TV right above them. I sipped my beer and tried to appear like I was really into the Tigers so no one would take the stool next to me and try to talk. My plan worked for about ten minutes.

"Excuse me. Jack Valentini, right?"

I looked over my shoulder, and there she was. Up close, she was even prettier than she'd looked across the kitchen, which did nothing to help my mood. "Yeah?"

She smiled, revealing perfectly straight white teeth between those painted lips. "I thought that was you." She held out a hand. "I'm Margot Lewiston. From Shine PR? We met today at Pete and Georgia's?"

I didn't want to touch her, but I saw no way to get out of it. I slipped my hand into hers. Her fingers were pale and slender, and mine wrapped around them easily. Our eyes met, and something strange happened in my chest—a hitch. I pulled my hand away. *What the hell?* Directing my attention back to the screen, I hoped she'd take the hint and leave me alone.

Nope.

"Is this seat taken? I'm dying for a cold drink." Without waiting for me to answer, she slid onto it.

Out of the corner of my eye, I saw those legs extending from short shorts and ending at sandals with straps that twined up her legs like vines. I shifted nervously in my seat as the bartender approached her with a smile.

"Hi, what kind of gin do you have?" she asked. He rattled off some names, which she apparently did not find up to her standards. "Hm. How about a wine list?" He handed her one, and she looked it over briefly before sliding it toward me. "Any recommendations? I see they have some local wine. Should I try one?"

"Get whatever you want." I tried not to look at her as she leaned toward me. Jesus, I could smell her perfume—something floral and summery and sexy and probably hundreds of dollars a fucking ounce. I held my breath.

She looked up at me a moment and then settled back on her stool. I exhaled.

"I can make a recommendation if you like," offered the bartender, fucking college-age sap who probably thought he could get in her pants tonight if he poured her the right Riesling.

"That would be lovely," she said, handing the menu back to him.

A few minutes later, she was sipping on a glass of local Pinot Noir, and I quickly finished my beer, feeling like I should get out of her presence sooner rather than later. Something about her made me uncomfortable. Well, not *her* exactly, but my body's reaction to her.

"You don't want me here, do you, Jack?" she said after I'd put a twenty on the bar.

"It's not that. I'm just done with my beer. I'm ready to go." I braved a glance at her.

"I don't mean here in this bar, I mean here in this town. At the farm. Working for your family." She smiled tightly. "It's pretty obvious. No use denying it."

I frowned as I pocketed the change and left a tip. "Look, it's not personal. I just don't think we need to spend money on publicity. There's plenty of real things we need."

"But publicity *is* a real need." She shook her head. "What good will all your investment do if you don't get the word out about your farm? The food you grow? The animals you raise? The benefits of eating and buying local from small, sustainable farms like yours? I spent the entire afternoon researching your practices, the costs and the benefits, the hazards of industrial farming. People don't know about this stuff, Jack. You can help teach them."

I opened my mouth to speak, but she cut me off, a hand in the air.

"Don't tell me. You don't want to be a teacher. OK, fine. So you let me do it." She touched her chest right below the pearl necklace she wore. (My mind immediately took an unauthorized detour.) "Or you let me map out the strategies for you, and family members can do it. Bottom line is, your brothers are right. Just from the initial research I've done so far, competition is only getting tougher and you need to set yourself apart."

"And do what?" I crossed my arms over my chest, which seemed to distract her for a moment. She stared at it for a solid five seconds, her cheeks coloring slightly, before she answered, looking me in the eye again.

"What about agritourism? Have you ever considered that?"

"You mean whoring out my farm so people can traipse all over it and complain about the high price of my funny-looking tomatoes when the ones at Meijer are a lot cheaper and prettier? *No*."

"It's one of the fastest-growing segments of the travel industry!" she went on, as if I hadn't spoken at all. She was tenacious, I'd give her that. "An opportunity not only to educate and increase profits but also to offer an *experience*. There's an entire generation of young people—which, by the way, is the most likely to be concerned about their food and more willing to pay more to get healthier options—who value *experiences* over things."

"What do you mean?" I asked, confused.

"I mean they prize *doing* things—and showing off pictures of themselves doing things—more than cars or jewelry or electronics. And they're willing to pay to do them. So they come to the farm, have whatever amazing and authentic and delicious experiences we come up with, and then they post pictures of themselves on social media with a bunch of fun hashtags that make all their friends and followers go, 'Hey! I want to do that or make that or eat that or buy that' or whatever. Then they're doing the PR work for you. For free!" Her smile lit up her face. "Doesn't that sound good?"

Good? The last thing on earth I wanted was a bunch of people at my farm looking for me to provide them with entertainment. Fuck that. Not that I'd have a choice—I could just see Brad and Pete and Georgia getting all turned on by this idea. It was enough to make me pissed and resentful again, plus I could still smell her, I couldn't stop looking at that pearl necklace at her throat, and every time our eyes met, my stomach tightened. I needed to leave.

"No. It sounds like a fucking nightmare. I gotta go." Ignoring the twinge in my gut when I saw the way her face fell, I strode down the bar and out the door.

I wanted her out of my sight.

chapter eight

Margot

"So how's it going?" Jaime asked. I'd called her on the walk home.

"It's going well, I think. I met the clients today and they were very nice—well, most of them were."

"Uh oh. Someone's not nice?"

"Not to me, anyway. It's the middle brother, Jack." I pictured him sitting next to me at the bar and my heart pumped a little faster. He filled out a t-shirt like nobody's business. Had he noticed the way I'd stared at his chest? I liked his eyes, too. They were dark but had flecks of gold in them. And I hadn't missed the way he'd looked at my legs, the care he took not to get too close, the spark when he took my hand. *Something* was there. Why'd he have to be such a jerk?

"Is that the hot one? I saw the family picture."

I bit my lip. "You think he's hot?"

"Yeah. Don't you?"

"I guess so," I said cautiously, then quickly followed it up with, "but he's not my type at all."

"Why not?"

"Uh, besides the fact that he's a scruffy, sweaty farmer who needs a haircut, he's stubborn, grouchy, and ill-mannered." Truthfully, I hadn't minded his hair, his scruff, or his sweat earlier in the day. And tonight, he'd been cleaned up, combed and trimmed and smelling faintly like a beach bonfire. I kept wanting to lean over and sniff him.

Jaime laughed. "What's he grouchy about?"

As I walked, I described my meeting with the family and what they'd told me about Jack. When I got to the part about his wife, she gasped.

"Oh my God, how?"

"Drunk driving accident."

"That's so sad!"

"Isn't it? He still wears his wedding ring." I'd noticed it right away tonight. "Georgia said they were so in love."

"God, that sucks. Poor guy. This is why people shouldn't get married. Bad things happen."

I had to smile. "Is Quinn hinting around about proposing again?"

"Yes. God, if he really does it, I'll fucking kill him."

"Don't be ridiculous. You guys are madly in love, you've been together for a year and a half, and you've lived together for months. Why not get married?"

"Because we're happy!" she exploded, as if that explained it all. "Why fuck with that?"

Sighing, I glanced around. Had the walk to the bar taken me this long? "OK, whatever. Don't get married. I think I'm lost."

"Lost where?"

I stopped walking and turned a full circle, positive I hadn't seen that park on the corner before. Nothing creepier than a playground in the dark. "Lost walking from town back to my cottage. What the heck, there weren't even that many turns."

Jaime laughed. "Hang up with me and use Google Maps or something. Then text me when you get there so I don't worry about you wandering alone in the dark somewhere."

"OK."

"And then call me tomorrow so we can talk more about what you're thinking for strategy."

"I will. I want to do some more research and brainstorming, but I have a few thoughts. Their budget isn't much."

She sighed. "I figured."

"But that's OK. You know what? I really want to help them. I'd do it for free."

"You need to stop doing things for free," Jaime scolded. "You're not working for Daddy anymore. You're a grown woman with her own company."

"And her own trust fund." I laughed a little. "I don't mind doing things for a good cause, and I like their cause. Plus it's not only for them, it's for the community and the economy and the common good! Did you know there's such a thing as food insecurity?"

"What the hell is that? Tomatoes with trust issues?"

"Lack of access to adequate, nutritious, affordable food. And it's not only in urban areas, it's in rural areas too. People who live surrounded by farms might never eat what's grown and harvested right in their backyard! We export what we grow and import what we eat. It's crazy!"

She laughed. "*You're* starting to sound a little crazy."

"Sorry. I got sidetracked today by poverty statistics when I was researching sustainable agriculture and food justice."

"Food justice?"

"The right of communities to grow, sell, and eat healthy food. It's a huge movement I had no idea existed, but now I'm really inspired. I want to get involved."

"Gah. You're such a softie. Let me know when you're home."

"I will. Night." I ended the call, and punched the address of the cottage into

Google Maps. While jabbering away to Jaime, I'd kept walking when I should have turned, and missed my street by about three blocks. I backtracked, found my way home, and texted her that I made it.

Fifteen minutes later, I turned off the lights and got in bed, curling up on one side. As soon as I shut my eyes, Jack Valentini popped into my head and stubbornly refused to leave. *How predictable of him.*

I flopped onto my back. He was so aggravating. Was he going to shoot down every idea I had? I wondered if he'd always been so crotchety. Did he ever laugh? Had he been different before his wife's death? Before the Army? Was it any one thing that made him so different than his brothers, or was it everything?

On a whim, I turned the lamp on again and got up to grab my laptop. I brought it back to the bed and sat cross-legged in front of it, trying not to feel creepy as I Googled Stephanie Valentini.

The first search didn't turn up anything enlightening, so I added Michigan and drunk driving death to the search words, feeling even worse about what I was doing. But it worked. Eventually I found a local news article about the accident, and I clicked on the link.

Two photos appeared at the top of the page, and I covered my mouth with one hand. On the left was a close-up of a pretty, dark-haired woman with huge brown eyes and dimples. On the right was a wedding picture of Jack and Steph, and it stunned me to see him smiling and happy, breathtakingly handsome.

The headline was chilling: **Man with 2 previous drunk driving convictions kills local woman in hit and run.** The details were sickening. She'd worked a shift waitressing at a bar just up the highway, and her car had conked out on the ride home. Her cell phone was dead, so she'd been walking the half-mile toward the farm when a drunk driver with previous convictions and an open container of alcohol in the car struck her. He drove away but drove into a ditch not two miles down the road. Another driver saw the accident, and called 911. Steph had been airlifted to the hospital but died several hours later of her injuries. The driver had been taken to jail and held on a $1 million bond.

I read the article once more and stared at the wedding photo for a long time. Finally, I closed the computer, plugged it back in to the charger, and slipped beneath the covers again.

No wonder, I thought. No wonder he was the way he was. That kind of loss, plus the loss of his father and whatever he'd experienced in the Army, could harden anybody.

I felt bad that my being here was causing him more distress. *I pushed too hard tonight. That was my fault.* I needed to convince him that I honestly cared about what he was doing and really did want to help, but I needed a less direct approach. What would it take to make him look at me differently? See me as a friend?

Or something more…

No. Just stop that train right there and get off, Margot. For God's sake, he's a client! And he's still wearing a wedding band! You're a little attracted to him, yes. You feel sorry for him, fine. You want to help his farm, sure. But leave it at that.

Sighing, I rolled onto my stomach and tried to stop thinking about him.

But I tossed and turned all night.

☙❧

At five thirty, I gave up on sleep and tugged on running shorts, a tank top, and running shoes. If I couldn't sleep, I might as well try to get a little exercise. I figured I'd make my way up to the highway, then head across and up the dirt road next to the Valentini farm. Scout it out a bit.

I put my hair up, locked the door, and tucked the cottage key into the little hidden pocket on my shorts before setting off at a light jog. Behind me, the sun was just peeking up over the lake, turning the sky a gorgeous orange-pink. The punishing heat of the day was hours away, and the air felt cool and refreshing against my arms and legs. I smiled at an early dog walker and an old couple out for a hand-in-hand sunrise stroll, but my spirits flagged when I reached the highway and realized I should have gone to the bathroom before I left.

Oh, well. I'd be OK for a quick jog, wouldn't I? I'd just loop around their property and head back. How big could a "small farm" be?

As it turns out, pretty fucking big.

I headed west on the dirt road—past the orchard, big plots planted with vegetables, a pasture, and finally thick woods. By the time I turned left at the far edge of their property, I had to go, and the pressure in my bladder quickly escalated from bad to worse.

Biting my lip, I eyed the woods behind the Valentini fence on my left and the open pasture of someone else's farm on the right before glancing back the way I'd come. I hadn't seen a single soul back here. But…but I was *outside*. Could I really?

I don't think I need to tell you I'm not a terribly outdoorsy type of girl. My idea of "roughing it" is a three-star hotel, I certainly don't camp, and the one time I had to use a port-o-potty at a concert Jaime dragged me to I thought I was going to die of disgust. Or a bacterial infection.

Would peeing outside like an animal be worse than the port-o-potty? What would I use to wipe myself? I'd heard stories about girls having to do this before, but clearly I'd never paid close enough attention! Did you drip dry like a boy? Use a leaf? But I had sensitive skin! And what if I used poison ivy by mistake? Or some other harmful plant? Wasn't there something called poison oak? I didn't know what those things looked like! Why hadn't I brought my phone? Throwing scones was one thing, but *this* was something I still found dreadfully unpalatable.

I hopped from foot to foot, desperately wishing for another solution to magically present itself so I would not have to relinquish my dignity or give my vagina a poisonous rash. But none appeared, so I climbed over the Valentinis' fence and ducked into the trees, cursing myself for being so out of it before I left the cottage.

Hurrying across the forest floor of dirt and pine needles and dry leaves, I moved away from the road until I couldn't see it anymore. I was about to squat (good grief, what an inelegant word) when I heard a splash nearby. Gasping, I straightened up and looked around, frantically yanking my shorts back into place. When I heard another splash, I cautiously made my way in that direction.

Oh my God!

Not far from where I'd been about to relieve myself was a clearing in the trees, and beyond it was a small lake. Jutting into the lake was a short wooden dock, on which stood Jack Valentini, dripping wet and *buck fucking naked.*

It was as if an electrical switch had been flipped inside me. Suddenly I was driven by one gut instinct: *I need a better view.* There was a weeping willow about twenty feet closer to the lake, and without giving it a second thought, I darted toward it and then scrambled up onto a low branch.

Yes, I actually *climbed a tree.*

Hanging onto a branch above my head, I carefully side-stepped out a little bit and peered through the leaves. Tongue caught between my teeth, I watched him push his wet hair back from his face and stretch a little, arms over his head. *Hmm, a farmer's tan is actually a thing.*

My eyes automatically went low, and my jaw dropped when I saw the size of his dick. If it was that big when it wasn't even hard, how big would it get when it was? Suddenly I felt like a kid who'd been told she could look at her birthday cake but not taste it. A hundred irrational—and frankly perverted—thoughts assaulted my brain.

I want to see him get hard. I want to touch him. I want my mouth on him. I want to watch him touch himself. Damn, he's huge. I want to be fucked with a cock like that. I bet it could tear me apart. Christ, he could probably fuck me from clear over there.

No! No, he should find me here. He should discover me in the woods and get angry. Then he'd have to punish me for spying on him. He'd be ruthless.

I realized I was panting.

What the hell was the matter with me? I'd never had these kinds of thoughts about anyone, let alone a veritable stranger. Was I having a midlife crisis at age twenty-nine?

He turned away from me, giving me a chance to appreciate the nice round butt I'd noticed in the photo, but also the muscular back and shoulders, the tattoos that snaked around to his ribs on his right side. What were they? I'd never known a man with tattoos before, not personally. And I'd definitely never seen one naked.

I hadn't seen that many men naked at all, really. Maybe that was my problem—fascination, sort of like he was a museum exhibit or exotic animal or circus sideshow. The male bodies I'd seen in the flesh were pale and thin—*nothing* like the beautiful work of art in front of me now, which had bulges and ridges and lines, the morning sun burnishing his skin to bronze. I wanted to—

CRACK!

The branch I was standing on snapped, and I hit the ground in an ungraceful belly flop.

(Also, I may have peed myself. Just slightly.)

I picked up my head and looked at Jack, shocked to see he'd quite literally hit the deck, his body flattened against the wood. A second later he looked up and saw me. *Not* the discovery fantasy I'd concocted by a long shot.

Oh, Jesus. This is worse than Sconehenge.

How the hell was I going to explain myself?

chapter nine

Jack

FIRST, TERROR. ADRENALINE-FUELED, HEART-POUNDING, BLOOD-PUMPING, GUT-wrenching terror.

Then, anger. That I hadn't been vigilant enough. That I'd missed some sign of danger. That I'd failed.

Finally, awareness. That I was OK. That everyone was safe. That nothing had happened.

Well, nothing dangerous.

My heart rate and breathing slowed as I took in the scene—Margot Lewiston, flat on her belly—and realized the noise that had startled me had been the snapping of a tree branch, which had apparently given out under her weight. "Fuck," I muttered, feeling foolish, like I always did when this happened.

And that's when I *wasn't* naked.

I jumped up and yanked on my sweaty running shorts, which were lying on the dock next to my socks and shoes. Since Pete was checking on the animals this morning, I'd decided to take a quick swim after my run. I hadn't counted on an audience.

Once I had the shorts on, I stood up straight, fists clenched, ready to rip into her for trespassing, for spying, for scaring me. *For refusing to get out of my head.* But one look at the way she hopped to her feet and started running toward me—on her toes, knees pressed together, hands over her crotch—and I was momentarily stunned.

"Oh hey, Jack," she said casually, like she just happened to be in the neighborhood, "I know you're probably wondering what I'm doing here. And I'm sure I can explain. But first, can I please, *please* use your bathroom?"

"Uh, OK." Annoyed as I was at the invasion of privacy, I nearly laughed out loud at her awkward rush for the cabin's back door. I jogged ahead of her and let her in, gesturing toward the bathroom.

"Thank you," she mouthed as she raced by me.

While she was in the bathroom, I stayed out on the back porch, uncomfortable with the thought of being in the cabin alone with her. What the hell was she doing here? Bad enough I'd spent an entire sleepless night trying not to think about her legs and her eyes and that fucking pearl necklace. She had to show up first thing this morning in those tiny shorts and a tight shirt? My dick started perking up, and I did my best to crush its hopes, thinking about crop rotations and drip irrigation systems and long range weather forecasts.

Thankfully, I had myself under control by the time she came out, a relieved smile on her face.

"Wow," she said, shutting the screen door behind her. "That was close. Thank you so much."

"You're welcome." I crossed my arms, wishing I'd thought to grab a shirt. "Want to tell me what you were doing out there?"

Her cheeks colored. "Um, I was taking a run."

"Up a tree?"

She laughed nervously. "No. Well, I didn't start out in a tree. That happened later."

I cocked my head, unable to resist giving her a hard time. *Not so sure of yourself now, are you, Barbie?* "Oh yeah?"

"Yes. See, I left the cottage I'm renting without using the bathroom by mistake," she began, twisting her fingers together, "and I was planning on running a loop around the farm, but it's bigger than I thought."

"Ah. So you were looking for a bathroom in the woods?"

"Well, yes." She swallowed. "Sort of. But then I heard a splash and saw you…" Her cheeks were practically purple now.

I played dumb. "Saw me what?"

"Saw you naked, OK?" she blurted, throwing her hands up. "I admit it—I saw you naked."

I had no hang-ups about nudity, but I was damn serious about my privacy, *and* about people sneaking up on me.

But her embarrassment was funny. The two times I'd seen her before, she'd been so polished and poised. It felt good to put her in her place a little. "So you climbed a tree for a better view, is that it?"

Bowing her head, she dragged the toe of one shoe across the wood planks of the porch floor. "Something like that." Then she looked up at me. Took a breath. "I'm really sorry. I shouldn't have done that. I was—I mean, I got—I couldn't—" She sighed, briefly closing her eyes. "I have no excuse. Will you accept my apology?"

She was prettier without makeup, I decided. And the way she wore her hair off her face emphasized the wideness of her eyes, the angle of her cheekbones, the arch of her brows. Her lips didn't need all that glossy crap, either. They were a perfect rosy pink, and I wondered if they'd feel as soft as they looked.

Fuck. I hadn't kissed anyone in three years.

Clearing my throat, I took a step back. "Yeah. It's fine." *Now get out of here.*

She didn't move. "So you're not going to fire me?"

"I never hired you."

"I know. But I really want this job. I think I can help, Jack. I know I can."

"Suit yourself." My name on her lips was trouble. Needing some distance from her, I started walking toward the dock to get my shoes and socks, but she followed me. God, she was a pest. It reminded me of the way Steph used to tag along after the boys when we were kids, wanting to get in our games.

"Are you going to be like this the entire time I'm here?" she asked.

"Like what?"

"Moody and uncooperative?"

"Probably."

"Why? Do you hate me that much?"

"I don't hate anybody. I just don't see why we should pay some city girl who's never set foot on a farm to advise us." We reached the dock, and I leaned down to get my stuff.

"I'm not even asking to be paid, so piss off!" she shouted, her voice carrying on the water.

I straightened. "Oh, you're working for free?"

"Yes!"

"Then you're an idiot. Or so rich you don't need the money."

"I'm not an idiot," she said through clenched teeth.

"So you're rich, then." I don't know why I was being such an asshole. But for some reason, I did not want to let her see another side of me, or see another side to her. "I should have guessed."

She crossed her arms. "And what's that supposed to mean?"

"It means you look like you've led a charmed life. Like you've had everything you've ever wanted handed to you. Like you've never gotten your hands dirty."

"So get them dirty."

I almost fell off the dock. "What?"

"Get them dirty. Teach me about working this farm. I want to learn."

Was she serious? The last thing I needed was to drag her ass around all day, explaining things. *Or stare at her ass all day, imagining things.* But one glance at her defiant face and I shook my head. "Why do I feel like if I say no, you'll just keep bothering me?"

She smiled and clasped her hands behind her back, rocking forward on her toes. "Because I will. I don't like being told no."

"Of course you don't." Jesus, she was trouble. A bad apple—smooth and shiny on the outside, spoiled rotten on the inside. But for no good reason, I found myself giving in. "Fine. Go change your clothes."

She grinned. "Where should I meet you? It will take me about a half hour to run home, change, and get back here."

"No idea where I'll be then. You'll have to find me."

"Fair enough." She glanced over her shoulder at the trees. "What's the quickest route back? Through there?"

"No. Take the path toward the house to get back to the highway."

She turned in a circle. "Which way is the house? I'm not very good with directions."

"Jesus. It's that way." Jabbing a thumb into the air over one shoulder, I decided I'd better get her going the right way or I'd be waiting around for her forever. "You can cut through the cabin. Come on."

We walked back to the cabin and she followed me from the kitchen into the front room. "Hey, I like your place. It's cozy. And so clean."

"Thanks."

The cat jumped down from the front windowsill and crossed in front of us, checking out the situation.

Margot knelt down to pet her. "How sweet. What's her name?"

I grimaced. "Bridget Jones."

She burst out laughing. "You have a cat named Bridget Jones?"

"Yeah. What's so funny about it?" I snapped.

"I don't know. Take it easy. You just seem more like a dog person, I guess."

"I am," I admitted, some of the tension leaving my voice. "The cat was my wife's." I opened the front door, hoping Margot would take the hint, but not surprised when she didn't.

"Have you always lived here?"

"Since I got out of the Army."

"When was that?"

"Six years ago."

She nodded, rose to her feet, and glanced around the room. Her eyes lingered on the framed wedding photos hanging on the wall. "Oh, how beautiful. Can I look at them?"

"I guess." I let the screen door swing shut as she went over to examine them. God, how long had it been since someone other than me had looked at those pictures? I felt nervous about it, but also pleased she'd noticed them.

There were three—one family photo; one of us during the ceremony, holding hands beneath a floral arch; and one taken in the barn where Steph stood on a bale of hay so her head would be level with mine when I kissed her. When Margot got to that one, she laughed. "That's adorable! Look how tiny she is—and she's wearing cowboy boots with her big wedding dress, I love it!" She pointed at the way Steph was holding up the bottom of her dress to show off her feet.

"Yeah. She loved her boots. She said she wasn't a heels type of girl in real life and didn't need to be one on her wedding day." I could still hear her proclaiming it with no apology in her voice.

Margot nodded. "I'm a heels type of girl."

"You don't say."

"But everybody should be free to be who they are on their wedding day. I love that she wasn't afraid to be herself."

"She wasn't afraid of anything." In general, I wasn't the kind of guy who opened up to people I didn't know. Or to people I did. But it felt good to talk about Steph in front of Margot. It felt safe.

"You don't look too bad yourself here. You wore boots too, I see."

"Yeah, I'm not much for fancy shoes. Or clothes. But Steph said I had to wear the suit."

"You wore it well."

"Thanks."

A beat went by. "I was sorry to hear about what happened." She kept staring at the picture. "You must miss her."

"Yeah. I do."

She sighed and turned around. "Well, I guess I better go get changed."

Nodding, I opened the door again, and as she went by me, her shoulder brushed my bare chest. Gooseflesh rippled down my arms, and my nipples puckered. Quickly, I shut the screen door in front of me before giving her directions. "Head for those trees straight ahead and stay on the path that runs through them. You'll see the house on the other side."

"Got it." She started down the steps.

"And be careful crossing the highway."

At the bottom of the steps, she stopped and looked back at me. "I will. Promise."

She took off running at a decent pace, and I tried not to look at her butt.

I had a feeling I'd be fighting that battle all damn day.

chapter ten

Margot

I HURRIED BACK TO THE COTTAGE, MORE EXCITED THAN I SHOULD HAVE BEEN ABOUT the day ahead. For heaven's sake—Jack and I could hardly spend five minutes together without getting on each other's nerves. But something about this felt like a victory to me.

I'd blown up at him by mistake—my plan had been to kill him with kindness, but instead I'd spied on him before calling him moody and uncooperative. But he was so frustrating! I was trying to help him!

The strange thing was, he hadn't seemed that angry about the whole tree incident. In fact, he'd seemed almost amused by the whole thing—I could've sworn I *almost* saw him smile at one point.

Why that had me grinning I had no idea.

Inside the cottage, I peeled off my damp running clothes and decided, in the interest of saving time, not to shower. I didn't want Jack to use tardiness as an excuse not to show me around today, and it's not like I had to worry about him getting close. I'd never met a man so uncomfortable being next to me. He was always backing up or moving away, crossing his arms over his chest.

I pulled on fresh underwear and socks, my skinny jeans and a plaid button-down, and tugged the elastic from my ponytail. In the bathroom, I brushed my teeth, braided my hair and unzipped my makeup bag.

Then I caught myself.

What are you doing, Margot? This isn't a date. You don't need mascara in a barn.

I zipped it back up, but I did put on my pearl necklace…and a spritz of perfume.

A girl's got to have a *hint* of pretty, right?

Right before I left, I yanked on my old riding boots, thankful I hadn't given them away. They were beautiful brown leather, and still had plenty of wear left.

I raced out the door just fifteen minutes after I rushed in, and headed out to the car, pleased with myself. Not only would I learn more about the farm, which would help me do my job, but I'd get the chance to prove to Jack that I wasn't the enemy. I respected his work and honestly wanted to help. And if it made him look at me in a more favorable light, well…so much the better.

I was determined to make him smile for real.

chapter eleven

Jack

"Are you sure about this?" Margot peeked into the first nesting box, where three eggs sat in the hay.

"Yes. You just reach in, take the eggs, and put them in your basket." I'd thought gathering eggs might be an easy place for her to start, but Christ Almighty, I was beginning to wonder if even that was too much for her. She was *such* a city girl—although she did look cute in her tight jeans and little plaid shirt, and I liked the way she wore her hair in one long braid down her back. Her boots were hilarious, though—some sort of equestrian riding boots that looked like they belonged in a movie about a rich girl who has her own show pony. At least she hadn't put makeup on.

But believe it or not, she *had* put on the pearl necklace.

It was killing me.

"Come on," I prodded, annoyed more with myself than her. "Get the eggs, we have work to do."

"Won't they get mad?" She looked around the coop, nervously eyeing the hens about our feet.

"No. They're used to it."

"OK." She reached in and took out two eggs, then laid them gently in the basket. "I did it!" she said, smiling proudly.

I nearly smiled back before I caught myself. "Good job. Now keep going. Or we're going to be here all day."

She took the third one out, gingerly placed it next to the others and studied them. "So do the brown chickens lay the brown eggs and the white ones the white eggs?"

"No. You can tell what color eggs a chicken will lay by the color of her ears."

Her eyes bugged. "No way!"

"Yes. Now come on, work faster. Like this." I reached into the next box, quickly pulled three eggs out with one hand, put them in the basket, and moved on to another.

"Wow, you're really good at this."

"I've had a lot of practice. Now you do the next one."

She moved in front of me, bent over, and looked into the box. "There's somebody in there."

"So reach beneath her and take the eggs." I struggled to keep my eyes off her ass.

"I don't think I should. She's giving me the evil eye."

"Jesus Christ. Move, I'll do the rest." I took her by the waist and swung her to the side to get her out of my way, but once I had my hands on her, I didn't want to let go.

And I'm a fucking weak-willed asshole, so I didn't.

I left them there a couple seconds too long.

"Jack?" She looked at me over her shoulder, her expression confused.

I dropped my hands.

What the fuck are you doing?

"Just give me the basket," I ordered roughly, yanking it from her hand.

She turned around. "Did I do something wrong?"

"No." I angled away from her and started grabbing the remaining eggs, angry with myself.

This was a bad idea.

◈

It was a long day.

As I'd suspected, Margot was clueless about everything and had a thousand ridiculous questions.

"So you don't milk a male cow?"

"Why do you need an electric fence?"

"How big is an acre?"

"Are those goats?"

"What's a CSA?"

"Why do you have to rotate crops?"

"Isn't it weird to butcher an animal you spent all that time raising? Do you ever want to keep the cute ones?"

"So chickens lay eggs from their butts?"

I did my best to answer her questions, figuring the more she realized she didn't know, the more likely it would be that she might decide she couldn't help. But she learned fast, and by late afternoon, her questions grew more thoughtful, her hands steadier, her pace quicker. I found myself admiring her curiosity about the farm, her willingness to tackle any job I gave her, and the fact that she never once complained about the sun or the heat or the smell or the dirt lodged under her fingernails and caked on her fancy boots.

But the worst thing was the way I kept wanting to *touch* her. I couldn't stop thinking about what I'd done in the chicken coop, and I stopped myself a dozen times from doing it again. What the hell was my problem?

Finally, I had to admit that for the first time since Steph died, I was seriously attracted to a woman.

It was almost a relief.

I wasn't happy about it, but logically, I knew it was just a biological urge and I shouldn't be too hard on myself, especially since her presence here was temporary. And who wouldn't be attracted to Margot? She was beautiful, smart, and kind. And aside from her ignorance about life outside the bubble she lived in, she was nice to be around. She could laugh at herself, tried again if she failed at something the first time, and was actually really good with the horses. I wondered if she'd had experience with them.

"Do you ride?" I asked her when we were in the barn at the end of the day.

"I had a horse growing up," she said, stroking the neck of the mare I'd been concerned about yesterday.

"Of course you did. Rich girl." I couldn't resist giving that braid a tug. What I really wanted to do was wrap it around my fist. Yank her head back. Kiss her neck.

Fuck. Stop it.

"Hey," she said, pouting. "None of that. I did everything you asked today, didn't I?" She looked so hopeful, a smudge of dirt on her sweaty forehead, I didn't have the heart to shoot her down.

"You did fine," I told her, giving the horse's nose a little rub, trying to keep my hands busy. But my dick was swelling in my pants, as if owning up to my attraction for her had woken a sleeping beast. And the voice in my head would not stay quiet. *I'd like to give you a little rub—right between the legs with my tongue.*

"Thank you. And thank you for taking me around today. I really appreciate it."

"You're welcome." *How'd you like to appreciate my big hard cock in your pussy?*

"And look!" She laughed. "I got my hands dirty!"

"Oh yeah? Let's see." I grabbed her wrists and turned up her palms between us, examining them. "Well, look at that. They're filthy."

She giggled. "All of me is filthy. I can't wait to take a hot…" Her voice trailed off as she stared at my fingers circling her wrists. Then she looked up at me. Those blue eyes wide. Those pink lips open. That pale white throat beckoning.

I knew what I was going to do before I did it.

I knew it was a bad idea. I knew I'd regret it.

And I still did it.

Heart pounding in my chest, I pulled her forward by the wrists until her mouth was so close I felt her breath on my lips.

And I kissed her—lightly at first, my lips barely resting on hers, and then harder, my mouth opening, my hands sliding around her back, over her ass. I pulled her in tight against my hips, my erection trapped between us.

She looped her arms around my waist and rose up on tiptoe, pressing her chest to mine. Our tongues met and I tasted her hungrily, like I'd never get enough. It actually reminded me of the time Pete and I ate all the vanilla ice cream our mom had bought for Brad's tenth birthday the day before his party. We knew we shouldn't and we were bound to get caught and punished, but damn if it didn't taste so good we couldn't stop. Margot tasted like that—sweet and forbidden at the same time.

Just let me have this, I thought as my conscience pricked. *Just this once.*

I wound her braid around one hand and pulled her head back, moving my mouth down her throat. I inhaled the scent of her skin, reveled in the velvety feel of it beneath my lips, the salty sweet taste. Slipping one thigh between her legs, I ran my tongue along the pearls resting against her neck. Her fingers dug into my back.

"Jack," she whispered.

My name—whispered by another woman.

The wrong woman.

This isn't right.

Get away from her.

chapter twelve

Margot

H E WAS KISSING ME LIKE I'D NEVER BEEN KISSED BEFORE. Like he was going to war. Like he didn't care about breathing. Like something in him needed something in me so desperately, he had to find it or die trying.

Not that I wasn't willing to give it up. At that moment, I'd have flung my panties across the barn like a scone at a political fundraiser.

He was so *different* from any man I'd ever kissed—everything about him exuded strength and raw masculinity. His chest was so broad, his arms so muscular, his cock so hard, his mouth so commanding as it moved down my throat. It was *intoxicating*. I'd have let him do anything he wanted to me, just to experience being at the mercy of such power.

Jesus Christ, where did this come from?

I'd sensed him warming toward me throughout the day, and there had been that electric moment in the chicken coop when he'd put his hands on me, but this… *This.*

He shifted my body so I straddled his thigh, pulled my head back and ran his tongue along the strand of pearls at the base of my neck. My clit pulsed. My hands flexed on his back.

Oh my God.

Oh my God, I'm going to have an orgasm. In a barn. With a farmer. Who I met yesterday.

And it's going to be SO. GOOD.

I whispered his name…and he pushed me away.

As if hearing his name had signaled the end of a scene we were filming, he put his hands on my shoulders and stepped back, separating us.

We stared at each other in silence, both of our chests rising and falling with rapid breaths. His eyes were clouded with something I couldn't read—I saw desire there, but pain too.

He dropped his hands. "You should go."

"Jack, please, can't we—"

"Go!" He roared, putting his hands on his head. "Just get the fuck out of here, Margot! Now!"

Hurt and confused, I turned and ran from the barn across the yard, tears burning my eyes. I cut a wide berth around the house, hoping Pete and Georgia wouldn't see me, and darted out to the road where I'd parked. When I reached the safety of my car without being seen, I pulled the door shut and collapsed against the steering wheel.

A few tears spilled over, and I wiped at them with my filthy hands, angry I was this upset over a stupid kiss. "Fuck you, Jack Valentini. I was right about you to begin with. You're nothing but a foul-mannered jerk."

So what if he was handsome underneath that scruff and dirt? So what if he had a big, broken heart somewhere inside that massive chest? So what if he had a big dick and probably knew how to use it?

He was an asshole.

And he was a *client*.

But that kiss…*that kiss*.

Why did the best kiss I'd ever had have to be with *him*?

"Dammit!" I banged my head against the steering wheel a few times, then pulled myself together.

In my purse, I found a handkerchief and dabbed at my eyes and nose, dismayed by the amount of dirt that came off my face. I stared at it, noticing how the embroidered navy blue M of my monogram was beginning to fray. Tossing the soiled linen aside, I started the car and drove back to the cottage, berating myself the whole way.

What the hell had I been thinking? It didn't matter what he looked like naked or how he kissed or why he'd pushed me away. I worked for him, and that was a boundary that shouldn't be crossed.

He probably realized that too. You should be glad he came to his senses before you started flinging your panties around.

Back at the cottage, I took a long, punishingly hot shower, vowing to put Jack out of my mind and concentrate on the work that needed to be done. I had a meeting with Pete and Brad and Georgia tomorrow, and I wanted to go in prepared. More than prepared—if Jack said anything to them about my less-than-professional behavior, I had to counter that with proof I was good at my job.

When I was finally clean, I put on my pajamas, pulled from the freezer a pitiful frozen lasagna that probably came off an assembly line six years ago, and opened a bottle of wine. While I waited for the lasagna to heat up in the microwave, I called Jaime.

"Hey," she said. "How's it going?"

"Great." I forced myself to be cheerful. "I'm fired up. I've got lots of ideas."

"Awesome. Hit me."

I told her about some of the ideas I had—beyond the obvious ones like creating a logo, revamping the website, and using social media, I described agritourism and why I thought it would work for them. "I've done the research and there aren't that many places around here offering unique experiences…I'm going to talk with Pete and Georgia tomorrow about the possibilities of a small restaurant on site with a chef's table, cooking classes, weddings and other special events. I think their place could be a real destination."

"Sounds great. What about the grouch? He gonna go for all that?"

I sighed as I pulled the lasagna from the microwave. It was still frozen in the center but bubbling at the edges. "Nope. Probably none of it."

"Ugh, what a pain. Can you work around him?"

"Who knows? He basically told me earlier he doesn't care what I do as long as I don't involve him. Of course, he might have been mad because I saw him naked."

"Excuse me?"

While I nuked the lasagna some more, I told her what had happened this morning, and she laughed.

"What's going on with you, anyway? For thirty years, you've lived this perfect, well-mannered life and now you're throwing scones and climbing trees to spy on naked men."

Pulling the entree out again, I stabbed at the lasagna, now burnt at the edges. "Maybe I'm tired of behaving properly all the time. I'm experimenting with letting my gut take over."

"I heartily applaud this experiment. You've always been way too well-behaved. Have some fun. Throw scones. Spy on naked men. Do more than that if you want."

As I chewed a bite of tasteless, rubbery lasagna, I considered confiding in Jaime about what had happened in the barn. I wasn't usually a kiss-and-tell kind of person, but maybe if I talked it out with Jaime, I could make more sense of it.

"Actually, I did a little more than that today." I filled her in, and she was silent the whole time.

"Wow," she said once I'd gotten to the part where he yelled at me to leave. "That is messed up."

"I know." Giving up on the lasagna for the moment, I took a bag of baby carrots out of the fridge and munched on them instead. They reminded me of the meal we'd had at Pete and Georgia's house today at lunchtime—a delicious beet salad, everything from their own garden except the goat cheese (but that was made at a Michigan creamery) and some grilled pork tenderloin in barbecue sauce made with local peaches. I eyed the carrots in the bag, perfectly uniform and lacking in any personality whatsoever. Perfect could be so boring.

"And he's a client," Jaime reminded me.

"I know. I keep telling myself that. It's just...I'm drawn to him for some reason, not that I could tell you what it is," I said irritably. "I can list *ten* reasons I *shouldn't* be."

She laughed. "I'll tell you what the reason is. He's fucking hot. Here's two more—he's got a big dick, and you haven't been laid since Tripp the Drip."

I groaned. "Thanks for the reminder." The memory of Jack's dick pressing into my pelvic bone made my insides tighten.

"Sorry, Gogo. I shouldn't tease. So what are you going to do?"

"Forget about him. What else is there to do?"

She sighed. "That's probably for the best. I fully support getting outside your comfort zone, but a widowed Vet farmer who's also a client might be *too* far out."

"Way too far." *So far it shouldn't matter this much.*

"You OK? You need me to come up there for the meeting tomorrow?"

"No. I'm fine." I tried to sound confident. "I promise this thing will not affect my work."

"I know it won't. You're a perfectionist. That will never change." She paused. "But did you really feed pigs today?"

That made me smile. "I sure did. And cows and horses and goats. And gathered eggs from chickens. Did you know they lay them from their butts?"

"No. And I really didn't need to."

I clucked my tongue. "Jaime Owens, you should really pay more attention to where your food comes from."

"In this case, I think ignorance is bliss. Call me tomorrow?"

"Will do. Night."

"Night."

I spent the rest of the evening preparing for the meeting and trying to keep thoughts of Jack from distracting me.

But it was impossible.

I relived that kiss a thousand times. I felt his hands around my wrists. His tongue on my neck. His thigh between my legs.

Closing my eyes, I pictured him in his little house. What was he doing right now? Was he thinking about me? Did he still miss his wife at night? Did he ever try to ease the loneliness with other women? I felt a vicious stab of envy for any woman who'd been with him, and a pang of longing so fierce it shocked me.

Yes, his mood swings made me dizzy, but he was masculine and strong and real. He was a soldier. A survivor. And he'd worked for what he had—worked long and hard with his own two hands. He wasn't afraid to get dirty.

That was sexy.

I'd never been so attracted to a man in my life.

But there was nothing I could do about it.

chapter thirteen

Jack

WHAT THE HELL HAD I DONE?
You know what you did. You let your guard down. You lost control. You fucked up.

I had fucked up. Badly.

I'd been a complete asshole to Margot, who didn't deserve it. I'd messed around with a woman who was working for me. And I'd betrayed Steph's memory.

I felt guilty about everything. I needed to talk to someone…someone who knew me, someone who would understand.

It wasn't that I sought forgiveness—I'd never have that—but more a need to remind myself who I was. So after I finished up in the barn, I went home, cleaned up, picked some of the wildflowers growing in front of the cabin, and drove out to the cemetery.

We'd buried Steph according to her family's wishes. She and I had never even talked about what we wanted in terms of burial—who thinks of death when they're young and newly married? And afterward I'd been in such a fog of grief and regret, I'd let her parents and sister make the decisions, everything from where she would be buried to what clothing she'd be buried in.

The only thing I'd asked was that they let her wear her boots.

"Hey, babe." I lowered myself to the grass in front of her stone and hung my arms over my knees. "Brought you these." Laying the wildflowers in front of the pink granite marker, I took a minute to pull some weeds that had sprouted around it since last week. *I bet Margot likes hothouse roses, not wildflowers.*

Tossing the weeds aside, I frowned and put Margot from my mind. Concentrated on imagining Steph here beside me, on all the familiar things I loved and missed about her until my heart ached. "I'm having kind of a rough time. August is always hard for me."

If I closed my eyes, I could hear her voice, and I always knew what she'd say.

Are you sleeping OK?
"Not much at all."
What about the meds?
"I don't take them."

She'd get exasperated. *Jack. You have to! They were helping! You were finally getting a full night's sleep on them.*

"Fuck sleep."

Did you come here to argue with me? We've been over this a thousand times.

"It's my fault. Everything is my fault."

You weren't driving the car that hit me.

I closed my eyes and saw her walking along the highway, headlights careening toward her in the dark, felt the guilt slam into me with the force of five thousand pounds of metal and glass.

You weren't driving the car that hit me, Jack.

I shook my head, tears in my eyes. "Doesn't matter how many times you say it. I'm to blame."

Why do you think that?

In my mind, another car moved through the dark—toward me this time. "You know why. You're the only one who knows why."

Stop it.

"'Just as he has done, so it shall be done to him.'"

Jack! I'll never believe that. Never. You did what you had to do.

My throat constricted. I tried clearing it, but my voice still cracked. "The price was too high."

She was silent. Of course she was.

She only ever saw the good in me. And yet what I'd done had cost her life—I was sure of it.

Even on my good days, I carried the burden with me.

The truth was, I didn't deserve to sleep peacefully. I didn't deserve the love and sympathy of my family. And I certainly didn't deserve to give in to my desire for another woman.

No matter how much I wanted to.

Later that night, I was sitting on my back porch watching the sun set with a beer in my hand when Georgia appeared around the side of the cabin. In her hands was a plate covered with foil.

"Hey," she said. "I brought you some dinner."

"Thanks."

She came up onto the porch. "I knocked in front but you didn't answer."

"Sorry. I didn't hear."

"Everything OK?"

"Fine." I kept my eyes on a family of ducks in the pond.

Georgia was silent a minute. "You go to the cemetery today?"

How the hell she knew, I had no clue. But I didn't have it in me to deny it. "Yeah."

She nodded slowly, and for a second I hoped she'd ask me about being there, or say something about Steph, or just acknowledge her existence—or even her memory—in some way. People rarely did. All they ever wanted to know was how *I* was doing, how *I* was feeling. Did they think by avoiding the subject, I wouldn't feel the pain?

Sure enough, Georgia moved on.

"Have you eaten, or should I throw this in the fridge?" She held up the plate and grinned. "It's fried chicken. Yum yum good."

"I ate. Fridge is fine." I hadn't eaten, but I wasn't hungry. I felt sick about what I'd done, but worse, I couldn't stop thinking about that kiss with Margot as I sat here. How much I'd liked the feel of her body against mine, her hair in my hands, her skin under my lips. How much I'd wanted to wrap myself up in her perfect, perfumed, pearl-necklace sweetness and forget for a while. How badly I wished I could.

You can't. So stop fucking thinking about it.

Georgia sighed, but she went into the cabin and I heard the fridge door open and shut. Then a bottle being opened. "Mind if I have a beer with you?"

"No." Actually, I wanted to be alone in my misery, but didn't want to be a dick to Georgia. She was always good to me. Maybe she could distract me from thinking about Margot.

She came back out and dropped into the chair next to me. "How was the rest of your day with Margot?"

So much for that idea. "Fine."

"She drive you crazy?"

Fuck yeah she did. She still is. "Yep."

Georgia took a long drink of her beer, then laughed. "I know it's not nice, but I keep picturing her doing chores in her little outfit with the fancy boots and jewelry."

A smile threatened. "Farmer Barbie."

Georgia slapped her leg. "Right? She's so sweet, though. And it was nice of her to be so interested and offer to help. Don't you think?"

"She wasn't that much help," I muttered wryly.

"I wasn't either when I first got here. You guys used to laugh your asses off at me trying to get on a horse. Remember?"

"Ha. Yes." But the memory of us laughing together actually made me a little sad. Steph had been there, too. "We thought you were hopeless."

She reached over and poked my arm. "But I learned."

"You learned." I tipped up my beer, thinking about Margot riding a horse. "Actually, I think Margot knows how to ride a horse."

"Oh?"

"Yeah, she said she owned one growing up. She was pretty comfortable with ours today."

She looked at me, her head cocked. "What do you know, you two have something in common. You should let her ride you while she's here."

I almost choked. "What?"

"I said, you should let her ride with you while she's here. Maybe one day this week."

"Oh." Jesus, now the thought of Margot riding me was stuck in my head. I couldn't get a moment's fucking peace! "Maybe."

"She'll be over tomorrow morning to go over some ideas." A not-so-subtle suggestion.

"Hmph."

Georgia sighed and sat back, evidently giving up for now. We drank in companionable silence as the sun went down, slapping at the occasional mosquito and listening to the crickets. When our bottles were empty, she stood.

"Well, I should get back. Thanks for the beer."

"Anytime. Thanks for bringing dinner." I rose too. "It's dark. I'll walk you back."

"You don't have to."

"Yes, I do."

She knew better than to argue. If it was dark, I never let a woman walk anywhere alone.

When we reached the house, she gave me a quick hug. "Think about coming tomorrow, OK? Nine o'clock. I'm making the French toast casserole you like."

I moaned. "With the brown sugar and banana? Now you're just being mean."

She laughed and patted my cheek. "Not mean, just smart. Maybe I'll see you in the morning."

"Maybe."

"Night."

I watched her go inside the house and shut the door before turning around to head back. As I walked through the trees, I remembered Margot falling out of the willow this morning, and shook my head. Now that I knew her a little better, I was amazed she'd even managed to climb it. *She must have really wanted that better view.* I smiled briefly, wondering what she'd thought once she got an eyeful. Had she liked what she'd seen? Then I wondered what she'd thought of the way I'd dropped to the ground when the branch snapped.

She probably thought you were a fucking lunatic, but what does it matter? What she thinks about anything—you, this farm, that kiss—doesn't mean shit.

But I couldn't stop thinking about her. About kissing her. About touching her. About getting to know her better. Was she just a spoiled rich girl intent on getting her way or was there more to her? Was she actually attracted to me or was she just messing around with the stable boy, so to speak? Did she think I was an asshole for grabbing her that way? Did she think I was a dick for pushing her away? What would have happened if I hadn't?

It doesn't matter. She doesn't matter. In a few days she'll leave town and go back to Detroit where she belongs and you'll never see her again.

Something tightened in my gut.

I'd never see her again…unless I went to that meeting tomorrow.

Don't. Seeing her again will only cause trouble.

Maybe. Or maybe by seeing her again and remaining in control of my temper and my desire, I could prove to myself—and to her—that yesterday was a fluke. I'd sit right across the table from her, look her dead in the eye, and force myself to feel nothing.

I was still a soldier, wasn't I?

I could do it. I had to.

chapter fourteen

Margot

THE FIRST THING THAT THREW ME OFF WAS THAT JACK WAS *THERE* WHEN I arrived at Pete and Georgia's house the next morning. Sitting at the kitchen table with a cup of coffee, looking a little tired but rugged and handsome and sexy as hell. His t-shirt hugged the muscles of his arms so tight, I went dry in the mouth and wet in the panties. All I could think of were those arms around me yesterday in the barn. Our eyes met—and both of us immediately looked away.

Frantic, I glanced around at everyone. Was it obvious there was awkwardness between us?

"Good morning, Margot," Georgia chirped, setting a giant glass pan of something that looked and smelled delectable on the table. "Hope you're hungry."

"Um, yes. That looks amazing." My heart was racing, and I turned away from the table to set my bag down in one corner of the room, telling myself to stay calm. This was a work meeting, and I was a professional. I had to act like it. *Come on, Margot. You're good at this. Grace under pressure.* A few deep breaths later, I went back to the table.

"Why don't you sit there, Margot?" Georgia said, indicating the chair across from Jack.

Great.

I lowered myself into the chair and smoothed my skirt. Patted my hair. Touched my necklace.

My necklace, where his tongue had been not even twenty-four hours ago. I risked a glance and caught him staring at my fingertips on the pearls. My stomach fluttered.

What the fuck? *Now* the butterflies made an appearance? I couldn't handle butterflies right now!

So stop looking at him.

But I couldn't help it. And when I looked again, I found him looking right back. Eyes hard. Jaw locked. Neck muscles tense. Almost as if he were angry with me. He swallowed. Sat up taller and squared his shoulders.

What the hell? What had I ever done to him?

Unexpectedly, my eyes filled and I furiously blinked the tears away. And something happened—his eyes softened for a second, his lips parting slightly before pressing together again. God, he was all over the place! Did he want to kiss me or punch me?

Just pretend he isn't here.

It wasn't easy. Although he said nothing, I felt his angry eyes on me constantly. I was so aware of his presence I might as well have been sitting on his lap. But I kept a mask of cheerful nonchalance on my face, praising the meal, sipping coffee with cream, and chatting with Pete and Georgia about New York. Beneath that mask, though, I was a nervous wreck.

"This is delicious! Is it French toast?" *Please don't let my cheeks be too pink.*

"Could you pass the cream, please?" *Oh God, I said that too loud, didn't I?*

"I love that restaurant! They have an amazing brunch." *Look at his forearms. Christ, they're huge.*

After breakfast was over and the table was cleared, I concentrated on pulling my notes from my bag and preparing to talk. *Don't look at him. Who cares if he's staring at you like he can't decide whether to tear your clothes off or tear you to shreds? He doesn't care about this anyway. Focus on the issues and strategies. You got this.* When everyone was seated again, I began.

I'd outlined a three-pronged strategy for building brand awareness as well as increasing revenue. The first involved the basics: they needed a logo, they needed a new website, they needed social media accounts and someone to run them. "I've listed contact information for a few graphic designers I know, but I encourage you to shop around for someone local as well," I said. Brad threw a few names out, Pete asked a couple questions and took notes, and Georgia smiled at me as she bounced Cooper on her lap. Jack, however, sat with his arms crossed and continued to give me the evil eye.

Ignore him. Keep going.

The second prong involved creating content—they had to be prepared to put a lot of work into engaging potential customers and getting people talking. "And I don't mean ads saying how great you are. I mean pictures and stories about what you're doing here—the messes *and* the successes. Show off those funny-looking vegetables! Talk about the time you failed at beekeeping or whatever! Admit your first attempt at homemade pie crust was a disaster! People relate to that. Make them *feel* something, make them laugh, make them wonder. This isn't about you—it's about them."

Jack snorted.

"I love that," Georgia said, shooting Jack a look over Cooper's head. "And I like to write, too."

"Perfect." I smiled at her with grateful relief. "Let them get to know you all. Be real, be fun, be visible. They'll associate your brand with you as people, make that human connection."

"Do we all have to be visible?" Brad frowned.

I shrugged. "Not if you don't want to be. But I think the whole concept of the family-owned and operated farm is stronger if the whole family is involved. Plus, the name is Valentini Brothers Farm." I didn't miss the way they glanced at Jack, but I kept my eyes off him.

"I like photography," Brad said. "My daughter Olivia does too. Maybe we could take pictures for the site?"

I snapped my fingers. "There you go. That's perfect. Maybe your daughter could even have her own little corner on the website, a blog where she talks about things for kids. Teaches them about eating local and organic."

"And easy recipes," Georgia added. "She likes to cook too. This is great, Margot."

Jack cracked his knuckles.

"Moving on," I said, this time giving him a pointed stare, "let's talk about agritourism. A lot of smaller farms are using it to supplement their income." I explained the concept, and everyone but Jack was excited about it.

"We can't do weddings here. We don't have the space." Even though what he said was argumentative, it was almost a relief to have him say something and not just sit there bristling.

"We had *your* wedding here," Pete reminded him.

"That was a one-time thing."

"He's right to be concerned about space, though," Georgia said. "For his wedding, they rented a tent. Would the client have to do that every time?"

Jack groaned. "Then we have people trampling everywhere to set up a tent every weekend? Catering trucks? Port-o-johns? No."

I tried to help. God knows I didn't like port-o-johns either. "What about a semi-permanent structure or space dedicated to that purpose? What if you invested in a huge tent that stayed up the whole summer?"

"We could do that," Pete enthused, earning a dirty look from Jack. "And we wouldn't need catering trucks." He sat up taller in his chair. "*We'd* want to cater it. But we'd need to get a license."

Georgia nodded grimly. "Kitchen inspection. And generally, a home kitchen won't cut it."

I thought for a moment. "When you imagine your farm-to-table restaurant, where is it? Somewhere on the premises?"

Pete and Georgia looked at each other. "We had this idea at one point," Pete began cautiously, "about buying the old house across the street. It's vacant, has been for years. And the property has enough space for a tent, maybe even a barn, for events."

"The Oliver place?" Jack sounded shocked. "The roof will cave in on your heads! That place is falling apart."

"Old houses have good bones, though," Brad put in. "That house is solid. I didn't know you guys were interested in it. My office has the listing."

"It's really just an idea we're kicking around at this point," Georgia said. "We can't afford it right now anyway."

"But I can see how it would work," I said, my mind filling with images of intimate dining tables in high-ceilinged rooms. "You'd have to put in a brand new kitchen, I'm sure, and—"

"This is ridiculous. Do you know what a new commercial kitchen costs? And that's on top of the price of the house!" Jack grumped. "And there's no guarantee people will even want to get married here."

"*You* did," I pointed out.

The look he gave me could have cut steel. "That's because I belong here. It *means* something to me. Other people want fancy halls with marble and glass, not some tent right next to a barn."

"Calm down. It's worth considering, Jack," Pete said. "That's all we're doing. Considering ideas."

"I know what you're doing. You're trying to change things around here, make this farm into something it was never intended to be, and you don't care what I say about it." He stood, his chair scraping the wood. "So go ahead and make your website and take your pictures or whatever if she's got you convinced that crap will make a difference, but she knows fuck-all about this farm and this family. She's been here, what—two days? You can't just show up somewhere and start messing with people's lives like that." He glared at me across the table, and suddenly I knew what this was about.

"Hey!" Pete stood up too. "Apologize to her, right now. She's a guest in this house and you have no right to treat her that way."

Jack's face went even darker, and his fists clenched at his sides. His expression was a mixture of anger and shame, but his posture was pure Fuck-You-I-Won't-Back-Down. No way would he apologize. Instead, he turned around and stomped out, slamming the back door behind him.

My own temper flared—and I didn't need a tray of scones to hurl at him, I had plenty of words to use.

"Excuse me," I said to everyone at the table. Then I raced out after him.

"Hey!" I yelled, my heels poking into the grass as I chased him across the lawn. "I want to talk to you!"

He didn't even turn around.

I broke into a run. "I said stop!" Catching up with him as he reached the path through the woods, I yanked on his arm.

He turned on me angrily, shook off my hand. "I don't want to talk to you, Margot. Get away from me."

"What the hell is your problem?" I demanded.

His eyes were dark and tortured. "My problem is you, OK? You come in here with your fancy ideas and expensive clothes and shiny hair and big blue eyes and everyone loves you and it's fucking with me. Everything about you is fucking with me. Just leave me alone." He turned and took off again.

"Get back here!" I yelled. "We're not finished!"

He didn't even glance back, just kept marching through the woods toward his cabin.

Dammit. *Dammit!* I stifled a scream that threatened to claw its way out of my throat and fisted my hands in my hair. He was so frustrating! So stubborn! So irrational! Why couldn't he see that his family wasn't trying to ruin his dream, they were trying to make it better? And I wasn't trying to fuck with him, I was doing my job. It's not like coming here had been my idea—they'd hired me!

And what the hell was that about my eyes and my hair? What did he want me to do, put a bag over my head? I couldn't help it if he was attracted to me! Did he think I enjoyed being attracted to him any better? Because I didn't! I wished to God I'd never laid eyes on him! Fuming, I watched him disappear around a bend in the woods.

Calm down, Margot. Pull yourself together.

After a few deep breaths, I walked slowly back toward the house, trying to think of a way to explain what I'd just done. Jesus, I was a disaster these days.

What was going on with me?

༺♡༻

As it turned out, the family members left at the table were twice as mortified as I was, and bent over backward apologizing for Jack's behavior, assuring me they loved my ideas, and begging me not to take his words to heart.

I said I was sorry for running out, promised I was OK, and asked them to contact me in a few days, after they'd had a chance to go over everything I'd proposed. "I have some vacation time coming, so I'll just be parked in a beach chair," I said, hoping my smile looked genuine.

Georgia walked me out and insisted on giving me leftovers. "Please, take it," she said, holding out the plastic container. "I'll feel better."

"You've got nothing to feel bad about, Georgia."

"I do, though." She shrugged helplessly. "I went to see Jack last night and pleaded with him to come today. I thought he'd listen with an open mind."

"Really?" *I could have told you he wouldn't.*

"Yeah. He's not always this bad, it's just..." She sighed, closing her eyes briefly. "I don't know what it is. Something is going on with him, but he won't talk about it."

"He's a tough nut to crack, I agree." And I wasn't going to waste my time trying. He might look like a grown man on the outside, but he had the temperament of a stubborn brat. "Thanks for the leftovers. Breakfast was delicious."

I went back to the cottage with every intention of changing into my bathing suit, grabbing some sunscreen, a towel, and my book, and sitting in the sand for hours. I'd earned it, hadn't I? I'd read, I'd swim, I'd relax—what I would *not* do was waste one more second thinking about Jack Valentini.

At least, I *tried* not to think about him.

I put on the suit, rubbed in the sunscreen, and sat on the towel with my book, but all I did was stare at the same page, cursing his name and letting my anger fester.

I mean, what an asshole! How dare he treat me that way! How dare he make those shitty remarks after I'd tried so hard to please him yesterday! And after that kiss—which *he'd* initiated! I'd been doing a good job keeping my hands to myself. This was on him, not me. Tossing my book aside, I crossed my arms and scowled beneath the floppy brim of my sun hat.

That's what his problem is. He's mad at himself, and he's taking it out on me. This isn't just about weddings on the farm. This is about him being unable to handle the fact that he's attracted to me—someone he sees as a spoiled rotten rich city girl who always gets what she wants. And even if he hated all my ideas, that doesn't give him the right to be rude.

Even a swim in chilly Lake Huron couldn't take the hot edge off my anger. That asshole owed me an apology—and he needed to hear what I had to say! Maybe the old Margot would have stayed cool, brushed it off, taken the high road, but she had been replaced of late by New Margot. And New Margot didn't hold back! She spoke her mind. She threw scones. She stood up for herself.

So after spending the entire day dying to tell Jack Valentini just what I thought of him (and the entire evening drinking wine and eating leftover French toast casserole), I showered off the sand and sunscreen, threw on some clothes, and stomped through the dark to his house to do just that.

chapter fifteen

Jack

I WAS LYING ON THE COUCH, DROWNING IN MISERY, WHEN I HEARD SOMEONE approaching the cabin. Immediately on edge, I sat up and listened. My windows were open, and I heard a voice. A female voice.

It was quiet at first, as if she were muttering to herself, but grew a little louder as she got closer. "...so you can go to hell, asshole. I've never been so mad at anyone in my entire life. How dare you say those things to me after what you did yesterday? You should be ashamed of yourself."

Margot.

Was she coming here to tell me off?

If so, I deserved it. I'd been way out of line this morning. But she had me so fucking worked up—I'd tried so hard to do what I said, look her right in the eye and feel nothing, and I'd failed. Everything about her got to me—the long blond hair, the blue eyes, the fair skin, the pearl necklace, the graceful hands. I couldn't see her legs beneath the table, but they drove me crazy anyway. Then there were other things, not even physical—the lilt of her voice, the excitement in her smile, the confidence she had in herself and her ideas, the genuine enthusiasm for our farm. Other than a few nervous glances early on, she'd hardly seemed rattled by my presence. And I'd been a fucking mess.

So I'd taken it out on her, on all of them. Tried to make them feel guilty for distorting my dream, when I knew they were just trying to build on it. But dammit! I didn't want things to *change* around here. I didn't want the farm to be something new and different. *I* didn't want to be someone new and different. And Margot, who'd never been told no in her life, didn't understand what it was like to feel like you were losing control of what mattered to you. None of them did! This wasn't just about weddings at the farm. It was about everything in my life feeling so slippery all of a sudden. About being unable to hold on to what mattered.

I sighed, closing my eyes as she drew closer.

But I shouldn't have treated her that way. It wasn't her fault I was so drawn to her. She had no idea that she was part of what was making me feel so unsteady. I owed her an apology, but after that, I needed to stay away from her.

I opened the door before she even knocked, and her mouth fell open in surprise. I was surprised too—she looked so different. Her hair was wet, and although she wore a flowery summer dress, she had no makeup or jewelry on. My heart knocked against my ribs. *She's so beautiful.*

Beautiful and fucking furious.

Her mouth snapped shut, her eyes narrowing. "I have something to say to you."

"So say it." I joined her on the porch, shutting the door behind me so the cat didn't try to get out. I figured I owed it to Margot to let her bitch at me. What could she say that I hadn't said to myself?

First, she parked her hands on her hips and then she poked a finger in my chest. "You're not nice."

I almost smiled. "No?"

"No. I don't know what you have against me, but I'm not here to make you miserable, I'm here to do a job. And I'm just as sorry about yesterday as you are, but you did not have to be such a jerk to me today."

"No, I didn't. And I'm sorry."

"And you—" She blinked at me. "What?"

"I'm sorry. You're right. I was a jerk today. You didn't deserve it."

She looked to the side and then back at me. "That's it? You're not going to argue with me?"

"Did you come here looking for a fight?"

She huffed. "I don't know. Yes."

"Well, there's nothing to fight about. I was a dick." I stuck my hands in my pockets and took a small step back. Margot sweet and bubbly in broad daylight was tempting enough—Margot feisty and looking for trouble in the dark was downright dangerous.

"Why'd you do it?" she asked.

"That's hard to explain."

"Were you getting me back for spying on you?"

"No."

She chewed her lip for a second. "What about that stuff about my shiny hair and blue eyes fucking with you? What about telling me *I'm* your problem?"

"You're not my problem. That came out wrong." *My problem is the way I feel standing so close to you.*

She didn't appear convinced. "What about what happened yesterday? In the barn. Are we ever going to talk about that?"

I shrugged. "It was a mistake."

That earned me an eye roll. "No shit."

"Then why'd you ask?"

Her brow furrowed. "I don't know. Because you confuse me. I never know whether I'm coming or going with you. One minute we're kissing, the next you're yelling at me to get out. This morning you're an asshole, tonight you apologize." She slapped a hand to her forehead. "I can't keep up."

"You don't have to. Aren't you leaving soon?" *Please say yes. I can't go on like this, wanting you this way.*

"In about ten days."

Fuck. I wasn't sure I'd make it.

Suddenly she clapped her hands over her face. "God, what am I *doing* here? I must be crazy. You're a *client.*" She stepped off the porch and started hurrying down the path away from the cabin.

"Margot, wait!" I was relieved she was leaving, but I couldn't let her go alone. "I'll walk you to your car."

"I didn't drive," she called, heading into the trees.

My chest got tight, and I sped up, following her into the dark. "Margot, stop! I'll drive you back. You shouldn't walk alone at night."

"I'm *fine.*"

"Hey." Catching up to her, I grabbed her elbow and spun her around. "I'm not letting you walk anywhere near that highway in the dark, do you understand me?"

Just enough moonlight spilled through the tops of the trees that I could see her eyes glitter with angry tears. "Let go of me."

"No." I started trying to drag her back toward the cabin so I could get my keys, but she fought me.

"Let go of me," she said through clenched teeth.

"No!" I roared, gripping her by the upper arms and drawing her in. "I can't."

And without even thinking about it, I crushed my mouth to hers.

She wiggled around in my grasp for a second, and I thought she was still trying to escape, but when I loosened my grip, she threw her arms around me.

I reached under the bottom of her dress and grabbed the back of her thighs, lifting her right off the ground. She wrapped her legs around me, threading her fingers through my hair, fingernails raking across my scalp. Chills swept down my arms and back. It felt so good to be touched this way again, wanted this way—I'd forgotten how good, and the heat of it ignited a fire inside me that had long been out. She stroked my tongue with hers, kissed my jaw, my forehead, my neck, and my entire body thrummed with the need to be inside her, to be surrounded by the warmth of her desire. It was enough to shut off my brain—all I did was feel.

Moving off the path, I put her back against a thick tree trunk, pinning her there, pressing the bulge in my jeans between her legs, rocking my hips to rub against her. She used her legs to pull me closer. Minutes flew by as our breathing grew heavier, our bodies more demanding. "Yes," she whispered. "I want it. I want it."

Ten seconds of fumbling around with clothing later, I was sliding into her, my hands beneath her ass, her forearms braced on my shoulders. Her mouth was open, just above mine. "Oh God," she whimpered as I lowered her onto my cock. "I want it, but don't know if I can take it."

"You're going to take it," I told her.

Her eyes closed as I buried every last inch inside her tight, wet pussy, her head turning to the side. "You're so big it hurts."

"Want me to stop?" *Don't say yes, don't say yes, don't say yes.*

Her eyes flew open and she stared me down. "Fuck you. I want this. I don't even know why I want this so badly, but I do."

It was enough for me. Because I *needed* this—needed to be this close to someone, needed to hear her sighs and moans, needed to feel her heat and softness, needed to release all the tension inside me. I needed it so desperately I couldn't see straight.

Pushing her back against the tree again, I drove into her, hard and fast and deep. She cried out at the peak of each thrust so loudly I put a hand over her mouth so that anyone within hearing distance wouldn't think someone was being attacked by an animal.

But I felt animalistic in my desire—almost bloodthirsty. She gasped for air against my hand, her eyes wide and wild. But I felt her tongue stroke my fingers, and when I slipped my thumb into her mouth, she sucked it, licked it, bit it. Every muscle in my body was tight and tingling, and I knew I couldn't hold out long. I put both hands beneath her again and concentrated with all my might on being less selfish, holding her tight to my body and flexing my hips to give her the best angle, rubbing the base of my cock against her clit. I'd missed this too—making a woman come, feeling that surge of power and pleasure.

"Yes! Just like that," she cried, her eyes closed. "Don't stop, please don't stop…" She dropped her head to my shoulder and sank her teeth into my flesh, one hand fisted in my hair, the other clutching my bicep. Her legs tensed up, her entire body going still, and I pulled her even closer, using my hands to move her in little circles on my cock. Her pussy pulsed rhythmically around me, and I lost control.

I rasped and growled through clenched teeth, my orgasm tearing through me with brutal force. I fucked her barbarically, passionately, like I hated her, like I loved her, like a man completely driven by instinct and not reason or emotion. And when I came, exploding inside her with violent bliss, her face buried in my neck, everything went silent and black.

Stumbling backward, depleted and dizzy, I sank to my knees taking Margot with me. She yelped and clung to my neck like a child, sending me tumbling onto my back in the dirt.

And I laughed.

chapter sixteen

Margot

I ENDED UP STRADDLING HIM, MY KNEES IN THE DIRT, MY ARMS AROUND HIS NECK.
He was laughing.
Laughing.
I had to smile. *So that's what it takes? An orgasm?*

And speaking of orgasms, my whole body was still humming from the one he'd just given me. I'd never felt anything like it—so deep and intense I couldn't even move while it happened. And it had happened so fast! I usually had to concentrate pretty hard to come during sex, and certain conditions had to be met for me to relax enough to let it happen. (Total darkness, soft sheets, complete privacy. Also, I didn't love being on top because it forced me to see a man's O face, and they were never dignified. It also made me feel sort of like being on display during a vigorous treadmill workout.)

But with Jack, it had struck me like lightning.

The reality of what had just happened started to sink in. I'd just been fucked against a tree. By a farmer. Without a condom.

Oh, God.

My sandals were missing. He'd seriously fucked me right out of my Jack Rogers. And tree bark had probably torn up the back of my Lilly Pulitzer shift.

But damn, that was good. Rough. Messy. Frantic.

Totally un-Margot, yet I'd loved every second.

I sat up, laying my hands on his chest and peering down at him. He looked so *different*. It was dark, but I could see the way his facial muscles had relaxed—no furrow in his brow, no tension in his jaw. His full mouth looked even more sensual, one side of it hooking up in a wry grin.

"That the fight you were looking for?" he asked.

I smiled ruefully. "Not exactly."

"You were pretty mad."

"I'm still mad."

He laughed again, and my toes tingled. I loved the sound of it—deep and warm and gratifying.

"But embarrassed too," I admitted.

"Why are *you* embarrassed? *I* started it." Some of the tension returned to his face. "Are you OK?"

"I'm fine."

"We didn't use anything..."

I pressed my lips into a line. "No, we didn't. But we're OK." I was on the pill, although I'd never had sex without a condom before.

Don't think about that.

Or with a client.

Don't think about that either.

"OK." He took a breath, his chest moving under my palms. His hands were still on my hips. "God, Margot, I'm sorry. I don't know what came over me."

"Don't be sorry." I started to get up, feeling like things were about to get awkward. "Really. It just...happened."

He helped me to my feet, located my shoes, and while I tugged my panties back into place (they were still looped around one ankle), he did up his jeans. "I guess I just..." He ran a hand through his thick dark hair. "Lost control. It's been so long."

"How long?" I asked before I could stop myself. "I'm sorry—you don't have to tell me that."

"Since Steph."

My jaw dropped. "That long? *Three years*? Wow, I thought I had you beat. But it's only been just over a year for me." Not that sex had ever been anything like what we'd just done. I hadn't even missed it, to be honest.

"That's a long time, too."

I lifted my shoulders. "Guess that explains it. We just needed to get something out of our systems."

He nodded, sticking his hands in his pockets. "Yeah."

We stood there for a moment as the crickets chirped around us. My heart was beating a little too fast for comfort as I looked at him in the dark, knowing I was the first woman he'd been with since his wife. It was messing with me... I wish I'd known. I might have tried to make it nicer or something, maybe not screamed so loud. Or bit him.

I mean...*the first woman since his wife.*

That *meant* something to me.

But I had no idea what to do with it.

"So," I said briskly, as if we were wrapping up a business meeting, "I think the best thing would be to pretend this never happened."

He nodded again. "I think so too."

"We'll just agree it was a moment of insanity, fueled by pent-up frustration," I suggested, needing to file this in my brain somewhere, and not in my heart.

"Right."

I put on a smile, but I didn't feel happy at all. "And now that the moment of insanity has passed, I'd better get going."

"Please let me drive you." His voice was quiet and serious. "I won't sleep tonight if I don't, not that I sleep very well anyway."

"You don't sleep well?"

"No."

It was something small but personal, and I was grateful for the admission. Still, I hesitated, glancing toward Pete and Georgia's house. "Won't someone see us and wonder what we're doing?"

"No. It's late. Pete goes to bed early, and Georgia is working tonight."

I nodded. "OK, then."

"I just have to get the keys. Come with me?"

"Sure." We walked toward the cabin in silence, Jack's hands still in his pockets and my arms crossed over my chest. I thought about asking to use his bathroom to clean up a little, but something about it didn't feel right. Instead I waited for him on the porch, and then we retraced our steps back through the trees toward Pete and Georgia's.

In the driveway, Jack opened the passenger door of his pickup for me and I climbed in. He got in the driver's side just as I was pulling the bottom of my dress down as far as I could. I thought about asking Jack if he had a handkerchief, but he didn't look like the type.

"What are you doing?" He gave me a funny look.

"Trying not to get the seat sticky," I said, feeling heat in my cheeks. So much about sex was embarrassing.

He chuckled and started the truck. "Don't worry about it. Really. Tell me where you're staying?"

I gave him directions, and we were silent again on the two-minute ride. *Thank God*, I thought. Because the more he talked to me in that sweet, serious voice or smiled or laughed or showed me there was a gentleman inside that rough exterior, the more I liked him.

I didn't want to like him.

When he pulled up next to the cottage, I opened the door. "Thanks for the ride."

"Margot, wait." He put a hand on my leg. "Don't go yet."

It's better if you don't touch me, Jack.

"Yes?"

"It's not personal, my objection to your ideas for the farm. I can tell you're good at what you do."

"Thanks."

He took his hand off my leg and rubbed his jaw. "I just don't want things to change."

"Even if the changes make sense? If they'll bring in more money eventually? If they'll make people happy?"

He didn't answer, but I saw the stubborn set of his jaw return.

Sighing, I pushed the door all the way open and got out. "Goodnight, Jack. Thanks for the ride." I shut the door and walked to the door, and he waited until I was safely inside before pulling away.

Another display of courtesy.

Damn him.

⁓⁓

Later, I lay in bed, listening to the waves through the screens and struggling to process tonight's surprises. The way Jack had apologized. The way he'd agreed he'd been mean and unfair. The unexpected—and vehement—insistence that he drive me home. The shock of that first kiss, when he'd grabbed me by both arms, his frustration giving way to passion all at once.

You're going to take it.

My stomach hollowed as I recalled the way he'd driven deep inside me, so deep it had hurt. Never in my life had I experienced anything like the way that sharp twinge had started to feel good. How could pain accompany pleasure like that? How had two opposite sensations merged inside my body, so seamlessly that I couldn't tell where the pain stopped and where the pleasure began? Which was which?

And I'd screamed and panted and gasped and clawed at him like an animal. He'd drawn something out of me, a part of myself I didn't even know was there, a part that existed only to *want* so ferociously, I could think of nothing else—not our crude surroundings, our nonexistent relationship status, not even our privacy. I never once worried about how loud I was or felt ashamed of my desire or stopped to fret that well-bred ladies should not appear to enjoy sex so unabashedly. (Bet I was the first Thurber woman to fuck a farmer in a forest.)

I'd loved every minute of it. Even his O face.

Was sex with Jack always like that? I wondered if the mad desperation of it was due to the fact that it had been so long for both of us or if he was always so rough and aggressive.

You'll never know. Understand?

Out of nowhere, Old Margot made an unwelcome appearance.

You both agreed it was a one-time thing. Leave it alone.

I frowned, waiting for New Margot to speak up and defend my right to another mind-blowing orgasm, but that scone cold bitch said nothing.

See? Even she agrees. There is no universe in which you and Jack Valentini make any sense whatsoever. Fine, he's not the jerk you thought he was this afternoon, but the reasons you need to forget about him still exist, not to mention that he's made no secret of the fact he'll be glad to be rid of you when you're gone. Finish up your work here and get back where you belong.

Sighing, I rolled over onto my stomach and closed my eyes. Old Margot was right. In ten days, I'd be back in my world, and this would just be that craziest-thing-I've-ever-done story I looked back on and laughed about.

Or cried about. One of the two.

chapter seventeen

Jack

I LAY IN BED THAT NIGHT, WAITING FOR THE GUILT TO ASSAULT ME. FOR MY conscience to prick me. For my ghosts to haunt me. For regret, for tears, for a bitter taste in my mouth. All the familiar things that usually accompanied a sleepless night.

But it didn't happen. Even Bridget Jones lay beside me, content and purring. Didn't she know what a horrible person I was?

Come on, I thought angrily. Someone needs to scream at me for this. Make me feel bad. Demand to know how I could do such a thing. *Make me answer for this, God. I shouldn't come away unscathed.*

But God was silent tonight.

Instead the voice in my head was Margot's. *I don't even know why I want this so badly, but I do.*

It was a mystery to me, too, this explosive chemistry between a beautiful, sophisticated city girl and a rough-around-the-edges country guy like me. Where did it come from? And why did it have such a grip on me? It drove me insane the way I couldn't stop thinking about her. All I could do was pray that giving in to that desire would get her out from under my skin.

I was likely out from under hers, anyway. She'd been pretty quick to decide we should just pretend it never happened. Not that I disagreed—I didn't need anyone in my family to know about it, and I certainly didn't want to pursue any kind of relationship with her. I wasn't free to do that.

My heart would always, always belong to someone else. I'd made a promise to Steph, and I intended to keep it. Not only that, I wanted to be the kind of man she'd be proud of. I wanted to honor her memory. I wanted to honor *her*.

Thinking about how to do that kept me up long into the night.

In the morning, after checking on the animals, I went up to Pete and Georgia's for coffee. I could have made it at the cabin, but I owed them both an apology and wanted to get a few things off my chest.

I knocked twice on the back door before letting myself in. "Morning."

Georgia looked over her shoulder at me from where she sat at the kitchen table helping Cooper with his breakfast. "Morning." Neither her tone nor her face was particularly welcoming.

I'd expected that. "Pete around?"

"He's out front."

"OK to have some coffee?"

"Help yourself."

I poured a cup, ruffled Cooper's hair, and went out to the driveway, where Pete was changing the oil on an ATV. "Hey," I said.

He glanced at me. Barely. "Hey."

"Almost done?"

"Not really."

"Can you take a break?"

"For what?"

"I have something to say, and I want to say it to you and Georgia at the same time."

My brother laughed, but it wasn't a happy sound. "I think you said enough yesterday."

I took a deep, slow breath, fighting my instincts to get angry and snap back. "I was wrong yesterday, and I'd like to apologize."

"You should apologize to Margot."

"I did."

He looked up at me in surprise, shielding his eyes from the sun. "You did?"

"Yes."

Turning his attention back to the oil filter, he was silent for a few seconds. "I'll meet you inside in five minutes."

"Thank you." I went back into the kitchen and sat across from Cooper, making goofy faces at him so he'd giggle. His little laugh was my favorite sound in the world.

"Jack, I'm trying to get him to eat," Georgia complained, but she was smiling too. "You're making it difficult."

"I'll do it. Go get some more coffee." I went around the table and nudged her out of her chair, then sat. "Cooper's gonna eat for me, aren't you buddy?"

"Bunny!" he said happily.

"I said *buddy*. Now open the barn door, because here comes the horsie!" I did my best at the horse, motorcycle, and airplane tricks to get him to open his mouth and managed to shovel in the rest of his blueberry pancakes by the time Pete came in.

"Good enough," Georgia said, taking away the little plastic plate and wiping his mouth and hands with a washcloth. "Thanks."

"Anytime. I can take him to the park later, if you want."

"That would be great." She set him down on his feet and I laughed when he took off running at full speed, face planted in the hall, then got right back up again. Kids were so resilient.

"You guys have a few minutes for me?"

Georgia nodded and sat down across from me, and Pete took the chair next to her. "So what's up?" he asked, bringing his coffee cup to his lips.

"I need to apologize for yesterday. I had a bad attitude right from the start and I was rude to a guest in your house. I'm sorry."

"And you apologized to her already?" Pete still sounded like he didn't believe me.

I nodded. "I did. Last night."

They exchanged a glance. "Last night? Where?" Georgia asked.

Be careful. "The cabin. She came over to talk about the meeting, and I told her I was sorry for being such a dick about things. I tried to explain myself better." *Then I fucked her right out of her shoes.*

"What reason did you give her?" Pete asked.

"I told her I can tell that she's good at what she does, but that I'm reluctant to make any changes on the farm that weren't part of my original vision."

"But Jack, her ideas can be in addition to your vision," he said. "No one wants to take the farm from you or stop you from doing what you love and what you're good at. This place is your dream. We know that."

Pressing my lips together, I forced myself to say what I'd come here to say. "You two deserve the same shot at *your* dream. So I won't stand in your way."

They were stunned silent for a moment. Then Pete said, "Are you serious?"

"Yes." I took a breath. "I did a lot of thinking last night. And if the situation were different, and it was Steph sitting here, not me, I know she'd tell you to go for it."

Georgia smiled, her eyes getting misty. "That's so true. She would have."

"And the best way to honor her is to do what she would do."

Pete cleared his throat. "That's great, Jack."

"I'm not promising to go along with just anything," I said quickly, "and I don't want anything to interfere with what I'm doing, but I'd be willing to discuss the possibilities of a restaurant, maybe look into buying the Oliver place. If that's impossible, I'd *consider* finding space on our property to put up a tent or barn for weddings or whatever. But you guys will have to do the legwork. Convince me it won't be horrible."

Georgia squealed and jumped up, coming around the table to throw her arms around my neck. She kissed my cheek and squeezed so hard I nearly choked, but inside I felt good. Deep down, I didn't think there was any way we could afford the Oliver place, and I still hated the idea of strangers trampling around my beloved farm, but something Margot had asked me last night stuck with me. *Even if the changes make sense? If they'll make people happy?*

The truth was, it wouldn't matter what changed or didn't on the farm— I'd never be happy, not after everything that had happened. So if they could, then I shouldn't hold them back. They didn't need to suffer for my sins.

"I'll call Brad," Pete said. "Maybe he can send us some info on the Oliver listing."

"I better get back to work. Thanks for the coffee." Rising from the chair, I took my cup to the sink before heading out the back door.

A few seconds later, I heard Pete's voice. "Hey, wait a sec." He jogged to catch up with me. "Thanks, man. Georgia is beside herself."

I shrugged, sticking my hands in my pockets. "I hope it works out."

"So why the change of heart?" he asked, lifting his cap off and replacing it. "I'm curious."

"I don't know."

"You get laid last night or what?"

I rolled my eyes, but my cock twitched. "Jesus, Pete."

"OK, OK. Just asking." He held up his palms. "You seem different today, that's all. More relaxed than you've been in a long time."

"So quit bugging me before I get tense again," I said, resuming my walk across the yard. Actually, I did feel more relaxed. A sense of relief and even peace had eased the tension in my mind and body. My steps were lighter. My shoulders looser. My fingers free of the urge to curl into fists.

Whether that was because of the sex I'd had or the conclusions I'd drawn or the apologies I'd offered, I wasn't sure. I had yet to suffer any debilitating guilt about having sex with Margot, which shocked me—I'd actually felt worse after the kiss. It had seemed more *personal,* somehow. Fucking her in the woods felt more like blowing off steam than anything else.

At least, that's what I told myself.

But the real relief would come in nine days, once Margot was gone for good.

chapter eighteen

Margot

I WAS ON EDGE THE NEXT MORNING. TOO MUCH COFFEE HAD ME JITTERY, TOO little sleep had me restless, and too much time thinking about Jack had me unsettled. I didn't feel right in my skin.

I spent the morning trying to catch up on work for other clients, but I struggled to focus. The tenderness between my legs, the soreness in my stomach muscles, the memory of my legs wrapped around his waist distracted me endlessly.

Stop it! It never happened!

After lunch, I took a walk on the beach, hoping a little exercise and Vitamin D might help.

It didn't.

I tried to take a nap, which was a disaster since what I actually did was lie there and picture every inch of Jack's naked body (good thing I'd gotten that view from the tree), and replay in my mind every second of The Fuck That Never Happened.

Irritated, I sat up and grabbed my phone. I felt like talking about it to someone, but I hesitated before calling Jaime for two reasons—one, I'd told her I wouldn't bang the client, and two, I was supposed to be pretending I hadn't. Telling her about it was *not* a step in that direction.

I could always call Claire instead, I thought. I'd have to start from the beginning since she didn't know anything about Jack yet, but—

My phone buzzed in my hand. *Mom calling.*

I cringed. My mother was the *last* person I wanted to talk to right now, but I dutifully took the call.

"Hello?"

"Hello, Margot. This is your mother."

No matter how many times I told her she didn't have to announce herself, she never failed to do it. "Hi, Mom. How are you?"

"Fine. I played tennis this morning and I'm about to meet Aunt Dodie for lunch."

"Sounds nice." *Nothing ever changes in her world.*

"So I have to run," she breezed on, as if she hadn't been the one to call me, "but I wanted to let you know you can come home whenever. Tripp was caught *in flagrante delicto* with a waitress at the country club. In the men's locker room, of all places! Why any woman would want to go in there is beyond me."

My jaw was hanging open. "Really?"

"Yes, it's all anyone can talk about. Mimi Jewett's beside herself, but if you ask me, she had it coming, the way she gossiped about you and The Incident."

"Right."

"So I don't know what your plans are, but do be back for the Historical Society fundraiser at the end of the month. We're hosting, and it's important for Daddy's campaign."

"What's the theme?"

"Gatsby."

"Again?"

"People like tradition, dear."

I sighed. It was useless to argue with Muffy on the subject of tradition. Her life was ruled by it. Mine was too, for the most part. "I'll be there. Bye, Mom."

I put my phone down and looked out the window at the lake. So thanks to Tripp (what an idiot), I could show my face again at home. And even though I was paid up here for nine more days, I knew hanging around any longer than necessary was probably a bad idea.

Because the more I thought about Jack Valentini, the more I wanted to see him again, get to know him better. Kiss him again. Touch him. Feel him inside me. Hear him whisper to me in the dark. Figure out why the chemistry between us was so good. Was it simply a case of opposites attract? Or was there more to it?

Sighing, I gave up trying to solve the riddle and admitted the truth.

There's no way this can work. I should just leave.

⁓

I tidied up the cottage, packed my bags, and called Georgia, explaining that due to a family emergency I was leaving earlier than planned, but I'd be available by phone or FaceTime or Skype or whatever she wanted to use to keep in touch moving forward. She thanked me for my time and said she'd contact me as soon as they'd had a chance to discuss everything.

I also contacted Ann, the property manager for the cottage, and told her I was leaving sooner than expected, but I understood I wouldn't get my money back.

"I'm sorry to hear that. I'll mail you a check for the security deposit."

"Thank you. I'm about to get on the road, so I'll leave the key on the counter."

"You're not leaving tonight, are you?" she said. "At least wait until morning. There's a huge line of storms coming through."

Frowning, I looked out the window but saw no evidence of impending doom. Maybe Ann was like my mother, who thought every drizzle was a monsoon. But I did drive an old car, whose windshield wipers weren't the best. I could wait until morning. "I suppose I could wait until tomorrow."

"I think you'd better, dear. If you shoot me a text when you leave, I'd appreciate it."

"I'll do that. Thanks."

Faced with an evening alone and no food in the fridge, I decided to walk into town and grab a bite to eat and a glass of wine. On my way out the door, I thought about grabbing an umbrella, but a quick hunt for one in the cottage turned up nothing. Oh, well. At this point, the skies looked relatively clear, the water was calm, and only a slight breeze ruffled the curtains. I wouldn't be out long, anyway.

I walked into town, proud of myself for remembering the way, and purposely chose a restaurant other than the one I'd seen Jack at two nights ago. It was right on the water, busy with a summer dinner crowd, and the hostess seemed a bit put out having to seat a table of only one. "I can sit at the bar," I told her. "It's not a problem."

She looked grateful. "Perfect. It's right through there in the next room."

The moment I walked in, I saw him. I might have turned right around and left, except he saw me too. Sitting at the bar, a beer in his hand, he turned and looked right at me, like he knew I was there. Our eyes met, and he slowly lowered the bottle. My pulse galloped.

Dammit. Now what?

chapter nineteen

Jack

PRETEND IT NEVER HAPPENED.

I knew that's what I was supposed to do, but the sight of her had caught me off guard, and I found myself staring at her, dumbfounded, my beer halfway to my lips.

I'd purposely chosen this place because she'd been at The Anchor last time, and I wanted to avoid seeing her. But I'd been sitting there thinking about her, when all of a sudden I'd looked up and seen her reflection in the mirror behind the bar—as if I'd conjured her up. I glanced over my shoulder, and sure enough, she was real.

Real and beautiful and walking right for me, a surprised smile on her face. "Well, hello. Guess we think more alike than it would seem."

Pretend those legs were never wrapped around your body. "Hey. How's it going?"

"Good. I was going to get a table," she said, gesturing behind her toward the dining room, "but they weren't too keen to seat just one person."

Pretend those hands were never in your hair. "Yeah. Busy in here tonight."

"Is there room for one more at the bar?"

Pretend you didn't come inside her so hard, your knees buckled. I recovered enough to look around, and noticed the chair next to me was empty. *Fuck.*

My hesitation flustered her. "I'm taking off tomorrow, and I already cleaned out the fridge at the cottage, so—"

"Tomorrow? I thought you were here longer than that." If she was leaving tomorrow, I'd be OK. Maybe.

"I was supposed to be here longer, but my mother called this afternoon, and there are some family issues…" She waved a hand in the air. "Anyway, I won't bore you with it. But yes, leaving tomorrow. So this is my last night."

"Oh." Some of my nerves evaporated, and I nodded toward the empty chair. Now I simply had to keep it casual. Light. No touching. "No one's sitting here. If you're not still mad at me, you can sit."

Laughing, she slid onto the seat and set her purse at her feet. "I'm not mad. You apologized. We can be friends."

"Friends, huh?" I side-eyed her. "I don't know if I can be friends with a city girl."

She smiled. "If I can be friends with a cocky, know-it-all farmer like you, you can handle a sweet little city girl like me."

"Sweet—ha." I took a long pull on my beer, and damn if she didn't stare at my mouth the entire time.

"Can I get you something?" the bartender asked her.

"Uh." Her cheeks grew a little pink as she realized what she'd been doing. "Can I see a wine list? And a menu?"

While she chose a drink and some food, I studied her covertly. She wore the sandals from last night, this time with pink shorts that made her legs look even longer, and a white blouse. Her hair was loose and wavy around her shoulders, and I had to stop myself from leaning over to smell it.

"Have you eaten already?" she asked me.

"Yeah. Earlier at home. I just came up here to get out of the house a little. Every now and then I have to remind myself to do it."

She nodded. "I get that."

"You live alone?" I asked her, feeling braver since her departure was imminent. No harm in getting to know her a little better at this point, right?

"Yes." She swirled her wine around in her glass. "But my family lives close. Not as close as yours," she said, grinning, "but close."

"They do live close—too close sometimes." I grimaced and lifted my beer again. "But I love having my nephew there. He's so fucking cute. I took him to the park today."

She placed a hand over her heart. "Awww. Did you?"

"Yeah, he loves the park. He never wants to leave."

"So cute. And you're so good with him—I heard you have the magic touch."

Our eyes met. "The magic touch, huh?"

The blush in her cheeks deepened.

I looked at her lips, and my thoughts strayed into dangerous territory. *It would be so easy to kiss her right now. So easy.* My entire body tightened up, and I gripped the beer bottle tight.

I couldn't. We were in public, this was a small town, and rumors would fly. They'd probably fly already, just because we were sitting together. I tossed back the rest of my beer, the moment passed, and she cleared her throat before taking a sip of wine.

Just talk to her, asshole. "You'll be glad to know I apologized to Pete and Georgia. Told them I'd be willing to consider their ideas. *Your* ideas."

She gasped as she set her glass down. "Did you really? That's great—I bet they were so happy."

"They were."

Her head tilted. "Can I ask about the change of heart?"

I took some time with my reply. "I did a lot of thinking last night. Some of the things you said sort of sank in."

"Really?" She sat up taller, her face lighting up. "What did I say?"

"You said something about changes making people happy, and I realized I didn't want to be responsible for standing in the way of their dreams." I studied the label on my empty beer bottle. "And I thought about what Steph would do if she were in my place."

"Oh."

I kept my focus on the bottle in my hand, tilting it this way and that. "I know she'd support them. She was completely unselfish."

Margot took another drink of wine and said, "Tell me more about her."

I blinked at her. Seriously? She wanted to hear about my late wife? Not only did it seem strange in light of what we'd done last night, but no one *ever* asked me about Steph. "What do you want to know?"

Margot shrugged and smiled. "Anything. I know she was short and cute and loved her boots, but what was she *like*?"

Exhaling, I tried to come up with words that would do her justice. "Feisty. Energetic. So damn smart. She was accepted at three different medical schools. Granted scholarships at all of them."

"Wow! I didn't realize she was a doctor."

"She wasn't. She didn't go to med school, said she'd changed her mind." Which her parents had always blamed on me, even if they never said it outright.

She drank again. "Tell me more."

"She was stubborn as hell. Once she made up her mind about something, she never wavered. None of us could talk her into going to school."

"She must have wanted something else more," Margot said pointedly.

"I guess." I shrugged, feeling guilty again. "Me. The farm."

"I take it you feel bad about that?"

I rubbed the back of my neck. "Sometimes. But she had me convinced it really was what she wanted. And if she wanted something, she never gave up, and she didn't care what people thought. She was a firecracker."

"Ha. I like her."

"Everyone liked her."

She smiled again, a little sadly. "Were you high school sweethearts?"

"No. She was two years younger than me, and I thought she was a pest. I'd known her since we were kids, though. And I knew she had a crush on me, but I never looked at her that way until I was out of school."

"Did *you* go to college?"

I nodded as the bartender offered me another beer. "For a year, but it wasn't for me. I hated being in a classroom. I was restless and bored. Then 9/11 happened, and I joined the Army."

"*Really*," she said, as if she'd never heard of such a thing. "And how long were you in the military?"

"Eight years."

"Wow. And she waited for you?" Her eyes went wide.

I nodded, smiling ruefully at the memory of her insisting she'd wait for me, even though I told her not to. "She did. Swore she would, and she did. I mean, she went to college while I was gone, but we kept in touch, saw each other when we could."

"And you got married when you came home?"

I nodded, taking a sip of the new beer. "We got married after my dad died. About five years ago."

She propped her elbow on the bar and her chin in her hand. "Tell me how you proposed."

I grinned at the memory. "Actually, she proposed to me."

Her head came off her hand, her lips opening in surprise. "No way. Really?"

"Really. She knew we were right for each other and I wasn't one for ceremony. I'd probably have just asked her in the chicken coop or something."

Margot rolled her eyes. "You and that chicken coop. Thank goodness she had more of a sense of romance than you."

"You don't think the chicken coop is romantic?" I slapped a palm to my cheek. "I'm shocked."

"No, I don't." She poked me in the chest. "Now go on."

"About what?"

"The proposal!" She slapped my shoulder this time, rolled her eyes. "Sheesh!"

"Oh, right." But I was distracted by the way she kept touching me. "Uh, she asked me at the cabin. Brought me breakfast in bed on my birthday and there was a little note on the tray that said 'Marry Me.'"

Again she put a hand over her heart, and her expression went wistful. "So sweet."

I felt some heat in my face, remembering how things had gone after that. I'd said of course I would—promised to love her and take care of her forever, the way she'd been taking care of me. We'd made love over and over again that day, on the bed, on the floor, in the shower, on the kitchen table. I never felt safer or more sure of myself than when I was lost inside her. I missed that feeling so much. And I missed taking care of someone. "Yeah. It was."

"Was she your first love?"

I hesitated before going on. It felt a little odd to be talking about this with Margot, but it was also kind of nice. And as long as conversation stayed on the topic of Steph and our marriage, I was safe from other, less honorable thoughts. "Definitely. I was a typical guy in my teens, totally uninterested in any emotional attachments. But when I joined the Army, it kind of forced me to reevaluate what mattered in life. I realized what I had in her. And when I got out..." I paused, nervous to reveal too much of myself but unable to deny that it felt good somehow. *Just keep it focused on Steph.* "I kind of struggled to adjust, and losing my dad made it worse. Steph was there for me. She pushed me to get better."

"She must have been really special," Margot said softly.

"She was. She saved my life, I have no doubt." I took a long drink. "But I couldn't save hers."

Margot's face fell, and she studied the base of her wineglass.

I groaned and set my bottle down. "What the fuck—I'm sorry, Margot. I didn't mean to unload that on you."

"No, no, it's OK," she said, touching my arm. "I'm glad you did. I'm sorry if asking about her made you sad."

"Don't apologize. I'm glad you asked. You know what?" I ran a hand over my scruffy jaw, wishing I'd trimmed it up a little. "No one does. No one ever talks about her in front of me."

"Maybe they're worried it's too painful."

"I guess. But I'd much rather talk about her than myself." I looked at Margot and realized I'd monopolized the entire conversation. "Actually, I don't want to talk at all, I want to listen. Tell me about you."

She smiled. "What do you want to know?"

I thought for a second. "Tell me about the horse you had growing up."

Her eyes lit up, and she told me about Maple Sugar, the thoroughbred she'd owned from the time she was eight years old until she left for college. When she teared up, she apologized and said it was silly to get sentimental about a horse she hadn't seen in more than ten years, but I understood the bond between humans and horses and told her so.

I learned about her family, her father's Senatorial race, the company she'd started with her friend. "Did you always want to go into marketing?" I asked.

"No. Not really." She smiled. "Actually, I'd have liked to be a social worker, but Muffy said that was out of the question."

I made a face. "Muffy?"

"My mother's nickname. You see, all the first-born daughters in her family, the Thurbers, are named Margaret or some variation thereof, the middle name has to be her mother's maiden name, and woe to anyone who tries to defy this tradition."

"Oh yeah?"

"Yes. You can go traditional, like Margaret or Marjorie. French like Margot or Marguerite, and you can even get away with changing up the spelling, like M-A-R-G-R-E-T, but don't you dare get cutesy and American and do something like Maisie or Maggie or Greta, at least not on the birth certificate. My cousin Mamie named her daughter Marley, and Great-Grandma Thurber died before she spoke to her again."

"Wait." I put out one hand. "Mamie and Muffy are OK, but Marley isn't?"

She giggled, flushed from two glasses of wine. "Mamie and Muffy are only nicknames, not on the birth certificates. We have to have nicknames, see, otherwise it would be mass confusion all the time. Plus WASPs love nicknames."

I propped my arm on the bar. "What's yours?"

She brought her hands to her mouth, laughing uncontrollably. The sound was girlish and playful, and sent a wave of heat rushing through me.

"Come on, tell me," I said, unable to keep a smile from my lips.

She dropped her hands in her lap and tried to keep a straight face. "It's Gogo."

"Gogo?" I burst out laughing, leaning back in my chair. "Seriously?"

"I'm afraid so." She looked at me, and her eyes were full of something good—wonder and warmth and affection.

My laughter died down and I found myself looking at her the same way. I loved that she could laugh at herself. *If only things were different.* I cleared my throat. "So Muffy said no to social work, huh?"

"Yes. She said, 'Don't be ridiculous, Margot. Thurber women go to Vassar and major in English.'" She shrugged. "So I did."

"Were you happy with that decision?"

"I guess. I never really thought about it. I got my degree, came home, took a job working for my father…and that was that."

"Did you like what you did?"

"Yes." She thought for a moment. "A lot of what I did involved charity work and fundraising, and I liked knowing I was helping people."

"How'd your parents take it when you left to start your own company?"

She chuckled. "They were kind of baffled by everything I did last year—I broke up with my boyfriend, took up yoga, quit working for my dad, started Shine PR…"

"Yoga?" I arched a brow at her.

She shook her head. "Didn't take."

"And the boyfriend?"

"Still gone. And he'll stay that way." Her dinner arrived and she laid her napkin across her lap.

"Why's that? Let me guess—Muffy didn't approve?"

She hesitated, her fork hovering above her planked whitefish. "That's a long story. Let's just say we've both moved on. I'm looking for something better."

"Like what? What is Margot Thurber Lewiston looking for in a man?" I was teasing, but I was also curious. "A certain number of zeroes in his bank account? A Rolls Royce? A house in the Hamptons?"

"No," she said. "I'm not *totally* shallow and pretentious, despite what you might think."

"So?" I prodded. "What then?"

She put a forkful in her mouth and chewed as she thought. "I don't know exactly," she finally said. "I'm still figuring that out."

"Fair enough."

"I know I want to get married and have a family. Actually, I sort of thought I'd have one by now, but..." Her voice trailed off and she shook her head. "But I was wrong."

"Life's full of surprises." I tried not to sound bitter.

She glanced at me. "What about you? Think you'll get married again?"

"No," I said, and I meant it. "I know what I had. And it doesn't happen twice."

"Fair enough."

We chatted a little more about the farm, about my family and hers, about places we'd traveled. She liked visiting big cities, and I preferred small towns, but we both agreed Mackinac Island was beautiful, perfect for a summer getaway. The more we talked, the easier I found it. Margot had definitely grown up in a different world, but she wasn't a snob. And she was so damn pretty. Even the way she ate and drank was graceful. I found myself mesmerized by little things—the curve of her wrist, the straightness in her back, the arch of her foot. She had the kind of beauty that resides in the bones. The creamy skin, perfect lips, and big blue eyes were just a bonus. Then there was the body—the endless legs, the narrow waist, the small round breasts that sat high on her chest.

What did they look like? I hadn't even gotten to see them last night. Were they even more pale than her face? And what about her nipples? Pale pink like cotton candy? Dark pink like a raspberry? Or maybe even deeper, like a cherry. As she chattered on about Mackinac Island fudge, my cock started to rise as I imagined licking my way up her vanilla skin to the cherries on top. *I can practically feel them under my tongue. I can taste her.*

God, why hadn't I done it last night? Why had I raced to the finish like a fucking teenager afraid of being caught? Why hadn't I taken my time with her? For fuck's sake, I'd barely touched her *anywhere*. I dropped my eyes to the napkin on her lap.

"Jack?"

"What?" I looked up sharply to see her slightly amused face.

"Do you want another beer?" She nodded toward the bartender, who was standing there waiting.

"Oh, sorry." I was completely torn. On one hand, I was having a nice time, and when was the last time I'd done something like this and enjoyed it? On the other, the longer I sat here with Margot, the more attracted I felt to her. "I shouldn't."

"Oh, come on. I will if you will. And then we can go our separate ways and you'll be rid of me forever."

I shook my head. "You really don't like to be told no, do you?"

She grinned devilishly, her blue eyes lighting up.

Sometimes I wonder if it was that smile that did me in.

chapter twenty

Margot

I'D THOUGHT IT WOULD BE AWKWARD, PRETENDING IT HAD NEVER HAPPENED. I'D thought it might be difficult, making conversation with him. I'd thought it would be safe, talking about his wife—I'd thought hearing about her would help me remember that he was off-limits.

But it was fun. And easy.

And deliciously, drastically dangerous.

When I'd first walked in, it had been slightly uncomfortable, not knowing exactly how it would go pretending we hadn't done what we did. But then he'd invited me to sit, and made a joke, and eventually, he'd smiled. And laughed—God, his laughter made me so happy. I wanted to roll around in it, get it all over me, like a pig in the mud.

He looked so *good*. I could hardly take my eyes off him. I loved the wayward curl of his hair, which I noticed for the first time had a little bit of gray. I loved the shape of his full mouth and had a hard time looking away every time he brought his beer bottle to his lips. I loved the way the cuffed-up sleeves of his blue shirt showed off those tanned, muscular forearms. He even wore a wrist watch tonight, with a large round navy blue face and a brown leather band with white stitching.

He also wore his wedding ring. And when he brought up Steph, I'd taken it as an invitation to ask about her, although I was surprised at how forthcoming he was. I got the feeling he was surprised, too, by how much he was revealing about himself, but it made me happy to think he felt comfortable confiding in me.

But instead of shutting down my attraction to him, the opposite happened—after hearing about their romance, I found myself even more intrigued. Here was this big, brawny, tough-as-nails ex-soldier talking about his first love, how grateful he was for her, how she'd saved him. And when he'd said he couldn't save her, my heart had cracked, and feelings for him had started to seep in.

Maybe if he hadn't asked about my horse. Maybe if he hadn't been curious about my family. Maybe if he hadn't told me he'd enlisted after 9/11 or talked so lovingly about his nephew or laughed so joyfully at my nickname. Maybe then, I'd have been safe.

But instead, I found myself wanting him again—badly—and regretting the circumstances that made it a terrible idea.

I tried not to flirt. I tried not to touch him. I tried to "pretend it had never happened," but by the time he paid the bill—he'd insisted on treating me to dinner—we were both half drunk and unable to remember the rules.

"OK, Magellan," he teased, turning me around after I headed the wrong way, looking for the exit. "Neither one of us should drive home tonight, so I'm going to walk you back to your cottage. Then I'll walk home."

"You don't have to walk me back!"

He held up a hand. "Please. If I don't help you, you'll probably end up in Deckerville."

I giggled. "What about your truck?"

"It'll be fine. Oh, shit." Thunder rumbled as we stepped out onto the sidewalk in the dark, the air warm and humid and smelling faintly metallic, but it wasn't raining yet. "We better hurry."

I had to work to keep up with him, and I was out of breath by the time we'd walked a block. "Slow down," I panted, then laughed. "You're always so fast at everything."

He groaned and grabbed my hand as we crossed the street, like he was the parent and I was the child. "Last night was not representative of my sexual skills."

"Hey, no complaints here," I said, stumbling up the curb.

He caught me by the elbows, and his touch electrified me. It must have had an effect on him too, because he let go of me as soon as I had my balance and put some distance between us. "Well, good."

"And anyway, it never happened." I bit my lip to keep from laughing.

"Nope, it didn't," he said.

"Not in a house."

"Not with a mouse."

"Not in a box."

"Not with a fox."

"It did not happen here or there."

"It did not happen anywhere." Lightning flashed, and he grabbed my arm and started to jog, dragging me alongside him. But he was laughing.

And I was giggling so hard, I could hardly breathe—the fact that Jack could recite Dr. Seuss was hilarious to me. Did he read to his nephew?

"Oh God, I have to go to the bathroom," I moaned, trying to run in sandals while squeezing my legs together. "Who told me to have that fourth glass of wine. Was it you?" I pointed at him accusingly.

"Don't blame me, Miss I Will If You Will. If you wet your pants, it will not be my fault. And I don't have a bathroom to offer you this time."

I groaned. "This is really embarrassing."

"I know. You're a mess." He looked both ways and led me across another street.

"I am, aren't I?"

"Yep. Look at you. Unattractive, not too clever, uneducated, *hopeless* at farm work, a Peeping Tom, and *serious* bladder control issues."

"Ouch." I made a face.

"And you're slow," he complained, tugging me along.

"Sheesh, I don't have much going for me, do I?" A few raindrops started to pelt us as he yanked me up the walkway to my cottage.

"Oh, I don't know." We stood at the door and faced each other as the drops fell heavier. "You might have a few things going."

"Like what?" The air around us hummed with electricity. He was so close I could smell his beach bonfire scent, feel his breath on my lips. *Kiss me, Jack.*

He slid his fingers into my hair, cradling my head in his hands. "You have beautiful eyes."

"Thank you."

"And lips." A flash of lightning lit his face briefly before thunder growled above us.

"Thank you." My voice trembled.

"And if things were different..." He closed his eyes as the rain made the metal gutters sing. "If I were different..."

"I don't want you to be different." Rising on tiptoe, I lifted my chin, let my eyes drift shut, waited to feel his mouth on mine.

But he pressed his lips to my forehead instead. "Goodbye, Margot."

One second later, he was racing away from me in the rainy dark.

I stood there in shock, stomach jumping, hands shaking, rain dripping from my hair and clothes. *He's gone. That's it.*

Disappointed, I let myself into the cottage and locked the door behind me. A lump formed in my throat, and I tried to swallow it away. *What did you expect? He is who he is, and you are who you are, and the two of you do not belong together.*

I used the bathroom and washed my hands, talking back to the voice of reason in my head. *Of course we don't belong together. I know that. But it was such a nice night, and I thought maybe...*

No. There is no maybe.

Sighing, I switched on a lamp in the front room and stood by the windows looking out at the lake. The rain drummed hard on the cottage roof, and I shivered again as lightning lit up the dark. The lamplight flickered, and I wondered what I'd do if the power went out.

Three sharp knocks made me jump. I hesitated for a second, then raced toward the sound. Was it him?

I yanked open the door, and there he was—dripping wet, breathing hard, body tense with restraint.

A second later, we lunged for each other.

Our mouths slammed together as his hands moved into my hair again, slanting my head as his tongue plunged between my lips. I ran my hands up the damp front of his chest and gripped the back of his neck. *He came back! He came back!*

He walked me backward without taking his lips off mine, kicking the door shut behind him. Frantically, we tore at wet clothing, our hands working as fast as the rain was falling. My fingers fumbled with the buttons of his shirt until I could push it from his shoulders. He broke our kiss only for the half-second it took to whip my blouse over my head. I undid his jeans and shoved my hand down the front of them, both of us moaning as I wrapped my fingers around his cock. It was hot and hard and grew thicker inside my fist. He unbuttoned my shorts and slid his hands down the back, inside my underwear, squeezing my ass.

Oh, God that *feeling* was back—that desperation to clutch and claw, to lick and bite, to scratch and pull. The way I wanted him gnawed at my insides like it was captive, determined to escape.

Part of me was dying to know what had made him change his mind, but no way was I about to stop and ask. And nothing about his actions suggested he wasn't sure about this—not the stroke of his tongue, not the strength in his hands, not the thrust of his cock through my fingers. The force behind his desire heightened my own, because I *knew* what it had taken for him to come back here tonight, to admit that we'd failed to smother the spark between us, to give it another chance to burn.

Howling winds pressed against the windows as we shoved off shoes and jeans and shorts and underwear and tumbled onto the rug. He caught himself above me, and I stretched out on my back, his hips between my thighs. For the first time, we stopped kissing and looked at each other. Lightning flashed a split second before a loud crack of thunder shook the floor beneath us. Then the power went out, leaving us in the near dark.

Jack looked sharply toward the corner of the room where the lamp was, and his body tensed. In my mind I saw him hit the ground after the branch I was standing on snapped.

"Hey." I took his face in my hands, forcing his eyes back to mine. "It's OK." I kissed his lips, his cheek, his lips again. "It's OK. Stay with me."

He pressed his mouth to mine and reached behind me with one hand, and I arched my back so he could unclasp my bra. The moment he'd tossed it aside, he descended on my breasts, kissing them, licking them, sucking them, kneading them with his hands. I wove my fingers into his hair, fisted them tight when he took one nipple between his teeth and flicked it with his tongue. The ache between my legs throbbed, and I sighed with pleasure when he slipped one finger inside me, then two. As his mouth traveled down my ribs and stomach, I rocked my hips against his hand, melting into his touch. His thumb moved gently over my clit, slow, rhythmic circles that made my skin hum and my stomach muscles tighten.

He moved down further, settling his head between my thighs. I closed my eyes and held my breath. No one had done this to me in *years*.

After what seemed like a lifetime, he treated me to one long, slow stroke of his tongue from bottom to top, his fingers pushing deeper inside me. I moaned louder than I intended to and caught my bottom lip in my teeth. But when he did it again, this time lingering at the top to tease my clit with the tip of his tongue, I cried out with even more abandon. Propping myself up on my elbows, I looked down at his dark head between my pale thighs. Was this even real?

"I had to taste you." His voice was low and gravelly, and I struggled to hear him over the storm. "I was halfway home, soaked to the bone, and determined to put you out of my head, but all I could think about was tasting you."

"I'm so glad you came back," I whispered. "I didn't want you to go."

"You taste as sweet as you look," he went on, pausing to circle his tongue in a slow, decadent spiral. "Like strawberries in June." He flicked my clit with quick, hard strokes. "Cherries in July." He sucked it into his mouth. "Peaches in August."

"Christ, you can even make fruit sound sexy."

"It's you." He tilted his head in a different direction, swirled his tongue from a new angle. "It's all you."

I wanted to tell him it wasn't—it couldn't be—wanted my hands on his body, wanted to lick him and suck him and taste him, wanted to drive him insane like he was doing to me—but I couldn't talk, couldn't move, couldn't breathe. Higher and higher he took me, until I teetered at the edge of bliss and then sailed over, my clit throbbing against his tongue.

Desperate to feel his weight on me, I grasped at his shoulders, trying to pull him up. He took his time, lingering between my thighs like I was his favorite dessert and he didn't want anyone to take the plate away, even though it was empty.

"Come up here," I said. "Please."

Reluctantly, he crawled up my body, his mouth hot and wet as he kissed a path up my stomach, between my breasts, up my throat, until his elbows were braced above my shoulders. I reached between us, positioned the tip of his cock between my legs, rubbed it over my clit, slipped it inside me. My entire body vibrated with need for him.

He lifted his hips, pulling out. "I didn't plan for this. I don't have—"

"It's OK."

"You're sure?"

I nodded. "Please. I want to feel you there again."

"Feel me where?" He slid into me, slow and controlled.

I smiled wickedly and moved my hands to his ass to pull him closer. "So deep it hurts," I whispered in his ear. "I want you to tear me apart. Leave me bruised. Mark tonight on my body."

"You shouldn't say that to me."

I gasped as he plunged in deep, the sharp twinge making me jump. "God, I love the way you move. Like you want me so badly you can't hold back."

"I can't. No matter how hard I tried—and fucking hell, I tried." He moved a little faster, rolling his hips over mine. "But you're under my skin."

Then I couldn't talk anymore because his mouth was on mine, and I let my desire take over—I raked my nails across his back, took his lower lip between my teeth, pulled his hair, writhed and panted and gasped. Pleasure zinged along every nerve ending in my body like a live current. When I came again, I cried out his name as my body pulsed around his driving cock, my fingers digging into his ass. I felt wild, untamed, untethered—free to say and do and feel *everything*.

As the rippling waves tapered off, Jack pulled out and flipped me over. "Get on your knees."

Heart still pounding against my ribs, I got on my hands and knees, wincing when he grabbed my hair. He yanked my head back as he pushed inside me—*yes*. He gripped one hip, holding me steady as he fucked me so hard, I could hear his hips smacking my ass—*yes*. He came fast, his body going stiff, a growl escaping his throat, his cock throbbing again and again inside me—*yes*.

He let go of me and fell forward, catching himself on his hands outside of mine. His forehead rested on the back of my head, his breath was warm and soft on my neck, and the rain still drummed against the cottage roof. Neither of us spoke.

A moment later he wrapped one arm around my stomach, holding me close to him.

My throat squeezed shut. I wanted to say things. I wanted to tell him that he was the best I'd ever had. I wanted to ask if he was OK. I wanted to know if I'd eased anything inside him. I wanted him to know how badly I too wished things were different. I wanted him to know I'd never regret this, I'd never forget him, I'd never stop wondering *what if*.

I opened my mouth, but he spoke first.

"Don't go home tomorrow, Margot," he said, tightening his arm around me. "Please. Don't go."

chapter
twenty-one

Jack

Her body went still beneath mine. *She's holding her breath.*

She swallowed. "You want me to stay? Are you sure?"

"Yes." I pulled out of her, and turned her gently onto her back. The way she looked up at me made my chest tighten. "If you want to."

"Jack." Her hands flew to my face, her thumbs brushing my cheekbones. "Of course I want to."

I smiled, feeling as if a massive weight had been lifted off my chest. "Good."

"But I know things are complicated."

"They are." I wouldn't lie to her. "And I can't make any promises."

"I don't need promises," she said quickly. "I don't have conditions, don't need to put a label on this, don't have to know how it ends. I just like being with you."

I kissed one of her palms. "Thank you."

She smiled, letting her hands trail over my shoulders. "You know, it's funny. This is the first time in my life I'm giving myself permission to just do what I want to do without worrying about how it fits in to the grand scheme of my life. Without caring if it's what Thurber women do."

That made me chuckle. "I'm gonna guess Muffy would not approve."

She giggled and shook her head. "Probably not. But guess what? I don't care." Her face lit up the dark. "I don't care. I just want to stay here for a while and enjoy myself."

"Me too." Although for me, *here* wasn't a physical place. It was a state of mind that allowed me to enjoy some time with Margot without feeling like I owed anyone an apology. Without feeling like it was a complete betrayal. Without the guilt. It was a place I'd reached as I'd run through the rain toward home, realizing that I could either spend another sleepless night alone and tortured by thoughts of her, or I could allow myself a brief reprieve from the loneliness.

And maybe for Margot, it was the same—a break from the expectations, the rules governing her behavior, a chance for her to indulge her less…*polite* side. Get her hands dirty. I could definitely help her with that.

But that's all it could be—a respite, a temporary relief. Anything more was out of the question.

"Wonder when the power will come back on." Margot came out of the bathroom carrying the candle we'd lit. She was still naked—I loved that. "Think it's on at the cabin?"

"No idea." The prospect of spending the entire night in the dark did not thrill me. Did I have candles to burn? I tried to remember as I buttoned up my shirt.

"Is it still raining?" We listened for a moment, and sure enough, the downpour hadn't let up.

"Yeah." Frowning, I glanced around the room for my socks, which were probably still soaked. Fuck, I hated wet socks.

"Want to stay here tonight?"

I looked at her, hesitated. Sex was one thing, but spending the night with another woman seemed like too much. Lying next to her. Watching her sleep. Waking up with her. *But I want to. Just this once would be OK, right?*

"No pressure." Margot walked toward me, the candle lighting her face from below. "But the invitation is there. Thinking about you trying to get home in the pitch dark makes me nervous."

Our eyes met, and I wondered if she was thinking about the highway. *It was raining that night too.* For one insane second, I wondered why the hell I shouldn't tempt fate. Would I get what I deserved?

"You wouldn't let *me* walk home in the dark, remember?"

The concern on her face moved me. "I remember."

"So stay." She set the candle on an end table and twined her arms around my waist. "For me. I know you're a big strong soldier and you're not afraid of the dark, but I'll be too scared here all alone."

I smiled and wrapped my arms around her. *You have no idea.* She rested her cheek on my chest, and I kissed the top of her head. Even her hair smelled sweet. *A whole night surrounded by her scent. By the sound of her breathing. By the knowledge I wasn't alone.* "OK. I'll stay."

"Good." She wriggled happily in my arms. "God, I love getting my way."

I pinched her butt. "You're a spoiled brat. Did you just trick me?"

"Maybe."

"Jesus, you could sell water to a drowning man. You should go into politics."

"No, thanks. But I was pretty good at fundraising, or at least getting rich people to write checks for good causes."

"I have no doubt." She yawned, and I hugged her tighter. "Tired?"

"Yes. You wore me out. Or maybe it was the wine."

"Let's say it was me."

She looked up at me and smiled. "It was totally you."

She went into the bathroom to brush her teeth, taking the candle with her, but she left the door open so I could find my way into the bedroom. By the time she came out, I was undressed again and under the covers.

Setting the candle on the bedside table, she slipped in next to me and then blew it out. We lay there for a moment, the rain softer now, the scent of smoke from the candle lingering in the air. Both of us were on our backs, no parts of our bodies touching.

"Is it strange?" she asked.

I looked over at her. "Is what strange?"

"Being in bed with someone else."

Returning my eyes to the ceiling, I put my hands behind my head. "Yeah. It is."

She turned onto her side to face me, tucking her hands beneath her cheek. "I'm glad you didn't lie and say it wasn't."

I focused on her again. "I won't lie to you, Margot. I promise."

"OK." Her voice was soft. "I was brushing my teeth and thinking that I shouldn't have pressured you to stay. I didn't think about it being strange for you that way. I feel bad."

"Hey. Come here." I reached for her, and she moved close, tucking herself along the side of my body. Her skin was warm and soft and smelled like vanilla. My cock stirred beneath the sheets. "I stayed because I want to be here with you tonight. Yes, it's the first time I've spent the night with anyone other than Steph in a lot of years, and yes, it's a little unfamiliar, but it's not uncomfortable."

"OK." She kissed my chest, slinging an arm over my torso. "Since we're being honest, I have to tell you how much I love your chest."

I smiled. "Yeah?"

"Yes." She rubbed her lips back and forth on my skin, slid her hand up my ribcage. "From the moment I met you."

I thought for a second. "In the kitchen?"

"Yes. You were so grouchy and mean, but you had this amazing body. I felt like you could snap me in half, and you looked like you wanted to." Her fingertips brushed over my nipple, and my dick jumped so high it made the sheets move.

"I think I did." Oh fuck, now she was circling my other nipple with her tongue, flicking it gently. Heat rushed through my body, prickled over my skin.

"Maybe you still will." She pinched the nipple beneath her fingers, and I inhaled sharply. It felt so fucking *good,* and it was one of those things I'd never ask for but loved. Her hand moved slowly down my stomach. "I've never seen a body like yours before. So tight and muscular. All these ridges and lines." She let her fingers ripple lightly over my abs, making them clench. "It's incredible how strong you are. It makes me think of all the things you could do to me."

Keep going, I thought, *and keep fucking talking.*

Her hand closed around my cock, now fully hard and aching. "And this," she said, her voice low and fluid. "When I saw you on the dock, dripping wet and completely naked, my eyes went right here." Working her hand up and down my shaft, she picked up her head to speak softly in my ear. "I had thoughts I've never had before."

"Like what?"

"I wanted to watch you get hard. I wanted to get my hands on you. I wanted to taste you."

"Fuck," I rasped, one hand seeking her breast, the other snaking down her lower back.

"I was *so bad*," she whispered. "I wanted you to touch yourself, and I wanted you to catch me watching you. I wanted you to punish me for it."

"Yeah? How would I do that?" I pinched her nipple hard enough to make her gasp and slid my middle finger along the crack of her ass.

She went still. "Actually, I don't know. I didn't get that far."

"Never mind. You couldn't dream up anything close to what I'd have done."

"Tell me," she begged. "I want to hear it."

"Nope. I'll let it come as a surprise."

A slow, sly grin stretched her lips. "Fair enough."

I moved fast, flipping her onto her back across the bed and pinning her wrists to the mattress, anchoring her body with my hips. "I don't always play fair."

The grin vanished.

But her eyes glittered.

When we were finally sated—no easy feat, Margot had an appetite for sex that nearly matched my own—we collapsed on top of the twisted sheets, her head on my chest, one arm and leg draped over me. I wrapped an arm around her shoulder and kissed the top of her head.

"This OK?" she asked. "I don't know if you're a cuddler or not."

"It's OK."

"Night," she murmured sleepily.

"Night."

She fell asleep in minutes, her breathing deep and rhythmic, her body relaxed. I lay awake for a while, listening to the rain, in awe of her and this night and myself. It hadn't been an easy decision, coming back here. It hadn't been easy asking her not to leave tomorrow. It hadn't been easy climbing into bed with someone other than the woman I'd married.

But everything else…everything else had been *so* easy. Talking to her. Touching her. Listening to her. Being inside her. Why was that? How was it possible I was this comfortable with someone I'd only met days before, someone so completely different from me? It didn't seem real.

So let it be a dream, then. Don't analyze it. Don't scrutinize it. Don't look for meaning that isn't there.

I closed my eyes, content to be with her in a temporary dream world where I wouldn't be judged—where neither of us would be judged—for what we wanted.

For the first time in years, I fell asleep in the dark.

And slept through the night.

chapter twenty-two

Margot

The mattress shifted, and I reluctantly opened my eyes. Blinked. In the pale gray morning light, I saw Jack sitting on the bed, dressed. His hair was a disaster.

I smiled. "Hey."

"Hey. I have to go."

"Are your animals missing you?"

He mussed my hair. "Yeah. And I have to get my truck still."

"Oh, right. What time is it?"

"Just after six."

The conversation we'd had last night filtered through my wake-up haze. "I need to tell them I'm not leaving today."

"I was hoping you'd still want to stay. How much longer do you have?"

I had to think for a second. "What day is it?"

"Wednesday. The twentieth."

"I'm here until the twenty-eighth. So eight more days." When I'd been faced with the prospect of eight more days here having to stay away from him, it had seemed an interminable amount of time. Now it seemed short.

"Good." He leaned down and kissed my cheek. "Don't get up. I'll let myself out and catch up with you later, OK?"

"OK."

After I heard the front door shut, I tried to go back to sleep but couldn't. Was it possible things had changed so much in just twenty-four hours? If Jack hadn't been here when I woke up, I might have thought I'd dreamt the whole thing.

Rolling onto my back, I stretched out my arms and legs, pointed and flexed my feet. I was sore in places I didn't expect to be—my back and arms and neck. I was also sore in the expected places. Holy moly, that man could fuck a woman into next year! And his tongue, oh my *god*, he was good with his tongue. I'd had four orgasms last night—four! That was more than I'd had in the last *six months* of my relationship with Tripp!

I had to tell someone. I had to.

My phone was still in my purse from last night, which meant it was probably dead. Was the power back on yet? Hopping out of bed, I darted naked into the front room, grabbed my phone and the charger, and plugged it in next to the bed. It took a minute, but eventually it buzzed on and began charging. As soon as it would let me, I hit Jaime's name in my recent calls.

"Hello?" She sounded nervous.

"It's me."

"Are you OK?"

"Yeah, I'm fine. Why?"

"Because it's not even seven."

"Oh! Sorry. I didn't think."

"Why are you awake? Aren't you supposed to be on a semi-vacation?"

"Yes. And I'm awake because I can't sleep. And I can't sleep because of what happened last night."

"What happened last night?"

"I had four orgasms!" I burst out. "Onetwothreefour!"

She gasped. "Hold on, let me go in the other room."

"But I want to hear about the four orgasms," I heard Quinn say.

"They're not for you, now hush." There was a pause and some muffled breathing before she spoke again. "OK. Go. Tell me everything."

"I will, but first…" I chewed on one knuckle. "Promise you won't get mad."

She sighed. "I'm going to pretend the fourgasm was from someone other than a client. Does that work?"

"Good idea." I filled her in on what had happened since I'd last spoken with her, everything from the disastrous meeting—she groaned—to the tree sex—she gasped—to the fourgasm—she sighed.

"That's awesome, Gogo. I'm happy for you. I'm also in shock."

"Believe me, I am, too." And I couldn't even tell her about some of the most shocking things—the bruises on my body, the bite marks on his skin, the scratches on his back. The way I'd begged him to be rough. The way he'd used his size and strength to subdue me. The need in me to explore a different side of myself. The need in him to lose control without fear. That took *trust*—and somehow we had established it in the short amount of time we'd known each other.

Maybe that was the biggest surprise of all.

"So now what?" Jaime asked. "Will you see him again?"

"God, I hope so. When he left, he said something about catching up with me later."

"Why'd he leave so early?" She laughed. "Is he a bolter like I was?"

"Ha. No, he had to go feed the animals, I think."

"I keep forgetting he's a farmer. You're fucking a *farmer*."

"I know, and he's so hot," I said seriously. "I mean, I don't know if there are others like him, but women seriously need to start checking out the farmers markets around them just in case."

"Hm. Maybe we should tell Claire."

"Yes! Do it! What's she up to this week?"

"House hunting, actually. I'm supposed to go look at one with her later today."

"Any more dates with the hockey player?"

"Not that I know of. I'll get the scoop tonight."

"That's right, it's Girls Night." I felt a little sad about missing our standing date. "I'm sorry I can't make it."

She burst out laughing. "Shut the fuck up, you are not. And I wouldn't be either."

I grinned. "OK, I'm not."

"Just give us all the juicy details when you get back. We'll forgive you."

"Scout's honor."

She sighed. "I better get in the shower. Keep me posted on the work end of things please. I'm going to keep pretending you're not sleeping with the client, though."

Guilt made me cringe a little. "Is there anything else you need me to be working on while I'm up here?"

"No, don't worry about it. I have things handled. Take a few days off."

"You're the best." I blew her a noisy kiss. "Bye."

"Bye."

I hung up and sat there for a moment, trying to decide if I was tired enough to go back to sleep. But I was wired—I felt like I'd already had six cups of coffee and a bowl of Froot Loops with a sprinkling of cocaine on top. Where was this energy coming from? I couldn't have gotten more than six hours of sleep, and I usually liked eight. I wondered if Jack was tired or if he felt the same kick I did this morning. Had he slept OK? I remembered how he said he didn't usually sleep too well. Had being in my bed made it better or worse? He'd seemed happy enough this morning, hadn't he?

Finally I decided I was too keyed up to lie around thinking about him. I got up, dressed in jeans and a t-shirt, and figured I'd head over to the farm and help him out today, or at least make the offer.

I had to laugh as I tugged on my boots, still caked with mud from the other day. If anyone would have told me I'd be spending a vacation day doing farm chores a year ago—even a month ago—I'd have said they were crazy.

But everything about me felt different.

Well…almost everything.

I still wore the pearl necklace, of course.

Since it was light out and not too hot, I decided to walk over to the farm. It had stopped raining, but the skies were cloudy and the air was muggy. On my way up the sloped, cottage-lined street toward the highway, I called Ann and was surprised when she answered, since it was still early.

"Oh, hi, Ann. I was just going to leave you a message and tell you that I've decided not to go home early."

"Oh good!" she said. "I'm so glad. You survived the little blackout last night?"

"I certainly did. I lit a candle and had a perfectly enjoyable evening." *Want to hear about my fourgasm?*

"Happy to hear it. You enjoy the rest of your stay, and let me know if you need anything."

"I will. Thank you."

I crossed the highway right in front of the Valentini house, and saw Georgia come out the front door, coffee cup in her hand.

"Good morning!" she called from the porch with a wave.

"Good morning!" I waved back and headed up the gravel path toward her.

"I saw you crossing the road. What brings you here so early?" She smiled at me over the brim of her mug.

Damn, what should I say? My cheeks warmed before I could formulate a response. "Uh, I thought I'd offer Jack a hand again." I gestured over my shoulder in the direction of the lake. "Not much of a beach day."

"Nope." She looked a little amused. "Jack know you're coming?"

"No." I stuck my hands in my jeans pockets. "Truthfully, he might have told me not to bother. Not sure I was that much help the other day."

She laughed. "Any extra pair of hands is a help. But why don't you come in for a cup of coffee first? He doesn't know you're coming, so he won't miss you yet, right?"

"Right." I smiled, even though I was kind of anxious to see him. "OK, thanks. Coffee sounds good." I followed her into the house and down the hall to the kitchen, where Cooper sat on the floor playing with plastic containers and lids.

I ruffled his curls. "Hey, cutie."

"Cream and sugar?" Georgia asked, pouring me a cup.

"Yes, please."

I took a seat at the counter, and she placed a steaming cup of black coffee, a pitcher of cream, and a sugar bowl in front of me. "There you go. Doctor it up."

I added some white stuff to my coffee until it was a shade of beige I could handle, and took a sip. "Perfect. Thank you."

Holding her cup in two hands, she leaned on her elbows across from me and smiled like the cat that hasn't eaten the canary yet, but knows where it lives.

She suspects something.

Again my face warmed, and I tried to hide the blush behind my coffee cup.

"I'm not good at keeping secrets," she blurted.

"Oh?"

"No, not when I'm this curious." She set her cup down and straightened up. "Last night when I came home from work, I noticed Jack's car wasn't there. Then this morning I saw him driving home. And I'm just wondering where he might have spent the night." The glint in her eye told me she had a pretty good idea.

I shifted in my seat, my eyes dropping to the ivory Formica countertop. "Uh…I'm not really, um, at liberty here to…" Shit! We hadn't talked about this at all. Did Jack want to keep our little fling a secret?

"It's OK." She held up one hand. "You don't have to tell me anything specific. Let me just say that yesterday when he came over to apologize, both Pete and I sensed something different about him. He was more relaxed, more willing to listen, less stubborn and crotchety."

"Interesting." I played it cool with a big sip of coffee.

"It was. Very." She smiled as she toyed with her cup. "Pete asked him flat out if he'd gotten laid."

I swallowed the mouthful of coffee too fast and ended up coughing. "And what did he say?" I asked when I could speak again.

"He neither confirmed nor denied."

Lifting my cup to my lips again, I struggled to keep my expression neutral. Her grin was huge. "OK then. Moving on."

"Moving on."

"Did Jack tell you the exciting news? We're going ahead with plans for catering and the restaurant—I mean, at least with exploring the options."

"That's wonderful," I said.

"I'm so excited. And I was thinking, once the new website is in place, I could start blogging about the project."

"Perfect! That's exactly the kind of story to put out there."

"Brad is supposed to call us today to tell us if we can get in to see the house this afternoon." She made a face. "But we usually do the Frankenmuth farmers market on Wednesdays from three to seven, so I'm not sure how that's going to work. We might have to wait."

"Can't someone else do the market?"

She shrugged. "It's not really Jack's thing, at least it hasn't been since—"

The kitchen door swung open and he appeared. My pulse raced. My arms and legs tingled. My stomach was wild with butterflies. I couldn't keep the smile off my face, especially when I saw his hair. He hadn't put a hat on, probably because it wasn't sunny today, and it was still a mess from last night. *From my hands.*

I crossed my legs.

"Hey," he said, offering a small smile, but a smile nonetheless. "What are you doing here?"

I smiled back. "Thought I'd see if you wanted some help today."

"Oh. I came in for some coffee." He gestured toward the pot but didn't move, just stood there looking at me with that little smile on his lips.

Georgia looked back and forth between the two of us. "Can I get you a cup, Jack?"

"Ah, I got it." He started for the cupboard but caught sight of Cooper and leaned over to scoop him up. "Hey, buddy!"

"Pahk!" Cooper said as Jack set him on his arm.

"You want to go to the park *again*?" Jack teased. "Aren't you tired of the park?"

"Never," Georgia said. "But no more ice cream when you take him. He refused to eat dinner yesterday."

Jack set Cooper down and tweaked his nose. "Don't worry, buddy. We can sneak the ice cream. That's what uncles are for."

Georgia flicked him on the shoulder as he passed her on his way to the coffee pot. "I was just telling Margot that Brad is trying to get us in to see the Oliver place later today."

He muttered something unintelligible as he poured himself some coffee, and Georgia and I exchanged an eyeroll.

"But there's a conflict because they're supposed to do a farmers market somewhere," I said.

"Frankenmuth." Georgia turned to Jack. "From three to seven."

"I was thinking, why don't we do it?" I said brightly. "I've never been to a farmers market before, and I'd like to learn more about them."

Jack turned around and leaned back on the counter. "No. I don't like those things."

"Why not?" I demanded.

"There are *people* there," he said in his grouch voice.

"Oh, for goodness sake. Of course there are—they're called *customers*," Georgia said. "I think it's a great idea! You should do it, Jack."

He brought his coffee cup to his mouth and mumbled into it before taking a sip.

"Please?" Setting my cup down, I clasped my hands and gave him my best smile. "I'll be good."

He exhaled, narrowing his eyes at me, but I saw a smile threatening. "I suppose I have to buy you an ice cream, too."

I clapped twice. "Yay! Ice cream!"

"This is great. Thank you," Georgia said. "I'll let you know for sure once I talk to Brad."

"Let's just plan on it!" I said excitedly. "No matter what, Jack and I will do it."

"Really?" Georgia blinked and looked at her brother-in-law. "That OK with you?"

"It's fine." Jack tipped up the rest of his coffee and set his cup in the sink. "I'd better head back out if I'm only getting half a day in. Is everything ready to go for this afternoon?"

"No, but I'll sort, wash, and package this morning, and maybe Margot will give me a hand getting the tables and signage together. That way I can show her how I set up. All you'll have to do is load the truck."

"Of course," I said. "Anything you need."

"OK." Jack looked at me. "Want to give me a hand with the egg collection before you do that?"

I wrinkled my nose. "Do I have to?"

"Yes."

"Have fun, you two," Georgia chirped, giving me a secret thumbs up while Jack was opening the door for me.

As we walked toward the coop, my boots sank in the mud, my nostrils were assaulted with the smell of manure, and my anxiety about reaching beneath an angry hen returned. But my heart tripped with excitement for the day ahead.

chapter twenty-three

Jack

As soon as we got around the side of the barn, out of sight from the house, I grabbed Margot's hand, spun her around, and kissed her. Our arms wrapped around each other, our bodies straining to get closer, as if it had been a lot longer than just a few hours since we'd seen each other. She smelled like last night—vanilla and sex.

Fuck, that's hot.

I hadn't thought of anything but this since I'd left her in bed. I was distracted as hell, too, moving slowly or standing still staring off into space when I was supposed to be getting shit done. "What the hell is with you?" Pete had asked me an hour ago when he found me standing like a statue in the barn, a length of rope in my hand. *Oh nothing, just thinking about tying up the nice lady who's working for us, maybe blindfolding her too. Fucking her mouth. The usual.*

Then when I saw her in the kitchen, my heart had knocked fast and hard against my ribs—a feeling I hadn't counted on. How long had it been since I'd felt so happy to see someone? She'd looked so pretty sitting there, with her hair off her face and no makeup, a simple white t-shirt. It would be filthy by day's end, but I didn't think she'd care.

"Wow," she said, coming up for air. "Is this because I said I'd help you with the eggs?"

"Nope. It's because I'm glad to see you. And also for the sleep I got last night."

Her face lit up. "I was going to ask you. You told me you don't sleep well the other night."

"I don't, not usually. But last night I did." I was trying not to think too much about it and simply enjoy the feeling of being well-rested. If I let my mind dwell on the *why* behind the *what*, I'd have to ask myself some questions I wasn't ready to answer.

"That makes me happy." She bounced on her toes.

I kissed her again, slow and soft this time, wanting to stretch out this moment in time as far as it would go. But when my hands started to wander and the crotch of my pants grew tight, I figured we'd better stop. "I'd much rather do this than work today, but I should probably get some things done before we have to leave."

She smiled. "I'm all yours. Put me to work."

Margot was still hopeless at gathering eggs ("I can't take that one under the hen…it seems personal, like she really wants to keep it."), but she remembered lessons from the other day and definitely worked faster. After that, Pete and I went out to check the fences and Margot stayed with Georgia to get things ready for the market. I hadn't done one in years, and when I had, Steph had been there to make everything look nice. Hopefully Margot would remember everything Georgia told her.

Just before noon, we loaded everything in the truck—including a picnic basket Georgia had packed for our lunch—and set off for Frankenmuth. "What kind of music do you like?" I asked her as we headed west. The sun was just starting to shine through the clouds, and it looked like we'd have good weather, which always meant a better turnout.

"Oh, I like whatever."

"Whatever, huh?" I played with the radio to see what stations would come in. "We'll see what we can find, but this truck is old and completely lacking in frills, like, say, a Mercedes."

She poked me in the ribs. "My Mercedes is from 1972. Frills as we know it weren't really an option then."

"True. And who needs 'em, anyway?" I turned up the radio and rolled down the windows, since the A/C didn't work. "Scratchy Hank Williams in a beat-up Chevy truck, driving down a back road, wind in your hair…" I thumped her on the leg and drawled, "It don't get more country than that, sweetheart."

She laughed and threw her head back. "Yeehaw!"

I laughed too. I hadn't felt this good in a long, long time.

We arrived at the pavilion around one-thirty, located our vendor spot, and unloaded the truck. Margot gamely did a bunch of the heavy lifting, wiping the sweat from her forehead with the crook of her elbow, and began setting up once we had everything ready.

"I can do that," I told her as she struggled to get a stubborn table leg unfolded.

She straightened up, blew a wayward piece of hair out of her face, and gave me a dirty look. "I'm not totally helpless, Jack. I can handle a folding table."

"OK, OK." I turned away from her to hide a smile as I unpacked the scale.

When the tablecloths were on and the displays done exactly how Georgia had specified, Margot stood back and eyed it critically. "I wish we had some different levels on the table. And more depth."

I frowned. "Depth?"

"Yes. I love the different-sized baskets on the ground and the old barrels.

But on the actual tables, I think we could use something more." She tapped her chin with one finger. "The banner needs to be redone once you have your new logo, and we should also get it on the tablecloth front. I'd like to see it be a little modern and a little old-fashioned at the same time. On-trend but authentic."

"What difference does it make? Shouldn't the quality of the product be what attracts people?"

She smiled indulgently at me. "That will bring them *back*. But look at how many people are setting up here right now. How are you going to stand out? People make decisions about first impressions in under a second, Jack. You need to catch their eye with something visually stunning. Lure them in."

I scratched my head. I had no idea how to do that, but if anyone knew visually stunning, it was Margot.

She came around the tables and grabbed her purse. "I'll be right back."

"Where are you going? Don't you want to eat lunch before it opens?"

"Give me ten minutes," she called over her shoulder as she hurried off.

She was back in five with potted herbs and flowers at varying heights, which she set up on the table, rearranging things to make room. Standing back, she studied it again and nodded. "Better. And that basil smells so good. Once we sell some things, I'll use the empty boxes to sort of prop up the little crates along the back of the table, but this will work for now."

I arched a brow at her. "You're the boss. Ready to eat?"

"Yes. I'm ravenous, actually."

We ate lunch at our stand, scarfing down the sandwiches, pickles, and cookies Georgia had packed. "I hope they get to see the house today," Margot said around a mouthful of cookie.

I uncapped my water bottle and took a drink.

She kicked my foot. "Hey. Don't you?"

"I guess."

She clucked her tongue. "You're such a poop. Well, *I'm* excited for them. It's their dream!"

"I know," I said grudgingly. "And while I can't say I like the prospect of them buying that peeling, splintering old heap, I do like knowing it's making Pete and Georgia happy."

"That is because underneath your grouchy exterior beats an actual heart." She gave me a superior look. "Admit it—you're really a softie."

I made a face. "A softie? I'm not sure I like the sound of that."

"Don't worry, Farmer Frownypants, your secret is safe with me." She patted my leg. "I won't tell anyone how sweet you really are."

I leaned over to whisper in her ear. "And I won't tell anyone how *dirty* you really are."

She gasped and giggled. "You better not."

"Jack?"

I looked up at the woman who'd spoken, and for a terrifying second, I thought I was seeing a ghost. *Holy shit.* "Suzanne." Immediately I sat back in my chair and moved it away from Margot's a little.

"I thought that was you. I saw the banner and expected it would be Pete and Georgia." Steph's younger sister looked at Margot and then back at me. "Haven't seen you here in forever."

"Yeah, I don't usually do them." Fuck, the older she got, the more Suzanne looked like Steph—same coloring, same height and build, even the same voice. They were three years apart, so Suzanne had to be thirty now, the age Steph had been when she died.

"Well, come here, you big lug." She opened her arms, and I stood up, coming around the side of the stand to give her an awkward hug. She went up on tiptoe the way Steph used to do to get her arms around me, and my stomach turned over. "It's good to see you."

"You too," I lied, letting her go and retreating behind the stand as quickly as I could. At least she didn't smell like Steph. Suzanne was wearing flowery perfume, and Steph had never touched the stuff.

"Hi. I'm Margot Lewiston." Margot stood and offered Suzanne her hand and a smile.

Did Suzanne hesitate before taking it? Maybe I only imagined it. My equilibrium was off, and I'd started to sweat.

"Suzanne Reischling." She shook Margot's hand, and though she wore sunglasses and I couldn't see her eyes, I sensed her sizing Margot up from heel to hair.

"Nice to meet you," Margot said.

"You too." Suzanne took her hand back. "Are you a new employee at the farm?"

Margot laughed. "Sort of. I'm doing some marketing work for them. Helping them with branding and PR, that kind of thing."

"Interesting." Suzanne folded her arms. "Are you from around here?"

"No, I'm actually from Grosse Pointe, which is just north of Detroit."

"I know where it is."

Suzanne's reception of Margot was so cool, it jolted me back to my senses. "Margot is visiting for a week or so and getting to know the business better," I said, feeling an odd need to defend her.

"Yes, and I just tagged along today to see what this was like. I've never been to a farmers market before." Margot's smile remained genuine, her tone friendly. Sticking her hands in her back pockets, she rocked onto the balls of her feet. "I'm excited."

"How nice," Suzanne said flatly.

"What about you? Are you here with your mom?" I turned to Margot. "Mrs. Reischling sells homemade jellies and jams and baked goods at these markets sometimes." Yet another reason I avoided coming to them. She never said as much, but how could she not blame me for everything that had happened? Wasn't she dying to scream at me? I knew exactly what she'd say: *If it weren't for you, she'd be a doctor right now, probably married to another doctor, living in a nice big house with a baby on the way.*

She'd be right about all of it.

"I *am* here with Mom, and I know she'd love to see you. Come over and say hi?" Suzanne cajoled.

I glanced at Margot. Did she realize who this was? If she did, her face didn't show it. She was so good at keeping calm, at holding her tongue. *I could use a lesson in that.* "Maybe later. We need to finish setting up here."

"OK. Don't forget, though. We're still your family, aren't we?" It almost sounded like an accusation.

"Sure." I stuck my hands in my pockets, hoping she wouldn't try to hug me again.

She smiled with Steph's mouth, and it made my spine stiffen. "See you later, then." Without another look at Margot, she ambled off.

When she was out of hearing range, I exhaled and dropped into my chair. Picked up my water bottle. Took a long drink.

Margot slowly lowered herself to the edge of her seat. "Steph's sister?" she asked gently.

"Yeah."

She nodded. "Thought so. They look alike, huh?"

"Yeah."

"That's gotta be tough."

I shrugged. "Steph was really different than her sister."

"How so?"

"Different personalities. Different interests." I looked at her. "And Steph never would have treated you that way."

Margot's lips tipped up in a sad smile. "I got the feeling she didn't like my being here with you."

"Probably because this is something I used to do with Steph."

Margot tilted her head side to side. "So her reaction is understandable."

"Maybe. That doesn't make it OK, though." I sighed, closing my eyes for a second. "You know, when Steph was alive, her family never even liked me that much."

"Really?" Margot sounded shocked. "Why?"

I shrugged. "They felt she could have done a lot better than stick around here and marry me. Fuck, she could have done better. I told her that a million times." Angrily, I chugged my water again, wishing it was whiskey.

"I find that hard to believe."

"I don't know why," I said bitterly. "You've seen firsthand what an asshole I can be."

"Because you're a good man, Jack. Yes, you get angry and lash out. You get pushed, you push back. And hell yes, I've seen you be an asshole." Her voice softened. "But I've also heard you apologize. I've seen you treat people and animals with love and kindness. I've seen you treat *dirt* with love and kindness."

I almost smiled, and she caught me.

"Plus," she said, leaning over to whisper in my ear. "You've got good hands, an *amazing* tongue, and a big dick. What more could a girl want?"

Reluctantly, I allowed a small grin and shook my head. Did she really believe a big dick made up for everything I couldn't offer? Margot, of all people? "Uh, stability? Financial security? A nice car? A big house? Expensive jewelry?"

"You told me yourself she didn't care about those things."

"But you do." It came out of nowhere. Why the hell would I compare Steph to *Margot*? "Fuck. Forget I said that."

"No, listen." She put a hand on my leg. "You're not wrong. I do care about those things. I've never lacked for them, or anything else money can buy. But you know what?"

Christ, we are so different. "What?"

"Something is missing from my life."

I looked at her. "Like what? What could possibly be missing from your life when you have everything you ever wanted? And if you don't have it, you can go out and get it?"

She rolled her eyes. "I hate to break it to you, but they don't sell happiness at Bloomingdale's, Jack. Plenty of wealthy people are miserable and plenty of poor people are content."

"I guess."

"Were you and Steph rich?"

I snorted. "No."

"But you were happy."

"Yeah, we were. Too happy."

She cocked her head. "What do you mean?"

Jesus, why had I said that? Working off sexual tension with her was one thing, but I didn't want to reveal too much of myself. "Nothing."

"You meant *some*thing, Jack. Tell me."

I exhaled, feeling weight return to my shoulders that hadn't been there all day. "I just meant that it can't last, the kind of happiness that we had."

"Why not?"

"Because it was too good to be true. I didn't deserve it." *Shut your goddamn mouth, Valentini! What the hell are you doing?*

She studied me a moment. "Why not?"

"Christ, Margot. Can we drop this, please? I really don't want to talk about it. You won't understand, and it has nothing to do with you." *And I can't start telling you things. I just can't.*

"But I—"

"Drop it, I said! Steph and I are none of your fucking business!" And because my temper was threatening to get the best of me and I had a habit of running my asshole mouth when that happened, I jumped out of my chair and stomped off.

I had no idea where I was going, I just wanted some distance between us. Marching past other vendors in a blind rage, I strode through a public parking lot and took off down the street.

Goddammit, why did she have to get into it with me? I'd been in such a good mood today. Happy, even. Why did she have to ruin it by prodding at my pain with a fucking hot poker? Just because I was fucking her didn't mean she had the right to ask me about my feelings. She and I weren't going to do feelings—it was sex for the sake of sex and that was it! We didn't need to complicate things by talking about our pasts or our pain or what was missing from our lives. The moment we started to do that meant this was turning into something else, something I didn't want and she didn't need.

Taking a few deep breaths, I stopped walking and locked my hands behind my head. Waited for my heart rate to slow. For my agitation to ease. For my raw edges to smooth over.

After a few minutes, I was calm.

And ashamed of myself.

I was the one who'd said too much. What was it about her that made me spill my guts like a slaughtered animal? I couldn't fucking do that. And again, I'd gotten mad at myself and taken it out on her. When would I learn that lashing out at people who were trying to help only made me feel worse? Margot didn't have any idea how guilty I felt about Steph's death or why I felt responsible. And I wasn't about to tell her—not only would it burden her unnecessarily and cast a pall over what was supposed to be an uncomplicated good time, but it was too big a betrayal. Sex was one thing, but our connection had to remain purely physical.

Friendly was fine, but romantic was pushing it, and intimate was out of the question. *The less she knows about me, the better.*

I had to be more careful. For both of us.

On my way back, I stopped to buy some flowers for Margot. Unsure what kind of blooms were her favorite, I chose a small arrangement of blue hydrangeas because the color reminded me of her eyes. They were nicely wrapped in brown paper and tied with twine, but when I saw her sitting alone at our table, looking a little nervous and a lot sad, I felt like I should have bought a bigger bunch.

I walked around the stand and dropped down beside her chair, balanced on the balls of my feet. "Hey."

"Hey." She kept her eyes on her hands, which rested in her lap.

"These are for you." I handed her the flowers. "I'm sorry."

She looked at the bouquet and then at me. Took a breath. "Me too."

"You've got nothing to be sorry about."

"I do, I do..." She shook her head. "I shouldn't have bugged you about what you said. I've never lost anyone like you have, and I don't know what it's like. I've never even *loved* anyone like you have." Her eyes met mine. "I have no business trying to give you advice. I don't blame you for getting mad."

"It wasn't you I was mad at. I know it seemed like it," I said quickly when I saw the doubt on her face, "but I promise you it wasn't. I was mad at myself and let it get the best of me. I apologize."

"Apology accepted." She smiled and then buried her nose in the flowers she held. "I love hydrangeas. Thank you."

"I'm impressed you know what they are."

Over the blooms, her matching eyes glittered. "Good."

"The color matches your eyes. That's why I chose them."

She lowered the bouquet and looked at me in surprise, her cheeks going pink. Her mouth opened slightly like she might say something, but then she closed it again.

Looking at her, my heart started to beat a little too quickly for comfort, so I checked my watch and saw it was coming up on three. "Market's about to open up. You ready?"

"Yes." Smiling, she set the bouquet gently under the table and stood. "What should I do?"

"Don't let them walk away without buying something." I straightened up, my joints cracking.

She grinned. "Easy peasy. I could sell water to a drowning man, remember?"

"I remember," I said. "And I'm counting on it."

She gave me a thumbs up as a few people approached the stand. I watched her charm them, smiled and shook hands when she introduced me, and gave her a high five after they left with a bag full of eggs and vegetables.

It happened again and again.

Margot was a natural. People were drawn to her. They listened to her. Talked to her. No wonder she was so good at her job—she was beautiful and sweet and sincere. People wanted to please her. And I could tell she'd done her research on sustainable farming and the benefits of organic eating. She even dazzled *me* with her knowledge, especially because I knew she'd acquired it in such a short time. She was smart. And was she really doing all this for free?

"This is awesome," I told her. "I just have to stand here and take money while you do the work."

"Don't be silly, this is nothing. You do the hard work growing everything! Honestly, I can't believe I never thought about where my food was coming from before, or what was on it." She blinked those blue eyes at me. "I'm in awe of what you do. Plus, I think this is fun!"

She turned her attention toward the next customers, and I couldn't resist catching her around the waist from behind. "Careful, city girl. I'll want to keep you."

She laughed as I let her go.

But the scary thing was, I was only half joking.

chapter twenty-four

Margot

After the market closed and we'd loaded the truck, Jack wanted to take me out for dinner to thank me for working today. I told him it wasn't necessary, that I'd truly enjoyed myself, but he insisted. I think he still felt bad about the little blow-up, too, although he didn't mention it again.

I still felt bad about it. I'd only been trying to reassure him that he was good enough for Steph and deserved to be happy, but I shouldn't have pushed like that. He'd asked me to drop it. It was so sad, though—why did he think he didn't deserve to be happy? I'd never heard anyone talk about himself that way. It made my heart ache.

After he'd left me at the table, I'd felt like crying. Here I'd practically forced him to come to the market, something he used to do with his wife, and he'd run into her sister, which had dragged up painful memories, and then I'd made it worse by digging where I didn't belong.

And what an asshole I was, offering platitudes like *money doesn't buy happiness!*

How could I compare my situation, which was probably just boredom, to his tragic loss? What a spoiled brat I was, complaining about "something missing" from my life. I'd never wanted for anything. God, I wanted to kick myself! I could just imagine how that sounded to someone like Jack, who knew what it was to fight and struggle and suffer. What did I know about any of those things?

And his apology was so sweet. I'd gotten roses from Tripp before, but he'd always had them delivered. And while I appreciated the classic formality of the gesture as much as any woman, there was something so endearing and personal about the way Jack had handed me the bouquet today. The way he wanted to take the blame. The way he hunched down next to me and offered the flowers. The way he'd chosen them because they matched my eyes. It meant something to me.

He meant something to me. I just wasn't sure what.

He never did go over and say hello to Steph's mother, which I was glad about. I believed in social niceties, but after seeing the way Suzanne had acted toward me, I didn't feel he owed her any favors. She'd made things uncomfortable for him when she could just as easily have been nice. After all, I was no threat to her sister's memory. I just wanted to make him smile and laugh and feel good, even if it was only for a little while.

"I know a place you'll like in town," he said as we left the parking lot.

"And how do you know I'll like it?"

"Because it has things on the menu like charcuterie and fromage and craft cocktails." He put his pinkie in the air. "Very chic."

I slapped his hand down. "Oh, stop. I'm fine with anything. And I certainly don't belong in a place that's chic." I held my shirt away from my body. "I'm sticky and sweaty and gross."

"On your worst day, you couldn't be gross."

I smiled. "Thank you. But are you sure we're dressed OK?"

"I'm sure. Not too many places have a dress code around here."

We opted to eat on the restaurant's patio, and we were seated at a table under a string of party lights and a black and white striped umbrella. It was a table for four, and I was glad when Jack sat next to me instead of across. We ordered drinks—a martini for me and a whiskey on the rocks for him—and while those were being made, we looked over the menu and chose some charcuterie, cheese, and other small plates to eat.

Our drinks arrived, and the logo on the cocktail napkins reminded me of something I wanted to ask him. "Hey, what does a beet look like when it's picked?"

He arched a brow at me over his whiskey glass. "Why?"

"Because I need to draw one." I flipped the napkin over and took a pen from my purse. "Show me. Draw three of them."

He gave me a funny look but sketched a trio of beets on the napkin. "Like this?"

"Perfect." Biting my lip, I added a little banner across them and inked the words *Can't Beet Valentini Brothers Farm* on it. A little shyly, I turned it to face him.

He groaned, but he smiled too. "What is that?"

"Just an idea for a logo. Wouldn't that be cute on your tablecloths and your banner? On t-shirts? Shopping bags?" I was getting excited.

"Are those beets me, Pete, and Brad?"

I nodded happily. "We could even give the beets little faces!"

"You're killing me."

"I'm branding you." I took the napkin back and stuck it and the pen in my purse. "And I had lots of ideas today."

"I had some too. But none of them involved beets."

Our eyes met, a hot little current passing between us.

He still wants me! My heart beat faster. I'd been nervous that seeing Suzanne today and the blow-up afterward might dampen the fire between us, but it still burned.

We ate quickly.

On the way home, I asked Jack what his favorite meal was. I had this crazy idea I'd try to cook it for him—that would probably give him a laugh.

"Hmm. Probably a steak on the grill. Twice baked potatoes. Some kind of vegetable from our garden."

Damn. That was a tall order. I'd have to learn to grill. And twice-baked potatoes? What the heck was that? Why would you bake a potato twice? Wasn't once enough?

He glanced at me. "Why do you ask? Are you going to cook for me?"

"You don't have to sound so amused." I frowned slightly. "I think I could do it, but I'm not sure how to work the grill at the cottage."

"Why? Is it complicated?"

"I don't know. I asked the property manager how to turn it on but she started talking about charcoal and lighter fluid." I shook my head. "That sounded dangerous to me."

He burst out laughing. I'd never get tired of that sound, even if it was at my expense. "Jesus. You really have led a sheltered life."

"Not *that* sheltered," I said defensively.

"Oh no? Let's play a game." He gave me a sidelong glance. "I'll name something, and if you've never done it, you have to take off a piece of clothing."

"What?" I said indignantly. "OK fine, but if I *have* done it, you have to."

"Fine with me," he said.

"OK, then. Go."

"Changed a flat tire."

"Oh, come on!" I scoffed. "Start with an easier one. Who does that for herself?"

"Plenty of people. You should learn how. You've got that old car, what are you going to do if you get a flat tire?"

"Call triple A."

"What if you don't have a phone?"

I sighed.

"One piece of clothing." He said it like a warning.

"Fine." I tugged off one boot. "Next."

"Pumped your own gas."

"Ha! I've totally done that." I pointed at him. "Take something off."

He grinned. "Take the wheel."

I did, and he whipped off his t-shirt. My mouth watered. Even in the shadowy dark of the truck's cab, I could see the bulges in his arms, the lines on his stomach.

He grabbed the wheel again. "Waited tables."

"Oh, Jesus." I took off the other boot. "I didn't have summer jobs. We traveled abroad."

Jack thought that was hilarious. "OK, OK. An easier one. Plunged a toilet."

Off came one sock.

"Mowed a lawn."

Off came the other.

"Smoked a joint."

There went my t-shirt.

"Slept in a tent."

I shimmied out of my jeans.

He was smiling. "This is fucking fun as hell."

"I hope we don't get pulled over," I said, crossing my arms.

"I might pull over anyway."

My bare toes tingled.

"Been in a fight."

I thought for a second. "Like what kind of fight?"

"A fight. Where punches are thrown."

"Punches, huh? Not scones?"

"What?" He glanced at me. "What the hell are you talking about?"

I started to laugh. "My weasel ex came over a couple weeks ago at two AM and proposed to me. I can't even believe it now, but I sort of said I'd think about it. The very next night, he and his stupid girlfriend showed up to a fundraiser for my father's campaign, and she was wearing the very diamond ring he'd proposed with. He'd gone right from my house to hers."

"That is *fucked up*."

"Yeah. Come to find out, his father said he had to quit dicking around with his life and get serious, and I guess getting married would show he was serious. If he didn't, he wouldn't inherit his trust fund, which he needs to pay off gambling debts."

"Man." Jack shook his head. "Guess having money doesn't solve your problems."

"Nope. Anyway, I was so mad that night at the fundraiser that I started screaming at him and throwing scones."

He looked at me. "Scones? That was the best you could do? There wasn't a vase or something? In movies, rich people throw vases around."

I slapped his bare arm. "I knocked over a vase. Does that count? Oh! I also accidentally set fire to a table cloth."

Jack shook his head again, but he was grinning. "Did you ever hit the target?"

"Once or twice."

"How many scones did you throw?"

I shrugged. "Maybe a dozen or so?"

The grin widened. "Hopeless. And it doesn't count as a fight."

Sighing, I reached behind my back and unclasped my bra. It dangled off my arms a moment while I looked around. We were on a rural highway that wasn't well lit, and I hadn't seen a lot of other cars, but still. I could just hear my mother saying *Thurber women do not disrobe in moving vehicles.*

"Well, come on, city girl. Show me what you've got."

I slipped off the bra. Struck a sex kitten pose. "Happy?"

A quick glance my way, and he frowned. "Oh, fuck. I didn't think this through. I don't know if I can drive with you naked."

"Ha! Should have thought of that before you started this little game."

Next thing I knew, Jack slowed the truck and made a sharp right turn down a narrow dirt road between two fields. He switched off the car, and everything went dark and silent. "Come here."

But before I could move, he slid toward me on the seat and flipped me onto his lap, my legs on either side of his thighs. Our mouths crashed together as his hands snaked down my back. He grabbed my ass and pulled me against the bulge in his jeans. I rocked my hips over him, feeling my panties go damp.

My hands moved over his chest and arms and abs, my head filled with the scent of him. I felt drunk with the idea of him, of us, of doing this crazy, spontaneous, probably illegal, definitely ill-advised thing on someone else's property. We could be seen. We could be caught. We could get in trouble.

I'd never really been in trouble.

"My cock is so fucking hard." He flexed his hips, lifting them off the seat.

"I love it." Words I'd never uttered before tumbled out easily, breathlessly. "I want you to fuck me with it. Right here." I reached for his belt.

Inside a minute I'd wiggled out of my panties and he'd shoved his jeans down just enough for his cock to spring free. I lowered myself onto it, watching his eyes close, feeling his fingers gripping my hips.

I felt powerful and solid and *physical*. I'd never been so aware of my body or felt so driven by its need. Never experienced hunger or thirst or exhaustion to the point where my body craved food, water, or sleep the way it craved to be filled by this man. Connected to him. Anchored by him.

When he was buried deep inside me, I stayed still for a moment, wanting to commit the feeling to memory.

He opened his eyes. "Sex in a car?"

I smiled as I began to move. "Never."

"Good. I'm a fucking pioneer." He moved his hands and mouth to my breasts as I rocked my hips above him, making me arch and gasp with his fingers and tongue and teeth.

I wasn't very experienced being on top, but somehow my body knew exactly what to do, how to circle and grind and writhe above him, rubbing my clit along the base of his cock, angling so he'd hit that perfect spot inside me. And when I came, it was unlike anything I'd ever felt—deep, hard, surging contractions as my entire core tightened around him, the world turning to gold behind my eyes.

"I can feel you." Words whispered against my chest. "I can feel you come, and it drives me fucking crazy."

"Let me feel *you*." I could hardly talk.

He took over, grabbing my hips and sliding me up and down his cock as he stabbed into me. Then he switched it up, holding me tight to his body and working me back and forth, making my clit start to hum once more. "Come again for me. Now."

Fuck, I loved it when he gave me orders like that, his voice as hard as his cock. "Yes," I breathed, letting him move my body like he owned it, surrendering completely. "Make me."

It was like magic, the way he knew how to move with me, the way my body asked and his answered. The way his body commanded and mine obeyed. We shared everything—the spiraling ascent, the dizzying peak, the spinning free fall...and as we clung and cursed and kissed and caught our breath, something in me began to unravel.

The slight sense of unease stayed with me as I dressed myself and we got back on the highway. But what was it? The sex had been incredible—each time was better than the last. Each time, I felt more comfortable letting instinct take over. Each time, I felt more pleasure in giving myself to him and taking what I wanted. What I needed. Was I worried he didn't feel the same way?

No, that couldn't be it. He was enjoying himself every bit as much as I was—I could hear it in the way he talked, see it in the way he looked at me, feel it in the way he moved. We felt free with each other. It was as if the temporary nature of our arrangement gave us permission to be as wild as we wanted to. We had nothing to worry about, no relationship drama, no complications.

But we did have a deadline. An expiration date. In a week, this thing between us would be over.

I looked over at him, and my stomach flipped.

What if I didn't want it to end?

chapter twenty-five

Jack

AS THE TRUCK SPED DOWN THE HIGHWAY THROUGH THE DARK, I KEPT MY EYES on the road but my mind was all over the place. Questions I'd avoided asking myself this morning now refused to be ignored.

Why was this so easy with her? Why was the sex so hot? Why did being with her feel so good? What was it about Margot Lewiston, rich city girl who didn't even know how to light a grill let alone use one, that appealed to me so much? When I looked at her, why did I feel like I *had* to have her?

Sex with Steph had been amazing, but it hadn't been like this. I hated to even compare because the two women were so different, and it wasn't as if I felt sex was *better* with Margot, but it satisfied a different need in me. Sex with Steph was passionate because we loved each other, understood each other, took care of each other. It was a physical expression of our emotional connection and our history. We'd been through so much, and I'd wanted to shelter her, protect her, cherish her, even during sex. I'd never even thought about being rough with her, pulling her hair, leaving bruises on her body. Maintaining control had never been an issue, because I always felt I had it.

Sex with Margot was passionate too, but in a completely different way—if being with Steph was like diving into a beautiful blue sea, being with Margot was like going over Niagara Falls without a barrel. It was rough and turbulent, fraught with panic and desperation. At any given moment, there might be pleasure or pain, fear or relief, stillness or chaos. I had to fight for control, assert myself over her, combat the feeling that I was powerless. Thankfully, that dynamic worked for her too. She liked that I didn't treat her as if she were delicate, breakable, and when I issued commands, she obeyed.

I loved the contradiction between the Margot everyone else saw and the person she was with me. I loved every dirty word she whispered, every scratch and bite mark she left, every animalistic moan and cry.

Maybe that was it—maybe it was so good between us because we could be someone with each other that we couldn't be with anyone else. Or maybe it was the short-lived nature of this thing, sort of like how vacation sex feels better than everyday sex. And maybe I'd been able to sleep next to her because for the first time in years, I'd been able to forget for a while, let go of some of the pain. That was OK, wasn't it? Because it was only temporary? I'd take it all back again as soon as she was gone. For now, I'd stay focused on the present. On her.

I looked over at her and saw her chewing on a thumbnail. "So serious. Are you worried about what I'm going to do next to unshelter you?"

She smiled, giving me a sidelong glance. "Should I be?"

"Definitely."

"Whips and chains?"

"Ha. You wish. I'm taking you camping."

The grin melted off her face. "What."

"You heard me."

"Like…camping where you sleep outside on the ground in the woods?" she asked, like she might not entirely understand the concept.

"Yes. Scared?" I reached over and poked her in the side.

"Yes! There are creepy-crawly things on the ground! And there are no bathrooms! Or room service! Or plush hotel bedding!"

I laughed. "Nope."

"And there are animals in the woods." She whispered it, like she didn't want to alert them she was coming.

"Sweetheart, the only animal in the woods you'll have to worry about is me." I glanced over at her. Her eyes were wide, her expression half-pleased, half-terrified.

"Couldn't we just go to a nice, quaint little B & B around here?"

"What fun is that?" I turned into Pete and Georgia's driveway. "No, I want to take you camping for real for one night. You can manage one night without luxury, can't you?" I put the truck in park and looked at her.

"One night?" she asked shakily.

"One night."

She thought for a second, then sat up straighter. "OK. Yes. I can handle camping for one night. And you," she went on imperiously, "can handle a black tie Great Gatsby-themed fundraiser for the Historical Society."

"Black tie?" I pretended to think. "I don't think I own one of those."

"Black tie means you wear a tuxedo."

"Well, I sure as fuck don't own one of *those*."

She patted my arm. "I'll take care of everything."

"No way. I'm not going to any fundraiser."

"Scared I'll throw a scone at you?" Cocking her wrist back, she pretended to take aim.

I laughed and opened the driver's side door. "Actually, I'd like to see you do that."

She jumped out and met me around the back of the truck, and we began to unload it. "Come on, please? It will be fun."

"You don't really think that."

Her turn to laugh. "Not really. But I don't think camping will be fun, either." We started to walk through the dark toward the shed, arms loaded with empty crates and boxes. "Actually, you know what? I think we would have fun at the fundraiser."

"Oh yeah, why's that?"

"I think we would have fun anywhere."

I smiled, wondering who'd feel more out of place—Margot in a sleeping bag or me in a tux? It was a close call, but I think I'd win. Plus, I was only comfortable spending this time with her because whatever was between us would end when she left. I didn't want to make any promises that extended beyond that day. "I'm sorry, Margot. But no."

She sighed. "You're so unfair. I have to leave my comfort zone for you, but you won't leave yours for me?"

"You're going to leave your comfort zone for *you*. I'm going to teach you valuable survival skills. Like how to light a match."

"And when is this happening?"

"Let's see. Today's Wednesday, tomorrow night I'm watching Cooper, so how about Friday night?"

"Deal. Do I need a certain kind of clothes for camping?"

We reached the shed, and I laughed as I pulled the door open, picturing her decked out head to toe in some kind of designer camping gear, all in white. "Nope. You can wear anything. Or nothing's fine too."

"Hey, you two."

I jumped, nearly dropping the armload I held, my nervous system kicking into high gear. It was Georgia walking toward us, and she hadn't meant to startle me, but it took a moment to breathe normally again.

"Hey, Georgia." Margot greeted my sister-in-law, but her eyes were on me.

"How'd it go?" Georgia asked, hands in her back pockets.

My heart was still beating too fast as I moved inside the shed and stacked boxes against the wall.

"Great," Margot said. "I had a ball."

A second later I felt her hand on my back—a brief, reassuring touch. She didn't say anything, didn't even make eye contact, but I knew what she was doing...and I appreciated it.

"A ball?" Georgia laughed as we came out.

"Yes. And I have a bunch of ideas for you."

We began to walk back to the truck, and Georgia followed. "Margot was a natural," I told her. "We sold out of everything we brought."

"Really? Wow!"

"Did you get to see the house?" Margot asked.

Georgia shook her head. "Tomorrow at ten. Want to come along?"

"I'd love to!" Margot looked at me. "Unless Jack needs me for something."

Fuck, she was cute. I smiled at her. "No, you can have tomorrow off."

We reached the truck and Georgia peeked in the back. "You really did sell well today, huh?"

"It was all Margot," I said. "I'm telling you. She's got some kind of magic in her smile. No one can say no to her."

Margot beamed. "That's very flattering, but all I did was sell what you grew. That's the real magic."

Georgia looked over her shoulder at us, and my face felt hot. Why had I said that about her smile? Now Georgia probably suspected something.

"Come on, let's get this done." I tried to sound businesslike, but I was positive my sister-in-law's mind was ticking. She stayed quiet the rest of the time it took us to unload the truck, and she's *never* quiet.

"Well, goodnight, you two," she said breezily when we were done. "Thanks again for working the market today. See you tomorrow. Oh Jack, you still on for babysitting tomorrow night?"

I nodded. "Yeah."

"Great, thanks. Night!"

"Night, Georgia," Margot called. As soon as we were alone, she looked at me. "She knows."

"Seems like it."

"Are you OK with that?"

Rubbing the back of my neck, I thought for a second. It wasn't so much I minded Georgia knowing, but I didn't want her telling my brothers. They'd have a field day. They'd ruin it. But that wasn't Margot's problem. "Yeah, I'm fine. Georgia gets me."

She nodded. "Seems like it."

We stood there for a moment while the crickets chirped and wind rustled through the birch trees nearby. Lonely, nighttime sounds. *But I don't want to be alone tonight. More than that—I don't want to leave her.*

"So." I took a step closer to her.

She smiled. "So."

"What would you like to do?"

"Honestly? I really need a shower."

I cocked a brow. "What a coincidence."

I stared at the tub. "Really? A bubble bath? I don't think I've taken one of these in thirty years." We'd stopped in at the cabin—Margot had waited on the porch—so I could grab clean clothes, then gone back to her cottage, where she'd filled up the bathtub with hot water and bubbles.

Margot giggled. "Then you're due. How old are you, anyway?"

"Thirty-three. You?"

"I'll be thirty next month."

"And you still take bubble baths?"

"As often as possible. And I never travel without my bath foam." She breathed in, closing her eyes. "Doesn't that smell good?"

I inhaled the scent of lavender. "I have to admit it does."

"See? A little luxury is nice sometimes." She looked pleased with herself.

We peeled off our clothes, and Margot got in, leaving me standing there staring at the tub. "There's no way I'm going to fit in there with you."

"Yes, there is." Scooting toward the back of the tub, she looked up at me and splashed the bubbles. "Come and play."

Somehow I managed to get in without falling, and we spent the next five minutes scrubbing up and rinsing off with some kind of fancy shower gel she'd also brought from home. It smelled delicious, just like her skin, but I couldn't resist giving her a hard time. "I'm going to smell like a girl tomorrow. What's the matter with plain old manly bar soap?"

She frowned. "It's not good for your skin."

"Oh." I started washing my hair with the gel and she looked appalled.

"Jack! That isn't shampoo!"

"What difference does it make? It made suds. I'm sure my hair is getting clean."

She reached for a bottle on the tub ledge. "Rinse that out. I'll do it."

I rolled my eyes but let her wash my hair with her fancy shampoo, which frankly didn't even foam up as well as whatever cheap shit I had in my shower. I told her so.

Sighing with exaggerated patience, she began to massage my scalp. "That is because your cheap shampoo has chemicals in it called sulfates that make it suds up. Frankly, I'm surprised at you, Jack. You know about avoiding chemicals in your food but you don't pay any attention to them in your skin and hair care products?"

I could hardly speak, her fingers on my head felt so fucking good. Every nerve ending in my body tingled, and my cock started to swell. I might have moaned.

"OK, turn around and tip your head back."

I had to stand up to turn around, and she started to giggle.

"What?"

"Your..." She pointed at my dick, which stuck straight out at her and was covered in foamy white bubbles. "It looks so funny."

I stuck my hands on my hip. "For fuck's sake, Margot. You can say dick. Just don't say it looks funny."

"I'm sorry," she said, laughing uncontrollably. "But I just never pictured you like this—standing in my tub all covered in lavender bubbles with half a hard-on—oh, God." She shook her head and tried to compose herself while I stared her down.

"I'm going to remember this when we're deep in the woods." Turning around, I sat down again and tipped my head back.

"No! I'm sorry. Don't torture me in the woods." She used a cup to pour water over my head, rinsing off the shampoo. "There. Now stand up again."

"Why? So you can laugh at me some more?" But I stood and faced her, making sure this time there were no lingering bubbles on my junk.

"No." Scrambling to her knees, she slid her hands up my legs. "I'm sorry." She kissed my right thigh. "Your dick isn't funny." She kissed my left. "It's very serious." She kissed the tip of my cock, making it jump like it wanted to kiss her back. "It's perfect."

My breath caught when I felt her tongue on me—soft, sweet little licks that made my insides quiver and leg muscles tighten. I was fully hard in seconds, and she ran her tongue from bottom to tip. Good fucking God, it had been so long...

I glanced down to see her look up and smile at me, that naughty little grin that always proved to be my undoing. "My turn."

"Your turn to what?" I managed as she took me in her hands, angling my dick toward her mouth.

"To taste you." She swirled her tongue around the tip. "To drive you crazy." She took the head between her lips, sucked gently. "To make you come with my mouth."

I groaned as her lips moved down my shaft, half my cock disappearing inside her mouth before she pulled back. Then she did it again, and again, never sucking too hard, never moving too fast, never making any sound.

Her tongue felt incredible on me, her mouth was hot and wet, and I loved the way she kept her hands on what she couldn't get in her mouth, but Margot was giving the most polite blowjob I'd ever had.

In contrast to the way she moved during sex, it almost seemed like she was scared of hurting me. Or maybe she was scared of *being* hurt. A girl like Margot probably hadn't done this very much. Maybe she didn't even like it and was only offering to please me.

Well, fuck—now what should I do?

My hands slid into her hair, and I forced myself to maintain control, to hold back, but every instinct in my body wanted to take over.

No, asshole! Let her be in charge! Just because she likes rough sex doesn't mean she wants to choke on your dick.

Oh fuck, now I'm thinking about that. I need to calm down.

I let go of her head, stared at the ceiling, counted to ten.

She knew what I was doing.

"Jack," she drawled. "Are you holding back on me?"

I looked down at her and saw those blue eyes gazing up accusingly as she rubbed the tip of my dick playfully against her lips. Her skin was wet, and her nipples were hard. Fuck, she was gorgeous. And sweet. What the fuck was the matter with me that I wanted to choke her with my dick? Was I an animal? "I don't want to hurt you."

"You won't."

"You don't know what I want to do to you right now."

"Tell me."

I groaned, knowing I was unable to say no to her.

"Teach me, Jack." Her cheeks colored as she placed her hands on my thighs. "I don't have much experience with this. But I want to learn. I want to make you feel good. Tell me what to do. Tell me what you want."

I swallowed hard. Tightened my fists in her hair. "Open your mouth." She widened her lips, and I pushed inside, as deep as I could go. "I want your mouth so full of my cock you can't breathe."

She jumped when I hit the back of her throat, and I thought she'd try to back away.

But she didn't.

She wrapped her fingers around my shaft again and looked up at me expectantly.

"Good girl. Now listen to me. I want you to stop being so fucking polite. Use your hands. Get messy. Make noise. Forget about being queen of the prom and suck me off like the greedy little slut under the bleachers. Got it?"

She got it. Oh my fucking God, she got it. She went at me like a porn star.

Five minutes later, I came so hard I saw galaxies born on her bathroom ceiling and thought my body might rocket into space, and she eagerly swallowed every last drop.

"So," she said, breathing hard. "Was that greedy enough for you?"

I reached under her arms and pulled her up to sit on the edge of the tub, then I dropped to my knees and pushed her legs apart. "Fuck yes, it was." Lowering my head between her thighs, I stroked her clit with my tongue. "But I'm about to get greedier."

chapter twenty-six

Jack

"Tell me about these." Margot's hands brushed over the ink on my side, sending a shiver down my spine. We'd probably been in this tub for an hour, the bubbles were gone, and the water wasn't even that hot anymore. But I was reluctant to get out. *It's not raining tonight. I have no reason to stay.*

"They're swallows," I said.

"Can I look at them?"

I turned around and sat so my back was to her.

"You have two of them." She traced them with her fingers.

"Two tours of duty."

"Ah. Did they bring you good luck?"

I closed my eyes. Heard shots fired. Saw bodies in the front seat. Smelled blood.

Swallowing hard, I clenched my gut and forced the ugly memory from my head. *Here and now. Here and now. Here and now.* "I didn't get them until I came back."

"So they're more of a symbol of a journey completed than a good luck charm?"

"Something like that."

"Are you glad that you did it? Joined the Army, I mean?"

"I've asked myself that question a lot. And I guess the answer is yes. I mean, if I had it to do over again, I know I'd still join up when I did."

"You know, you're the first person my age I've ever met in the military."

I looked at her over my shoulder. "Seriously?"

"Yeah. I think someone in my graduating class went to the Naval Academy, but I've never personally known a real soldier unless you count Veterans of World War II or something."

"Wow." Her life had been so different from mine. So different.

She kissed my shoulder blade. "I've never met anyone as brave as you."

I snorted, but I liked the compliment. "Thanks."

"Or someone who works as hard or knows so much about things I don't."

"Or someone whose hands get as dirty as mine do every day. I bet most people you know wear suits to work. Have their shoes shined. Get regular haircuts." *Own boats, golf clubs, and stock portfolios.* It was hard not to compare myself to those guys.

"Hey." She poked me in the back. "I like that you get your hands dirty every day."

I didn't quite believe her. "Yeah?"

"Yeah. It makes you different from other guys I know. Same with your tattoos." Sighing, she looped her arms around my neck and leaned back against the tub, taking me with her. "I don't have any tattoos."

My back rested against her chest, my head in the crook of her neck. The tension drained from my muscles. *If only I never had to leave this bathtub.* "I didn't think you would."

"Why not?"

"You just didn't strike me as the kind of girl who'd have them is all."

"I'm not," she said after a moment. "You're right. The truth is, I think they can be beautiful, but they seem very exotic and forbidden to me. Something for people who are braver than I am."

"Why? Are you scared it will hurt?"

"No, not exactly. More like I'd be scared of what people would think about me."

"Fuck people."

She sighed again. "Muffy would die."

"No, Margot. She wouldn't."

"Maybe not. But she'd think I'd gone crazy."

"So let her. Don't spend your life worried about what people think of you, Margot. That kind of fear is like a cage—it will trap you forever if you're not careful."

She didn't speak right away. Then a question. "What are you scared of?"

I didn't answer, because I knew I'd say too much. She was too soft, too sweet, too warm tonight. It would be too easy to tell her things she didn't need to hear, too selfish of me to reveal things just to share the burden of my truths. She'd only try to reassure me I wasn't the monster I thought I was, just like Steph had done.

But it would feel so good.

"Probably nothing, right?" She squeezed me. "You're a big tough soldier. Not scared of anything."

I spoke without thinking. "I'm scared of becoming unrecognizable."

A pause. "What do you mean?"

"Nothing," I said quickly. What the fuck was I doing? I even tried to get up, but she held me in place, wrapping her legs around me from behind.

"What would make you unrecognizable, Jack?"

Exhaling, I allowed myself to surrender, just a little. Just this once. "Letting go."

"Of what?"

"My past."

"You don't have to let go of your past—it will always be part of who you are. But you don't have to let it shackle you, or prevent you from moving on."

Yes, I do. She didn't know, didn't understand.

"Hey." She squeezed me again. "Talk to me."

God help me, I wanted to. My secrets were pushing up against the underside of my heart so hard I thought my chest might burst open with them. I wanted to admit my guilt. Open my wounds. Bleed for her.

The temptation overwhelmed me. "The accident. It was my fault."

"I don't understand."

I tried to swallow but couldn't. "Steph's accident."

"What are you talking about? You weren't driving the car that hit her."

"No. But...there was a different car." My voice was weak, and my body started to tremble. "Years ago. In Iraq."

Margot's hand began rubbing my chest in slow, soothing arcs. "I'm listening. Tell me."

My throat was dry and tight, but the story forced its way out. "My convoy was moving through the country and we'd stopped to rest. Three of us set up a checkpoint. Cars were being used as rolling bombs, so we had to stop every vehicle from coming into the zone where soldiers were resting."

She shivered, as if she knew what was coming. Pressed her lips to my head.

"We had signs in Farsi instructing drivers to stop, and if a vehicle didn't stop, we fired warning shots at six hundred meters. It was rare that cars tried to go through, unless they carried IED's. But one night..." I paused. Inside my head was a voice screaming at me to stop talking, but I couldn't. Every word out of my mouth relieved some kind of pressure inside me. I had to get it all out.

"One night someone didn't stop?" she prompted. "Was there a bomb in the car?"

I shook my head, swallowing the sob threatening to choke me. "No. But it's possible the driver thought the warning shots were coming from behind, because the car sped up as soon as they were fired. So I fired directly at the vehicle. I didn't even think twice."

"Of course you didn't." Her voice was strong. "Jack, no one would ever blame you. You did your job. You protected people."

"I didn't even see who was in the car until morning and it was time to move from that position." My eyes filled.

She went completely still. "And?"

"The driver was a woman. And there were children with her."

"Oh, my God."

"Three of them." My voice cracked, and tears dripped from my closed eyes.

"Oh, Jack." Margot's voice was splintering too. She held me tight. "That must have been horrible for you."

I inhaled, regaining control. "You know what? It wasn't. It barely registered. At the time, I remember feeling proud for doing what I had to." The words were bitter in my mouth. "Later, after I got home, it hit me what I'd done. I was a wreck. I couldn't talk to anyone, didn't feel safe, couldn't make myself feel normal. Every single minute I was just waiting for the retribution, you know? I was positive there was no way what I'd done could go unpunished. I *wanted* the retribution. I nearly brought it on myself."

She hugged me even tighter, and I felt the trembling in her body as she wept. Kissed my shoulders, my head, my neck. Ran her hands over my chest and stomach, as if she had to reassure herself I was still here. "I'm so sorry. And I'm so glad you're here. You didn't do anything wrong."

I didn't deserve her sympathy or her tears.

"Do you know how many fucking nightmares I've had about that woman?" I touched my thumb and index finger to the insides of my eyes. "She's right there in front of me and I'm begging and begging her to stop, and she doesn't. I wake up shaking and screaming."

"Do you still have the nightmares?"

"Sometimes. For a while, they got better, after I went to the doctor. I started taking meds that would make me forget what I'd dreamt. I didn't dread going to sleep so much. But I stopped taking them after Steph's accident."

"Why?"

"Because it was my fault." I retreated into the truth that tortured me, repeated the words that haunted me. "'Just as he has done, so it shall be done to him.'"

"No, Jack. You're wrong." She sniffed and sat up taller. "What you did saved lives, and it had nothing to do with Steph's accident. You are *not* responsible."

I closed my eyes. "It's the only way I can make sense of it."

"No one could *ever* make sense of a tragedy like that."

"Sometimes I dream about the checkpoint, and it's Steph driving the car," I whispered. "In my subconscious, they're connected forever."

Gently she rocked me, her words laced with quiet sobs. "It wasn't Steph, Jack. She was the love of your life, and you never would have harmed her. You made her happy."

"I wanted to. God, I wanted to."

"You did. And if she were here right now, I *know* she'd be saying the same thing to you that I am—it wasn't your fault."

I knew she was right—Steph would say that, and she *had* a thousand times in my mind. But I just couldn't believe her.

"And she'd probably be angry that you blame yourself," Margot went on. "She'd want you to forgive yourself so you could be happy again. Don't you think?"

Of course she would. She'd stand right there and argue with me just like she used to. But forgiving myself would mean giving myself permission to move on, to be happy when I didn't deserve it. I'd never make that mistake again. "I can't."

She rocked me again, her arms wrapped around me, her lips pressed to my skin. When she spoke, her voice was soft. "Have you ever told anyone about this?"

I hesitated. "Steph and my therapist knew about Iraq. But I've never talked to anyone about feeling responsible for her death until you."

She let that sink in—both of us did. I'd just shared a part of me with her that I hadn't shared with any other living soul. I wasn't even sure why I trusted her so much, but I did. Again, I figured it had to do with her temporary presence in my life. It freed me to be my real self around her.

"I wish there was something I could do for you," she said.

I exhaled. The truth was out. And while I didn't exactly feel better or hopeful, I did feel less alone. I put my hands over hers on my chest. "You're here. You're listening. That's something."

"I *am* here. And I'm glad you told me."

"I am too." It was startling to realize I meant it. I hadn't intended to reveal so much of myself, but it had been so long since I felt this kind of closeness to someone, the kind that compelled you to share your secrets.

She sighed as she leaned back again. "Want to hear something ridiculous?"

"Sure."

"The entire reason I took the job up here was because my mother made me leave town after the scone-throwing incident."

I craned my neck so I could see her face. "What?"

"It's true. I had to leave town until the rumors died down."

"Jesus. And have they?"

"Yes. She called yesterday and said I could show my face again."

"That's why you were going to leave yesterday, huh?"

"Yes."

God, I was glad she hadn't. "But you're still here."

"I'm still here," she whispered.

I kissed her, felt her fingers stroking my jaw. Her lips were warm and soft and tasted like lavender, and I wanted nothing more than to live in that kiss with her forever, to trap it under glass and stay safely inside, cut off from memories that haunted me and a future that could never be.

I wanted it so badly I didn't stay the night.

chapter twenty-seven

Margot

The next morning, I walked to Pete and Georgia's house just before ten. I hadn't slept well, so I felt a little groggy as I made my way, but the sunshine felt good on my arms. Inhaling deeply, I hoped the fresh air would succeed in perking me up where three cups of coffee had failed. But I caught the scent of manure on the breeze, and wrinkled my nose. Was that fertilizer? Ugh, how did people who lived near farms ever get used to that smell? *That's one thing I will not miss when I go home.*

But there was something I would miss—being with Jack. The last twenty-four hours had been incredible. Something had changed between us. What we shared no longer felt like a meaningless little fling. I felt close to him. Protective of him. Proud of him. Fascinated by him and how he made me feel.

I was falling for him so fast, everything around me was a blur.

It was mind-boggling. We weren't even dating! In the past when I'd developed feelings for someone, it had taken a while. And those feelings had stemmed from times spent together enjoying common interests rather than intense physical attraction. For heaven's sake, it had taken me six months to sleep with Tripp! And I'd never even had a one-night-stand, let alone an extended fuckfest with someone *not* my boyfriend. I'd never had an extended fuckfest, period!

And last night had been *insane*. I could still hear him telling me to act like a greedy little slut—was it terrible that it turned me on so much? How had he known that's what I'd needed—permission to act that way *with the lights on, while he watched*? That's what had made me nervous. Prior to that we'd always been in the dark, and letting that other side of me take over hadn't seemed so daunting. I'd gotten stage fright, especially since I wasn't that experienced with oral sex to begin with. But I'd wanted to do it for him. I wanted to make him feel good in every possible way.

And the things he did to me... I stopped walking for a moment. Put a hand on my stomach. Caught my breath.

Everything felt different with Jack. Now I knew what Jaime had been talking about when she said things like *mind-blowing physical chemistry*. And since I'd gotten a taste of it, I didn't want to let it go.

It wasn't just physical either. Not anymore. When I thought about the way he'd opened up to me last night, sharing something with me he'd never told anyone else, shedding tears in front of me, making himself that vulnerable...

God, I just wanted to hold him and kiss him and cry for him, make everything better for him, make him happy.

But how?

I'd been hoping he might stay over again, especially since he'd said he'd slept well in my bed the night before, but I hadn't wanted to pressure him. I'd asked, he'd said no, I dropped it. He'd revealed so much of himself to me, he probably needed the time alone to come to terms with that. I understood that about him, and I'd learned not to push his buttons that way—he snapped and pulled back when I tried to get too close, almost like a skittish horse.

So after kissing him goodbye, I'd said goodnight and climbed into bed, hugging the pillow he'd used the night before. Sleep eluded me for hours, which I spent replaying every moment of the day and night in my mind, struggling to keep my feelings under control, and choking up all over again when I thought about what he'd told me.

By morning I had to face the truth.

I had feelings for him, and I didn't want this to end.

I wanted there to be a way for us.

Was it out of the question? People dated long distance all the time, didn't they? Two hours was practically nothing! I could work from anywhere most of the time, and I liked this little town. It didn't have designer shops or three-star restaurants or glamorous salons, but Main Street was charming, the beach was uncrowded, and the farms were beautiful. I could even start riding again! Being with the horses the other day reminded me how much I'd missed it.

As I waited for highway traffic to clear so I could cross, I thought about an even bigger problem than distance: Jack didn't want to get married again. Didn't think he could love someone again. Didn't want to let go of his past. Part of me thought I was crazy to even worry about getting married, since I'd met the guy less than a week ago, but another part of me insisted.

Look how intense things were between us after just five days. What if we started dating, and things continued to go well? Did I really want to invest time and energy and feelings in someone who didn't want what I wanted in the end? And I was almost thirty—I didn't want to wait that much longer to start a family. If there was no chance of that, what was the point?

As I hurried across the two lanes and started up Pete and Georgia's drive, I saw that wedding band on Jack's finger, heard his voice in my head.

I know what I had. And it doesn't happen twice.

My heart dropped. How on earth could I argue with that?

Jack was right about the Oliver house in many ways—it needed a lot of work, including a new roof, but Brad was right, too. Like all aging beauties, it had great bones beneath layers of dust, mold, peeling wallpaper, flaking paint, smelly carpet, and rot. It would take time and money and loving care, but it could be restored.

Georgia was beside herself as we walked back. "I knew it. I knew I'd love it that much." Brad and Pete were up ahead, Cooper in his dad's arms.

I smiled at her. "It could be great. And so easy to bump out the back wall, extend the kitchen."

"Pete and I have been talking about making it a bed and breakfast in addition to a restaurant," she said.

"A B and B, I love it! And it totally makes sense if you host weddings on the property."

"Exactly. And if we bumped out the back wall for an extended kitchen, we could put living space for us above. That would leave the five bedrooms in the old part of the house for guests."

Her enthusiasm was contagious, and I found myself brimming with new energy. "Yes! Oh, Georgia, that's perfect. Just imagine decorating that place—it could be so beautiful."

"I know!" Her eyes lit up. "Antique beds, a big old table in the dining room, vintage dishes and silver pieces..." Then she sighed. "But that takes money. And we haven't got it."

"What about selling your current house?" I asked.

Georgia shook her head. "We couldn't. It's been in the family too long. Plus it's mortgaged with the farm, which is owned equally by Pete, Brad, and Jack. Any money we got for it would technically have to be split between the three of them."

"Would Jack move into it if you left?" I wondered where he was working this morning and if he was thinking about last night as much as I was. "Maybe he'd buy you out."

"I don't think so. He doesn't have the cash, and he loves that damn cabin."

"You'd think he might want to leave, though, given the chance. Aren't the memories kind of painful there?" As soon as I said it, I realized that it wouldn't matter—staying in that cabin was one of the ways he prevented himself from letting go of his past.

"Yeah." She sighed as we reached the path leading to their front porch. The others had gone inside already. "He baffles me sometimes, you know? The way he refuses to move on? He chooses to be unhappy, and I don't know why."

I dropped my eyes to the ground. I knew why, but Jack trusted me with his feelings. I couldn't betray him.

"I mean, Steph's clothes are still in the closet."

I gasped and met her eyes again. That was a detail he hadn't mentioned. "Wow."

She shook her head. "I've offered to get rid of them so many times, but he won't let anyone touch them."

"God, it's so sad." My hand covered my heart. "How can he live like that?"

"He says that's how he wants it. And whenever any of us try to help, he lashes out."

"He does do that," I agreed, remembering how he'd snapped at me yesterday at the market. "But it's hard not to try, because once you get to know him, you see how sad he is. And you want to help."

Georgia looked at me for a moment. "I will say this. He's been different since you've been here. Better."

"Me?"

She rolled her eyes. "Yes. You guys were like two googly-eyed teenagers when you got back last night. Let's not pretend there's nothing there."

"What could be there?" I tried for innocent, but it came out more coy than anything.

Georgia laughed. "I don't know exactly what it is you're doing, but he's never called *my* smile magic. I haven't seen him that way in years. It's a shame you live so far away."

"Yeah." Frowning, I played with the braid trailing over one shoulder. "But I don't know if it would make a difference anyway. I mean, does he ever date?"

"Never," she admitted.

"And he told me the other night he'll never get married again. Doesn't want a family."

"Yeah, that's what he says to us too, any time we suggest he try getting out there again. It's sad, because he'd make such a great father. And he's still young."

Exhaling, I dropped my hands to my sides. Tried to cover up my disappointment with a lie. "Oh, well. I don't think I'm his type anyway, and he's not really mine."

"Oh, I don't know," she said airily. "I think you two could be good together. And sometimes opposites attract, right? Maybe you can change his mind."

I smiled. Opposites attracted, sure, but attraction wasn't our problem. We had *all* kinds of that. Our problem was that the attraction was getting stronger. It was bringing us closer. It was making me feel things with my heart and not just with my body.

But he wasn't interested in my heart.

⸎

Georgia and I chatted a little more about the branding and social media strategies I'd outlined for them, and I was happy to hear they'd contacted a web designer and had filled out her project questionnaire. Again she asked me to please send her a bill for my time, but I politely refused. "You're going to need every extra dollar to buy that house," I told her. "Consider it my donation."

She hugged me and went inside to discuss things with Pete and Brad. Presumably Jack would be in on the discussion eventually, but he hadn't come to see the house. I hoped he'd be reasonable on the subject of buying it.

I also hoped I'd see him today. We hadn't made any plans, but he had put my number in his phone before leaving last night. Maybe he'd call.

In the meantime, I didn't want to sit around doing nothing, since that would just mean more time spent fretting over him. Instead, I researched some of my ideas for their market stand and displays, then drove to the nearest craft store for materials. I hit the grocery store too, buying fresh items for the next few days. When I saw the potatoes, I wondered again about baking them twice and made a mental note to look that up. Maybe I could take a cooking class or something—that would be getting out of my comfort zone for sure.

Learn to cook. Start riding again. I started a mental list of things I could do to change up my life, be happier and more fulfilled. *Stop obsessing over my thirtieth birthday. Get involved with the food justice movement.*

After a peanut butter and jelly sandwich lunch, I spent the early part of the afternoon working on the display projects and mulling over possible solutions for Pete and Georgia's cash flow problem. A small business loan maybe? But I knew next to nothing about the loan process since I'd never needed to take one out.

I was printing a price list on a chalkboard when my cell phone buzzed with a text. **Hey you. It's Jack. Want to meet Cooper and me at the park?**

I picked up the phone, grinning at it like a goofball. **Sure. What time?**

Twenty minutes?

That was perfect—I'd have time to finish what I was doing first. **See you then!**

I set the phone down and hummed a tune as I completed the list, then held it out to make sure the writing was even and legible. When I was satisfied, I quickly put everything away, used the bathroom, brushed my teeth, and touched up my makeup. At the last minute, I decided to wipe off the lipstick I'd applied and put on some honey lip balm instead. It looked more natural and tasted better.

As I walked to the park, my feet felt a hundred times lighter than they had this morning. Nothing had changed since then, but just the prospect of seeing him was enough to excite me. And when he came into view, standing behind Cooper, pushing him on a swing, the butterflies in my stomach multiplied. *This feeling*, I thought as I crossed the playground toward him. *I don't want to lose it.*

He looked up as I approached and the smile he gave me turned my legs to jelly. "Hi."

"Hi."

He glanced over his shoulder. "Didn't you come from the cottage?"

I cringed. "Yes, but I walked one block too far, so I came from the other side. I wasn't paying attention."

He laughed, shaking his head. "It's like three blocks away. Only you could screw that up."

"I know, I know." I'd let him tease me as much as he wanted as long as I could stand there watching him push his nephew on that swing. His fitted black t-shirt showed off his arms and chest, the tight jeans hugged him in all the right places, and his aviator sunglasses worn without the usual hat made him look a little more polished, a little more military. It did things to me. In the panties.

"Did you hear about the house?" I asked.

He harrumphed and mumbled.

"I take it that's a yes."

"I heard about it. They've got some crazy idea about running a motel there?"

I rolled my eyes. "Oh, Jesus. It's not a motel, Jack, it's a bed and breakfast."

"Whatever. I won't stand in their way, but there's no way they'll come up with the money they need."

"That's what Georgia said. Could they get a small business loan or something?"

"I guess they can try." He didn't sound too hopeful.

"I wish there was a way I could help," I said wistfully. How terrible to have your dream within reach and not be able to afford it. I'd been so spoiled my entire life. Not that I'd spent frivolously or irresponsibly, I hadn't—but I also didn't know what it was like to go without something I really wanted because I couldn't afford it.

"That's nice of you, but they'll figure it out. *We'll* figure it out."

"So you have Cooper tonight?" I ruffled the little boy's hair as he swung near me.

"Yeah. Pete and Georgia are both working."

"What will you do with him?"

"Feed him ice cream for dinner, buy him a bunch of candy, let him watch a bunch of TV until he falls asleep." He smiled at me. "The usual uncle stuff."

"Sounds like fun."

"Want to join us?"

My heart stuttered. "Sure. I'd love to."

We spent another hour at the park, and I was amazed at how good Jack was with Cooper. He went down the slide with him, spun him on the merry-go-round, helped him climb up the old-fashioned jungle gym. When Cooper fell and scraped his knee, Jack brushed him off, dried his tears, and hugged him close. When it was time to leave and Cooper insisted on one more time down the slide, Jack raced him to it. When we walked to the ice cream parlor, Jack swung the little boy up onto his shoulders and held his tiny hands the whole way there.

Later, I watched him make dinner for Cooper and spoonfeed him every bite. I watched him give his nephew a bath—we'd exchanged a fun look as he started to fill the tub—careful not to get any water in his eyes when he rinsed the shampoo from Cooper's hair. I watched him put a diaper and clean pajamas on the tired toddler, brush his baby curls off his forehead in an adorable imitation of his own hair. "There," he said. "Just like your Uncle Jack."

All I could think was, *This man should be a father.*

When it was time to turn off the light and put him in bed, I said I'd wait downstairs, said goodnight to Cooper, and headed down to the kitchen.

As soon as I entered the room, I heard Cooper fussing for "Mama" and then Jack's voice on the monitor. "OK, Buddy, time to settle down. Let's get Bunny." Smiling, I stood in front of the little screen and watched Jack grab something from the crib and cradle the weepy Cooper against his chest.

"You want to rock a little bit? OK, OK." He disappeared from view. A few seconds later, the fussing stopped. And the singing began.

It was soft at first, and I leaned toward the monitor to hear it better. At first, I didn't recognize the song—something about a whippoorwill—but after another line or two, I clapped a hand over my mouth, my heart pounding. It was the Hank Williams song that we'd heard in the truck yesterday on the way to the market. He'd sung along then, too. He had a nice voice—deep and melodic with just the right amount of grit.

Goosebumps blanketed my arms. I put a hand over my heart, surprised my chest was still flesh and bone since I felt as if I were melting. I'd never heard anything so sweet.

A lump formed in my throat.

Give me a chance to make you happy, Jack.

Let me try.

chapter
twenty-eight

Jack

I ROSE TO MY FEET, CAREFUL NOT TO JOSTLE MY SLEEPING NEPHEW. CURSING THE wood floor that creaked beneath my feet, I tried to avoid the spots I knew made noise as I made my way to the crib. After laying him down on his back, I kissed my fingertips, touched his forehead and quietly slipped out of the room.

I found Margot sitting on a kitchen chair, one hand over her heart. When she saw me, she clapped the other one over it. Looked as if she were about to burst into tears.

"Fuck. I forgot to turn off the monitor, didn't I?"

"I can't talk, I'm a puddle."

Groaning, I went to the fridge and grabbed a beer. All I wanted to do was get my hands on her (and various other body parts) but it didn't feel right in Pete and Georgia's house, so I needed to find something to occupy them.

"Don't worry, don't worry. Your secret sweetness is still safe with me."

I eyeballed her as I uncapped the bottle and took a drink. "It better be. Want a beer?"

"No, thanks."

"Glass of wine?"

She hesitated. "I hate to drink Pete and Georgia's wine."

"Why? They got free babysitters tonight." I pulled a bottle down from the rack above the fridge and showed it to her. "This OK?"

"Looks great. Thank you."

I uncorked the bottle and poured her a glass. "You hungry? I was going to order pizza."

"Pizza sounds perfect." She smiled, and it was perfect. Her hair in that long blond braid was perfect. The way she held her wineglass was perfect. The way she'd kissed my shoulder last night and told me I was the bravest person she knew was perfect. Pizza was fucking dough and sauce and cheese. It didn't even taste as good as she did.

I'd lain awake the entire night thinking about her. About us. I thought I'd feel good that I hadn't given into the urge to stay with her again, that I'd been strong enough to resist that temptation, but instead I just felt miserable. Restless. Lonely. In the past I'd found a kind of solace in those feelings, but not last night.

Last night, I'd just missed her.

I thought about the days we'd spent together, the way she made me laugh, the way she listened to me. I wondered when I'd see her again, what she'd be wearing, what we'd do. There were places I wanted to take her, things I wanted to show her, songs I wanted her to hear, foods I wanted her to taste. There were curves on her body I wanted to kiss, filthy words I wanted to whisper to her, things I wanted to do to her. But I wanted to listen to her, too. Wanted to know about her dreams, her hopes, her memories. And I didn't have a lot of time—a week, that was it.

I made up my mind not to waste any more of it.

Because when she left, that would be it. I'd sleep alone again every single night for the rest of my life. I'd suffer for my sins. The loneliness would be all the worse for having had these days and nights with her, so in a way, *she* would become part of my punishment.

A friend in the Army once lent me a copy of *The Prophet* by Khalil Gibran, and it resonated with me so much, I'd bought my own copy when I came home. I thought about this one particular line a lot: *The deeper that sorrow carves into your being, the more joy you can contain*. At the time, it had brought me hope.

Later, I realized the reverse was also true: The greater your joy in something, the deeper your sorrow will be when it's gone.

And loss, I'd learned, was inescapable.

After we ate, I dug out a deck of cards and taught Margot to play gin rummy. In contrast to her egg-gathering efforts, she was a quick learner at cards and improved fast. A few times my mind waded into deeper waters, imagining how nice it would be to have her around during the winter, when nights were long and cold and there wasn't much to do but light a fire and play cards or curl up on the couch and watch a movie. I'd had to scold myself.

Don't. She's leaving next week, and it's for the best.

If Pete and Georgia were surprised to find her there with me when they got home, they didn't say it. We chatted with them for a few minutes, then said goodnight and exited out the back door.

"Come here." I pulled her into the shadows behind the house, away from any windows, and crushed my mouth to hers. Her arms came around my neck, and I lifted her right off her feet. Her lips on mine felt like rain after a drought.

"Wow, you been saving that up?" she asked once I let her catch her breath.

I set her down. "Yes. I was afraid if I started in there, I wouldn't be able to stop."

"Mmm. Don't stop," she whispered, rising up on her toes and kissing my neck. Her tongue on my skin sent bolts of lust straight to my cock, which twitched uncontrollably. It was as if my body knew the clock was already counting down the hours we had together. She moved one hand to my crotch, rubbing the bulge through my jeans while she sucked my earlobe, licked her way down my throat, sank her teeth into my shoulder.

"Oh, fuck." I grabbed her arm and took off across the moonlit yard. I barely even thought about where I was going, I just knew I had to get her somewhere alone before I came in my pants like a teenager.

We ran through the trees to the cabin, pounded up the porch steps. It wasn't until I opened the front door and pulled her through it into the darkened front room that it struck me I'd brought her to a place full of memories. I froze, my fingers still clasped around her wrist. Could I do this?

"Hey." She spoke softly. "It's OK."

I turned to her, my chest a battleground. "Fuck," I whispered.

She put a hand on my jaw. "It's OK. I understand."

"Margot, I'm sorry."

"Don't be. I know this is hard."

Exhaling loudly, I circled both her wrists and tipped my forehead to hers. "It shouldn't be this hard. I want you so badly."

"I want you too." Her voice was strained.

The dark was so thick I couldn't see anything in the room. But I heard her breathing, sensed the rise and fall of her chest. Felt her skin, warm beneath my palms. Smelled her hair, the scent evoking memories of last night. And then my mouth was on her throat, because I had to taste her.

"Jack," she whispered. "We don't have to—"

"I don't want to be alone tonight," I heard myself saying. "I'm so fucking tired of being alone."

"You don't have to be." She slid her fingers into my hair, covered my face with kisses. "I won't leave you."

Her words stayed with me as we hurriedly removed clothing and tumbled to our knees. *I won't leave you.* As I laid her down gently on the rug and stretched out above her. *I won't leave you.* As I moved my hands and lips and tongue over her breasts, her ribs, her stomach. *I won't leave you.* As I buried myself inside her, rhythmic and deep, her arms around my neck, her lips a whisper away.

I won't leave you.

God, what would that be like? What would it feel like to let go of the guilt, let go of the pain, let go of the fear? To look forward, and not back? What would it feel like to be happy again? To believe that I deserved it? To think that it could last?

I fought back against the crazy seed of hope taking root inside me, but its hold was already frighteningly deep and strong.

Something that had long been closed off inside me was opening up, and I felt a rush as it was filled with her presence, her trust, her understanding. The idea that she could feel something for me. The hope that all would be forgiven. The promise of a new life. A new beginning. A new love.

No. This is not about love. It's not absolution or even acquittal. It's a temporary stay, a bandaid on a wound. Soon it'll be ripped off, and you'll bleed again. Oh, God...

I felt like two halves of me were splitting apart—one wanted so badly to be granted that second chance at loving someone and allowing myself to be loved, while the other demanded I serve out my life sentence alone in the prison I'd built for myself.

Desperate to regain control, I focused on the heat and friction between us, on the sound of her voice saying my name, on the sting of her nails raking down my back. I concentrated on making her come, grinding against her the way she liked, whispering dirty words in her ear. I was rough with her, like I had been before.

But it was different this time—how could it not be? I'd told her everything. I was vulnerable to her in a way I'd never been to anyone. Everything was bare to her now, all my secrets, all my suffering, all my scars.

And she still wanted me.

I felt myself falling.

Frantically, I fought off my orgasm, panicked that coming together would only strengthen our sexual chemistry and bring us closer. But she held me so tightly, like she'd never let me go, and she took me so deep, and her cries were so helpless and my cock was so hard and I couldn't hold back, couldn't hang on, couldn't stop myself from crashing through the gates and careening over the edge with her, my willpower no match for my feelings.

Don't leave me, I thought with every thrust and throb inside her trembling body, every pounding beat of my heart. *Don't let me go. I need you to feel alive.*

As our bodies stilled and our breathing slowed, I opened my eyes—and realized what I'd done.

I'd let her in. I'd let her get close. I'd let myself feel again.

Worse, I'd brought another woman into sacred space. I'd broken a promise. I'd dishonored a vow.

I had no right. No right.

The hope I'd felt moments ago was crushed by the weight of shame.

I forced myself to stop justifying my behavior and admit the truth.

This had to end. Tonight.

I didn't say anything as we put ourselves back together. My chest felt like a cannonball had lodged within it, and my throat was tight.

"Can I use your bathroom?" Margot asked timidly.

"Of course." Already my voice was stiff.

While she was in the bathroom, I sat on the couch in the dark, hating myself for letting it come to this. *I never should have kissed her. Never should have touched her. Never should have asked her to stay.*

Now I had to get her to leave, and I only knew one way to do it and make sure she left for good—put up walls around my heart and be a complete and utter asshole. Blow her off. Hurt her. *Make her hate me like I hate myself.*

She came out of the bathroom, leaving the light on, and sat next to me on the couch, but not touching me. "You OK?"

Fuck, Margot. Don't be sweet to me now. "Yeah."

"That was kind of…intense."

I shrugged. My stomach churned.

"You didn't think so?" She looked at me, probably trying to read my expression.

"Not really."

Her body deflated. "Oh. Well…maybe it was just me then."

"Maybe." I couldn't bear to look her in the eye, so I stared at her knees, which were pressed together tightly, her hands clasped around them. Someday, some rich bastard with a trust fund and a Porsche would put a big fat diamond on her finger. She'd have the huge, fancy wedding of her dreams, followed by a luxury honeymoon. After that, he'd buy her a mansion, which they'd fill with beautiful children who went to private schools and called her Mummy. She'd have everything she wanted. *She'll be where she belongs, and she'll be happy.*

I looked down at my wedding band. *And I'll be here.*

"Jack, what's wrong? Something is off, I can tell."

"Nothing." I stood up. "I'll take you home."

I grabbed my keys from the shelf and went out the front door, so she didn't have much choice but to follow me. I pulled it shut behind her and started down the porch steps, but she grabbed my arm.

"Hey. Wait a minute."

I steeled myself and looked at her. "What?"

"Are you mad at me?"

"No." *I'm mad at me.*

"Are you mad that we…did what we did in there?" She dropped her hand. "Because we didn't have to do it. I told you I understood."

"It's not that."

"Well, it's something." She stuck her hands on her hips. "I know you're moody, but this is like a complete one-eighty. An hour ago you couldn't keep your hands off me, and now you're freezing me out. Tell me what I did."

"You didn't do anything," I snapped.

"Then tell me what you're thinking. Tell me what went wrong. Tell me something, Jack!" Her voice broke. "You can't just shut down on me."

"Yes, I fucking can!" I yelled, furious with myself for letting my guard down and with her for penetrating my defenses. "This is me, Margot. This is who I am. And it's why we never should have gotten involved in the first place."

Her body seemed to wilt. If I could have seen her eyes, I knew they'd be shiny with tears. "This isn't you. I know you."

I put up another wall. "You think because we fucked a few times that you know me? You don't. It was just sex."

She shook her head again, like she couldn't believe what she was hearing. "Why are you doing this?"

"Because it's time, OK?" My hands were shaking. "We both knew this thing couldn't go on, so we might as well end it now."

"Why couldn't it go on? I don't live that far away, and…" She took a breath. I had the feeling I wouldn't want to hear what she said next, and I was right. "I feel something for you, Jack. I don't want it to end."

I had to be ruthless. Rip off the bandage. "Well, I do."

She started to cry. "Don't you feel anything for me? Have the past few days meant nothing to you?"

I shrugged, and she cradled her stomach as if I'd struck her. She believed the lies so readily. Fucking hell, this was torture.

"God," she wept, rushing past me down the steps. "I was so wrong about you."

Cursing myself, I followed her through the trees, past the spot where we'd first combusted, and into Pete and Georgia's yard. I saw her glance at the spot where I'd kissed her so passionately just a couple hours ago, and wanted to put my fist through a wall. *Godammit, you weren't wrong about me. But I can't handle my feelings for you. I have no place to put them, they don't fit inside me, don't fit inside the life I have to live. I have no choice, Margot! Can't you see?*

She didn't even try to walk home—she knew me too well, another punch in the gut—but marched right to the driveway and got into my truck, slamming the door so hard I thought it might fall off.

Moving slowly, as if the air around me was mud, I got behind the wheel and started the engine. She sat as far away from me as she could, arms crossed, legs together, jaw set. How insane that an hour ago, I'd been inside her, and she'd welcomed me in. I'd never feel that again.

My walls started to crumble.

"Margot, look. I—"

"Don't. Don't say my name, don't talk to me, don't even fucking look at me."

Exhaling, I put the truck in reverse and backed out of the driveway. I should have been relieved that she wasn't crying anymore, that she wasn't going to make this any harder for me, that she was going to go back to her pretty world and forget I ever existed.

It was exactly what I wanted, wasn't it?

chapter twenty-nine

Margot

THE RIDE BACK TO THE COTTAGE WAS AGONY. I COULDN'T BELIEVE THE WAY HE'D turned on me. My head was spinning!

It was just sex.

It was?

But he'd waited three years. He'd come after *me*. He'd asked me to stay. He'd confided in me. He'd shared deeply personal feelings. It wasn't just sex! So what the hell was this sudden withdrawal? I racked my brain, trying to piece it together.

Had he just pretended to be a good guy? Was this asshole next to me the real Jack Valentini? Had the entire week been one big charade just to get in my pants? I found that hard to believe, but I was reeling. A couple hours ago, we'd been laughing and kissing and talking.

What had gone wrong? Were all men just manipulative bastards? I couldn't accept that Jack was like Tripp.

Maybe having sex in the cabin had been too overwhelming. Maybe it felt like cheating for him. Maybe he felt guilty for enjoying it so much. Despite what he'd said, there *had* been something different about it tonight. Something intense and real and big. Something *good*. I'd felt it, and he must have, too.

I stole a glance at him and caught the usual stubborn body language and expression out of the corner of my eye. But there was something else…his right hand was nervously tapping on his thigh. I'd never seen that before. Something had him wound up. Something was making him nervous—scared, even.

That's it.

It hit me all at once. His biggest fear—letting go of his past.

Maybe he started to let go. And it terrified him.

A little sadness tempered my anger. Why did he torture himself this way? Why wouldn't he forgive himself and move on? Why wouldn't he let me help? Why was he so fucking *loyal* to his pain? And after everything he'd told me, did he think I couldn't see what he was doing?

I wanted to shake him. Hug him. Scream at him. Plead with him. Hurl accusations at him until he admitted the truth—he felt something for me.

But what good would it do? He'd never admit it. In fact, pushing him like that would only make him retreat further. It was hopeless. Until he made a conscious decision to move on, there was nothing I could do. And if the last few days hadn't been enough to convince him, I had to face the fact that maybe it wasn't going to happen. Blinking away fresh tears as he pulled up at the cottage, I had my hand on the door handle before the truck even stopped moving.

"Margot."

I froze. Refused to look at him.

"I just...want you to know. I've..." He struggled for words. "I've had a good time with you."

"Oh my God." Now I glared at him. His words felt like a slap in the face. "Really? That's what you have to say to me right now?"

He jerked his chin at me. "What do you want me to say?"

"I want you to admit the truth, Jack!" I yelled, cursing these damn tears that wouldn't quit. When had I become so emotional? "You feel something for me, and you're scared of it."

"Don't tell me what I feel," he said angrily, fidgeting in his seat. "You have no idea what it's like to be me."

"You're right, I don't. But I know you're *choosing* to be that way. Closed off. Miserable. Lonely." I wiped my nose with the back of my wrist and softened my voice. "It doesn't have to be that way, Jack. We could be good together if you'd let yourself move on."

He started to say something, then stopped. His right hand clenched into a fist. "The night I asked you to stay, you said you didn't need promises."

"I didn't! And I don't—I'm not asking for a promise, Jack. I'm asking for a *chance*. That's all. A chance." My heart beat frantically in my chest as he weighed my words against his misguided convictions. His lips trembled and slammed shut. His forehead creased. His fingers curled and flexed. I could see the struggle in him, the temptation to give in to me versus the strength of his guilty conscience. Which would prevail? Our eyes met, and for a second, I thought he'd choose me.

But he didn't. He looked away. "I've got no chance to give you."

Devastated, I got out of the truck and ran into the cottage, choking back tears. When the door was closed behind me, I locked it and ran to the bedroom, throwing myself onto the bed. Gathering his pillow in my arms, I sobbed into it for what felt like hours.

I cried for Jack, for the life he lived and the life he was wasting. I cried for myself, because I hadn't been enough to change his mind. I cried at the thought of going home and trying to forget we'd ever met, kissed, touched each other.

And I cried for what would never be, a chance that would never be taken.

chapter thirty

Margot

I WAS UP THE ENTIRE NIGHT. EVEN AFTER THE TEARS RAN DRY, QUESTION AFTER question nagged me. Was this my fault? Had I pushed too hard? Had I rushed things? Had I imagined something between us that wasn't there? Was I crazy to be this upset over someone I'd known for a week? Had the amazing sex clouded my judgment?

Then there were the maybe's. Maybe I'd romanticized the whole hot farmer thing. Maybe I was only attracted to him because he was the anti-Tripp. Maybe the affair was just one big rebellion against rules for Thurber women. Maybe I'd get home and realize he'd never have fit into my life, I'd never have fit into his, and thank God he'd broken things off when he had.

But there were what if's too.

What if I'd come here for a reason? What if he was the something missing from my life? What if I wasn't supposed to give up on him? What if he needed me to help him heal? What if I never met anyone who made me feel the way he did? What if we were supposed to be together?

The mental and emotional anguish was too much. I craved the familiarity of home, the feeling that I belonged somewhere. At six the next morning, I packed my bags, left a message for the property manager and the key on the counter, and drove home.

On the two-hour drive, I chugged crummy gas station coffee and cringed repeatedly at the memory of his rejection. It was like reliving the breakup with Tripp all over again! What was the matter with me? Why didn't anyone want me? Was I fundamentally unloveable? Was the prospect of a future with me so terrible? Did I smell? I sniffed my armpits.

Since it seemed like my deodorant worked, it had to be something else, and by the time I got home, I was convinced of my general worthlessness and repugnance.

Dumping my bags at the door, I went straight to my room, traded my shorts and blouse for pajamas, and flopped into bed. But I'd had so much coffee on the drive that sleep was impossible. I lay there, getting more despondent by the minute, until I finally gave up and called Jaime.

"Howdy," she said when she answered. "How's life on the farm? You get your four orgasms already today?"

"Not even close. I'm not even at the farm anymore." I pictured the sun coming up over the lake, shining on the horses in the pasture, creating shadows behind the barn perfect for kissing in. Was Jack awake? Had he even slept? Was he doing chores and remembering when I'd helped him?

"What happened? You sound miserable."

"I am." I closed my eyes. "Maybe I shouldn't be, but I am."

"Want to talk about it?"

"Yes. Where's Claire? Can you have lunch?"

"Crap, I can't. And Claire's looking at houses this afternoon. How about drinks right after work? Around six?"

"Where?"

"Bar at Marais? You probably missed your fancypants martinis."

"Not really," I said glumly.

"Damn, you *are* depressed. I'll text Claire."

"OK. Hey, can you do me a favor?"

"Of course!"

"Can you call Georgia Valentini and tell her I had to come home suddenly but I'll be in touch tomorrow? I'll forward her contact information." I couldn't bear to talk to her.

"Consider it done. Now go get a massage or something. A mani-pedi. Or a blowout! Those always perk you up."

"I'll be fine. Maybe I'm just tired." It wasn't exactly a lie. "I'll take a nap and see you after work."

We hung up, and I messaged her Georgia's number before tossing my phone aside. I didn't want a massage or a manicure or a blowout. None of those things would make me feel better, and in fact it kind of made me feel shallow and vain that I was the sort of person who regularly enjoyed those luxuries. Why didn't I use my resources for more meaningful things? What was I even doing with my life? How was I contributing to the greater good? Millions of people lived in poverty and I did nothing to help them! No wonder no one loved me!

I curled into a ball, knees tucked under my chest, butt in the air. "I'm a terrible, useless person," I moaned into my pillow. "My life has no purpose."

Eventually I got hungry, so I went downstairs to find something to eat, but even the contents of my fridge depressed me—suspicious cheese, expired milk, a jar of pickles, rotting lemons, mysterious takeout containers—and the freezer contained only ice cubes, a bottle of gin, and some frozen meals for one that spoke of my sad single status and inability to cook. "This is my life," I said as clouds of cold air billowed out. "Gin, loneliness, and Lean Cuisine." Sorta sounded like a country song.

In the pantry I managed to find a box of crackers that had probably been left over from a cocktail party in 2014, and I ate them while sitting on the kitchen floor. They were stale and tasteless. I sniffed at the cheese and decided

I wasn't that desperate, so I ate the entire jar of pickles instead. After that, I went back to bed and hid under the covers, where I eventually fell asleep.

I woke to the ring of my phone around five. *Georgia Valentini calling.* Chewing on my lower lip, I debated taking it. Could I fake cheerful well enough to fool her? Old Margot wouldn't have thought twice. Was she still inside me somewhere?

I did my best to summon her. "Hello?"

"Oh, Margot, hi. I thought I'd get your voicemail. Your business partner called a bit ago and said you had a family emergency. I hope everything is OK." Georgia sounded concerned, and I felt guilty about the lie.

"Yes, everything's fine. It turned out to be no big deal." *Just my own existential crisis.*

"Glad to hear it. I just wanted to tell you how grateful we are that you took the time to come here and jumpstart our efforts at marketing more effectively. You did your research, came prepared, got to know us, and really delivered."

"Thanks."

"And you inspired us to get moving on our restaurant dream, too. Even if the Oliver place doesn't work out for us, we're motivated to keep pushing toward it."

"I'm glad to hear it. Any news on the house?"

"Nothing too encouraging," she said. "But we're getting some estimates on what it would take to renovate the place, and Brad's helping us come up with a plan to apply for a business loan."

"I'm keeping my fingers crossed for you."

"I appreciate that, thanks." She paused for a minute. "Margot, I hope it's not out of line to ask if you're OK? You sound different."

I sighed. "I'm OK. I mean, I'll *be* OK. I guess."

She laughed sympathetically. "That does not sound good."

"I just…got my hopes up about something I shouldn't have."

"I understand." A few seconds went by. "Margot, he's sad too."

"I doubt that."

"Why?" Georgia sounded genuinely surprised.

"Because he's the one who broke things off. He doesn't want me. Not enough, anyway."

She sighed exasperatedly. "He *does*, though. I can see it. He's just so damn stubborn."

"Anyway," I said, "it's done. And it's what he wanted."

"I'm sorry, Margot. I really wish things were different."

"Me too." I needed to hang up before I started bawling again. "Bye."

She said goodbye and we hung up. Flinging an arm over my eyes, I wondered how she knew Jack was sad. Was he moping over coffee this morning?

Had he been short with her? Lashed out? The thought made me angry. How dare he take it out on other people! He did this to himself!

Grumpy and depressed, I wandered into the bathroom, and looked at myself in the mirror. Yeesh. My hair was matted and tangled, my face was puffy, and my eyes were red-rimmed with circles underneath. "You know what?" I said to my reflection. "This is the real me, and if people don't like it, they can fuck off." I snapped a pony tail holder around my hair, threw on some old jeans with my Vassar T-shirt, tugged on some socks, and shoved my feet into sneakers. I didn't feel like the old me, so why should I look like her?

The Mercedes was a bit of a problem with my new image, but I'd think about that tomorrow.

"Wow." Jaime blinked at me. "That's a different look for you."

I'd gotten to the bar first and was sitting on one of the velvet sofas along the wall. My friends had just slid in across from me. "I feel different," I snapped. "Why shouldn't I look it?"

"No reason," she said with false brightness and a glance at Claire. "Want to tell us what's going on?"

"What's going on is that I've come to the conclusion that my life is meaningless."

"Margot, what on earth?" Claire asked, brows furrowed. "Your life isn't meaningless. Why would you say such a thing?"

"Because it's true," I said, lifting my expensive gin martini to my lips. After struggling with it for a few minutes, I'd decided a life without purpose was no excuse to drink cheap booze. "I don't contribute to society in any meaningful way. The world is full of terrible things like poverty and hunger and disease and abuse, and I don't do anything about it. I will live and die, and humanity will not be any better off."

"Wow," Jaime said again as the waitress approached. "Hold on, I'm going to need a drink for this." She and Claire gave their orders and sat back again. "OK. What happened?"

I didn't even know where to start.

"Is this about the farmer?" Claire's expression was quizzical. "Jaime told me about him, but last I heard, things were going well."

"They were." I took another drink. "But then he must have realized I'm a spoiled rotten city girl who doesn't care about anyone but herself."

"Oh, Jesus." Jaime rolled her eyes and sat forward. "Do I need to remind you of the work you do *for free* while I am trying to keep the lights on at our office? You're the most generous person I know, Margot!"

Claire nodded in agreement. "You're constantly attending charity lunches and volunteering at things. I don't know how you find the time!"

"OK, so your family has bags of money," Jaime allowed, "but there's a reason the hospital has a Lewiston wing and the art museum has a Thurber gallery. It's because they give so much."

"And remember last year when I mentioned the fundraiser at my school for that family who lost everything in a fire?" Claire said. "You were the first in line to write a check, and I happen to know it was the biggest one."

"But it's all so impersonal," I complained. "I don't feel like I'm really doing anything worthwhile except writing checks. And I've led this completely sheltered life. I don't know how to mow a lawn, change a tire, or grill a burger!"

"What the hell difference does that have to do with anything? You're a good person, Margot." Jaime reached across the table and touched my wrist. "You're loving and smart and funny and successful and beautiful."

I arched one brow at her.

"Well, yes, you're looking a little ragged at the edges right now," she conceded, "but any other day, you're what every woman aspires to be."

"Then why didn't he want me?" I closed my eyes and felt tears on my lashes. "Why doesn't anyone want me?"

"I hope you're not talking about Tripp," Jaime said. "You wasted enough time on him. And as for Jack, I don't know, honey." Her voice got softer. "Maybe he just wasn't ready to want you. Maybe he's not over his wife yet."

"I guess that could be it. But I don't get that feeling." I chewed my lip for a moment. "He talked about loving her, and I have no doubt that losing her broke his heart. But he never said anything like 'I'll never get over her.' Although," I went on, the corners of my mouth turning down, "he did say he'd never get married again."

"Why not?" Claire asked.

I sighed. "He said he knew what he had, and it doesn't happen twice."

"Maybe he's crazy." Claire reached out and patted my arm. "Because I cannot imagine why any man wouldn't jump at the chance to be with you."

"Well, he didn't." Sighing, I lifted my glass to my lips again. "And it's got me messed up in the head. I really felt something for him, you guys."

"So soon?" Jaime asked as the server set their drinks on the table between us.

"Yes. At first I thought it was just a really intense physical thing, but..." I shivered, remembering the night he'd bared his troubled soul. "It was emotional, too. And it felt good, at least to me."

"So why did he break it off?" Claire wondered.

"Honestly, he didn't really give me a reason. We had a great day yesterday, and then..." I lowered my voice. "Last night we had sex on the living room floor of his house, where he'd lived with his wife, and it was really intense. Right after that, he suddenly ended things. Said we never should have gotten involved in the first place."

"Aha. You scared him." Jaime sounded confident as she sat back. "That's what I used to do, before Quinn. As long as it was just sex with a guy, I was fine, but if there was any chance of an emotional attachment, I was out of there."

"You even tried to do it with Quinn," Claire reminded us.

Jaime nodded. "Totally. And I didn't have the baggage Jack has. Maybe he just needs some time and distance. Gain a little perspective. That's what I needed."

"Maybe," I said. "But we exchanged some pretty harsh words last night. And I flat out asked him to give me a chance, and he said no."

"Well, don't give up. He might surprise you." Jaime sipped her drink. "And if he doesn't, it's his fucking loss, because you're amazing."

"And strong." Claire patted my arm again. "You're one of the strongest women I know."

"I'm not," I said, feeling like a fraud. "I've spent my entire life just doing what I'm told Thurber women do, playing the role of dutiful daughter and society debutante. I can't think of one decision I made for myself that I'm proud of or one risk I took."

"I can," Jaime said loyally. "You quit your job and came to work with me. That was a risk."

"Not really." I wasn't going to let them talk me into liking myself. "I was never going to be poor."

"When Tripp said he didn't want to get married last year, you broke things off. *And* you said no to him when he proposed, even though part of you wanted to say yes," Claire added. "That was not easy."

"I didn't want to marry that jerk," I said. "I just liked the ring, which makes me shallow."

"Well, you should be proud as hell that you threw those scones. *I'm* proud of you." Jaime shook her head. "God, I wish I'd been there."

I allowed a tiny smile to work its way onto my lips. "I guess I'm proud of that."

"See? And you can still make changes to your life. You don't have to play any role you don't want to," she went on. "If you don't want to work at Shine anymore, tell me. We can figure things out."

"No, I do. I like the work. I like helping people grow their dreams." I sighed, swirling the last sips of gin in my glass. "It's not that I don't like my life. I love my family, my friends, my work. And I'd be lying if I said being Margot Thurber Lewiston is really that tough. It's not. I mean, what do I actually lack? It's selfish to want more than I have, isn't it?"

"Margot, it's OK to want to share your life with someone," Claire said. "No one thinks you're selfish just because you want someone to love, and someone to love you back."

The lump was back in my throat. "I do want that. And crazy as it sounds,

I had this gut feeling Jack could have been that someone. I'm just so frustrated and sad he doesn't see it."

My friends looked at me sympathetically. "I wish I had more advice," Jaime said. "But love is strange. When you're looking for it, it knows just where to hide. When you're not, it jumps out and clobbers you on the head."

"Don't I know it," said Claire, tipping back her drink. "Maybe that's what we're doing wrong, Gogo. We're looking."

I shook my head. "I'm sorry, you guys. I'm being a complete downer and I'm totally monopolizing the conversation. I had a disappointment, but I'll survive." A shaky smile made its way to my lips. "I actually started making this list of things I want to do while I was up there."

"Like a bucket list?" Jaime ate one of the olives from the stick in her martini.

"No, more like Margot Thurber Lewiston's To-Do List for Having a Funner, More Fulfilling Life."

Claire grinned. "What's on it?"

"Stop fearing 30. Ride horses. Learn to Cook. Get involved with the food justice movement. Get a tattoo." It came out of nowhere, but as soon as I said it, I realized it was true.

"Wow," Jaime said for the third time today. "It's like a whole new Margot. What happened to you up there?"

"It wasn't just up there," I said. "I mean, it was definitely an intense week, but looking back over the last year or so, maybe even longer, I think this awakening has been a long time coming."

Jaime nodded and held up her drink. "To Funner and More Fulfilling Lives."

Claire and I lifted our glasses to hers and clinked. I felt better, and grateful for my friends, but a little piece of my heart still ached for Jack.

Maybe it always would.

chapter thirty-one

Jack

The morning after I broke things off with Margot dawned sunny and warm. It aggravated me, since I wanted the weather to match my glowering mood. I did the morning chores sluggishly, my bones weary, my muscles lax. No pride in my work. No feeling of contentment or accomplishment. No hope that I might find something about today to enjoy.

Just emptiness.

I'd spent the entire night hating myself for what I'd done. But I'd had no choice—I'd known all along I couldn't have her. It didn't matter that she was willing to give me a chance…I couldn't take it. And she deserved someone whole, someone perfect, someone like her. She shouldn't waste that chance on me. I was too broken, too flawed.

But God, I could have loved her. Easily. Deeply.

If I were someone else, if my life had gone differently, if I'd met her sooner. What would that alternate life look like? Would we be married? Would we have children? For a moment I let myself picture them, a little boy with curls like Cooper, a little girl with blond hair and blue eyes.

I swallowed hard, imagining tucking them in at night, reading them a story, giving in to their pleas for one more song, one more kiss, one more hug. Then I'd share the rest of my night with Margot, share my thoughts, share my body, share my soul.

I could have taken care of her in all the ways she needed. We were different, but maybe our differences would have complemented each other. We could have fit together like two jigsaw pieces. She had book smarts and business savvy; I had physical strength and common sense. She had a gift with people; I had a gift with nature. I knew how to grow; she knew how to sell. She was smooth where I was rough, articulate where I was tongue-tied, social where I was aloof.

I could have loved her.

Sheltered her. Cherished her. I could have done the things for her she didn't know how to do, taught her things she didn't know, shown her things she'd never seen. And she could have been my link to the outside world, offering me refuge when I needed it. She could have taught me things too—she knew about art and literature and history. Things I'd never paid attention to, but didn't want to leave the world without learning.

I could have loved her.

I could have let her love me. I could have been a father. I could have been happy.

Instead, I was alone. But at least it had been my choice.

~

I didn't want to go to Pete and Georgia's that morning since they'd likely ask about Margot, but I'd run out of coffee, and I needed the caffeine badly enough to risk it. From the moment I walked in, I made it clear I wasn't in the mood for talking.

"Morning, Jack," Georgia called as I entered the kitchen. She was feeding Cooper at the table.

With barely a harrumph in greeting, I crossed the room to the coffee pot and poured a cup. Even this damn kitchen reminded me of Margot. I could still see her sitting at the counter last night with her wine, eating at the table, laughing over cards. *Maybe this would have been our house.*

"What's going on today?" she asked.

"Nothing." *She'd be feeding our baby at the kitchen table.*

"Have you and Margot gone riding yet?"

"No." *We'd go riding together all the time.*

"Might be a nice day for it."

"I don't have time," I snapped. But she was right—it would have been a nice day for it. *I was going to take her camping tonight.*

She glanced back at me, her brows arched. "OK. Just a thought."

I swallowed mouthfuls of coffee, letting it scald my throat, glad for the pain. I wondered if Margot was still sleeping, if she'd go home today or stick around. Hopefully, she'd leave…I didn't think I could stay away if I knew she was here, and I had to. I had to.

"Do you and Margot want to do the market tomorrow? She seemed to really enjoy it the other day."

"No."

Georgia looked at me again, a little longer this time. "Everything OK?"

"Fine," I said. But I wasn't fine.

I couldn't stop thinking about her. No matter where I went on the farm, something reminded me of her—the chicken coop, the barn, the pasture. The woods, the lake, the cabin. I went to the hardware store, and I swear to Christ, the cab of my truck even *smelled* like her. On a whim, I drove by the cottage, telling myself I wouldn't knock on her door, I'd just see if her car was there.

It wasn't, but a minivan was, and as I idled past, a woman came out of the front door carrying what looked like a bucket of cleaning supplies. *She's gone.*

I was angry at myself for being disappointed. Annoyed at the way my chest caved. Alarmed at the ache in my heart.

What the hell? This was better, wasn't it? I didn't want her hanging around, tempting me at every opportunity. I wanted her out of town, out of reach, out of my life.

Later I took Cooper to the park, hoping that would boost my mood, but even that reminded me of Margot. Christ, would she never get out of my head? I'd done the right thing! When would I be rewarded with a little peace of mind?

That night I was so exhausted I fell asleep early, but I woke at two in the morning from a nightmare, yelling and shaking, the sheets soaked with sweat. I sat up, my heart beating furiously, my chest tight. Frantically, I looked around the room for danger, but it wasn't there.

When my heart rate slowed, I swung my legs over the side of the bed, and sat still for a moment to catch my breath, cursing my fucking subconscious for its unrelenting assault.

Minutes later, I stripped the bedding and tugged new sheets over the mattress. I thought about Margot's hands clutching at them. Leaving them twisted and shoved aside. Holding her beneath them. I got back into bed and lay awake, blinking at the ceiling. I wondered if I'd ever see her again. I wondered if I'd ever be able to forget her. I wondered if she missed me as much as I missed her.

I wondered if I'd ever stop asking myself *what if?*

⁂

A few miserable days later, I broke down and called her.

It was after midnight, which made me an even bigger asshole, but I couldn't go another minute without at least hearing her voice. I'd gotten into the habit of pulling up her picture on the Shine PR website, and the image was driving me crazy—I wanted those blue eyes looking at me. I wanted that smile to be flashed in my direction. I wanted that long blond hair slipping through my fingers. I wanted her light, her laughter, her lips on mine.

More than that, I wanted the feeling she gave me—that heart-pounding, gut-clenching, blood-rushing feeling that made me feel alive and vital and virile. I wanted to feel *wanted* again. I craved it.

But that was impossible, wasn't it? She'd never agree to see me. Not unless I apologized and admitted I'd made a mistake, and there was no way I could. It didn't matter that I wished things were different—they weren't. This wasn't a fairy tale. This beast wasn't going to turn into a prince, and she deserved a prince.

But I was starving for her. I needed a taste.

I paced next to my bed as I listened to the ring. *Please, please answer, Margot,* I begged silently. Voicemail would be OK, because at least I'd still get to hear her, but a conversation would be better. I wanted to feel close to her again.

She didn't pick up right away, and my hopes started to dwindle. *Why should she answer your call, asshole?* But then it stopping ringing, and I heard her breathing. Goosebumps blanketed my arms and legs.

"Hi," I said quietly.

"Hello."

"I wasn't sure you'd answer."

"I almost didn't." Her voice was hushed, and I wondered if she'd been asleep. My blood ran warmer as I thought of her under the covers.

"Did I wake you?"

"No."

"Good. I'm…" Shit. Now that I had her on the line, I couldn't think of anything to say. "I'm sorry to call so late."

"It's fine."

"So…how are you?" *Fuck. So stupid.*

"OK. You?"

She wasn't OK. I could hear it. And neither was I. "OK."

An uncomfortable silence followed, during which I thought of nothing I could say and ten things I couldn't, starting with *I miss you. I miss you so much I can't breathe.*

"Are you really OK?" she asked.

"No," I admitted.

"Me either."

"I want to see you so badly," I blurted. "I miss you."

"I miss you, too." She paused. "Does this…does this mean you changed your mind?"

I wanted to say yes so badly, I felt strangled by it. "No," I choked out.

"Then I can't see you, Jack. It wouldn't do either of us any good."

"Please," I whispered before I could stop myself. "I need you."

"No. I'm hanging up. This hurts too much."

"No, wait!" Panicked, I held out one hand as if she could see me. "Please don't go, Margot. I miss you so fucking much. All I do is think about you."

She said nothing at first, and then I heard soft, quiet sobs. "Why are you doing this to me? I'm trying to forget you."

My heart broke for both of us. "I'm sorry, Margot. I know I shouldn't have called. I'm just…" I closed a fist in my hair. "…so fucked up about this. I don't know what to do."

"What do you *want* to do?"

I exhaled, lowering myself to the bed. What I wanted was so simple. "I want to feel alive again." My throat thickened. "The way I felt with you."

She was openly crying now, and it was torture knowing I could make her stop. But the words wouldn't come—something inside me held them captive. Fear? Guilt? Shame? All of the above?

"Jack," wept Margot, "I can't do this. I want to be with you, but not unless you're ready to move on. I don't know what that would take, but it's something *you* have to figure out."

She was right, of course. It was on me to find a way out of the cold, lonely dark and into her light. But I felt immobile, chained to the past and unable to break free, even for her.

A moment later, she whispered goodbye.

Cursing, I set my phone aside and dropped forward, elbows on my knees, head in my hands. Instead of feeling better, I felt worse. Sad and angry.

What I *wanted* was one thing; what I was capable of was another.

Why the hell couldn't she see that?

chapter thirty-two

Margot

If I'd made any progress getting over Jack in the last few days, the phone call set me back that much and then some.

What was he trying to do to me? To himself?

The tone of his voice, tender and sorrowful, told me how miserable he was. The things he'd said tore me to shreds—*I miss you, I want to see you, I want to feel alive again.* It was agony knowing we both wanted to be together and it was just his stubborn head getting in the way. Never in my life had I simultaneously wanted to hug someone and hit him with a scone at the same time. Did he just need more time?

But how much? How long would I be willing to wait? At some point, it would be pathetic rather than patient to keep holding out for someone who was never going to want me that way.

I had to get over it. Pick myself up, dust myself off, and try again with someone who wasn't so hell-bent on being alone forever. Someone who wanted everything I had to offer. Someone who recognized that the kind of chemistry we had didn't come along that often in life.

I started to get angry.

Damn him for not seeing what we could be. Sitting up in bed, I reached for a tissue from the box on my nightstand. *Damn him for being a coward when I need him to be brave. Damn him for being stubborn when all he wants is to give in.* I blew my nose, threw the tissue on the floor, and grabbed another.

I hope you're even more miserable than I am, Jack Valentini. Because this is your fault. I never rushed you. I never pushed. The only thing I did was care, and fuck you for being too scared to care back. I deserve better.

By the time I fell asleep that night, my nose was raw, my eyes were puffy, and my head ached, but I made up my mind not to waste any more time crying over Jack. Yes, it was sad that he didn't think he deserved to be loved because of his past, but that was his choice.

Plenty of people don't get to even make that choice, Jack. They never experience what we have.

Damn you for giving it up so easily.

My anger simmered throughout the day Sunday. I felt like I needed to keep busy so I wouldn't think about Jack, and I spent the day doing things like laundry, cleaning out the fridge, reorganizing kitchen and bathroom cupboards, and grocery shopping. It kept me occupied, but it didn't necessarily take my mind off Jack. Clothing I'd worn at the farm reminded me of him. Food and drinks reminded me of him. My bubble bath and shampoo reminded me of him. The damn produce section at Kroger reminded me of him.

Later in the afternoon I went to the bookstore and bought some beginner cookbooks, and for dinner that night I attempted lemon chicken. It turned out pretty well and gave me a dose of confidence, even if I did feel a little lonely celebrating my first culinary triumph by myself.

Later that night, I was in bed reading a new romance I'd picked up at the bookstore (which I'd chosen for its premise and *not* because the guy on the cover looked like Jack, I swear) when my phone rang.

Jack Valentini calling.

I refused to answer it. It refused to stop ringing.

"Fuck you," I said. But my heart throbbed. I wanted to hear his voice so badly.

What if he'd changed his mind? What if he was calling to apologize? What if he'd realized we deserved a chance?

I grabbed the phone. *Whoa. Stay calm.* Summoning Old Margot, I took a breath and accepted the call.

"Hello."

"Hey." His voice cracked, and so did some of my composure. "How are you?"

Be strong. No tears tonight. "Fine," I said coolly.

"That's good."

Silence. My patience wore thin. "What do you want, Jack?"

"Just to hear you."

I closed my eyes and swallowed. So this wasn't an apology call. *Damn him!* "Why? To torture yourself?"

"I guess."

"I'm not playing these games, Jack." My voice wavered. "If you want to wallow in your own pain, you go right ahead, but I will not contribute to it. It hurts me too much."

"I'm sorry, Margot. I never meant to hurt you. I want so fucking badly to be someone else right now."

I bit my lip so hard I expected to taste blood. "I wouldn't want anyone else! How can you not see that?"

"You say that now, but you don't know what it's like to be with me." His voice was stronger. Angry, even.

"Because you won't *show* me! You're a coward! I don't even know what it is you're so afraid of! All I know is that you're throwing away the chance to be happy, and you're *taking* it away from me."

"I'm sparing you!" he blurted.

"You're sparing yourself! It's going to take work to move on, Jack. I know that. And I know it wouldn't be easy." I softened my voice. "But I'd be there for you. Don't you want to try?"

Silence. "You'd never be happy with me."

I took a breath and put my heart out there one more time, praying he didn't crush it. "Give me the chance to prove you wrong, Jack. I won't ask again."

"I can't," he whispered. "I want to, but I fucking can't."

I lost the battle not to cry, and hot tears spilled down my cheeks. "Then say goodbye, because this is all we will ever be."

"Margot, please—"

"Hang up!" I yelled. "I want it very clear that it's you who's walking away, Jack. It's *you* who thinks you couldn't love me."

"I know I could love you," he said without hesitation, his voice full of anguish. "I just don't deserve to."

I steadied myself. Willed myself to stay calm. "Then say goodbye, and hang up."

I held my breath, hanging on to one tiny thread of hope that he'd say something—anything—other than goodbye.

But he didn't.

chapter thirty-three

Jack

MARGOT'S WORDS CUT DEEP. THE TRUTH ALWAYS DOES.
You're a coward.
You're sparing yourself.
You're throwing away the chance to be happy.

I was a coward. And a fool. And an asshole. I knew calling her a second time was the wrong thing to do, but I was so damn lonely and depressed, I couldn't think straight. I hurt, and I wanted to feel better—she was the only one who could make it better, so I called her.

The logic of a fucking child.

I didn't blame her for getting angry or calling me names. Some part of my brain probably hoped that she would, I was so fucked up. And I was mad as hell at myself. What right did I have to call her, say those things to her, hurt her all over again? I'd only thought about *my* pain. But hers was real, too. I could hear it in her voice. I'd told myself a thousand times over the last few days that my agony was the price I had to pay for letting her get close, but what about the price she was paying? It killed me to think that she was half as miserable as I was. Did she really think I was walking away because I couldn't love her? It was exactly the opposite!

I lay back on my bed and covered my face with my hands. What the hell was I going to do? I couldn't live like this, torn between the past and the future, between two lives, between two selves.

It was like standing at a fork in the road—one path went nowhere, simply circled back upon itself in a never-ending spiral of solitude and sameness. The other went forward, and while I couldn't see what was at the end of that road, I knew it offered the possibility of being happy again.

But what would it take for me to feel I deserved a second chance?

⁂

A few nights later, Georgia invited me to dinner at the house. I accepted, grateful to escape the lonely silence of the cabin. Brad and Olivia were there too, and after dinner we went out to the front yard, where my brothers got on the trampoline with their kids.

Georgia and I sat on the porch rockers, drinking whiskey on the rocks and watching Pete try to do a flip. "He's going to break his neck," I said, chuckling a little.

"Oh God, don't even think it." She glanced over at me. "It's good to hear you laugh. Been kinda down this week."

I tipped back some whiskey. "Yeah."

"Probably no point in my asking this, but I will anyway. Want to talk about it?"

On the trampoline, my brothers bounced and laughed and took pictures of their grinning kids in mid-air. *I want that—I want it so fucking badly.* "I envy you guys," I said.

From the corner of my eye, I saw her nod slowly. "I get that."

"I thought I'd live in this house eventually, raise a family, all that."

"It's not too late, you know."

"You don't think so?"

"Not at all."

I thought for a moment, willed myself to be brave. "Georgia, can I tell you something?"

"Of course."

"I've been thinking lately, I served with guys who didn't make it back. Guys who were stronger than me. Braver. Smarter. Sometimes I wonder why I survived and they didn't. What was it for?"

She looked at me but didn't say anything.

"I used to think it was for Steph. For the family we'd have. But once she was gone, it seemed pointless again."

"You don't think you could fall in love again? Have a family?"

I hesitated. "I never used to."

"And now?"

"Now..." I inhaled and exhaled slowly, met her eyes. "Now there's Margot."

She smiled, her eyes lighting up. "So what's holding you back?"

"A lot of things." I stared at the ice cubes in my glass. "I fucked things up really badly, Georgia."

"I know."

Something hitched in my chest. "You've talked to her?"

Georgia paused, and I sensed she didn't want to betray Margot's confidence. "Yes."

"I mean it when I say I fucked up. I hurt her."

"Ask forgiveness."

She made it sound so easy. "What if she says no?"

"What if she says yes?" Georgia countered.

"She could have so much better. Someone with money and cars and—"

"She wants you. Trust me."

I looked her in the eye and spoke the truth. "I'm scared."

"I know you are. And it's gonna take some hard work, but I bet it'll be worth it. I *know* it'll be worth it, Jack. Even if Margot isn't the one, you have to do this for you. It's time."

Nodding, I let her words sink in. "It's three years tomorrow."

"I know," she said softly, her eyes tearing up. "But Jack, Steph would be the first one to tell you that you're not honoring her by refusing to move on." She reached out and touched my arm. "You've been using her to punish yourself. It's time to let her go. I know it hurts, but it's time."

My throat closed, and I had to look away from Georgia's tears before my own started to fall.

The following day, I went to the cemetery. Sitting in front of the stone the way I always did, I imagined Steph beside me and concentrated on the memory of her voice.

"Hey. I need to talk to you."

What's up?

My throat tightened. "This is hard."

Talk to me.

I swallowed hard. "I met someone."

Good.

"Is it?"

Why wouldn't it be?

"Because she's making me doubt myself. She's making me reconsider things I'd already decided."

Like what?

"Like getting involved with someone again. Letting myself fall in love again. Spending my life with someone instead of being alone."

Sounds serious. What's she like?

"She's impossible. Spoiled rotten. A know-it-all city girl."

Laughter bounced off the stones. *Someone to put you in your place, huh?*

"She loves to try." I took a breath. "She's also kind and smart and beautiful. She makes me laugh."

You have feelings for her?

"I do, but…I don't know if I want them."

Why not?

"For one thing, it drives me crazy that she's nothing like you. I feel guilty—like I'm betraying your memory by falling for someone so opposite everything you were."

You're not betraying me, Jack. I want you to move on and be happy.

Tears sprang to my eyes and I touched my eyelids with my thumb and forefinger. "I want to be happy too, I just can't seem to figure out how to get there and be OK with it."

Well, first, you need to go back to therapy. It's time to admit you stopped going because it was helping and you didn't want to get better.

I blinked. I'd never thought about it that way. In my mind, I'd stopped going because it was too painful to talk about my feelings anymore. Was Steph right? Had I let myself off the hook? Was quitting therapy just another way I'd sabotaged my recovery?

You know I'm right. Next, you need to clean out that cabin. Give my clothes away. Throw out my junk. Take my pictures off the damn wall. Better yet, move out. It's all just part of the prison you created for yourself, and you know what? It's imprisoning me, too.

It felt like a punch in the gut. "What?"

You heard me. You have to let me go, Jack.

Gooseflesh rippled down my arms. The back of my neck prickled. "But I—"

No backtalk, you. If you loved me—

"You know I did. More than anyone. You were the love of my life, Steph."

I was the love of the life you had then, Jack. I was your first love...but I'm not your last.

The breeze rustled through some nearby trees while I let her words sink in and dissolve the final doubts inside me. She was setting me free, and I had to do the same for her. A weight was lifted. "You're right."

Of course I am. Now I have one more request: Call that woman and take her out for dinner. Poor thing is probably tied in knots wondering what the hell is going on in that thick skull of yours. You tell her I understand. You drove me crazy, too.

"I'm sorry, Steph. For everything."

I know you are, Jack. I forgive you. You ready to do this?

I nodded. "I think so. I can't say I'm not scared, but I think I know what I have to do."

Good. Go live the life you were meant to. You've got a lot of love to give, Jack Valentini. Don't you forget it.

"OK," I whispered, a shiver working its way through my body. "And Steph...thank you. You're an angel."

I listened for a response, but she was gone. I felt her absence as strongly as I'd felt her presence just moments ago. Somehow I knew she wouldn't be back.

I kissed my fingertips, touched the top of the stone, and said goodbye.

Later that night, I stood in my bedroom and looked around. It looked the same as it did every other night, but it felt different. For the first time, I recognized it as what Steph had called it—a prison. Steph was so *present* here—her clothing in the closet, her books on the shelves, her shampoo in the shower, our photos on the wall. But it wasn't entirely in memory of her; it was punishment. A lifetime sentence of solitary confinement.

Yet I'd brought Margot here. Kissed her. Touched her. And when she'd offered to stop, I'd been the one to press on. I'd wanted her more than I'd wanted to preserve the sanctity of this space.

Would she forgive me? Would she still want the chance she'd asked for? I pictured her, and something in my stomach went weightless. I wanted to be happy again. For the first time in years, I felt like it was possible.

I glanced down at my left hand, where my wedding band still circled my finger. Slowly, I twisted it off, looked at it for a moment, then placed it in my nightstand drawer. I was slightly sick to my stomach for a moment, but after a few deep breaths, I was OK again.

It was time.

Over the next week, I made four important phone calls. One to my therapist, who was glad to hear from me, and scheduled an appointment for me within days. The second call was to Georgia, who said she would be happy to help me sort through and remove Steph's things from the cabin. The third call went to Suzanne Reischling's voicemail. I left a message saying I was finally cleaning out the cabin and told her to call me if she wanted to come by one night this week and see if there was anything she wanted. And the fourth call was to Brad—I wanted to sit down with him and see if there was anything I could do to help Pete and Georgia buy that house.

It made the most sense for me to buy them out and live there, especially since I was planning on moving out of the cabin anyway—too many memories there, and I was serious about moving on—and I wanted to have a place I was comfortable inviting Margot to.

Brad said he'd be glad to meet with me, and he'd be thrilled if I could buy him out. "Let me talk to the bank," he said. "I'll explain the situation, get the numbers, and we can sit down sometime this week."

"Sounds good," I agreed. "But don't say anything to Pete and Georgia yet. I don't want to get their hopes up."

My first therapy session was painful, but I'd promised myself I was going to be honest. For the first time, I told him how I really felt about Steph's death, the way it was connected to the incident in Iraq in my mind, and how that guilt had prevented me from moving on. While he couldn't ease my conscience completely, he did give me some strategies for coping with my feelings and dealing with the guilt, and urged me to use the meds to get more sleep.

He also told me about a weekly group therapy session for Veterans that he'd organized within the last year, and I began attending them. Hearing others talk about their feelings, tell their stories, admit to struggling with guilt and anxiety just like I did made me feel like I wasn't alone. Sometimes I didn't even talk at those sessions, and that was OK too.

Cleaning out the cabin was tougher. I got through it with Pete and Georgia's help, by remembering Steph's wish to be set free, and by watching Cooper play with Bridget Jones while we worked. But it wasn't easy or quick. We worked Wednesday evening and throughout the day Thursday. There were moments I choked up, moments I teared up, moments I had to walk outside and take a few deep breaths. Even so, there was no uncertainty. I knew in my heart I was doing the right thing.

On Thursday night, Suzanne came by, and her eyes misted when she saw the bags and boxes in the front room. "You really did it," she said, putting a hand over her heart.

"I had to," I said quietly, but firmly.

Her eyes scanned the room. "You took down the pictures. Why?"

"Because they were making it too difficult to move on with my life, Suzanne." I met her eyes directly, and noticed she didn't appear to resemble Steph quite so closely tonight. It was a relief.

"Oh." She trailed the fingers of one hand along a box. "Are you moving on with that blond woman?"

"That's none of your business."

"Sorry," she said meekly. "It's just hard this week."

Sympathy softened my tone. "I know. But she wouldn't want us to sit around and grieve her again. She'd want us to celebrate her life by moving on with our own."

She nodded sadly. "My mother wants everything, but she was too upset to come."

"I'll help you load it. I've got a four wheeler here, and we can take it to your car."

"OK." Closing her eyes, she sighed. "I really am sorry about what I said. You're right. Steph would want us to move on. I just miss her, and it helps to think that you miss her like I do."

"Apology accepted. And it's OK to miss her, Suzanne. I miss her too. But it took me a long time to get where I am now, and I like thinking she'd be proud of me for that."

"She would be. I'm sure of it." Suzanne sniffed, and then laughed a little through her tears. "She was a much nicer person than me."

Three weeks after she'd gone home, I was ready to apologize to Margot and ask for another chance, but I wasn't sure how to do it. An apology over the phone wasn't the same as coming face to face with someone and asking their forgiveness. Admitting you'd been wrong. Putting yourself out there. If I was going to ask for a second chance, I needed to do it in person.

But how? What could I say that would convince her to see me again without giving myself away? All day Friday I thought about it, trying to come up with something romantic and clever—but romantic and clever had never been my thing. I needed help.

Swallowing my pride, I went to Georgia.

She grinned. "I'm not sure what you should do, but I know someone we can ask." Scooping up her phone from the counter, she tapped the screen a few times. My own phone buzzed in my pocket, and I took it out.

She'd shared a contact with me. "Jaime Owen?" I asked. "Who's that?"

"It's Margot's close friend and business partner. Call her."

I frowned. Involve another woman in this? "I'm not sure."

"*Call her.*" Georgia squeezed my arm. "I'm positive she'll know exactly what you should do."

I told her I'd think about it, stuck around to play with Cooper a little bit, then went home to brood about making the call. Georgia was probably right, but this was fucking embarrassing...it was one thing to call Margot and explain myself. She *knew* me. Calling this Jaime woman was another thing entirely. God only knows what kind of stories Margot had told her, what she thought about me.

That's your own fault. Make the call, asshole.

Groaning childishly, I dialed the number.

"Hello?"

"Hello, is this Jaime Owen?"

"Yes, it is. Can I help you?"

"My name is Jack Valentini. I'm—"

"Oh."

'*Oh?*' What does that mean? "I'm a friend of—"

"I know who you are." Her tone wasn't rude, just a bit aloof, but I'd expected that. She probably had a whole headful of things she'd like to scream at me, but I was technically still a client.

I wasn't sure how to proceed. "Georgia gave me your number."

"Did you have a question about your account?"

"No, it's not that. It's..." I took a breath. "I need to see Margot."

"Why?"

"To apologize."

"Why aren't you calling her?"

"Because I need to do more than apologize—I need to make up for the way I treated her, for the things I said."

"You hurt her, you know."

I closed my eyes. "I know. I'm sure she told you I was a total dick to her. But it was the only way I could get her to leave."

"And you needed her to leave because you didn't care about her anymore?"

"No, because I cared too much," I blurted, wondering how I was going to explain that. But she surprised me.

"I knew it!"

"What?"

"I knew that's what it was." She sounded happy all of a sudden. "You started falling for her so you had to back off—or in your case, you had to scare Margot off so she wouldn't get too close. But you didn't really mean the things you said."

"Yeah," I said, mystified. I held the phone away from my face and stared at it a second. Was this woman psychic?

"You were scared," she went on. "Because letting her in meant you had to let go of yourself in a way. And you didn't think you were capable."

"Jesus," I said. "Who are you?"

She laughed. "Someone who understands. So now what?"

"I need to see her. I'd like to surprise her somehow, but I'm not sure how to do it."

"Surprise her, huh? Hmmmm."

"Yes. And I think I should go to her. Prove to her that—"

"Oh my God!" she burst out suddenly. "What are you doing tomorrow night?"

Other than work, I had nothing planned. "Nothing," I admitted, feeling a little pathetic.

"Good. Margot is attending a cocktail reception at the DIA. It's a fundraiser for the opening of a new exhibit in the Lewiston Gallery."

"DIA?" I wasn't sure what that was.

"Detroit Institute of Arts. Her family donates a lot of money every year."

"Ah." Of course they did. I braced myself for where this was going. "And?"

"And what better way to show her that you want to be part of her life than to introduce yourself to it? I have a ticket but I'll give it to you. I won't say anything to her."

"Isn't there a less…socially awkward way for me to see her? I'm not good with crowds, and I don't own the right clothes or anything."

"Do you own a suit?"

I cringed. "No. I guess I could buy one tomorrow, but…would it even fit right? What if I have to have it altered?" The last thing I wanted to do was show up at a fancy cocktail reception in a suit that didn't fit. I'd be uncomfortable enough in one that did.

"Listen, I know some people," she said. "Leave it to me. Can you meet me downtown tomorrow morning?"

This was clearly going to be an all-day thing, probably a two-day thing, and I'd definitely need Pete and Georgia's help with things around here. But I was pretty sure they'd pick up my slack for this cause. "I think so."

"Good. I'll text you time and place in a bit. Do you need a haircut or anything? I could book you an appointment."

I ran a hand through my hair and frowned. "Probably. Thanks."

"No problem. I'm really glad you called me, Jack. You're doing the right thing."

I thanked her again and told her I'd see her tomorrow. After we hung up, I called Pete and Georgia's and asked if they could cover the farm work for two days. Georgia was scheduled to work this weekend, but Pete said not to worry, that Brad could always pitch in. "You're doing the right thing," he said, echoing Jaime's words. "Good luck."

"Thanks," I said. "I'll need it."

chapter thirty-four

Margot

Having a funner, more fulfilling life was easier said than done, especially with a broken heart.

After Jack rejected me a second time, I vowed to do exactly what I wanted *him* to do—move on. He had feelings for me, but clearly he wasn't willing to let go of his past, and I wasn't sure he ever would. Every time I thought about it, I felt like crying, but I couldn't save him from himself. I could only work on me.

I focused on my list.

I signed up for cooking classes. Watched online tutorials. Read my cookbooks. Made lists of things I needed in the kitchen and filled my cupboards and drawers with cookware and gadgets. I grocery shopped with a critical eye, choosing local and organic whenever I could. Stopped eating out so much. Invited my friends over to try my pesto, my piccata, my potatoes au gratin. A hundred times, I stopped myself from taking pictures of my culinary triumphs and sending them to Jack so he could see my progress and be proud of me.

I went riding three times and made up my mind to buy my own horse. There was something about that relationship I truly missed. Again I fought the urge to call Jack and share my excitement—there was no one in my life who understood the bond between a horse and human like he did.

Through a friend, I got involved with the Fair Food Network, a nonprofit dedicated to supporting farmers, strengthening local economies, and increasing healthy food access. One of their goals was to increase funding to Double Up Food Bucks, which helps low-income families make healthy food choices and purchase from local farmers. I used my family's connections to secure funds and support, and I also volunteered to create marketing materials to help spread the word about the program, teach people about the economic and health benefits of eating and shopping local, and advertising the days, locations, and hours of local markets that accept benefits. Was I single-handedly abolishing poverty? No, but the work was rewarding and I felt like I was contributing to the greater good.

And…I got my tattoo. It was mainly inspired by one of my favorite stories, *The Awakening*, by Kate Chopin. At first I was only going to get a little bird somewhere on my back—a tiny symbol of my own awakening. But then I realized I'd never be able to see it. I decided on my inner arm instead, and I also decided to go with words instead of a symbol. It made the tattoo bigger and more noticeable, but wasn't that the point? Now when I looked down, I saw these words inked on my fair skin:

*The bird that
would soar
above the plane
of tradition
and prejudice
must have
strong wings.*

Seven lines of elegant script that reminded me not to let myself be caged by the fear of what people thought or expected. I was my own person, and I could make my own choices. Strength was a beautiful thing.

Of course, it was inspired by Jack too, and I wanted nothing more than for him to see it. Night after night, I went over everything in my mind, trying to find the place where we'd gone wrong, but I could never find it. We were different, but that's what had given us our spark. I still felt that kick whenever I thought about him. Still craved his skin on mine. Still missed the way he'd talked and laughed and teased me. Still cried sometimes when I thought about his past.

Once, when I was talking with Georgia about new family photos for the website, she made a vague reference to Jack "working on himself." Though she offered no specifics, my hopes bloomed fresh.

But as the days turned into weeks and I still hadn't heard from him, they started to wither.

Muffy, as expected, nearly fainted when she saw my tattoo. "What on earth have you done to yourself? Will that come off?"

"I don't want it to come off, Mother. I like it." We were having cocktails in the Rivera Court at the DIA, and she looked around frantically, trying to shield me as if I were naked. The cavernous room was full of wealthy, well-dressed people sipping drinks and listening to a string quartet, but only one of them appeared scandalized by my ink.

"I just don't understand you these days, Margot. First the scone thing, then this volunteer business at a homeless shelter, and now a tattoo?" She shook her head. "Whose daughter are you?"

"Calm down, Mom." I patted her taffeta shoulder. "You should be happy about the tattoo. You wanted me to major in English, didn't you? *The Awakening* is a classic."

"Margot Thurber Lewiston, that is not the point. Your erratic behavior *is*."

"I've explained and apologized for the scone thing a hundred times. And I started volunteering at the shelter because I like helping people. And it only costs my time."

Muffy looked at me like I was nuts. "We donate money to those places so we don't *have* to spend time there."

I sighed. There was no use trying to explain it to her. "Well, I don't mind the time. What else have I got to do?"

"I'd rather hoped you might start dating again."

I took another sip. "It's not that easy."

"It is. You're simply too picky."

"What's wrong with picky?"

"Nothing, when it comes to hiring a cook, gardener, or maid. But finding the right husband shouldn't be that difficult."

I clenched my teeth. "I'm not going to settle, Mom. I want to fall in love."

"Don't be ridiculous. *Everyone* settles in marriage, Margot," she said, rolling her eyes like I'd said something childish.

"Even Thurber women?"

"*Especially* Thurber women." Again she looked at me as if I were crazy. "Every Thurber woman I've ever known has settled. Marriage isn't about being in love. It's about merging two families to create a better one. It's about preservation and lineage. It's about tradition." She sniffed. "Love is for children and poor people."

If I hadn't grown up listening to such ridiculous bits of Muffy's "wisdom," I might have been horrified. But she couldn't help the way she was. In her mind, falling in love was probably akin to Causing a Scene. Loud, messy, and indiscreet. But I didn't have to perpetuate her strange notions, and I'd teach my daughter differently.

"I'm sorry you feel that way, Mother. But *this* Thurber woman isn't settling." It was a small thing, maybe, talking back to Muffy like that, but for me it was huge. It had taken me years to find the voice to do it. "I'm holding out for what I want."

"And what is it you want?" Muffy sounded miffed. "The Prince of Wales?"

"Not even close. I don't need a prince, Mother. Just a good man. Someone who—" Over Muffy's shoulder, I noticed someone moving toward me. Someone tall, dark, and handsome. Someone dressed in a black suit. Someone who took away my ability to speak, think, or breathe.

My skin prickled with heat. My mouth fell open. I blinked. It couldn't be. Could it? What was he *doing* here?

Dizzy, I swayed on my feet, and my mother grabbed my arm. "Margot, are you all right?"

"I'm not sure," I said, still watching in disbelief as Jack drew nearer. Our eyes locked. "I feel a little dizzy."

"Dizzy? You never felt dizzy before you got that tattoo," she said, studying it suspiciously. "Maybe it's poisoning you."

"It's not the tattoo," I said. "Excuse me for a moment." I started to walk toward him, and my heart clamored faster with every step. Jesus Christ, he was gorgeous. The cut of the suit emphasized his slim torso and broad chest. His shoulders looked even wider. He'd gotten his hair cut, and it had been styled with some kind of product, slicked away from his face. His scruff was trimmed way back too. He looked polished and sophisticated.

And nervous as hell.

I felt a rush of protectiveness. *He hates crowds. He hates dressing up. He's doing this for me.*

But I also nursed some lingering anger and doubt. Was this just another 'I need to see you' thing? Was he here just to get a fix? Or punish himself? I wasn't going to play that game.

We met in the middle of the room and stood nearly chest to chest. My emotions were all over the place, my breath coming fast. Someone behind me dropped a glass, and at the sound of the crash, he glanced around sharply. My heart ached at his anxious expression, the tension in his neck, the sheen on his brow.

"Hey." Compassion moved me to slip my hand into his, lock our fingers. I was angry with him, but I also recognized how difficult this was. "Look at me."

His facial muscles relaxed slightly as he refocused on me. "Sorry."

"What are you doing here, Jack?"

"I came to apologize."

"For what?" I held my breath.

"For lying to you. For breaking things off. For being a coward." He grimaced. "You were right. I was afraid of what I was starting to feel. Of what it meant."

Hope was exploding like fireworks inside me. "What did it mean?"

"It meant letting go of things—my past, my guilt, my pain—and giving myself permission to move on. I wasn't ready to feel that way about myself. And I probably still wouldn't if I hadn't met you." His eyes skittered across the room again, and he swallowed. "Margot, I have so many things I want to say to you, but I'm not very good in a crowd."

"Then let's get out of here."

He frowned. "I promised myself I wouldn't do that—if this is important to you, then it's important to me."

"Jack, there is nothing more important to me right now than hearing what you have to say."

Relief eased his features. "OK."

"I have some things to say too."

He looked tense again.

"Follow me. We'll find a quiet place to sit down." My heart thumped wildly as I led him out of the room.

We held hands as we walked down the promenade and through galleries, searching for the right spot. Finally we found an empty room with a bench in the center, and I let Jack lead me to it. It was dimly lit to protect the art, and the deep red walls made it seem warm and romantic. The butterflies in my stomach were out of control, and I had to remind myself to stay calm. He was saying the right things, but was he really ready to be with me?

Jack kept my hand in his as we sat, and he looked down at our fingers laced together on his lap. "You got a tattoo?" He held my arm up and angled it so he could read the words. "It's beautiful. I love it."

"Thank you. I do too."

"What prompted that?"

"I decided you were right. It was time to stop worrying about what other people think. I was tired of being afraid of what people would say if I did something different."

He nodded slowly and he lowered my arm and took my hand again. "What did Muffy say?"

"She thinks I'm crazy."

He met my eyes and we both smiled. Some of my doubt dissipated. *This feels so good. Please let it be real.*

"You know, it's funny you decided *I* was right about something," he said. "I've been wrong about most everything." He looked down at our hands for a moment, stroked the back of mine with his thumb. *"You* were right. That night in the cabin." His eyes met mine. "I did feel something for you."

I couldn't breathe.

"I'd started to feel so much for you that it scared me. I felt like I was losing control, like I was losing myself. I panicked. Retreated. Tried to put up walls. But…" He lifted his shoulders. "It was too late."

"It was?"

"Yes. What I felt didn't go away just because I tried to shut you out. I didn't feel stronger or more in control after you left. Hurting myself was one thing, but hurting you made me feel cruel and weak. I felt like I'd crushed something frail and young and beautiful that couldn't fight back."

"That's exactly what you did." He needed to know how I felt too. "And all I could do was watch. I *felt* something for you. I felt something between us. But what could I do? I asked you to take a chance on me, and you said no. Twice!" My nose tingled and I fought against tears.

Jack shook his head, his eyes full of pain. "I'm sorry, Margot. I hated myself for saying no. I wanted to say yes so badly. I missed you constantly. I kept thinking about the way I felt when I was with you. I imagined what my life would be like with you in it, and I agonized over the choice I'd made to be alone." He closed his eyes briefly. "Finally, I realized how stupid I was being. How wrong I'd been to walk away from you. How much I wanted to give you that chance you asked for." He took both my hands in his and squeezed tight. "I came here hoping you'd still be willing to give me one."

My fears were unraveling, but I had to ask. "How do I know you're serious now? How do I know you're not going to panic and put up walls again?"

He squeezed my hand. "You don't. That's a chance you'll have to take on me. But I'm begging you to take it."

I swallowed against the lump in my throat. "You're ready? To move on, I mean?"

He nodded, looked me right in the eye. "Yes. In the last few weeks, I've made some really good progress."

"Like what?"

"I went back to therapy. I cleaned out the cabin. And I said goodbye," he finished quietly.

I knew what he meant, and it made me smile through tears.

He smiled too. "I want a new start, Margot. And I want you there with me. Say you'll give me a chance."

"Oh, Jack," I said softly. "That's all I ever wanted. I know I can't be your first love, but—"

"Shh." He put a finger over my lips. "I'm not looking for my first love. I'm looking for my last."

He leaned over and put his lips on mine. It was a sweet, soft, still kiss—but it was more than that. It was an apology, a promise, a new start. It spoke of letting go, of moving on, of falling in love. I shivered, and Jack put an arm around me. "You cold?"

"Not at all," I said, feeling warmth flow throughout my body. "Now I want to know how you found me."

Jack grinned sheepishly. "Your friend Jaime."

"Jaime!" I yelped. "She said she was too sick to come tonight!"

"She gave me her ticket."

I shook my head, trying to piece it together. "So you called her?"

"Yes. Last night. I was trying to think of a way to surprise you, and Georgia gave me her number."

I giggled, my whole body tingling. "Oh my God, this happened in one night? It worked. I'm surprised."

He just smiled at me for a moment, almost a little sadly. "I missed that laugh. I was scared I'd never hear it again."

"Now you can hear it as much as you want."

"I wanted to tell you." He cleared his throat. "I'm moving into the house. I decided to buy out Pete and Georgia so they can afford the Oliver place."

Squealing, I threw both my arms around his neck. He smelled delicious, and I breathed him in deeply. "Oh my God, that's amazing! I'm so proud of you."

His arms closed around me. "Thanks. I wouldn't have done any of it if it wasn't for you."

Unwilling to let go, I kept my chest pressed to his. "I feel like we have so much to catch up on."

"It's all good stuff."

"Pete and Georgia must be so happy."

"They are. And it's only possible because of Brad. He said he'd wait a little longer for me to buy him out so that I could afford to make this happen."

Reluctantly, I stopped strangling him and sat back. "I'm so happy for you. And for them. That's wonderful about Brad, too."

Jack nodded. "For the first time in years, I feel like I can breathe. Like I have something to look forward to."

I couldn't stop smiling. "You don't know how happy this makes me."

He hauled me across his lap, and I looped my arms around his neck. "You don't know how beautiful you are when you're happy. I want to put that smile on your face every day." His brow furrowed. "But I'm hoping I don't have to wear this suit to do it."

Laughter bubbled out of me. "You can do it in nothing, believe me—and you're going to."

"Hell yes I am," he drawled. "The sooner the better."

"Not so fast, cowboy. You're wearing the hell out of that suit, and I need to get my fill before I take it off you, one piece at a time." I leaned back and admired him, my belly fluttering. "I didn't even think you owned one."

"I didn't."

My eyebrows shot up. "Jaime?"

"And Quinn. Nice guy. Knows a lot about clothes." He shook his head. "Mostly I just stood still and let them dress me."

"They did it well. When I saw you walking across the room toward me, I swooned. Nearly fell right over."

"I'd have caught you." His arms tightened around me. "I'll always catch you."

I'll always catch you, too, I thought as our lips met again. *Now let yourself fall.*

chapter thirty-five

Margot

I DIDN'T WANT TO STAY AT THE EVENT VERY LONG, BUT I DID WANT TO INTRODUCE Jack to my family. We found my father schmoozing a few voters in the Great Hall, and he shook Jack's hand enthusiastically when he heard Jack owned a farm. Dad probably thought I was helping him "shore up the base" with the introduction, but that was OK. Eventually I'd explain to him that Jack wasn't Big Ag and probably didn't have the same views on farming policy he did, but for now it was enough that they'd met.

My brother Buck raised an eyebrow at me when I introduced Jack as my date, maybe because I hadn't brought a date to a function like this since Tripp. But ever the charmer, he gave Jack his hand and a slap on the back like he was an old prep school buddy. When my brother learned Jack lived near Lake Huron, they talked for a few minutes about fishing on the Great Lakes, something they both enjoyed. Never mind that as kids Jack had *worked* on the boats while Buck had chartered them—it was something they had in common, and I was glad for it. Flashing Buck a grateful smile, we moved on to my mother.

Muffy was still in the Rivera Court. Near the bar, of course. "Mother, this is my friend Jack Valentini. Jack this is my mother, Muffy Lewiston."

"Nice to meet you." Muffy extended a hand, and Jack took it as she scrutinized him. "Valentini, did you say? Good heavens, what a lot of syllables."

I rolled my eyes. Muffy had a thing about syllables in a last name. One or two was ideal, three was fine as long as it didn't end in a vowel, but four—plus the vowel at the end—was just too much.

"Uh, yes." Jack looked at me for help.

"Jack owns and runs Valentini Brothers Farm in Lexington. That's where I was earlier this month."

Muffy reacted as if I'd said something absurd. "You were on a farm?"

"Yes. Doing some work for Shine. I told you that, Mother."

She studied him again. "He doesn't look like a farmer."

"I thought the same thing when I met him." I gave him a quick smile. "Would you excuse us? I think we're going to head out."

"Of course." Muffy dismissed us with a nod.

"Nice to meet you," offered Jack. "Wow," he said when we'd left the room. "For a small woman, she looks like she's got bones of steel."

I laughed as we headed for the museum valet. "She might."

"How'd I do?"

"Fantastic. Were you nervous?"

"I'm sweating bullets. I kept feeling like everyone was looking at me."

"Aww." Hooking my arm through his, I hugged it to me. "You have nothing to worry about. They were dazzled by your looks, and by the fact that there was a new face here. These things are always attended by the same people."

"Yeah?"

"Yeah." After we handed our tickets to the valet, we went outside to wait for them to pull our cars around. I turned to Jack and smoothed his lapels. "Thank you for coming tonight. I know it wasn't easy in there."

"It's a different world for me, that's for sure."

"Like me in the chicken coop."

He laughed and dropped a quick kiss on my lips. "Right. And you know what this means, don't you?"

"What?"

"Camping."

I wrinkled my nose. "Oh yeah. But not tonight, right?"

He laughed again, and I knew I'd never get tired of that sound as long as I lived. "Not tonight. Tonight I have a Luxury King room at the MGM Grand," he teased. "Would you like to stay with me?"

"Did you say luxury? That's like my favorite word." I fanned myself and whispered, "I'm so turned on right now."

"Good." He pulled me close. "Because I've got plans for you."

I shivered. "What kind of plans?"

"The kind where I make you come all night long, scream my name and beg for more."

I swooned.

This time he caught me.

The elevator at the MGM was crowded, and Jack pulled me back against him. "So many people," he said low in my ear. I thought he meant that there were too many people for him to be comfortable, but then he said, "Do you think they know what I'm going to do to you?"

I froze, my face growing hot.

"Do they know how soon I'm going to have my tongue between your legs?"

My mouth fell open.

"Do they know how loud I want to make you scream?"

I couldn't breathe.

"Do they know how deep you're going to take me?"

My legs started to shake.

"Do they know I'm getting hard right now, thinking about all the ways I want to fuck you tonight?"

Sweet Jesus. I spun around and whispered in his ear, "If I was wearing panties, they'd be soaked."

He inhaled sharply.

Ten seconds later, the doors opened and he grabbed my arm roughly, yanking me out behind him. He moved down the hall so fast I could barely keep up in my heels, and the moment the hotel room door shut behind us, he pushed me back against it. My evening bag hit the floor.

His mouth covered mine, his tongue driving between my lips as his fingers hitched my dress up to my hips. He groaned when he realized I'd told the truth, running his palms down over my bare ass and up the sides of my thighs. I pushed at his jacket, forgetting about taking my time to undress him and thinking only about what was beneath the layers of dress clothes. I needed to feel his bare skin on mine, needed those hard muscles flexing above me, needed his power and strength and size to overwhelm me.

He let his jacket fall to the ground and my fingers fumbled with the knot in his tie. But it was hard to concentrate because he moved one hand between my legs and his touch paralyzed me—he slid his fingers back and forth along the slick seam at my center and circled them gently over my clit. I finally got the damn knot to come loose just as he slipped two fingers inside me, and I clutched his shoulders, melting against him.

"I want to be right here." His voice was low and raw and intense. He pushed his fingers deep.

"Yes," I whimpered, riding his hand. "I want you there." I ran my palm over the bulge in his pants, wishing I could rip that gorgeous suit to shreds with my teeth like a wolf. God, I'd missed this feeling, this side of myself. Letting it take over was a relief and a pleasure and a high better than any I could imagine.

Jack dropped down and buried his face between my thighs, his tongue swirling over my clit. My legs trembled, and he slung one then the other over his broad shoulders. Then *he stood up*, my back sliding up the door, my hands flattening on the ceiling. Holy fuck, he was strong! Holding me there on his shoulders, his hands gripping my waist, he sucked my clit, flicking it with his tongue until I was writhing and gasping and making so much noise, I was positive the people in the elevator could hear us, no matter what floor they were on. Probably the people in the lobby too, and maybe even the people still at the DIA.

And yes—I screamed his name and begged for more.

He set me on the floor and I went at him like a cyclone, yanking off his tie and shirt and shoving down his pants. After wriggling out of my shoes and dress, I pushed him backward into the room and onto the bed, where I dragged off the rest of his clothes. Climbing onto his body, I straddled his hips, took his dick in my hand, and rubbed the tip between my legs. "You don't know how much I missed this."

"You're fucking crazy if you think that," he said, groaning as I slid onto him. His hands moved to my breasts, his thumbs flicking my nipples.

I bit my lip as I took him in deep and rocked my hips over his. He sat up, his mouth closing over one tight, hard peak, his fingers pinching the other. He sucked and bit and teased, lifting his hips to match my rhythm, both of us moving faster and faster. When he said my name, I knew he was close.

"Jack," I whispered. "I want you on top."

In two seconds, he'd flipped me onto my back and covered my body with his. *Yes, yes, yes*, I thought as his weight pinned my hips to the bed, as his cock drove deep and hard, as the muscles of his arms and chest and back and ass worked beneath my roving hands. I loved the gravity of him, the power he wielded, the punishing thrust of his hips. I loved the growl in his voice, the sweat on his skin, the roughness of his hands in my hair. I loved that he'd come here for me, that he wanted me in his life, that he was willing to make such drastic changes to have me.

And as all the coiled-up tension in our bodies released in powerful, rippling contractions that stopped our breath and stole our sight and splintered every last wall between us, somehow I knew in my heart and soul that I would love this man forever.

I would heal him, cherish him, adore him. I would believe in him, support him, work with him. He would be a lover, a husband, a father. And I would stay with him for the rest of my life.

But for now, I'd enjoy the fall.

epilogue

Jack

I WOKE UP EVEN EARLIER THAN USUAL, BUT I WASN'T SURPRISED.

Today was a big day.

After checking to make sure that Margot was still asleep, I slipped out of our bed without even kissing her cheek like I wanted to. I couldn't risk waking her up.

Quickly and quietly, I hurried down the hall. When I passed the room that used to be Cooper's, I smiled. It was empty right now, and Cooper was asleep in his new "big boy" room across the street, but I hoped it would contain a crib and rocker again soon. Maybe even within a year.

My heart tripped with excitement as I took the stairs down a few at a time, careful not to hit any of the ones that creaked. I knew this house so well—its familiarity was a comfort to me. When I'd first moved out of the cabin, I'd been worried it would feel too big for me. I'd thought living there alone might make me sad, remind me I had no family of my own to fill it with.

But I hadn't been alone for long.

For a few months, Margot and I had dated long distance, but by Thanksgiving, I'd asked her to move in with me. She already spent several days a week up here, had clothes in the closet, a toothbrush in the bathroom, a table she used as a desk in a spare bedroom.

Hell, she had a horse in my barn.

I loved when she was here and hated when she left. My days were always better when I kissed her good morning, and my nights were always better when I held her close. I still battled anxiety and nightmares sometimes, but Margot took it all in stride. She was my calm, my rock, my haven. She pushed back when I needed it and let me breathe when I didn't. She understood me. She loved me.

And I loved her.

Silently closing the kitchen door behind me, I remembered when we first said the words, not too long after we began dating seriously. She'd come up to help me move into the house, and after a long day of cleaning and hauling and unpacking and organizing, she said she had a surprise for me.

It was a bubble bath.

I had to laugh as she undressed me and told me to get in the tub. But the scent of those bubbles and the feel of her wet skin beneath my palms took me back to a night months before, when I'd felt close enough to her to tell her everything.

Something in me must have known even then.

And as she rested her body on mine, her head on my chest, I wrapped my arms around her and felt an overwhelming sense of peace and warmth and gratitude that I was alive and well and here with her.

"I love you," I said out of nowhere.

She went completely still and then picked up her head. Her eyes searched mine and saw I was serious. "Jack," she whispered.

"Those are words that have never come easy to me, and I probably won't say them nearly as often as I should, but I want you to know that I do."

Her eyes filled. "I know. And I love you, too."

Margot didn't seem to mind that I didn't say the words much, even though I thought them—felt them—all the time. In fact, she told me she liked that it wasn't something I threw out there casually. It meant more to her when she heard them, she said, knowing that they didn't come easy.

And maybe the words didn't, but the feeling sure as hell did. I'd only loved one other woman, and I'd known her so long I couldn't remember falling for her this way—fast and hard and head over heels. I'd loved Steph deeply, but I loved Margot with a kind of intensity that shocked me. I hadn't known I was capable of it.

It made me want things—a ring on her finger, my last name on her driver's license, a house full of kids.

I'd never be rich, never be able to give her all the things she'd grown up with, never own a vacation home in L'Arbre Croche or a Mercedes Benz. But I knew Margot well enough by now to know that she didn't care about those things as much as she cared about me. About us. Oh, she was still a city girl, even when she wore her jeans and boots, but dammit, she was my city girl, and I loved her beyond words.

I smiled as I let myself into the chicken coop and slipped my hand into my pocket.

I didn't like surprises, but Margot did.

I wanted to give her the surprise of her life.

Margot

I woke up and reached for Jack. He'd promised me he'd stay in bed a little longer this morning, since it was kind of a special day—the anniversary of the day we met.

Sometimes we looked back on that day and laughed at the way we'd stood there staring at each other across the kitchen, him broody and mean, me trying to be charming. "Was it love at first sight?" people sometimes asked us.

"Hell, no," Jack would tease. "I didn't want any rich city girl hanging around."

"And I couldn't stand him," I'd say. "He was dirty, sweaty, and rude."

But we belonged together, and it hadn't taken us that long to figure it out, all things considered. I'd gone back and forth for a while, but I'd been thrilled when he'd asked me to move in. Farm life was a bit of an adjustment at first—the smells, the early mornings, the never-ending list of chores to be done—but I grew to appreciate things about living in the country. I loved the quiet mornings, the lack of traffic, the charm of the small town, the sun rising over the lake and setting over the trees, the skies full of stars at night. When I missed the shops or bars or salons or restaurants, I'd zip down and meet my friends for an afternoon or evening. But I found I didn't miss city life too much, and I loved being around horses again.

The hardest thing had been leaving Jaime and Claire and our weekly Girls Night Out, but I saw them at least once a month, and they were happy for me. At first, I kept my job at Shine but cut back my hours, spending a lot of time helping Georgia with the new house, preparing to open the Valentini Farms Bed & Breakfast, and making sure the new marketing push went as planned. Once the B & B opened in May, I left Shine and dedicated myself completely to marketing duties at the farm and inn. I also volunteered for the Fair Food Network, reaching out to farmers and families in the region and continuing to help spread the word.

I'd never been happier, which befuddled my parents a little bit, but they seemed content to focus on my father's political career—he'd won his election—and give me a break.

Jack seemed happy too, and we'd grown infinitely closer since I'd moved in. His moods and silences grew easier to understand, his anxiety easier to manage. His nightmares were infrequent but terrifying, and I always wished there was more I could do for him, but he swore just having me there was enough. He loved me—I felt it, even if he didn't say it too often.

I sat up in bed and looked around. He'd left the blinds down, so it was still pretty dark in the room, but sun peeked around them. I glanced at the clock, which told me it was just after eight. "Jack?" I called.

Nothing.

There was no way he'd forgotten, because we'd talked about it before going to sleep. It wasn't like Jack to break a promise. I lay back again and gave it about ten minutes, then I sighed and threw back the covers. Maybe there was an emergency across the street?

I pulled on some jeans and a t-shirt and went downstairs. The front door was open, so I looked out on the porch. No one was there, although I noticed his truck was gone.

What the hell? It's like he forgot all about me.

Grumpy that a morning in bed was not on the horizon, I went into the kitchen. He hadn't even made coffee!

Angrily I poured the water and scooped the grounds, then crossed my arms and pouted while it dripped. The dumb old thing took forever, but Jack was funny about letting me replace things around here. Not because he was attached to them, but because he had a hard time letting me buy things for his house. "I live here," I kept telling him. "Isn't it my house too?"

He always said yes, of course it was, and hugged me in apology. Recently we'd had a long talk about redoing the kitchen, and when he balked at the cost of stone counters and tile floors, I'd put my foot down. "Listen. I am not trying to buy your love. I am trying to add a little bit of luxury to our lives because I like it and I can afford it and I'm spoiled, OK? You won't let me buy Brad out, so at least let me buy the damn countertops."

He'd grumbled about it but eventually caved, and a man was coming to take measurements this week. I was excited about it—I loved living up here with Jack, but I did miss a *few* things from my old life. And some high-end finishes in this beautiful old farmhouse could only make it better. I'd sweet talk him into things. I was good at that.

The smell of fresh coffee perked me up, and I turned around to reach for a mug. That's when I noticed the note on the counter.

Had to run out. Back later. Can you collect the eggs?

I groaned. Not only had he forgotten about his promise, he'd asked me to do my *least* favorite farm chore. For some reason, I could not get comfortable with it. Those hens hated me, I could tell.

But I dutifully put on my boots, grabbed a basket, and trudged over to the coop.

The hens clucked at me as I entered. "Yeah, I know. Good morning to you, too."

I checked the first box, and there was only one egg in there. I reached for it, scooped it up, and put it in the basket. The second box only had one as well, and when I went to place it next to the first, I noticed it had something written on it.

You're beautiful.

It made me smile. I turned the first one over, and the smile widened.

Good morning.

The writing was undeniably Jack's, and I looked around, expecting to see him standing there. He wasn't.

I went to the third box and pulled out the egg.

Did you think I forgot?

I started giggling, my pulse picking up. He did remember! And look at him being clever and romantic!

Grinning, I reached into the next box and took out the egg.

I love you.

And the next...

I will always love you.

My hands were shaking as I reached into the last box in the row.

Turn around.

Gasping, I spun around.

And there he was—going down on one knee.

My heart stopped.

He opened a ring box and held it out, his expression surprisingly calm, his dark eyes glinting. "I'm not saying I deserve you, Margot Thurber Lewiston, only that I'll keep trying as long as you'll let me. I've never loved anyone or anything the way I love you. You brought everything good back to my life—you brought *me* back to life, and I want to spend it with you. Will you marry me?"

I stood there, literally shaking in my boots, while I tried to find the wherewithal to move, talk, breathe, anything. A few tears slipped down my cheeks. "Yes," I squeaked, still clutching the basket.

"Want to put the eggs down, baby?" he asked, a smile tugging at his lips.

Nodding, I set the last egg carefully in the basket and put it on the ground. Then I moved closer to Jack and held out my hand, sobs working their way free from my chest. The ring winked at me from a black velvet Tiffany cushion, a gorgeous round solitaire set in a platinum band. My hand trembled as he slipped it on my finger.

I'd thought the ring that Tripp had chosen was perfect, but this one—this one—was *my* ring. Simple yet exquisite. Modern yet classic. Perfection.

"I love it," I sobbed, unable to stop myself.

He rose to his feet, laughing a little. "I'm glad. The way you're crying, I might have wondered."

I threw my arms around him and he held me tight, lifting me right off my feet. "I love you," he said in my ear. "I want this forever."

"Me too," I said, burying my face in his neck. My heart was so full it spilled over. "Forever."

The End

Thank you so much for reading! I hope you enjoyed Jack and Margot's story. If you'd like to read bonus scenes from their wedding day (and night!), use the link below to sign up for emails about twice a month from me! The first thing you'll get once you confirm is a link to the bonus material.

www.melanieharlow.com/get-after-we-fall-bonus-wedding-scenes

also by MELANIE HARLOW

The Frenched Series
Frenched
Yanked
Forked
Floored

The Happy Crazy Love Series
Some Sort of Happy
Some Sort of Crazy
Some Sort of Love

The After We Fall Series
Man Candy
After We Fall
If You Were Mine
From This Moment

The One and Only Series
Only You
Only Him
Only Love

The Cloverleigh Farms Series
Irresistible
Undeniable
Insatiable
Unbreakable
Unforgettable

The Bellamy Creek Series
Drive Me Wild

Co-Written Book*s*
Hold You Close (Co-written with Corinne Michaels)
Imperfect Match (Co-written with Corinne Michaels)
Strong Enough (M/M romance co-written with David Romanov)

The Speak Easy Duet

The Tango Lesson (A Standalone Novella)

Never miss a Melanie Harlow thing!

Want new release alerts, access to bonus materials and exclusive giveaways, and all my announcements first? Subscribe to my once or twice monthly newsletter!

Want to stay up to date on all things Harlow day to day, get exclusive access to ARCs and giveaways, and be part of a fun, positive, sexy and drama-free zone? Become a Harlot!

Amazon shopper? Follow me there!

Want a chance to become a Top Fan and win exclusive prizes? Check out my Facebook page!

Want to be notified about freebies and sales? Try Bookbub!

Interested in excerpts and little bites of my romances so you can read more before buying or borrowing? Try Book + Main!

acknowledgments

I am so grateful to the following people:

Jaime and Charles Collins, for talking so openly and honestly about PTSD and military matters.

Amanda Williams Brown, for answering my "city girl" questions about life on a small farm.

Lindsay Way, for an abundance of information on the Fair Food Network.

Cheryl Guernsey, for being Jack's biggest champion day to day.

Melissa Gaston, for everything she does to keep me organized, sane, and productive.

Kayti, Laurelin, and Sierra, for being the best squad of snakes ever.

Jenn Watson, for being superhuman publicist, reader, and friend.

Candi, Nina, Hilary, and the entire Social Butterfly PR team for all you do.

Rebecca Friedman, agent and friend, for honest advice and encouragement.

Tamara Mataya, for fantastic edits that always make me smile.

Laura Foster Franks, Amanda Maria at AM to PM Book Services, and Angie Owens for proofreading with eagle eyes.

Letitia Hasser, for another gorgeous cover.

Joseph Cannata, for the excellent visual inspiration.

Laurelin Paige, Lauren Blakely and Corinne Michaels, for sage advice; Staci Hart for amazing feedback and long talks; Helena Hunting, for good times and colorful play money.

The Peen Queens for feedback, laughs, and inspiration.

The Harlots, for all your love and support.

The bloggers who share my work and invite me to signings and review my books simply for the love of reading—THANK YOU.

All my readers, for your support and enthusiasm—this is only possible because of you.

Finally, thank you to my husband and children, for your love, patience, and understanding.

about the author

Melanie Harlow likes her heels high, her martini dry, and her history with the naughty bits left in. In addition to AFTER WE FALL, she's the author of over twenty additional contemporary romances and a historical duet.

She writes from her home outside of Detroit, where she lives with her husband and two daughters. When she's not writing, she's probably got a cocktail in hand. And sometimes when she is.

Find her at www.melanieharlow.com.

pucked love

HELENA HUNTING

dedication

For my Pucked Series readers: this one is like reading with your seatbelt off.

prologue

NDA Coffee Date

Charlene

I breathe into my palm to check for freshness. I brushed my teeth less than ten minutes ago, but I pop two Altoids anyway. Fresh breath is crucial. I crunch down and spread the fiery-cold bits over my tongue. The burst of mint makes my eyes water, so I have to dab at the corners with my sleeve and breathe through my nose to avoid making it worse.

Darren Westinghouse is picking me up for a coffee date. *The* Darren Westinghouse, Chicago's NHL right wing and the most mysterious man in the league. There are loads of rumors about him. His dating history is unclear and based mostly on speculation and conjecture. I'm excited to get to know the man behind the intense, stoic mask.

My palms are sweaty, and my panties are inappropriately damp as I wander around my kitchen. My reaction to anxiety is weird. And rather inconvenient. I've already changed my panties once in the past half hour.

"It's just coffee," I scold my crotch.

It doesn't seem to matter, though. She's preparing for all possible scenarios.

I introduced myself to Darren when I went with my best friend, Violet, to an away game. He was gentlemanly and sweet, offering to walk me back to my room. I went in for a goodnight kiss that turned into an epic make-out session. We kissed like teenagers until my lips were raw. It took a week before they finally stopped peeling.

Today I'm wearing shiny gloss that tastes like cotton candy—my hope is that Darren likes the flavor and will want to kiss it off more than once. I smooth my sweaty palms down my jean-covered thighs. I'm going for casual—except under my jeans I'm wearing a nice pair of lacy panties, just in case his hand happens to find its way into them. My bra matches, of course.

I check the time. It's nine forty-nine in the morning. He's picking me up at ten, but those eleven minutes feel like they're taking an eternity to pass. I mentally scroll through the approved topics of conversation: obviously hockey, weather, my job, and my college experience are all approved.

I've learned that it's best to give people the barest of facts and then shift the topic away from the really personal stuff. People usually love to talk about themselves, so it's not all that hard to do. At nine fifty-three I do another breath check and startle as my doorbell chimes.

"He's here!" I whisper-shriek to no one. Or maybe I'm addressing my anxious vagina. I take two deep breaths and count to three before I open the door.

I'm still not adequately prepared for the vision taking up my front porch.

Darren's in jeans and a long-sleeved shirt—so different than the suit he was wearing the last time I saw him. His short hair is styled neatly, and his hard, icy blue eyes move over me in a casual sweep that I feel everywhere. Darren is intense. He's lightness and darkness fused together. And he's unearthly beautiful. It's a lot to process.

A half-grin tips his mouth and quickly becomes a disarming full smile that transforms his face from severe to stunning for as long as it lasts.

"Hi." It's almost a moan it's so breathy.

"Hello, Charlene."

I have tingles below the waist from those two words.

"Hi." I'm repeating myself. Not smooth.

"I'm a little early," he says. "I hope that's okay."

I snap out of my Darren-induced daze. "Yes! Yeah, of course. Just let me get my purse." I turn, prepared to grab it from the kitchen, when I realize it's already hanging from my right arm. "Oh, never mind. Looks like I'm all set." I hope he doesn't think I'm a complete idiot.

I shrug into my coat with Darren's help—so courteous—grab my keys from the hook, and step out onto the porch. It's a crisp morning, but the sun is shining, so it takes the edge off the chill in the air.

Darren is ultra-polite, opening the passenger door and helping me in before he rounds the hood and takes the driver's seat. We make small talk as we drive toward the water.

I'm a little surprised when Darren pulls into a Starbucks and heads for the drive-thru. This isn't quite what I had in mind when he proposed a coffee date. I figured we'd go to some quaint, cozy little café and stare into each other's eyes.

"I thought we could go to the park."

"Oh, sure. That would be great," I say. Parks can be romantic. Especially since it's kind of chilly today. Maybe he'll have to put his arm around me to keep me warm. I can totally get on board with that.

Once we have our coffees, Darren drives to the water. He parks the SUV, but leaves the engine running. I assume we're going to get out and stroll the boardwalk, but instead we stay where we are and chat while we people-watch. Also not what I was expecting, but he smells great, so I guess I'll take it.

He's a quiet guy, so I end up doing the majority of the talking. Instead of rambling about myself, I regale him with Violet stories, which make him chuckle—a sound I like a lot.

After an hour or so, during which my stomach starts to grumble since I was too nervous to eat this morning, he shifts to face me. He skims my cheek as he sweeps my hair over my shoulder.

I lean into that touch, willing him to lean in, too. And he does. His thumb rests against that soft spot under my chin.

"I would like to kiss you," he says.

"I have coffee breath."

"As do I."

I consider offering him a mint, but decide I don't care. I tip my chin up. "Okay then."

His smile is soft and warm, in stark contrast to his hard features and icy eyes, and his lips feel like silk against mine. I have no idea how long we kiss, but it's enough that my neck starts to get a kink. He finally pulls back, those icy eyes heavy with the same lust that's ruining my underwear.

"Would you like to have lunch with me?"

In my head I turn lunch into extended foreplay, but either way, spending more time with him is on my yes list. "Definitely."

"Great." That smile of his makes another appearance, shorting out all the connections to my brain and redirecting the energy to my lady bits.

He reaches into the backseat and retrieves a messenger bag. He then produces a file folder with my name printed neatly on the front of it. Well, that's kind of . . . odd. Although that seems to be the way this date is going: nice, but odd.

"What's that?" I ask, the lust and excitement I was feeling a few seconds ago transforming into anxiety.

"A non-disclosure agreement," he says breezily, as if he's telling me the name of a flower.

I've signed plenty of non-disclosure agreements during my time at Stroker and Cobb Financial Management. It's necessary when working with famous hockey players and managing their finances. But unless I've read this whole thing incorrectly, Darren isn't going to ask me to manage his finances. At least I hope he's not.

"I'm sorry, why would a non-disclosure agreement be necessary?"

His brow furrows, making the sharp lines of his face even more severe and slightly ominous. "Because I'd like to have lunch with you."

I surreptitiously place my hand on the armrest, near the door handle. Just in case. "You need a non-disclosure agreement for lunch?"

He runs his hands down his thighs. "I'd like to take you to my house."

"For lunch?"

"Yes."

"Is *lunch* code for something?"

I get more of his furrowed brow. "Code?"

Maybe the rumors about him are true. Maybe he really is some kind of Dom and he's looking for me to be his next submissive. I'm not sure how to feel about that. I've read all the Fifty Shades books, and sure, some of that stuff sounds like a fun time, but I don't like to sign contracts for anything outside of work and banking. Even then, it makes me uncomfortable.

"Yeah, like, is *lunch* a code word for some kinky sex games or something?"

His furrow turns into an arch, and a slightly sinister smile tugs at the corner of his sinfully sexy mouth. The same mouth that was recently suctioned to mine.

"No. Although I'm certainly not opposed to kinky sex games if that's what you'd prefer in lieu of lunch."

I pick up the folder, which he's left on the dash between us and flip it open. The agreement is several pages long.

I glance at Darren and raise my own eyebrows.

"Take your time. I can wait." He smiles again, but it seems more like a grimace.

I scan the contents. It's incredibly thorough, with a whole bunch of clauses. There's even one pertaining to a credit card and a budget for clothing and lingerie. *What in the actual fuck?*

I close the file folder and pass it to him. "I'd like you to take me home."

He grins widely and produces a pen. His smile is so pretty I almost forget why I want to go home. Then I remember the pre-date paperwork.

I hold up a hand. "No, you're not understanding. I'd like you to take me to my house, not yours. I'm not signing an NDA agreement for a lunch date—especially this type of NDA."

That smile of his drops, and he blinks rapidly, fingers tapping against the manila file folder. "But I thought we were enjoying each other's company."

"We were. But there's no fucking way I'm signing this, so if you want to have lunch with me, you'll have to do it without an NDA."

He's clearly experiencing some conflict over this because he stares at me long enough that my skin grows hot before he finally says, "It's meant to protect us both."

"It's not a condom, Darren. It's an NDA. The next thing I know I'll have some kind of tracking chip and I'll be tied to your bed."

He tips his head to the side and seems to be fighting a smile. "Would you like to be tied to my bed?"

"Not if I have to sign an NDA."

"And if you don't have to sign an NDA?"

The answer to that question is still *no*, I think, but I shrug, because even him asking makes things happen in my panties.

"I'm a very private person, Charlene."

"So am I. Doesn't mean I make all the people in my life sign an NDA because of it. If you want to have lunch with me, you can do it without asking me to sign away my rights."

He regards me for several long, intense moments in which I have to fight to hold eye contact. Jesus, I'm nervous.

"Okay, no NDA," he finally concedes. "But I have rules for dating, Charlene."

"So do I, and we can discuss them over lunch."

chapter one

Miscommunication

Darren
Two years later

WE ARRIVE AT MY HOUSE, TWO HUGE VEHICLES FILLING UP THE DRIVEWAY. Normally, we'd go to Alex's house after practice (my best friend and teammate), but his wife, Violet, is working from home today, and he doesn't want us to pose a distraction. My place is the second closest to the rink, and I don't live with anyone, so I'm the default.

My house is a modern build with solar panels and floor-to-ceiling sound-proof windows you can see out of but not into, because I like my privacy. I also like having sex with my girlfriend against the ones that overlook the front lawn.

Our teammates, Lance, Randy, Miller, and Rookie, pile out of Lance's Hummer while I grab my stuff from the trunk of Alex's muscle car. I key in the code, and they follow me into the foyer, where I dump my hockey bag.

"I'll grab some beers, and we can head out back."

It's early April, but the weather has been unusually warm, so at least we can get some fresh air while we discuss the impending expansion draft. Vegas is starting a new team, which means they'll be cherry picking a player from every established team in the league. So far, only Alex and Randy are safe from the draft with their no-trade clauses.

I stop short and breathe a curse when I reach the living room. My erection is nearly instantaneous. It's also very confused because I shouldn't be seeing what I'm seeing.

"Holy shit," Alex says from my right.

"What the fuck?" Randy bumps into me from behind.

"I *knew* you were into some kinky shit!" Lance's thick Scottish accent makes me acutely aware that what's supposed to be for my eyes only is *not*. I consider, very briefly, the ramifications of scooping out my teammates' eyes with a melon baller. I decide it's in my best interest not to act on that impulse. I don't think prison suits me, and it's hard to play hockey without eyeballs.

A low whistle comes from my right. I glance over to find Rookie blinking rapidly, his bewilderment apparent. "Dude, are you having some kind of fucked-up party? 'Cause if you are, I might want to get back on the bunny train for a night."

Randy smacks him across the back of the head. "That's not a bunny, asshole."

He's referring to puck bunnies, the groupies of the hockey world.

"Ow! Fuck!" Rookie rubs the spot.

In the middle of the room, halfway between kneeling and standing, is Charlene. My girlfriend. Naked. Well, apart from her pearl necklace and a pair of fuck-me heels. Her gorgeous hazel eyes are deer-in-the-headlights wide as they meet mine, and then they dart down to her naked form. Seeming uncertain how to proceed, she stumbles a few steps and drops back to her knees on the pillow. She bars one arm across her chest, the other moving to shield the apex of her thighs.

Rookie seems unable to process the scene with anything but stupidity. "Is that a ball gag? Who the fuck wears that mask? How do you even breathe with that on?"

"Shut it, Rook," Miller says.

I hadn't even noticed everything else. But I pull my gaze from Charlene and look at the items littering my living room. This is pretty damn far from ideal.

"Everybody out," I snap as I cross the room, nab the throw from the reading chair—*Charlene's* reading chair—and step over the dragon dick dildo Charlene purchased when she was in her *Game of Thrones* phase. I drape the blanket around her, which sends some of the light, lacy pieces of lingerie fluttering across the floor. But the blanket does the job, hiding every inch of bare skin covered in goose bumps.

That my teammates have now seen.

I grit my teeth against the possessive anger and exhale a slow breath, trying to find some calm.

Here's the thing, finding Charlene mostly naked in any given room in my house is not necessarily out of the ordinary.

Even the selection of lingerie arranged in a very neat circle around her—everything from virginal satin to a studded leather corset—isn't particularly unusual. Charlene enjoys dressing up, and her choices often tell me a lot about what she'd like to have happen in the bedroom—or whichever room we're having sex in—and prove helpful in allowing me to gauge her expectations. Leather often indicates she's feeling feisty. It's cute when she thinks she wants to be in charge.

What *is* highly atypical is the second circle, which consists of a wide variety of assistive pleasure devices, many of which have been on Charlene's *I think I might want to try that eventually* list. It's a long list. Almost as long as her *I thought it would be fun but I changed my mind* list.

Charlene and I have been extraordinarily careful about keeping what she feels is our *sometimes colorful* sex life private. What happens behind closed doors should remain behind closed doors, as far as I'm concerned. It's the reason I've always insisted on an NDA—until Charlene, anyway. Not particularly romantic or enticing when starting a new relationship, but my privacy has always taken precedence.

In lieu of signing a non-disclosure agreement, Charlene promised not to discuss our details with her girlfriends. Those women love to share, especially her best friend, Violet, and I have a feeling they might not fully understand the complexities of our relationship, since sometimes even I struggle with that.

"I'm sorry," Charlene's voice shakes along with her hands as she clutches the ends of the throw.

"Stay here, please." I bend and press a kiss to the top of her head, hoping the simple gesture helps dispel some of her anxiety.

Her bottom lip trembles. "Okay."

I want to assure her my dark mood isn't directed at her, but I need to deal with my teammates before they run their mouths to someone besides each other, like their girlfriends or wives. This is why relationships are tricky. I may trust Charlene to maintain our privacy, but I can't be sure anyone else will—especially when we live in a world where people like to color inside the lines, and Charlene believes she likes to scribble in all the margins, when really she likes to get close to the margins and then run away from them.

I step over the sex toys, noting exactly how many are from her *I thought it would be fun but I changed my mind* box. Apparently she had big plans. I wasn't expecting her until much later, as she'd messaged earlier to let me know she had to work late. She must have rearranged her schedule to accommodate me.

I drag a hand down my face and follow my teammates outside as they head for their respective vehicles.

"Wait." It's more bark than word.

They turn as a collective, expressions ranging from curious to downright disturbed. I need to do triage and smooth this over. I slip my hands into my pockets, conscious to remain calm on the outside, unaffected. I think it's pointless to tell them it isn't what it looks like, because it honestly is exactly what it looks like, just not quite the way they think.

Instead I go with, "It would be ideal if we could all keep this between us."

"And you all think *I'm* fucked in the head? What the fuck is wrong with *you*?" Lance waves a hand in the air as I open my mouth to speak. "Never mind. I don't want to know." He spins around and stalks to his Hummer. "I'm out."

"It's really not . . ." I don't know how to finish that sentence without compromising Charlene more than she already has been, so I don't.

"We'll talk to Lance. You don't have to worry about him saying anything." Miller thumbs over his shoulder and then motions between himself and Randy.

Randy lifts a finger, looking like he has something to add, but he stops and strokes his beard, gives me a nod, and follows Miller to the Hummer. Of all the guys, Randy is probably the least likely to get on my ass about this. Last month he and Lily did five grand in damage to a hotel bathroom when they ripped the sink off the wall during one of their own sexy funtimes and flooded the room.

"I always thought you were so . . . normal." Rookie rushes after them. He doesn't even have the door closed before Lance starts backing up.

Alex is the only one left. We watch Lance's Hummer peel out of the driveway.

"What was that about?" I ask.

Alex glances at me, his expression flat, lips mashed into a line. "I don't know."

I don't like the way he's looking at me, like he doesn't know me. And in some ways, he doesn't. He only knows the sides of me I let him see. And now he's seen one that's not easy to explain.

"Let Charlene talk to Violet, please."

He huffs out a small laugh and shakes his head. "What Charlene tells Vi isn't your problem right now, Darren."

"It's not what it lo—" I stop, because it's pointless to say that. "It's complicated."

"Well, it just got a fuckload more complicated." He runs a hand through his hair. "I'm gonna see if I can catch up with the guys and make sure they keep this to themselves, maybe find out what's got Lance so riled."

"I should come with you."

I take a step toward his car, but Alex slaps a palm against my chest. He gives me a look, somewhere between disbelief and disgust. "Are you fucking serious right now? You can't leave Charlene in there on her own after that. Where are your priorities? Manage your relationship, Darren, or whatever the hell it is."

He's right. Of course. But what he doesn't understand is that Charlene is my priority, and making sure the guys keep their mouths shut is more about her than it is about me.

chapter two

Oh, No.

Charlene

WELL, THIS CERTAINLY DIDN'T GO AS PLANNED. I HAD GREAT INTENTIONS when I came here today. Violet is the one who made the suggestion. Well, she didn't suggest I surround myself with weird sex toys and hang out naked in Darren's living room. She thought it would be a good idea for me to be here when he arrived home so I could offer to relieve some of his stress. With sex.

I glance around at the sex wheel of fortune. Individually, the toys might not be that shocking—except maybe the dragon dildo, the crotchless black latex bodysuit, and possibly the mask that looks like it belongs to the lizard man or something—okay, maybe it's a bit more shocking than I originally thought. On a scale of one to ten, I would classify this as an eleventy-billion of epic clusterfuck.

Playoffs begin in a few short days, which is both exciting and stressful. Chicago has had a great season and is in a good position points-wise. But the excitement over making it into the playoffs this year is dampened by the looming expansion draft.

Today they had a team meeting about it, and Darren doesn't have a no-trade clause like Alex, so he must be worried. I know I am. It doesn't matter that he's older than a lot of his teammates; his stats are great—better than they were last year, which puts him at risk. Especially since the owner of the expansion team has been interested in Darren before.

So I came up with an awesome plan to surprise him. Or it would've been awesome if he hadn't brought half his team home with him. I'd wanted to provide all the best distractions for Darren tonight in the form of every single sex toy and apparatus he's ever seemed remotely interested in. In hindsight, my choices might have been a little over the top.

I clutch the blanket Darren draped around my shoulders and stare at the empty space where his teammates—our friends—stood moments ago. The front door closes with a slam. I jolt and clench below the waist, as if it's echoed in my clit.

Which it kind of is. Whenever I get anxious, I feel it in my vagina, like my clit is the Grand Central Station for my nervousness. It's rather inconvenient, and it can be embarrassing. It's also not a normal reaction to stress. I know this, but there's nothing I can do to stop it.

I finger the pearls at my throat, their smooth surface strangely calming as I debate whether I should clean up the kinky evidence, or wait for Darren as he requested. Another wave of anxiety slaps me right between the thighs. My eyes roll up, and I exhale a shuddery breath.

I don't have a chance to make a decision about putting away the sex toys, because the front door opens and closes—much more gently this time. Darren appears at the threshold of the living room a few moments later.

"I didn't think you'd be by until later," he says, low and even, despite the dark look he's wearing.

I swallow thickly as he approaches, my body lighting up like an arcade game. A bead of sweat trickles down my spine and I shiver, clutching the blanket tighter.

"I wanted to surprise you. I thought it would be okay since the guys never come here. I'm so sorry."

"You've already apologized." He steps over the dragon dick again—it's ridiculously huge, and not at all useful—and skirts a pale lace teddy until he's standing in front of me. His rough finger rests gently under my chin, and he tips my head up. His expression is intense, as is typical of Darren. "And you're certainly a surprise."

Instinctively, I want to issue yet another apology. My lips part of their own volition, and Darren tilts his head ever so slightly. It feels like a warning. I have to remind myself to breathe. Shadows dance across his face, sharpening the angles and making them more severe. He's terrifyingly beautiful. Quietly stunning.

He caresses my cheek, the touch so gentle it's entirely possible I imagine it. "We need to talk about how this changes things." He holds out his hand. "And I would prefer if you weren't on your knees for this discussion."

My panic takes over, and the worst possibilities bubble up in my head. The weight of his words feel like anchors wrapped around my heart. The only thing Darren has ever asked of me is to keep our private life private, and now it isn't anymore.

I slip my shaking, clammy fingers into his warm palm. I'm stiff from kneeling for so long, and I wobble unsteadily as Darren helps me to my feet.

The uneasiness that's settled low in my belly flares and claws its way up, twisting through my stomach, into my chest, until it clamps around my throat. My pearls feel too tight and not tight enough.

What have I done? What if he breaks up with me over this?

My lashes wet with each frantic attempt to blink back the tears. All it took was one mistake to unravel two years. I feel as though I've tried to build a house of cards on the precipice of a mountain.

"It was an accident." The words crack like shattering glass.

"I'm aware it was unintentional." Darren frowns. "Why are you crying?"

"I broke a promise."

He inclines his head—it's more acknowledgement than it is agreement. "And what do you think that means?"

I lick my lips, my mouth dry, palms sweaty. "That you're going to . . ."

"I'm going to?" he prompts.

The words stick in my throat, like I've tried to swallow a pill without water. "I shouldn't have listened to Violet. I should've messaged you first. I didn't think. I-I-I—"

"Charlene, stop." He places his wet thumb against my lips, and I taste my own sadness.

Darren takes my face in his palms. I memorize the feel of his fingers sliding along the edge of my jaw, consider what the absence of his touch will be like. Remember how the fear that Darren could be traded at the end of the season has plagued me all day.

I brace myself as he tips my head up. "Look at me."

I have no choice but to comply. I try to stop my chin from quivering, but I'm too unnerved to manage my emotions.

He sweeps his thumbs under my eyes as new tears free themselves. "Do you think I'm angry with you?"

"I don't know."

"Then what are you so upset about?"

Now it's my turn to frown. "I-I—" I have to take several deep breaths to calm down and organize my thoughts. "You didn't want anyone to know." I motion to the lingerie and surrounding sex toys. "And now they do. So I thought maybe . . . it might mean that you'd—"

He waits for me to go on.

"End this." The words barely carry.

"End this?" His expression shifts to confusion.

"Us. End . . . us." My stomach churns at the thought. Losing Darren would mean giving up a lot more than a boyfriend. He's connected to almost every single important person in my entire world.

His eyes flare. "Do you honestly believe I would walk away from you over something so trite?" His jaw tics. "Have I ever been that rash in my decision making?"

"No, but—" I bite my lip and drop my gaze. It's hard to look at him when he's this intense. His severe beauty is more than I can handle sometimes.

"Is it unfortunate? Yes. Will it create unpleasant questions? Most likely, yes." He traces the contour of my eyebrow, sweeping along my temple. "Help me understand what's happening in this beautiful head that would make you come to such an extreme conclusion."

"I just thought, I don't know. I broke a promise. The *only* promise. I guess in my head it's the same as if I'd gone back on an NDA."

I've taken great pride in my ability to keep our private life private. Well, I mean, obviously I talk to Violet about the things I can, but I never tell her what *really* happens behind closed doors.

"Did you happen to write an exposé chronicling our sex life in an attempt to blackmail me in addition to this?" He makes a sweeping motion to encompass the circle of toys and lingerie.

"No, I just gave all of your closest friends a very vivid peek into what we do when no one else is watching." Now that I'm not quite so worried about Darren breaking up with me, embarrassment is setting in.

His cheek tics, not with a smile exactly, but a hint of mischievous humor makes his eyes glint. "I'm sure they're having a very interesting conversation about it at this precise moment. And I'm even more certain questions will follow for both of us, which is why we need to discuss how this changes things."

"Oh." Wow. I went way overboard with the internal drama on this one.

"Come. You're shaking; you need to sit." He keeps hold of one hand and wraps his other around my waist, guiding me to the couch.

I drop to the cushion and immediately spring back up, face mashing into Darren's chest. His fingers curl around my arms. "Are you okay?"

"Fine. I'm fine." *Shit*. I forgot how thoroughly I prepared for *any* possible scenario this evening, which is saying something about my state of anxiety and might explain why it's been bouncing around in my clit so hard.

"Between the tears and how jumpy you are, I'm going to disagree that you're fine." He smooths a palm down my back. I try to shift away before he reaches my ass, but my calves are pressed against the couch and I'm wearing sky high stilettos—which accounts for the sore ankles—so my coordination is somewhat lacking. I accidently step on the end of the blanket, tugging it free from my grasp, which means I'm once again naked—apart from shoes, and pearls. At least this time there are no other witnesses.

"Maybe I should get dressed before we talk about how to deal with this," my suggestion is super pitchy.

Darren's eyes narrow as I attempt to untangle my heel from the blanket. It's one of those soft, hand knitted ones from a super-cute store downtown. I pointed it out to Darren once when we were out for dinner, and the next time I came over it was draped over the reading chair he bought me last year. The chair doesn't often get used for reading, and the blanket doesn't match Darren's décor, but it's sweet that he bought it for me.

Unfortunately, I'm now caught up in his thoughtfulness. Literally.

"Turn around for me, Charlene." Darren's voice is low, commanding.

My entire body flashes with goose bumps. *Oh shit*. His expression is no longer serious. Instead a dark smile appears briefly. I can't decide right now if that's a good or a bad thing.

I turn slowly, fighting the urge to crane my neck so I can see his face. I shudder as he drags a single knuckle from the top of my spine to my tailbone and then lower. Fanning out his fingers, he skims the pink, fuzzy bunny tail—which is attached to a butt plug that's currently parked in my ass.

"I see you had expectations for tonight," he murmurs.

"No expectations," I breathe.

"I don't think that's true." His lips are at my ear, his fingers spread across the underside of my jaw, palm resting against the base of my throat as his other hand trails along my hip, palm flattening under my navel as his chest comes flush with my back.

His shirt is cotton, soft and warm, his belt buckle is a cold shock resting against my low back. I exhale on a whimper when Darren's fingertips graze the crest of my pubic bone, the heel of his palm pressing firmly against my low belly, his thick erection putting pressure on the plug through the barrier of his jeans.

"I wanted to be prepared for whatever you needed tonight," I whisper.

"Ah, you were being thoughtful, then?"

"I know today was stressful for you." It sure was stressful for me, even more so in the past twenty minutes.

"All this trouble you went to." His teeth graze the sensitive skin at the side of my neck. "It was definitely a stressful day, and you would've been the perfect surprise had circumstances been different."

"I'm sorry." I need to stop saying that.

"Actions always speak so much louder than words, don't they?" His voice is a shadow looming. "Why don't you show me how sorry you are?"

chapter three

Anxiety Orgasms

Darren

It's a good thing Charlene can't see my face right now. It's difficult to not smile, which is the reason I have her in this position. Of all the relationships I've been in—which isn't all that many considering most women aren't excited about signing an NDA before the first date—Charlene is hands down my favorite sexual partner. She's my favorite everything, really.

Her throat bobs with a nervous swallow under my palm. I bite the shell of her ear. "Whatever shall I do with you?"

She stumbles forward a step when I release her. She doesn't turn around, doesn't ask any questions, simply waits for instructions. It looks like she's giving me the reins tonight. I bite my knuckle as I consider the plethora of sex toys and then Charlene. She really is gorgeous, with her long auburn hair piled on top of her head to expose the gentle line of her neck, slender shoulders rolled back, and that pink bunny tail peeking out from between her ass cheeks is just . . . adorably sexy. If there was a sex toy that could encapsulate Charlene's personality, it's that goddamn butt plug.

Here's the thing about Charlene: I know what she wants better than she does. And it sure isn't that fucking mammoth dragon cock sitting in the middle of the living room floor. Charlene has an incredibly wild imagination, and she loves to read every dirty, smutty book she can get her hands on.

She also thinks she wants to try everything, but sometimes she jumps in head first and then realizes what she thought, and what truly is, are not the same. So she'll come at me with the most extreme of extremes, and I've learned from experience and trial and error to feed into it, then dial it all the way back until we're a few shades out from vanilla. That way she's not at risk of having a full-on panic attack over the possibility that I might try something she's not ready for.

It's clear my needs were her priority when she set this up today, which tells me more about her frame of mind than she realizes. Charlene is worried, just as I am, about the expansion draft. I know better than to expect her to say it outright, but her concern is laid out in the offerings surrounding us. What Charlene doesn't understand is that my needs end and begin with only her.

Starting at her shoulder, I drag my finger along her skin, following the contour of the pearl necklace, and slowly circle her.

Her hazel gaze rises to meet mine, lashes fluttering. It's filled with need and uncertainty and desire. My worry is echoed in the parting of her lips, in her shallow breaths and her tiny hum of longing. I want to take her to the edge and hold her there. I want to make her understand that there is no end to us, that I will never willingly walk away from her—not unless that's what she wants.

Charlene is like a firefly, and sometimes that's what I call her. She's elusive, and if you catch her she'll burn bright, but keeping her trapped dulls her fire and dims her beauty.

So I don't trap her. Not for long, anyway. I might enjoy watching her burn for me, but in the end I always set her free. Over and over, I let her fly away, even though it goes against every instinct I have.

So far she always comes back. I keep waiting for that to change, and hoping it won't. The expansion draft could be a potential threat to this thing we have, and it makes me edgy.

I dip down and press my lips to hers, flicking my tongue out to taste her, but not slipping inside as I'm sure she wants. Her lips are like candy, but I taste the salt of her uncertainty, tracked in tears over her cheeks. Charlene stumbles forward, chest meeting mine as she grips my shirt.

I drop one hand to her hip to prevent contact from the waist down, and to help keep her upright. She moans against my lips, the sound sweet and needy. As much as I'd like to deepen this kiss and make it last for hours—and I truly would—she needs to be taken care of. And so do I.

I pull back, stroking her cheek as she whimpers her displeasure. "You should choose something from your circle of sex toys so we can play."

I allow a half-smile to form as I drag a finger from the center of her clavicle, down between her breasts, going lower to circle her navel before I finally dip between her thighs. She sucks in a tremulous breath as I skim past the hood piercing—the one she opted to get during a long stretch of away games. Her legs shake as I brush the inside of her thigh.

"What are you waiting for?" I cup between her legs. "Make a choice, little firefly. Or maybe I should call you little bunny, all considering."

"But I—" Her eyes roll up as I drag my fingertips past her entrance. She's so wet. I can feel myself unraveling—the stress of this day, the possibility of potential loss too much to handle. I need to drown myself in the certainty of her.

"Unless you'd prefer I make it for you."

She exhales a quick breath as I remove my hand from between her legs. I grip her hips to keep her steady and glance to the right. Her eyes follow mine, landing on the ball gag, and dart back to my face.

She tips her chin up, so determined, even though her voice wavers. "I want whatever you want."

I tap the end of her nose and smile darkly. "I guess we'll find out whether that's true or not, won't we?"

Two hours later, Charlene is stretched out along my side, her head resting on my chest. Her manicured nails trace the dips in my abs. When she reaches my navel she circles, the sensation sending a rush of goose flesh over my skin. She flattens her palm and smooths it all the way back up, as if it will erase the imaginary lines she draws on me.

"Keep doing that and you're going to wake the beast," I warn.

She lifts her head, resting her chin on my pec, her wide hazel eyes meeting mine as she drags her finger back down the center of my chest.

Somewhere downstairs a cell phone buzzes across a hard surface.

I grab her hand before she reaches my navel and thread my fingers through hers. "We need to discuss how to handle our friends." I bring her fingers to my lips, kissing the tips of each so she doesn't take it as rejection.

"I'm spending tomorrow afternoon with Violet and the girls."

"Which means you'll be fielding questions, I'm sure." I understand that asking the guys not to say anything excludes their significant others. Charlene is always the exception to every rule, it seems. I'm aware it's no different for my friends, hence the reason I asked Alex to allow Charlene a chance to talk to Violet—I'm not sure that was a reasonable demand, considering.

Charlene chews on the inside of her lip. "What should I tell them?"

"What do you want to tell them?"

She lifts a shoulder. "I don't know. I mean, it's not like we're superfreaks or anything."

I fight a smile. We're far from superfreaks, although Charlene's collection of toys, outfits, and props would lead some to believe otherwise. "So maybe that's what you tell them."

"Violet might be upset."

"Why?" Violet doesn't strike me as judgmental. From what I understand, she likes to dress up Alex's cock as a super hero, which is fucking weird. But then Alex is also a little off center, so there's that.

"Because she's always been open with me, and I haven't been the same with her. I sort of let her come to her own conclusions. I let all the girls come to their own conclusions, but now they're going to have all these ideas. It's one thing for them to speculate when there was no evidence to support it, but this is different. It was kind of fun to keep them guessing, and I never figured they would take me seriously. Now they'll want to know what's really going on."

I trail my fingers down her spine, enjoying her shiver. "I can take the blame for all the secrecy."

"I like the secrecy. I liked that what we had was just ours." Charlene murmurs, eyes on my chin. "I just don't want Violet to be hurt."

"And you're worried about that?" I prompt.

"It'll be fine. She'll be fine," she says, possibly as much to herself as to me.

"You're sure?" I don't understand why Violet would be hurt, but then she's a woman, and sometimes I don't understand their reactions to things. Even Charlene, who I can read fairly well most of the time, has odd reactions on occasion.

She nods pensively. "I mean, I guess the most awkward part is that all my girlfriends' significant others have seen me naked. But it could be worse, right? At least it wasn't the whole team."

Charlene is referencing the time Alex and Violet were caught fucking in the locker room. Alex had been ejected from the game for beating the shit out of a Toronto player. The guy had been taunting him, so it was somewhat understandable. The entire team walked into the locker room as a woman was screaming her way through an orgasm. That woman turned out to be Violet, now his wife.

All I saw were her legs wrapped around his waist.

In this case, all of our closest friends have seen Charlene's pierced nipples, so it's a little different, but I'd prefer to lessen her anxiety over this, rather than make it worse, so I don't point that out. "Fortunately it was only a few of the guys."

"What're you going to tell them?"

I lift a shoulder. "I don't have plans to tell them anything."

"But won't they ask questions?"

It's my turn to shrug. "They can ask, doesn't mean I'm going to answer."

"But you can't tell them nothing."

I don't understand her sudden panic. "Is there something you want me to tell them?"

"No. I don't know. Just . . . all that stuff in the living room sort of paints its own picture, doesn't it?"

"And that concerns you?"

"They're going to think you use all that stuff on me."

"You're the one who surrounded yourself with it."

"It was all stuff I thought you might be interested in," she mumbles.

"Ah, now the truth comes out, but I'll keep that little detail to myself, if that's what you prefer." I untwine our hands and hook her leg over my hip. "We can discuss details later, over dinner. Right now I have plans to fill you up again."

chapter four

Girls Be Gossiping

Charlene

Ever have one of those dreams where you know it's not real but you can't seem to pull yourself out of it? It happens to me all the time. I have this recurring nightmare where I'm locked in an RV and there's no way out. The RV gets smaller and smaller, like I'm Alice in Wonderland and I've eaten the wrong thing. I'm growing, growing, growing while everything else is shrinking, shrinking, shrinking.

I wake up and instantly go into panic mode because I can't move. It takes me several blinks and just as many seconds to realize I'm not in my bedroom, I'm in Darren's, and it's him I'm trapped under. Well, I'm not exactly under him, but he's wrapped completely around me, which is . . . abnormal.

Usually Darren sleeps like Dracula, on his back with his arms crossed over his chest, and I starfish on the other side of the bed. But not today. Today we're spooning.

I try to slip out from under his arm, but it tightens around me. "Oh no you don't." His voice is gravelly in my ear, and his lips brush my neck. "I'm taking full advantage of the fact that you being here means I don't have to rub one out in the shower."

"I'm so glad I can be helpful."

He smiles against my shoulder. "Tools are helpful, Charlene. You in my bed this morning is a treat."

My heart flutters at his words and the warmth of his lips on my skin. That fluttery feeling echoes through my body as his palm glides down my stomach.

"And I plan to enjoy you as I would the most decadent dessert," he whispers in my ear before he bites the lobe.

By the time we're done I've had two more orgasms, which Darren happily adds to his running tally. He quite literally keeps track of my orgasms, like they're part of our sex stats.

I curl up against his side, blissed out enough that my brain and my mouth are on a disconnect, so I ask a question I'm not so sure I want the answer to. "Did you find anything out about the expansion draft?"

"Just that Alex and Randy are safe. The rest is up in the air until they announce the other players they want to hold on to."

"Do you think you'll be one of them?"

He runs his fingers through my tangled hair. "It's hard to say. At thirty-four I'm closer to the end of my career than I am to the beginning, but that doesn't necessarily mean anything."

"Because the Vegas team owner has a hard-on over you?"

Darren sighs. "Yeah. Here's hoping he doesn't throw away one of his picks on me, but if he does, I guess I spend a year in Vegas playing like shit so they don't renew my contract."

I don't know whether he's intentionally left me out of the equation or not.

He checks the clock on the nightstand. "Fuck. I didn't realize it was so late. I need to go. I have practice in half an hour."

I regret bringing up the expansion draft when we don't have time to really talk about it. He rushes to get dressed and gives me a quick peck on the lips as he shoves his wallet and phone in his back pocket.

"Your face smells like my pussy!" I shout as he rushes out of the bedroom.

"It's my favorite cologne," he calls back.

I expect to hear the door slam shut, but instead he pounds his way back up the stairs. He appears in the doorway, expression unreadable as he tosses my phone on the bed and then climbs up after it. "You have a thousand messages from Violet. She'd like to know if you're being kept in my lair and if so, do you have a cage, or are you allowed to sleep in my bed." He straddles me, eyes dark as he leans down, fingers sliding into my hair at the nape of my neck. His lips ghost over mine. "Feel free to answer that however you like."

I wait to see what he's going to do. Apart from a few brushings of lips and teasing of tongues, there wasn't much kissing last night. Our mouths were too busy on other things.

He sucks my bottom lip between his and then his tongue flicks out, stroking along the roof of my mouth, causing me to jerk and flail. He pulls back, eyes searching my face as one side of his mouth twists in a malevolent smile. "Change the setting on your phone so there's no preview of the messages, Charlene. Unless you want me and the rest of the world to know the content of your conversations with Violet."

With that he releases me. I flop back down on the mattress as he gracefully rolls off the bed. He pauses at the door. "Next time I'll kiss you for hours before I let you come."

And with that, he disappears down the hall. I cover my mouth with my palm and smile behind it. I don't care if our relationship is weird; I wouldn't trade it for all the normals in the world.

I pick up my phone and key in my password. Darren wasn't lying. I have a million and one messages from Violet. Half of them are gifs of the Fifty Shades movies. Most of them feature Christian Grey half naked, so I get distracted by the pretty as I scroll back through them. They stopped from midnight until eight this morning, and then started up again. The most recent ones are requests for proof of life.

I'm about to take a selfie, but then I realize I look like I could be a kidnapping victim with how messed up my hair is, so instead I search the internet for pictures of sex dungeons and send that to her instead.

I love Violet, and she knows more about me than anyone else in this world—except maybe my mother, and in some ways, Darren. But after my mom and I left The Ranch when I was a teenager, it was drilled into me to gloss over personal details. The less I share, the easier it is to keep myself and the people around me protected from my past. It's part of the reason Darren and I work so well. We're both private people when it comes to our pasts, and that makes him safe in a way a lot of other people are not.

Almost as soon as I hit send, my phone rings. "You do realize Darren and I have been dating for two years. I think you'd know by now if he chained me up and kept me in a cage," I say by way of greeting.

"Alex said the living room looked like a BDSM porn set."

"It was just a few toys and some lingerie." I'm downplaying it, by a lot, but Violet is prone to exaggeration, and those two are pretty vanilla—apart from the costumes she makes for Alex's penis, anyway.

"Lies. Go wash Darren's pearl necklace off your chest and get your ass in your car. I need to know exactly how much you've been keeping from me so I know how angry I'm supposed to pretend to be when the rest of the girls get here. Oh, and pick me up a dairy-free latte on the way over." With that she hangs up.

I'm relieved that she doesn't seem nearly as upset as I expected. I take a quick shower, not because there's jizz on my chest—although there might be some in my hair—but because there was a lot of sweating between last night and this morning, and I'm a little ripe. I also smell like I bathed in sex perfume.

I put on my dress from yesterday since my bag with extra clothes is still in the car. I have an extra outfit or two in the trunk of my car at all times. And an emergency escape kit, just in case. I think it might be a PTSD thing from the whole fleeing The Ranch when I was a teenager, but I'm not willing to unload it on a therapist, so all I can do is hypothesize.

For years after we left, my mom and I always had a bag of essentials packed: three changes of clothes, hair dye, toiletries, Miss Flopsy (I will love that stuffed bunny forever), five thousand dollars in cash—obviously small bills, a burner phone and new identification, and a few other essentials. Was it overkill? Probably. But then my mom isn't playing with a full deck. She's missing pretty much every face card there is. But I still love her.

I'm on my way downstairs when I hear a code being punched into the front door. I freeze on the stairs. It can't be Darren coming back; he has practice. The front door opens, and the warning alarm beeps.

"Mr. Westinghouse! It's Gertrude. I am here for the housekeeping!"

I let out a relieved sigh. Gertrude has been Darren's housekeeper for years. I take the rest of the stairs at a light jog, my calves tight from last night's awkward, but fun, sex positions. Gertrude appears in the hallway as I reach the bottom of the stairs.

Now here's something interesting about my relationship with Darren: we don't have a lot of sleepovers. He's a light sleeper, and I'm a flailer, so I feel bad when I wake him up with my acrobatics routine in the middle of the night—at least this is the excuse I usually give him.

I mean, I do feel bad when I accidentally elbow him in the face, and once I charlie-horsed him with my knee, but sleeping beside someone else is . . . strange. You really need to trust someone to be unconscious next to them for a lot of hours in a row. Waking up the way I did this morning, with Darren wrapped around me, makes me feel vulnerable, and also protected, which doesn't make a lot of sense, but there it is.

"Hey, Trudes!"

Gertrude startles and nearly drops her cleaning gear. "Oh! Miss Hoar! I am sorry to surprise you!" She looks past me, up the stairs. "I can come back later if now is a bad time."

I wish she would just call me Charlene. She always forgets the H in my last name—Hoar—is silent. "You're good," I sigh. "Darren's at the arena, and I'm on my way out."

She smiles, looking a little relieved. I don't think she likes cleaning when Darren's home. He makes her nervous. He makes a lot of people nervous because he's so quiet and intense, sometimes even me. But it's the good kind of nervous.

"I will get started right away then." She heads for the living room. Two seconds later, she shrieks.

I rush to find out what happened and cringe. The remains of the kinky sex toy wheel of fortune are still scattered around the living room. The dragon dick stands majestically in the middle of it all, right beside the ball gag and the latex body suit. I don't know what I was thinking when I pulled all that stuff out yesterday, other than I wanted to erase my fear and make Darren happy.

I scramble for a reason all of this stuff to be here. "I'm so sorry! We had a party last night."

She glances at me with wide, horrified eyes.

"I mean with my girlfriends."

Now she looks downright disturbed.

"Shite McCockslap," I mutter. "It was a joke. One of my girlfriends is getting married, and we had one of those bachelorette sex toy parties, but the host brought all this stuff. Crazy, right? I'll just put it all away for you." I put my hand on her shoulder and turn her away from the sex prop trainwreck. "You can start in the kitchen."

She nods mutely, lids fluttering as she fans her face with her feather duster. I snap a photo of the living room before I put everything away. Darren has more than one special trunk in his walk-in closet, complete with padlocks, where we store all the toys for exactly this reason.

Gertrude is in the kitchen with her cell phone plastered to her ear, speaking in German, since that happens to be her mother tongue. I lean casually against the doorjamb, don an icy smile, and clear my throat. She startles, again, and drops her phone on the floor.

"Oh! Miss Hoar! I did not realize you were still here." She bends to pick up the phone, says something into the receiver, and ends the call.

"I'm on my way out now." I tip my head to the side, exactly the way Darren does when he's measuring his words. "I think now might be a good time to remind you of the NDA you've signed and how it pertains to all facets of Darren's life within these walls."

Her eyes flare until I fear she'll be unable to blink ever again. "Of course, Miss Hoar. I will not breathe a word of your sex party to anyone."

"Bachelorette party. Have a lovely day, Trudes."

I spin on my heel and sashay to the garage, where my car is parked. I waffle for a moment over what I should do about the Trudes situation.

I don't typically text Darren directly after a sleepover. I don't ever want to appear clingy, so I try to wait until he messages me, but it isn't easy. By the twenty-four-hour mark, my anxiety gets pretty bad, and no amount of marble rolling seems to calm it down.

I decide it's in my best interest to let Darren know what Trudes saw this morning. I send him the picture of the living room pre-cleanup, along with a message to check his voicemail. Then I leave him a voicemail and fill him in on Gertrude, suggesting he call and remind her of the NDA himself, because he's a fuckton scarier than I am.

I stop on the way over to Violet's, pick up coffees for us, and order myself a breakfast sandwich, which I scarf down in less than a minute. I'm always super hungry after a night with Darren. It's better than a boot camp workout, that's for sure.

I pull into Violet's driveway and take a deep breath, aware that I'm walking into a conversation that's going to be awkward, especially with Violet.

The door opens before I can even knock. "Took you long enough. Did you have to free yourself from Darren's elaborate restraint system to get here?"

I pass her the dairy-free latte. "Haha. There was a line at Starfucks."

She checks the label before she takes a sip, since there have been occasions when they've gotten the order wrong and Violet has paid the price for consuming dairy. She arches a brow at me over the lip of her cup, moaning her latte love.

"Thanks for this. Now get in here and give me some details."

I follow her down the hall to the kitchen, where a pile of takeout bags sit unopened on the counter. Violet doesn't cook, which is a good thing because she's horrible at it. She and Alex would starve to death if she were in charge of meals.

She plunks down on a chair and slaps the counter. "Well?"

"Well what?" I'm not going to make this easy for her.

Darren suggested I tell the girls whatever I damn well please, but I don't know how much I want to share. I've enjoyed how private our relationship has been up until now. Darren definitely has a commanding presence, so it's not hard to imagine that extending beyond his performance on the ice.

"Alex said there was a ball gag, and some weird latex stuff, and a fucked-up giant dildo, or butt plug—he wasn't sure. I hope you're happy with yourself because thanks to you, Alex spent an hour on some online sex toy shop and asked me fifty times if I wanted an anal training set." She taps the counter with her manicured nails.

"You're going to need a hell of a lot more than an anal training set to get that dick in your ass," I scoff.

I've accidentally seen Alex's hard-on—through the barrier of boxer shorts, but still. It was enough to know Violet isn't exaggerating his size. Darren is well-endowed, above the national average for sure, but Alex's dick is terrifying. I have no idea how Violet walks without crying most days.

"No shit." Violet wrinkles her nose. "Anyway, Alex's Area 51 mission aside, I'm kind of pissed at you. I can't believe you've kept this from me all this time."

I sigh. This is what I was worried about. "There really isn't anything to tell."

"Uh, pretty sure that's a lie with all the freaky deaky Alex saw. Clearly there's a lot more to it than Darren jizzing on your chest and getting into your Access Denied hole."

"I promised Darren I wouldn't say anything."

She frowns. "But I'm your best friend. Those promises don't apply to me."

I give her an apologetic smile. It's not fair to use Darren as a copout. "Darren is private about this kind of thing, and so am I."

"But we always talked about boyfriend stuff before Darren."

"Before Darren it was different. I didn't want to risk him getting asked questions by anyone, so . . ."

"I wouldn't have said anything if you'd told me not to."

I give her a look. "Not even Alex?"

She starts to speak but makes a face. "Okay, you have a point. I'd probably tell Alex because husbands fit under the same cone. Alex was pretty freaked out last night. I mean, those guys have been besties for as long as you and I have been besties, and he had no clue Darren was such a kinky fucker. We thought you might be a little off-side, but not all the way out in left field."

"It looked a lot more extreme than it is," I offer. "Most of it is the stuff my mom sends me from all her dominatrix conventions, and the majority of it I haven't even considered trying out. I guess I went a little overboard yesterday."

"Well, that's going to take all the fun out of the kink inquisition."

"Kink inquisition?"

"Yeah, the girls are freaking out over this. They started a group chat last night asking me all sorts of questions. I didn't pull you in because I figured you didn't want to be bombarded with text messages, and you were probably busy with Darren, doing whatever." She crosses over to the fridge and produces a couple of bottles. She holds out the champagne. "Pre-inquisition mimosa?"

"That's probably a good idea."

"I figured."

She hands me a glass and pours herself some sparkling grape juice since she and Alex are actively trying to get her knocked up, and she doesn't want to drink until or unless she gets her period. Then the doorbell chimes. I exhale a nervous breath. This is probably going to be uncomfortable, but if I can deal with wearing a butt plug for several hours, I'm pretty sure I can handle a few questions and dispel some misconceptions.

Sunny, Lily, and Poppy appear in the kitchen a minute later. It's awkward times a million. Especially since the first thing out of my mouth is, "Sorry all your significant others saw me naked yesterday."

"Everyone except Lance has heard me come," Violet says, because she's my best friend and is happy to offset my humiliation with her own.

"Um, Lance has heard you come, Violet, and so have the rest of us," Poppy, Lance's fiancée, says quietly.

Her face turns the color of her name. She's so stinking cute. It's amazing that someone so sweet could end up with one of the most volatile players in the league, who was also dubbed a notorious womanizer—although the media likes to twist things around. And from what I know, Lance is actually a little broken, kind of like me and Darren both seem to be. His childhood wasn't the best either.

Violet looks confused. "Since when?"

"When we went to the cottage over winter break and you and Alex had sex in the outdoor shower," Lily replies when Poppy doesn't respond right away.

"Ooooh, right. Lesson learned on that one, I guess."

"And only Darren and Miller haven't seen me naked, so don't feel too bad." Lily gives me a side hug.

"Wait, what?" Poppy suddenly looks like she's ready to go a round. As sweet as she is, she's a massage therapist, so she's strong, and dating Lance means she has to have a backbone of steel. She also has a fiery personality to match her hair.

"It was an accident. Randy came home from an away series, and I answered the door wearing a bow like a necklace. I didn't know Lance was with him until it was too late," Lily explains.

"And Alex saw her naked when she was six, so that doesn't really count," Violet adds.

"Oh. Right." That seems to calm Poppy down.

"My boob popped out when I was breastfeeding Logan at a team BBQ last summer." Sunny pats her little baby bump. "But only Miller saw, so I guess that's not the same."

"It's a good one, though." Violet claps her hands. "Okay. Who needs a drink before the sex-quisition?"

"The what?" Sunny asks.

"The sex-quisition. The sex inquisition. I'm sure everyone has questions for Charlene after last night. I figured nothing goes better with uncomfortable questions about our sex lives than booze! Sunny, I have dealcoholized champagne for us. It basically tastes like fizzy grape juice, but we can drink it out of fun glasses and pretend we're getting drunk, too."

Sunny shrugs. "I don't need to pretend to be drunk, but I like fizzy grape juice."

Violet serves everyone drinks, and we all head to the living room. This whole thing makes me nervous. I mean, they're all my friends and we're all pretty open with each other, but with all the focus on me, I realize that *they're* open, while I've spent the past two years saying little about my sex life. I wish we could go back to the way it was before all my secrets were spilled out with the dragon-shaped plastic schlong.

I root around in my purse for one of my candies and pop it into my mouth. I need all the calm I can get. I don't care that the candy is going to make my mimosa taste like crap.

"I have a question." Lily drops into the chair parallel to mine.

"Oh, I bet you do." Violet grins.

"Randy wants to know where you go lingerie shopping."

That seems to break the tension a little. "Depends on what I'm shopping for, but I can give you a list of places."

"Or maybe we can go together," Lily says.

Poppy raises her hand. "I would like to go lingerie shopping."

"I need new maternity lingerie. I don't think the ones from Logan's pregnancy are going to fit for much longer." Sunny blinks a few times and then sniffs.

Lily and Poppy are out of their chairs with tissues and hugs before the first tear falls.

It's another minute of consoling before Sunny is okay again. "Sorry," she sniffs. "I'm already showing, and I just found out there's a baby in there. I can't imagine how big I'm going to be this time around."

Lily and Poppy murmur their understanding, even though Lily is the size of my wrist. Poppy is curvier, but being able to see her toes isn't an issue, and likely won't be for a while yet. At least I don't think she's going to jump on the baby train, but then who knows?

Darren and I have never talked about kids. He held Logan when he was born for, like, a minute and a half or something. He doesn't seem to have anything against kids, but he's never mentioned wanting them. Personally, I'm on the fence, mostly because my childhood was seriously fucked up, and I worry no matter what I do, I'll mess my own kid up by default.

Darren grew up in a very strict house with a lot of rules about what constituted acceptable behavior, which may account for how private he is and his sometimes commanding presence in and out of the bedroom.

Sunny's mini-breakdown seems to have shifted the subject away from my unconventional sex life. For a few minutes, anyway.

"Once the playoffs are over, we should plan a trip to the cottage," Violet says.

"That would be so great! I want them to do well, but it would be nice if they were finished before June so they get a bit more of an off-season and Miller can spend more time with Logan," Sunny agrees.

"We could roll it right into a birthday celebration for Charlene or something!" Violet flaps her hands excitedly and nearly topples her sparkling grape juice.

"Aren't there a million black flies up there at the end of May?" I ask.

Once we left The Ranch, my mom and I never made a big deal about birthdays.

"Fine," Violet says. "We have the party here and plan a weekend at the cottage for later in June."

I wave off that idea. "I don't need a party."

"That's what you said last year. You're turning twenty-six. It's your champagne birthday, so we need to do something fun." Violet bounces, making her boobs shake and my mimosa slosh perilously. "It should be themed! We can all wear leather chaps!"

"Could you be any more cliché?" I roll my eyes. "Just to be clear, Darren doesn't own chaps."

"Just a ball gag and a mask with no eye holes, according to Alex."

And we're back to my sex life. I knew I was getting off so easy.

I wonder if Darren is catching this kind of heat today. I seriously doubt it's worse than what I'm getting since I don't think his friends are likely to push his buttons, but I'll have to ask when I speak to him next. I'm not sure when that will be, either. The message I sent about Gertrude was pretty straightforward and doesn't necessarily require a response. Maybe I should've worded it differently.

Sunny raises her hand, like we're all still in middle school and she's waiting her turn to speak. "Wouldn't a mask with no eyeholes be dangerous? You wouldn't be able to see where you're going." Her eyes widen, and she looks around the room. "And what's a ball gag?"

I honestly love that Sunny has grown up in this highly overinformed society and still manages to be innocent. I was sort of like that, at least until we left The Ranch. Then I went from blissfully innocent to exceptionally knowledgeable in a very short span of time. The internet, while helpful for finding information, is also not the best place to learn about things like sex. It was a rough transition.

"Yeah, Char, wouldn't a mask with no eyeholes be dangerous?" Violet props her fist on her chin and smiles. "And please, do explain what a ball gag is."

"I'm not sure you really want the answer to that, Sunny." Poppy gives me a look I can't quite decipher.

Sunny twirls her hair around her finger. "Why not?"

"Where's the harm in a little bondage-sex education? It's not like Miller's ever going to go out and buy either item for her. First of all, Alex would murder him, and secondly, I don't think that's Miller's thing."

Sunny's face lights up, and she does jazz hands. "Oh! I think I know what Miller's thing is!"

Lily grins. "Eating your cookie?"

"He really likes to do that, a lot. When my belly gets too big I'll have to watch from the mirror." She gets a faraway look in her eyes. "But he has another thing! Kind of like how you and Randy are always getting it on in bathrooms, except I think it's a bit more sanitary."

"And it doesn't cause thousands of dollars of damage," Violet adds.

Lily throws her hands up in the air. "That sink was already falling off the wall. It's not my fault it broke!"

"That was one expensive orgasm," I say.

"And Randy says it was worth every penny." Lily's smile is devious as she bites her knuckle, then turns to Sunny. "Anyway, back to Miller's thing."

Sunny wiggles around excitedly in her chair. "So Miller paints my toenails for me."

"Miller's thing is painting your toenails?"

"Yes. Well, no. I think he likes my toes." Her fingers go to her lips, and she looks around the room, her cheeks flushing.

"Say what now?" Violet asks.

"Sometimes he kisses them." She covers her mouth with her palm and says something unintelligible.

Violet sits forward in her chair. "Hold on a second, does Buck have a foot fetish?"

"Um, I don't know." Sunny looks worried now. "Is that weird? Is it, like, mask with no eyeholes kind of weird?"

I dig my toes into Violet's calf, a warning for her to keep her mouth shut. "No, Sunny. It's not weird. Lots of people like feet."

"All our nerve endings are in our feet," Sunny says matter of factly.

"That's actually true," Poppy confirms. "I've taken a course on foot massage."

"Miller gives the best foot massages! Anyway, he didn't say anything about what happened yesterday apart from that he saw your boobs and some things he shouldn't have, so I want to hear more about that, especially the face mask and ball gag thing. Who else wants to know what they are?" She raises her hand again and looks around, expecting everyone to raise their hand, too.

"Am I the only one who doesn't know what this stuff is?" Sunny frowns.

"It's okay not to know," I tell her.

"But all of you know." Sunny sits up a little straighter and flips her hair over her shoulder. "I want to know then, too."

I look to Poppy and Lily, who both shrug. They spend more time with Sunny than me. They would know what could potentially upset her, which is not something I want to do to a pregnant woman—especially not one as sensitive, and obviously naïve, as she is. I'm almost sad that I'm taking this little piece of innocence from her. "I guess a ball gag is exactly what it sounds like. It's a rubber ball that goes in your mouth."

Sunny looks horrified. "Isn't that dangerous? You could choke!"

God, I love her. "It has straps attached to it, so you can secure it at the back of your head," Lily explains.

Sunny blinks a few times. "Why would you strap a rubber ball to your face? I don't get it."

"Maybe a picture would help." Violet performs a quick search on her phone, but I grab it from her before she can show Sunny the image. I would like it to be the least potentially scarring ball gag picture out there—which seems like an oxymoron. I find one that doesn't look too awful and show it to Poppy first. Her eyes flare, but she tips her head to Lily.

I pass the phone to Lily, who grins. "I think my question is, who wears it? You or Darren?"

Sunny throws her hands in the air. "Will someone show me what it is!"

Lily holds the phone out to Sunny. "Remember to keep an open mind."

Sunny peers at the small image on the screen. She frowns and brings it closer to her face. She twists her hair furiously around her finger until she's either at risk of knotting it or ripping out the entire chunk. "Wouldn't it be hard to talk?"

Lily coughs. "I think that's kind of the point."

Sunny looks from the phone to me and back to the phone. "But . . . why?"

"So no one can hear her scream." Violet's grin is evil.

"Don't be a jerk!" I jump in. "It's about trust, and heightening the experience. When you remove the ability to communicate through words, your partner has to be able to read your body and your reactions. Just like if you remove sight, it heightens touch, smell, and taste. You focus on feeling and being in the moment." I'm fidgeting with my pearls, nervous about the way they're all looking at me, maybe judging, seeing me differently. "Not that I have personal experience or anything."

"Wait, what do you mean, you don't have experience? Does that mean Darren is the one who wears the ball gag?" Violet's eyes light up.

I snort. "I'd have better luck getting a porcupine to wear a T-shirt."

"So what do you do with it if you don't use it?" Lily looks like she might be interested in taking that ball gag off my hands.

I don't want to explain where it all came from, but I've kind of boxed myself into a corner. I mean, some of the stuff I bought myself, but the majority came in the form of gifts—not from Darren. Violet and Darren know about my mother's unconventional career, but I generally don't broadcast that she's a Dominatrix. Usually I say she's in the entertainment industry, which is categorically true.

I have never worn that ball gag. It was one of my mother's gifts that ended up in my *this sounds interesting* pile on the heels of a super-smutty read. It always sounds so hot in books, but then when I tried it on, I didn't like the way the rubber tasted, and it was awkward. Also, I don't like not being able to talk. And I couldn't stop drooling, which is completely unsexy, so it went in my box of *no thanks* toys. It's a big box.

"We use some things."

"Like the mask with no eyeholes?" Sunny asks.

"Well, no, not that either."

"Wait a hot damn minute!" Violet slaps the arm of the couch. "Does this mean Darren doesn't actually have Area 51 access?"

"Oh, he definitely has Area 51 access, but I get why you don't want Alex in there."

"It's not that scary. You just need to work up to it," Lily says.

"Hold the fucking phone, you let Balls and his giant dick in your backdoor? How does that even happen?" Violet looks shocked.

"Lots of patience and lube," I reply.

Lily smiles. "Exactly. How do you think that hotel bathroom got destroyed?"

"I guess we know the value Balls puts on anal," Violet says. "All right, my butt is clenching just from talking about this. Let's move on, shall we? You know what I'm curious about?" She looks to me. "That necklace you always wear."

I finger my pearls. "This?"

"For a while there I thought maybe it was a collar and Darren was your Dom or something."

I roll my eyes. "That's because we went on a BDSM reading spree in our book club."

"What's the significance, then?" Violet asks.

"I bought them a long time ago, when I was a teenager, and I wore them until they broke. I loved them so much that I put them in a little bag and carried them around with me all the time anyway." Which I'm sure sounds silly, but they were the first thing I bought after we left The Ranch. I found them at a thrift shop and fell in love with them.

"Anyway," I continue. "One day Darren found them and had them restrung for me, and I've been wearing them ever since."

"Oh, huh. I made that into something a lot bigger than it was." Violet seems a little disappointed.

I'm relieved when no one brings the conversation back to the wheel of sex toys. Maybe it was the mystery and secrecy of what Darren and I do or don't do in the bedroom that made it more intriguing than it really is.

Phones start pinging mid-afternoon, signaling the end of practice. Poppy checks her messages, a frown tugging at her mouth. "This whole expansion draft is crazy."

"It really is," Sunny agrees.

"Between that and playoffs, Randy's super stressed."

"At least he's safe, though," Poppy says. "I'm still trying to figure it all out, and getting Lance to explain it is maddening."

"What do you mean?" Violet asks.

"I don't get how it works."

"Oh, well, every team in the league can keep nine players safe from the draft. Players with no-trade clauses can't be picked up by Vegas, so Alex and Randy are automatically safe. That leaves the team with seven additional players they can keep safe." Violet pops a grape into her mouth and pushes it to the side, making a lump in her cheek. "There's no way they'll let Lance go."

"You can't be sure of that, though, since he doesn't have a no-trade clause." Poppy's anxiety is obviously shared collectively.

"From a pure numbers perspective, it makes sense, though, right, Char?" Violet looks to me, and I nod.

As an accountant and financial portfolio manager of NHL players, we know not just what kind of money they make and how to invest it, but also trends, stats, and player viability. We need to be able to look at career trajectory and performance in order to help make smart short- and long-term financial goals.

I've also been obsessed with hockey since I watched my first game, so I know a lot about this.

"Can you explain that? Because Lance is kind of freaking out a lot about this whole thing. I think he's worried he's going to be moved to Vegas and he'll have to start all over again."

I tap on the arm of my chair. "I can't promise I'm right, but based on Lance's stats over the past two years, he's likely to be safe. He's too valuable to the team for them to let him go. Same goes with Miller. They're the best defense on the team. They're not going to risk either of them."

"You think so?" Sunny twirls her hair around her finger.

"Logically, yes. When you take in points, age, team dynamics, and all that other stuff, it makes sense to keep them safe."

"What about Darren? He has to be safe then, too, right?"

I finger my pearls and shrug. "I don't know. It could go either way." I've reviewed Darren's stats incessantly since they announced the expansion draft, and the conclusion I've come to isn't great; despite his age, his stats have improved over the past two seasons, rather than declined.

"But he's been Alex's wingman for years. They can't trade him," Lily says.

"Who'll take us lingerie shopping if you move to Vegas?" Violet jokes, but her expression reflects my own worry.

I have no idea what will happen to me and Darren if he's traded, and our brief conversation this morning left me with more questions than answers.

Beyond that, Violet has been my only constant since freshman year of college. The idea of leaving behind the stability of my job, my best friend, and my independence is terrifying. Besides, I don't even know if Darren would want me to come with him. We don't have the same kind of relationship as the rest of our friends.

I'm independent, and so is he. I have my little house, and he has his big house. Hell, we haven't even met each other's parents. Until now it wasn't something I worried about.

With the expansion draft looming and the possibility that Darren could end up traded, I feel uncertain about everything. I don't want to lose him, but I don't want to lose anyone else either, or my job and my independence. It's been easy up until now, and suddenly it isn't anymore.

Even Poppy, the newest addition to our group, knows that no matter what, she's going where Lance goes. It's secured in the diamond she wears on her ring finger. Lily and Randy might not follow the wedding-and-babies path, but they live together, too, and they have a dog together, which is almost like having a kid. All I have is the pearl necklace Darren had restrung for me, and no real certainty that he'd want me to come with him. Or whether I'd be able to leave all of the other people I love behind for him.

I feel off kilter when I get home, listless and uncertain. While all the other girls had messages from their boyfriends or husbands this afternoon, I had silence from Darren. Normally it wouldn't be an issue, but with what happened last night and the discussion about the expansion draft, I'm feeling less than secure, which is not like me.

The reason Darren and I work so well is partly because he's never pushed to get serious. He seems content to keep doing what we're doing. Which is fine with me—or at least it was.

I drop my purse on the kitchen counter and scrub a hand over my face. I need something sweet. Well, what I really need is Darren and an orgasm. But since I saw him last night, that's not an option unless I want to look clingy—which is something I pride myself on not being—so I'll have to settle for hot chocolate.

I fill my milk frother, because I'm not ruining nice hot chocolate by using boiled water, and pick one of the gourmet tins my mom likes to send me. Every month I get a care package from her. Mostly it's herbal stuff likes teas and candles and creams for endless youth, but she also likes to send me whatever new sex toy she's found at whatever Dominatrix conference she's attended recently. She means well, but it's awkward.

I check the tin with the candies my mom sends me and frown. My supply is dwindling, which is yet another thing to worry about. I haven't been this anxious since . . . well, since we left The Ranch. I tap on the counter, waiting for the milk to froth. I could maybe try giving myself an orgasm to take the edge off, but I'm not sure that's going to be helpful.

I've just poured the frothy milk into my mug when my phone buzzes on the counter. I snatch it up, but my smile fades as *Mom* flashes across the screen. I feel bad for being disappointed, but I'd hoped Darren might check in. I put a pin in my disappointment because it's nice to hear from my mom. She keeps busy, so sometimes it's difficult to find time to catch up.

"Hi, Mom."

"Char-char, how's my baby girl?"

"I'm good." I prop the phone on my shoulder, dump a handful of marshmallows into my hot chocolate, and head for the living room. "How are you?"

"Fantastic. Just wonderful! I can't talk long because I'm in between clients, but I wanted to let you know I'll be in town next week."

I sit up straighter, fingers of unease raking down my spine and slithering lower. It's such an uncomfortable feeling, especially when I'm talking to my mom. "In Chicago? When?"

"Probably not until later in the week. I'll know more soon, but I want to spend some time with you! I haven't seen my baby in almost a year, and I miss you. Oh! And I have some new fun things for you, too! Early birthday presents and such. You'll be around? I know sometimes you travel for work."

I hold in my sigh of relief. Darren leaves for the first two away games of the playoffs in a couple of days, so I don't have to worry about my mom being in town at the same time he is. So far I've been lucky that her infrequent visits have coincided nicely with his away games.

Also, I don't actually travel for work, but sometimes I go to away games with Violet when they're on the weekends or we can get a day off, especially on the long stretches when the guys are gone for more than a week. It's nice to break up the separation a little. I don't talk to my mom about relationships since she's very much against them. She hasn't had a real boyfriend since we left The Ranch, and that was over a decade ago.

"That would be great. What's in Chicago, other than me?" My mom wouldn't just come for the sake of visiting me. It's not that she doesn't love me—she does—but her life is . . . strange. She doesn't stay in the same place for long, moving around the country and refusing to set down any roots. She's not designed for parenting, something I learned once we left The Ranch. She's really good at a few things: getaways, making candies, and being a career Dominatrix.

"I have a work conference. It should be a lot of fun. Oh! My five o'clock is here! I'll call you when I'm in town."

"Okay. Oh, and Mom?"

"Yes, Char-char?"

"Can you bring me more candies? I'm almost out."

"Of course, honey. I'll bring lots."

I end the call and flop back on the couch. It's close to dinnertime, but I don't feel like making anything. I wonder what Darren's doing now. For the first time ever, I consider what it would be like to have someone to come home to, how I might like to curl up in that reading chair in Darren's living room and wait for him to walk through the door.

Sometimes I think it might be nice to be less independent and not quite so afraid of being trapped in someone's jar.

chapter five

The Sauna Inquisition

Darren

Practice is tense, as expected. I follow Alex to the sauna and drop down on the bench. Half the team is in here, and most of them are talking about the upcoming playoff game against Nashville. Not knowing who's safe and who isn't only adds to the stress.

After a while, the sauna clears out until it's me, Alex, Miller, Randy, Lance, and Rookie.

"So . . ." Rookie slaps his bare thighs. "You and your girl get freaky, huh?"

Of course he's the one to start off the conversation.

I shrug. "I guess it depends on your definition of freaky."

"Whatever floats your boat, right?" Miller glances nervously at Lance when he scoffs.

I don't know his whole story, only bits and pieces from time spent with him. But based on his previous on-ice behavior, his penchant for fights, his occasional destructive meltdowns, and his former reputation with women, I can take a stab in the dark.

I wonder if the ability to intuit brokenness in other people is a sixth sense only other damaged people are privy to. Like me and Charlene. Sometimes the most broken souls find each other, as if their missing pieces exist in another person. It doesn't matter what form the abuse takes. The holes it leaves in the psyche fracture the soul, too. It probably accounts in part for my instant attraction to Charlene. She's guarded and open at the same time. I might want more from her, but I won't take it at the risk of pushing her too far and losing her entirely.

"As long as you're both into it, it's cool, yeah? Consenting adults and all that." Randy runs his fingers through his beard thoughtfully. "Do you buy Charlene's lingerie, or does she do the shopping?"

I try not to envision all the lace and satin and leather we left in the living room last night. "I buy the lace, she buys the leather."

Randy's eyebrows pop. "Who's in control?"

"Who's in control in your bedroom, or bathroom, as it were?"

Randy rubs his bottom lip. "Both of us?"

"Why would you think it's any different for me and Charlene?"

"Good point."

"I gotta get home," Lance grumbles and pushes up off the bench. The massive cross tattoo on his back shifts as he punches the door open and disappears through it.

"He gonna be all right?" I ask.

Miller runs a hand over his buzzed head, then taps his temple. "I think he has some messed-up ideas about what's going on with you and Char." He turns to Randy. "I'll ride home with him."

"Mind if I come with you?" Rookie asks.

"If you want, sure." Miller shrugs.

"You think I need to talk to Lance?" I ask as Miller and Rookie get up to leave.

This is the exact reason I like my privacy, because people tend to jump to conclusions. Often the wrong ones.

"He'll come to you when he's ready," Randy says. "I'm hoping whatever conversation the girls have today will get relayed by Poppy and he'll relax a bit."

"If that's what you think is best."

Miller and Rookie take off, leaving the three of us.

"So, I have a question." Alex's knee is going a mile a minute.

"Fire away."

"What exactly are you and Charlene?"

"I don't understand the question."

Alex rolls his shoulders. "Like, is this a real relationship or is it contractual?"

"Contractual?"

"Like those books they all read—you know, they made some of them into movies, and those girls binge watch the fuck out of them every time a new one comes out, and then Violet wants to—" He pauses, maybe realizing it's not just the two of us, and he should probably censor. "Anyway, in the beginning the girl signs all these papers about what she will and won't do. Is it like that?"

"No, Alex. It's not like that."

"So then what's it like?" I can see the challenge in his eyes, and maybe a little mistrust, because I haven't been upfront with him about this, and we've been friends for a long time. But explaining how it really is exposes Charlene, and I'm not willing to do that, because it could compromise what we have.

"It's a real relationship. There's no contract, and whatever you think is going on, it isn't." I reconsider that, since Alex and Vi are pretty strait-laced, apart from the locker room sex and the dick dress-up games. "Well, it probably is going on, but not quite the way you think."

"I'm not judging. I'm trying to understand what this is. I mean, you and Char have been together almost as long as me and Vi, and it all seems pretty casual. What's your plan if you get traded—to Vegas or another team?"

This is the exact question that's been eating at me since the expansion draft was announced. I shrug, because I don't have answers to that. "I guess I'll have to wait and see what happens."

Do I want it to end? No. Not at all. Would I want her to come with me if I was traded, yes and no. Selfishly, I want to keep her, but is it reasonable? I don't know. I can give her what she needs physically, but I'm unsure if I'm capable of providing her with more than that, or if she'll even let me try.

Is it fair for me to take her away from everything she knows, everyone she cares about and keep her all to myself? I know Charlene, maybe better than she knows herself. If I took her with me, I'd be her everything, and she's made it very clear that's not what she wants. And I respect that.

Her childhood was bad enough that her mother took her and ran in search of a better life, and Charlene shuts down every time I try to talk to her about it, which admittedly hasn't been often. Most of the time it's enough that I know she's broken. But sometimes I want to know how closely our broken parts match.

Alex's brow furrows. "Haven't you ever talked about it?"

"About what?" I ask.

"The future, asshole. Your future with Charlene."

"She doesn't like being tied down."

"Uhhh . . . We've moved on from your sex life, Westinghouse." Randy snorts.

I shoot him a look. "I'm not talking about my sex life. Charlene is . . . complex."

"She's a woman; of course she's complex," Randy says.

"Do you think I should talk to her about the future?" I look between Alex and Randy, who are both more than half a decade my junior, yet still manage to have a better handle on relationships.

"Probably? I have a hard time believing she's hanging around just for the orgasms at this point, man," Randy offers.

We hit the showers. The locker room is empty, everyone else long gone. I think about what's waiting at home for me—which is a whole lot of nothing—and how I'm going to be away soon and unable to see Charlene.

Typically after Charlene spends the night at my place, she's scarce for a day or so, depending on how the night went and whether or not I got all up in her personal space like I did last night with the accidental spooning. I don't like the space, but I also understand she sometimes needs it. Staying at my place makes her nervous. I'm not exactly sure why, but I sense it's because she feels trapped, much like a firefly in a jar.

Whenever she comes to see away games, I expect at least one day of silence for each night we've slept in the same bed. It's fucking torture, but I'm not the easiest person to be with, so I usually accept what she's willing to give.

It's a fine balance with Charlene, but with everything that's going on, I don't feel like toeing the line. Even if it makes her uncomfortable, I want to push, and honestly, it doesn't even matter if I do, because I won't be here for the fallout anyway. By the time I get back from the away games, she should be fine again.

I open my locker and find my boxer briefs. I look around and note that both Alex and Randy have their phones in their hands, and they're awkwardly trying to text and get dressed at the same time.

I scroll through my alerts—there aren't many since my people are all here, apart from Charlene. I freeze when I see that I have both texts and a voicemail from her. This has never happened before. Ever.

It's been less than twelve hours since I left her in my bed. That she's messaging *me* this soon afterwards is unheard of. I fight the initial shot of panic that something bad has happened and check the message.

The one from this morning is an image of the living room post wheel of sex toys and requests that I listen to my voicemail. Another came an hour ago asking how practice went. I can't decide if that's a good or a bad thing because it's so atypical.

"Dude, you okay?" Alex asks. "You look like you're gonna puke."

"Charlene messaged me."

"Did something happen?"

"I don't know." I listen to the voicemail, relieved it's just about Gertrude. I can handle that, but Charlene messaging hours after we've had a night together is . . . different. I can't explain that without it being strange to Alex and Randy. Which makes me question how fucked up my own perception of relationships is, and whether I've been doing Charlene a disservice all this time.

I care for her. About her. I don't want to be without her. But I have no idea if she feels the same way, and it's setting me off balance. Like I'm riding the Tilt-a-Whirl after drinking a bottle of scotch.

I send her a response:

Practice was fine. Please let me know if you are okay.

"Just go see her if you're that worried," Alex says when she hasn't messaged back fifteen seconds later.

"Go see her?"

He makes a face, the same one he makes when one of our teammates makes a bad play. "Yeah. Like, if she said she needed you right now, you'd drop your shit and go, right?"

"Well, yeah."

"So go."

"But she hasn't messaged me because she needs me."

Alex exhales a slow breath. "Look, man, she's not going to say it outright. Is she messaging and calling when she doesn't usually message or call?"

"Well, yeah."

"Then she's asking you to be there when she needs you."

"But she hasn't asked me to be there for her at all," I argue.

Alex rubs the space between his eyebrows. "Look, I get that maybe this isn't familiar to you, but you can't tell me you don't know when Charlene is asking you to be like . . . on for her." At my confused expression he shakes his head. "Do I even fucking know you?"

I scrub my hands over my face. "Look, I'm emotionally stunted. I don't understand how this whole thing works. I want Charlene, and I don't want to lose her. The possibility is actually my worst fucking nightmare. I didn't grow up in a home with two parents who cared about me and whose entire existence was based on my success as a human being. You had that. I didn't. I don't know how to do this and be successful, and Charlene is just as fucked up as me, so any normalish perspective you can give, without judgement, would be really helpful right about now."

"I don't—"

I grab him by the shoulders. "Just tell me what the fuck to do!"

"Go to her house. Go see her. Make her happy, however you do that."

"Make her happy?"

"Yeah, man, like, however that works for you, make her feel good."

"You mean sexually, right?"

Alex frowns again. I don't like that expression on his face. It makes me question things. "If that's what works, then yes. But considering how long you've been together, I'd say it's probably beyond just where your dick goes."

"My dick goes in a lot of places." I figure honesty is important here.

Alex scoffs. Maybe that was the wrong thing to say. "Can we think beyond your dick, Darren?"

"Of course. What would you like me to think in terms of?"

"Charlene. Think about her."

"What about her, specifically?"

Alex stares at me and says nothing for a long time. "Other than your weird-ass sex life, what does she like? How do you show her you care about her and that she's on your mind? What do you do for her?"

"I buy her things."

"Such as?"

I consider that for a moment. "Usually clothes or lingerie. Sometimes I take her out for dinner, and there was that time I sent her to the spa with Violet. That was good. She liked that."

"Aside from clothes and lingerie, is there anything else?"

"I bought her a chair."

"Please don't tell me it's some kind of fucked-up sex chair."

"There are fucked-up sex chairs?" Randy asks, reminding me this conversation isn't private. Jesus, I'm offering up an awful lot of personal details to these guys in the name of making sure my relationship with Charlene doesn't get messed up.

"No. Well, yes, there are fucked-up sex chairs, but I didn't buy one of those for Charlene. I bought her a chair to read in. And a blanket for when she gets cold."

"Which I bet is pretty often if she's only allowed to wander around your place naked, eh?" Randy says.

"She doesn't need my permission to put on or take off clothes." I turn back to Alex, because Randy's commentary is unhelpful. "Should I buy her something else along those lines—maybe a footstool, or a pillow, or a side table for her tea? That could be good, right? It'll show her I'm thinking about her for reasons that don't pertain to sex."

Randy shakes his head. "Or you could just buy her some fucking flowers."

"Chocolate is always nice, or candy," Alex adds. "Unless she's feeling bad about her body; then chocolate is a bad idea."

"Charlene never feels bad about her body."

"Not that she's mentioned to you," Alex grumbles and slams his locker closed. "What's her favorite color?"

"I like her in purple."

"No, dickweed, not *your* favorite color on her, *her* favorite color. What color does she like the most?"

When she's the one picking the lingerie for the evening, she tends to go for dark and dangerous, even though she's anything but. "Black or silver, I guess."

"Jesus Christ, Westinghouse, if there was a boyfriend test, you'd be failing like a motherfucker," Randy laughs.

"Why?"

"Because you and Charlene have been together for two years, and you don't even know what her favorite color is. Think about the clothes she wears when you're with her—the color of her purse, her favorite mug, her goddamn fucking shoes," Alex snaps.

"Oh. Yellow?"

"Why are you asking me? Is it or isn't it yellow?" Alex asks.

"I think it's yellow. Or maybe it's peach. I could ask her." I pull up her contact on my phone, but Alex smacks my hand.

"For fuck's sake, don't ask her." Alex angrily thumb-types a message on his own phone.

"Are you asking Charlene?"

He gives me a look. "No, I'm asking my wife because she's your girlfriend's best friend, and girls know this kind of stuff about each other."

"Oh. Right. That makes sense. What's Violet's favorite color?"

"Red, most of the time." His phone buzzes. "Yellow is the correct answer for Charlene, so what you need to do is buy her some yellow flowers."

He thumb-types another question as he speaks, and Violet answers right away. "She also likes mint and chocolate-covered candied ginger, so I'd get her some of that, too. Then go over to your girlfriend's house and make sure she's okay. All of your friends saw her naked yesterday, surrounded by a bunch of whacked-out sex toys. She might need some emotional support that extends beyond last night."

"I can do that. I can buy her flowers and chocolate and provide her with emotional support if she needs it."

Alex rubs the back of his neck. "I don't know whether to pat you on the back or punch you in the face."

I'm not sure which I deserve more at the moment.

chapter six

The Best Boyfriend Award Goes To . . .

Darren

I drop Alex off at his place. Before he gets out, he programs a flower shop into my GPS. "You don't have to get all yellow flowers."

"What?"

"The flowers—when you buy them for Charlene, they don't all have to be yellow. And, stay away from yellow roses. They mean friendship."

"How do you know this?"

"Google."

"Maybe you should come with me."

Alex claps me on the shoulder. "You can buy flowers for your girlfriend, Darren. Just tell the sales girl what you're looking for, and she'll be able to help you out."

"So tell her my girlfriend's favorite color is yellow?"

"And that you want to convey you like her for more than her ability to be a jizz depository." I'm not sure what my expression must be, but he tacks on. "Don't say that last part to the sales girl."

"I'm relationship-stunted, not a social idiot."

"Just making sure. There's a Godiva store down the street. You'll be able to get everything you need. And under no circumstances are you to stop at a lingerie store."

"But—"

"No buts. Do not buy her something you plan to take off her body. You need to show Charlene that you think about her beyond just sex."

"But I'd like to have sex with her tonight. We have away games."

Alex punches me in the shoulder. "Christ, Darren, how the hell have we been friends this long and I had no idea you were this relationship challenged?"

I roll my shoulder. "Because I've never had an actual girlfriend before Charlene."

"How is that even possible?"

"I don't know. Usually there's an NDA and lot of rules."

"Because of the freaky sex shit?"

"No, because I'm trying to protect myself and them from all the media bullshit."

"Did Charlene sign an NDA?"

"No. She promised we would keep our sex life private." I wanted to date her more than I needed an NDA.

"Look, I don't care what your sex life looks like. I mean, thanks to Charlene I've gained Area 51 access. It's limited, but more than Violet would probably allow otherwise."

"You have what?"

Alex waves me off. "Never mind. I'm just saying, as long as it's consensual and everyone's enjoying themselves, I don't give a shit what you two do. But if you want to take this relationship to the next level, and I'm pretty sure you do, then you need to make it clear it's not limited to orgasms. So let Charlene initiate."

"She only does that when she's wearing leather."

Alex blows out a breath. "I did not need that information. I'm getting out of the car. Go buy your girlfriend some flowers and chocolate."

"Okay." I pop the trunk as he gets out of the car. "Alex?"

"Yeah."

"Thanks."

"For what?"

"Helping me."

"All you need to do is ask, Darren."

I wait until he's closed the trunk before I follow the directions to the flower shop. The girl helps me pick flowers for Charlene, which is something I decide I'm going to do more often. Flowers are a lot like lingerie, full of beauty in different forms and textures. Some are lacy, silky, frilly, soft and pale, dark and heavy. It takes me nearly an hour before I have a complete bouquet, which costs almost as much as lingerie and contains everything from purple night lilies to yellow dahlias with petals that look like the tips have been dipped in red ink.

I stop at the Godiva store and fight the urge to browse the lingerie shop next to that. Alex is right. Buying lingerie for Charlene will give the message that I would like sex. Which is true. However, as soon as I choose lingerie for Charlene, she also believes I'm choosing how things will happen in the bedroom. Sometimes it's fun, but I would like to avoid that tonight.

I fire off a text to Charlene before I get in my car, but she doesn't respond right away, so I drive over, hoping I'm right and she'll be home. I can leave the presents for her if she's not, but it defeats the purpose.

My palms are sweaty as I pull in to her driveway. Her car is here, which means she should be home. Christ, I'm nervous, which is ridiculous considering I'm just bringing her flowers and chocolate. It's not like I'm asking her to marry me.

I contemplate that, the idea of marriage. Would I marry Charlene? The institution as a whole doesn't mean much to me. It's one's actions that dictate devotion. Words mean nothing if there's no conviction behind them.

Do I think Charlene would want to marry me? I don't know. But I'm not here to ask Charlene to marry me. I'm here to show her that I can be a normal-ish boyfriend. I can be thoughtful and buy her unnecessary and frivolous things.

It's with that in mind that I get out of the car, bouquet and chocolate in hand. I check my phone before I slip it in my pocket, noting that she still hasn't responded to my messages from earlier.

Her front walk is lined with pretty flowers in a variety of colors, but yellow seems to dominate, along with some purple and white, so the ones I've chosen should go over well. I hope.

Maybe she's in the bath. That would be nice. I like Charlene fresh from the bath. She'll be relaxed. I could let myself in since I have a key, but I rarely come to Charlene. My house is more convenient, and my bedroom is much better equipped for sex and sleepovers. And since I'm surprising her, I figure it's a good idea to knock and wait to be let in, setting a precedent and all.

Charlene opens the door the requisite three inches the chain latch allows. Her hazel eye widens. "Darren? What're you doing here?"

"I wanted to see you."

"Oh." Her hand flutters to her throat.

Hmm. I expected a slightly different reaction. "Can I come in? Have I caught you at a bad time?"

"What? Oh! No. Yes, I mean. You can come in. Just a sec." The door closes and the sound of the latch disengaging follows. A few seconds later she opens it again and steps back to allow me inside.

"This is a surprise." She pulls at the bottom of her shirt with one hand and pats her hair again with the other.

"That was my intention."

I look her over. She's wearing a pair of teal leggings covered in a donut print and a pale purple tank with a donut on the front holding a cup of coffee. Her hair is piled on top of her head in a messy bun, and her face is free of makeup. She's not wearing socks. Her toes are naked apart from the big one on the right foot, which is painted the same shade of purple as her tank. I don't believe she's wearing a bra based on her perky nipples.

Her gaze darts down where my hands are tucked behind my back in an attempt to conceal the massive bouquet of flowers and the box of chocolates. Actually, there are two boxes of chocolates since ginger chocolate and mint chocolate should be separated, according to the lady who assisted me.

I reveal the bouquet of flowers first.

Charlene blinks several times, eyes darting from the flowers to my face and back again. "You brought me flowers?"

"I did." I'm not sure what kind of response I expected, but again, this isn't quite it. She seems shocked. "Should I not have?"

"What? Oh! I, uh . . . they're just . . ." She traces the satiny petals. "So beautiful."

"Yes. Like you."

A soft smile lights up her face. I wonder at her sweetly unguarded surprise. I'm certain I tell her she's beautiful all the time. I know I think it every single time I see her. Maybe the words get stuck in my head and never actually make it out of my mouth.

"You can take them. They're for you."

Charlene's bun flops around as she gives her head a little shake and takes the bouquet. "Oh, wow, this is heavy." She buries her nose in the blossoms and inhales deeply. I want to frame the image.

"I brought you something else as well." I hold out the Godiva bag.

Charlene's expression shifts to childlike excitement. "You brought me flowers *and* chocolate?"

"I did." I smile. "And based on the samples the saleswoman provided, I will attest that they're delicious—just like you, as well."

My smile widens at her blush.

"This is really sweet of you, and very unexpected," Charlene clutches the flowers and chocolates to her chest. "Um, I should go upstairs and change and then put these in some water." She makes a move toward the kitchen, which she'll have to pass through to get to her bedroom.

"No! I mean, I like you exactly as you are."

She glances down at her outfit.

"Please don't change on my account. I'm rather fond of this." I skim the strap of her tank and watch goose bumps rise along her arm. "Why don't I help you put the flowers in water, and you can try the chocolate? Unless you have plans this evening?"

"I don't have any plans."

"So it would be okay for me to stay and spend some time with you." I shake my head at how awkward I sound. "That was meant to be a question."

Charlene bites her bottom lip. "You can stay and spend some time with me, if you want."

"Yes. I want." I nod, then realize I haven't completed the thought. "To spend time with you."

I retrieve a vase from Charlene's pantry and help her arrange the flowers. She has trouble deciding where she wants them, and eventually settles on the kitchen table, which she can see from the living room and the front door.

Charlene's house is small, as one might expect for a single woman living on her own. She makes good money as an accountant for sports professionals, but she's still managing all of her costs on a single income, which is why I insisted on giving her a credit card to make special purchases.

She adjusts the vase, turning it half an inch to the right and then to the left, determining placement. Her ass looks fantastic in leggings, and I decide I need to find out where she gets them so I can buy some for her, and she can wear them more often.

When she comes to my place, her visits are always arranged in advance, which means her makeup is flawless and she's impeccably dressed. But I like this version of her as well. She looks relaxed and comfortable, something I would like to experience more of.

"What do you want to do now?" she asks.

"What were you doing before I arrived?"

"Just watching TV."

"Well, we could do that together."

"Uh, we can, but I was watching bad reality TV."

"That's okay." I'm likely going to be watching Charlene and not the TV, so the content is basically irrelevant.

I follow her to the living room, which is cozy, like the rest of her house. It looks like she was sitting on the couch, curled up with a blanket. I drop down at the end that's blanket free and adjust the pillow behind me.

Charlene folds the blanket and drapes it neatly over the back of the couch, then takes a seat on the other end. She fidgets. Picks up her half-consumed hot chocolate and takes a sip while she unmutes the TV.

I glance at the screen. "What is this?"

"*Teen Baby Daddy*. I told you I was watching bad reality TV."

"Wow. So this is really a show?"

"I can change it." She reaches for the remote, her cheeks flushing.

I cover her hand with mine. "No. Don't do that. It's fine."

"Sometimes I like to watch reality TV because it reminds me how easy my life is in comparison. But we can do something else if you want." She sets her hot chocolate on the side table and shifts closer. She looks shy and uncertain as she leans in, brushing her lips over the edge of my jaw. "Thank you, for the flowers and the chocolate. That was a nice surprise."

I have to fight with my body not to turn my head, slip my fingers in her hair and taste her mouth. I imagine she's sweet like chocolate right now. I remind myself that I have another purpose for being here that isn't supposed to be about sex. If it's offered, I don't want to say no, though, especially since I'm going to be away for a few days and all I'll have is my hand to keep me company.

"I wanted to make sure you were okay after last night and your afternoon with the girls."

She sits back, putting distance between us again. I don't like it. Maybe I should've sat in the middle of the couch, then she'd have to sit next to me. "Oh. Right, of course. Do you want to know what I told them?"

"Only if you want to tell me." I pick up the nail polish sitting on the coffee table and tap the end of her single, painted toe. "Don't you usually go to the spa for this?"

"I was going to make an appointment for when you're away."

"Would you like me to make one for you?" I shift and set her foot in my lap. "I could arrange to have Violet join you."

"You don't have to go to the trouble."

"It's no trouble. You could have a whole day at the spa if you'd like." I run my thumb along her instep. "In the meantime, I could paint these for you while you get your TV fix." I wiggle her big toe.

"Just as long as this isn't the beginning of a foot fetish, have at it," she says.

"I think you know all of my fetishes by now." I start to unscrew the cap but Charlene stops me.

"You have to shake it first."

"Like real paint."

"Exactly."

Charlene's feet are delicate, much like the rest of her. I definitely don't have a foot fetish, but I can appreciate that even her feet are pretty. While Charlene indulges in brain candy, I focus on the task of painting her toenails. It isn't exactly easy. I have to use a Q-Tip dipped in polish remover a couple of times when I mess up, since Charlene's toes are small, and my hands are not.

"I think Miller has a foot fetish," Charlene says as I finish the first coat. She's informed me already that they'll require two, which is fine with me. I'm touching her, and I'd like to continue doing so in a way that doesn't make it seem like I'm here just for sex.

"How do you know that?"

Charlene arches an eyebrow. "Sunny mentioned that he likes to paint her toenails."

"I'm painting your toenails, and I don't have a foot fetish."

"She also told us he likes to kiss her toes, and her face went completely red when she said that, so I have a feeling he might like to do more than that."

"You girls certainly like to share."

Her eyes stay fixed on her mug. "I keep it pretty vague. Violet always draws her own conclusions."

I wonder how much harm I've done her in asking to maintain such a high level of privacy. In doing so, I'm responsible, in part, for creating some of the distance in this relationship. My own secrets don't make it any better.

"And that's how you managed today?" I ask.

"No one made a big deal out of it. Except Violet and her Area 51 fears, but those are kind of justified, so . . ."

"Area 51?" Alex used the same term earlier. I have no idea what aliens have to do with sex.

"Anal invasion."

My smile is automatic and likely lecherous. "Ahh. Violet is opposed, then?"

"She's a little wary of Alex's size."

I've played hockey with Alex for years. There's a lot of time spent in the locker room showering and getting changed when you're on an NHL team. You get used to seeing a lot more of people than you would in most professions.

Charlene must read my confusion. "He's a grower, not a shower."

"And you know this how?"

"I accidentally got a peek in Vegas when we had to pry Violet away from Alex for the wedding. You would not be granted access if you were packing a cannon like that."

I'm not sure if I should be offended or not. "I'm above average." I know this because I've read the articles and taken the necessary measurements.

"Trust me, I'm very aware of how above average you are. But Alex is scary huge."

"Huh. Well that's . . . interesting." I accepted a long time ago that Alex is the better player on the ice, but I always thought I had a leg up—proverbially speaking—in this department. As a competitive person, I'm displeased to find out he's winning in that area, too. So far he's more accomplished in hockey, relationships, cock size, and who the fuck knows what else.

"How were the guys today? I'm sure they had all kinds of things to say." Charlene bites her lip and dips a finger in her hot chocolate before slipping it in her mouth. I'm not sure if it's meant to be intentionally sexual or not. I choose to pretend it didn't happen rather than offer her something significantly larger to dip in there.

"Randy wanted to know who wore the ball gag."

Charlene's eyes widen. "What did you say?"

"Why does it matter?"

"I don't know. Just curious, I suppose."

"I told them no one wears it."

"That's it?"

"And that you don't like the way it tastes."

She traces the edge of the donut on her knee. "I could try it again if you want."

Would I like to see Charlene wearing a ball gag? I mean, I wouldn't be opposed. But is it something I need? Absolutely not.

"I don't ever want you to do anything you don't one-hundred percent enjoy. My concern today is that you weren't overwhelmed by questions, or a sense of responsibility or ownership for what happened. I don't want you to feel as though you have to tell me anything you talked to the girls about today, but I hope if there's something that isn't working between us, you would come to me so I could try to fix it."

She tips her head to the side, eyes locked on mine. "I like how we are together. And I like that you're here now."

"As do I."

She takes another sip of her drink, licking away the marshmallow foam that sticks to her lip. She manages to leave a little behind.

"You missed some." I rub my thumb over the spot.

I'm not disappointed when Charlene's fingers wrap around my wrist and her lips close over my thumb, swirling slowly, eyes locked on mine. These kinds of real conversations aren't always easy with Charlene because we're both so guarded. But we can communicate incredibly well in other ways.

When she releases my thumb, I replace it with my lips. I didn't kiss Charlene last night, except for maybe once or twice. Which drives her crazy.

Charlene loves making out. She would kiss until her lips are raw if I let her. Sometimes I deny her, so the next time we're together I can capitalize on how much she seems to love the simple act of kissing.

I stroke inside her mouth on a leisurely sweep. Charlene moans, low and sweet, fingertips dragging softly down my cheek as she opens wider, inviting me deeper. Which is the exact moment I disengage and retreat to the other side of the couch.

"Your toes should be dry now. I can put on a second coat."

She's still clutching her mug in one hand. Her eyes dart down, and she exhales a shaky breath.

I take my time with the nail polish, making sure each toe is perfect before moving on to the next. I know Charlene is still trying to figure out what's going on here. My being here, unannounced, bringing her flowers and chocolate, painting her toenails for fuck's sake—I've never done any of this before. Not in two years. And I'm starting to see very clearly how that needs to change. Because tonight I've realized something very important. Up until now, I've only seen the side of Charlene she thinks I want.

And while I adore that she likes to try new things and experiment with sex positions and ridiculous toys, I think I might enjoy this just as much.

Once I'm done, I clean up the discarded Q-tips and tissues and take them all to the kitchen. I toss everything in the garbage and wash my hands, then root around in Charlene's cupboards for a snack. She has an odd balance between holistic stuff and junk food. I hit the jackpot when I find a bag of Cool Ranch Doritos stuffed in the back of the cupboard. I check the fridge for beer, but Charlene isn't big on it, so I'm unsurprised to come up empty handed. She has ginger ale and lots of milk. She also has a container of onion dip, which will go perfectly with the Doritos. I snatch the Godiva bag from the counter and bring it with me to the living room.

Charlene's expression goes from hopeful to crestfallen. "What're you doing?"

"I thought you might want a snack."

"Doritos and onion dip? Why did you even come here if you're going to eat that?" Charlene seems annoyed, angry even.

"Would you like me to find something else?"

She throws her hands up in the air. "Yes! You ruin making out when you have Dorito breath."

"I didn't come here to make out. I came here to spend time with you."

Her brows pull down. "Why can't we do both? Why does it have to be one or the other? Or do you not . . . want me like this? Do you need me to change?" She motions to her attire, her confusion endearing, and painfully understandable.

I drop the snacks on the coffee table and sit down beside her. "I always want you, Charlene."

"So why the Doritos? I don't get it. You come here with gifts, paint my toenails, tease me with that kiss, and then pull out gross-breath snacks like it all makes some kind of sense. What the hell?"

She's definitely angry, which seems to defeat the entire purpose of me showing her I want more than sex. "You know that I care about you, don't you?"

She purses her lips, eyes roaming over my face as if she'll find some kind of explanation there. "Yes. I know that."

"How?"

"What?"

"How do you know?" I ask, because I want to understand what I do to make her see that, since I honestly don't know.

"You take care of my needs before your own. You understand when I take things farther then I mean to, and you always know where my limit is. You'll let me try new things even if it's not always something you're keen on. And you bring me flowers and chocolate because you think that's what I need based on someone else's idea of what constitutes normal. That's how I know."

It doesn't escape me that most of these references apply to our sex life, except for the last part, which only serves to reinforce how change is necessary, but it may need to be a bit more gradual. I have until the end of June, which should give me lots of time to make Charlene see that we're supposed to be more.

That way, if I'm traded at the end of the season, asking her to come with me won't be something she'll balk at. Broaching that subject now doesn't make sense, not when flowers and chocolate cause this kind of reaction.

"Darren? Did I say something wrong?"

I realize I've been staring at her, saying nothing in response. I smile in what I hope is reassurance. "No, firefly, you didn't say anything wrong."

She skims my knuckles and scoots a little closer. "This morning you threatened to kiss me for hours the next time we were together."

"I did say that, didn't I?" I drag a single finger along the column of her throat. "Would you like me to make good on that now?"

"Mmm. I would like that very much."

I shift until I'm in the center of the couch and move Charlene to straddle me. I press the softest kiss to her lips, then trail my fingers along her throat. I don't go back to her mouth like she wants me to. Instead I start at her fingertips, kissing each one, working my way over her knuckles, following the vein on the inside of her wrist all the way to her elbow. I keep going, up the inside of her arm, over her shoulder, across her collarbone, along the side of her neck and the edge of her jaw to her chin.

The entire time Charlene grinds over me, rubbing herself on my erection through the barrier of clothing. If we were naked, I'd be inside her already. For some reason, restraint is difficult to find and hold on to tonight. Maybe because everything is shifting for me, and I want it to be the same for Charlene.

I'm about to continue the kiss torture, starting with the neglected fingertips of the other hand, but Charlene grabs my chin to keep me from moving away. She doesn't try to kiss me. Instead her eyes meet mine, uncertainty flickering there. "Stay here for a minute, please."

I lean in and kiss the corner of her mouth before I brush my lips over hers. I curve my finger around the shell of her ear and ease my thumb along her throat until I reach the soft spot under her chin. Her pulse hammers there, hard and steady with untended need.

I angle her head slightly and tip my own in the opposite direction. Breathing in the warmth of her shaky exhale, I taste chocolate and marshmallow before our mouths are even connected. I press my lips to hers, reveling in the softness before I stroke along the seam. She tastes sweet, as she always does, and that little buzz of lightning always follows, much like the shock of light that appears in the sky when a firefly makes its presence known.

I don't stay for a minute. I linger at her lips, sweeping inside her mouth over and over, slow and languorous, as if there is no other place to be, and we're speaking through kisses that never end.

I have no idea how long we make out, but Charlene's lips are swollen and her chin is red from stubble burn by the time I disengage.

"Should we go upstairs? Do you want me to change now?" she asks on a breathless whisper.

I skim her bottom lip with a fingertip and shake my head. "I want to stay right here." I brush her nipple through her tank. "But I'd like to see more of you, if that would be all right."

She nods. "Please."

I find the hem and tug it up, exposing first her decorated navel, then the gentle curve of her belly to the swell of her breasts. I sigh when I reach her nipples. I had the barbells custom made for her. They boast the Chicago logo and my number on the little balls that hold them in place. She had them pierced a few months after we started dating. Avoiding them during the healing time was a torture worth enduring for both of us.

Charlene lifts her arms, and I pull the tank over her head.

"You're so beautiful." I meet her heavy, needy gaze. There's something else there, not the anxiety and anticipation that comes with wondering what's next, but a different kind of wanting.

A small smile curves her pouty lips. "So are you."

"I think only to you," I mutter, then dip down to pepper kisses along her jaw and neck and then lower until I reach the swell of her breast. I capture her nipple between my lips, tonguing the barbell before I tug it between my teeth.

Charlene arches and moans, that delicate sound sending a bolt of heat down my spine. The ache in my balls is damn near violent, but I'm accustomed to delayed gratification and determined to make good on this morning's promise.

I lick and suck and kiss one nipple and then the other, moving back and forth between them until Charlene's fingers are fisted in my hair and she's grinding aggressively, fighting her way toward an orgasm. I wrap my hands around her waist and lift so she can't achieve friction.

She whines my name.

"I'm pretty sure I said I was going to kiss you for hours before I let you come."

"It's been long enough, don't you think?" she pleads.

I glance at the clock on the wall, ticking away our evening. We've been making out for far longer than I realized. I pull her closer and kiss the space below her navel, and along the waistband of her leggings. I plan to kiss every inch of her body—eventually—but I'd like to play with her a little longer.

I settle her ass on my thighs again, but away from my erection so she can't rub on me. Her expression is pained, desperate, her need for release overwhelming. I keep one hand on her hip but slide the other palm up her stomach, between her breasts, until my fingers drift over her throat, tracing the edge of the pearls. Moving higher, I curl a finger along the shell of her ear and follow the curve of her jaw with my thumb.

As soon as I release her hip, Charlene tries to slide forward. I tip my head to the side, and she stops.

I follow the waistband of her leggings with a single finger. "I like these. Why don't you wear them more often?"

"I wear them all the time," she says breathlessly.

"I would like it if you wore them for me."

"Okay. I can do that."

I trace the outline of a donut that ends conveniently at the apex of her thighs. She sucks in a raspy breath as I run my knuckle over the bump of steel piercing her hood.

"I bet I can make you come like this."

"I'm sure you can."

I find the steel with my thumb and press gently. Charlene's grip on my knees tightens, and she rolls her hips. I decide this is how I want her tonight:

in my lap, close like this, so I can see every emotion as it crosses her perfect, expressive face.

I keep circling the piercing, slow and gentle, aware that softness pushes Charlene to the edge the fastest, and that the lack of direct contact is going to make her even needier.

And just as I predict, she comes, body shaking hard, nails digging into my knees through my jeans. Her elbows give out, and I have to tighten my grip on the back of her neck to keep her in place as she rides out the waves of pleasure, her soft moans growing louder as the orgasm drags her under.

When she's over the crest I pull her close again. She's drunk on her orgasm, uncoordinated and fumbling as brings our mouths back together.

"Thank you," she mumbles, tongue already in my mouth.

She grabs the hem of my shirt and pulls it roughly over my head. Her satin fingertips drift down the sides of my neck to my chest. Charlene comes back to suck on my bottom lip as she circles my nipples, but when she attempts to go lower, I stop her. At her questioning expression, I grip her by the waist and lay her out on the couch.

"I want to taste how much you need me," I explain.

I drag her leggings down and toss them to the floor, then pause when I hook my fingers in her underwear. Most of them are some combination of lace, satin or leather. Sometimes it's all three, and occasionally there are buckles and chains and metal clasps—those are her choice, not mine.

But her panties tonight are different and nothing I've ever seen on her before. They're cotton—that boy short style I've never been particularly fond of. Until now. These are lace trimmed at the waist, with tiny polka dots. Sweet and sexy, just like Charlene.

"Do you have a lot of these?"

"A few pairs." Her cheeks flush.

"I can buy you more," I offer.

"They're not expensive. I get five pairs for twenty-five dollars." She lifts her hips, possibly encouraging me to remove them.

"We could shop for them together. Do they come in different patterns and styles?"

"They do. I can show you my other ones after."

I shimmy them over her hips and drop my head, pressing my lips to the crest of her pubic bone before I remove them and drop them on the coffee table.

I shoulder my way between her legs and make her come with my mouth. She smells like need and tastes like want. By the time I'm done, the ache in my stomach is damn near killing me. I let Charlene pop the button on my jeans and drag the zipper down. I shove my jeans and boxers over my hips and down my thighs. Charlene stands between my legs and pulls them off the rest of the way, then pushes the coffee table back and sinks to her knees between my parted thighs.

My erection is pretty much pulsing. Even the air hurts at this point. The head is an angry shade of purple usually reserved for eggplant emojis, and the tip is weeping.

"Oh God, Darren." Charlene runs her hands up my thighs, tongue sweeping across her bottom lip.

I cover her hands with mine before she can put them on me. "No hands, no mouth." Jesus. I can't even form sentences that make sense anymore. "Stand, please."

She braces her palms on my knees and rises. Then she starts to turn.

I grab her hips to keep her facing me, then slide my palm down the outside of her thighs until I reach the back of her knees. When I tug her forward she has no choice but to brace her hands on my shoulders and straddle my lap.

I meet her confused gaze, which is understandable. Usually sex is an elaborate event for Charlene. "Should we go upstairs now? I could—"

"I want you like this, please." In two years, we've never had sex like this: on her couch, the TV still droning in the background.

"Okay." Her eyes are glassy with the same need I feel. "I can take you now?"

I smile at her phrasing and grit out a *yes*.

Charlene's palms rest on my shoulders and she shifts forward, lining us up without touching me. I position my thumb at the base and angle it toward her. When her hood piercing skims the tip, I groan.

Charlene's eyes dart to mine and then back down as the head nudges at her entrance.

"Slowly, please. I want to savor the feeling of you surrounding me."

She places a gentle palm on the side of my neck. Every part of me is burning with need so extreme I feel as if my nerve endings are on fire. She eases down, legs trembling as I disappear inside her.

I let my head drop back against the cushions, eyes still on her, and take a moment to absorb the sensation. It's different tonight. Like it's weighted with something new.

I could come right now, without even moving, but that would be embarrassing as hell, so I hold her hips to keep her steady, close my eyes to block out the sight and just breathe. Charlene's fingertips brush along the edge of my jaw, and I have to tell her to stop.

I open my eyes and find hers. "Everything is magnified right now. Give me a few moments."

"Okay."

Recognizing how much I need her, all the versions of her, even the ones she might not want me to see, makes this experience so much more intense than usual. While I battle my response to being inside her like this, I trace the delicate lines of her body, distracting myself with the way her skin dampens under my touch and her muscles flex and tighten when I hit a sensitive spot. All of it threatens to push me over the edge, despite not having moved at all. I drop a hand between her thighs and draw tight circles, shifting under her just enough to make her come and keep myself balanced on the painful edge.

As soon as the orgasm tips her into bliss, I move to the edge of the couch, wrap her legs around my waist and pull her close until our chests meet. I rock her over me, the ache in my balls bitingly vicious as it expands, shooting down my legs and forcing its way up my spine.

"Ah, fuck." I press my face into her neck, sucking on the skin, nipping my way up to her mouth. I kiss her, fighting to stay gentle, but need takes over and our teeth clash. I pull back, and Charlene's nails bite into the back of my neck.

Her eyes are soft but her words are not. "You gave, now take."

I hold her hips, lift and lower, over and over, faster, harder until I come—the whole world a wash of white and stars, the fusion of pleasure and pain so violent I nearly black out.

Charlene runs her fingers through my hair, the rhythmic action soothing. Eventually I lift my head from the crook of her neck.

"Hi." Her voice is hoarse.

"Hey."

"Feel better?"

"Mmm." I kiss her tenderly. She'll need lip balm for days after this. I make a note to do some research and have some sent to her while I'm away. "You?"

"Mmm. Better times four, I think."

"I would like to spend the night, if that's all right with you."

Her eyes flare with surprise, and her smile makes my chest tight.

"That's all right with me."

Charlene's bed is a double, so it means we spoon most of the night. My sleep might not have been the greatest, but the night was excellent, so I consider it a fair trade.

We sleep in late and have lazy morning sex. I'd like to spend the entire day with her, but apparently she has yoga with the girls this afternoon. We shower together, which turns into another round of sex, the slippery kind. Afterward, I watch her get dressed. She wears black yoga pants and a sports tank, her long auburn hair pulled into a ponytail. Like last night, her face is makeup free. She's always stunning, but I've decided I like her best like this. I want her without the mask.

I fold a hand behind my head as she slips on pair of flip flops. "What are your plans after yoga?"

"We usually go out for shakes afterwards. Would you like me to cancel?"

The answer to that is yes. I would very much like her to cancel, but I'm also aware it might be pushing Charlene too much, too quickly.

"I don't want to interfere with your plans. We fly out early tomorrow, so it's best if I get ready this afternoon and get a good night's sleep." I don't like that the first two playoff games of the series are away, but there's nothing we can do about it, other than come in prepared.

I throw the covers off and swing my feet over the edge of the bed. Crooking a finger I beckon her over. When she reaches me, I pull her between my legs and run my hands down her arms. Even with all the fabric in the way, she shivers.

"I'd like to speak with you tonight, if that's all right."

"Speak with me? About what?"

A furrow creases her brow, so I smooth it out with my thumbs.

"To find out how your day was. To hear your voice."

"Oh." The furrow returns.

"Is that okay?"

"Of course it's okay."

"Great." I take her face between my palms and kiss her until she has to push away and rush out the door for fear of being late.

I flop back down on the mattress. I could upgrade it for her. Get her something better and bigger, but I don't want to make her place more comfortable.

I meet up with Alex for an afternoon workout since I have nothing else to do and then head home. As I pack a bag for tomorrow's flight, I check my messages and frown when I note a voicemail from my grandparents. My good mood is dunked in a bucket of shit when I find out my parents are supposed to be in town this week for some kind of conference. I never hear from them directly. Technically I don't consider them my parents at all since my grandparents officially adopted me when I was four. At least I won't be in Chicago at the same time they are, so that's a relief.

I want to brush it off as meaningless, but it shines a dark light on the progress I made with Charlene last night. Because as much as I want things to change, one thing I want to keep her away from is my family, and I'm not sure I'll be able to do that forever.

Which is exactly how long I want to keep Charlene.

chapter seven

Momma Domme

Charlene

TONIGHT THE GIRLS ARE COMING OVER TO WATCH THE HOCKEY GAME. I TIDY UP the living room, having passed out on the couch last night. I'll blame it on lack of sleep prior to Darren going away and the *Hoarders* marathon. The whole him showing up unannounced, flowers and chocolate thing was a shock, not to mention the normal-people sex and the all-night spooning. But I'll admit, I enjoyed every moment of it, and I'm not opposed to a repeat.

I go about setting out all the snacks—the Doritos and onion dip are perfect since the boys are away—and make sure I have wine and sparkling juice for Sunny and Violet. The doorbell rings in the middle of setting up. It's only five-thirty, and the girls aren't supposed to arrive until closer to seven, but Violet often shows up early, bestie privileges and all.

I open the door, ready for the shenanigans to begin, and Violet's snide comments about pearl necklaces and anal. Except it's not my bestie.

"Mom?"

"Char-char!" She drops her bag and throws her arms around me, enveloping me in a tight, painful hug.

I pat her back, glancing over her shoulder. Laverne, the old lady next door is busy tending her garden—or was. She's currently staring slack jawed in our direction. It takes me a moment to realize why. My mom is dressed in her work gear.

"Why don't you come in?" I maintain the hug while dragging her inside the house and away from the neighbor's eyes. I hope Laverne's pacemaker is working these days, because she looks like she might be going into shock.

I grab my mom's bag from the front porch, give Laverne a quick wave, and disappear inside.

"I didn't realize you were arriving today." My voice has that high-pitched quality to it, much like a prepubescent boy who's accidentally zipped up his man noodle.

My mom is decked out in a black leather corset, complete with buckles and chains—hence the painfulness of the hug. Her skirt is short and barely covers her butt, and she's wearing fishnets and huge heeled boots with buckles that end mid-calf. Her makeup can only be described as *goth*, or maybe *emo*.

Her hair has been dyed jet black, and her lipstick is the color of a rich cabernet sauvignon.

"Oh! Did I forget to tell you I was coming in today? I swore I left a voicemail for you, or maybe that was in my head. I thought it might be nicer to stay with you than at a hotel. We can catch up and have some real quality mother-daughter bonding time!"

"Right. Sure. I have a spare bedroom. How long are you going to be in town?" I'm beyond relieved that Darren has already left Chicago for a variety of reasons.

"Just three days, so I want to make the most of it. It's been so long since I've seen you. You look . . ." She seems to struggle to find the right descriptive word and finally settles on "Good." Her pinched expression tells me she does not, in fact, think I look good.

I would describe my outfit as cute. As soon as I arrived home from work, I changed into my Westinghouse jersey and a pair of black and red leggings boasting the Chicago logo.

My mom flits around the kitchen, adjusting the dishcloth draped over the edge of the sink. "Anyway, tonight's a bit of a rush. I have a client meeting at eight that will probably take a few hours, depending—" She's interrupted by another knock.

Shit. It's still too early for the girls to be here.

"Oh! That's for me." My mother struts to the door.

"Did you invite your client here?" I choke the words out, mortified by the possibility.

She throws a look over her shoulder. "Of course not, Char-char. I'll explain it all. Just give me a moment."

She throws open the door and a swarm of people flood my kitchen. With video cameras. And there's some guy wearing one of those latex face masks with only eyeholes and a mouth hole, dressed in leather chaps, his entire ass on display. Thankfully his penis isn't hanging out.

"Mom?" There's that high pitch again.

She turns and claps her hands excitedly. "They're casting for a reality show this weekend. It's called *Momma Domme*! Isn't that cute? Anyway, I thought it was a great opportunity. This is my audition video. It's so much classier to film it in a house, you know? It'll only take half an hour."

And this, right here, is one of the many reasons I have never introduced Darren to my mother.

I pull her aside. "Is that a good idea, Mom? Being on a reality show? I mean, you'll be putting your face out there for everyone to see."

"I'll be wearing a mask, so it'll be fine. Plus, I dyed my hair for the show. You worry too much." She pats my cheek.

This coming from a woman who cut a hole in a barbed-wire fence, taught me how to hotwire a car, and drove me across continental middle America to escape a whole pile of crazy. Then she legally changed our names—not the best names, and not the best changes, but then, my mom doesn't always think things through. Who willingly chooses the last name Hoar?

"I have friends coming over soon," I tell her.

"Don't worry, Char-char. They'll be in and out within the hour."

I sure as hell hope so. Explaining my sex life with Darren is one thing, but explaining my mother is another entirely.

I make myself tea as the crew takes over the kitchen and starts moving furniture out of the way. The chair from my living room is relocated to where the table once was. A footstool is brought in while my mother opens her bag and sets out a vast array of sex toys, many of which I'm familiar with since she likes to send me every new prototype she gets her hands on.

"Nice place," Mask Guy says. He's doing that head-nod thing people do when they're uncomfortable and don't know what else to say. He also hitches his thumbs in his chaps, probably wishing he had pockets.

"Uh, thanks."

"So that's your mom, huh?" He inclines his head in her direction. She's using eyelash glue to attach a mask to her face. All it covers is the area around her eyes, so it's not particularly great at concealing her identity. I'd like to point this detail out to her, but there are currently too many people here.

"Yup." I bring my mug to my lips and blow. Later I'm drinking wine, or shots. Right now I'm trying to calm myself with chamomile.

"Do you ever tag team?"

I choke on a mouthful of hot tea and cough, trying to clear my airway. I set my mug on the counter as Mask Guy slaps me on the back. But when I keep coughing, he starts the Heimlich on me, and several flashes go off.

"Stop! Please don't touch me," I yell at both the photographer and the mask guy as I smack at his hands. He releases me and drops to all fours.

"I'm prepared to accept my punishment, mistress daughter."

I flail around. "Mom! Can you come deal with this?"

This is way more than any daughter should have to handle when her mom comes for a visit.

My mom steps in and slaps Mask Guy on the ass a couple of times. She gives me a patient smile while she pats his head like he's a dog, not a person.

"I brought you fresh candies. They're in my bag. Why don't you have one and relax, sweetie? I also brought you presents, but we can open them together if you want to wait."

I grab my mom's bag and take it to the living room, where there is no camera crew. I find the bag of candies in one of the side pockets—which is the only place I check because going through my mom's overnight bag isn't for the faint of heart, and I'm sure I'll find a few things I'd rather not see.

As promised, the camera crew is able to wrap things up within the hour. But of course, Mom has to chat them up, so they're on their way out the door when Violet and Poppy arrive.

Mask Guy pulls it up over his head on his way out the door. His hair is wet from being encased in latex for the past hour, and his face is red. He might be okay looking, but I'm too distracted by Laverne sitting on her front porch, witnessing the porn parade exit my house.

"If you ever get into the biz, and you need someone to practice on, I'd love to bottom for you," maskless Mask Guy says.

"I have a boyfriend."

"Of course you do." He slips his hand down the front of his assless chaps and withdraws a baggie. Inside are his business cards. "Here's my card, should that change."

"Uh, thanks."

Violet and Poppy stand at the edge of my garden as the porn parade disperses. They both check out maskless Mask Guy's ass as he passes. It's a pretty nice ass; I'll give him that. I glance the card—apparently his name is Rodney Steele. Of course. Steel rod, how clever.

Violet and Poppy give each other a look before they rush up the walkway and I usher them into the house. "Uh, you wanna explain that?" Vi asks as I close the door behind them.

"Hi girls! You must be Char-char's friends! I'm Whensday! Her mom!"

When we changed our identities, my mom wanted to make sure our names were easy to remember. Her real name is Wendy, so she decided on Whensday, spelled incorrectly—W-H-E-N-S-D-A-Y. Although she says it was on purpose. My life was a lot weird. Clearly it still is.

Poppy flashes one of her sweet smiles and extends a hand. "It's so nice to meet you."

"Mom, this is Poppy, and you remember Violet."

"Oh, yes, of course! And you're both flowers! How fun is that?" My mom is still wearing her fetish gear. The last time Violet met my mom she was wearing normal-people clothes, so this is a bit of a shocker, I think.

"Um, are you planning to change now that the camera crew is gone, or . . ." I let it hang, hoping she'll take the hint.

"I have to leave soon to meet with a client, so I'll change when I get back. What're you girls doing tonight?"

"We're watching the hockey playoffs."

The doorbell rings again, forcing me to leave my mother unsupervised with my friends.

Sunny and Lily are standing on my front porch. They look like a couple of bag ladies with all the stuff they're carrying, including a sleeping Logan strapped into his car seat. He could be a professional napper. When he isn't bumbling around being super cute, he's sleeping on any available surface: chairs, couches, laps, the floor, Lily's wiener dog's dog bed.

"Look, girls, I need to tell you some—"

Before I can finish the sentence, my mom makes her presence known. She appears behind me, holding a box of wine—the kind with the spout. "Hi, girls! Oh! This is so fun! Char-char, you have so many friends!"

"Lily, Sunny, this is my mom." I'm not sure if this is much better than when the guys saw me naked surrounded by crazy sex toys.

Sunny's eyes go wide, and her mouth forms an "o". Lily nudges her, and Sunny clamps her mouth shut. Her bag-laden arm shoots out toward my mom. "It's so nice to meet you, Ms. Hoar." Like Gertrude, she forgets that the H is silent.

Lily chokes back a cough, but my mom doesn't so much as flinch. "It's Whensday, darling."

Sunny's brow pulls down. "I thought it was Friday."

My mom throws her head back and cackles. She sounds like a crow being eaten alive. "Aren't you adorable? My *name* is Whensday."

"Like the Addams' Family girl?" Lily supplies.

"Almost! Except it's spelled like 'when are we going to go to the party', not Wed-ness. Anyway, *The Addams Family* is my favorite movie in the entire world!"

Sunny looks appropriately confused by this explanation.

My mom claps her hands and looks to me. "We should have a movie night while I'm here and watch it together!"

"Sure, Mom." Better than Dominatrix training videos, I guess.

I need to pull my mother aside and make sure she doesn't say anything to my friends about my childhood, because that's not something I'd like to explain. To anyone. Ever. I don't think she'll mention it, as we've spent the past decade pretending it never happened, but her behavior today is concerning, so I'm unsure what to expect.

"I wish I could hang out with you girls, but I have a client meeting, and I still have to figure out how to get there." My mom waves her hand in the air, like the life of a Dominatrix is painfully trying. "Maybe you'll all still be here when I get back." She taps her lip. "Although, this client is a bit difficult, so I might be several hours."

My mom sashays across the kitchen and grabs her bag. "I'll give you your presents now, Char-char."

"That's okay, Mom. They can wait."

She waves me off. "It's so much more fun to open presents when you're with friends, though, isn't it? And I think your friends will get a kick out of this. We're all adults here!"

"Sure are," Violet's expression is gleefully malevolent.

Usually when Darren buys me things, they're professionally wrapped, or they come in a pretty bag with nice curly ribbon. Not gifts from my mom. They come in nondescript plastic bags.

I reluctantly peek inside the bag. Oh yeah, this is going to be . . . stranger than usual. I should've gotten out the tequila in preparation. I reach inside and pull out the least offensive item.

"What is that?" Sunny tips her head to the side.

"It's a vibrating cockring. Watch." My mom plucks it from my hand and puts it in Sunny's palm before she turns it on.

Sunny's face turns an even brighter shade of red. "Oh. That would feel . . ."

"Great, right?"

Sunny nods uncertainly.

"Go ahead. There's more." My mom motions for me to keep going. When I'm not fast enough, she grabs the bag from me and dumps it on the table.

I sigh as I stare at the weirdness in front of me.

Violet screams and hides behind me. "What the fuck are those?" She points from her place over my shoulder.

"You mean these, or this?" My mom holds up two separate items, both of which are equally freaky.

Violet makes a gagging sound from behind me. "Either, both? Is that real?"

"These are Ben Wa balls, and this a Spidergasm. They're prototypes for this year's Halloween Dominatrix party in Vegas! Fun, aren't they?"

That's not quite the way I would describe them. The Ben Wa balls—weighted balls that hang out in your vag for pre-sex stimulation—look like actual eyeballs, the kind you find on those creepy dolls, and the Spidergasm looks like a black widow spider.

Violet shudders. "So fun. Can we put those away now?"

"Are you afraid of spiders? This might help you get over your fear."

"I'm fine. It's okay." Violet uses me as a shield.

"No really, you should try it out."

"I can do it." Lily steps forward.

We all look at her like maybe she's lost her mind, but she smiles and holds her hand palm up.

"Okay. So imagine this is your clitoris." My mom turns on her sexy Dominatrix voice and runs one of her talon nails along the length of Lily's middle finger.

Lily shivers, but nods, eyes darting questioningly to me. I can't save her now.

My mom picks up the black widow and makes it pretend crawl across Lily's palm and up her finger—yes, it's creepy.

"And this little spider is about to fire off all eight thousand of those nerve endings!" My mom wraps the little spider around the end of Lily's finger and taps the butt.

Lily shouts her surprise, and then her jaw clamps shut. "Does it . . . bite?"

"Yes! And it vibrates. Research tests are showing that it takes the average woman four minutes to achieve an orgasm through the Black Widow Spidergasm model. That's one minute faster than their previous model." My mom maintains her Dominatrix sex sales voice through the entire spiel.

"Huh. That's—"

"—incredible, right?"

"This explains a lot," Violet whispers in my ear, still clutching my shoulder.

"I know," I mumble.

Thankfully my mom's phone alarm chimes. She pulls her pouty face. "Duty calls. That's too bad. I would've loved to chill with you girls tonight." She grabs my arm. "I know! Maybe you and all your girlfriends would like to come to the convention tomorrow."

"Convention?" Lily asks. The spider is still attached to her finger. She keeps pushing on its butt, increasing and then decreasing the vibrations.

"Sexapalooza! It's a great convention. I can get you all free tickets since I'm a presenter." She puffs out her chest, clearly proud of this accomplishment.

"Will there be more stuff like this?" Lily holds up her spider finger.

"Oh yes! If it has to do with sex, it's there." My mom roots around in her purse and pulls out a handful of tickets. "Char-char will fill you in. I must be on my way." She kisses me on the cheek. "I'll be back later. You girls have fun!"

And with that she's out the door.

Sunny raises her hand as soon as she's gone. "Um, what does your mom do for a living?"

Usually I say she's in the entertainment business, which is kind of true. "She's a Dominatrix."

"So what does she do, exactly?" Sunny wraps her hair around her finger.

"Basically she bosses men around until they have an orgasm." That's not totally accurate, but for the sake of simplicity, it works.

"Oh."

"I'm going to have a glass of wine. Anyone else feel like a glass of wine? Or some shots? We could do shots."

Poppy helps with the wine, and Lily pours sparkling juice into champagne flutes so Sunny and Vi don't feel left out. I do two shots of Patron, and Lily joins me, because shots.

Once we all have drinks, we head for the living room. Lily still has the black widow spider attached to her finger, so Violet sits as far away from her as she possibly can. The game has already started, but the score is still zero on both sides.

Lily's only half paying attention, still fascinated with the clit-biting spider. "We're going to the convention tomorrow, right? Randy's been talking about lingerie shopping and ball gags so . . ."

"You'll be able to get your very own ball gag there for sure. And lingerie." I mean it to be snarky, but based on their expressions, I don't think anyone takes it that way.

Violet raises a brow. "I can't wait to see your mom in action. She makes mine look like a dream."

"I think your mom is interesting," Sunny offers.

"Will they have these at the sex show?" Lily wiggles her spider finger in the air.

"Probably, but you can have that one if you want it."

"Really?" Her eyes light up. I know Lily and Randy get it on, like, every five minutes or whatever, but I didn't realize they were into the freak-a-leak business. Or it's possible Lily is just now discovering her inner freak. It'd be nice to have a friend who's freakier than me. Violet believes Vagazzling makes her adventurous.

"Sure." I gulp my wine. "But I should warn you, it's probably been used."

Lily's elation deflates like a balloon. "Seriously?"

"Yeah, like once or something? Especially if it's a prototype," I explain.

"Prototype?"

"Yeah. Sometimes my mom tests out products before they hit the market."

"So your mom might've used this?" Lily peels it off her finger and drops it on the coffee table.

"Uh, it's possible? I mean, it could've come out of the package, but I have no way of knowing, unless you want me to ask her."

"That's okay. If they have them at the sex show, I'll buy one there."

"I don't think Miller would like that very much," Sunny says, thoughtfully. "He's not a fan of spiders."

"Understandable, really." Violet smiles behind her glass.

"Ever since he had his scrotum drained after that spider bite, he makes me get rid of all the eight-legged creatures. I don't kill them, though. I always take them outside when he's not looking."

"Whoa, Miller had his—" Poppy motions to her groin area. "—*drained?*"

"Oh my God! I forgot that was pre-Poppy days! So when Miller and I were still trying to figure things out, he went up to a Canadian hockey camp with Randy and they volunteered to train with the kids. It's so sweet, and special, really. But Miller was bitten by a spider, and he had an allergic reaction."

"His balls were the size of my boobs." Violet motions to her girls.

"Well, not quite that big, but there's a picture somewhere out there. They were very swollen. So he had to have them drained," Sunny explains.

"That's just . . . awful."

"It was. Poor baby. Anyway. His balls are fine now, obviously." Sunny pats her belly.

We half pay attention to the game while the girls exchange stories about the beginnings of their relationships. Which are a lot different than the way Darren and I started.

Chicago wins the first game. We all pick up our phones and send congratulatory messages that won't be seen for a while yet. Half an hour later, phones chime around us with replies. Sunny excuses herself to take a call from Miller. Lily gets a message from Randy asking if she's alone. Violet and Poppy both field short calls, and I sit with my phone in my hand, waiting for something, anything.

Eventually I get a message. It's simple. Short. A *thank you*. I remind myself that Darren doesn't engage in extensive texting, and any response is a good one. Most of the time it's enough, but in this moment it makes me feel a little too different, like I don't quite fit and maybe never will. I used to be fine with that. Tonight it makes my heart ache.

chapter eight

Meet the 'Rents

Charlene

The following afternoon, Lily picks me and Violet up at my place since she stayed the night.

I follow Violet outside and hit the lock button on the door—Darren didn't feel my previous lock set was sufficient, so he had a keypad installed with a code and an alarm system. It's another way I know he cares and wants to keep me safe. Although my neighborhood is pretty quiet. It's mostly older couples and a few young families.

I start down the front walk and scream at the sight of a mini Winnebago—the kind one pulls behind a car—parked in my driveway. "Holy fuck!" I rush back to the door and punch the keypad, but I'm too frantic to get it right, so it squawks at me in protest.

"Oh shit—" Violet mutters. "I should've warned you, but I figured you already knew it was here.

I shield my eyes. "Where did that come from? Why is it here? Who's in it?"

"I think it's your mom's?"

I stop freaking out. "What?"

"It was here when I came over yesterday, and the SUV it was hooked up to is gone, so it's just a guess. But I'm thinking it's a pretty solid one. Are you going to be okay?"

"What?" It feels a lot like I can't breathe properly. "Oh. Oh yeah. I'm fine."

"Should we go?"

"Yeah. Yeah. Sure." I've taken two shuffly, unsteady steps down the walkway when the alarm goes off in the house. "Shit. Hold on."

By the time I get the door unlocked, the alarm company is calling. I explain that I accidently hit the wrong code, give them all the personal details they require to ensure someone hasn't broken into my house and taken me hostage, and lock up a second time.

I keep my eyes averted as I speed walk to Lily's truck—well, technically it's Randy's truck, but she always drives it when he's out of town—and throw myself into the backseat.

"I didn't know you were a camper," Sunny says from the front seat.

"I actually hate camping."

"What's with the camping trailer, then?" Lily asks.

"It's her mom's," Violet supplies when all I do is sit there, dry mouthed and anxious.

"Oh, did you have a bad experience? When Lily and I went tree planting, it was awful." Even Sunny's frown is cute.

"I think it might've been the people we went with," Lily replies. "But it can be fun. If you're with the right people."

I don't say anything, because my experience with RVing is probably not like most people's.

Less than two minutes after getting into the truck, my phone rings. I'm surprised to see it's Darren. We don't have a lot of phone conversations when he's away. I bring the phone to my ear.

"Charlene? Is everything okay? Are you all right?"

His concern is even more surprising than the out-of-the-blue phone call. "I'm fine. Why?"

"Oh. Okay." He exhales a long breath. "Okay. That's good. I received a message from the alarm company that was . . . concerning. I wanted to make sure nothing happened and you were safe."

I hadn't realized Darren would be contacted if my house alarm went off.

"I'm fine. I put in the wrong code one too many times, and it went off. Sorry if I worried you."

"As long as you're safe, that's all that matters. It sounds like you're in a car. Are you driving?"

"I'm with the girls, and I'm not driving."

"Ah. That's good. Okay. Well, I won't keep you, then. Maybe, uh, we could talk later? Or I'll text if that isn't convenient for you."

My stomach flips. Darren doesn't usually suggest phone calls unless we're making a plan to see each other and texting will take too long. "I'd love to talk. I can message when I'm home and see if you're around?"

"That would be perfect. Have a fun day with your friends."

I finger my pearls, smiling at how formal and awkward he can be when he's unsure how to approach a subject. It's endearing. "Okay. I will."

"But not as much fun as you'd have with me."

I laugh. "Of course not."

I end the call with a smile.

"Everything okay?" Violet asks.

"Oh yeah. Darren got the message from the alarm company and wanted to make sure I'm okay."

"He gets alerts when your house alarm goes off?" Lily asks.

"He's the one who had it installed, so yeah. I guess he wanted to make sure I'm safe."

"That's sweet, isn't it?" Sunny smiles. "That he wants to make sure you're taken care of when he can't be with you."

"Yeah." I roll the pearls over my lips. "It is."

∽

It takes half an hour to get to the convention center, and another twenty minutes to find parking. Violet is absolutely shocked when Lily manages to back into a spot without hitting anything. Most of the time when we go out as a group we don't allow Violet to drive because she's so bad at it. She can manage to drive in a straight line, but parking, backing out, and turning all seem to be a challenge for her.

We hand our tickets over and head inside. I've been to plenty of sex shops to buy lingerie, and sometimes toys and fun stuff. But in the past I've tried to avoid these kinds of sex conventions because of my mom's job, so it's new, even for me.

Lily meanders from display to display, checking everything out. Poppy's face is an interesting shade of perma-red, and Sunny, well, I think this whole experience is going to scar my poor friend for life. At least I tried to shield her from it, which is more than I can say for the rest of them.

Violet is . . . Violet. She stops at a table with strap-ons and picks one up. "Can I test this out?" she asks the guy manning the booth. He looks like he probably watches a lot of internet porn and doesn't often see the light of day.

"Uh, test it out how?" he asks.

"Like, can I try it on? See if it fits?"

"Oh, yeah. For sure." He nods at her boobs. Although to be fair, she is wearing a v-neck Chicago shirt with the logo stretched across her chest. On the back is Alex's last name and jersey number. She has a lot of Alex-inspired gear.

She tosses one at me. "You should try this on, too."

I snort and roll my eyes. "I'm good."

"Oh come on! Aren't we in your favorite playground right now? Have a little fun!"

Before I can protest, Lily grabs it from me.

I think the guy manning the booth is going to have a coronary watching the two of them fasten each other with strap-ons. In fact, pretty much every guy in the general vicinity has stopped what they're doing to watch.

"You really can't take Violet anywhere, can you?" Poppy asks with a smile on her still-red face.

"Not really, but she's definitely entertaining."

As soon as Violet has Lily's strap-on in place, they have a dick sword fight, which draws more attention—the kind where people take pictures on the sly that are for sure going to end up on social media.

I drag Vi behind a display of dildos suctioned to the wall, and Poppy does the same with Lily.

"People are taking pictures," I scold. "Take off your dongs and act normal for once."

Violet's face is red from laughing and exertion. "But I like my dong."

"Pictures are probably going to be posted all over the place, and you're wearing an Alex shirt. He's going to get tagged, and then he's going to see you and Lily having a strap-on sword fight."

Her smile drops and she cringes, the red spots on her chest grow progressively blotchier. "Shitballs." She tries to unharness herself, but she's too frantic to manage it. "I can't get my dong off!"

"Here, let me help." I free her quickly while Lily unbuckles her own.

"You're awfully good with the buckles and stuff," Vi observes.

"Don't even go there," I tell her. "If it wasn't for you and the rest of the girls, I wouldn't be here."

"It's fun though, and it demystifies a lot of the stuff we read about in BDSM, right? Besides, this one is loving all the porny stuff." She thumbs over her shoulder at Lily, who shrugs and grins.

We come back out from behind the wall of dildos, thank the guy who's probably going to be blue balling it for the rest of the day, and go in search of Sunny. Which is when we run into Skye, Violet's mom, and Daisy, who is Alex and Sunny's mother.

"Shit!" Violet tries to pull me behind a display of latex-body-suit-wearing mannequins.

"Vi! Charlene! Girls!" Skye shouts.

Violet cringes and drops her head in defeat. "Hey, Mom. Daisy, what are you doing here?" She peeks inside the stroller Daisy's pushing. "With Logan?"

Skye wraps her arm around Violet's shoulder and gives her a big hug. "Sunny mentioned you were going to this 'palooza thing today, so Daisy and I looked it up and thought it would be fun if we came, too!"

"With a baby?" Violet asks.

"Logan is too little to remember any of it, so it's fine. Isn't that right, my favorite little chubbie-wubbie?" Daisy gets all up in little Logan's face and tickles his feet. He giggles and swipes at her swinging hair.

"You should've told us about this! We could've made it a whole mother-daughter bonding experience!" Skye flails around excitedly.

"Yeah, 'cause shopping for sex toys with my mom is exactly what I want to do on a Saturday afternoon."

"Oh, come on, Vi! We had so much fun when we went in Vegas, didn't we?"

"I think they have a maternity sex section," Daisy tells Sunny, who's finally wandered over. She looks a little disturbed to find her mother here. At least hers is just shopping and not part of the event.

This day keeps getting better and better. Especially when we finally stumble upon my mom, performing a Dominatrix demonstration. There's a different masked, assless chaps guy following her around on all fours wearing a leash. I know it's a different guy because this one has a massive back tattoo, and the guy from yesterday did not.

Thankfully, we arrive at the tail end of the demonstration.

Skye does her dejected-four-year-old flaily thing. "Too bad we missed that. It looked like fun. I wonder if Sidney would like those kinds of pants." She turns to Daisy. "I bet we'd look hot in that leather business. That woman looks to be about our age." She gestures to my mom.

It's then that my mother notices me and starts waving. She struts—she's actually incredibly adept at the whole strut deal—over to us. "Char-char! Are you and the girls having fun?"

I slip my hand into my pocket, feeling around for my candies. I'm a little worried about introducing Skye to my mom. Individually they're embarrassing enough, but together, the humiliation could be epic.

"Oh my God!" Skye shrieks like a teeny bopper at a boy band concert. "You two know each other?" Skye's hand shoots out, and my mom takes it. "I'm Skye, Violet's mother."

"I'm Whensday, Charlene's mother!" my mom replies with exactly the same level of enthusiasm. "But my stage name is Climaxica."

Maybe I can sneak away while this happens. My mom threads her arm through mine and hugs me to her, killing that idea.

"I was mentioning to Daisy how amazing you look in this ensemble!" Skye motions beside her. Daisy's still in charge of the stroller.

My mom runs her hands over her leather corset. "I have half an hour between performances. I'd be happy to show you around and take you to a few of the BDSM-wear booths."

Daisy pats her hair. It used to be more helmet-like, but since Violet's wedding, it's moved into the twenty-first century. Her clothes are a slower transition out of the eighties, but at least she's not wearing shoulder pads anymore. "I'm not sure leather would work with my complexion."

"Are you kidding me? Blond hair and black leather are a lethal combination." My mom threads her arm through Skye's as well, and the girls follow her as she woman-swaggers through the crowd, waving hello to the other vendors and performers. She air kisses about twenty people and stops at one booth to paddle some random guy's ass.

As I observe my mother in her element, I recognize how she and I are very much polar opposites. Where she's spent the years since leaving The Ranch flitting from town to town, putting men in their place, I've put down roots, found stability, and tried to build a somewhat normal relationship. I'm not so sure I'm ever destined to be successful at the last part, but I'm certainly trying. I created a non-traditional family of my own so I wouldn't have to be alone.

We stop at a boutique called Leather & Laces and browse for a while. Lily takes an armful of outfits and disappears into a changing room. They have all sorts of sexy leather corsets and fun stuff. Darren prefers pretty and lacy. It's not that he doesn't like the leather, he clearly does—the peen doesn't lie—but his eyes light up in a different way when I'm in lace or satin. I always end up the recipient of an insane number of orgasms on those occasions.

The curtain beside us sweeps open a bit, and Lily's head pops out. "I need an opinion."

"What's going on in there?" I try to peek around her, but she's holding it like she's in *The Shining*, wearing the same creepy smile.

"You have to come in."

We've all been in various stages of nakedness on multiple occasions with each other, so it's not a big deal. I slip through the curtain, and Violet follows. The changing room is cramped with three bodies.

Vi's eyes go wide. "Holy shit."

"Is that good holy shit or a bad holy shit?" Lily tugs at the collar around her neck. "Is this overkill?"

I actually have almost the exact same corset ensemble. I've worn it a couple of times for Darren. I'm a big fan of the collar with the metal ring at the throat. There's something empowering about letting someone you care about deeply take control of your body and cater to your needs. And this outfit screams submission and trust.

"There's only one way to find out, isn't there?" I cock a brow.

"Uhh . . ." Lily glances from me to Violet and back again.

"Send a picture to Balls and see what he has to say?" Violet asks.

Lily chews on her lip and then hands me her phone. "Okay."

She strikes sexy poses while I snap a bunch of pictures. We scroll through them and comment on how it makes her cleavage look great before she picks one to send to Randy.

It takes all of thirty seconds before he responds.

1. Where the fuck are you? 2. Buy that if you haven't already. 3. Who took that picture and am I going to prison for murder?

Lily grins as she types her reply, and Violet and I leave her to change back into normal clothes. Skye is already at the register with her own purchase.

"I gotta say, I'm super glad I don't live in my parents' pool house anymore," Violet says.

"Right?"

We find Poppy and Sunny huddled with sleeping baby Logan over by the sweeter sexy things in pinks and greens and florals. I glance around, wondering how soon we can get out of here now that I've seen my mom. I note a couple in the porn star area. There are actual stars signing posters and old school DVDs, and even some VHS tapes for the serious diehard fans. Which is kind of sad.

"Hey." Violet elbows me and points to the right. "Doesn't that guy look like an older version of Darren?"

I follow her gaze and note the couple, probably in their fifties, posing for pictures. The woman is outfitted in a silver mini-dress and has definitely had her boobs done, and likely a lot of other things, including her face, but she still looks mostly human. The guy is tall, wearing only black leather pants with a zebra stripe down the side. He's still rocking a pretty decent body for being older, complete with four pack, even if it's the tiniest bit saggy.

I scan all the way to his face and take in his dark, slicked-back hair. "Huh. That's weird. He does look a lot like him."

"You need to take a picture with that guy. Tell Darren you found his future self—and he's a porn star! The resemblance is uncanny, isn't it?" Violet turns to Poppy and Sunny, who both nod their agreement.

I give in and let her drag me over. My mom seems to know them personally, so she flits on over and introduces us. "Rod and Cherry, this is my daughter, Charlene. She needs a photo with you!" Rod and Cherry. I guess subtlety isn't their thing. My mom squeezes me between them and snaps a million pictures.

I send one to Darren with a laughing emoji and the caption: *Your next profession could be a porn stunt double for this guy.*

"So you're a Chicago hockey fan, Charlene?" Rod's smile is blindingly white and eerily like Darren's.

"I am."

Rod leans in closer. "Can you keep a secret?"

It's starting to creep me out how much he looks like Darren. His voice is even deep like Darren's, and he has the same icy eyes.

"Uh, sure?" I'm hit by an odd sense of foreboding.

"My boy plays hockey in Chicago." Rod's grin grows even wider as he looks over my shoulder. "And you're wearing his name on your back."

chapter nine

Mom's Approval

Darren

I typically sleep on the flight home, but this time all I can do is tap on the armrest and count down the minutes until we land.

My worries revolve around Charlene. After the picture and caption, I fired back a message telling her not to talk to them. I tried to follow it up with a phone call, but it went right to voicemail. In my panic, I made some irrational demands, to which she responded that this certainly wasn't a phone conversation, let alone one to be had over text messages.

I honestly never thought there would be a reason to tell her about my birth parents since they had almost no hand in raising me.

I go directly to her place from the airport, even though it's unlikely that she's home from work so we can have a discussion. The Uber drops me off in front of her house. I have my hockey gear with me, which is somewhat inconvenient, but I didn't want to stop at home first. Charlene's car is missing from her driveway, and in its place is a mini red Winnebago hooked up to a small SUV.

The Winnebago is a shock, mostly because Charlene has a thing about RVs, regardless of size. I know this because once on our way to Alex's cottage we stopped at a gas station and she nearly had a panic attack when one pulled into the bay next to us. She refused to let me get out of the car until it left.

When I tried to pry more information out of her, she mumbled something about where she grew up and how she associated RVs with bad men. At that point I knew little about her upbringing, but I'd never seen her in such a state of panic.

So seeing this Winnebago in her driveway brings up all sorts of questions. Ones I'd like some answers to. I run my sweaty hands down my thighs and gather myself before I finally ring the bell. When it swings open, I'm face to face with a woman dressed in a black leather corset and a pair of heels that could double as murder weapons.

She slides her hand up the doorframe and the other one goes to her hip, which she juts out. Her brow arches and a grin forms on her wine red lips. "Well, hello there. If you're trying to get me to go to your church, I'm afraid I'm far too sinful for that. Would you like a demonstration?"

I look down at myself. I'm wearing dress pants and a button-down shirt.

I suppose I can see how she might mistake me for a church type, but...did she just proposition me? I slip my hands in my pockets and glance over her shoulder, trying to see past her, but she takes up most of the doorway.

"I'll have to pass on that. I'm here to see Charlene."

Her smile falters as she inspects me in a new way. "Oh? Is that right? And who might you be?"

"I'm . . . uh . . . her boyfriend?" For some reason it comes out as a question.

"Oh! Yes, of course! Char-char can be so secretive about stuff like that." She gives me a conspiratorial wink.

Char-char? "I guess?"

She motions for me to come inside. "She should be home soon. Would you like to come in?"

"Sure. Thank you." When I enter the kitchen, I freeze. The counter is covered in sex toys. More specifically, the kind I typically find in Charlene's *I thought I might like it but I changed my mind* trunk. What the hell is going on here? "May I ask how you know Charlene?"

"I'm so sorry. I'm so distracted. I haven't even introduced myself properly. I'm Whensday, Char-char's mother." She extends a hand.

"Oh! I didn't realize you were visiting Charlene. It's nice to meet you."

I'd tell her mom I've heard a lot about her, but the truth is, I haven't. I know the basics. That she's a Dominatrix, and has been since Charlene was a teenager. Before that they lived in a rural community, and Charlene's father wasn't a good man, so they left. Aside from those details, I know little about Charlene's family or her early life. Neither of us is particularly keen to talk about our childhoods, so we don't.

"It's always nice to meet Char-char's friends. A mother worries, you know."

"I'm sure you do."

I agree even though I wouldn't know what that's like. My parents gave zero fucks about me. I'm fairly certain that hasn't changed in the past decade. And my grandparents, who did raise me, are about as warm as ice.

Charlene's mom crosses to the counter where a plethora of dildos and other sex toys are laid out on dishtowels. I make a mental note to throw out every dishtowel in the house.

"It's such a small world, isn't it? Char-char had quite the adventure meeting your parents this weekend! The resemblance between you and your father is actually rather uncanny. So smart that they went into directing since porn stars have such a short shelf life. No one wants to watch boobs flop around when they're trying to get off, do they? And don't get me started on old balls, am I right?"

I'm not sure if she honestly expects me to respond. I'm also suddenly very aware that as fucked up as I might think I am, based on what I'm seeing and hearing, Charlene is just as much a mess. It doesn't appear that her mother sheltered her in any way from her chosen profession. It makes me want to protect Charlene from all the bad things in this world, myself excluded.

"So how long have you been dating Charlene, exactly?"

I go with vague. "We've been together for a while."

"Really? Hmm... Well, enjoy her while you can."

What the hell does that mean? "I'm sorry?"

"Char-char doesn't often let people get too close to her. Well, apart from her girlfriends, anyway."

My mouth is suddenly dry. I contemplate how well I really know Charlene, because there's some truth in what her mother has said. Charlene has always been the one to pull back in our relationship. I've allowed it because I don't want to risk losing her by pushing her, but we're two years into this, and I don't have the sense of security I'd like to.

"It's been nice visiting her. She has such fun friends. They all enjoyed themselves at the convention. You know, I tried to raise Charlene in a very sex-positive, shame-free lifestyle, at least once it was just the two of us."

"That's important." I'm not sure what else to say to that.

"It really is, but sometimes I think it might have been better for Char-char if she'd had a more normal childhood. She was always so sweet, and smart as a whip! My God, she could recite her times tables up to twelve by the time she was four. It's no surprise she works with numbers. If I'd had her smarts, maybe I would've made better choices." She gives me a rueful smile. "I'd always thought maybe one day Char-char might want to travel the world with me, but she seems settled and happy here."

"She is happy, and very much settled." Her house is homey, her life has a routine and comfort in it, and I'm part of that.

She tips her head. "You play professional hockey, yes?"

"I do."

"That means you travel often?"

"During the season, yes."

"Mmm..." She says something that sounds like *close but not too close.* "That must make relationships challenging."

"I'm in Chicago during the off-season, and Charlene is very independent, as I'm sure you know." I force a smile, aware that even if she doesn't have the most conventional job, she's still a mother making sure her daughter is taken care of. "She also has good friends who are always here when I'm away."

"Those girls she spends her time with seem like a family," Whensday observes.

"They're very much like sisters," I agree.

"That's good. She needs that. She was always surrounded by a lot of—"

The door slams before Whensday can finish that thought. "Mom? I'm home!"

Charlene's voice is the balm I've needed since the plane landed, even if her words aren't directed at me. I'm simultaneously calm and anxious. I wonder if this is how Charlene feels on a regular basis when I return from away games.

She comes to a halt as soon as she sees me. Her eyes dart to Whensday, then to the sex toys in the drying rack before they swing back to me. "What're you doing here?"

I guess we're ignoring all the awkward. "I wanted to see you. I thought we should talk."

She arches a brow. "You could've called first."

Her mom seems to be oblivious to the sudden tension. "Darren and I were talking about professions. We have a lot in common with all the traveling we do, don't we?" She looks to me for confirmation.

It's really the only thing we have in common apart from Charlene. "I suppose—"

Charlene directs a withering glare at her mother. "Well, that's nice. I don't like living out of a suitcase, so I guess that makes me the odd one out." She motions to the sex toys in the drying rack, refusing to look my way as her cheeks flush. "Why is this stuff sitting out like this? Can't you put it away?"

"I couldn't pack them wet. And honestly, Char-char, it's not as if Darren hasn't seen it all before." Whensday turns her bright smile on me.

How would she know what I've seen and what I haven't? And suddenly it all clicks. Charlene wanting to try new things and then deciding against it. Charlene's box of *I thought I might* toys. They were never her idea; I just didn't realize that until now.

With her mother's traveling sex shop lying all over the kitchen, I can see exactly how Charlene came to believe this is normal, expected even. Prior to this moment, it hadn't occurred to that her mother might influence those choices, mainly because I'd believed she and her mom weren't all that close. This alters my perception of the antics she often pulls, and I have to wonder if she only suggests half the things she does because she's been brainwashed to believe I won't want to have sex with her otherwise.

A phone buzzes from somewhere amid the sex toys on the counter, and Whensday moves things around until she finds it. "Oh my! I didn't realize it was so late. I have to get going!"

Charlene helps transfer the toys into Ziplock bags, which her mom dumps into a small suitcase. I don't offer my assistance until everything is packed up since this whole situation is uncomfortable enough as it is. I carry the suitcases out to the little RV. Charlene is extra skittish once we're outside, close to the Winnebago. I might need to push for more information about the whole RV thing considering the way she keeps pulling at the collar of her shirt as I load her mom's bags. Once I'm finished, I get a hug from her mother and head back inside so they can say their goodbyes.

I pace the kitchen for a minute, then peruse her fridge for something to drink. Charlene has wine, but it's in a box. I'm not sure I've ever consumed wine in such a fashion, but I believe the conversation we're about to have requires alcohol, so I retrieve two glasses from the cupboard and fill them. Generously.

A minute later Charlene returns. Her back is to me, so she hasn't noticed me yet.

I don't say anything as she stands there, facing the door, fingers flexing on the knob, the other hand at her throat. Eventually she turns, working the buttons of her blouse free.

"Shit!" she yells when she sees me standing on the other side of the kitchen, leaning against the counter.

"I didn't mean to startle you." I hold out the glass. "Would you like some wine?"

Her lips flatten into a thin line, but she crosses the kitchen and grabs the glass. Some of the wine sloshes over the edge and lands on my foot, soaking my sock. She either doesn't notice or doesn't care. She tips her head back and chugs the contents. A dribble of wine spills down her chin, and she swipes it away with the back of her hand.

"Your mother seems . . . nice." Based on the glare I get, I'm not sure that was the best conversation starter.

"Really, Darren? That's what you're going with? My mom seems *nice?*" She steps around me and heads for the fridge. Wrenching it open, she pulls out the box of wine and slams it on the counter beside me. There's a fine sheen of sweat on her brow and her neck. Her hands shake as she fills her glass and drains it, again.

As she fills it a third time, I would like to point out that it typically only takes her three glasses of wine to get a buzz, but I don't want to make her more upset.

"I'm sorry."

Charlene freezes with the glass halfway to her mouth. "What are you sorry about? That my mom is a lunatic? That you lied about your parents? That you tried to boss me around over text messages?"

I'm not sorry about meeting her mother. If anything, it gives me a much better idea of who Charlene is. But I'm also uncertain if I can explain fully what I am sorry about, so I address the parts of that question that I can. "I didn't lie, and I was concerned."

"Really? Because I've seen a picture of you with your parents, and neither of them looked like Cherry or Rod."

"Rod and Cherry may have created me, but they didn't raise me. My grandparents did. They actually adopted me."

Her defiant, suspicious glare changes to confusion. "I don't understand.

You told me you were raised in a strict house that lacked affection, and privacy was not permitted. Those were your exact words."

"And that is very much the truth."

"Why didn't you tell me you were raised by your grandparents?"

"I didn't think it was necessary." I swallow down the panic that comes with being forthcoming about my family history. I've never told anyone about this. Not even Alex knows. Well, I'm sure he does now, but I've kept this terrible secret my entire life. Because it's very much the reason I'm as fucked up as I am. And the reason for the NDA agreements. "Please come sit with me so I can explain."

She exhales a shaky breath, but allows me to take her hand and lead her to the living room. She waits until I sit on the couch before moving to the love seat. I'm disappointed but unsurprised that she wants space.

I sip my wine and try not to allow the displeasure to appear on my face. I make a mental note to have a couple cases of good wine delivered to her house so she doesn't feel compelled to drink this shit. Running my hand up and down my thigh a few times, I take a deep breath. "I've never shared this with anyone, Charlene. I had hoped I would never have to."

I take her in, noting the protective way she cups the bowl of the glass in her palms, warming the white. When I reach her throat, I note her missing pearls and my chest constricts. Charlene always wears them, and the significance of their absence is like a razorblade slice across my heart. Her expression and her posture are both guarded. I hope I haven't lost all my gains because of this.

I hate my parents so much for making me feel secrecy is necessary.

"I was raised by my mother's parents."

"Because your parents are porn stars."

"Yes."

She doesn't ask for more information, but silence will only widen the gap between us. She wants me to tell her without having to prod.

"My parents started dating in their last year of high school. They were eighteen and careless."

"And your mom got pregnant," Charlene says softly.

In a lot of ways our stories are similar. Young adults making mistakes and having kids—us—way before they were ready. "She did. And because of my grandparents' beliefs, she kept me. They agreed to support her *if* she broke it off with my father."

"But she didn't."

"She did not. They ran away together—such a romantic notion, isn't it?" I smile at the irony and glance at Charlene, who looks sad. "They learned very quickly how difficult it is to afford a child with no education and no support from family, so they found a way to make money. And they made a lot. But with certain professions, there's a lifestyle." I look down at my hands and a disjointed series of memories that never made much sense until I was older flicker like an old movie behind my eyes. "At a young age I was exposed to things I shouldn't have been."

Charlene's teeth press into her lip as she puts together what I mean. "Oh," she breathes.

"It was . . . damaging in more ways than I can count, which is why I don't like to talk about it. Most of the memories are vague and indistinct, like wisps of a dream I can't quite catch and hold."

She nods. "I understand that. Sometimes I feel the same about my childhood, like it's shrouded in a fog I can't sift through."

"Exactly." I worry what telling her this will do to us. I worry more that we're too cumulatively messed up to be good for each other. "When I was four, I was removed from my parents' home and sent to live with my grandparents. I was raised in two very extreme households. The first was expressly permissive and overly sexual. The second was suffocatingly oppressive. There were restrictions put on me that weren't always reasonable."

"What kind of restrictions?" Her voice is a whisper.

I consider how much I want to tell her and decide I might as well let her in all the way. "As soon as puberty hit, the door to my room was removed."

She frowns. "Why?"

"My grandparents wanted to eradicate the perversion out of me."

"And they thought they could do that by taking away your privacy?"

"Mmm."

"God, you must've had to take a lot of long showers."

I give her a rueful smile. "They put a timer on the thermostat in the shower. The hot water shut off after five minutes."

"How did you even manage?"

"I lived and breathed hockey. I spent hours at the rink every single day, and I became very accustomed to being uncomfortable. Thankfully I was drafted at eighteen. But sometimes, when you've been oppressed for so long, freedom causes more pain. I think you might understand that."

Charlene nods, and her fingers drift up her throat, but stop when she doesn't come in contact with her pearls. I want to ask where they are since they rarely come off.

"It's hard to trust," she murmurs.

I edge closer to her, my knee nearly touching hers. "Yes. That's it exactly. The only people I could safely place faith in were my teammates."

Charlene drops her head, her fingers dragging down the side of her glass. "Is it like that still?"

Charlene is just as broken as I am. Someone whole would be better for her, but I don't think I'm selfless enough to let her go if she's damaged enough to want to stay.

"I covet privacy because it was something I was never permitted. I didn't tell you about my parents because I never anticipated you would have the misfortune of meeting them. I took my grandparents' last name because it separated me from them and removed the threat of association. They didn't want people to know, and frankly, neither did I."

I exhale slowly, hating the tightness in my chest, wishing I could control it. "I'm not normal, Charlene. I don't feel things the same way other people do. Relationships are difficult for me because I genuinely struggle to understand where the boundaries should be. Mine were always too close or too far away. Real intimacy is unfamiliar and terrifying because I have not allowed it. Until you."

She startles when I trace the edge of her jaw without making physical contact.

"And I'm beginning to see I haven't done a very good job at conveying that, or making it easier for either of us with all of this secrecy," I say.

"I understand the need for secrets."

"I know you do." I skim the back of her hand, a whisper of touch that helps calm me. "The only good thing about my childhood was hockey. I learned very quickly that people like to use my past for their own personal gain, hence the NDAs and the lack of relationships."

"I understand that a lot better now." She flips her palm over, the ends of our fingers meeting.

"My childhood fucked me up, Charlene, and I would like very much if it didn't have the same impact on what we have. I didn't tell you because I didn't want to drive you away."

"Well, if you haven't noticed, my childhood was pretty fucked up too, so I guess our broken parts sort of fit together, don't they?"

"They seem to." I stroke along her throat, where her pearls should be.

She covers my hand with hers. "I was fidgety today, and I couldn't stop playing with my necklace. I worried I was going to break it again, so I took them off." Reaching into the pocket of her skirt, she withdraws the pearls. "Will you help me put them back on?"

"Of course."

She drops them in my palm.

Charlene gives me her back as she piles up her hair and bows her head, exposing the gentle slope of her neck. I clasp them around her throat and place a kiss just above where they lay. "I'm sorry if my secrecy hurt you, Charlene. I'll try my very best not to do that to you again."

chapter ten

Love Games

Charlene

WHO KNEW FINDING OUT YOUR BOYFRIEND'S PARENTS ARE PORN STARS COULD take a relationship to the next level? Not this woman, that's for damn sure. It's been three weeks since Darren met my mom, and he hasn't decided my crazy is too much for him. In fact, for the past three weeks, I've seen more of him than usual. We've had more sleepovers in the past couple of weeks than we had in the two months before that. It's weird. I like it. But it also makes me nervous.

Because I still have a secret, and Darren doesn't anymore. I've considered telling him about The Ranch, but I don't want to upset this new balance. I'll tell him eventually—maybe after the playoffs are over and the expansion draft is out of the way.

I pull into the underground parking lot at Stroker and Cobb Financial Management and groan as I hoist myself out of the driver's seat. My legs ache. So do my arms. Actually, my entire body hurts thanks to the marathon of sex Darren and I engaged in. Chicago lost last night's game, and Darren needed a way to get out some of that pent-up negative energy. Obviously I offered to help. Hence I'm underslept and achy, but sated.

I take the elevator to the third floor. Six months ago I was offered a senior accounting position. Aside from Violet, I'm one of the youngest on staff in a senior position. Jimmy and Dean, who were hired around the same time as me and Violet, weren't all that happy about it, and for a couple of weeks they were real dicks, but things have settled down. Mostly.

One of the perks of my promotion is that it came with a sweet office instead of a shitty cubicle and an extra forty grand a year. While I may only make a fraction of Darren's salary, I'm doing pretty damn good for an almost twenty-six year old.

I drop my purse beside my desk and turn on my monitor so I can check emails. I've just finished logging in when Violet peeks her head in the door. "Do you have any snacks? I'm so freaking hungry this morning."

"I should have something in this drawer." I tap my desk and motion her inside while I pull up my emails. My mother has sent me a million. She still hasn't figured out that she can text me pictures and doesn't have to send them individually by email. "I didn't know you were coming in today."

"I wasn't, but Alex wants me to come to Toronto this weekend if they go to game seven of the series, so I'm shuffling days around, just in case." Violet only comes in to the office two or three times a week at most. The rest of the time she works from home. As awesome as it is for her, I miss having my best friend around every day. Jimmy and Dean can be fun, but they're not Violet.

She digs around in the drawer, tossing items on my desk. "What is all this shit? Why don't you have any good candy?"

"Probably because you ate it all the last time you were here."

"It looks like I have to settle for this." She sighs and unwraps a chocolate-coated granola bar. Taking a huge bite, she makes a face. "The oats totally ruin this. We should hit the Thai buffet for lunch."

"Sure. Sounds good. I have a meeting from ten to eleven. Other than that I'm catching up on emails and reviewing accounts." I click on an email from my mom. I assume it's another picture from the sex convention.

Violet choke coughs at the image on the screen.

"Darren can never see this," I say.

It's an action shot of the masked dude administering the Heimlich maneuver when my mother auditioned for the reality show thing. It looks like he's trying to hump me from behind. Darren would break the guy's knees with his hockey stick for putting his hands on me. It's worrying that the idea makes me a little excited in the pants.

"Yeah. You should tell your mom to delete that, and then you should delete it, too. Forever."

"Yeah." I move on to the next email, cringing as I open it. This time it's a video of the dude giving me the Heimlich, but there's no sound, so it really does look like he's trying to hump me fully dressed. I rub my forehead. "I don't know why she insists on sending these to my work email."

Violet pats my shoulder. "Two days ago Skye told me she wore that fetish gear for Sidney. She also told me she slipped him a Viagra and his hard-on lasted so long they had to go to the emergency room. You're welcome for that horrifying visual."

"Is Sidney okay?"

"I think so? Skye was pretty proud of herself, so there must not be any lasting damage."

We're interrupted by a knock on the door. I quickly close my browser, expecting maybe Jimmy, Dean, or my boss, Mr. Stroker, but it's none of them, and I can't see the person on account of the huge bouquet of flowers.

"Delivery for Charlene . . . Hoar?"

"The H is silent," Violet says with a grin.

The delivery guy lowers the bouquet enough so he can see us. "Sorry 'bout that. Where would you like these?"

"Oh, right here would be great." I clear some papers from the corner of my desk, and he sets them on the edge.

I nearly choke on his cologne. It smells like he dumped the entire bottle on himself. My eyes are watering.

Violet coughs into her arm. "Fred?"

He adjusts his baseball cap, which sends another waft of cologne in our direction. "Violet?"

He seems familiar, but I can't place him.

"Hey! How are you?" She coughs again.

"Good, good. Still delivering flowers. Still single." He shoves his hands in his pockets and rocks back on his heels. "I, uh, saw in the news that you married Alex Waters a while ago, so, uh . . . congratulations, I guess."

Well, this is awkward.

"Thanks."

"That offer to take you to the movies doesn't have an expiration date, so if you ever get divorced, you can always look me up."

"I'm taking my wedding vows pretty seriously—the whole 'til death do us part thing. Besides, he's got a huge dick, so you know, lots of incentive to stick around." Violet cringes, likely because she's gone too far with her sharing.

"Right. Yeah. The, uh, condom endorsements made that pretty obvious. I guess if you're looking to downsize to something more average, I could be your man." He takes a step back, toward the door.

"I'll keep that in mind."

Fred's pager goes off, and he blows out a breath. "It was really nice to see you, Violet. Hopefully I'll deliver flowers again here soon." He continues to back out of the office, knocking his elbow against the doorjamb. He frees one of his hands from his pockets so he can wave and disappears down the hall.

Before I can say anything, he peeks his head in the office again. "Oh, those flowers should be in direct sunlight. They'll last longer that way."

"Thanks, Fred."

"Okay. Well, bye." He disappears again.

Violet waits a few seconds before she tiptoes across my office, but she's wearing heels, so she's not stealthy or coordinated about it. She almost trips and falls into the hallway. She manages to catch the doorjamb before she goes down and sticks her head into the hall.

"Coast is clear, but the hallway smells like an entire high school of teenage boys doused themselves in cologne at the same time." She smacks her lips together as we open all the windows in my office. "I'm probably going to taste that for the rest of the day."

It's not particularly warm out, but I'd rather freeze my nipples off than continue huffing cologne. I suck in several lungfuls of fresh air. "I think my olfactory senses are destroyed. Who the hell was that guy?"

"He used to deliver Alex's flowers when I lived in the pool house."

"Oh my God! I remember him! Didn't he ask you out right after you told him you'd had Alex's dick in your mouth?"

"That's the one."

"I don't remember his cologne problem being that bad before." I have to dab under my eyes to wipe away the tears since they're still stinging.

"Maybe it's gotten worse over time, like prolonged exposure to the flowers has made him incapable of smelling things." Violet motions to the bouquet. "Are those from Darren?"

"I don't know. Maybe?" I pluck the card from the bouquet, which is almost entirely comprised of yellow flowers with a few pinks and oranges thrown in. It's like a sunrise. I dab my eyes again, telling myself it's because they still sting from the cologne.

I slip the card out of its tiny yellow envelope. Darren's neat writing fills the space.

A little something beautiful for my beautiful someone.

Violet's chin rests on my shoulder. "Wow. That's super sweet."

"It really is." And not like anything he's ever done before. I mean, the flowers, yes. He surprised me with that bouquet and candy before, just never at work.

"Did you let him in your backdoor last night or something?"

"Seriously?" I elbow her and accidentally get her in the boob.

"Ow!" She staggers back, gripping it in both hands. "That really fucking hurt, Char!"

I roll my eyes. "Oh, come on."

She keeps kneading her boob. "No, really. It feels like you tried to shave off my nipple with your pointy-ass elbow." She looks down her shirt, as if she's checking to make sure her nipple is indeed still attached to her body. "Remember how sore your boobs were when you were a teenager and they were just busting out?"

I shrug. "I guess."

"It's like that, but worse. They've been like this all week. Alex is getting frustrated that he can't slide his dick between them." She's still kneading her boob with one hand and fingering the petals of a dahlia with the other. "I have a meeting in twenty, but I expect to hear all about what you did to inspire those flowers at lunch." She nabs another granola bar from my desk and leaves me to it.

Darren calls before I have a chance to reach out and thank him for the flowers.

"I was about to message you," I tell him.

"Were you now?"

I can almost see him smiling, and it makes my heart flutter.

"Someone sent me something beautiful."

"Is that right? What kind of something beautiful?"

"Some very stunning flowers. They look like a sunrise."

"So you like them?"

"I love them. They're gorgeous. I'm not sure what I did to warrant them, but they're certainly appreciated." Why are there butterflies suddenly flitting around in my stomach?

"You don't need to do anything to warrant something nice. If it was reasonable, I'd send you flowers every day." He clears his throat, and I can hear water running in the background. "I wanted to check in with you before I head out this afternoon. Would it be okay for me to call you later tonight, once I'm settled in Toronto?"

"Of course."

"And when I'm home, you'll stay over again? If you're not busy?"

"I'm available whenever you need me."

"That would be always, Charlene. I'll touch base when I'm in Toronto. Enjoy the flowers."

"I will. Bye, Darren."

He never ends a call with goodbye. I don't know why. I stare at my phone for several long seconds as I roll what he said around in my head. *That would be always.*

With the recent revelation about his family, I've come to a few new realizations. Darren was essentially starved of affection as a child, and likely for his entire life, so his asking for my time is him trying to restrain his neediness. All those nights spent in his bed with him lying like Dracula was as much about giving me space as it was about being afraid to seek intimacy and be denied. It isn't control he's seeking, so much as a way to let go of the restraints placed on him.

Part of me loves being needed by him like this, but the other part worries that need turns into dependency, and that's when things get dicey. Until now I've never allowed myself to get involved with someone to the point of needing them so acutely.

I don't have time to fixate on it, though. My morning meeting and deleting my mom's emails keep me too busy to be able to obsess. At noon, Violet peeks in my door and declares it's lunchtime and she needs to eat all the Thai food because she's starving to death.

I shoulder my purse. "Should we invite Jimmy and Dean?"

She gives me her cringy face. "Only if we run into them on the way out?"

"Sure."

We're barely seated at a table before Violet is beelining it to the buffet, loading her plate with things she normally wouldn't. She barely utters a word as she shovels food into her mouth.

Violet slows down about halfway through her plate. "Okay, I think I got a little overexcited." She slumps back in her seat and rubs her tummy. "I hope Chicago doesn't shit the bed this game."

I pause with my fork half an inch from my mouth. "Vi! You can't say things like that. You're pretty much ensuring they lose with that kind of talk."

"Toronto has been solid this season, and they're fighting to win, you know? They haven't seen the Cup in more than half a century. Besides that, and you can't repeat this to anyone, but Alex hasn't been on top of his game. That injury last season has slowed him down, and the only reason he's been managing is because Darren is picking up the slack. Everyone knows that. All the guys, and Darren I'm sure, but none of them will say anything."

"Alex has been playing well," I counter. But even as I say it, I know it's a half-truth. Normally Alex is one of the top players in the league, but this year has been different. His stats have taken a serious hit, and he hasn't been playing as well as usual, whereas Darren's stats have been on the rise, particularly his assists. It's like he's handing goals to Alex instead of taking them for his own. Which says a lot about him as a person.

"Well, in the general sense of the word, but not like he used to. Promise me this conversation stays between us."

"Of course. I promise."

"You can't tell Darren."

Violet has been my best friend for almost a decade, so when she asks me to keep a secret, it's usually a no brainer. But since Darren and I just dealt with the fallout of one of his secrets, I hesitate for a second before I respond.

"I won't tell Darren."

I hold out my pinkie and Violet grips it with hers. "Imagine if you unzipped a pair of pants and found a dick this small inside. How sad would you be?"

"So sad."

"Darren seriously hasn't said anything about Alex's performance this season?"

I consider what she's asking, and weigh it with how freely I should share my private conversations with Darren. "He mentioned that recovery can be slow and Alex was playing his best."

Violet nods and pushes her food around on her plate. "He really is. But he's also aware that his shoulder doesn't feel the way it used to. He doesn't want to wreck his body. He's been thinking about the future a lot, about what he sees for himself after the NHL, so when his contract is up with Chicago, he's considering retirement."

"What if Chicago wants to renew again?" I ask.

"We'll see, but it really depends. I don't think he wants to go out with tanked stats, you know? He's been at the top of his game for a long time, and it's hard for him to put in so much extra work and not see the payoff."

"What will he do when he retires?" Darren's plan once his hockey career ends isn't something we've discussed.

"He's talked about sportscasting or coaching. I'm hoping for the former since he'll probably be able to get on in Chicago, and then I won't have to quit my job."

"You're serious about this, aren't you?" This makes me intensely aware of how different my relationship is with Darren. We don't plan past next weekend, let alone next year. That he asked me to be available when he returns from the away game in Toronto is a big deal.

"The concussion last season scared him. He still has holes in his memory, Char. Sometimes he has difficultly remembering simple things, and he gets flustered. It's not anything really worrying, but it's there. He doesn't want to take the risk anymore, especially now that he's actively trying to knock me up. He doesn't want to compromise his family for his career."

"I can understand that, but retirement? It seems so final."

I have to wonder what that's like to have someone love you so much that they weigh choices in favor of who, not what they love.

There's a pit in my stomach, and every time we have one of these heavy conversations, it gets a little deeper. Everyone else is settling down, creating their own microcosm of family, and here I am getting excited over Darren wanting time with me next week.

Violet folds her napkin until it sort of resembles a diaper. "I know, but Alex wants to be involved, and traveling would made that hard. Besides, Alex doesn't want to leave Chicago, and I know Buck has plans to settle here once his career is over."

She smiles wistfully. "It'd be nice if our kids could all grow up together, wouldn't it? I can kind of see what the future would be like if all of us stayed here. Wouldn't it be awesome if we both had girls and they were best friends like we are?"

I don't even know if Darren is going to be in Chicago next year, let alone if we're still going to be together, and already Violet is planning our kids' futures.

Violet wipes under her eyes and stares down at the wetness as if she can't understand how it got there. "Oh my God, I'm not even pregnant yet, and I'm already crying about everything."

I hand her a clean napkin, and she blots under her eyes. "Are you sure you're not pregnant? I mean, you're eating like you're trying to win some kind of competition. And the breast tenderness . . ."

I mean it as a joke, but she pulls out her phone and flips through her calendar. "Oh shit."

My stomach does a little flip.

"I should've gotten my period five days ago." Violet's eyes are huge. She grips the edge of the table. "What if I'm pregnant?"

"Isn't that what you want?"

"Well, yeah, I mean, I guess that's the whole point. I figured it would take a while—like, more than a couple of months, you know? I thought I'd be able to have a glass of wine this weekend. If I am preggers, it's going to be a year before I do that again."

"At least you'll have Sunny to keep you company?" It's meant as reassurance for her, but it causes a twinge of jealousy because it's another way I'm not like the rest of the girls.

"Yeah, there's that." Violet taps her lips. "You know what we should do?"

"Stop at a CVS on the way home and get one of those pee-stick tests to find out if you're knocked up?"

"No—well, yes, but that's not what I was going to say. If they go to game seven in this series, we should *all* go to Toronto. And if I'm not pregnant, I'm totally going to drink my face off."

"Either way, that would be fun." It would be nice to get away for a couple of days.

I feel bad that I'm almost hoping Violet isn't pregnant. I'd like to get smashed with my best friend.

"Right? We can start looking at flights. Maybe go in a day early and do some shopping? Stock up on all the mapley deliciousness."

"I'll ask Darren if he'd be okay with that."

Violet's eyes light up. "Or you could surprise him!"

"Uh . . . I'm not so sure that's a great idea, considering what happened the last time I did that." My face heats at the memory.

"This is different, though. You're not planning a BDSM bash. You'd just be coming to see him play hockey and ride his joy stick."

I give her a look. "I should still ask him first. Just to make sure."

"Why? I mean, he's going to want you there regardless, isn't he? If Chicago wins, they move on to the next round of the playoffs, and you get to have fuck-yeah sex." She pumps her fist almost like she's jerking off a pretend penis. "If they lose, you get to have condolence sex. You're the one who told me this back when Alex and I were doing our mating dance."

"I'll talk to Darren about it. In the meantime, let's find out if you'll be able to drink something other than ginger ale for the next nine months, unless you want to wait until Alex gets home and do it then."

"I can't wait until tomorrow. We're doing this now."

We stop at the CVS on the way back to the office. Violet makes me come into the private wheelchair bathroom with her while she pees on a stick. I face the wall while she does the honors, letting out a crazy squeal.

"Holy shit—are you pregnant?"

"No, I just peed on my hand!" After she's finished her business, she sets the stick on the edge of the sink and washes her hands three times, breathing like she's practicing Lamaze. "Has it been two minutes yet? Jesus, I'm so nervous. You look for me." She closes her eyes and thrusts the stick at me.

I look at the little window and swallow down the lump in my throat. "It's a plus sign."

Her eyes pop open. "What does that mean? Does that mean I'm preggers?"

I nod and show her the test, smiling softly at my best friend even though a part of me is so very sad.

She grabs the test and stares down at it, slack jawed. "Look at how blue that is. I went off the pill two freaking months ago. Alex is going to be so proud of his magic sperm. Fuck. Shit. I'm pregnant, Char. What if I make a terrible mother? What if I'm like Skye and I embarrass the fuck out of my kid? What if it hates me, and we become estranged, and it writes a tell-all book about how horrible I am—"

"You're an amazing best friend, Vi. You're going to make an even more amazing mother."

She throws her arms around me, hugging me hard. "I don't know if I'm ready for this," she mumbles into my shoulder.

"You've got this. You're going to be fabulous."

She steps back, holding my shoulders, maybe for balance or support. "I'm going to get so fat, and my boobs are going to be huge."

I laugh, but tears threaten to spill over. "Alex is going to love that."

She cups her hands over her mouth. "Oh my God, he's going to be so excited."

"Are you going to call him?"

"I don't know. I mean, he'll be home tomorrow. Maybe I should wait and tell him in person. I should wait. I want to see his face. And I don't know if I want to tell anyone else yet. It's still so early, so much can happen." She takes my hands in hers. "Can we keep this between the two of us for now? I'll tell Alex tomorrow, and we'll figure out when we want to tell everyone else. But for now, it'll just be us who know, okay?"

"Of course."

"Oh my God, Char. I'm going to be a mom, and you're going to be an aunt, because let's face it, you're as close to a sister as I'm ever going to get."

She hugs me hard again, and I let the tears fall, because as happy as I am for her, I'm a little sad for me and how this is going to change things.

chapter eleven

Shift

Charlene

CHICAGO ENDS UP LOSING THE GAME IN TORONTO, WHICH MEANS THEY'RE COMING home to play game six in the series. If they lose again, Toronto moves on to the next round, and they're out of the playoffs. If they win, they go back to Toronto to play game seven.

The second Darren lands in Chicago, he calls to make sure I'm still coming over after work, which is good, because I need a distraction from Violet's not so little secret.

That anxious feeling settles in my stomach and moves lower. Too bad sneaking off to the bathroom at work to get myself off is frowned upon. "If you still want me to, yes."

"Definitely. Yes. I want you." There's a short pause before he continues. It sounds like he's opening and closing drawers. "To come over after work."

"What are you doing? You sound distracted."

"I can't find any of your clothes in my dresser. I mean, apart from lingerie. You must have a few articles in here somewhere," he says.

"Oh, uh, I always bring my things home with me after I spend the night."

"Oh." He exhales heavily. "I didn't realize that. You should leave things here for the nights you plan to stay."

"Okay. I can do that."

"Good. Great. I'd like that. You'll stay tonight, then?"

"You have a game tomorrow night; you need your rest. You know I'm an active sleeper." I can't be responsible for interfering with his game when Chicago is so close to making the finals again.

"I suppose I'll just have to wear you out so you don't pose a threat to my sleep."

I laugh at that. "Are you sure?"

"Positive. I would like more rather than less of you, and you staying the night solves that problem."

"I'll stop at home before I come to you after work and pick up some things, then."

"I can do that. I have errands to run so I'll be out anyway. I could stop by your place and pick up a suit and whatever else you need, That way you can come straight to me—if that works for you, of course."

"Are you sure? It's kind of out of your way, isn't it?"

"Not at all, and it means you'll be at my place that much sooner. We'll order dinner in." He almost sounds giddy.

"Sure. That sounds great."

"Perfect. I'll see you soon."

I leave work promptly at five, my body humming with nervous excitement as I head to the parking garage. I need Darren tonight as much as he seems to need me. Violet's pregnancy news is hitting me harder than I expected. It's another thing she and Sunny will have in common, and another way our relationships are just so different. I wonder how Violet's doing. I'm sure I'll get a message from her tonight at some point, or maybe she'll be too busy celebrating.

In my head I'm already filtering through the lingerie drawer at his place. Since they lost the last game, I'm thinking Darren will want sweetly sexy tonight. Something soft to distract him from a hard loss. I imagine I'll end up in pale purple.

Before I leave the garage, I decide it would be a good idea to let Darren know I'm on my way. Normally he's quick to respond, but I don't get anything from him between getting in the car and arriving at the security of his gated community. The guard lets me in, and I pull into Darren's driveway. It's empty, but he often keeps his cars in the garage, so it's not out of the ordinary. I check my appearance in the visor and take a deep breath. The pinging ramps up in my lady bits as I cut the engine and grab my purse from the passenger seat.

I ring the doorbell and wait, but after a minute, there's still no answer. I check my messages again and find I have a new one from Darren. My stomach drops at the possibility that he might be canceling, but as I scan the text, I smile.

Had to run out. Make yourself comfortable. I'll be back soon.

He gave me the code to his house a long time ago, but since most of our dates are planned, I've never needed to use it. It feels odd to let myself in, but I punch the numbers and open the door. The first thing that catches my attention is the massive bouquet of flowers on the side table to the right. Flowers aren't a typical decoration for Darren. In fact, knickknacks and decorations in general aren't Darren's thing.

His house is pretty much on the extreme side of minimalist. There's generally no evidence of clutter, or that he even lives here, apart from the occasional mug in the sink or a pair of boxers that missed the laundry basket in his walk-in closet.

Much like the ones that arrived in my office several days ago, this bouquet seems to be keeping with the sunrise theme. It's filled with pale and vibrant yellows, soft peaches, pinks, and purples. There's a card beside the vase with my name written neatly on the front. I flip it open and smile at the note inside.

Charlene,

I'm sorry I'm not here. Upstairs you'll find something more comfortable to change into.

The restless pinging down below ratchets up a few notches as I consider what exactly his something more comfortable might consist of. Taking the note with me, I head upstairs to his bedroom, which is where I'm assuming the something more comfortable will be.

I bark out a quiet, shocked laugh when I step inside his bedroom and turn on the light. The very first thing I notice is a second bouquet of flowers, which contrasts perfectly with the one downstairs. Instead of a sunrise, this is more sunset with a cascade of yellow, darkening to vibrant peach and nearly black purple lilies and dahlias at the base.

The flowers aren't the only addition to the room, though. Laid across the end of the bed are several clothing options. I expected lace or satin, or possibly some combination of the two. But that's not what I'm looking at.

It appears Darren has done some shopping at my favorite legging store. There are five new pairs. Two of them are ridiculously adorable and firefly themed, and the others are covered in fun pastel prints reflective of the season. He's also gone to the trouble of buying matching tanks and shirts, and a vast array of new cheekies in every color, pattern, and fabric available.

In addition to those, there's a black gift bag tied with a bow. I'm not sure if I'm supposed to open that now or wait, so I leave it and pick a pair of leggings, a shirt, and a pair of panties to change into. They're freshly washed, as evidenced by the distinct smell of Darren's fabric softener.

I head back downstairs to wait for him and find yet another surprise in the living room. Set up on the table beside the reading chair he bought for me is a bucket with a bottle of white wine chilling and a glass waiting to be filled. Several books are stacked on the seat of the chair, their spines creased from my excessive reading and pages folded over. Sometimes, when I love a book I'll earmark certain chapters or passages so I can find them easily and read them over.

Darren must have scooped them from my nightstand and brought them here for me. I press my fingers to my lips, my chest light and heavy at the same time. His attentiveness is endearing, and while part of me loves it, the other part worries about what it means. So many things are changing, and I don't know quite how to handle it. The neat lines we'd drawn seem to be erasing themselves, and I don't know how to do this without them. It makes me feel unsteady.

With shaking hands, I pull the cork free and pour myself a glass of wine. I take a small sip and moan. This is way better than that boxed stuff my mom brought with her. I actually considered tossing the rest of it, but figured it was too much of a waste, so I mixed it with ginger ale and juice. Then it wasn't so bad.

I grab my phone and my ear buds, because I might as well enjoy the lengths Darren has gone to for me.

Moving the books to the table, I relax into the chair, cover myself with the throw, and sigh contentedly. On the next inhale, I note the faint scent of Darren's cologne clinging to the fabric. I turn my head and press my nose against the backrest. I'm not sure if I'm imagining things, but I swear it smells like his shampoo, which means he's been using the chair when I'm not here.

I slip in my ear buds, pick a playlist, and settle in with a book, flipping to one of my many favorite chapters. I like to read romance, maybe because my childhood was such a mess and the kind of relationships I witnessed weren't normal. I like the smutty ones as much as the sweet ones, but my favorite stories have the most broken characters. Even though it's fiction, it gives me hope that even the most messed up people can find someone to love them.

I'm on my second glass of wine, rereading my second favorite chapter when a shadow passes over my book. I startle as I look up to find Darren standing in front of me, and I nearly douse myself in wine.

He grabs the glass before I dump it in my lap, a wry smile forming as he tugs my ear buds free.

"I didn't hear you come in." I look him over. He's wearing black jeans, and a T-shirt that hugs his biceps and stretches tight across his chest.

"I gathered that from your reaction. You look cozy." He takes a sip from my glass.

"So cozy." I close my book and set it on the table.

"Can I see which ones you picked?" He tugs at the end of the blanket so it slips down a few inches.

"You went a little overboard, but thank you." I pull the throw off, and Darren's grin widens.

I grip the arms of the chair to push myself up.

He raises a hand. "No, no. Stay right here."

"Okay?" I draw the word out as I drop back down.

He drags a finger from my ankle to my knee. "This is nice—you right here, looking like it's where you belong."

I shift over and pat the seat cushion. "Why don't you join me? There's plenty of room." The chair is huge, and round. There's more than enough room for two bodies, even if one of them belongs to a huge hockey player.

"Let me get a glass."

"Or we could share mine?"

"We could definitely do that." He adjusts my legs so they're draped over his and stretches one arm across the back. Sliding his palm up my thigh, he runs his nose along my neck and follows with his lips. "I like you being here when I get home."

I laugh and then sigh as his lips trail along the edge of my jaw and across my cheek. When he reaches the corner of my mouth I turn toward him, our lips brushing.

His rough fingers glide gently up my arm and thread into the hair at the nape of my neck. The kiss starts slow, the warm soft drag of his tongue becoming a sweet tangle. I have no idea how long we kiss, but eventually Darren pulls back, his thumb sweeping back and forth across my bottom lip, his breath coming hard.

"How was your day?" he grinds out.

I laugh and twist in his grip so I can straddle his thighs. "Long." Knowing he was back in Chicago but having to wait to see him made the day pass more slowly than usual.

"Same." He settles his palms on my hips. "But this makes it worth it."

"Making out in my reading chair?" I reach for the glass of wine and take a sip.

"Just you being here period. But the making out is nice too." He watches as I take another sip. "I'd like some of that."

I raise the glass, expecting him to take it, but he doesn't. Instead he parts his lips and cocks one sinister eyebrow.

"I might spill it on you," I warn.

"It's white. I'll take the risk."

I tip the glass up until the wine reaches the edge, wetting his lips. My tongue is caught between my teeth, my smile wide as I lift the tiniest bit too high and it trickles out of the edge of the glass and down his chin.

"Told you." I set the glass on the side table, nearly missing since I'm paying more attention to Darren's mouth than what I'm actually doing. I catch the drip with my tongue, then kiss the wine away, but when I get to his lips I pull back.

Darren's apparently not having it, because I suddenly find myself airborne. I land on my back on the chair, Darren's mouth on mine as he parts my legs with his knee and sinks his hips into mine.

Half an hour later, I've had three orgasms and I'm back in my spot on the chair with my legs thrown over his, except now we're both mostly naked. Well, I'm totally naked, but Darren put his boxers back on. He tucks the blanket around me. "I'd planned to take you upstairs before I got inside you."

"So I could dress up in whatever's in that black bag on the bed?"

His brow pulls down. "Haven't you opened it?"

"Was I supposed to? I thought since it was wrapped I would wait until you were here."

"You can open it before we go to sleep since that's when it'll come in handy." He reaches over and picks up the single wine glass, offering it to me before he takes a sip.

I run my fingers through his hair and his head drops back, eyes falling closed. When he's like this, unguarded and at ease, he looks much less severe. "How are you feeling about the game tomorrow night?"

He runs one hand slowly up and down my thigh. "Truthfully?"

"Unless you feel like you need to lie to me about it to make yourself feel better."

He cracks a lid and a smile, then lifts his head. His smile disappears and his eyes seem to trace over my face. "Worried."

"You played really well last night."

"Not well enough." He blows out another breath.

"You can only be as good as your teammates allow, though." I drag my nails down the back of his scalp and goose bumps flash across his arms.

"It's not *my* game I'm worried about."

"Alex is struggling." It's not a question. I've seen it during the games, and then there's the conversation Violet and I had.

Darren chews on the inside of his lip for a few seconds before he gives me a reluctant nod. He's incredibly loyal, and even though it's the truth, I know all Darren wants to do is protect him.

"He needs to go into this game with a positive frame of mind, and my biggest concern at the moment is that he's beating himself up over the loss."

"Home ice advantage should help, shouldn't it?"

"Theoretically, yes. We have a great team, and Randy is an excellent front line player. Rookie is pulling his weight, and Miller and Lance are holding defense, but Alex has always been the best for scoring, and he's just not making the shots the way he used to." Darren drops his head and mutters a quiet *fuck*.

"Hey." I take his face between my hands and force him to look at me. His expression is pained, and I want to take that away for him. "It's okay to talk to me like this. You're not being disloyal for saying what's true. I'm sure he knows this and it's eating at him that you're the one picking up the slack. I know it's hard to separate your friendship from the welfare of the team and Alex's ego, but you might need to start taking some of the shots you've been passing."

"It's not that simple, Charlene."

"I know Alex likes to be the best at everything, but surely he must see how it would be better for the team—"

"It's not Alex; it's me."

"That's untrue. You've been incredible out there. I realize I'm biased—"

He presses his lips to mine to stop me. "You don't understand. Alex doesn't want me to pass to him. He knows he's not playing like he used to, and it's killing him because he feels like he's letting down his team. He wants me to take the shots, but I've been passing anyway, so it's my fault we lost last night, not his."

"Why would you pass to him if he asked you not to?"

"Goals get more points than assists," he says.

As if I don't know this. "And that matters why?"

He mumbles something else.

"I'm sorry, I didn't catch that."

"Can we just drop this? It's a real fucking downer, and that's not what I wanted tonight to be." His jaw tics and his throat bobs, fingers tightening on my thigh briefly before they skim up and in. I twist away from his wandering hand and cross my legs so he can't get between them.

He purses his lips, and I mirror the expression. His sigh is heavy as he trails his fingers down the side of my neck, pushing away the blanket. "Please, Charlene. Not tonight. Any other night." He drops his head, lips finding the place his fingers just were and gliding up to my ear. "I just want to get lost in you."

There's such vulnerability in his words and his tone. I pull back, wanting to see his face, trying to understand the sudden shift, the shutting down when we're finally making progress.

"I need you to let this go tonight. We can come back to it." His pained eyes search mine. "But for now, I need this. You. Please."

"Okay, Darren." I press a palm to his cheek. "If that's what you need."

He kisses me, softly at first, and then greedily. It's late when we finally make it upstairs to bed. I don't flail in my sleep. I can't with Darren wrapped around me like a human blanket.

We're shifting again, and I worry too much change too fast is dangerous. It creates fault lines and cracks. The kind I'll get lost in and won't find my way back out of.

chapter twelve

Sisterhood

Charlene

CHICAGO WINS THE GAME AGAINST TORONTO WITH DARREN SCORING THE winning goal. He should be happy about it, but he's stoic instead. I want to chalk it up to game seven being in Toronto, but I'm sure it has to do with Alex.

We're sitting at the bar after the game, and Darren has me tucked into his side, one arm thrown over my shoulder. He's been quiet, smiling when people pat him on the back, but not saying much else. Which isn't unusual. What is unusual is the number of times he tucks my hair behind my ear, or leans in to kiss my neck.

"So we're all going to Toronto to cheer our boys on, right?" Violet says from across the table.

She told Alex last night that she's pregnant, but she wants to keep it quiet until she's through the first trimester. Considering how many weeks away that is, and how much he's fawning over her like she's an injured bird, I'm not sure the secret is destined to be kept.

I find out how right I am about five seconds later. "We can celebrate the end of the series and the fact that I'm going to be a dad!" Alex shouts. He's a few beers into the night, so it's hard to hold him too accountable.

Violet slaps his chest. "Alex!"

He cringes, then turns to her. "Sorry. Shit. I'm just so fucking excited. You're going to be the sexiest pregnant woman in this history of the universe."

There's a flurry of excitement, and I stand, along with Darren. His mouth is at my ear. "Did you know?"

"I was with her when she took the test. Violet didn't want me to say anything until she told Alex." I feel as if I should apologize.

He squeezes my hand and nudges me forward. "You don't have to explain. Alex told me this morning."

I look into icy eyes that seem somehow soft and warm. "You're not upset that I didn't tell you?"

"She's your best friend. You keep her confidence, as you should." He strokes my cheek and presses a gentle kiss to my lips.

A moment later I'm swallowed up in Alex's bear hug while Darren gives

Violet a much gentler version of the same affectionate congratulations. I step back to let a teary Sunny hug her brother.

Darren slips his fingers between mine and pulls me into him. "It's a weekend game; can you get an extra day off? I want the time with you."

It's as if he knows that this good thing is in some ways bad—like it separates us from them in yet another way.

"I can talk to my boss tomorrow," I tell him.

"He'll say yes."

He's not being cocky, not really. Our firm represents a number of Chicago players. Violet is married to the top earner on the team, and only two other players in the league have bigger contracts than Alex. Darren isn't a slouch either, and Stroker handles his account directly. He'll let us go.

By ten the following morning, we have the green light from Stroker, much to Jimmy and Dean's dismay, and our plane tickets are booked. Darren wanted me on his flight, but I have to work on Friday, as do most of the girls, so we're leaving in the evening, which means we'll have all day Saturday to do fun girl things before the game.

When we arrive Friday night, the boys swarm the lobby and claim their significant others, leaving only the parents—of course Skye and Sidney came along, and Daisy and Robbie drove out from Guelph to be here—at the bar. It's late, but Darren needs some release before I force him to go to sleep.

I check my phone around midnight to see what the rest of the girls are up to. Looks like I'm the last one to be done putting my hockey man to bed. I slip out from beneath the covers, find my clothes, and tiptoe to the bathroom so I can change without disturbing Darren.

It's after two by the time I come back to the room. Lily and I drank too many cocktails while we talked lingerie. Skye and Daisy were far more sauced than us though, having been in the bar all evening. I'm not as quiet or coordinated as I'd like to be as I strip down. I try to find my pajamas, but it's too dark, and I don't want to risk waking Darren, who's curled around my pillow.

I pull his discarded shirt over my head and slip between the sheets as stealthily as possible. He shifts as soon as I'm under the covers, but he's still hugging the pillow, so it bars his way. Darren grunts his displeasure, groggy and only half aware as he struggles to get near me.

I turn to face him, settling a gentle palm on his cheek. "Let me help."

He hums and his limbs go lax, eyes fluttering open for a second before falling closed again as I replace the pillow with myself. Darren sighs and buries his nose in my hair. His arm comes around me, fingers splayed across my stomach. They travel up, between my breasts, skimming my collarbones until he reaches the pearls. He follows the strand, curling his fingers around my shoulder, thumb resting in the hollow of my throat.

I close my eyes and relax into his warmth. I want to hold onto this protected feeling, but it's terrifying. I crave this closeness with him, and when he's sleeping it feels safer, because it's unconscious on his part. I don't have to face it the way I do in the waking hours.

I fall asleep wishing I could erase my past so I could be a better version of myself, one that didn't have her innocence blown apart at the age of fourteen when I learned my life had been a fucked-up lie in a fucked-up world.

I wake up to Darren's hard-on pressed against my hip and his lips at my ear asking to get inside me. There's no chance I'm saying no to him, so we follow morning sex with room service while he gets ready for his pre-game skate, and I prepare to explore Toronto with the girls until game time.

He's quiet, which isn't unusual for Darren, but he's tense and restless, even after the morning orgasm.

"You okay?" I smooth his shower-damp hair away from his face.

"Mmm." He sits on the edge of the bed, pulls me between his legs, and tucks his head under my chin.

"That's not really an answer," I point out.

"Keep touching me, please."

"We're supposed to be downstairs in two minutes."

"I'm not asking for sex, Charlene. I just need you close to me."

"You're going to be amazing tonight."

His nose brushes my throat at his nod, and his fingers flex on my hips. His palms slide up my back, wrapping around my shoulders as he pulls me in tighter. He tips his head and his lips press against the side of my neck and part. The soft, wet touch of his tongue warms my body, and heat settles low in my stomach.

"Darren." It's warning twisted with desire.

He stands quickly, one palm curving around my nape. I tilt back as he looms over me, his gaze hot and needy.

"What—"

He cuts off the question with his mouth. His tongue pushes past my lips, and he finds his way under my shirt with his free hand. We need to be downstairs now. His team is leaving for their pre-game skate in minutes. We don't have time for another round of morning sex, and I don't want to be the reason he's off his game tonight.

I put my palms on his chest with the intention of pushing, but his fingers dip into the waistband of my leggings—it's pretty much all I packed for the weekend—and slide into my panties.

I gasp and grip his shirt when he finds the barbell piercing my hood and circles it roughly. He goes lower and thrusts two fingers inside me. Finding the magic spot, he curls fast and hard, making my knees buckle. His grip on the back of my neck tightens, preventing me from sinking to the floor.

He curls his fingers one more time before he withdraws to circle my clit again. It won't take much to make me come. Just a bit more friction and I'll go tumbling over the edge. But his hand disappears, and he wrenches his mouth away from mine.

I cry out at the loss of his touch and try to pull him back to me with his shirt. His name is a whine on my lips. My clit is throbbing, and my knees are weak.

"Please, Darren." The high pitch should be embarrassing, but dear God, the muscles are already clenching with the promise of an orgasm, if only he would touch me again.

His hot, almost angry gaze stays locked on mine as he lifts his hand, fingers glistening. I groan as he slips them into his mouth, sucking loudly.

Somewhere to the right a phone buzzes with a message.

One corner of his mouth tips up in a sinister smile as his fingers slide out of his mouth. He licks between the webbing, and my eyes roll up. I attempt to shove my own hand down my pants to finish what he started.

"No," he barks and grabs both my wrists. He spins me around until my knees hit the back of the bed and I drop to my ass. He straddles my legs, clamping them together as he hovers over me once again. "How do you feel right now, Charlene?"

The sound that comes out of me is somewhere between a whimper and a growl.

"That's not an answer, little firefly."

I fight against his hold on my wrists and swivel my hips.

He dips down until his face is an inch from mine. "Are you on the edge?"

"Yes."

"Are you angry?"

"No."

"No?" He quirks a brow.

"Yes!" This time it's a moan.

"Restless? Needy? Wanting? Desperate?"

I nod fervently. "All of those things."

"This is how I feel every time I'm away from you."

His eyes stay on mine, unblinking as he waits for me to process what he's just admitted. We don't talk feelings, and yet here he is, telling me more in these few words and actions than he has in the past two years.

"Don't make yourself come today. Whatever happens tonight, this is how I need you so we match when we're back together. Do you understand?" His voice is hard, but his expression is vulnerable.

"Yes, Darren. I understand."

His smile turns soft and his lips are softer still as they brush over mine. He releases my wrists and steps back, setting me free. I feel like I've been shot up with adrenaline and tranqued at the same time.

"Come on, baby. The girls are waiting for you, and I'm going to be in trouble with my team if we don't move our asses." He extends a hand and winks.

"You're an asshole," I gripe, but take his hand because I don't think I'm capable of standing on my own.

His chuckle is dark as he pulls me to my feet. I stumble and end up mashed against his chest. I might try to rub myself on him during that brief contact. He kisses my temple. "But I'm your asshole."

I snort, but he's right. He hands me my purse and phone, then pockets his own and grabs his bag. I'm less than coordinated as he opens the door and ushers me into the hall. I have to concentrate on putting one foot in front of the other rather than slamming him into a wall so I can hump him until I come.

He punches the elevator button, and I stare at the numbers as they rise. The churning in my stomach grows the closer it gets to our floor. I don't know what I want more—the elevator to be empty or full. If it's empty he's going to torment me, as he sometimes likes to do. I'm aware that this is tied to his stress level over the game tonight.

The elevator dings, and the doors slide open. *Shit.* It's empty.

"Come on, firefly." Darren links our pinkies and tugs. I stumble forward, my mouth dry. Expectation and anxiety make the ache between my legs flare. I catch a glimpse of my reflection in the mirrored walls. My eyes are wide and glassy, cheeks flushed, lips swollen from his kisses.

He presses the button that will take us to the lobby, and I watch as the doors slide closed. Darren drops his bag on the floor and crowds me into the corner, pressing his hips into mine.

I groan and let my head fall back against the glass, waiting for him to do something, anything. His lips find my neck and trail up to my ear. "Feeling trapped?"

I shake my head.

"Still needy?" Now his lips are on my cheek.

I exhale a shuddering breath and nod.

His smile makes the harsh angles of his face even more severe rather than softening them. "I bet your panties are already soaked through."

I swallow hard and clench my thighs harder. His knee presses against mine, and I open, letting him in. I glance up. We have thirty more floors, but the elevator could stop anytime to pick up people. He rolls his hips, his erection pressed against my stomach, his thigh providing the friction I'm so very desperate for.

The orgasm is like an aura in the air, the glitter of a sunrise on the water—close but not quite within reach.

"What are you waiting for? Chase it. See if you can catch it before it's too late."

I fist his shirt and grind shamelessly on his leg, not caring how desperate I must look and sound as I whimper and roll my hips while he stands immobile, one hand gripping the bar on either side of me, eyes fixed on mine. He's not helping, but he's giving me a chance to help myself.

I glance over his shoulder. *Shit.* Only fifteen more floors to go. I grind harder, moaning loudly as sensation builds and funnels, a tornado gaining momentum.

His gaze follows mine in the mirror. "Better hurry. Time is running out."

I'm right there—bliss a lit firecracker ready to explode in my clit—when the elevator dings. Darren covers my hand with his and steps back, even as I try to follow his thigh. He shakes his head, his expression almost remorseful, and he uncurls my fingers from his shirt and brings my knuckles to his lips. He kicks his bag to the wall and leans against it.

He's quick to wrap an arm around my shoulder and pull me into his side. He drops his head, lips finding my temple as he whispers, "Sorry, firefly, you almost had it."

The doors slide open and a family enters, giving us half smiles while their kids press their faces against the glass and the youngest one tries to push all the buttons. My knees feel weak all over again, and I want to cry. My clit is still singing "I was *that* close."

When the elevator finally reaches the lobby, Darren laces our fingers together and guides me to where his bus is waiting and the girls are huddled around their phones.

"Finally!" Violet holds up her phone, showing us the time. "They were about to leave without you." She thumbs over her shoulder to where Alex is standing outside. Darren's phone rings as Alex brings his to his ear.

"I gotta run. I'll see you tonight. Have fun today." Darren brushes his lips across mine in a very uncharacteristic public display of affection.

I stare after him as he heads for Alex, who throws his hand up in the air. All I catch is "What the fu—" before the doors close and cut him off.

Darren holds up a hand, probably telling him to settle down. He claps him on the back and Alex shakes his head, shoulders rolling as he turns and climbs onto the bus. Darren looks over his shoulder as he brings two fingers to his lips and holds them up in my direction.

I smile until I realize it's the fingers that were inside me not that long ago—the same ones that did not provide me with an orgasm. As my grin falls, his rises. And then he disappears onto the bus.

As soon as he's out of sight, I turn to the girls, ready to issue a somewhat insincere apology for holding them up. They're all staring at me, eyes wide.

"What?" I touch my face and pat my hair, making sure it's not all messed up.

"What the hell was that?" Violet makes wild hand gestures.

"What was what?" *Why are they all looking at me like I've grown another head?* I look down to make sure I'm not flashing a nipple or have a wet spot on my crotch.

"I didn't think Darren was big on PDAs," Violet says.

I shrug. "He usually isn't." Until now, I guess.

"Well, I think it's sweet," Sunny says, rubbing her bump. "Can we get something to eat before we go shopping? I'm starving."

I'm grateful that she takes the attention off me.

"I second that!" Violet says, and we pour out onto the Toronto street.

We stop at a breakfast place that has vegan options. Violet orders a full breakfast and a side of bacon and devours everything. We stroll down the street, stopping at a candy store, and then of course we find a sex shop, so it's imperative that we go inside, at least according to Violet and Skye.

Violet's eyes light up as she rummages through the penis-themed party favors. "Oh! Poppy, we need to start planning your bachelorette party!"

"I don't think that's necessary quite yet since we're not getting married for at least another year, maybe two, depending."

"Unless Lance knocks you up," Lily wags her brows.

Poppy rolls her eyes. "He's not going to knock me up. I'm on the pill."

Sunny raises her hand. "I was on the pill, and I got knocked up."

"Yeah, but you were on antibiotics and forgot that makes the pill ineffective," Lily reminds her.

"Oh, right. Oh well, at least this time around it was planned. Might as well have them all now so they can grow up together." She pats her tummy.

Lily smiles softly, but there's a sadness there, too. Her mom got pregnant by an NHL player when she was eighteen. He took zero responsibility and never paid a dime in child support. Randy's dad, a former NHL player, had a bad habit of sleeping with women who weren't his wife while he was on the road.

While Lily and Randy seem to have a great relationship, they're both a little skittish about marriage and kids. She's still young and not in a rush to start a family of her own, but I think part of her is sad that if she does end up having kids, they'll be much younger than Sunny's.

I can relate, I guess—not that I want to get married and have kids. I mean, I guess maybe I would eventually consider the kid part, but marriage seems a lot like a prison sentence from my experience growing up.

On the way back to the hotel, we're forced to stop again because Sunny needs more food. The game doesn't start until seven, but we arrive back at the hotel around four in the afternoon. It appears housekeeping has been by to tidy up, and Darren has come and gone. On the bed is huge black box tied with a red ribbon and a small black card with my name written on it in silver ink.

The ache between my legs that finally dulled into something tolerable this afternoon becomes sharp again as I consider the contents of the box.

I'd message Darren, but I don't like to distract him before games. I pick up the card and flip it open.

So we match in all the important ways.
xo Darren

I shiver at the memory of what he said this morning when he left me hanging. It's been a long time since he's brought me to the edge like that—twice even—and kept me wanting all day. What if it's some kind of sex toy in there? How the hell am I going to make it through the rest of the night without an orgasm?

I'm still standing at the edge of the bed, staring at the box, when there's a knock at my door.

I glance through the peephole, thinking maybe he organized room service—which is totally something he would do—except it's Violet standing in the hall with the rest of the girls.

I flip the lock and open the door. "Hey, what's going on?"

"We're getting ready for the game, and you weren't answering your messages, so we all came to you," Violet replies.

They file into the room toting bags. Lily has champagne, and Sunny is carrying a bottle of that sparkling grape juice she's in love with.

All of them are already dressed and ready for the game, wearing their jerseys and leggings.

"Ooooh! You have a present!" Violet picks up the box and shakes it around. It doesn't make a sound, so clearly there's nothing metal in it. She thrusts it at me. "Open it!"

"Uhhhh . . ." I look around at their expectant faces.

"Oh, come on, we already know you and Darren aren't nearly as freaky as you pretend to be. How bad could it be?" Violet reasons.

"Remember you said that if it's something you don't expect." I take the box from her.

"You don't have to open it in front of us if it makes you uncomfortable," Poppy says softly.

I wonder if it makes her uncomfortable. She was pretty quiet when we were at Sexapalooza, and she mostly looked at the funny condoms when we were in the sex shop. For as horrible a reputation as Lance had with women, he's incredibly tender with Poppy. He treats her like she's a delicate flower, even though I think she's kind of a badass with the way she handles him.

I take a seat on the end of the bed and pull the red ribbon, then nervously flip open the box. I press my fingers to my lips and suppress a grin. Now the note card makes more sense.

Inside is a brand new jersey to replace the one I've had for nearly two years.

There's also a pair of leggings covered in a team logo and WESTINGHOUSE 26 pattern. He even went so far as to get matching socks. But it's what I find under the jersey and leggings that makes me fight back a thick swell of foreign emotion. I'm not sure if I want to laugh or cry.

I pick up the small card sitting on top of the bra and panties set and flip it over.

I'll probably be lynched for going against team colors, but I thought this suited you better.

I run my fingers over the pretty pale yellow cheekies, edged in lace and decorated with not only the Chicago logo, but a tiny firefly print. I have a feeling they might be glow in the dark. I flip them over and laugh. They read WESTINGHOUSE on the butt. The bra is the same fabric, minus the text.

"He really is sweet, isn't he?" Poppy says.

"He is," I agree.

He's always been big on gift giving. Mostly it's been lingerie and sometimes more practical things, like upgrading the alarm system in my house and buying me that reading chair. But these kinds of gifts are new. And I think I like it, even though it scares me. I should be bracing myself for the possibility that he's going to be traded at the end of the season, not holding on tighter.

"You look like you might need this." Lily hands me a glass of champagne, which I gladly accept.

I take a small sip at first, then a much larger one since it's so delicious, and she's right. I do need it. This whole coming to away games with Darren isn't new. I've been invited plenty of times. It's how the dynamics have changed that's freaking me out.

I've always come prepared and with a plan. Or Darren has mentioned specific lingerie or toys he'd like me to bring. This time he offered to pack the leggings and shirts he purchased and keeps at his place—in the third drawer he cleared out for me. The first and second contain all the lingerie he or I have purchased over the past two years.

I chug the rest of my champagne and head to the bathroom so I can freshen up a little and change before I start the whole makeup process. The bra and panty set are adorably perfect. If I'd brought my phone in with me I'd consider taking a selfie and sending it to Darren, but that's not something I've done before, and I'm not sure if he'd appreciate it or be put off by it. Besides, I have a feeling it will be more impactful if he sees this on me in person.

When I come out of the bathroom, fully dressed in my brand new, freshly washed outfit—I know this because the clothes smell like Darren's laundry detergent—Lily hands me another glass of champagne.

Violet and Sunny are arguing over what color eye shadow will look best on

Poppy. Well, not arguing so much as holding up different color palettes and debating what will look more natural. Poppy doesn't need to wear makeup at all, and neither does Sunny. They have those natural, flawless faces that look best with a hint of lip gloss and maybe a coat of mascara.

I don't go crazy on the makeup, but pictures from the games often end up online, so I won't go out with a naked face, either. While my relationship with Darren got a lot of press and questions when we first started dating—which was unnerving for a lot of reasons—it was difficult to really qualify it since physical contact in public has never been our thing. It kept everyone guessing as to what was going on.

If Darren pulls another PDA like he did this afternoon, that could change things again. So of course I want to look decent if my picture ends up splashed on hockey sites for the bunnies to rip apart.

At six we meet Alex and Violet's parents in the hotel lobby and head to the arena. It's a short walk, but it's clear both Daisy and Skye have been drinking already—and possibly engaging in other activities that are legal in Canada.

The champagne has loosened me up a little, but I'm still nervous about the game. I root around in my purse for one of my mom's candies. I'm grateful when I find several at the bottom. I pop one in my mouth and sigh as the minty flavor coats my tongue. I know it's probably the placebo effect, but I immediately feel the tiniest bit better after a couple of sucks.

The stadium is full of blue and white jerseys, so we stick out like sore thumbs with our screaming red and black. Not that any of us gives a flying fuck. Violet figures Toronto would've picked Alex up—as a Canadian player—if they'd been on their game and realized what a formidable opponent he was going to be. Even with an injury he plays better than most, though he's been a lot more cautious recently, and I see that now in a way I wouldn't have before the conversation with Darren.

We have the kind of seats people want to shank you for. We file down our row, drinks in hand, and settle in while we wait for the teams to be announced. While the girls were in my room I'd almost forgotten about the discomfort between my thighs, but it's back with a vengeance. Part of it comes from knowing I'm wearing those pretty panties with his name on the ass.

I reach into my purse for another one of my calming candies.

"Are you coming down with something?" Lily asks from my right.

"Huh?" I pop the candy into my mouth and try not to groan out loud as the minty taste coats my tongue for the second time in the past hour.

"Is that a cough drop?"

"No. Why? Do you need one? I might have some." I don't want to part with my mom's candies.

"I'm good. It probably won't taste great with my beer." She clinks her can against mine, and we both take a sip.

Yeah, it's not all that delicious when you combine mint and beer.

A few minutes later, the teams take the ice, first Toronto, then Chicago. The apprehension I've been holding on to all day drops from my stomach to settle lower, between my thighs, making the pervasive ache that much worse. It's going to be a long game.

We all wave as the boys skate past, warming up before they take the bench. Violet's knee is bouncing, and she chews on her thumbnail.

"You okay?" I ask.

She nods. "Just nervous. I want them to win."

"Me, too."

Alex and Darren have their heads together as they take the bench and wait for the ice to be cleaned, Darren's hand on his shoulder. I lift my pearls to my lips as Darren glances in my direction.

He raises two fingers, the hint of a smile appearing as he taps his lips. I drop the pearls and mirror the movement.

The buzzer sounds, and his smile fades. He puts on his helmet and gloves and takes the ice. The first period isn't great. Darren passes the puck instead of taking shots, and Alex can't seem to get it past the net. Toronto steals the puck from Alex more than once, and by the end of the first period, Chicago is down one.

In the second period, Alex narrowly avoids getting slammed into the boards by Cockburn, the same guy who took him out last season and nearly cost him his career.

Darren puts himself in the way and takes the hit for Alex. He and Cockburn crash into the boards, the sound echoing through the arena.

"Fucking Cockburn!" Violet jumps out of her seat and starts yelling at the ref to call the dirty play.

Darren shakes it off, and Toronto takes a penalty, giving Chicago a two-minute power play. They switch out Alex for Randy, and he takes control when the puck drops, barreling down the ice toward the net with Darren on his right. At the last second, Randy passes to Darren who takes the shot, sliding the puck past the net, tying the game.

He doesn't smile as his teammates pat his back, eyes on the scoreboard and the minutes counting down the second period.

"Holy shit." Lily nudges my arm and points to the screens above us. Darren and Randy's faces flashes across it. While Randy wears a cocky smirk in his picture, Darren's eyes are dark, mouth almost set in a scowl. Their stats flash across the screen. Darren's sitting just below Randy this season, which makes him an incredibly valuable player—the kind who is covetable despite his age.

It's the reason he's been passing when Alex has asked him not to. He hasn't wanted all the points because of the draft. It all makes sense now.

The heavy feeling I've been carrying all day grows as the game continues. Randy scores a goal in the top of the third period, giving Chicago the lead, but Toronto ties it again halfway through. Alex and Darren are back on the ice together with three minutes left in the game. I can barely breathe when Alex gains control of the puck and skates down the ice toward the net, Darren parallel to him.

I cross my fingers as Alex makes the shot, but it goes wide. Darren catches the puck as it glides past the net and skates around behind it. It looks like he's going to pass to Alex, but he takes the shot instead, scoring his second goal of the game.

Toronto fans give a collective groan as the Chicago fans go crazy. It's a matter of keeping the puck away from the net while the final seconds tick down, securing Chicago's place in the next round, bringing them that much closer to the finals again.

TV crews swarm the players once they're off the ice. Darren looks uncomfortable with cameras on him, especially when they start talking about how his stats are the best of his career and then ask questions about the expansion draft and trade possibilities. Alex plasters on a smile when they turn the mic on him, but there's tension in the set of his jaw. He's unhappy with his performance.

"Guess I better get the Epsom salts ready. Tonight's going to be hard on the beaver," Violet says as we file out of the arena and pour onto the street, heading for the hotel.

We go directly to the bar, aware that it'll be a while before the guys arrive. Daisy and Skye appear to be three sheets to the wind already, and they've ordered a round of shots. They're having an inappropriate conversation—not unusual for those two—about their husbands and their sexual prowess.

Violet turns to Sunny. "That could be us one day."

Sunny rubs her belly. "I wonder if this one will be another boy. I'm getting really big really fast this time."

Violet leans her head on Sunny's shoulder. "Wouldn't it be great if we both had a boy or a girl at the same time? They'll have so much fun together, and when they're older we can have the kind of conversations our moms have and embarrass them."

I watch their sisterly exchange and selfishly fear that this new bond they're forming is going to usurp all the years of friendship between me and Violet. They'll have so much more in common now that they're both pregnant, and Sunny will be able to give Violet new-mom advice. They'll have stories and experiences to share that I can't be part of.

She'll have new responsibilities. I've seen how motherhood has changed Sunny this past year, and I worry it will be the same for Violet. She'll settle into her new role, and I'll won't fit into her life quite the way I did before.

Poppy pulls me out of my personal pity party when she hands me a drink.

Daisy and Skye's conversation seems to have moved away from doing the dirty to hockey, which is a little better.

"Robbie used to play hockey in college. I loved going to the games." Daisy sighs wistfully.

"I went out with a hockey player once," Skye blurts.

"Really?" Daisy perks up.

Violet rolls her eyes.

"Mmm. In my first year of college I used to waitress at this little bar. It was near the stadium, so sometimes we'd get fans and players in there." She waves a hand around in the air. "Anyway, this guy came in and sat in my section. He was a real hottie, and he played professional hockey—I think maybe for North Carolina? I can't remember now, but he was charming, and one thing led to another." Skye grimaces. "Sadly, he was terrible in the sack, and he had a tiny penis."

"I love your mom," I snicker.

"Wanna trade?" Violet grumbles. "Wait, it's pretty much the same thing, so never mind."

"Oh no!" Daisy puts a comforting hand on Skye's arm. "That's awful."

"It was such a disappointment. The condom slipped off in the middle, and I ended up having to fish it out after." Skye shudders, and Violet makes a gagging sound. "One good thing came from the experience, though." She turns to Violet and pats her on the cheek. "I got you."

Violet's mid-sip, so she spit-sprays ginger ale all over her mother's face and also gets my cheek. "What?"

Skye wraps her arm around Violet's shoulder. "I was almost five months along before I realized I was pregnant. In hindsight, I should've figured it out sooner, but sometimes things happen for a reason. I had zero interest in that hockey player, so I raised you on my own until I met Sidney and we fell in love."

"My dad was a professional hockey player?" Violet asks.

"He was. Not a very good one, mind you, but a hockey player nonetheless."

"I can't believe this is the first time I'm hearing this! Why didn't you tell me before now? I always thought he was some random."

Skye gives Violet a patient smile. "He was a random, honey."

"Does this random have a name?"

"Of course he does."

"Do you remember it?"

Skye makes a face. "Well, yes."

Violet arches a brow. "Care to share?"

Skye sighs, maybe realizing she's not going to get out of this. "His name is Dick, which is kind of ironic really, considering his was so small and all."

"My father's name is Dick?" Violet looks unimpressed.

"Sidney is your father, Violet. He gave you away at your wedding. I think that trumps being a sperm donor."

"Agreed, but still—even if Dick is a dickless dick, he's my biological father, and I think I have a right to know who he is, Especially since he's contributed half of my DNA, and I'm pregnant, and who knows what effect his genetic bullshit will have on this kid." She motions to her stomach, eyes wide with horror. "What if we have a boy and he has a tiny little penis?"

"You're almost exactly like me, and nothing like your biological dad. I'm sure Alex's DNA will win out in this case."

"Still, it'd be good to know. Does dickless Dick have a last name?"

"Of course." Skye grimaces and mutters something.

"What was that?"

"His last name is Head."

Violet blinks. And blinks again. "Come again?"

"Head. His last name is Head."

"My dad's name is Dick Head?"

"Technically it's Richard, but yes." Skye takes a healthy gulp of her drink. "Maybe we should talk about this later."

"Richard Head? And he played for North Carolina?"

"Yes, honey. Are you okay? You're really pale." Skye gives me a worried look.

"Maybe you should sit down." I put a hand on Violet's shoulder and urge her to the closest stool. Something about this conversation is very familiar, and I can't place why that is.

Lily appears, having returned from the bathroom. "Is everything okay? What's wrong with Violet?"

"Skye just told her who her birth father is."

"What?" Lily's eyes go wide.

"She's pretty drunk," I say.

Lily frowns. "I thought Violet was pregnant."

"Oh, Violet's not drunk, Skye is."

"And I thought Butterson was a bad last name." Violet shakes her head. "I guess Head isn't the worst, unless you name your kid Richard, and even then, you could go by Rich, or Richie, Why go by Dick?" She looks like she's hovering between shock and horror. "You're just setting yourself up for a world of ridicule. What kind of person, other than a dickhead, goes by the name Dick Head? My fucking father, that's who."

Lily grabs her shoulders. "What did you just say?"

"My sperm donor's name is Richard Head, but he goes by Dick. Seriously, he must be the biggest asshole in the history of the world with a sad, tiny dick," Violet replies.

And then I remember why this conversation is so damn familiar; two New Year's ago, before Randy and Lily were super serious, we talked about Lily's biological father, and Violet couldn't get over his stupid name.

Both Violet and Lily's eyes go wide. "Oh my God!" they say in unison.

"Your bio dad's name is Richard Head?" Lily asks.

"And your deadbeat dad's name is Richard Head," Violet replies. "Did he play for North Carolina?"

Lily nods slowly.

"What are the chances . . ." Violet trails off. "Holy shit. Does this mean you're my half-sister?"

chapter thirteen

I Got You

Darren

I'm not sure if the cost of winning this game will be worth it. The only thing that's going to make me feel better is Charlene. I want to put the lid on her jar and never let her go.

I realize, very clearly, that I'm in a terrible frame of mind. I've kept her on edge all day and probably shouldn't have since she was already there to begin with. I'm also aware that having done this to her is fucked up, but it seemed better than telling her things she's not ready to hear, especially when I'm not sure if I'm ready to say them.

Alex is quiet and in a shit mood as we make our way to the bar. He's not angry that we won the game; it's *how* we won that he's upset about. It's not jealousy, it's bigger than that. It's about his worth to the team. It's the position he feels he's putting me in. It's knowing that my chances of being pulled in the expansion draft get higher the more I pick up the slack he can't manage. It's the nine-million-dollar-a-year salary he doesn't think he's worth anymore.

The bar is loud and busy. I look around for Charlene and the rest of the girls, but they're not easy to find since pretty much every female in the place is decked out in our team gear. Loud shrieking and jumping draws my attention.

"There they are." I point to where Violet and Lily are hugging.

"I'm glad Vi can't get wasted. I need in my wife tonight," Alex says.

I scan the area around them and finally find Charlene. Her pearls are at her lips, her expression reflecting none of the excitement Violet, Lily, and the other girls seem to be experiencing. Which makes me question what's going on.

We weave through the crowd slowly because of the volume of people. Thankfully, not many attempt to talk to me, probably because I don't come across as friendly, and I don't often engage in conversation with people I don't know.

I step up behind Charlene, who's still worrying her pearls against her lips, and drop my mouth to her ear. "What's happening here?"

She startles and nearly fumbles her drink as she spins around. She tips her head back as I straighten, eyes finding mine. Emotions flit across her face, pain floating around in there. I'm unsure if it's physical, emotional, or both, and I regret keeping her hanging all day.

"Violet and Lily just found out they have the same father," she says softly. "Is this a joke?"

Her voice cracks, along with her forced smile. "I wish it was."

I want to ask her to explain, but Violet is jumping around, screaming at the top of her lungs. It's drawing a lot of attention. "Isn't this awesome? Both of our moms made terrible choices!" Violet motions between herself and Lily. "Can you see the resemblance? Boobs aside, of course."

Lily rolls her eyes. "Maybe I should put on one of your bras and stuff it with socks so it's easier to see the resemblance."

Randy comes up to stand beside me, observing the spectacle. "Did I hear that right? Vi and Lily have the same dad?"

"Apparently."

He runs a hand over his beard, looking from one woman to the other. "I don't see it."

I shrug because neither do I. Apart from the fact that they're both female and on the petite side, that's all the similarity I can find. Violet is busty and curvy where Lily is narrow and lean. Lily also has a couple inches on Vi. "Does Lily look more like her mother?"

Randy nods. "Yeah, kind of like Vi looks like hers." He tips his head in Skye's direction. She really does look like Violet, plus about twenty years. She also dresses very much like her daughter.

I'm grateful for the soap-opera-style family drama, because it takes the focus off tonight's game. I should be happy that we're going to the next round, and for the team I am, but the call I received this afternoon before I went on the ice worries me. My agent let me know that Lucas, the owner of the Vegas team, had contacted him for the third time, wanting to talk numbers. There's been interest from other teams too, and I'm still unsure where Charlene and I are headed. I feel like I'm just figuring out how to do this new version of us right, and I don't want to screw that up.

It's another hour before I finally manage to get close to Charlene again. She's drunk, and based on the empty glasses scattered over the table, someone thought shots were a good idea. She's positioned herself at the end of the table, slightly apart from the other girls, quiet instead of engaged in the lively conversation. She reminds me of how I get when there are too many people and I feel exposed.

I bend so I'm at her ear and don't have to yell. "You want to go up to the room now so I can take care of you?"

I back up enough so I can see her face. Her expression is a mixture of relief and desperation, so intense that for a second I think she's going to burst into tears, which is very unlike Charlene. The only times I've seen her cry were when Alex had his accident last year and Violet was a mess, and when my teammates found her surrounded by sex toys.

Her lips move, forming the word *please*, but it's not accompanied by sound, and I'm uncertain if it's because she hasn't made any or because it's too loud to hear.

I straighten and pull her chair out, giving her space to stand up.

"You're going?" Violet frowns. "Come on! Just stay a little longer."

"I apologize, Violet, but I need her." Which is true. I very much need to get lost in her for a while, and I have a feeling Charlene needs the same.

Violet jumps up and rushes around the table so she can hug Charlene. I don't understand why women feel the need to hug each other all the time. It's not as if they won't see each other again soon, like in the morning.

When all the hugging is over, I link our fingers, marveling at how much softer and smaller her hand is than mine and how much I crave this innocuous contact. I keep her close as we weave through the bar. Alex holds up a hand when he sees us leaving. I nod but don't stop to talk. This whole thing with Violet tonight has taken his mind off of the game, but soon he'll want to sit down and figure out how to manage the next series.

We're not alone on the elevator ride up to the penthouse floor, so I simply keep our hands joined, sliding my thumb back and forth over her knuckles. Charlene's free hand is at her throat, fingering her pearls.

She exhales a shuddery breath when the last couple exits the elevator at the twentieth floor. When the doors close, I lift our twined hands and bring them to my lips. "Are you okay?"

She nods, but her bottom lip trembles, and her breath comes sharp and fast.

"You don't seem okay," I observe.

She opens her mouth to speak, but the doors slide open. A couple of women wearing Chicago jerseys fall into the elevator, giggling, clearly drunk. One of them pushes the button for the lobby while the other leans against the rails opposite us.

I'm annoyed at the interruption.

"Oh my God!" one of them shrieks. "You're Darren Westinghouse! You were incredible tonight!"

The high-pitched, exclamation-point-laden yelling makes me want to pull out a roll of duct tape, but instead I smile and tuck Charlene in tighter to my side. This is part of the reason I've never tried to be better than I am. Because it draws unwanted attention. Stay solidly average and out of the limelight, and people don't recognize you on the street. Play better than most, and people start to notice.

I've been content to be Alex's wingman for the past six years. He loves the accolades and thrives on it. He manages it better than I can. I don't want this overwhelming level of notice. I don't want these drunk screaming girls, looking for autographs. I don't want to be nice and open and friendly. I want privacy and Charlene. I want some semblance of normal in a life that's never been that way.

One of the girls roots around in her purse for a pen so I can sign something for her. Neither of them acknowledge Charlene. It's as if she doesn't even exist. So when one of them finally manages to find a pen and her game ticket, I tip Charlene's chin up and press an unexpected kiss to her lips.

"This will just take a moment," I murmur, lips still touching hers.

"Okay." It's more breath than word.

I just want to be alone with her. I want these fans and my worries to disappear. I want to drown in her taste and her scent and her soft, sweet moans.

But first I need to sign some shit.

The women gawk unapologetically as I tuck a loose tendril of Charlene's hair behind her ear. It's unnecessary. Her hair is perfectly fine the way it is without me messing with it. I just want a reason to touch her, to indicate on some base level that she's mine, and I'm hers.

I sign their tickets, then sign the back of their jerseys, even though one has Ballistic and the other has Waters, which makes sense since they're the star players on the team. Thankfully the elevator chimes. I reach for Charlene's hand, tugging her along as I hit the close door button and slip out into the hall. I don't want them following us. When the door stays closed, I exhale a sigh of relief and walk quickly toward our room, rooting in my pocket for the key card, but Charlene is already prepared. She swipes it across the sensor, and I throw it open, ushering her inside.

The door barely has a chance to lock before Charlene launches herself at me. She forces me back against the wall—which is no easy feat considering I have a good six to eight inches on her and I outweigh her by a hundred pounds. I'm attributing it partly to her catching me off guard.

Her fingernails cut into my shoulders as her mouth connects with mine, and she tries to hoist herself up. I spin so she's against the wall and lift her by her ass, positioning her so my erection is finally where it's supposed to be, albeit covered by clothes. I plan to remedy that soon.

She rolls her hips and moans, head hitting the wall as she arches. Her nails bite my scalp, and her teeth sink into my bottom lip. Charlene is a lot of things in the bedroom—uncertain, curious, semi-adventurous, adorably sort-of commanding when she's decked out in leather—but she's rarely, if ever, aggressive like she is now, which tells me I've either pushed her too far, or something is wrong.

Possibly both.

I also think her prolonged anxious state means she needs to come, badly.

Pinning her against the wall with my hips, I press a palm to her chest and splay my fingers out to frame the pearl necklace.

"Darren, please." The words draw out on a plea.

This is about so much more than delayed gratification. She's not just wanting, she's desperate and sad and panicked, and I need to understand why. But first I need to take care of her, for both our sakes.

I run my free hand down her side and under the waistband of her leggings. "After I make you come, you're going to tell me why you're so upset."

"Whatever you want."

I slip my fingers into her panties, which are practically soaked through. All day I left her in this state—too many hours and too much uncertainty. It's my fault she's out of control, and I'm right there with her.

She jerks as soon as I find her clit. Her legs go lax, along with the rest of her, as if she's been dosed with Valium. I ease her down the wall, wishing I'd made it to the bed, but aware that stopping now would be an even worse kind of torment. So I push two fingers inside and curl forward, fluttering fast and hard.

Charlene is lost in all the sensations, chasing down bliss. My name is a guttural groan as she comes in waves, and I keep pushing her, dragging it out because I can, and she needs it.

She sags against me, hot breath fanning across my skin, and I kiss her temple. "Do you need me to keep going?"

She makes a noise, but I can't tell if it's a yes or a no. I skim her clit, and she sucks in a gasping breath, fingers tightening in my hair again. So I keep circling, light and slow, pulling her to the edge and pushing her over gently. This orgasm is much less violent, but no less intense.

I ease my hand out of her panties, grab her thighs and hoist her up, keeping her wrapped around me as I carry her to the bed. A stream of light from the bathroom cuts across the floor, illuminating the way.

"I won't do that to you again," I promise as I lay her out on the bed, kissing along her temple and down her cheek. "I won't leave you needing that long ever again."

She's shaky and clumsy as she tries to unbutton my shirt. I cover her hand. "Let me get it."

I kneel between her legs and shrug out of the suit jacket, unfasten the first three buttons and pull my shirt over my head, tossing it somewhere on the floor. Charlene's already managed to get her jersey over her head and her leggings off.

"Leave the rest for me, please." I unclasp my belt, pop the button on my pants and get my zipper halfway down before Charlene pushes them over my hips, taking my boxers with them.

My erection springs free, and Charlene wraps her soft, warm hand around the length. Her eyes flash up to mine, glassy and desperate as she leans forward and parts those gorgeous lips, engulfing the head.

I groan out a low *fuck* and close my eyes for a second, because seeing her like this is almost too much.

The head bumps the back of her throat as I shove my fingers into her hair.

But I don't try to control her. I don't need to. She knows me well enough to anticipate what I want. She pulls back, sucks the head, and then draws me in, over and over, again and again, eyes locked on mine.

I trace her bottom lip. "If you take me deep one more time, I'm going to come down that pretty, sweet throat of yours." It's as much a warning as a promise.

As fun as it is to make a mess on her chest, I'd prefer not to do that tonight, mostly because I don't want to take the time to clean it up before I get into those pretty panties of hers with more than my fingers.

I'm right there, balls tightening, the ache merging with the promise of release. She sucks hard, her hot mouth surrounding every inch of me, and I let go, pulsing as she swallows. I fold forward, groaning her name, struggling not to thrust since I'm already as deep as I can go.

When I'm finished coming, I ease out gently and bend to brush my lips over hers. "I didn't deserve your mouth tonight."

"I didn't do it for you. I want you in me for a long as possible tonight, and this guarantees that."

I chuckle and kiss her softly. "Well, I'm going to need a few minutes before I can do that, and I have a really great idea about how to pass the time." Charlene smiles against my lips. I'd like to stay where I am for a while, but I've tortured her enough for one day, and there's little I love more than watching her unravel for me.

I drop a kiss between her breasts and one below her navel. The custom bra and matching panties are perfect on her gorgeous body. "I want to see the back of these," I murmur.

Charlene slides up the bed and flips onto her stomach, craning to look her over shoulder. Her lip is caught between her teeth. I run my hands down her sides to her hips.

"I don't know why it took me this long to come up with these, but they're my new favorites."

"I think Violet has a pair for every day of the week with Alex's name stamped on her butt."

As soon as I get home, I'm going to order them in every color combination, style, and pattern I can. Fuck lace and satin. Cotton boy shorts are where it's at.

I regret how I handled her this morning, because now I want to take my time, but I'm aware I can't. I open the clasp on her bra and kiss the space between her shoulder blades, then the dip in her spine before I pull the panties over her hips and bite the swell of her ass, smiling at her gasp. I drag my thumb along the divide, and she jolts and moans. Slipping my fingers between her thighs, I skim the length of her slit, passing her entrance to find the steel piercing her clit. Her hips lift as I circle once.

"On your back baby, I want to spend some time kissing you."

Charlene is quick to comply, flipping over and tossing her bra on the floor.

I stretch out between her legs, hooking my arms under her thighs and lick up the length of her pussy. Charlene writhes against my mouth when I take her clit ring between my teeth and tug. The first orgasm comes hard and fast, the second only minutes behind the first. And I keep going, pushing her higher so I can watch her spiral down, down, down.

I lose track after orgasm number three. And eventually I can't and don't want to wait any longer. It's not just about getting lost in her, which I admittedly want. But more than that, I need her. I need the closeness. I need to know she's mine and that no matter what happens at the end of the season, that's not going to change.

I prowl up her body, position myself at her entrance and ease in.

I drop my forehead against her neck and groan. "Only you make me feel this alive."

Charlene's knees press against my ribs, and links her hands behind my neck. "I felt empty all day," she whispers.

Her words make the hairs on my arms stand on end. Something about her tone tells me this isn't just about withholding orgasms. It's more.

I kiss my way up her neck and across her jaw. "And how do you feel now?" I push up on my arms so I can see her face.

"Like you're under my skin, but I can't get you deep enough."

I roll my hips, and she moans quietly. I don't know what's happening here, but I want to give her everything she needs. I want to be everything she needs.

I slip my fingers into the hair at the nape of her neck, cradling her head in my palm as I drop my lips to hers. I can still taste her on my tongue, so when she licks at my mouth and moans, I know it's because she can taste herself.

I kiss her the same way I move inside her. I'm in no rush for this to end, and somewhere inside my head, I fear what will happen when it does. Things between us are shifting again. And as close as I feel to her in this moment, I worry that outside of it, there will be distance I don't know how to bridge.

Charlene grabs my biceps, fingernails digging in while she moves with me. I pull back in time to see her eyes flutter open and meet mine as she starts to pulse around me.

Charlene spends a great deal of energy trying to make sex into some kind of event, as if she feels l need to be entertained to enjoy her. But nothing compares to this. There are no distractions, nothing to get in the way as I watch her light up under me. She lifts her hand and drags gentle fingers down my cheek.

I close my eyes for a second, absorbing the sensation before I catch and hold Charlene's gaze again. The orgasm is painfully intense as it burns through me. White spots blank out of my vision, taking away Charlene's perfect face for the briefest moment. It feels as if I'm drowning in pleasure so extreme the possibility of never having it again is agony.

I drop my head, nuzzling into her neck, breathing in the salty sweet scent of her skin. My body feels weighed down with satiety. I want this every day. I want to wake up to this, go to sleep to this, come home to this, and I'm not sure why it took this long for me to realize it. My limbs are heavy and uncoordinated as I ease out. I slip an arm under her and roll to the side, taking her with me.

Charlene tucks her head under my chin, a shiver ripping through her. At first I think it's the aftermath of such a powerful, drawn-out orgasm, or maybe she's cold. I try to shift away so I can tuck us under the covers, but she mumbles *no* against my neck and tightens her hold.

"Let me get a warm cloth so I can make you more comfortable," I murmur against her temple, once again trying to extricate myself.

She clings tighter and shakes her head, shuddering again.

I pull back enough so I can see her face, but she twists her head away, tucking her chin against her shoulder, eyes screwed up tight.

"Are you okay?" I stroke her cheek, hoping to calm her, but her lips twist as if she's fighting whatever emotions are swimming to the surface, ones she's clearly trying to hide.

"I'm fine," she whispers brokenly, still not looking at me.

"You seem the opposite of fine."

"I need a minute. Please."

I don't know what to make of this reaction, or the way she's clinging to me. This isn't typical Charlene behavior, and I don't know how to handle it.

A tiny whimper hums across my throat.

"Did I hurt you?" I don't think I did. I'm always extraordinarily careful with Charlene.

She shakes her head into my shoulder, which should be a relief, but the fact that she's breaking down emotionally after sex seems bad. The sound of her pain tears at my heart, her ache my own.

I want to be better at this, at caring for someone. A wave of emotion slams into me, the kind I've guarded against my entire life. I shift her body so I can sit up and keep her in my lap. She wraps her legs around my waist, arms locked around my shoulders with her face buried against the crook of my neck.

She feels like she could break apart in my arms, and I'm forced to finally accept the truth I've been hiding from: I'm in love with Charlene, and have been for a very long time.

Jesus. I'm so emotionally stunted by my fucked-up family, I couldn't even recognize love until it punched me in the face.

I rub circles on Charlene's back with one hand and smooth my free palm over the back of her head. "Breathe, baby," I murmur in her ear and press my lips to her temple. "Let me make it better."

She sucks in a high-pitched breath, and I worry I'm making it worse. Eventually she seems to calm, and then her lips find that sensitive space behind my ear. She trails kisses up my neck and along the edge of my jaw.

For a moment I'm confused, until I realize her mouth is meant to be a distraction. It almost works.

I cup her face in my hands and lift, forcing her to look at me. Charlene's eyes are red rimmed, her cheeks flushed, and her expression is pure panic.

"What's going on?"

"Nothing. I'm fine. I want you again." She tries to come back to my mouth, but I hold her still.

"What is this about?" I smooth away her tears.

"That was intense. Today was intense."

"And that's the only reason for the tears?" I press. "I need you to talk to me, Charlene."

"I waited all day for you." She sighs and lifts her gaze, vulnerability leaking through. "I know the game was stressful for you, and it's the same for me. You wanted me on edge, and I was. I was worried and anxious. It was a lot."

I still think she's leaving things out, purposely or not, so I try to pull them out of her however I can. "What exactly are you worried about?"

"I don't know. Everything? You? What you're not telling me."

I sigh. I'm going to have to give to get here. "My stats are too high, and I'm getting too much attention. I don't like it, and I don't want it. But I don't have a choice, and I won't tank our team because I dislike the press I'm getting."

She blinks a few times, maybe stunned that I'm being so forthcoming for once. It's about fucking time, I suppose. Buying her new clothes and nice things only goes so far. I have to let her into my head if I want her to let me into hers.

"Now can you tell me why you're so upset, other than the fact that I'm an asshole for having kept you on the edge all day?"

Her fingers go to her pearls. "Now I feel stupid."

"What? Why?"

"Because you're worried about your team, and I'm worried about myself."

I want to erase the sadness that pulls her mouth down. I want to take the ache away. "Trust me when I tell you it's not just my team I'm worried about, Charlene. I'm not that selfless."

"What else are you worried about?"

I shake my head, aware this is yet another diversion tactic. "Not understanding why you're so upset."

She runs her fingers through my hair, eyes fixed there, maybe so she doesn't have to look directly at me. "It feels like I'm losing things that are important to me."

"How do you mean?"

"Violet's always been my best friend. And maybe it's petty and stupid, but she's going to get closer to Sunny because they're both pregnant, and Sunny and Lily have always been close, and now Violet and Lily are *actual* sisters, and I feel like I'm on the outside with no way in. And then there's this whole expansion draft, and what if you're traded and I . . ." She sucks in a deep breath, trying to keep herself in check. "I don't want to lose all the people who mean the most to me."

I skim the hollow of her eyes, brushing away more tears. As much as I don't like to see her upset, I'm almost relieved we're on the same page, at least about not wanting to lose the people we care for. I can't control what's happening with Violet or Alex, but I can try to keep hold of what we have.

"Whatever happens with everyone else, I'm in this with you. We can be on the outside together."

She drags her fingers along the edge of my jaw, eyes sad. "Everything's changing, and I want it to stay the same. I need this to stay the same."

My stomach bottoms out. "This?"

"Us. How we are."

Is it a warning? Was tonight too much for her? The closeness is something I want more of. And it has to be gradual, something that happens so slowly she won't even recognize the change is happening at all. So I don't ask for clarification, because I don't want an answer I won't like. Instead I tell her what she needs to hear.

"It's always going to be me and you, Charlene. Whatever you need, I'll be that for you."

chapter fourteen
All Good Things

Charlene

THINGS SEEM TO STABILIZE AFTER WE RETURN TO CHICAGO. My panic over losing my best friend because she now has a real half-sister wanes as I realize things haven't changed all that much. I mean sure, Violet and Lily might be a little closer because they literally share DNA, and she and Sunny can gripe about sore boobs, but it hasn't changed how much time Violet and I spend together. In fact, once we're home, Violet and I are together more, rather than less. Darren and I spend a lot of time in coupley situations with Vi and Alex, so I don't feel like my best friend position has been usurped.

Things between Darren and me are good—great even. He hasn't shifted from a quiet, introverted, sometimes guarded man to the kind of guy who shares all of his feelings and loves being around lots of people. But there are shifts, and not all of them are subtle.

I now have a rack in his walk-in closet filled with brand new business wear, the kind I can't afford unless I switch careers and become a high paid escort who works every night of the week. The price tags are always missing, but I've done my research. I know what a Fendi suit costs—especially if it's this season and has been custom tailored to fit me.

One side of the bathroom vanity now houses duplicates of the stuff I keep at home.

Darren also purchased a second dresser to match his, which is where all of my lingerie, new leggings, sleep sets, and panties now reside. When he has home games, he requests that I stay with him almost every night. He's grown particularly fond of returning from a game or practice to find me snuggled up in my reading chair with either a book or account files I've brought home with me. Although admittedly, that chair ends up being used for sex almost as much as it is for reading.

Series three of the playoffs is intense, once again going to game seven, and putting Chicago into the finals. Darren's stats continue to rise, and with them his anxiety, *and* his requests for me to stay at his place. I can't and don't want to say no, but I worry, more than I let on, about what's going to happen at the end of the season when the expansion draft finally happens.

I'd like to believe he's not going to end up on the chopping block, but the truth is, his game keeps improving. Which tells me something incredibly important about Darren. He adapts to his environment and the people in it.

He played only as well as he needed to in order to keep Alex in the limelight. And now he's playing better to keep his team afloat. As I settle into this new us, I've begun to realize this is who he is and how he operates, whether consciously or not. He adjusts himself and his expectations based on someone else's need.

When his grandparents took away his privacy as a teenager, he found ways to adapt—physically, mentally, emotionally. In his career, he always puts his team's needs in front of his own, and I believe, in a lot of ways, he does the same with me.

I'm the reason our relationship never progressed. I'm the reason we've stayed the same all this time. Whatever I wanted, Darren gave me. He never tried to open the doors I kept locked. Until recently.

He's always very careful and calculated in the way he manages me. Us. Except now we're transforming, and I don't know how to stop it—or if I can, or if I even want to.

Chicago wins the first two home games of the finals, but loses the first away game in Tampa. I worry this will be another seven-game series, making their off season that much shorter, when they could use the extra time to recuperate. I'm relieved when they win the second away game by one goal, and even more relieved when it's Alex who scores it, and Randy who handles the assist.

I'm already at Darren's place when he arrives home. For the first time in a long while, he picks out lingerie. I'm unsurprised when he chooses to dress me in lavender satin and lace. But when he opens the *I thought it would be fun but I changed my mind* toy box, my nervousness immediately skyrockets.

"What are you doing?"

It takes a few seconds before he finally shifts his attention away from the contents of the box. "Looking for something."

His expression is flat. I don't know how to read him tonight, and that nervous feeling drops low in my tummy and settles between my thighs.

He stops what he's doing and crosses to where I'm standing in the middle of the doorway. He caresses my cheek and bends to press his lips to my forehead. "Wait for me on the bed, please."

I search his face, but all I get is the tiniest hint of a smile before he turns me around, pats me on the butt, and sends me out of the closet.

I sit on the edge of the bed, nervously toying with my pearl necklace. Several minutes pass, or at least that's how long it feels, before he finally appears, carrying an armload of toys.

I swallow hard as I take in the items he's chosen, and the heaviness between my thighs expands with each toy he carefully places along the end of the bed on either side of me. I recognize several of them as items I'd foolishly surrounded myself with when his teammates walked in on me.

Darren comes to stand in front of me. I look up—taking in his dress shirt, the sleeves rolled up to his elbows, the top two buttons undone—until I reach his face.

He stares, unblinking as he taps my knee. "Open, please."

He tips his head to the side, eyes roaming over my body, pausing between my legs where everything is already tight and pulsing. He reaches out and skims my jaw, making every single muscle in my body clench and quiver.

"Are you nervous, firefly?"

"Yes."

He exhales slowly and runs his fingers up the inside of my thigh. I suck in a shallow breath when he slips one under the edge of my panties. If I wasn't wearing lingerie, I'm sure I'd be leaking all over his comforter.

I bite back a moan and eye the items on the bed.

"Tell me why," he whispers, voice low with gravel.

"You know why."

He shakes his head. "I don't think I do."

I look at the ball gag on the right and then that creepy facemask with only a mouth hole on the left.

"Darren," I moan when he circles my clit.

"Why do we still have all of this if we're never going to use it?"

I'm not sure why he wants to have this conversation right now. I expected him to walk in the door and get me naked on my reading chair, as has been typical recently.

"Does that mean you want to use it?" I ask.

I have to admit, as unnerving as it's been to have Darren focused solely on me and not any of the stuff I usually bring into our sex games, I actually love sex without all the distractions. I thought maybe he did, too.

He withdraws his fingers, trailing them down the inside of my thigh, leaving a streak of wetness that makes me blush as he sinks to his knees front of me. "I'd like you to answer my question before you pose one of your own."

I don't know what's happening here. Or how I'm supposed to answer that because the truth is at odds with my actions over the past two years.

"I thought maybe one day I'd change my mind."

"Is that really true?" he asks.

I bite my lip and shake my head.

"So all of this serves what purpose?" He gestures to the array of toys. "Apart from being a distraction."

"I thought maybe it was what you wanted."

He skims the pearls at my throat. "And I thought I was showing you that you're more than enough. I will give you almost anything you want, but I only need you. *You* are all I want, Charlene."

I motion to the items surrounding me on the bed. "Do you want me to get rid of all this stuff?"

"That's entirely up to you. I'm just telling you I can take it or leave it. Could it be fun? Maybe. But only if it's what you want. Otherwise it's unnecessary." He runs his hands up my thighs. "Now, I've been without you for four days. I'd like spend some time enjoying all the things I missed."

⁂

The night that follows could possibly end up being the championship game. I'm not as on edge as I was at the end of the last series, even though there's more at stake with this game. As usual we're all seated in close to the ice, behind the bench

Darren is as worried about winning as he is losing. The beginning of the game is rocky, with Tampa scoring twice in the first period, but Chicago evens it out by the end of the second. Alex scores a goal, which is good for his ego and team morale. Randy owns the second goal, with Darren as the assist for both, taking them into the final period tied. That doesn't last long, though.

They're less than five minutes into the third when Darren circles close to the net with the puck. He passes to Alex, who I'm sure is going to take the shot, but at the last second he fakes right and shifts the puck to Randy who scores another goal for Chicago.

They hold onto the lead through the third, and with less than three minutes left in the game, Darren gets hold of the puck and sprints down the ice on a breakaway, scoring again for Chicago.

Tampa is down two points with less than two minutes left in the game, and one of the players gets in Alex's face. The ref calls a roughing penalty, giving Chicago a power play for the final minute of the game, and of course they take the opportunity to score again, ending the game, and the season, with a 5-2 win for Chicago.

Chicago took the Cup home when Darren and I first started seeing each other, but this is different. Back then Darren had a no-trade clause, and we weren't as serious as we are now. So much is tied up in him, and our friends are interconnected, so this monumental win is both something to celebrate and fear.

Change is coming no matter what. Someone is going to Vegas at the end of the season, and hopefully it won't be Darren, whose stats are the best they've ever been.

Sunny passes Logan to Miller so he can skate him around the ice while they celebrate the win. The sports journalists clamor for interviews. Darren is never comfortable in front of the camera, unlike Randy and Alex. His answers are always short and to the point, almost as if he's annoyed. When one of the journalists asks him how he feels about the expansion draft, he mutters something about being at the end of his career and younger, better players being a safe bet. Then he turns around and stomps down the hall toward the locker room.

The journalist turns to Alex who defends Darren, saying they've been playing together for a long time, and any trade would be a big change.

Darren is quieter than usual at the bar, but he doesn't shy away from the celebration, maybe because it's possible this is the last time he'll get to do this with his Chicago teammates. I hope that's not the case.

The expansion draft won't happen for a few more weeks, so there will be unease while we wait for the outcome. Plus, losing one team member could have a domino effect. I try not to worry, but it's not easy.

We're all sitting around a long table in the back of the bar, chatter making it hard to focus on any one conversation. Also, Darren's hand is under the table, kneading my thigh and slowly moving higher.

"We need to have a party for your birthday this year, Char!" Violet shouts.

"Yes!" Lily agrees. "A real one since it's your champagne birthday!"

I shoot them both a look. Birthday parties have never been my thing. I don't like being the center of anyone's attention, except maybe Darren's.

"I've been thinking about your birthday," Darren says so only I can hear, in a tone that sends a shiver down my spine.

I wave Violet and Lily off. "It doesn't need to be a big deal."

"So how about a BBQ at our place? We can celebrate all the things! Your champagne birthday, winning the Cup, and the end of the season," Violet suggests.

Lily pulls up her calendar on her phone. "What about next weekend?"

"That's perfect!" Violet turns her smile on me. "Plus it's a holiday weekend, so a BBQ is essential anyway. We can eat burgers and lactose-free ice cream and cake and all the delicious things. And I need to wear a bikini and take pictures before this baby takes over my body!"

I don't have the heart or the desire to argue. Besides, with the trades still looming, I have no idea if this is the last birthday I'll get to celebrate with all of our friends. Will one of them will be somewhere else next year? I don't want to miss out on making memories, even if they might hurt in the future.

"Okay," I tell her. "Let's do it."

⁓

When your best friend is married to one of the top earners in the NHL, she can pull together a pretty damn sweet party in a very short span of time. Violet hires a caterer and buys all the decorations online.

Darren must ask me a million times, in a hundred different ways, what I want for my birthday. What I really want is for him to stay in Chicago and not be traded to Vegas, or anywhere else. But he doesn't have control over that, so I tell him I don't need anything and the party is enough.

My birthday begins with orgasms from Darren and a promise that he'll see me later. He leaves my bed, much to my dismay, just after ten in the morning and is replaced by Violet.

"I brought breakfast!" She wrinkles her nose as she takes a few steps into my bedroom. "It smells like Darren and sex. I vote we eat downstairs."

I roll out of bed, not caring about my messy hair or the discarded lingerie—I'm wearing one of my many shorts-and-tank sleep sets—as I follow her downstairs.

"You didn't have to go to all this trouble, especially since the party is at your place."

"Are you kidding? I wanted a couple of hours of you-and-me time before I have to go sharing you with all our friends. Remember when we used to eat pints of ice cream and have *Hoarder* marathons on your birthday?" She turns the bag over and two half-pints of Ben & Jerry's roll onto the counter. Her smile is questioning. "We don't have time for a marathon, but we could do an episode or two."

I don't know why I'm suddenly emotional, but I throw my arms around her.

When we finally release each other, Violet puts her hands on my shoulders. "I know a lot has changed recently, especially with me and Sunny both being pregnant, and then Lily and me finding out we're half-sisters—which is, like, so daytime soap opera, by the way. But there's only one you, Char. We've been best friends for almost a decade. We went through frosh week together and survived for Christ's sake."

I laugh at that. "You'd think we would've learned shots were bad back then."

"Academic intelligence isn't the same as social smarts. How the two of us made it through college without a criminal record is beyond me." Violet snort-laughs and then grows serious. "No one is ever going to replace you, Char. When we're old and saggy and we have to yell to hear each other, we'll still be best friends."

Of course that's the moment I burst into tears, because as much as I don't want to admit it, those are exactly the words I need to hear. And that sets off a whole chain reaction in which Violet starts crying, too. So we hug some more and cry a bunch like sappy idiots.

"I'm probably going to cry a hundred times today because my hormones are insane," Violet sniffles.

"At least you have an excuse."

Violet and I spend the next two hours eating crap and half-watching TV. It's good to have a little time with just her before the party.

My mom calls around noon to wish me a happy birthday, and she promises to visit soon. I'm a little disappointed, especially since she uses the reality show she auditioned for as the reason she's so busy. But then, we never made a big deal out of birthdays at The Ranch, likely for reasons I didn't understand at the time. Afterward, it sort of stayed that way, so the fact that I've agreed to a party at all is kind of a big thing.

Early in the afternoon, Lily and the rest of the girls come by to pick me and Violet up—apparently Alex dropped Vi off this morning. I don't need an overnight bag because I'm staying the night at Darren's, so all I bring is my beach bag with my bathing suit, sunscreen, and a hairbrush.

Lily is parked across the end of the driveway in Randy's huge Ford F-150. This one is new, and though I'm not all that big into cars, or trucks for that matter, even I can appreciate how cool it is with its chrome everything and grill guard on the front.

Violet bounces down the front walk for a few steps before she grimaces and holds on to her boobs. "Sweet Jesus, you'd think my bra was made of sandpaper with how sensitive my damn nipples are these days." She threads her arm through mine. "It's party time! You better do some shots for me tonight to make up for the fact that I'm incubating Alex's future hockey legacy."

I give her a side hug. "Shots are never a good idea, Vi. We both know this."

"Agreed. But there are Jell-O shooters, so you have to do at least one of those."

Violet makes a move to get in the backseat. I offer to help her in, because it's a long way up even with the running boards thanks to the huge tires on this truck, but she slaps my hand away. "I'm pregnant, not incompetent. I can do it myself."

Violet is uncoordinated at the best of times, but add height, her center of gravity being thrown off, and an additional cup size to her already huge boobs, and she's a walking disaster. Still, she somehow manages to get her ass in the backseat without damaging herself or anyone else.

"Happy birthday!" The girls call out as I drop into the passenger seat. They're all wearing birthday hats with a set of champagne glasses, my name, and the number twenty-six on them. Lily blows one of those birthday horns, and the thing that rolls out hits me just above the eye. It's followed by a burst of gold raining down on the front seat.

Lily's eyes go wide. "Vi! Not in the truck!"

The dash and the front seat are littered with gold glitter and tiny sequins. I cover my mouth with my palm, trying to decide if I should laugh or not, based on how horrified she looks.

Violet makes her apologetic face. "Sorry. I got excited and forgot."

"Randy's going to kill me!"

"We can stop by a car wash and vacuum it out," Poppy suggests.

"We don't have time. Everyone's supposed to arrive around two, and it's already one thirty. The birthday girl can't be late." Lily runs her finger along the dash. "Glitter is the worst. It never comes out. I'm pretty sure I still have glitter stuck to my vag from the last time Randy wanted to play figure skater," she says.

"Was that last night?" Violet asks.

"Last week." Lily puts the truck in gear. "Roll down your windows, girls, let's see how much gets sucked out the windows on the way to Vi's. And you're totally taking the heat for this. Randy can't get mad at a pregnant woman."

As Lily drives down the street, I spot an enormous RV parked not far down the road. I point and scream.

Lily puts on the brakes, maybe thinking she's accidentally almost run over my neighbor's cat, who has a terrible habit of playing chicken with cars. I swear he's maxed out his nine lives.

I unbuckle my seatbelt and try to tuck myself under the dash.

"What's wrong?" Lily asks.

"It's the RV, just keep going," Vi says.

Lily glances down at me uncertainly, but takes her foot off the brake and hits the gas. A cloud of glitter whirls in the air, and everyone sputters and waves their hands in front of their faces as they get pelted with it.

I cover my eyes with my palms as much to protect myself from the glitter as to hide from the RV. "Tell me when it's safe, Vi!"

We slow as we round a corner and then speed up again.

"Okay. You're good," Vi calls out.

"Are you sure?" My God. My heart feels like it's part of the backbeat to a techno track. It was bad enough when my mom parked her stupid mini Winnebago in my driveway for three days, but a full-sized RV is a whole different bag of no-fucking-way.

"I'm sure. We can't see it anymore."

I uncover my eyes and slowly pull myself back up, checking to make sure Violet isn't lying. The girls are looking at me like I've lost my mind.

"Are you okay?" Lily asks.

"Fine. Good. Sorry about that."

"Once when Lily and I were little, we went to the park and there was a guy in a white van with no windows and he offered us candy. Remember that, Lily?" Sunny asks.

Lily nods and shudders. "Sure do."

"Thankfully Alex was there playing hockey with some of the boys in the neighborhood. They started shooting their pucks at the van and broke the windshield." Sunny twirls her hair. "Ever since then, white windowless vans give me the willies."

"That's totally reasonable." I nod my agreement. "I feel the same way about RVs."

"Bad people are everywhere," Sunny says softly, still rubbing her belly. "I'm glad this one will have an older brother to protect him or her."

Violet and Sunny start talking about what it's like to have an older brother. Violet's experience is a lot different than Sunny's. Skye and Sidney married when Violet was a teenager, and she and Miller only had to go to the same high school for a year. But Miller and Vi really do act like brother and sister, and always have, as far as I know.

We pull into Violet's driveway a few minutes later. There are yellow balloons tied to the trees with Happy Birthday written on them.

I give Violet the eye. "I thought this was going to be more like a Memorial Day Weekend party."

She shrugs. "We're celebrating all the things, and as your best friend, I reserve the right to make a big deal out of your birthday even if you won't. Plus, Darren can be pushy when he feels like talking and making demands."

"He's good at that, the making demands part," I agree.

The guys are already in the backyard, playing Frisbee in the pool.

"The birthday girl has arrived!" Violet yells.

Darren turns as Lance lets the Frisbee go and ends up getting clocked in the back of the head. He nabs it before Randy can and hurls it back at Lance.

"Aye, fucker! It's nae my fault yer no payin' attention!" Lance's usually mild Scottish accent grows thick, and he winks in my direction as Darren wades to the shallow end. He pulls himself out of the pool, wearing a sinister smile as he rushes me.

"Don't you dare! I don't even have my bathing suit on yet!"

"You should've been better prepared, firefly." His smile widens as he hauls me against him. My yellow sundress soaks through and I push on his chest, trying to get free, but it's impossible.

"You're not supposed to run on the pool deck!" I shriek as his lips find my neck, and then we're airborne. The water is warm, but still a shock when we go under.

Darren brushes my hair away from my face and bubbles burst out of his mouth as he laughs, possibly at my expression. He launches us skyward when our feet touch the bottom of the pool.

Before I can yell at him for ruining my hair and the only outfit I brought with me, he grips the back of my neck and locks our mouths together. Someone whistles, and I'm pretty sure Randy tells us to get a room.

"You're a jerk," I mumble around his tongue.

He laughs and swims me to the shallow end. "I'm your jerk."

"You could've waited until I was wearing a bathing suit! I don't even have a change of clothes."

"Don't worry, I've got you more than covered." He grabs a towel from the edge of the pool. "Want some help changing out of your wet clothes?"

"From you? Nope." I push on his chest, biting back a grin as I climb out and wrap myself in the towel.

"We'll get him back for you later, Char," Miller calls after me.

"Oh, don't you worry. I'm more than capable of making him pay for his transgressions, and I'm sure my punishment will be far worse than anything any of you can dream up." I arch a brow at Darren and grab my bag, smiling at the chorus of laughter that follows me into the pool house.

Darren and I both know any kind of "punishment" I'll be doling out will be of the teasing variety, but they don't need to know that, and sometimes it's fun to keep them guessing.

It's a hot day in late May, and the air conditioning is on in the pool house. Goose bumps flash over my skin as I pad across the cold tile floor to the bathroom. On the counter is a yellow gift bag tied with a bow. My name is written on the little card in Darren's neat cursive.

Before I open the gift, I strip out of my clothes and wrap myself in the towel. I pull the satin ribbon, wondering if the whole dragging-me-into-the-pool business was an orchestrated move. I assume so. Darren doesn't do anything without plan or purpose. I remove the tissue paper, noting the firefly print.

Inside is a small package wrapped in more tissue paper; this time lavender. I pluck at it from the back and gently tear the paper.

A soft knock is followed by the twist of the doorknob. "Charlene?" I'm unsurprised that Darren has followed me. I'm curious as to what his plan is—whether it's going to be a delayed-gratification day, or the kind where we sneak off and satisfy our cravings for each other in short bursts of need and want. I'm banking on the latter since it's my birthday, and I should be able to call all the shots.

I clear my throat, my body already warming. "I'm getting changed."

"I came to assist with that."

I bite back a smile as I open the door and peek through the gap. Darren grips the doorjamb, eyes moving down my neck to where my pearls lie, then dipping lower to where I clutch the towel.

"What if I don't want your assistance?"

"I can just watch if you'd prefer." His smile is full of dirty promises as he pushes on the door, and I step back, allowing him in. He closes it and flips the lock. "It's your birthday. Whatever you want, you get."

"Whatever I want?" I tap my lips. "Hmm. You know, I've been looking at those new Teslas. I think I'd look pretty great in the driver's seat."

"We can go car shopping later."

"Haha."

I'm clearly joking. It's a two-hundred-thousand-dollar car. I would actually be terrified to drive it. Darren is quite sensible about his purchases. He has two vehicles—an SUV and a sweet sports car—neither of which cost an excessive amount of money. It's one of the many things I appreciate about him. His most frivolous purchases are usually lingerie related, or at least they were until a couple of months ago when he discovered his love of cotton panties that retail at five dollars a pair.

I turn back to the lavender tissue paper so I can finish unwrapping what I suspect is the first of many gifts. I find a brand new bikini in a soft, pale purple—one I've looked at more than once over the past month or so.

"This one is as much for me as it is for you, hence the color." He drops his head, lips finding my shoulder. "Are you sure you wouldn't like my assistance?"

"Everyone is going to know what's going on in here." I point out as he kisses up the side of my neck.

"I don't mind if they know I'm apologizing for throwing you in the pool." He untucks the edge of the towel, and it falls to the floor.

"Is that what you're doing? Apologizing?"

He skims the curves of my hips, making fresh goose bumps flash over my skin again. "You mentioned something about a punishment. I thought it might be a good idea to get that over with now." His lips lift against my cheek.

"You're welcome to serve your penance on your knees."

His mouth touches mine for the briefest moment before he drops to the bathmat.

Lifting me onto the vanity, he hooks my legs over his shoulders and shows me exactly how sorry he is with his mouth, and then again when he gets inside me.

It's a good half hour before we come out of the pool house. I'd be embarrassed, but this happens quite regularly with my group of friends—although usually it's Randy and Lily who make use of the various bathrooms. Hockey players have high sex drives, and watching their girlfriends or wives wander around in bikinis gets them excited. There are worse problems to have.

Lily passes me a glass of champagne as soon as I settle myself in one of the loungers.

"Oh! I like this!" She motions to my new bikini. "Do you know if they have the bandeau-style top?" Lily is modest in the chest department. She's incredibly lean and so fit she has a four pack.

"I think they might. I'll text you a link to the site."

Violet lowers herself into the lounger beside me. She adjusts her bikini top with a frown. "What the hell am I going to do if these get bigger? I'm already busting out of these tops as it is."

"Doesn't Alex buy you a new bikini every week?"

"I have some from my last pregnancy that might fit you," Sunny says from under her sunhat.

"Yeah, I might have to take you up on that. I'm constantly at risk of flashing a nipple here." Violet leans back in her chair, and then checks to make sure the movement hasn't exposed anything it shouldn't.

Lily, Poppy, and I drink champagne while Violet and Sunny drink fizzy grape juice with strawberries floating in the glass. I survey the pool, smiling as the guys play volleyball and Lily's and Sunny's dogs—Weiner, Titan, and Andy—run up and down the length of the pool, waiting for someone to throw them a ball or a Frisbee. As far as birthday celebrations go, this is my idea of perfect. I have almost all the people I care about right here.

About an hour later, commotion in the driveway draws my attention. Darren pulls himself out of the pool and heads for the gate. Robbie and Sidney appear, both carrying coolers, and behind them are Daisy and Skye.

When they move to the side, I shriek and jump out of my chair. "Mom?"

She grins and gives Darren a nervous smile before she does jazz hands. The best part is she's dressed like a normal person. "Surprise!"

I rush around the pool and throw myself into her arms. "I thought you were in the middle of filming."

"I might have fibbed a little. As if I could miss my baby girl's champagne birthday." She hugs me tight. "Darren called me last week and arranged to fly me out here."

He shoves his hands in his pockets and smiles. "I thought it would be a nice surprise."

After I'm finished hugging my mom, I launch myself at him. He catches me as I wrap my arm and legs around him. His smile grows, and he chuckles. "I did okay?"

"You did amazing. Thank you." Other words I want to say get trapped in my throat, so I kiss him instead.

The afternoon is full of appetizers, dips in the pool, crazy conversations between the moms about pregnancy, sex, and other things I've never wanted to know about Violet or Alex's moms, or mine. But I wouldn't trade the crazy for anything in the world.

We're in the middle of setting the table for dinner—I could use the food thanks to the amount of champagne I've consumed this afternoon—when another commotion at the gate draws my attention.

"What's going on over there?" I ask Violet, who's busy trying to attach pickled pearl onions to baby gherkins and wrap them in ham so they resemble mini Super MCs.

Violet looks over her shoulder and shrugs. "Maybe it's another delivery, courtesy of your boyfriend?"

"I'm going to check it out."

Darren has bought me a ridiculous number of gifts, and apparently there are more waiting at his place. I've unwrapped a new closet's worth of shirts and leggings this afternoon.

I tiptoe stealthily across the patio in hopes that I can catch a glimpse of whatever is being delivered.

"What the fuck is going on?" Darren mutters. "Why is this thing parked in your driveway? We need to get it gone before Charlene sees it."

Darren is standing shirtless with his arms folded across his chest, Alex beside him, adopting the same pose. I suppress a shudder when an RV comes into view. It's parked in the driveway. It looks eerily similar to the one that was parked on my street earlier today.

The door to the RV opens with an ominous creak. Anxiety ricochets awkwardly through my entire body as a man appears in the doorway.

I break into a cold sweat as memories I've spent the past decade trying to keep locked away and buried claw their way to the surface. I've never been more terrified of beige khakis with an elastic waistband and an off-white golf shirt. I feel like I'm being pulled into a nightmare. This can't be happening—not now when everything is so perfect. Not when I finally have all these good things in my life.

I fight for breath as he searches the faces of my friends, his combover lifting in the air like a hand waving. I take a step back, seeking cover, my knees wobbling perilously as his wild eyes land on me and a creepy-ass wonky-toothed smile spreads across his pale, doughy face.

"I knew the signs would lead me to you!" He spreads his arms as if he expects me to run into them. "I've come to bring you back into the fold!"

I'm pretty sure my scream can be heard all the way to Canada.

chapter fifteen

Daddy Frank

Darren

EVERYTHING AWESOME ABOUT TODAY DIES A HORRIBLE TRAGIC DEATH WHEN SOME pasty fucker steps out of the massive RV parked in Alex's driveway and starts yelling about signs and "the fold."

I question whether this is someone's idea of a practical joke, and whether or not I'm going to have to kick some serious ass, because it's sure as fuck not funny.

An ear-piercing scream startles us all, and I turn to find Charlene standing about ten feet away, eyes wide with terror, one hand clutching her pearls, the other covering her mouth as she continues to scream, and scream and scream some more.

I know she has some kind of RV-related PTSD, much like I have a complete aversion to open doors—especially in the bathroom—but this reaction is extreme. I'm also concerned she's going to pass out from lack of oxygen. I don't know how a person can scream that long or that loud without taking a breath.

"Charlotte! I've come to save you!" Khaki Man yells.

Who the hell is Charlotte?

Charlene lurches forward and squeezes between me and Alex. I reach out to stop her, but she pushes away, careening toward Khaki Man. She corrects herself, stumbling as if she's drunk. She grabs my arm, eyes bouncing around my face as she motions to the RV.

"Tell me this is a nightmare. Tell me this isn't happening."

"Are you okay? Do you know that man?" I try to wrap her up in my arms, but she pushes away again.

"No, no, no, no, no!" She grabs two fistfuls of hair, clutching hard as she shakes her head. "This isn't happening. This can't be happening." She spins around to face Khaki Guy. When she speaks her voice is clear, but shaky, "What the hell are you doing here, Frank? How did you find us?"

He makes some random hand gestures while waving around a cell phone. "I saw your mother on the devil's box, and I knew it was a sign to harvest again. I've been searching for you for so long. It's time to come home." He opens his arms wide. "Come give your Daddy Frank a hug."

"Daddy Frank? Is that Charlene's father?" Alex asks.

"I have no fucking clue," I reply.

Everyone from the backyard starts to trickle out in the driveway. "What the hell is going on?" Randy asks from somewhere behind me.

"Oh! Did Charlene's whole family come to celebrate her birthday?" Daisy asks.

This Frank guy claps his meaty hands twice and a woman appears at the door of the RV. She's wearing a white long-sleeve blouse buttoned all the way to her throat and at her wrists, despite it being eighty degrees today. She's also wearing a white bonnet, like she stepped off the set of *The Handmaid's Tale*. It's one of the few shows I've watched recently.

She hesitates on the last step, but when he motions her forward, she hikes up her long beige skirt, revealing a pair of white Keds, and takes a tentative step down. She scans the crowd, eyes falling on Charlene, and her expression is a mixture of fear, sadness, and envy. "I thought I'd never see you again," the woman says softly.

"What the fuck is happening here?" Lance asks from the other side of Alex.

Charlene takes a halting step. "Carrie?"

"Come see your sisters. They've missed you, Char-char!" Frank the fucker claps his hands again, and several more women follow the first one off the RV.

I notice several things: they're all wearing the exact same outfit, as if it's a uniform, and the rest of them keep their eyes fixed on their white Keds. They all also have medium to light brown hair that falls to the middle of their backs, which makes them look eerily like Charlene.

"Do you want me to call the cops?" Miller asks. "I think this guy has a few screws loose."

Based on Charlene's horrified expression, I'm pretty sure Miller is right about that. I step up, because Charlene's welfare is my first priority and my responsibility. "You need to leave before we call the police."

Khaki Man turns his wide, freaky-ass smile on me. "I can't leave. The devil's box sent me a sign and brought me here to save my Char-char from a life of excess and corruption." He motions to Alex's house and all of us standing there in bathing suits, beach coverups, and swim shorts, and finally to Charlene, as if that's all the explanation he needs to give. "I knew it was too late for her mother when I saw that awful show." He turns to Charlene. "But I can still save you. Don't you see? It's fate that I've found you again. It's time for you to come home and take your rightful place in the co-op."

Charlene shakes her head furiously and side steps toward the house, away from him. "This has to be a nightmare," she mutters. "You can't be here. This isn't happening. This can't be real."

"Oh, shit." Charlene's mom pushes through the crowd holding a huge bowl of potato salad, which she hands off to Poppy, who looks confused and alarmed. She stomps across the interlocking stone toward Khaki Pimp Daddy. "Frank! What in the ever-loving fuck are you doing here?"

He puffs out his chest. "I've come to save Char-char from your poor choices!"

"Poor choices? For the love of Christ, falling for your bullshit was the poorest choice I made. Now get your pasty ass back in that RV and go back to your subpar greenhouse operation where you belong!" She nods at the women. "Carrie, Cassie, Clara, Clair, Cara, Caddie, so sorry, no offense."

"Production really took a dive when you left," one of the women says with a shrug. The rest of them nod in silent agreement.

"Enough!" Frank puts a hand out as if he's some kind of magician and can stop Charlene's mom from advancing on him. "Cendy, you're no longer welcome in the fold."

"My name was never Cendy, you crazy dickbag! It was Wendy, and I had to change it to keep your psycho ass from finding us! And newsflash, Frank, I don't want to be in your fold, and neither does Charlene. Now get the hell out of here, or I'm going to file a goddamn restraining order."

"I won't leave without Char-char! It's time to bring her home!"

Frank pushes Whensday, or Wendy, or whatever the hell her name is, out of the way and lunges at Charlene.

His rash, ill-thought-out move spurs a series of actions. Charlene flails and screams as he grabs for her elbow. The women from the RV let out a collective gasp of surprise, and one of them yells for Charlene to run.

Poppy, Violet, Sunny, and Lily all converge on Charlene as she stumbles back. She trips on an uneven stone and lands on her butt. The ping of something hitting the interlocking stone and rolling across the driveway barely registers.

"Poppy! Get away from that guy!" Lance yells.

It's followed by shouts from Randy, Alex, and Miller, but the only thing that resonates is Charlene's desperate shriek.

I stop thinking. Instead I react, launching myself at him. I take him to the ground before he can put his hands on anyone else. He's soft and doughy, and clearly not built for a fight. He lands on the ground with a loud *oomph*.

"Run, beige ladies! You're free! Run while you can!" Miller yells.

The first punch hits Khaki Man's soft middle, and he groans and tries to curl into a ball.

"She's not yours to touch—not fucking ever. Do you understand me?" I yell in his pale, now somewhat greenish face.

"She belongs with me! She belongs with the co-op!" He tries to shove me off. "We need you back to make us whole again, Char-char!"

"She's mine, motherfucker. You can't have her." This time I punch him in the mouth to shut him the hell up.

Before I can give him a black eye, several sets of hands latch onto me, pulling me up. I fight against the restraints, because all I want to do is destroy this fucking lunatic who's a threat to my girlfriend.

Alex's voice is in my ear. "You gotta calm down, Darren. You're scaring the shit out of Charlene, and everyone."

I glance at the terrified faces of the beige-clad women and then at the cluster of women huddled protectively around Charlene. Behind them is a semi-circle comprised of Alex and Violet's parents, while my teammates act as a barrier between me and them. I note the nervous, unsettled expressions that color every single one of their faces.

I look back at Frank the fucker whose nose is bleeding. He struggles to sit up while holding his hand to his mouth. Blood streams down his chin and drips onto his pristine white shirt.

A few of the beige women gather around him and help him to his feet. They throw dirty looks over their shoulders at me as they usher him back in the RV. He starts it up and rolls down the window as he throws it into gear. "I'll be back for you, Char-char! I'll save you yet!"

"Come back and I'll run you over with your own goddamn RV!" I yell and try to rush the vehicle, but Lance and Randy grab me.

"I don't think you're helping the situation." Randy inclines his head to where Charlene sits on the driveway, trembling violently. Her knees are pulled up to her chest, clenched fists pressed to her lips. Violet wraps a towel around her, and Lily brushes her hair away from her face while Sunny tries to pry her hands from her mouth. Poppy picks something up off the ground. Multiple somethings.

I turn to Charlene's mom. "Can you tell me what just happened? Was that Charlene's father?"

"I suppose he functioned as one during her childhood, but no. That's my . . . ex for lack of better terminology, but it's a long story." She glances around and wrings her hands nervously. "One I'm assuming Charlene hasn't shared with any of you."

I shake my head, and there's a murmur of agreement from everyone else. I look to Violet, almost relieved that she seems to be similarly shocked, and swallow down the huge lump in my throat as I try to process what happened. I need to understand a lot of things right now, starting with what Charlene's childhood actually looked like, because the picture she painted for me wasn't *this*.

I make a move toward her, wanting to . . . I don't know, understand? Comfort her? I need something, anything to replace the strange state of disbelief I'm currently suspended in.

Alex puts a palm on my chest. "Look at your hands."

I cringe at the blood coating my knuckles. "Fuck."

"We'll get her inside and keep her safe until you've cleaned up and calmed down," Alex says.

Charlene's mom helps her up and wraps a protective arm around her, and all I can do is watch as the woman I'm in love with, but don't even know, walks away without looking back.

chapter sixteen

The Answers Aren't Always In Your Favor

Darren

Lance looks at me, lips pressed into a thin line. He puts a hand on my shoulder, his expression almost piteous. "This makes our parents look like they should be up for family of the year award, aye?"

I don't know much about Lance's family situation, other than the fact that he doesn't have a relationship with his mother and he only sees his father once a year at most. But based on his history with women, I can certainly make an experienced guess. Porn star parents and being raised by grandparents who were determined to eradicate the inherited perversion out of me seems pretty decent in comparison to what I now suspect Charlene went through.

And now my mind is reeling out of control. I want to hunt that fucker down and torture him in ways that would make horror movies look like they were produced by Disney.

I feel almost like I'm walking through a fog as Lance takes me to the pool house bathroom to wash up and throw on a shirt. I don't pay attention to much as I head for the house, feeling exposed and uneasy.

Violet meets me at the door, her face pale and eyes wide with the kind of disbelief that makes a stomach turn. "I had no idea. Not about any of this. I mean, I knew she grew up in a trailer park and it was bad, but I didn't realize it was this kind of bad."

"I don't know if that's supposed to make me feel better or not," I tell her.

"I'm sorry, Darren. If it's any consolation, we're all as shocked as you are."

"It isn't, but thanks."

"There's obviously a reason she didn't tell anyone, including you and me." Violet gives me a sad smile. "Alex and I are going to send everyone home. She's in the living room with her mom."

"Okay."

I don't know what to do with any of this. It explains everything and nothing at the same time. And even though I should probably be angry, all I am is sad that I wasn't safe enough to confide in.

Before I cross the threshold, her mom appears in the doorway.

"I need to ask you something before I talk to Charlene," I say in a hoarse whisper.

"Of course. I'll answer if I'm able, but this is Charlene's story to tell."

I nod and take a deep breath, my stomach rolling. "Did anyone ever—" I swallow down the bile. I don't know that I'll be able to refrain from killing Frank if the answer is yes. "Did Frank—was she ever in physical danger?"

"Oh, Darren." She settles a palm on my forearm and shakes her head. "Her childhood was a lot of messed-up things, but it wasn't that. I got us out before she was ever at risk."

I pinch the bridge of my nose, fighting against the sting behind my eyes and the tightness in my throat. "Okay. That's good."

She hugs me, and I stiffen for a moment, not expecting the embrace. But I accept it anyway, because for some reason knowing Charlene's innocence was kept intact makes me feel marginally better.

Her mom steps back and looks up at me. For being as small as she is, she certainly has a dominating presence, so I can see how she ended up where she did. Sort of.

She tips her head to the side. "Does she know?"

I frown. "Know what?"

Her smile is soft. "That you love her."

"I'm afraid I'll push her away if I'm honest with her."

She pats my cheek. "You're quite perfect for each other, despite the odds."

I find Charlene curled up in the corner of the couch, having changed into one of the new outfits she unwrapped this afternoon. It's a Chicago T-shirt with her first name on the back, because I avoid using her last name whenever possible, and the number twenty-six, since it's her birthday. I like that it's also my number. Despite how warm it still is, she's also wearing leggings.

She looks up when I enter the room, her eyes wary and her bottom lip caught between her teeth. I guarantee it'll be chewed raw by the end of the day if it isn't already.

"Are you okay?" I ask, advancing slowly, as if I expect her to bolt. She certainly looks like she wants to.

She lifts her shoulder and lets it fall. "Are you?"

"Not particularly, no." I'm a lot of things at the moment, but okay is definitely not one of them.

She bows her head and raises her hand to her bare throat, but drops it right away when there's nothing to fidget with. "I'm sorry."

"For what?" I want to rewind time and make us both different, not two irreparably damaged people trying to figure out how to be together without imploding.

"I should've told you," she whispers.

"Were you ever planning to?" I let her into all my darkness, but it hasn't been willingly. She's had to drag it out, and now I'll have to do the same with her.

She sighs and focuses on her hands. She's holding something, rolling it between her palms. "I wanted to. I was going to, especially after I found out about your parents. But it seemed like too much all at once, and trying to explain . . . I thought I could wait until after playoffs were over, but then with the expansion draft still looming, there was always a reason to wait. I didn't want to risk it."

"Risk what?"

"Losing you before I had to."

"Why would you think you'd lose me?"

She looks up, her expression guarded. "Nothing about me is normal, Darren. My childhood was messy and fucked up."

"I'm just as messy and fucked up. I thought we'd already established that."

Charlene scrubs a hand over her face. "I know, but my mom's already so much crazy—I didn't know if you could handle any more. I mean, who raises their child in a commune and thinks it's okay? And not just any commune, but a batshit crazy one where women are treated like property. The whole thing is like a bad talk show episode."

"Did you think I wouldn't be able to handle it?"

She sighs. "It wasn't you specifically. I've never told anyone, ever. We never talked about it after we left. It was like . . ." She pauses, maybe searching for the words. "It was all a terrible nightmare. My mom told me not to say anything because we didn't want Frank to find us and bring us back there."

She runs her hands up and down her legs. "I remember the night we ran. My mom woke me up in the middle of the night, and we escaped through a hole in the barbed-wire fence."

"Barbed-wire fence?" It sounds more like prison than a home.

"Yeah, it was meant to keep the bad guys out. Anyway, there was a car waiting for us down the road. I had to hotwire it because she was too panicked to find the key. I didn't even know what we were running from at the time."

Her eyes are the kind of haunted I associate with old memories made new again.

"We drove for hours before we finally stopped at a little diner somewhere in Nebraska. I'd never been to a restaurant, never seen a TV before, never shopped in a grocery store, never even worn a pair of pants, Darren. It was such a shock to realize the world was so much bigger than what I knew. It was too much to process. I don't remember it clearly at all—more like it was some messed-up recurring dream. And reliving it, trying to explain it . . . My extremes were the opposite of yours, Darren. I went from isolation to inclusion so quickly it was impossible to reconcile."

Charlene explains how her mom got pregnant before she graduated from high school. The guy was a year older, and they ran off together. She always wanted to travel, and he was a trucker. Turns out babies cramp the trucking lifestyle. So one day he dropped her off at a place called The Harvest Co-op, or what Charlene has always referred to as "The Ranch," located in the middle of Utah, and left her there with her infant baby. Penniless. With no identification.

And Frank took them in with open arms. He welcomed her into "the fold." It was fantastic. They were a self-contained unit. They earned their own way and functioned like a family, and for a woman who came from a small, isolated town where her parents threatened to help her get rid of the baby without seeing a doctor, it's not hard to understand why she ran, and why she stayed where she was for as long as she did.

While her mother might've known her situation wasn't normal or conventional, it was certainly preferable. Until apparently it wasn't anymore.

"So how did you get out, and what prompted leaving?" I ask, still trying to figure that part out.

"I started my period," Charlene mumbles, and her cheeks flush.

"I don't think I understand."

"My mom worried it wasn't going to be safe for me anymore. We were in extreme isolation, and there were a lot of restrictions. I never left the compound. I'd been told it was dangerous and forbidden. We didn't have identification. We were dependent on Frank for everything, and I was getting older."

It finally clicks as to what she means. "I should've killed that fucker when I had the chance."

Charlene ducks her head. "Don't say that."

"Charlene, that shit is fucked up. Far worse than anything I went through as a kid. That guy needs to be put behind bars or six feet under."

She rolls whatever she had between her fingers faster and faster until it pings on the table. She scrambles to grab it, but I catch it mid-bounce. It's a pearl. I glance up to where her fingers dance nervously around her throat.

"It broke when Da—Frank tried to grab me." She presses the heels of her hands against her eyes, and her shoulders curl forward.

I run a gentle palm over the back of her head. "It's okay. We'll get it restrung again."

"I think I lost half the pearls in the garden this time, or between the stones. We'll never find them all."

"So I'll add new ones until it fits." I never told her that the first time I had the ancient, broken necklace restrung for her, I replaced all but a few of the original pearls since none of them were real. These were. And I definitely won't be sharing that with her, either.

"You've already done that once. You shouldn't have to do it again."

"It's not about *having* to do anything, Charlene. It's about *wanting* to. Whatever you need, whatever you want, I'll do it for you. Don't you get it? I l—"

"Don't!" She scrambles away from me.

Her terror over the RV has nothing on her panic now. She shakes her head, as if she's erasing thoughts, words, and memories. "Please, Darren. Whatever you think you should say right now, please don't. I can't. I can't do this. There's too much. I don't even know." She stands up, smoothing her hands down her thighs. "I need to go home. I have to go home."

I stand too, wanting to reach out and hold on, to keep her where she's supposed to be, which is with me. "I can take you home. Why don't you stay with me? It's safe, and I'll take care of you."

"My mom is here," she says quietly.

"She can stay with us. I have spare bedrooms. If you need your space, you can stay in one of the other rooms, too." I sound desperate. Maybe because I am. I have no idea how to manage this situation, but I feel like I'm losing her, as if I've opened the glass jar and this time when she goes free, she won't come back.

That's not acceptable.

But I can't lock her away or I'm just as bad as the man she ran from.

Everything suddenly fits—the puzzle orders into a picture I couldn't ever piece together properly.

I finally understand how much she hates being tied down to anything, literally and figuratively, apart from her job. She seeks stability in things, not people.

Except for Violet. She's the only constant person I can see. Not even her mother holds that kind of sway with her. I want to know how to be that. I want to know what I need to do in order to be that for her. Because as she shuts down on me and pulls into herself, and the fire I love so much flickers and dies, I'm certain of one thing: if I'm traded, there's a good chance I'll lose her forever. Violet will be the anchor that keeps her from coming with me.

And after everything I've learned tonight, I'm not sure I can blame her for wanting to stay, even if it means I have to leave half my soul in Chicago with her.

chapter seventeen
Better Love

Charlene

THE NIGHT I CAME HOME FROM THE PARTY, THERE WAS A BOX ON THE FRONT stoop. I assumed it was from Darren, so I didn't open it right away. But the next morning a pamphlet from The Ranch had been shoved through the mail slot, possibly as some kind of messed-up, highly ineffective enticement. All it did was make me never want to leave my house again.

I learned a very important lesson on my twenty-sixth birthday. Burying the past and pretending none of it happened in no way erases it. In the wake of Frank's reappearance, the carefully crafted façade and the world I'd built for myself crumbled. In its place, I'm left with a past I can't escape, even though I ran from it, a present that terrifies me, and a future that's disturbingly unstable.

The number of memories I'd blocked out, or maybe hadn't been able to process with any kind of reasonable perspective as a fourteen year old, are now alarmingly clear. I see myself through a new lens, without the rose-colored glasses of youth to soften and smooth it all out.

I'm angry at my mother, my father—the real one, and Frank, who preyed on the weak and disadvantaged. They're the people who made The Ranch seem like the better option. In the wake of Frank's reappearance, I feel more alone than ever, even though I have perpetual calls and messages from my friends.

I feel extremely *other*, alien, like I no longer fit where I used to, and I'm embarrassed and humiliated by a past I had no control over. I don't know how to blend in anymore, or even just exist.

On Monday I stand at the front door, dressed for work even though my head is in a fog. I want to ground myself in this slice of normalcy. My hand is on the doorknob, but I can't seem to turn it. I sift through all the memories of The Ranch and fixate on the fence that surrounded the compound, meant to keep us all safe, but all it did was trap us in a life so narrow it was like living in a pinhole.

My head aches as things start to make sense in a way they haven't before. My fear of being trapped, of needing stability, the importance I place on my friendship with Violet, not wanting to leave Chicago and my built-in family, my inability to let Darren get too close. My head is a mess of memories, and my heart is bleeding with emotions I can't filter.

"Sweetheart?" My mom puts her hand on my shoulder.

"I'm afraid to leave. I'm afraid Frank is going to be out there, and he'll take me back to The Ranch, and I'll never get out again."

"That's not going to happen, honey. I won't let that happen, and neither will any of the people who love you." She leads me away from the door and takes me to the kitchen, where she pours hot water over one of her homemade candies.

I stir the water, watching the candy dissolve at the bottom of the mug. "I want to be normal. I want everything to go back to the way it was before all the memories came back."

"I'm so sorry, Char-char. If I could do it all over again I would make different choices. I would find a different way."

"I know."

I understand, sort of, why she chose the path she did. She put herself in control of her own life, she took the reins so no one else could, and she never stayed in one place so Frank couldn't catch up with her.

I call Mr. Stroker and request to work from home this week. I only have a few client meetings, so it shouldn't be too difficult to reschedule them. I also never ask to work from home, so he is more than accommodating—and concerned, of course.

I flounder for an excuse. Telling him I've suddenly developed acute agoraphobia as a result of being stalked by my not-real cult leader father sounds farfetched and could lead to more questions. So I tell him I had an allergic reaction to a new lotion, and it caused a full-body rash.

In the wake of the Daddy Frank episode, Darren has upped my security from the alarm system to a live bodyguard. So far he remains parked outside at night, and during the day he sits on my front step and makes sure the only people who come to my door are ones I want to see.

My mom leaves on Wednesday, very apropos, after my insistence that I'll be fine on my own, especially now that I have a bodyguard and Violet's been stopping by on a daily basis. I love my mom, but she gets antsy staying in one place for more than a few days at a time, and she's driving me crazy. Besides, I'm not keen on rehashing all the memories from The Ranch or hearing again how sorry she is that Frank found us on account of her audition. It's not like she could've known that Frank had finally jumped into the twenty-first century by getting a laptop and a Facebook account.

I don't even feel like I know myself anymore, and trying to explain that is difficult. My mom thinks the answer is to get out of Chicago and travel with her. The idea of running certainly has it's appeal, but then what would I have? I don't want to leave behind all the people I care about, the family I created for myself in Violet and the girls, and even Darren.

I don't know what to do about him, either. I've made such a mess of things.

He calls several times a day, but I can't answer. I'm afraid to. I know what he was going to tell me. But I can't decide if it was coming from a place of honesty, or if he was simply trying to give me a balm that would somehow soothe me, erase the pain and fear and uncertainty of everything that made me who I am. And I'm unsure who that even is anymore.

I want too much to let him love me.

But admitting it won't prevent him from being traded. Loving him won't stop him from moving halfway across the country. And if he goes, he takes half my heart with him.

He will regardless. So I don't know why the words scare me so much.

Maybe because all the love I've known has been tied up in so much weirdness and instability. Maybe I think as soon as it's real, it will fall apart. And if he stays, I have to acknowledge all the ways I've kept us in this constant state of stasis.

I spend all of Thursday watching terrible reality TV, trying to feel better about my shitstorm of a life. I don't know how to unbreak myself enough to be able to love the way I want to. I mentally unpack my childhood at The Ranch, followed by the freak show that was my teenage years, until I stumbled upon Violet in my first year of college. And in doing so, I see all the pieces of myself and how they fit together in a jagged-edged puzzle of crazy.

I'm sheltered but not. I created normal where there wasn't. I made a family so I wasn't alone. And then I found Darren, the man who molded himself into what I needed, who changed as I required, who kept his emotions locked down to protect me from myself, who never once put the lid on my jar. In a lot of ways we were safe for each other, until it all came crashing down, as happens when emotions are given room to breathe and grow.

I can't allow things to continue like this, with him constantly altering his needs to suit mine. But now that I see things clearly, I realize that how I operate is exactly what he's used to. I put restrictions on us, and he abided by them.

If I keep doing this, I'm just as bad as the people who raised him. And that's not what I want to be. Because I love him, and as scared as I am of what's coming, I don't want to lose him.

By Friday I'm restless. I've binge watched every terrible reality TV show available. After six straight hours of *Garage Wars*, I clean my house from top to bottom and fall asleep at four o'clock in the morning, only to have nightmares about being trapped at The Ranch again. Except there's no way out anymore because instead of a razor-wire-topped fence, the perimeter is lined twenty feet deep with recycled junk, and every time I try to climb to the top, the stacks fall and bury me.

I decide to switch to game shows after that for a few hours. Every time I nod off I have another nightmare, though, so I consume a pile of my candies, hoping to find some calm. I miss Darren. All I want is to curl up in his arms and let him protect me. But I worry as soon as I do, he'll turn into another Frank, and then I'll be trapped for the rest of my life.

It's not rational. It might not even be sane, but the fear takes hold and roots itself in my brain.

Around noon my stomach rumbles, and I make my bleary way to the fridge. The box of wine my mom left for me has probably turned into vinegar by now, and I've eaten all the food Violet left me yesterday. She's supposed to stop by after work with fresh donuts, which is all I want to consume right now, but that's still hours away.

There's a convenience store down the street. They'll have Twinkies and Ho-Hos. I can make it there and back in less than twenty minutes, especially if I drive. Nothing bad will happen.

I get a load of my reflection in the mirror. I look like I've been on a serious bender. My eyes are bloodshot, and my pajamas are a wrinkled mess. I end up taking a very long shower and changing into a pair of leggings and a shirt Darren bought for me. I brush and braid my hair, because drying it would take too much effort. Then I grab my purse, phone, and keys and open the door.

I've forgotten about the security detail—don't ask me how, he's there all day every day—and I suck in a sharp breath and grab for my pearls. But of course they're not there because they broke, again, all because of crazy fucking Frank.

"Miss Charlene, I apologize if I've startled you. Do you need something? A ride to Mr. Westinghouse's perhaps?" he asks, polite and formal.

I consider it for half a second as I glance around at the wide open space and all the potential for danger. All the worst possible scenarios bounce around in my head, such as Frank popping out from behind some bushes with a chloroform rag and dragging me back to the RV with the help of all the co-op women.

"No. No, I'm fine." I back up and slam the door closed, fixing the lock with shaking hands. I'm sweaty, and my mouth is dry. I pop one of my candies, even though I'm not sure they're effective at keeping me calm anymore.

The soft knock at the door makes me scream.

"Miss Charlene? I apologize again for startling you. Is there anything I can do for you?"

"How do I know you're not part of Frank's RV gang?" I shout through the door.

"I've been hired by Mr. Westinghouse to ensure your safety, Miss Charlene."

I know he's telling the truth. He's been standing outside my door all week. Also, Darren texted me his picture and his personal details.

"Prove it!" I yell. My voice is super pitchy. Clearly I'm losing it. Again.

Less than a minute later, there's another knock on the door. "Miss Charlene, I'm going to slide my phone through the mail slot. Mr. Westinghouse is on the line and he'd like to confirm that I am indeed here for your safety."

I catch his phone before it hits the floor and stare at the screen. Shit, Darren Facetimed. I take a few deep breaths, wishing I was more put together and that my hands would stop shaking.

"Charlene?"

I keep the phone pointed at the ceiling and drop to the floor. "One second." I put my head between my knees because I feel dizzy. I haven't spoken to Darren since my birthday, although he calls and leaves messages on a daily basis to make sure I'm okay.

"Firefly?"

The nickname makes me want to cry because I finally understand what it means. I'm his firefly. The one he wants to catch and keep, but can't.

"Just another moment."

"You're worrying me."

I lift my head and tilt the phone down until his face comes into view. I'm unprepared for the rush of emotion that comes with seeing him. I want to reach through the screen and touch him. I want the safety of his arms and the warmth of his lips against my skin.

"Hi." My voice is raspy and tremulous, like the rest of me.

He scans my face, assessing, his icy eyes dark and lips turned down. "Are you okay? Did something happen?"

I have so many things I want to say to him. Questions, admissions, fears I want to unload so he can assuage them. But all of those get stuck in my throat, and I go with stupidity instead. "I . . . no. I need groceries."

Relief is followed by a wash of sadness. "What do you need? I can pick it up and bring it over." He pauses and clears his throat. "Or have it sent if you'd prefer. You can order online if that's easier and use the credit card I gave you to pay for it."

I don't know why I didn't think about ordering groceries. Maybe because my mom was here until a couple of days ago, and between her and Violet, they've been taking care of feeding me. Not that I felt like eating much. Donuts are my go to. I want Doritos with onion dip, but they remind me too much of Darren.

"I have my own credit card."

I look down, away from his sad eyes and the lost look on his face.

"I know this is difficult for you, Charlene, and I understand your need for space, but when you're ready to talk, know I'm here, waiting for you. In the meantime, whatever you need, please don't hesitate to ask either myself or Luther."

"Luther?"

"It's his phone you're holding."

"Oh. Right." I feel bad that I didn't even remember his name.

After a few more moments of quiet he finally asks, "Are you okay?"

"I . . . no."

His voice hardens. "Has Frank tried to make contact?"

"No." But I don't trust he won't try again. He's too crazy not to. I'm sure he's laying low, biding his time, waiting until I let my guard down.

"Okay, that's good. If he does, will you call me? Or at least tell Luther?"

"Yes, Darren." I raise my eyes to the ceiling, hoping to keep the tears floating instead of falling.

"Charlene." When I meet his two-dimensional gaze, he gives me a small, strained smile. "I waited my entire adult life for you to come along and make sense of my world. I'm prepared to wait as long as I need to for you to accept that."

"I'm not ready." *I need you.*

"I understand."

"I have to go." *I'm in love with you.*

"I'll be here when you're ready to stay." He ends the call before I can.

After a few minutes, I open the door and pass the phone back to Luther, thanking him.

"Can I take you anywhere?"

"I'm fine, thank you." I go back inside. I'm not hungry anymore. I touch my throat, wishing I had more than a few unstrung pearls, the reminder of Darren that I've carried with me over the last several days. I don't know how to do this without him, or with him.

⁓⁓

Violet stops by after work with supplies. I should probably buy stock at Krispy Kreme donuts considering how many I go through these days.

"How you hanging in there?" She passes over the box of donuts, which I hug as if they're my best friend, rather than the person who brought them.

I lift a shoulder and set the box on the counter. Flipping it open, I admire the beautiful array of donut magic. I'm starving since I polished off the last box in the middle of the night. I should probably consider ordering groceries like Darren suggested, but I'm worried Frank will intercept and find a way to get to me, even with Luther standing guard outside my door.

"Have you talked to Darren yet?"

"This afternoon, yes."

She looks surprised. "How'd it go?"

"It was . . . okay."

She taps her nails on the counter. They're pink and blue with Alex's number on the index finger. "Okay how? What did you talk about?"

"Groceries."

"Really? You talked about groceries?" Violet sighs. "I know this has to be hard for you, Char, but you can't cut him out, or everyone else for that matter."

I swallow a massive chunk of donut. "I'm not cutting everyone out. I just need time. You don't understand what it's like."

"No. You're right. I don't, not at all, and I never will if you don't talk to me about this. I'm your best friend, Char, and considering what I witnessed the other day, I think maybe I can understand why you would never want to talk about what life was like when you were growing up. But I'm not sure hiding from it is going to make it any better, either." She takes me by the shoulders, forcing me to look at her. "We all love you no matter how fucked up your childhood was, just like you love me despite the fact that I'm clearly unable to censor myself *ever*, and I constantly embarrass myself and everyone around me. Let me do what a best friend is supposed to. Let me help you through this. Please don't shut me out."

"I'm not trying to. There's so much I don't want to remember, so many things that make sense now but never did when I was a kid."

"You don't have to try to make sense of it alone, though, do you?"

"I'm scared."

"Of what?"

"I don't know who I am anymore."

Violet's eyes are glassy. "You're my best friend, and you've been like a sister for almost an entire decade. You're loyal and fun and always up for an adventure. You think you like to try new things, but really you like routine and predictability. And you're terrified of accepting help, so you carry the weight of the world on your shoulders, which is pretty annoying for the people who love you and want to help. But I'll forgive you for that since you deal with me on a regular basis and I can be a pain in the ass too." She hugs me hard. "You're still you. Nothing has changed except maybe now we can all understand you a bit better than we did before."

chapter eighteen
Open the Jar

Darren

I'M A MISERABLE ASSHOLE WITHOUT CHARLENE. I KNOW THIS BECAUSE ALEX HAS TOLD me more than once this week to stop being a dick. It's not intentional. I'm not trying to be a cocksucker of epic proportions, but it's off season, and my plan was to have Charlene at my place almost full time by this point. I'd been on track before her birthday, and now she's not here at all.

Alex has tried to get me to talk on numerous occasions over the past week, but he can't help me, and he can't understand, not really. So I've mostly been stewing in my own frustration at not being able to protect Charlene the way she needs me to.

Her chair is empty. The book she was reading the last time she was here is still sitting on the table. When I'm really desperate for some piece of her—which is pretty much every waking moment of every day—I'll sit in her chair with her blanket and flip through to the earmarked parts.

Ironically, none of her favorite parts are smut, despite the content of the books she reads. It's all the sweet moments—the first kisses, the grand gestures, the breakups and the reunions—that she reads over and over.

I'm currently at the gym, trying to run out the frustration that comes with not having what I want or need. Lance jumps onto the treadmill next to mine, and I give him a nod, then up the speed to nine miles an hour. He cocks an eyebrow and starts off at a leisurely six and a half miles an hour jog.

"You doing okay?" he asks.

I make a sound, no commitment either way, because I'm actually pretty fucking shitty right now, and I don't feel like talking about how fucked up my life is, or my girlfriend's life, if she's even still that.

We run in silence for a few minutes. Lance slows his speed while I sprint. My lungs are about to explode, but I'm unwilling to slow down because that will mean talking.

"You were raised by your grandparents, aye?"

I glance over at him for a split second and nod, then stare at the TV hanging above me.

"I don't know if you're aware, but my aunt became my legal guardian when she found out my mum was beatin' the shit outta me fer missin' goals. Or whatever pissed her off, really."

I stumble a step and grab the rails, lifting my feet from the belt, I straddle the edges, this time giving him my attention and dropping the speed on my treadmill so I don't end up flying into the wall. "I'm so—"

He lifts one hand to stop me and drops his speed even more with the other until he's walking. "Don't apologize. It is what it is. Some people are just fucked up and they shouldn't be parents."

"Tell me about it."

I'm not sure why he's sharing this with me, of all people. I like Lance well enough, but I think he tolerates me more than anything else.

"I didn't understand how you and Charlene worked, but, uh, Poppy kind of set me straight on a few details."

"How so?"

He rolls his shoulders. "I had it in my head that you liked to . . ." He exhales a long breath. "Hurt her."

This time I punch the stop button. "What?"

He does the same, but instead of looking at me, his eyes are on the flashing numbers of his screen. "Like . . . hit her."

"You think I would hit Charlene?"

He runs a rough hand through his hair. "No, like spank her and shit."

That hot, tight feeling in the back of my neck eases up a bit. "Oh. That's not how things are with Charlene. Despite how it may seem, she's very . . . innocent, which I'm only starting to understand better these days."

I've probably just spoken more consecutive words to Lance than I have in the past three years he's been on the team. And my newfound understanding isn't helping me out much, considering yesterday's brief Facetime conversation with Charlene is the only one we've had in the past week.

"So, uh, based on the way you seem like you're either trying to murder that treadmill or yourself, I'm guessing things aren't all that good with Charlene right now."

I grit my teeth, annoyed that I'm so transparent, and that he's calling me out on it.

He nods, as if he understands my silence. "I don't know how things went down for you as a kid—like, when you went to live with your grandparents or what—but I was fifteen when the beatings finally stopped. From what I know, Charlene was a teenager when she went from one fucked up situation to another. I'm not saying it's the same thing."

He runs both hands down his face. "Fuck. Poppy should be the one having this conversation with you. She's a fuckton better at this. Look, what I'm trying to say is that I spent a lot of years trying to forget all the bad shit by keeping it locked up here." He taps his temple. "I'm pretty sure some of it is blocked out, at least that's what my therapist says, like my brain is trying to protect itself from the worst of it."

He exhales a long breath. "Look. I know I'm rambling, but maybe it's the same for Charlene? Or maybe it isn't." He rests a hand on my shoulder, his eyebrows pinched, a heavy swallow making his throat bob. "All I'm saying is that sometimes we shut ourselves off from the things we need when we're afraid to lose them the most. We're all kind of broken, and we all need a little saving sometimes, aye? Poppy seems to think you two are meant to save each other." He rolls his eyes. "I sound like a fuckin' asshole, but Poppy's usually right about this kind of thing." He nods, more to himself than me. "All right. Good talk, Westinghouse. I'm gonna get outta yer face now before you give me a beatdown."

He drops his hand and walks away, leaving me to ponder what he's said, and how much I want him to be right. Part of the reason I haven't been pushing myself on Charlene is my uncertainty about whether I'm all that good for her. But maybe Poppy's right and all of our broken parts do fit together.

It's with that thought in mind that I drive to Charlene's after my workout, with a quick stop on the way. When I arrive, Luther is posted outside the front door. He has a twin brother named Damien, and they've been trading off shifts this week at her house.

It's the middle of the afternoon, and Charlene should technically be at work, but I know from Alex that she's taken the week off. I'm also aware she hasn't left her house since her birthday party.

Luther nods his acknowledgement as I knock.

"Charlene?"

Her muffled voice comes through the door after a long minute. "Darren?"

I press my palm against the warm steel, aware she's almost close enough to touch. "Can I see you?"

It takes a minute before the door opens the three inches the chain latch allows. Her eye appears in the crack and darts down and back up, shooting around my face.

I hold up the bag. "I brought some things for you."

She stares at me for a few seconds before she bows her head and closes the door. The lock clicks, and she steps back as she opens it so I can come inside. She looks exhausted. Her eyes are red rimmed, hair piled on top of her head in a messy bun. She's wearing a pair of the leggings I bought her and a shirt. I try not to think about whether or not she's wearing cotton cheekies under those leggings.

Charlene's fingers go to her throat, but drop right away when she doesn't find her pearls.

"I wasn't expecting you."

"I know." I'd apologize for coming unannounced, but it would be insincere.

I set the bag on the counter and start emptying it so I have something to do with my hands that doesn't include hugging Charlene, which is what I want more than anything. That and to kiss her.

Charlene frowns as I set the bag of Cool Ranch Doritos on the counter. "What is this?"

"I picked up a few things I thought you might like."

"Oh." She seems genuinely shocked, which is odd.

"I also picked up some takeout in case you wanted something aside from snacks." I pull out the Styrofoam and Saran-wrapped box containing her favorite penne alfredo from the restaurant we frequent close to my place.

"You came here to feed me?"

"And talk, but Luther mentioned that you hadn't had a real meal in several days, so I felt it might be a good idea to bring you your favorites, soften you up a little after my arriving unannounced." I'm nervous, so I start peeling the cellophane from the takeout. "Are you hungry?"

"Not right now." She wrings her hands.

I imagine this level of anxiety is overwhelming for her, so I decide to cut to the chase and spit it all out. I prop my fists on the counter and take a deep breath. "Look, I know you think you're a mess, Charlene—"

"I don't *think* I'm a mess, I am one."

"But you're my mess, and I'm yours, and nothing has changed that. Not for me. Has it changed for you?"

"No, but—"

"If it hasn't changed, there shouldn't be a but. Why can't we be a mess together? Why do you feel like you have to go through this on your own? Let me be here for you."

"But what if you leave?" she asks softly.

I frown. "Why would I be here if I was planning to leave?"

Her fingers go to her lips. "What about the expansion draft?"

"You mean if Vegas takes me?"

"Yes. What happens then?"

No one ever gets what they want if they don't ask for it. "First of all, I don't think it's going to happen. There are two other players who are younger, faster, and better than I am, and they've brought on someone new to Vegas to keep Lucas, the owner, from making a bunch of stupid-ass decisions, which includes pulling someone as old as me over to a brand new team. But, should the unthinkable happen and I do have to go to Vegas, I want you come with me. But only if that's what you want. And if you don't, we try to make the long distance work, or maybe I take early retirement so I can stay right here."

"But you'd have to break your contract."

"The money doesn't mean anything, Charlene. Nothing means anything without you. I want you however you come—broken, messed up, in leather, lace, satin, cotton pajamas . . . However you are, it's just you I want." I step around the island, closing the distance between us. "I keep telling you that, waiting for you to hear me."

Charlene's eyes are wide. She pulls her bottom lip between her teeth, looking every bit the elusive firefly she often is. I understand it better now. I get her in a way I never could have before.

I cup her face in my hands. "I know you want to run from this. I know this whole thing scares you, but understand this, Charlene, I love you. That's the only truth you need. Everything else in that head of yours is white noise. All the worries are pointless. I want this with you, and I don't care if it's messy and fucked up and no one understands it but us." I smooth my thumbs over her cheeks. "Be with me in this, Charlene. No more of this you live at your house and I live at mine. If we're going to be together, let's just be together."

"Wait, what?" She frowns. "You want me to move in with you?"

That her first reaction appears to be confusion isn't reassuring, I drop my hands and step back, giving her space. "You were staying at my place more than here over the last couple of months. Moving in is the next logical step, isn't it?"

Her fingers go to her mouth. Her panic isn't what I want to see, but I've dropped a pretty huge bomb on her without any kind of warning, after a week of not seeing or speaking to her beyond daily texts to see if she's okay. Maybe pushing my entire agenda on her wasn't the best plan.

"You're asking a lot all at once," she murmurs.

"I'm not asking you to do much more than you already were." Except give up her house and share my space with me on a permanent basis. Not unreasonable after two years. Although maybe just managing our relationship and making sure we're stable first would've been a good start. It's possible I've jumped the gun here, but then again, sometimes Charlene needs to be pushed.

"What if we fight?"

"I expect that might happen on occasion, since I can be an asshole. There are four bedrooms in my house. I anticipate there may be nights I have to relocate, depending on how badly I piss you off."

"I'm not joking, Darren."

"Neither am I." I try to smile, but I'm sure it falls a little flat.

She closes her eyes and turns her head away. I don't know if I'm winning her or losing her. I'm about to tell her she doesn't have to decide in this moment, that she can have more time if she needs it, mostly so she won't say no.

"This isn't easy for me," she says softly.

"It's not easy for me either, but what specifically is so difficult about this for you?"

Charlene drags her fingers back and forth along the neckline of her shirt. "For all the years you spent with no doors or privacy, I spent the same amount of time locked away from the world. Love and dependency were imprisonment." She lifts her gaze. "I'm afraid to be trapped again."

"I'll never put the lid on your jar."

As soon as I say the words, I understand that's exactly her fear—that she'll lose her freedom again. I can only imagine how she felt after she and her mom left the compound, and they only had each other. It would've been a new kind of prison—one created from the fear of being dragged back to the hell they'd escaped. Although from what I understand, Charlene didn't perceive it as hell until she was out of it.

"I don't know what I have to do to prove to you that I'll love you and take care of you in whatever capacity you need me, but I won't walk away unless you tell me to." I press my lips to her forehead. "You know where to find me when you're ready."

My feet feel like they're weighted with lead soles as I head for the door. I've said what I came here to say. There's nothing else I can do to convince her.

She grabs my sleeve. "Where are you going?"

"Home."

"That's it? You're not staying?" She seems confused again.

"I'm not going to push you more than I have, Charlene. I know what happens when I do, and I'm not willing to take that risk." I pull her to me. All her broken pieces and bent edges fit with mine. "Call me when you figure out what you want." I inhale the scent of her shampoo and press my lips to her skin for the briefest moment before I untangle myself.

I don't want to leave, but I can't stay—not unless she's ready to let me in all the way. Luther is on the front step when I open the door, staring out at the neighbor's yard. There's an older woman in a pair of booty shorts weeding the garden. I'm pretty sure it's for Luther's benefit. He's a good looking motherfucker.

"Wait!" Charlene grabs my arm and yanks me back inside. She pauses to wave at Luther before she closes the door in his face.

I stare down at her. Even with her messy hair and wrinkled outfit, she's flawlessly flawed. It doesn't matter if she tells me the only reason she wants me to stay is because the apocalypse is coming; there's a reasonably good chance I'll say yes.

She grips my shirt as if it will keep me from moving. "I don't want you to go."

"Then give me a reason to stay."

She stares at her feet—her toenail polish is chipped—and slowly looks back up. "Can we ease into this?"

"You can't lube up for moving in."

She rolls her eyes at my terrible joke. "I wasn't expecting this. I was ready to deal with the feelings part of us, but then you blindsided me with the whole moving-in thing."

"I figured I might as well lay it all out there for you, so you know where I'm at."

She chews her bottom lip and nods. "I can't give up my night with Violet and the girls. They come over to my place, and we hang out and stuff, and if I live with you, we'll have to do that at your place."

"Those are the same nights I'm out with the guys, and we never come to my place."

"Maybe that should change."

"Do I need to remind you what happened the last time they ended up at my place?"

She manages to blush and give me the evil eye at the same time. "I don't want to sell my house right away."

"Property is a smart investment. You can rent it out indefinitely." I run my fingers through her hair, the need to touch her too overwhelming not to give in. "Whatever you need to make you feel safe, Charlene, you can have it. If you need a house in your own name, then keep it. But don't expect me not to buy you things. You're everything I need, and I'm going to give you everything I think *you* need."

Charlene seems to fight back a sob as she wraps her arms around my neck. "I love you, in case you weren't sure."

"I hoped." I press my lips to hers for a moment and then pull away. I slip my hand into my pocket and retrieve the necklace I've been carrying with me the past few days. I went in search of all the fallen pearls after her mother took her home and brought them to a jeweler the very next day. I picked up the necklace three days ago and have been carrying it around with me ever since.

Charlene's eyes soften, and a lone tear slides down her cheek as I clasp it behind her neck.

"I love you more than you can comprehend. I'll give you anything you want, Charlene. Just stay with me, let me love you like I'm supposed to, let me be exactly what you need."

"You already are."

I kiss her, and my whole world seems to come together and fall apart at the same time. She's everything. She's all the missing pieces I need to feel whole.

chapter nineteen
Candy Addict

Charlene

Darren and I don't make it farther than the kitchen counter before we're naked and all over each other. Make-up-slash-love-declaration sex is the best. Not that I want to have more arguments or breakups, but love declaration only happens once. All the anxiety and stress of the past week is erased by each kiss and touch. I believe Darren when he says he'll never put the lid on my jar. He's always been exactly what I need, and now that he knows about all the good and bad parts of me, it feels like he's truly mine.

An hour later we're stretched out on the couch in the living room. Darren has on boxers, and I'm wearing the shirt he arrived in. The rest of our clothes are scattered around the kitchen. I reach into the bowl next to me and unwrap a candy. I'm already relaxed, thanks to all the orgasms, but I'm a little hungry post sex, and too lazy to go to the kitchen for a snack. And too comfortable wrapped up in Darren.

I pop the candy in my mouth and settle back against his chest. I toss the wrapper, aiming for the coffee table, but I miss, and it flutters to the floor.

Darren reaches down and picks it up, inspecting the opaque square. "What kind of candy is this?"

"It's herbal." I pull myself up a little higher so I can kiss his neck. His skin is salty in contrast to the sweetness in my mouth.

He twists a little so his mouth is close to mine and sniffs while frowning. "Where'd you get them?"

"My mom makes them." I don't usually eat them when I'm with Darren, since I like the kind of anxiety he evokes in me.

Darren curves his palm around the side of my neck and presses his lips to mine. When his tongue sweeps out I part my lips, allowing him inside. He strokes against my tongue a few times before he pulls back, still frowning. He repositions us so we're sitting up. "Stick your tongue out for me."

"What?"

"Your tongue, stick it out."

"They're an acquired taste," I mumble, but I do as he asks, the candy sitting on the end of my tongue.

He pops it in his mouth, rolling it around, which could be kind of gross since it's been in my mouth, but then again, he does put his tongue in there, among other places.

After a few seconds he spits it into the wrapper. "How often do you eat these?"

I shrug. "I don't know. Usually a few a day."

His eyes go wide. "A few a day? How long have you been eating these?"

I don't understand why he's so shocked. "I don't know. My mom has been making them as long as I can remember."

I didn't think it was possible for his eyes to be any wider. "You ate these as a kid?"

"They're calming." Now I'm defensive about it. I love these candies.

"Uh, yeah, they would be since I think they're made from weed."

"No they're not," I scoff.

"I'm pretty sure they are. How do you think they get that green tinge to them?"

"They're herbal."

"And the herb they're made with is *weed*."

"How would you know that? You're not allowed to use recreational drugs," I point out.

"Correct, but I've spent enough time around Alex's dad to know what weed smells like, since he's a chronic pothead." He doesn't say anything else, possibly waiting for me to process this information.

I have to cover my mouth with my palm since I'm incapable of closing it. The greenhouses at The Harvest Co-op, aka The Ranch, flash through my mind—endless rows of gorgeous green plants, the smell of skunks, the barbed-wire fence, how we were located out in the middle of Buttfuck, Nowhere. All of it suddenly makes sense.

"Holy fuck," I say from behind my hand as the truth settles in. "Oh my God. My mother turned me into a pothead."

"Maybe there isn't any THC in them," Darren offers.

I think about how I've been this week—all the candies I've eaten and how much I've been zoned out and napping like it's my job. How many donuts I've consumed.

I consider how I'm relaxed for hours after I eat those candies, and how they always seem to heighten that tingly feeling in my body, particularly the one between my thighs when I'm nervous. I have to wonder if they're somehow related.

I almost always have one with my tea right before I go to bed when I'm at home. I can still sleep like the dead—the flaily dead—even with all my afternoon naps.

I drop my hand from my mouth. "I'm a pothead."

"There are a lot worse things to be."

"I've been carrying those around with me everywhere. I've taken them on planes, Darren! Oh my God, what if I'd been arrested? My mother is my dealer!"

Then it dawns on me that Darren had one in his mouth. "Shit. Now you have weed in your system! What if you test positive at the next drug test?"

"It's off season. There aren't any mandatory tests anytime soon, and I had, like, three sucks of a candy."

A little of the unease dissipates, but it fires right back up. "What if I'd offered them to Sunny and Violet? They're both pregnant!"

"You haven't given them any, have you? Or any of the guys?"

"Well, no, my mom said it was best not to share them, but I could've ignored her, and then I'd be feeding a baby weed, or ruining NHL careers!" I'm starting to feel lightheaded even though I'm sitting down. "I need to get rid of them!"

"Whoa." Darren grabs my arm before I can reach the bowl of candies. "I don't think it's a good idea to throw those out."

"Well, I can't keep them now that I know what they are!"

Darren pulls me back into his lap. "Calm down, firefly."

"I don't think I can." *Shit*. I'm at risk of hyperventilating. And all I want to do is simultaneously eat all of those candies and flush them down the toilet.

He kisses me softly. "Take a deep breath and listen to me, okay, Charlene?"

I nod and do as he asks, sucking in as much oxygen as my lungs will allow, then breathing my weed-candy breath in his face.

"You said you've been eating those as long as you can remember?"

"Since I was a teenager, I guess?"

He tucks a few hairs behind my ear, tracing the shell with his fingertips. They're softer than usual because he's not training as hard.

"So you've been eating these every single day for the past decade?"

He picks up the discarded candy from the coffee table. Peeling it off the wrapper, he holds it to my lips. "I think you should eat this."

My mouth waters in anticipation. "Oh, God. I'm an addict."

"It's just weed, Charlene. It's not like you've been shooting heroin your entire life, but I wouldn't suggest quitting cold turkey. It might be a good idea to cut down a little, though." He taps my lips, and I open my mouth, allowing him to pop the candy back in.

I feel instantly better, which I realize is not possible.

"Okay, so tell me about these candies. Your mother's been making them since you were a teenager?" Darren rearranges me so I'm straddling his lap, facing him.

I think back to when it all started. "Earlier than that. When we were at The Ranch, we grew all our own food. We had greenhouses, and there were some I wasn't allowed in, but I caught a few glimpses here and there. Harvest time was always busy. My mom would be gone all day and sometimes late at night. Then they'd make candies and box them all up, and trucks would come and take them away. Jesus . . ." I pause for a moment, remembering very clearly the night we escaped. "When we left the compound, my mom had a car waiting for us, and we had three backpacks—two of them filled with candies and some money, and the other had my stuff. That's how we survived until she found a job."

"That was pretty resourceful and a lot fucked up."

"This is crazy." I can't believe I've been eating weed candies for years and didn't know it, and that my mom failed to mention it.

"Do you think they're still making those candies?" Darren asks.

"Yes. Definitely. There was a box of them on my front porch on my birthday. I thought it was a birthday present from you, so I left them on my counter and finally opened them the other day. I was going to throw them away on garbage day because there's no way I'd ever eat anything from The Ranch, but I haven't had a chance yet. Let me get them."

I find them in the garage and bring them back to the living room. Darren opens the box and peeks inside. My mom's candies have a tiny logo on the wrapper. I'd never thought anything of it until I note the letters stamped on these mint green wrappers. Darren unwraps a candy, inspecting it.

He looks up at me. "If I'm right about any of this, we might've found a way to get rid of Frank."

chapter twenty
Going Down

Darren

WHEN I LOOK BACK ON THE NIGHT I MET CHARLENE, I DON'T THINK I EVER would've pegged her for a pothead who was raised in a commune, but then people only let you see what they want you to, until they take their masks off.

Still, this is the kind of thing they base reality TV shows on. In fact, if they haven't already, I'd be surprised.

"I should call Robbie," I tell Charlene.

She looks a hell of a lot shell-shocked. I can't say she doesn't have a right, considering she just found out she's been carrying around illegal narcotics in the form of candies for over a decade. And that her mother is a manufacturer of weed edibles, and may very well be a dealer.

I call Alex to see if his dad is around. They've been visiting Chicago a lot lately with Sunny and Violet both being pregnant.

"Yeah, man, my dad's here. What's up? Everything okay?"

"Yeah, things are okay. I have some questions for him, though. Would it be okay if Charlene and I stopped by?" I check the time. It's the middle of the afternoon.

"You're with Charlene?"

"I am."

"That's good news. And yeah, of course you can come over—both of you, obviously. Miller and Sunny are here with Logan, and Skye and Sidney are supposed to be over soon for a barbeque. We're all hanging out by the pool, so bring a suit."

"Great. Thanks. We'll be by in a bit."

Charlene packs a beach bag with a bathing suit and changes into a lavender sundress, with my help, of course. She seems to be on autopilot, which isn't all that surprising. We take my car to Alex's place with the box of candies from The Ranch and a few of the ones her mom makes, for comparison's sake.

Violet meets us at the front door. She looks from me to Charlene and cocks a brow. "Please tell me this means I don't have to stop at Krispy Kreme tomorrow."

"No more trips to Krispy Kreme," Charlene replies with an embarrassed smile.

"I'm glad that's over, because it was getting awkward. The same kid works every morning, and he was starting to remember my order." She rubs her still mostly flat belly. "So does this mean you're officially back together?"

Charlene looks up at me, so I put my arm around her shoulder and pull her into my side. She feels good there, right, like she fits. "Even better. I dropped the L-bomb on her."

Violet does some weird little dance and shakes her hands around in the air. It almost looks like a toddler who has to pee. "It's about fucking time! We all knew you two loved each other. I'd say I don't understand why it took so long to figure it out, but considering how screwed up you both are, I'm just glad you got there without turning into Bonnie and Clyde and going on a murder spree."

"It could still happen," I deadpan.

Violet points a finger in my face. "Don't do that. Remember, I'm the one who knows how not-sinister you really are, so that face isn't going to work on me. Also, I'm prone to nightmares at this stage in my pregnancy, and I would appreciate it if that didn't include my best friend starring in them as some kind of female version of *Dexter*."

"You're the one who mentioned murder sprees."

"Right. Okay. Topic officially dropped. Come on in. Alex and Miller are trying to teach Logan how to use a hockey stick. The poor kid has barely mastered walking." She shakes her head and motions for us to follow her to the backyard.

Logan seems more interested in hitting Miller in the shins and smashing flowers than the red foam puck they keep pointing out, but he seems entertained, if nothing else.

Sunny's reclined in a lounger with Daisy and Skye on either side of her. Their conversation comes to a halt when they notice us, and I realize Charlene probably hasn't seen them since her birthday. I lean in and press my lips to her temple.

"Don't worry, firefly, they love you exactly as much as they did before, if not more."

She tips her chin up, eyes meeting mine. "How did you happen to me?"

"I believe your best friend hooked up with my best friend, which likely wouldn't have happened had Alex not won a bet and room to himself."

"I remember Violet telling me about that. What was the bet, anyway?"

"Who could come up with the longest word in an online game of Scrabble."

"Seriously? I expected something so much more . . . interesting."

"It was a long bus ride. We were bored. Alex got lightning. It was impressive." I press a kiss to her perfect lips, promising myself we're going to make out later. For hours. Like teenagers.

I step back as Skye and Daisy converge on Charlene. Sunny's still working on sitting upright. She's looking really pregnant these days.

"Darren!" Robbie motions me over to where he and Sidney are sitting in the shade, watching their sons be dads.

"They're starting early, huh?" I nod to Alex and Miller.

"Pretty sure Miller thinks Logan's going to be drafted by the time he's in pre-school," Sidney says with a smile.

Alex takes a break from getting slammed in the shins with the hockey stick to grab me a beer. "Everything okay?" He glances over at Charlene who's corralled in a corner with Sunny, Violet, and the moms.

"With Charlene? Yeah. We figured it all out. Just took me getting my head out of ass to make it happen."

"That's good. Vi was worried about both of you this week."

"So was I, but I think we've got it all sorted. She's agreed to move in with me, which I'm taking as a good sign."

Alex's eyebrows pop up. "Whoa, that's a big step."

I nod and rock back on my heels. "Yeah. It's about time, right?"

He laughs. "It really is."

"Thanks for sticking by me. I know I'm not the easiest person to understand, but I don't think Charlene and I would be where we are if it wasn't for you."

"I didn't really do anything except give you some advice."

"You've done a lot more than that, Alex. Watching you and Vi grow together, being part of this family—" I motion to his backyard, full of the people Charlene and I both care about. "This is how I figured out how to love Charlene. So yeah, thanks." Jesus. I sound like an asshole.

Alex frowns, brows pulling down, and he blinks repeatedly before he claps me on the shoulder. "I'm gonna hug you now, so don't punch me."

I laugh, but it gets caught in my throat with a whole bunch of other emotions when he really does pull me in for a hug. He slaps me on the back a few times, though, just to keep it manly.

◦∽◦

Eventually I manage to get around to talking to Robbie about the weed candies. I want to make sure I'm right about the ones from The Ranch—or The Harvest Co-op as it says on the wrapper—before I go calling it in to the cops. I also want to verify that the candies Charlene's mother makes are the same, and that we can keep her out of this.

Of course Robbie is only too happy to check out the stock. He opens the box of candies, almost giddily, and picks one up. His expression turns serious. "Where did you say you got these?"

"I'm guessing someone from the RV left them on Charlene's doorstep the day of the party."

"Would Charlene know where they got these from?"

"They're the ones who produce it, according to Char."

"Really?" Robbie's eyes light up, and he calls Charlene over.

This prompts the entire group to congregate around the two of them while she explains what happened when she was growing up at THC—the acronym now making a lot more sense. Robbie listens raptly, as does everyone else.

"This is all very interesting," he murmurs once she finishes explaining what used to go down at THC. "And how old were you when you and your mom left?"

"I was fourteen and a half." Charlene chews on her bottom lip. "My mom took a couple of bags of candies with her. I think maybe she sold them, and I started eating them, but I'm not sure if these are like the ones my mom makes."

Robbie perks up. "Makes? As in still?"

"Um, yeah. She sends them to me every month. I didn't realize they were weed candies. She said they were herbal, and I thought it was more like a cough drop, but apparently I'm a pothead, so . . ." She stops rambling and looks around the group, her cheeks flushed.

"Nothing wrong with being a pothead." Robbie smiles. "Unless you're a professional hockey player. Then you have to wait until you're retired to enjoy that kind of relaxation." He taps on the arm of his chair. "You wouldn't happen to have one of the candies your mom makes, would you?"

"Um, sure. I have some in my purse." Charlene roots around in her bag and retrieves a handful of candies. "These are from the last batch, so they might be a bit stale."

Robbie unwraps one made by Whensday and one from THC and sets them side by side on the table, inspecting them closely. "Very curious," he murmurs.

"What's curious?" Charlene leans in to get a closer look.

"See how the coloring is slightly different."

"Mmm-hmm, the ones my mom makes are greener."

"It could be a purity thing." He pops the one made by Whensday in his mouth.

"Robbie! What're you doing?" Daisy asks.

"Research, darling." He grins. "I have a few theories about these candies, and I should know in about forty-five minutes if they're correct or not."

"What's the theory?" Charlene asks.

"A little over twenty-five years ago, right when I took the position at MJ Labs, edibles were growing in popularity. There was a company we'd been struggling to locate that began producing candies much like the one I'm eating. They cornered the market, but we didn't know where they came from and couldn't track the supplier. The recipe was flawless—the perfect balance to induce relaxation but maintain productivity. No matter how much we studied them, we couldn't replicate the recipe. Then a little more than ten years ago, the quality began to suffer. Something about the production had changed, and we couldn't figure it out. I may have the answer now."

"Which is what?" I ask.

"Charlene's mother leaving is the reason the quality suffered. I think she may very well have been the pioneer of the ultimate in edible candies."

Forty-five minutes later, Robbie is pretty much convinced this is the case. And based on his ridiculous smile, and the coveted bowl of chips he keeps stuffing in his face, I'm thinking Charlene has developed quite the tolerance for those.

He says he has to do a few more tests to make sure he's correct, and he'd like to bring the candies back to the lab in Canada so he can compare them, but it appears as though Frank has been funding the co-op through illegal marijuana manufacturing.

chapter twenty-one
Life on the Upswing

Darren

All it took was one anonymous tip—I placed the call because Charlene couldn't bring herself to do it—and Frank's entire operation fell apart. The media were all over THC like rabid dogs. Charlene couldn't handle watching any of it. Part of it had to do with the memories, but she worried a lot about the girls she'd grown up with, and how they would handle suddenly being thrust into a world that had changed so radically while theirs had remained narrow and isolated.

I learned a lot about how Charlene dealt with their escape, and how the internet and her mom's job formed the basis of her sex education, which explains pretty much everything about her bedroom antics.

I couldn't stand to see Charlene upset, so I pulled some strings and set up an anonymous fund to help the khaki ladies reintegrate into society. We were able to secure housing where they could all remain together, if that was what they wanted. Unsurprisingly, most of them opted to work at a local greenhouse facility.

Charlene's mom decided not to participate in the *Momma Domme* reality show, thank fuck, and instead she took an external consulting role with Robbie's Lab, which pays well enough that she decided she would retire from being a career Dominatrix, except for a couple of her favorite clients, anyway.

But the best news came at the end of June—well, it was the best news for me, but not for King, our goalie, who ended up traded in the expansion draft. This means I have two years left with Chicago, and then we'll see what happens after that. I won't take Charlene away from Chicago or the people she loves, so if they don't renew my contract, I'll retire. Alex knows that, my agent knows that, and most importantly, Charlene knows that.

I climb the steps to my front door and key in the code, having just finished a morning workout with Alex. We'll be getting together again later in the afternoon for a barbeque at his place.

"Charlene? I'm home!" I smile a little. The new-car smell hasn't worn off on saying that in the month since she moved in.

I wait for her reply, but all I get is silence. Her car is in the garage—her new car, the one I bought for her as a move-in gift—so she has to be around here somewhere. Excessive? Maybe, but it's a nice car, and she deserves nice things for putting up with my shit on a daily basis.

I drop my hockey bag by the laundry room door and head for the living room. Sometimes she listens to music while she reads or works in her chair, but she's not there. I find her in the kitchen—she is wearing ear buds—concentrating on something.

I pull one of the buds free and she startles, nearly falling off her stool.

"You know we have a whole house sound system. You could save your hearing and some heart palpitations if you used that to rock out to..." I lift the bud to my ear to catch the tune. "Madonna?"

She snatches the ear bud from me. "It's retro."

I smile at her pink cheeks and survey the counter. "What's all this?" The surface is covered in various candies and boxes of Fruit Roll-Ups. Maybe she's been into her candy stash and has the munchies or something.

Charlene claps her hands together excitedly. "I thought we could try something new!"

I raise a brow. Since moving in, Charlene has started pulling out the *I thought I might like it but I changed my mind* toy box. Fifty percent of the time she decides she still hasn't changed her mind, but the other half . . . well, let's just say it's been a stimulating transition.

I motion to the array of candies. "You want a sugar high before we have sex?"

She purses her lips, then licks them as her eyes dart around. She squares her shoulders, apparently finding her resolve. This should be interesting.

"No. I thought maybe we could play dress up."

I look at her and then the counter, trying to figure out what the fuck she's talking about. "I don't get it. What are we dressing up?"

"Your cock." Her tongue hits the roof of her mouth when she says cock, purposely making it sound liquid. So of course mine hardens, until her meaning finally registers.

"No."

She pouts. "Come on, it could be fun!"

I cross my arms over my chest. "Absolutely fucking not."

She opens her mouth, likely to argue her case, but I put up a hand to stop her. "I don't give a shit if Alex lets Violet emasculate his dick with costumes. That's their thing. It's not going to be ours."

"But I worked so hard on this." She holds up what appears to be some kind of cape.

I've heard about this—not because I want this kind of information, but because sometimes Charlene shares things she probably shouldn't with me. Apparently living together gives me *extra* information privileges. I'd be fine without them, but Charlene is chatty before bed at times.

As I take in the array of cape-like designs, I'll admit—in my head and never out loud—that she's been very creative. "Still no."

She bites her lip, clearly trying to come up with a way to convince me to let her dress up my dick like a fucking superhero. Her eyes light up, and a coy smile appears. "I'll let you tie me up."

For half a second I get excited by this prospect, and then I cock a brow. "No you won't."

She runs a hand up my chest. "With the yellow satin ribbons."

As enticing as her offer may seem, I know Charlene. "I'll get one wrist tied to the bed and you'll change your mind like last time." She was so cute, and anxious as hell by the time I freed that one wrist. It took me about thirty seconds to make her come. I also got a sweet blow job as a concession.

"I won't change my mind this time, I promise." She parts her legs and pulls me between them.

She really doesn't want to give up on this, apparently.

"Okay," I concede. "I get to use the yellow satin ribbons. *Then* you get to dress up my dick with an edible costume."

Her brows pull together, and I fight a smile. This is clearly not going the way she expected.

"Do we have a deal?"

She huffs. "What about anal instead?"

I scoff. "Baby, you love me in your ass. If I'm going to let you make a fool out of my dick, I better be getting something phenomenal in return."

She chews on the inside of her lip and starts slipping buttons free on my shirt. Her knees press against the outside of my legs. "What about anal against the window in the front room?"

I like everything about that idea, except the landscapers are here. Usually the whole point is the illusion of an audience, but I have an issue with that today. "No."

"No?" She tips her head to the side, regarding me curiously. "Why not? The landscapers are working on the garden right under the window, aren't they? You love that."

She hops off the stool before I can stop her and rushes for the front room, stripping off her shirt as she goes. I chase after her, her bra smacking me in the chest and dropping to the floor.

Charlene's all giggles as she glances over her shoulder and pulls her shorts and panties down, kicking them off.

"You're not playing fair, firefly."

"Says the man who likes to make me wait all damn day for an orgasm." She wiggles her ass and slaps her palms against the glass, causing the landscapers to look up. Which is when the reason I said no becomes obvious.

The company who does my landscaping hired a new kid. He's in his early to mid-twenties and has full sleeves.

She spins around, wearing an amused smile, and thumbs over her shoulder. "So it's okay when it's the Ramsbottoms and their poodle wandering by, or ancient Bob, but this new guy is a problem?"

"You're not checking him out while I'm fucking you."

"You think I'm going to check him out?"

"I've seen the way you eye my tattoo artist. This kid looks almost the same, except less broody."

"I was trying to figure out the design on his arm, not check him out."

"Still no."

She throws her hands up in air. "Oh come on! Stop being so difficult."

I laugh and thread my fingers in her hair. "I'm always difficult." I brush my lips over hers. "I appreciate your creativity, but you already own my balls. You're not dressing up my dick."

"I'm trying to be fun, Darren." She pouts. It's cute. And she's obviously already worked up, considering the way she's rubbing her thighs together.

"Stay right here, and don't move."

I go back to the kitchen and grab one of the bar stools. Charlene is exactly where I left her when I return, rolling her pearls over her lips. I give her a dark look as I set the stool down in front of the window and hold out a hand. "Have a seat, Charlene."

She releases her pearls and slips her palm into mine, allowing me to guide her to the stool where she sits, facing the front yard. The landscapers are working on the bushes to the right. I adjust her position so her ass is hanging over the edge and I have the access I need.

"Hands on the window," I whisper in her ear.

She complies, palms flat on the glass.

I slide a palm under her chin and tip her head back so she has to look at me. I run my other hand down her spine and between her thighs to circle her entrance.

I bend to touch my lips to hers. "Hands stay on the window and eyes stay on mine or I stop."

"Okay." She nods and arches her back, probably trying to get me to finger her. Too bad I'm not in a hurry to make her come. I spend the next ten minutes making painfully slow figure eights around her clit and entrance, but not penetrating. I know exactly the moment to back off so she doesn't go over the edge.

"Darren," she whines and lifts her right hand from the window.

"Hands, firefly. Yours stay where they are if you want mine to stay where mine are."

She moans and slaps her palm against the window. The landscapers have moved on at this point, but she doesn't know that.

I go back to doing figure eights around her clit. "It's a good thing the floor is hardwood. You're making quite the mess right now." She's dripping down my fingers.

"You're so mean," she grumbles.

I laugh. "Weren't you the one who wanted to play?"

"I wasn't expecting orgasm torture," she shoots back.

That's the moment I push two fingers inside her, find the sweet spot and start pumping, hard and fast. She can't keep her hands on the window, and for a second I consider stopping again, but we're spending the afternoon with friends, and I don't want her pissed off at me. So I keep pumping, and she starts coming. She latches onto my arm, nails digging in as her mouth falls open and a low moan bubbles up.

I drop my mouth to hers. "Does it feel good?"

"Oh my God, yes." The S draws out, long and low. And still, I keep pumping, and she keeps coming.

I could have her like this, but I want her wrapped around me, so I spin the stool and fumble with the button on my jeans. Yanking down the zipper, I free my cock, part her legs, line myself up, and push inside.

"We're finishing this upstairs so I can fuck you like I love you."

"Whatever you want, Darren."

"And you're not dressing up my dick. Ever." I grab two handfuls of ass and pick her up.

Her lips find the edge of my jaw as I carry up the stairs. When she gets to my ear she whispers, "You have to sleep sometime."

I chuckle ominously as I stretch out on top of her on our bed and grind my hips into hers. "I think you've forgotten who the lighter sleeper is between the two of us."

Her eyes flare, and she starts to tremble again, likely a combination of the sudden spike of uncertainty and the grinding. I dip down and press my lips to hers. "I love you, little firefly."

"I love you, too."

"Don't forget that when you wake up tied to the bed one day soon."

Another nerve shattering orgasm steals her breath. I wait until she comes down again before I kiss her, and love her, and tease and torment, and love her some more.

epilogue

Fireflies Forever

Darren
One summer later

"**S**OMEONE SMELLS LIKE HE COULD USE A DIAPER CHANGE!" Sunny scrunches up her nose and passes off baby Lane to Miller. "It's your turn this time."

"You gotta keep an eye on Logan and make sure he's not feeding Wiener all the cocktail wieners or we're going to have bigger problems than this stinker right here." Miller holds the screaming baby at arm's length, his face contorted into a grimace. "I think it's the broccoli soup that does this to him." He heads for the cottage.

"Logan!" Sunny calls out, and I follow her gaze to the table of food set up about twenty feet away.

Her son is indeed feeding cocktail wieners to Wiener. He pulls the treat away every time Wiener gets close so the dog has to jump for them, making his ears flap and Logan burst into a fit of giggles. It's cute, but if the dog gets the human treat, the cottage is going to smell like rotten dog fart for the rest of the weekend.

"I'll take Liam; you deal with Logan," I offer. Turns out the reason Sunny looked so pregnant at the end of last season was because she was incubating two babies instead of one.

Sunny glances from Logan to the squirming kid in her arms to me.

"I can handle it," I assure her.

Prior to all of my teammates having babies, I hadn't had much exposure, but when your best friend has a kid, it sort of forces you to figure out how to become an honorary uncle. I may not be one-hundred-percent natural around kids, but I can definitely watch one for a few minutes without the world coming to an end.

Sunny passes the little guy off to me. "Thanks. I'll be right back!"

"Take your time." He's half asleep, or at least he is until he's out of his mom's arms and into mine. "How's it going, buddy?"

He shouts nonsense in my face and cranes to find his mom.

"She'll be back. She's dealing with your older brother. He's getting up to no good over there." I have no idea how much he understands, but his little fists jab out, reaching for my sunglasses.

I find a lounger and rearrange Liam so he's stretched out in my lap, feet pushing into my stomach.

"Look at you." Charlene smiles as she crosses the lawn, a beer in one hand and some kind of girly drink in the other. She drops into the chair beside mine and pulls out her phone, snapping a bunch of pictures. "You better be careful, Mr. Westinghouse."

"Why's that?" I tickle the bottom of Liam's feet, and he bursts into a fit of giggles.

"It almost looks like you're enjoying this. People will start asking when you're going to knock me up."

"You let me know when you're ready for that, and we can jump on the baby bandwagon."

She laughs, but her expression shifts to contemplative. "Are you serious?"

"I want whatever you want, Charlene. You know that." I give his little tummy a tickle, and he giggles again and then farts. It doesn't sound dry. "Oh, you just did that, didn't you? I guess I better trade off with Miller." I lean over to give Charlene a quick kiss. "I'll be back in a few."

She grabs the front of my shirt, keeping our lips locked together long enough for her to get her tongue in my mouth for a stroke or two before she pulls back. "I love you."

"And I love you, firefly." I kiss the end of her nose, and she releases my shirt. I take Liam to the cottage and run into Violet on the way.

She's cradling a sleepy-looking baby Robbie. She raises a brow when she sees me holding Liam at arm's length. He definitely crapped his pants—the smell is getting worse, not better.

Violet's all smirky. I assume it's because I'm holding him like he's a nuclear bomb, not a kid, but if the diaper starts leaking, I don't want to wear his crap, thank you very much.

"Better not let Charlene see you with Liam."

"Why not?"

"Because it's baby central in here, and it's only a matter of time before her ovary clock starts ticking."

"Oh, well, nothing to worry about there. She's already seen me, and I already told her I'm happy to knock her up whenever she's ready."

Liam lets another fart rip, and Violet and I grimace at each other.

"Come on," she says. "Let's get that taken care of before he explodes all over the place."

I follow her down the hall to Robbie's bedroom, which is right next door to hers and Alex's. She pats the changing table, and I lay Liam down. He's started squawking, probably annoyed because he's marinating in his own crap. Violet puts Robbie in his crib, and I step back.

"Oh no, this is all you." She motions from me to Liam.

"What? I can't—"

"Seriously, Darren? It's poop. If you knock my bestie up, you're going to need to learn how to do this. Might as well start now. Don't worry. I'll walk you through it." She pats me on the shoulder.

I give her the eye.

"You don't scare me, Westinghouse. Deal with the poop."

I sigh. I guess she has a point. If Charlene decides she wants to have kids, I'm going to have to change some shitty diapers along the way. I unsnap the onesie that reads *iPood*, ironically enough.

"Okay, let's get the wipes ready. Liam is notorious for his ass explosions, aren't you, buddy?" Violet coos at him, and he smiles and claps his hands together.

I prepare the wipes and look to Violet. "What next?"

"Time to get your hands dirty. Okay, you're going to pull the tabs on the diaper, and the trick is to slide the top of the diaper down and then grab Liam's ankles and lift them before he can jam his foot in the dirty business. Got it?"

"I think so?" I follow her instructions and gag a little as I get a glimpse of the damage. Violet walks me through cleaning him up, which is just . . . fucking nasty. Liam seems to think it's hilarious, though.

Violet's all smiles as I go for wipe number fifty. "Did you bring the ring this weekend?"

"Yeah."

"You gonna pussy out again?"

I've had the ring for a few months. "I'm waiting for the right time. I don't want to push Charlene into something she's not ready for."

"Seriously? If she didn't run screaming at the offer to be knocked up by you, I'm pretty sure it means she's ready. Besides, I hear Randy's been looking at rings, and he and Lily are the co-founders of the Anti-Marriage Brigade. If you propose first, it means you get dibs on wedding dates."

"You think Randy's going to buy Lily a ring?"

"Make sure his wiener is pointing down," Violet instructs as I slide the fresh diaper under Liam's butt. She nudges me out of the way and finishes up. "I think what people want can change with time and perspective. You and Char are a perfect example of that. We can all make ourselves scarce tonight if you want. It's supposed to be nice out. There are always fireflies by the water when the sun goes down."

I mull that over. "You really think she'll say yes?"

Violet fastens the snaps and picks up Liam, patting his little fresh butt. "When I met Charlene, she didn't date a guy for more than three weeks. She never settled down and wasn't interested in long-term boyfriends, which, considering what she's been through, isn't much of a surprise. But everything changed with you, Darren. If you ask, she'll say yes."

"Okay." I nod, resolved.

She smiles and pats my cheek. "Now go wash your hands so they're not covered in crap residue, and maybe your face, too."

By nine o'clock, Alex and Violet still haven't reappeared from putting Robbie to bed. I have my doubts that Sunny and Miller will be back since the twins were fussy at dinner. Lily and Randy are likely doing what Lily and Randy do best, and with Poppy in the early stages of pregnancy where all she seems to want to do is take naps, she might be done for the night, as well.

I'm not sure Violet had to work all that hard to give me and Charlene some privacy.

Charlene snuggles into my side on the glider, and we watch the sun disappear behind the trees from the deck outside our bedroom. "Remember when we used to stay up until three in the morning and drink our faces off?"

"I certainly do. My favorite part was always getting you up to the room at the end of the night. You're such an adventure in the bedroom when you're drunk." I run my nose up her temple and kiss her cheek.

"I always went into it with the best of intentions."

I can feel her smiling. "Let's try all the things!" I mimic her voice.

"I do not sound like that when I'm drunk!"

"You do, and I love it. You're so fucking adorable when you're trying to be a little firefly." I chuckle. "We could do shots if you feel like letting your freak out."

Charlene snorts. "I think I'll pass. Those babies are like roosters at the crack of dawn. I can't imagine nursing a hangover and dealing with all of that craziness." She motions to the sounds coming from inside the cottage.

We're silent for a few minutes, enjoying the peace and the quiet—apart from the occasional burst of crying coming from one of the bedrooms, anyway.

"Alex said the cottage next door is for sale."

Charlene shifts so she can look at me. "You want to buy it."

It's not a question.

"This place isn't going to be able to handle all of us for much longer."

"Not with the way Sunny and Miller keep populating the future NHL draft," Charlene agrees.

Sunny's currently pregnant with baby number four, and very determined to have a girl. Based on Alex's competitive nature, I'm pretty sure he and Violet will be trying for baby number two soon. Even Randy seems to be warming to the idea of having a family. Although I think it's a lot easier to picture it when you're surrounded by your teammates, who are essentially your family. Which is something I've started to do lately.

"It might be nice to have a second cottage for summer get-togethers, especially since my contract expires at the end of next season."

"Chicago could renew."

"Maybe, but if they do, I think it'll be for a year at a time." I stare out at the lake, considering all the options for our future. Charlene and I have talked about this often over the past year—what I'll do when my contract with Chicago ends. "I don't know if I want to play without Alex."

Charlene kisses the edge of my jaw. "You are such a sentimental softie."

"I'm pragmatic."

"You can call it that if it helps you feel better about it. There's no shame in loyalty."

"I'm pretty sure he's going to retire at the end of next season."

"He has too much to lose now."

"He does. He'll go into sportscasting, and I can try coaching, and we can stay here where all the important people are." They're too much a part of both of our lives—the stability we both need, the good example of what a family should look like that neither one of us had growing up.

"I don't like to think about any of the guys getting traded," Charlene says softly.

"I know." I press my lips to her temple. The idea of anyone not being here is difficult to fathom, but it's a reality we'll all have to face. "They'll all be back eventually. Chicago is home."

"I hope you're right."

"I think I am."

The sound of babies finally settling gives way to crickets. I'm nervous now, edgy, this thing I want to ask her making my throat tight and my palms damp. I think we're at the place we need to be.

"Oh!" Charlene sits up and points out into the darkness. "Fireflies."

I take the opportunity for what it is and stand, holding out a hand to her. "Let's go catch one."

We take the stairs down and cross to the beach where it's darkest. Charlene is still, her eyes scanning the inky night for a tiny green glow. When she spots it, she jumps and claps her hands around it.

"Did you get it?"

"I don't know."

I come up behind her, ducking down to rest my chin on her shoulder, and we wait, patient and quiet to see if her palms light up.

"I think I missed it," she whispers when it seems to be taking too long.

"Just wait." I slip one arm around her waist and kiss her neck. And sure enough, a minute later her palms glow green in the inky night. She opens them immediately, and the firefly rises into the air, giving me the opportunity I need.

I clap my hands around empty air. "I think I got something," I whisper.

I hold my clasped hands out in front of her, lifting the top one to reveal the small velvet box.

"What is that?" Charlene strains to make out what's in my palm in the darkness.

I flip the lid open, the moonlight catching on the ring, making it sparkle as I come around to stand in front of her.

She lifts her wide, uncertain gaze to meet mine. "Darren?"

In my head I've done this a million times, practiced all the words I want to say to her. I drop to my knee in the sand, hoping I've got this right, that I know her as well as I think I do.

"I'll never put the lid on your jar, Charlene. I love you too much to do that. I know I already have you in all the ways that count, but I want this with you. I want your fire and your softness, your innocence and your adventure. I want to love you and protect you and take care of you, exactly as you do for me. I want to watch you glow every day for the rest of my life. Say you'll marry me. Be the only forever I need. Please."

Charlene's fingers lift to her lips and then drop to her pearls. Her eyes are soft and glassy as she takes my face between her hands and bends to kiss me. "Of course I'll marry you. You're my only forever."

note to my readers

In 2008 I started writing what would become my first published novel (duet, actually). It wasn't Pucked, it was Clipped Wings & Inked Armor. If you've read it, you'll know it's the polar opposite of Pucked; heavy instead of funny. I needed a break from all the depressing, snot sobbing angst, so I started writing what eventually became Pucked. The year I wrote it, Chicago won the Stanley Cup, and then the year I published, they won again. Not saying I had anything to do with that, just kind of a cool coincidence.

If you've made it to this note, then you've been on quite the journey with me and the Pucked gang. I have loved every minute of writing this series and I'm so proud of this bag of WTF that came out of my brain.

The other day Debra Anastasia, who has been on this very wild ride with me the entire time I've been writing, told me that Pucked Love was me writing with my seatbelt off. And that's pretty damn accurate.

The Pucked Series is where I let all the crazy out. It's outlandish, wild, ridiculous and just so much fun. Of course there are ups and down. Of course there are challenges to overcome, but I think the best part of writing this series has been how much these characters feel like a family. It's Violet's insanity and her lack of filter, it's Alex's Zero Fucks Given attitude that she sometimes says and does embarrassing things. It's in the way this unlikely group of characters supports and loves each other through all the good times and the bad that makes them difficult to say goodbye to.

Pucked Love is . . . nuts. I'll be honest, when I started outlining this pile of crazy I was like OH SHIT. What the hell have I done? I don't write BDSM. I might make little jokes about it, but that is not my wheelhouse. I write super consent-y sex where everyone is in control at all times—I mean, no one is actually in control during an orgasm, but there was no way on earth I was going to write BDSM with any kind of seriousness, so I had to get creative. I think Darren and Charlene are my favourite couple (although I say that with every book). I'll always love Alex and Violet because they're where this all started. Obviously I love all the couples for very different reasons, Miller and Sunny for being so freaking sweet, Randy and Lily for ruining all those bathrooms, Lance for being so broken and Poppy for saving him from himself with love and kindness and her quiet strength. But Charlene and Darren are a successful couple because of the people they have in their lives, not just because they're right for each other and to me, that makes them extra special.

I hope you loved this finale as much as I did. I hope the epilogue gave you a look into everyone's happy future. This Pucked family will take up a big place in my heart and I'm so glad I've had an opportunity to share so many laughs and tears with all of you over these past three years.

    Don't worry, it doesn't end here. There are always new stories, new characters and new families to build and fall in love with. Thank you, though, for being a part of this, no matter when you jumped on the crazy train with me.

Endless Pucking Love,

Helena

acknowledgements

This was quite a journey, from Violet and Alex all the way to Charlene and Darren, I've had an amazing team of people supporting me through this series. Sebastian, you said this was the book and you were right. Sometimes I just need to write with my seatbelt off and The Pucked Series has given me that freedom.

Huge love to all the people who have made this possible. Mom, Dad and Mel, your love and support mean so much to me. Debra, for being my rock, Leigh for being my faith when I couldn't manage it on my own, Kimberly for letting me write all the crazy on with this book.

Endless love to Nina and Jenn and the team at SBPR, (Sarah F and Bex, you rock my socks) for all your hard work with me on this series.

Sarah P, you're a gem and I'm lucky to have you and the Hustlers with me on this.

Shannon, I know this cover was tough, but I think you rocked it ;) thank you for making these covers truly shine, Teeny, thank you for always making the inside so pretty and Jessica, thank you for always cleaning up my grammar and commas and all the other things I'm so terrible at.

Bloggers, without you, the love for Alex and Violet wouldn't have had a chance to blossom, so thank you from the bottom of my heart for following this cast of characters all the way here with me. Readers, you're amazing. Thank you for embracing the insanity of the Pucked Family. I love your love for them, which makes it hard to say goodbye.

To all my author friends who have been with me along the way, through the ups and downs and all the in-betweens, thank you for holding my hand. Kellie, thanks for the brainstorming session that started this all, Deb, Leigh, Tijan, Kelly, Susi, Ruth, Erika, Katherine, Marine, Julie, Kathrine, Karen, Marty, you're my tribe. Thanks for pointing out I'm Violet and loving me anyway.

also by

HELENA HUNTING

PUCKED SERIES

Pucked (Pucked #1)
Pucked Up (Pucked #2)
Pucked Over (Pucked #3)
Forever Pucked (Pucked Book #4)
Pucked Under (Pucked #5)
Pucked Off (Pucked #6)
Pucked Love (Pucked #7)

PUCKED SERIES EXTRAS

AREA 51: Deleted Scenes & Outtakes
Get Inked

THE CLIPPED WINGS SERIES

Cupcakes and Ink
Clipped Wings
Between the Cracks
Inked Armor
Cracks in the Armor
Fractures in Ink

SHACKING UP SERIES

Shacking Up
Getting Down (Novella)
Hooking Up
I Flipping Love You
Making Up
Handle with Care

STANDALONE NOVELS

The Librarian Principle
Felony Ever After

FOREVER ROMANCE STANDALONES

The Good Luck Charm
MEET CUTE

ALL IN SERIES

A Lie for a Lie
A Favor for a Favor

about the author

NYT and USA Today bestselling author, Helena Hunting lives on the outskirts of Toronto with her incredibly tolerant family and two moderately intolerant cats. She writes contemporary romance ranging from new adult angst to romantic sports comedy.

Connect With Helena Hunting

AMAZON: www.amazon.com/Helena-Hunting/e/B00HHM5MLQ

FACEBOOK: www.facebook.com/helena.hunting69

WEBSITE: www.helenahunting.com

TWITTER : twitter.com/HelenaHunting

INSTAGRAM: www.instagram.com/helenahunting